KU-519-986

CHASM CITY
Alastair Reynolds

GOLLANCZ
London

Copyright © Alastair Reynolds 2001
All rights reserved

The right of Alastair Reynolds to be identified as the author
of this work has been asserted by him in accordance with
the Copyright, Designs and Patents Act 1988.

First published in Great Britain in 2001 by

Gollancz
An imprint of the Orion Publishing Group
Orion House, 5 Upper St Martin's Lane, London WC2H 9EA

A CIP catalogue record for this book is available
from the British Library

Typeset at The Spartan Press Ltd, Lymington, Hants
Printed in Great Britain by Butler & Tanner Ltd, Frome and London

C2000002998122

CHASM CITY

TOWER HILL LIBRARY
Tower Hill B42 1LG
Tel: 0121 464 1948

Loans are up to 28 days. Fines are charged if items are
not returned by the due date. Items can be renewed
at the Library, via the internet or by telephone up to
3 times. Items in demand will not be renewed.
Please use a bookmark

Date for return		
27 SEP 2012	1 3 SEP 2016	
	1 6 AUG 2017	
2 9 JUN 2013		
NR		
1 6 AUG 2014		
3 0 JUL 2016		

Check out our online catalogue to see what's in stock,
or to renew or reserve books.
www.birmingham.gov.uk/libcat
www.birmingham.bov.uk/libraries

Birmingham City Council

B
Birmingham
Libraries

50706

Also by Alastair Reynolds in Gollancz

Revelation Space

Dear Newcomer,

Welcome to the Epsilon Eridani system.

Despite all that has happened, we hope your stay here will be a pleasant one. For your information we have compiled this document to explain some of the key events in our recent history. It is intended that this information will ease your transition into a culture which may be markedly different from the one you were expecting to find when you embarked at your point of origin. It is important that you realise that others have come before you. Their experiences have helped us shape this document in a manner designed to minimise the shock of cultural adjustment. We have found that attempts to gloss over or understate the truth of what happened – of what continues to happen – are ultimately harmful; that the best approach – based on a statistical study of cases such as yours – is to present the facts in as open and honest manner as possible.

We are fully aware that your initial response is likely disbelief, quickly followed by anger and then a state of protracted denial.

It is important to grasp that these are normal reactions.

It is equally important to grasp – even at this early stage – that there will come a time when you will adjust to and accept the truth. It might be days from now; it might even be weeks or months, but in all but a minority of cases it will happen. You might even look back upon this time and wish that you could have willed yourself to make the transition to acceptance quicker than you did. You will know that it is only when that process is accomplished that anything resembling happiness becomes possible.

Let us therefore begin the process of adjustment.

Due to the fundamental lightspeed limit for communication within the sphere of colonised space, news from other solar systems is inevitably out of date; often by decades or more. Your perceptions of our system's main world, Yellowstone, are almost certainly based on outdated information.

It is certainly the case that for more than two centuries – until, in fact, the very recent past – Yellowstone was in thrall to what most contemporary observers chose to term the Belle Epoque. It was an unprecedented social and technological golden age; our ideological template seen by all to be an almost perfect system of governance.

Numerous successful ventures were launched from Yellowstone, including daughter colonies in other solar systems, as well as ambitious scientific expeditions to the edge of human space. Visionary social experiments were conducted within Yellowstone and its Glitter Band, including the controversial but pioneering work of Calvin Sylveste and his disciples. Great artists, philosophers and scientists flourished in Yellowstone's atmosphere of hothouse innovation. Techniques of neural augmentation were pursued fearlessly. Other human cultures chose to treat the Conjoiners with suspicion, but we Demarchists – unafraid of the positive aspects of mind enhancement methods – established lines of rapport with the Conjoiners which enabled us to exploit their technologies to the full. Their starship drives allowed us to settle many more systems than cultures subscribing to inferior social models.

In truth, it was a glorious time. It was also the likely state of affairs which you were expecting upon your arrival.

This is unfortunately not the case.

Seven years ago something happened to our system. The exact transmission vector remains unclear even now, but it is almost certain that the plague arrived aboard a ship, perhaps in dormant form and unknown to the crew who carried it. It might even have arrived years earlier. It seems unlikely now that the truth will ever be known; too much has been destroyed or forgotten. Vast swathes of our digitally stored planetary history were erased or corrupted by the plague. In many cases only human memory remains intact . . . and human memory is not without its fallibilities.

The Melding Plague attacked our society at the core.

It was not quite a biological virus, not quite a software virus, but a strange and shifting chimera of the two. No pure strain of the plague has ever been isolated, but in its pure form it must resemble a kind of nano-machinery, analogous to the molecular-scale assemblers of our own medichine technology. That it must be of alien origin seems beyond doubt. Equally clear is the fact that nothing we have thrown against the plague has done more than slow it. More often than not, our interventions have only made things worse. The plague adapts to our attacks; it perverts our weapons and turns them against us. Some kind of buried intelligence seems to guide it. We don't know whether the plague was directed toward humanity – or whether we have just been terribly unlucky.

At this point, based on our prior experiences, your most likely reaction is to assume that this document is a hoax. Our experience has also shown that our denying this will accelerate the process of adjustment by a small but statistically significant factor.

This document is not a hoax.

The Melding Plague actually happened, and its effects were far worse than you are currently capable of imagining. At the time of the plague's manifestation our society was supersaturated by trillions of tiny machines. They were our unthinking, uncomplaining servants, givers of life and shapers of matter, and yet we barely gave them a moment's thought. They swarmed tirelessly through our blood. They toiled ceaselessly in our cells. They clotted our brains, linking us all into the Demarchy's web of near-instantaneous decision-making. We moved through virtual environments woven by direct manipulation of the brain's sensory mechanisms, or scanned and uploaded our minds into lightning-fast computer systems. We forged and sculpted matter on the scale of mountains; wrote symphonies out of matter; caused it to dance to our whims like tamed fire. Only the Conjoiners had taken a step closer to Godhead . . . and some said we were not far behind them.

Machines grew our orbiting city-states from raw rock and ice, and then bootstrapped inert matter towards life within their biomes. Thinking machines ran those city-states, shepherding the ten thousand habitats of the Glitter Band as they processed around Yellowstone. Machines made Chasm City what it was; shaping its amorphous architecture towards a fabulous and phantasmagoric beauty.

All that is gone.

It was worse than you are thinking. If the plague had only killed our machines, millions would still have died, but that would have been a manageable catastrophe, something from which we could have recovered. But the plague went beyond mere destruction, into a realm much closer to artistry, albeit an artistry of a uniquely perverted and sadistic kind. It caused our machines to evolve uncontrollably – out of *our* control, at least – seeking bizarre new symbioses. Our buildings turned into Gothic nightmares, trapping us before we could escape their lethal transfigurations. The machines in our cells, in our blood, in our heads, began to break their shackles – blurring into us, corrupting living matter. We became glistening, larval fusions of flesh and machine. When we buried the dead they kept growing, spreading together, fusing with the city's architecture.

It was a time of horror.

It is not yet over.

And yet, like any truly efficient plague, our parasite was careful not to kill its host population entirely. Tens of millions died – but tens of millions more reached some kind of sanctuary, hiding within hermetically sealed enclaves in the city or orbit. Their medichines were given emergency destruct orders, converting themselves to dust which was flushed harmlessly out of the body. Surgeons worked furiously to tear implants from heads before traces of the plague reached them. Other citizens, too strongly wedded to their machines to give them up, sought a kind of escape in reefersleep. They elected to be buried in sealed community cryocrypts . . . or to leave the system entirely. Meanwhile, tens of millions more poured into Chasm City from orbit, fleeing the destruction of the Glitter Band. Some of those people had been amongst the wealthiest in the system, yet now they were as poor as any historical refugees. What they found in Chasm City could hardly have comforted them . . .

– Excerpt from an introductory document for newcomers, freely available
in circum-Yellowstone space, 2517

ONE

Darkness was falling as Dieterling and I arrived at the base of the bridge.

'There's one thing you need to know about Red Hand Vasquez,' Dieterling said. 'Don't ever call him that to his face.'

'Why not?'

'Because it pisses him off.'

'And that's a problem?' I brought our wheeler to near-halt, then parked it amongst a motley row of vehicles lining one side of the street. I dropped the stabilisers, the overheated turbine smelling like a hot gun barrel. 'It's not like we usually worry about the feelings of low-lives,' I said.

'No, but this time it might be best to err on the side of caution. Vasquez may not be the brightest star in the criminal firmament, but he's got friends and a nice little line in extreme sadism. So be on your best behaviour.'

'I'll give it my best shot.'

'Yeah – and do your best not to leave too much blood on the floor in the process, will you?'

We got out of the wheeler, both of us craning our necks to take in the bridge. I'd never seen it before today – this was my first time in the Demilitarised Zone, let alone Nueva Valparaiso – and it had looked absurdly large even when we'd been fifteen or twenty kilometres out of town. Swan had been sinking towards the horizon, bloated and red except for the hot glint near its heart, but there'd still been enough light to catch the bridge's thread and occasionally pick out the tiny ascending and descending beads of elevators riding it to and from space. Even then I'd wondered if we were too late – if Reivich had already made it aboard one of the elevators – but Vasquez had assured us that the man we were hunting was still in town, simplifying his web of assets on Sky's Edge and moving funds into long-term accounts.

Dieterling strolled round to the back of our wheeler – with its overlapping armour segments the mono-wheeled car looked like a rolled-up armadillo – and popped open a tiny luggage compartment.

'Shit. Almost forgot the coats, bro.'

'Actually, I was sort of hoping you would.'

He threw me one. 'Put it on and stop complaining.'

I slipped on the coat, easing it over the layers of clothing I already wore. The coat hems skimmed the street's puddles of muddy rainwater, but that was the way aristocrats liked to wear them, as if daring others to tread on their coat-tails. Dieterling shrugged on his own coat and began tapping through the patterning options embossed around the sleeve, frowning in distaste at each sartorial offering. 'No. No . . . No. Christ no. No again. And this won't do either.'

I reached over and thumbed one of the tabs. 'There. You look stunning. Now shut up and pass me the gun.'

I'd already selected a shade of pearl for my own coat, a colour which I hoped would provide a low-contrast background for the gun. Dieterling retrieved the little weapon from a jacket pocket and offered it to me, just as if he were passing me a packet of cigarettes.

The gun was tiny and semi-translucent, a haze of tiny components visible beneath its smooth, lucite surfaces.

It was a clockwork gun. It was made completely out of carbon – diamond, mostly – but with some fullerenes for lubrication and energy-storage. There were no metals or explosives in it; no circuitry. Only intricate levers and ratches, greased by fullerene spheres. It fired spin-stabilised diamond flèch-ettes, drawing its power from the relaxation of fullerene springs coiled almost to breaking point. You wound it up with a key, like a clockwork mouse. There were no aiming devices, stabilising systems or target acquisition aids.

None of which would matter.

I slipped the gun into my coat pocket, certain that none of the pedestrians had witnessed the handover.

'I told you I'd sort you out with something tasty,' Dieterling said.

'It'll do.'

'Do? Tanner; you disappoint me. It's a thing of intense, evil beauty. I'm even thinking it might have distinct hunting possibilities.'

Typical Miguel Dieterling, I thought; always seeing the hunting angle in any given situation.

I made an effort at smiling. 'I'll give it back to you in one piece. Failing that, I know what to get you for Christmas.'

We started walking towards the bridge. Neither of us had been in Nueva Valparaiso before, but that didn't matter. Like a good many of the larger towns on the planet, there was something deeply familiar about its basic layout, even down to the street names. Most of our settlements were organised around a deltoid street pattern, with three main thoroughfares stretching away from the apexes of a central triangle about one hundred metres along each side. Sur-rounding that core would typically be a series of successively larger triangles, until the geometric order was eroded in a tangle of random suburbs and redeveloped zones. What they did with the central triangle was up to the settlement in question, and usually depended on how many times the town had been occupied or bombed during the war. Only very rarely would there be any trace of the delta-winged shuttle around which the settlement had sprung.

Nueva Valparaiso had started out like that, and it had all the usual street names: Omdurman, Norquinco, Armesto and so on – but the central triangle was smothered beneath the terminal structure of the bridge, which had managed to be enough of an asset to both sides to have survived unscathed. Three hundred metres along each side, it rose sheer and black like the hull of a ship, but encrusted and scabbed along its lower levels by hotels, restaurants, casinos and brothels. But even if the bridge hadn't been visible, it was obvious from the street itself that we were in an old neighbourhood, close to the landing site. Some of the buildings had been made by stacking freight pods on top of each other, each pod punctured with windows and doors and then filigreed by two and a half centuries of architectural whimsy.

'Hey,' a voice said. 'Tanner fucking Mirabel.'

He was leaning in a shadowed portico like someone with nothing better to do than watch insects crawl by. I'd only dealt with him via telephone or video before – keeping our conversations as brief as possible – and I'd been expecting someone a lot taller and a lot less ratlike. His coat was as heavy as the one I was wearing, but his looked like it was constantly on the point of slipping off his shoulders. He had ochre teeth which he had filed into points, a sharp face full of uneven stubble and long black hair which he wore combed back from a minimalist forehead. In his left hand was a cigarette which he periodically pushed to his lips, while his other hand – the right one – vanished into the side pocket of his coat and showed no sign of emerging.

'Vasquez,' I said, showing no surprise that he had trailed Dieterling and me. 'I take it you've got our man under surveillance?'

'Hey, chill out, Mirabel. That guy doesn't take a leak without me knowing it.'

'He's still settling his affairs?'

'Yeah. You know what these rich kids are like. Gotta take care of business, man. Me, I'd be up that bridge like shit on wheels.' He jabbed his cigarette in Dieterling's direction. 'The snake guy, right?'

Dieterling shrugged. 'If you say so.'

'That's some cool shit; hunting snakes.' With his cigarette hand he mimed aiming and firing a gun, doubtless drawing a bead on an imaginary hamadryad. 'Think you can squeeze me in on your next hunting trip?'

'I don't know,' Dieterling said. 'We tend not to use live bait. But I'll talk to the boss and see what we can arrange.'

Red Hand Vasquez flashed his pointed teeth at us. 'Funny guy. I like you, Snake. But then again you work for Cahuella, I gotta like you. How is he anyway? I heard Cahuella got it just as badly as you did, Mirabel. In fact I'm even hearing some vicious rumours to the effect that he didn't make it.'

7

Cahuella's death wasn't something we were planning on announcing right now; not until we had given some thought to its ramifications – but news had evidently reached Nueva Valparaiso ahead of us.

'I did my best for him,' I said.

Vasquez nodded slowly and wisely, as if some sacred belief of his had just been proved valid.

'Yeah, that's what I heard.' He put his left hand on my shoulder, keeping his cigarette away from the coat's pearl-coloured fabric. 'I heard you drove halfway across the planet with a missing leg, just so you could bring Cahuella and his bitch home. That's some heroic shit, man, even for a white-eye. You can tell me all about it over some pisco sours, and Snake can pencil me in for his next field trip. Right, Snake?'

We continued walking in the general direction of the bridge. 'I don't think there's time for that,' I said. 'Drinks, I mean.'

'Like I said, chill.' Vasquez strolled ahead of us, still with one hand in his pocket. 'I don't get you guys. All it would take is a word from you, and Reivich wouldn't even be a problem any more, just a stain on the floor. The offer's still open, Mirabel.'

'I have to finish him myself, Vasquez.'

'Yeah. That's what I heard. Like some kind of vendetta deal. You had something going with Cahuella's bitch, didn't you?'

'Subtlety's not your strong point, is it, Red?'

I saw Dieterling wince. We walked on in silence for a few more paces before Vasquez stopped and turned to face me.

'What did you say?'

'I heard they call you Red Hand Vasquez behind your back.'

'And what the fuck business of yours would it be if they did?'

I shrugged. 'I don't know. On the other hand, what business is it of yours what went on between me and Gitta?'

'All right, Mirabel.' He took a longer than usual drag on his cigarette. 'I think we understand each other. There are things I don't like people asking about, and there are things you don't like people asking about. Maybe you were fucking Gitta, I don't know, man.' He watched as I bridled. 'But like you said, it wouldn't be my business. I won't ask again. I won't even think about it again. But do me a favour, right? Don't call me Red Hand. I know that Reivich did something pretty bad to you out in the jungle. I hear it wasn't much fun and you nearly died. But get one thing clear, all right? You're outnumbered here. My people are watching you all the time. That means you don't want to upset me. And if you do upset me, I can arrange for shit to happen to you that makes what Reivich did seem like a fucking teddy bears' picnic.'

'I think,' Dieterling said, 'that we should take the gentleman at his word. Right, Tanner?'

'Let's just say we both touched a nerve,' I said, after a long hard silence.

'Yeah,' Vasquez said. 'I like that. Me and Mirabel, we're hair-trigger guys and we gotta have some respect for each other's sensibilities. Copacetic. So let's go drink some pisco sours while we wait for Reivich to make a move.'

'I don't want to get too far from the bridge.'

'That won't be a problem.'

Vasquez cleaved a path before us, pushing through the evening strollers with insouciant ease. Accordion music ground out of the lowest floor of one of the freight pod buildings, slow and stately as a dirge. There were couples out walking – locals rather than aristocrats, for the most part, but dressed as well as their means allowed: genuinely at ease, good-looking young people with smiles on their faces as they looked for somewhere to eat or gamble or listen to music. The war had probably touched their lives in some tangible way; they might have lost friends or loved ones, but Nueva Valparaiso was sufficiently far from the killing fronts that the war did not have to be uppermost in their thoughts. It was hard not to envy them; hard not to wish that Dieterling and I could walk into a bar and drink ourselves into oblivion; forgetting the clockwork gun; forgetting Reivich; forgetting the reason I had come to the bridge.

There were, of course, other people out tonight. There were soldiers on furlough, dressed in civilian clothes but instantly recognisable, with their aggressively cropped hair, galvanically boosted muscles, colour-shifting chameleoflage tattoos on their arms, and the odd asymmetric way their faces were tanned, with a patch of pale flesh around one eye where they normally peered through a helmet-mounted targeting monocle. There were soldiers from all sides in the conflict mingling more or less freely, kept out of trouble by wandering DMZ militia. The militia were the only agency allowed to carry weapons within the DMZ, and they brandished their guns in starched white gloves. They weren't going to touch Vasquez, and even if we hadn't been walking with him, they wouldn't have bothered Dieterling and me. We might have looked like gorillas stuffed into suits, but it would be hard to mistake us for active soldiers. We both looked too old, for a start; both of us pushing middle age. On Sky's Edge that meant essentially what it had meant for most of human history: two to three-score years.

Not much for half a human life.

Dieterling and I had both kept in shape, but not to the extent that would have marked us as active soldiers. Soldier musculature never looked exactly human to begin with, but it had definitely become more extreme since I was a white-eye. Back then you could just about argue that you needed boosted muscles to carry around your weapons. The equipment had improved since then, but the soldiers on the street tonight had bodies that looked as if they had been sketched in by a cartoonist with an eye for absurd exaggeration. In the field the effect would be heightened by the lightweight weapons which were now in vogue: all those muscles to carry guns a child could have held.

'In here,' Vasquez said.

His place was one of the structures festering around the base of the bridge itself. He steered us into a short, dark alley and then through an unmarked door flanked by snake holograms. The room inside was an industrial-scale kitchen filled with billowing steam. I squinted and wiped perspiration from my face, ducking under an array of vicious cooking utensils. I wondered if Vasquez had ever used them in any extra-culinary activities.

I whispered to Dieterling, 'Why is he so touchy about being called Red Hand anyway?'

'It's a long story,' Dieterling said, 'and it isn't just the hand.'

Now and then a bare-chested cook would emerge from the steam on some errand, face half-concealed behind a plastic breathing mask. Vasquez spoke to two of them while Dieterling picked up something from a pan – dipping his fingers nimbly into the boiling water – and nibbled it experimentally.

'This is Tanner Mirabel, a friend of mine,' Vasquez said to the senior cook. 'Guy used to be a white-eye, so don't fuck with him. We'll be here for a while. Bring us something to drink. Pisco sours. Mirabel, you hungry?'

'Not really. And I think Miguel's already helping himself.'

'Good. But I think the rat's a touch off tonight, Snake.'

Dieterling shrugged. 'I've tasted a lot worse, believe me.' He popped another morsel into his mouth. 'Mm. Pretty good rat, actually. *Norvegicus*, right?'

Vasquez led us beyond the kitchen into an empty gambling parlour. At first I thought we had the place to ourselves. Discreetly lit, the room was sumptuously outfitted in green velvet, with burbling hookahs situated on strategic pedestals. The walls were covered in paintings all done in shades of brown – except that when I looked closer I realised they were not paintings at all, but pictures made of different pieces of wood, carefully cut and glued together. Some of the pieces even had the slight shimmer which showed that they had been cut from the bark of a hamadryad tree. The pictures were all on a common theme: scenes from the life of Sky Haussmann. There were the five ships of the Flotilla crossing space from Earth's system to ours. There was Titus Haussmann, torch in hand, finding his son alone and in the darkness after the great blackout. There was Sky visiting his father in the infirmary aboard the ship, before Titus died of the injuries he had sustained defending the *Santiago* against the saboteur. There, also rendered exquisitely, was Sky Haussmann's crime and glory; the thing he had done to ensure that the *Santiago* reached this world ahead of the other ships in the Flotilla, the ship's sleeper modules falling away like dandelion seeds. And, in the last picture of all, was the punishment the people had wrought on Sky: crucifixion.

Dimly I remembered that it had happened near here.

But the room was more than simply a shrine to Haussmann. Alcoves spaced around the room's perimeter contained conventional gambling machines, and there were half-a-dozen tables where games would obviously take place

10

later that night, although no one was actually playing at the moment. All I heard was the scurrying of rats somewhere in the shadows.

But the room's centrepiece was a hemispherical dome, perfectly black and at least five metres wide, surrounded by padded chairs mounted on complicated telescopic plinths, elevated three metres above the floor. Each chair had an arm inset with gambling controls, while the other held a battery of intravenous devices. About half the chairs were occupied, but by figures so perfectly still and deathlike that I hadn't even registered them when I entered the room. They were slumped back in their seats, their faces slack and their eyes closed. They all bore that indefinable aristocrat glaze: an aura of wealth and untouchability.

'What happened?' I said. 'Forgot to throw them out after you locked up this morning?'

'No. They're pretty much a permanent fixture, Mirabel. They're playing a game that lasts months; betting on the long-term outcome of ground campaigns. It's quiet now due to the rains. Almost like there isn't a war after all. But you should see it when the shit starts flying around.'

There was something about the place I didn't like. It wasn't just the display of Sky Haussmann's story, though that was a significant part of it.

'Maybe we should be moving on, Vasquez.'

'And miss your drinks?'

Before I had decided what to say the head cook came in, still breathing noisily through his plastic mask. He propelled a little trolley loaded with drinks. I shrugged and helped myself to a pisco sour, then nodded at the décor.

'Sky Haussmann's a big deal round here, isn't he?'

'More than you realise, man.'

Vasquez did something and the hemisphere flicked into life, suddenly no longer fully dark but an infinitely detailed view of one half of Sky's Edge, with an edge of black rising from the floor like a lizard's nictitating membrane. Nueva Valparaiso was a sparkle of lights on the Peninsula's western coastline, visible through a crack in the clouds.

'Yeah?'

'People around here can be quite religious, you know. You can easily tread on their beliefs, you're not careful. Gotta be respectful, man.'

'I heard they based a religion around Haussmann. That's about as far as my knowledge goes.' Again, I nodded at the décor, noticing for the first time what looked like the skull of a dolphin stuck to one wall, oddly bumped and ridged. 'What happened? Did you buy this place from one of Haussmann's nutcases?'

'Not exactly, no.'

Dieterling coughed. I ignored him.

'What, then? Did you buy into it yourself?'

Vasquez extinguished his cigarette and pinched the bridge of his nose, furrowing what little forehead he had. 'What's going on here, Mirabel? Are you trying to wind me up, or are you just an ignorant cocksucker?'

'I don't know. I thought I was just making polite conversation.'

'Yeah, right. And you just happened to call me Red earlier on; like it just slipped out.'

'I thought we were over that.' I sipped my pisco. 'I wasn't trying to rile you, Vasquez. But it strikes me that you're an unusually touchy fellow.'

He did something. It was a tiny gesture which he made with one hand, like someone clicking their fingers once.

What happened next was too fast for the eye to see; just a subliminal blur of metal and a breezelike caress of air currents being pushed around the room. Extrapolating backwards, I concluded that a dozen or so apertures must have slid or irised open around the room – in the walls, the floor and the ceiling, most likely – releasing machines.

They were automated sentry drones, hovering black spheres which split open along their equators to reveal three or four gun barrels apiece, which locked onto Dieterling and me. The drones orbited slowly around us, humming like wasps, bristling with belligerence.

Neither of us breathed for a few long moments, but it was Dieterling who chose to speak in the end.

'I guess we'd be dead if you were really pissed off at us, Vasquez.'

'You're right, but it's a fine line, Snake.' He raised his voice. 'Safe mode on.' Then he made the same finger-clicking gesture he had done before. 'You see that, man? It looked pretty similar to you, didn't it? But not to the room it didn't. If I hadn't turned the system off, it would have interpreted that as an order to execute everyone here except myself and the fat fucks in the gaming seats.'

'I'm glad you practised it,' I said.

'Yeah, laugh about it, Mirabel.' He made the gesture again. 'That looked the same as well, didn't it? But that wasn't quite the same command either. That would have told the sentries to blow your arms off, one at a time. The room's programmed to recognise at least twelve more gestures – and believe me, after some of 'em I really get stung for the cleaning bill.' He shrugged. 'Can I consider my point adequately made?'

'I think we've got the message.'

'All right. Safe mode off. Sentries retire.'

The same blur of motion; the same breeze. It was as if the machines had simply snapped out of existence.

'Impressed?' Vasquez asked me.

'Not really,' I said, feeling prickles of sweat across my brow. 'With the right security set-up, you'd already have screened anyone who'd got this far. But I suppose it breaks the ice at parties.'

'Yeah, it does that.' Vasquez looked at me amusedly, evidently satisfied that he'd achieved the desired effect.

'What it also does is make me wonder why you're so touchy.'

'You were in my shoes, you'd be a fuck of a lot more than touchy.' Then he did something that surprised me, taking his hand from his pocket, slowly enough that I had time to see there was no weapon there. 'You see this, Mirabel?'

I don't know quite what I was expecting, but the clenched fist he showed me looked normal enough. There was nothing deformed or unusual about it. Nothing, in fact, particularly red about it.

'It looks like a hand, Vasquez.'

He clenched the fist even harder and then something odd happened. Blood began to trickle out of his grip; slowly at first, but in an increasingly strong flow. I watched it spatter on the floor, scarlet on green.

'That's why they call me what they do. Because I bleed from my right hand. Fucking original, right?' He opened the fist, revealing blood pouring out of a small hole somewhere near the middle of his palm. 'Here's the deal. It's a stigma; like a mark of Christ.' With his good hand he reached into his other pocket and pulled out a kerchief, wadding it into a ball and pressing it against the wound to stench the flow. 'I can almost will it to happen sometimes.'

'Haussmann cultists got to you, didn't they,' Dieterling said. 'They crucified Sky as well. They drove a nail into his right hand.'

'I don't understand,' I said.

'Shall I tell him?'

'Be my guest, Snake. The man clearly needs educating.'

Dieterling turned to me. 'Haussmann's cultists split up into a number of different sects over the last century or so. Some of them took their ideas from penitential monks, trying to inflict on themselves some of the pain Sky must have gone through. They lock themselves away in darkness until the isolation almost drives them insane, or makes them start seeing things. Some of them cut off their left arms; some even crucify themselves. Sometimes they die in the process.' He paused and looked at Vasquez, as if seeking permission to continue. 'But there's a more extreme sect that does all that and more. And they don't stop there. They spread the message, not by word of mouth, or writing, but by indoctrinal virus.'

'Go on,' I said.

'It must have been engineered for them; probably by Ultras, or maybe one of them even took a trip to see the Jugglers and they screwed around with his neurochemistry. It doesn't matter. All that does is that the virus is contagious, transmittable through the air, and it infects almost everyone.'

'Turning them into cultists?'

'No.' It was Vasquez speaking now. He had found a fresh cigarette for himself. 'It fucks with you, but it doesn't turn you into one of them, got that? You get visions, and you have dreams, and you sometimes feel the need . . .' He paused, and nodded towards the dolphin jutting from the wall. 'You see that fish skull? Cost me a fucking arm and a leg. Used to belong to Sleek; one of the ones on the ship. Having shit like that around comforts me; stops me shaking. But that's as far as it goes.'

'And the hand?'

Vasquez said, 'Some of the viruses make physical changes happen. I was lucky, in a way. There's one that makes you go blind; another that makes you scared of the dark; another that makes your left arm wither away and drop off. You know, a little blood now and again, it doesn't bother me. At first, before many people knew about the virus, it was cool. I could really freak people out with it. Walk into a negotiation, you know, and start bleeding all over the other guy. But then people started finding out what it meant; that I'd been infected by cultists. '

'They started wondering if you were as razor-sharp as they'd heard,' Dieterling said.

'Yeah. Right.' Vasquez looked at him suspiciously. 'You build up a reputation like mine, it takes time.'

'I don't doubt it,' Dieterling said.

'Yeah. And a little thing like this, man, it can really hurt it.'

'Can't they flush out the virus?' I said, before Dieterling pushed his luck.

'Yeah, Mirabel. In orbit, they've got shit that can do it. But orbit's not currently on my list of safe places to visit, you know?'

'So you live with it. It can't be that infectious any more, can it?'

'No; you're safe. Everyone's safe. I'm barely infectious now.' Now that he was smoking again he was calming down a little. The bleeding had stopped and he was able to slip his wounded hand back in his pocket. He took a sip from his pisco sour. 'Sometimes I wish it was still infectious, or that I'd saved some of my blood from back when I got infected. It would have made a nice going-away present, a little shot of that in someone's vein.'

'Except you'd be doing what the cultists always wanted you to do,' Dieterling said. 'Spreading their creed.'

'Yeah, when instead I should be spreading the creed that if I ever catch the sick fuck who did this to me . . .' He trailed off, distracted by something. He stared into the middle distance, like a man undergoing some kind of paralytic seizure, then spoke. 'No. No way, man. I don't believe it.'

'What is it?' I said.

Vasquez's voice dropped subvocal, though I could see the way his neck muscles kept on moving. He must have been wired for communication with one of his people.

'It's Reivich,' he said finally.

'What about him?' I asked.

'The fucker's outsmarted me.'

TWO

A maze of dark, damp passages connected Red Hand's establishment to the interior of the bridge terminal, threading right through the structure's black wall. He led us through the labyrinth with a torch, kicking rats out of the way.

'A decoy,' he said wonderingly. 'I never figured he'd set up a decoy. I mean, we've been following this fucker for *days*.' He said the last word as if it should have been months at the very least; implying superhuman foresight and planning.

'The lengths some people'll go to,' I said.

'Hey, ease off, Mirabel. It was your idea not to waste the guy the instant we saw him, which could easily have been arranged.' He shouldered through a set of doors into another passageway.

'It still wouldn't have been Reivich, would it?'

'No, but when we examined the body we might have figured out it wasn't him, and then we could have started looking around for the real one.'

'Guy's got a point,' Dieterling said. 'Much as it pains me to admit it.'

'One I owe you, Snake.'

'Yeah, well, don't let it go to your head.'

Vasquez sent another rat scurrying for the shadows. 'So what really did happen out there, that made you want to get into this vendetta shit in the first place?'

I said, 'You seemed reasonably well informed already.'

'Well, word gets around, that's all. Especially when someone like Cahuella buys the big one. Talk of a power-vacuum, that kind of shit. Thing is, I'm surprised either of you two made it out alive. I heard some extreme shit went down in that ambush.'

'I wasn't badly injured,' Dieterling said. 'Tanner was a lot worse off than me. He'd lost a foot.'

'It wasn't that bad,' I said. 'The beam weapon cauterised the wound and stopped the bleeding.'

'Oh yeah, right,' Vasquez said. 'Just a flesh wound, then. I can't get enough of you guys, I really can't.'

'Fine, but can we talk about something else?'

My reticence was more than simply an unwillingness to discuss the incident with Red Hand Vasquez. That was part of it, but an equally important factor was that I just didn't remember the details with any clarity. I might have before I was put under for the recuperative coma – the one in which my foot was regrown – but now the whole incident felt like it had happened in the remote past, rather than a few weeks ago.

I'd sincerely believed that Cahuella would make it, though. At first he seemed to have been the lucky one: the laser pulse had gone right through him without cleaving any vital organs, just as if its trajectory had been mapped in advance by a skilled thoracic surgeon. But complications had set in, and without the means to reach orbit – he would have been arrested and executed as soon as he left the atmosphere – he was forced to accept the best black market medicine he could afford. It had been good enough to repair my leg, but that was exactly the kind of injury the war made commonplace. Complex damage to internal organs required an additional level of expertise which could simply not be bought on the black market.

So he'd died.

And here I was, chasing the man who'd killed Cahuella and his wife; aiming to take him down with a single diamond flèchette from the clockwork gun.

Back before I became a security expert in the employment of Cahuella; back when I was still a soldier, they used to say that I was such a proficient sniper that I could put a slug into someone's head and take out a specific area of brain function. It wasn't true; never had been. But I'd always been good, and I did like to make it clean and quick and surgical.

I sincerely hoped Reivich wouldn't let me down.

To my surprise, the secret passageway opened directly into the heart of the anchorpoint terminal, emerging in a shadowed part of the main concourse. I looked back at the security barrier which we'd avoided; watching the guards scan people for concealed weapons; checking identities in case a war criminal was trying to get off the planet. The clockwork gun, still snug in my pocket, wouldn't have shown up in those scans, which was one of the reasons why I'd opted for it. Now I felt a tinge of irritation that my careful planning had been partially wasted.

'Gents,' Vasquez said, lingering on the threshold, 'this is as far as I go.'

'I thought this place would be right up your street,' Dieterling said, looking around. 'What's wrong? Scared you'd never want to leave again?'

'Something like that, Snake.' Vasquez patted the two of us on the back. 'All right. Go and bring down that postmortal shit-smear, boys. Just don't tell anyone I brought you here.'

16

'Don't worry,' Dieterling said. 'Your role in things won't be overstated.'

'Copacetic. And remember, Snake . . .' He mimed firing a gun again. 'That hunt we talked about . . . ?'

'Consider yourself pencilled in, at least on a provisional basis.'

He vanished back into the tunnel, leaving Dieterling and me standing together in the terminal. For a few moments neither of us said anything, overwhelmed by the strangeness of the place.

We were in the surface-level concourse, a ring-shaped hall which encircled the embarkation and disembarkation chamber at the base of the thread. The concourse's ceiling was many levels above, the intervening space criss-crossed by suspended walkways and transit tubes, with what had once been luxury shops, boutiques and restaurants set into the outer wall. Most of them were closed now, or had been converted into minor shrines or places where religious material could be purchased. There were very few people moving around, with hardly anyone arriving from orbit and only a handful of people walking towards the elevators. The concourse was darker than its designers must have intended, the ceiling scarcely visible, and the whole place had the quality of a cathedral in which, unseen but sensed, some sacred ceremony was taking place; an atmosphere that invited neither haste nor raised voices. At the very edge of hearing was a constant low hum, like a basement full of generators. Or, I thought, like a room full of chanting monks holding the same sepulchral note.

'Has it always been like this?' I said.

'No. I mean, it's always been a shithole, but it's definitely worse than the last time I was here. It must have been different a month or so ago. The place would have been heaving. Most of the people for the ship would have had to come through here.'

The arrival of a starship around Sky's Edge was always something of an event. Being a poor and moderately backwards planet compared with many of the other settled worlds, we were not exactly a key player in the shifting spectrum of interstellar trade. We didn't export much, except the experience of war itself and a few uninteresting bio-products culled from the jungles. We would have happily bought all manner of exotic technological goods and services from the Demarchist worlds, but only the very wealthiest people on Sky's Edge could afford them. When ships paid us a visit, speculation usually had it that they had been been frozen out of the more lucrative markets – the Yellowstone-Sol run, or the Fand-Yellowstone-Grand Teton run – or they had to stop anyway to make repairs. It happened about once every ten standard years, on average, and they always screwed us.

'Is this really where Haussmann died?' I asked Dieterling.

'It was somewhere near here,' he said as we crossed the concourse's great, echoing floor. 'They'll never know exactly where because they didn't have accurate maps back then. But it must have been within a few kilometres of here; definitely within the outskirts of Nueva Valparaiso. At first they were going to burn the body, but then they decided to embalm him; make it easier to hold him up as an example to others.'

'But there was no cult then?'

'No. He had a few fruitcake sympathisers, of course – but there was nothing ecclesiastical about it. That came afterwards. The *Santiago* was largely secular, but they couldn't engineer religion out of the human psyche that easily. They took what Sky had done and fused his deeds with what they chose to remember from home; saving this and discarding that as they saw fit. It took a few generations until they had all the details worked out, but then there was no stopping them.'

'And after the bridge was built?'

'By then one of the Haussmann cults had gained possession of the body. The Church of Sky, they called themselves. And – for reasons of convenience, if nothing else – they'd decided that he must have died not just near the bridge but right under it. And that the bridge was not really a space elevator at all – or if it was, that was just a superficial function – but really a sign from God: a ready-made shrine to the crime and glory of Sky Haussmann.'

'But people designed and built the bridge.'

'Under God's will. Don't you understand? It's nothing you can argue with, Tanner. Give up now.'

We passed a few cultists moving in the opposite direction, two men and a woman. I felt a jolt of familiarity when I saw them, but I couldn't remember if I had ever seen any in the flesh before. They wore ash-coloured smocks and both sexes tended to wear their hair long. One man had a kind of mechanical coronet fixed on his skull – maybe some kind of pain-inducing device – while the other man's left sleeve was pinned flatly to his side. The woman had a small dolphin-shaped mark on her forehead, and I remembered the way in which Sky Haussmann had befriended the dolphins aboard the *Santiago*; spending time with the creatures that the other crew shunned.

Recollection of that detail struck me as odd. Had someone told it to me before?

'Have you got that gun ready?' Dieterling said. 'You never know. We might walk round the corner and find the bastard tying his shoelaces.'

I patted the gun to reassure myself that it was still there, then said, 'I don't think it's our day to be lucky, Miguel.'

We stepped through a door set into the concourse's inner wall, the sound of chanting monks now quite unmistakably human; sustaining a note that was almost but not quite perfect.

For the first time since entering the anchorpoint terminal, we could see the thread. The embarkation area into which we'd stepped was a huge circular room encircled by a balcony on which we stood. The true floor was hundreds of metres below us, and the thread plunged from above, emerging through the ceiling via an irised entrance door, then stretching down towards the point where it was truly anchored and where servicing machinery lurked to refurbish and repair the elevators. It was somewhere down there that the sound of the chanting was coming from; voices carried higher by the odd acoustics of the place.

The bridge was a single thin thread of hyperdiamond stretching all the way from ground to synchronous orbit. For almost its entire length it was only five metres in diameter (and most of that was hollow), except for the very last kilometre which dropped into the terminal itself. The thread here was thirty metres wide, tapering subtly as it rose. The extra width served a purely psychological function: too many passengers had baulked at taking the journey to orbit when they saw how slender the thread they would be riding really was, so the bridge owners made the visible portion in the terminal much wider than it needed to be.

Elevator cars arrived and departed every few minutes or so, ascending and descending on opposite sides of the column. Each was a sleek cylinder curved to grip nearly half the thread, attached magnetically. The cars were multi-storeyed, with separate levels for dining, recreation and sleeping. They were mostly empty, their passenger compartments unlit as they glided up or down. There were a handful of people in only every fifth or sixth car. The empty cars were symptomatic of the bridge's economic woes, but not a great problem in themselves. The expense of running them was tiny compared with the cost of the bridge; they had no impact on the schedule of the inhabited cars, and from a distance they looked as full as the others, conveying an illusion of busy prosperity which the bridge owners had long given up hoping would one day approach reality, since the Church had assumed tenancy. And the monsoon season may have given the illusion that the war was in its dog days, but plans were already drawn for the new season's campaigns: the pushes and incursions already simulated in the battle-planners' wargame computers.

A dizzyingly unsupported tongue of glass reached from the balcony to a point just short of the thread, leaving enough space for an elevator to arrive. Some passengers were already waiting on the tongue with their belongings, including a group of well-dressed aristocrats. But no Reivich, and no one in the party who resembled any of Reivich's associates. They were talking amongst themselves or watching news reports on screens which floated around the chamber like square, narrow-bodied tropical fish, flickering with market reports and celebrity interviews.

Near the base of tongue was a booth where elevator tickets were being sold; a bored-looking woman was behind the desk.

'Wait here,' I said to Dieterling.

The woman looked up at me as I approached the desk. She wore a crumpled Bridge Authority uniform and had purple crescents under her eyes, which were themselves bloodshot and swollen.

'Yes?'

'I'm a friend of Argent Reivich. I need to contact him urgently.'

'I'm afraid that isn't possible.'

It was no more than I was expecting. 'When did he leave?'

Her voice was nasal; the consonants indistinct. 'I'm afraid I can't give out that information.'

I nodded shrewdly. 'But you don't deny that he passed through the terminal.'

'I'm afraid I . . .'

'Look, give it a rest, will you?' I softened the remark with what I hoped was an accommodating smile. 'Sorry, it wasn't my intention to sound rude, but this happens to be very urgent. I have something for him, you see – a valuable Reivich family heirloom. Is there any way I can speak to him while he's still ascending, or am I going to have to wait until he reaches orbit?'

The woman hesitated. Almost any information she divulged at this point would have contravened protocol – but I must have seemed so honest, so genuinely distressed by my friend's omission. And so clearly rich.

She glanced down at a display. 'You'll be able to place a message for him to contact you when he arrives at the orbital terminus.' Implying that he hadn't yet arrived; that he was still somewhere above me, ascending the thread.

'I think perhaps I'd better just follow him,' I said. 'That way, there'll be the minimum of delay when he reaches orbit. I can just deliver the relevant item and return.'

'I suppose that would make sense, yes.' She looked at me, perhaps sensing something in my manner that was not as it should have been, but not trusting her own instincts sufficiently to obstruct my progress. 'But you'll have to hurry. The next departure's almost ready for boarding.'

I looked back to the point where the tongue extended out to the thread, seeing an empty elevator slide up from the servicing area.

'You'd better issue me with a ticket then.'

'You'll be needing a return, I presume?' The woman rubbed at her eyes. 'That'll be five hundred and fifty Australs.'

I opened my wallet and pinched out the money, printed in crisp South-lander bills. 'Scandalous,' I said. 'The amount of energy it actually costs the Bridge Authority to carry me to orbit, it should be a tenth the price. But I suppose some of that gets skimmed off by the Church of Sky.'

'I'm not saying that doesn't happen, but you shouldn't speak ill of the Church, sir. Not here.'

'No; that was what I heard. But you're not one of them, are you?'

'No,' she said, handing me the change in smaller bills. 'I just work here.'

The cultists had taken over the bridge a decade or so back, after they had convinced themselves that this place was where Sky had been crucified. They had stormed the place one evening before anyone realised quite what was happening. Haussmann's followers claimed to have rigged the whole terminal with booby-trapped canisters primed with their virus, threatening to discharge them if there was any attempt at an eviction. The virus would carry far enough on the wind to infect half the Peninsula, if there was as much of it in the bridge as the cultists said. They might have been bluffing, but no one was prepared to take the risk of the cult forcing itself on millions of bystanders. So they held the bridge, and allowed the Bridge Authority to continue running it, even if it meant that the staff had to be constantly inoculated against any trace contamination. Given the side-effects of the anti-viral therapy, it obviously wasn't the most popular work on the Peninsula – especially as it meant listening to the endless chanting of the cultists.

She handed me the ticket.

'I hope I make it to orbit in time,' I said.

'The last elevator only left an hour ago. If your friend was on that one . . .' She paused, and I knew there was no *if* about it. 'The chances are very good that he'll still be in the orbital terminal when you arrive.'

'Let's just hope he's grateful, after all this.'

She almost smiled, then seemed to give up halfway through. It was a lot of effort, after all.

'I'm sure he'll be blown away.'

I pocketed the ticket, thanked the woman – miserable as she was, I couldn't help but feel sorry for her having to work here – and then walked back to Dieterling. He was leaning on the low glass wall that surrounded the connecting tongue, looking down at the cultists. His expression was one of detached, watchful calm. I thought back to the time in the jungle when he had saved my life, during the hamadryad attack. He had worn the same neutral expression then: like a man engaged in a chess match against a completely outclassed opponent.

'Well?' he mouthed, when we were within earshot.

'He's already taken an elevator.'

'When?'

'About an hour ago. I've just bought a ticket for myself. Go and buy one as well, but don't act as if we're travelling together.'

'Maybe I shouldn't come with you, bro.'

'You'll be safe.' I lowered my voice. 'There won't be any emigration check-points between here and the exit from the orbital terminal. You can ride up and down without getting arrested.'

'Easy for you to say, Tanner.'

'Yes, but still I'm telling you it'll be safe.'

Dieterling shook his head. 'Maybe it will be, but it still doesn't make much sense for us to travel together; even in the same elevator. There's no guessing how well Reivich has this place under surveillance.'

I was about to argue, but part of me knew that what he said was right. Like

Cahuella, Dieterling couldn't safely leave the surface of Sky's Edge without running the risk of being arrested on war crimes charges. They were both listed in systemwide databases and – save for the fact that Cahuella was dead – they both had hefty bounties on their heads.

'All right,' I said. 'I suppose there's another reason for you to stay. I'll be away from the Reptile House for some time now: three days at the very least. There should be someone competent looking after things back home.'

'Are you certain you can handle Reivich on your own?'

I shrugged. 'It takes only one shot, Miguel.'

'And you're the man to deliver it.' He was visibly relieved. 'Fine then; I'll drive back to the Reptile House tonight. And I'll be watching the newsfeeds avidly.'

'I'll try not to disappoint. Wish me well.'

'I do.' Dieterling reached out and shook my hand. 'Be careful, Tanner. Just because there's no bounty on your head, it doesn't mean you'll be able to walk away without doing a little explaining first. I'll leave it to you to work out how to dispose of the gun.'

I nodded.

'You miss it so badly, I'll buy you one for your birthday.'

He looked at me for a long moment, as if on the point of saying something more, then nodded and turned away from the thread. I watched him leave the chamber, exiting back into the shadowed gloom of the concourse. He began to adjust the coloration of his coat as he walked; his broad-backed figure shimmered as it receded.

I turned around myself, facing the elevator, waiting for my ride. And then slipped my hand into my pocket, resting it against the diamond-hard coolness of the gun.

THREE

'Sir? Dinner will be served on the lower deck in fifteen minutes, if you intend to join the other passengers.'

I jumped, not having heard anyone's footsteps on the staircase which led up to the observation deck. I'd assumed I was completely alone. All the other passengers had retired to their rooms immediately upon boarding – the journey just long enough to justify unpacking their luggage – but I had gone up onto the observation deck to watch our departure. I had a room, but nothing that I needed to unpack.

The ascent had begun with ghostly smoothness. At first it hardly seemed like we were moving at all. There had been no sound, no vibration; just an eerily smooth glide moving imperceptibly slowly, but which was always gaining speed. I had looked down, trying to see the cultists, but the angle of the view made it impossible to see more than a few stragglers, rather than the mass that must have been directly below. We had just been passing through the ceiling iris when the voice had startled me.

I turned around. A servitor had spoken to me, not a man. It had extensible arms and an excessively stylised head, but instead of legs or wheels, its torso tapered to a point below the machine's waist, like a wasp's thorax. It moved around on a rail attached to the ceiling, to which the robot was coupled via a curved spar protruding from its back.

'Sir?' It began again, this time in Norte. 'Dinner will be served . . .'

'No; I understood you first time.' I thought about the risk involved in mixing with real aristocrats, then decided that it was probably less than that involved in remaining suspiciously aloof. At least if I sat down with them I could provide them with a fictitious persona which might pass muster, rather than allowing their imaginations free rein to sketch in whatever details they wished to impose on this uncommunicative stranger. Speaking Norte now – I needed the practice – I said, 'I'll join the others in a quarter of an hour. I'd like to watch the view for a little while.'

'Very well, sir. I shall prepare a place for you at the table.'

The robot rotated around and glided silently out of the observation deck.

I looked back to the view.

I'm not sure quite what I was expecting at that point, but it couldn't have been anything at all like the thing that confronted me. We had passed through the upper ceiling of the embarkation chamber, but the anchorpoint terminal was much taller than that, so that we were still ascending through the upper reaches of the building. And it was here, I realised, that the cultists had achieved the highest expression of their obsession with Sky Haussmann. After his crucifixion they had preserved the body, embalming it and then encasing it in something that had the grey-green lustre of lead, and they had mounted him here, on a great, upthrusting prow that extended inward from one interior wall until it almost touched the thread. It made Haussmann's corpse look like the figurehead fixed beneath the bowsprit of a great sailing ship.

They had stripped him to the waist, spread his arms wide and fixed him to a cross-shaped alloy spar. His legs were bound together, but a nail had been driven through the wrist of his right hand (not the palm; that was a detail the stigma-inducing virus got wrong) and a much larger piece of metal had been rammed through the upper part of his severed left arm. These details, and the expression of numb agony on Haussmann's face, had been rendered mercifully indistinct by the encasing process. But while it was not really possible to read his features, every nuance of his pain was written into the arc of his neck; the way his jaw was clenched as if in the throes of electrocution. They should have electrocuted him, I thought. It would have been kinder, no matter the crimes he had committed.

But that would have been too simple. They were not just executing a man who had done terrible things, but glorifying a man who had also given them a whole world. In crucifying him, they were showing their adoration as fervently as their hate.

It had been like that ever since.

The elevator tracked past Sky, coming within metres of him, and I felt myself flinching; wishing that we could be clear of him as quickly as possible. It was as if the vast space was an echo chamber, reverberating with endless pain.

My palm itched. I rubbed it against the hand-rail, closing my eyes until we were free of the anchorpoint terminal; rising through night.

'More wine, Mr Mirabel?' asked the foxlike wife of the aristocrat sitting opposite me.

'No,' I said, dabbing my lips politely with the napkin. 'If you don't mind, I'll retire. I'd like to watch the view while we climb.'

'That's a shame,' the woman said, pursing her own lips in a pout of disappointment.

'Yes,' said her husband. 'We'll miss your stories, Tanner.'

I smiled. In truth, I'd done little more than grimace my way through an hour of stilted smalltalk while we dined. I had salted the conversation with the odd anecdote now and then, but only to fill the awkward silences which fell across the table when one or other of the participants made what might, within the ever-shifting loom of aristocratic etiquette, be construed as an indelicate remark. More than once I had to resolve arguments between the northern and southern factions, and in the process of doing so I had become the group's default speaker. My disguise must not have been absolutely convincing, for even the northeners seemed to realise that there was not automatically any affiliation between me and the southerners.

It hardly mattered, though. The disguise had convinced the woman in the ticket booth that I was an aristocrat, making her reveal more than she might have done otherwise. It had allowed me to blend in with these aristocrats, too – but sooner or later I would be able to discard it. I was not a wanted man, after all – just someone with a shady past and a few shady connections. There had been no harm in calling myself Tanner Mirabel, either – it was a lot safer than trying to come up with a convincing aristocrat lineage out of thin air. It was, thankfully, a neutral name that had no obvious connotations, aristocratic or otherwise. Unlike the rest of my dinner companions, I couldn't trace my lineage back to the Flotilla's arrival, and it was more than likely that the Mirabel name had arrived on Sky's Edge half a century after that. In aristocrat terms I was posing as a parvenu lout – but no one would have been gauche enough to allude to that. They were all long-lived, tracing their lineages not just back to the Flotilla, but to the passenger manifest, with only one or two intervening generations – and it was perfectly natural to assume that I possessed the same augmented genes and access to the same therapeutic technologies.

But while the Mirabels probably had arrived on Sky's Edge sometime after the Flotilla, they hadn't brought any kind of germline longevity fix with them. Perhaps the first generation had lived a longer-than-normal human lifespan, but that advantage had not been passed to their offspring.

I didn't have the money to buy it off the shelf, either. Cahuella had paid me adequately, but not so well that I could afford to be stung by the Ultras to that extent. And it almost didn't matter. Only one in twenty of the planet's population had the fix anyway. The rest of us were mired in a war, or scraping a living in the war's interstices. The main problem was how to survive the next month, not the next century.

Which meant that the conversation took a decidedly awkward turn as soon as the subject matter turned to longevity techniques. I did my best to just sit back and let the words flow around me, but as soon as there was any kind of dispute I was pushed into the role of adjudicator. 'Tanner will know,' they said, turning to me to offer some definitive statement on whatever had provoked the stalemate.

'It's a complicated issue,' I said, more than once.

Or: 'Well, obviously there are deeper issues at stake here.'

Or: 'It would be unethical of me to speak further on this topic, I'm afraid – confidentiality agreements and all that. You do understand, don't you?'

After an hour or so of that, I was ready for some time on my own.

I stood from the table, made my excuses and left, stepping up the spiral staircase which led to the observation deck above the habitation and dining levels. The prospect of shedding the aristocratic skin pleased me, and for the first time in hours I felt the tiniest glow of professional contentment. Everything was in hand. When I reached the top I had the compartment's servitor prepare me a guindado. Even the way the drink fogged my normal clarity of mind was not unpleasing. There was plenty of time to become sober again: it would be at least seven hours before I needed an assassin's edge.

We were ascending quickly now. The elevator had accelerated to a climb rate of five hundred kilometres per hour as soon as it cleared the terminal, but even at that rate it would still have taken forty hours to make it to the orbital terminal, many thousands of kilometres above our heads. However, the elevator had quadrupled its speed once it no longer had to punch through atmosphere, which had happened somewhere during our first course.

I had the observation deck to myself.

The other passengers, when they had finished dining, would disperse through the five compartments above the dining area. The elevator could comfortably carry fifty people and not appear crowded, but there were only seven of us today, including myself. The total trip time was ten hours. The station's revolution around Sky's Edge was synchronised to the planet's own daily rotation so that it always hung exactly over Nueva Valparaiso, dead above the equator. They had starbridges on Earth, I knew, which reached thirty-six thousand kilometres high – but because Sky's Edge rotated a little faster and had a slightly weaker gravitational pull, synchronous orbit was sixteen thousand kilometres lower. The thread, nonetheless, was still twenty thousand kilometres long – and that meant that the top kilometre of thread was under quite shocking tension from the deadweight of the nineteen thousand kilometres of thread below it. The thread was hollow, the walls a lattice of piezo-electrically reinforced hyperdiamond, but the weight of it, I had heard, was still close to twenty million tonnes. Every time I made a footfall, as I moved around the compartment, I thought of the tiny additional stress my motion was imparting to the thread. Sipping my guindado, I wondered how close to its breaking strain the thread was engineered; how much tolerance the engineers built into the system. Then a more rational part of my mind reminded me that the thread was carrying only a tiny fraction of the traffic it could handle. I stepped with more confidence around the picture window.

I wondered if Reivich was calm enough to take a drink now.

The view should have been spectacular, but even where night had yet to fall the Peninsula was hidden under a blanket of monsoon cloud. Since the world huddled close to Swan in its orbit, monsoon season came once every hundred days or so, lasting no more than ten or fifteen days each short year. Above the sharply curved horizon the sky had darkened through shades of blue towards a deep navy. I could see bright stars now, and overhead lay the single fixed star of the orbital station at the high end of the thread, still a long way above us. I considered sleeping for a few hours, my soldiering years having given me an almost animal ability to snap into a state of total alertness. I swirled what remained of the drink and took another sip. Now that I had made up my mind, I felt fatigue rushing over me like a damburst. It was always there, waiting for the slightest relaxation in my guard.

'Sir?'

I flinched again, only slightly this time, for I recognised the voice of the servitor. The machine's cultured voice continued, 'Sir, there is a call for you from the surface. I can have it sent through to your quarters, or you may view it here.'

I thought about going back to my room, but it was a shame to lose the view. 'Put it through,' I said. 'But terminate the call should anyone else start coming up the stairs.'

'Very well, sir.'

Dieterling, of course – it had to be. He wouldn't have had time to get back to the Reptile House, although by my estimate he should have been about two-thirds of the way there. A shade early for him to try and contact me – and I hadn't expected any contact anyway – but it was nothing to feel any anxiety about.

But instead, the face and shoulders that appeared in the elevator's window belonged to Red Hand Vasquez. Somewhere in the room a camera must have been capturing me and adjusting my image to make it seem as if we were standing face to face, for he looked me straight in the eye.

'Tanner. Listen to me, man.'

'I'm listening,' I said, wondering if the irritation I felt was obvious in my voice. 'What was so important that you needed to reach me here, Red?'

'Fuck you, Mirabel. You won't be smiling in about thirty seconds.' But the way he said it made it seem less like a threat than a warning to prepare for bad news.

'What is it? Reivich pulled another fast one on us?'

'I don't know. I had some guys make some more enquiries and I'm damn sure he's on that thread, the way you think he is – a car or two ahead of you.'

'Then that isn't why you're calling.'

'No. I'm calling because someone's killed Snake.'

I answered reflexively, 'Dieterling?'

As it it could be anyone else.

Vasquez nodded. 'Yeah. One of my guys found him about an hour ago, but he didn't know who he was dealing with, so it took a while for the news to get back to me.'

My mouth seemed to form the words without conscious input from my mind. 'Where was he? What had happened?'

'He was in your car, the wheeler – still parked on Norquinco. You couldn't see there was anyone in it from the street; you had to look inside deliberately. My guy was just checking out the machine. He found Dieterling slumped down inside. He was still breathing.'

'What happened?'

'Someone shot him. Must've waited near where the wheeler was parked, then hung around until Dieterling got back from the bridge. Dieterling must have just got in the wheeler, getting ready to leave.'

'How was he shot?'

'I don't know man; it's not like I'm running an autopsy clinic here, you know?' Vasquez bit his lip before continuing, 'Some kind of beam job, I think. Close range into the chest.'

I glanced down at the guindado I still held. It felt absurd to be standing here talking about my friend's death with a cocktail drink in one hand, as if the matter was only a piece of easy smalltalk. But there was nowhere nearby to put the drink down.

I took a sip and answered him with a coldness that surprised me. 'I prefer beam weapons myself, but they're not what I'd use if I wanted to kill someone without making a fuss. A beam weapon creates more flash than most projectile weapons.'

'Unless it's very close range; like a stabbing. Look, I'm sorry, man, but it looks like that's how it happened. The barrel must've been pushed right into his clothes. Hardly any light or noise – and what there was would've been hidden by the wheeler. There was a lot of partying going on anyway tonight. Somebody started a fire near the bridge, and that was all the excuse the locals needed for a wild night. I don't think anyone would've noticed a beam discharge, Tanner.'

'Dieterling wouldn't have just sat back and let someone do that.'

'Maybe he didn't get much warning.'

I thought about that. On some level the fact of his death was beginning to register, but the implications – not to mention the emotional shock – would take a lot longer. But I could at least force myself to ask the right questions now. 'If he didn't get much warning, either he wasn't paying attention or he thought the person who killed him was someone he knew. He was still breathing, did you say?'

'Yeah, but he wasn't conscious. I don't think we could have done much for him, Tanner.'

'You're sure he didn't say anything?'

'Not to me or the guy who found him.'

'The guy – the man – who found him. Was he someone we'd met tonight?'

'No; he was one of the men I had tailing Reivich all day.'

This was how it was going to carry on, I thought: Vasquez just didn't have the initiative to expand on an answer unless it was dragged kicking and screaming out of him. 'And? How long had this man been in your service? Had Dieterling ever met him before?'

It was painfully slow, but he must have seen the way my questioning was running. 'Hey, no way, man. No way did my guy have anything to do with this. I swear to you, Tanner.'

'He's still a suspect. That goes for anyone we met tonight – including you, Red.'

'I wouldn't have killed him. I wanted him to take me snake hunting.'

There was something so pathetically selfish about that answer that there was a good chance it was true.

'Well, I guess you've blown your chance.'

'I didn't have anything to do with it, Tanner.'

'But it happened on your turf, didn't it?'

He was about to answer, and I was about to ask him what he had done with the body and what he intended to do about it when Vasquez's image dissolved into static. At the same instant there was a powerful flash that seemed to come from everywhere at once, bathing every surface in a sickly white radiance.

It lasted for only a fraction of a second.

It was enough, though. There was something unforgettable about that hard burst of tarnished light; something I had seen once before. Or was it more than once? For a moment I wondered: remembering carnations of white light blossoming against stellar blackness.

Nuclear explosions.

The elevator's illumination dimmed for a few seconds, and I felt my weight grow less and then return to normal.

Someone had let off a nuke.

The electromagnetic pulse must have swept over us, momentarily interfering with the elevator. I hadn't seen a nuke flash since my childhood, one of the war's small sanities being that for the most part it had stayed in the conventional realm. I couldn't estimate the burst yield without knowing how far away the flash had been, but the lack of a mushroom cloud suggested that the explosion had taken place well above the planet's surface. It didn't make much sense: a nuke deployment could only have been the prelude to a conventional assault, and this was the wrong season for it. Elevated bursts made even less sense – military communications networks were hardened against electromagnetic pulse warfare.

An accident, perhaps?

I thought about it for a few more seconds, then heard footsteps racing up the spiral staircase between the elevator's vertically stacked compartments. I saw one of the aristocrats I had just been dining with. I hadn't bothered remembering his name, but the man's levantine bone structure and golden-brown skin almost certainly identified him as a northerner. He was dressed opulently, his knee-length coat dripping shades of emerald and aquamarine. But he was agitated. Behind him, his foxlike wife paused on the last step, eyeing both of us warily.

'Did you see that?' the man asked. 'We came up here to get a better look; you've got the best view from here. It looked pretty big. It almost looked like a . . .'

'A nuke?' I said. 'I think it was.' There were retinal ghosts, pink shapes etched across my vision.

'Thank God it wasn't any closer.'

'Let me see what the public nets say,' said the woman, glancing at a bracelet-shaped display device. It must have tapped into a less vulnerable data network than the one which Vasquez had been using, because she connected immediately. Images and text spilled across the device's discreet little screen.

'Well?' said her husband. 'Do they have any theories yet?'

'I don't know, but . . .' She hesitated, her eyes lingering over something, then frowning. 'No. That can't be true. It just can't be true.'

'What? What are they saying?'

She looked to the man and then to me. 'They're saying they've attacked the bridge. They're saying that the explosion's severed the thread.'

In the unreal moments that followed, the elevator continued to climb smoothly.

'No,' the man said, doing his best to sound calm, but not quite managing it. 'They must be wrong. They've got to be wrong.'

'I hope to God they are,' the woman said, her voice beginning to crack. 'My last neural scan was six months ago . . .'

'Damn six months,' the man said. 'I haven't been scanned this decade!'

The woman breathed out hard. 'Well, they absolutely have to be wrong. We're continuing to have this conversation, aren't we? We're not all scream-ing as we drop towards the planet.' She looked at her bracelet again, frowning.

'What does it say?' the man said.

'Exactly what it said a moment ago.'

'It's a mistake, or a vicious lie, that's all.'

I debated how much it would be judicious to reveal at this point. I was more than just a bodyguard, of course. In my years of service to Cahuella there were few things on the planet which I had not studied – even if that study had usually been motivated by some military application. I didn't pretend to know much about the bridge, but I did know something about hyperdiamond, the artificial carbon alloptrope from which it was spun.

'Actually,' I said, 'I think they could be right.'

'But nothing's changed!' the woman said.

'I wouldn't necessarily expect it to.' I was forcing calm myself, clicking back into the crisis-management state of mind my soldiering years had taught me. Somewhere in the back of my head was a shrill scream of private fear, but I did my best to ignore it for the moment. 'Even if the bridge had been cut, how far below do you think that flash was? I'd say it was at least three thousand kilometres.'

'What the fuck has that got to do with it?'

'A lot,' I said, managing a gallows smile. 'Think of the bridge as being like a rope – hanging all the way down from orbit, stretched out by its own weight.'

'I'm thinking about it, believe me.'

'Good. Now think about cutting the rope midway along its height. The part above the cut is still hanging from the orbital hub, but the part below will immediately begin falling to the ground.'

The man answered now. 'We're perfectly safe, then? We're certainly above the cut.' He looked upwards. 'The thread's intact all the way between here and the orbital terminus. That means if we keep climbing, we'll make it, thank God.'

'I wouldn't start thanking Him just yet.'

He looked at me with a pained expression, as if I were spoiling some elaborate parlour game with needless objections.

'What do you mean?'

'I mean it doesn't mean we're safe. If you cut a long rope hanging under its own weight, the part above the cut's going to spring back.'

'Yes.' He looked at me with threatening eyes, as if I was making my objections out of spite. 'I understand that. But it obviously doesn't apply to us, since nothing's happened.'

'Yet,' I said. 'I never said the relaxation would happen instantly, all along the thread. Even if the thread's been cut below us, it'll take some time for the relaxation wave to climb all the way up to us.'

His question was fearful now.

'How long?'

I had no exact answer for them. 'I don't know. Speed of sound in hyperdiamond isn't different than in natural diamond – about fifteen kilometres a second, I think. If the cut was three thousand kilometres under us, the sound wave should hit us first – about two hundred seconds after the nuke flash. The relaxation wave should move slower than that, I think . . . but it will still reach us before we reach the summit.'

My timing was exquisite, for the sonic pulse arrived just as I had finished speaking, a hard and sudden jolt, as if the elevator had just hit a bump in its two-thousand-kilometre-per-hour ascent.

'We're still safe, aren't we?' asked the wife, her voice only a knife-edge from hysteria. 'If the cut is below us . . . Oh God, I wish we'd been backed-up more often.'

Her husband looked at her snidely. 'It was you who told me those flights to the scanning clinic were too expensive to make a habit out of, darling.'

'But you didn't have to take me literally.'

I raised my voice, silencing them. 'I still think we're in a lot of danger, I'm afraid. If the relaxation wave is just a longitudinal compression along the thread, there's a chance we'll ride it out safely. But if the thread starts picking up any kind of sideways motion, like a whip . . .'

'What the fuck are you,' the man asked, 'some kind of engineer?'

'No,' I said. 'Another kind of specialist entirely.'

More footfalls on the stairs now as the rest of the group came up. The jolt must have convinced them something was seriously wrong.

'What's happening?' asked one of the southerners, a burly man a foot taller than anyone else in the elevator.

'We're riding a severed thread,' I answered. 'There are spacesuits aboard this thing, aren't there? I suggest we get into them as quickly as possible.'

The man looked at me as if I were insane. 'We're still ascending! I don't give a damn what happened below us; we're fine. They built this thing to take a lot of crap.'

'Not this much,' I said.

By now the servitor had arrived as well, suspended from its ceiling rail. I asked it to show us to the suits. It should not have been necessary to ask, but this situation was so far beyond the servitor's experience that it had completely failed to detect any threat to its human charges. I wondered if the news of the severed thread had reached the orbital station. Almost certainly it had – and almost certainly there was nothing that could be done for the elevators still on the thread.

Still, it was better to be on the upper part of the thread than the part below the severing point. I imagined a thousand-kilometre-high section below the cut. It would take several minutes for the top of the thread to smash into the planet below – in fact, for a long while it would seem to hang magically, like a rope trick. But it would still be falling, and there was nothing in the world that could stop it. A million tonnes of thread, slicing down into the atmosphere, laden with cars, some of them occupied. It would be a slow and quite terrifying way to die.

Who could have done this?

It was too much to believe that it didn't have something to do with my ascent. Reivich had tricked us in Nueva Valparaiso, and if it hadn't been for the bridge attack I would have still been trying to assimilate the fact of Miguel Dieterling's death. I couldn't imagine Red Hand Vasquez having anything to do with the explosion, even though I hadn't completely ruled him out of the frame for my friend's murder. Vasquez just didn't have the imagination to attempt something like this, let alone the means. And his cultist indoctrination would have made it very hard for him to even think of harming the bridge in any way. Yet someone appeared to be trying to kill me. Maybe they had put a bomb aboard one of the elevators rising below, thinking I was on it, or would be on one of those below the cut point – or maybe they had fired a missile and misjudged the point to aim for. It could have been Reivich, but only in the technical sense – he had friends with the right influence. But I'd never figured him as someone capable of an act of that ruthlessness: casually wiping out of existence a few hundred innocents just to ensure the death of one man.

But maybe Reivich was learning.

We followed the servitor to the emergency space suit lockers, each of which held one vacuum suit. They were of antique design by spacefaring standards, requiring the user to physically insert themselves in the garment rather than have it enfold around them. They all appeared to be one size too small, but I donned my suit quickly enough, with the dexterous ease with which one might slip on a suit of combat armour. I was careful to hide the clockwork gun in one of the suit's capacious utility pockets, where there should have been a signal flare.

No one saw the gun.

'This isn't necessary!' the southern aristocrat was saying. 'We don't need to wear any damn—'

'Listen,' I said, 'when the compression wave hits us – which it will do any second – we could be flung sideways with enough force to break every bone in your body. That's why you need to be wearing a suit. It'll offer some protection.'

Maybe not enough, I thought.

The six of them fumbled with their suits with varying degrees of confidence. I helped the others, and after a minute or so they were ready, except for the huge aristocrat, who was still complaining about the fit of the suit, as if he had all the time in the world to worry about it. Troublingly, he began to eye the other suits in the closet, wondering perhaps if they were all truly of the same size.

'You don't have time. Just get the thing sealed and worry about cuts and bruises later.'

Below, I imagined the vicious kink in the thread racing toward us, gobbling the kilometres as it climbed. By now it must have already passed the lower elevators. I wondered if it would be violent enough to fling the car off the thread.

I was still thinking about it when it hit.

It was much worse than I had imagined it would be. The elevator jerked to one side, the force of it slamming all seven of us against the inner wall. Someone broke a bone and started screaming, but almost immediately we were flung in the opposite direction, crashing against the clear arc of the picture window. The servitor broke loose from its ceiling rail and fell past us. Its hard steel body daggered into the glass, but though the glass fractured into a webwork of white lines, it managed not to break. Gravity fell as the elevator decelerated on the thread; some element in its induction motor had been damaged by the whiplash.

The southern aristocrat's head was a vile red pulp, like an over-ripe fruit. As the whiplash oscillations died down, his body tumbled limply around the cabin. Someone else started screaming. They were all in a bad way. I might even have had injuries of my own, but for the moment adrenalin was whiting them out.

The compression wave had passed. At some point, I knew, it would reach the end of the thread and be reflected back down again – but that might be hours from now, and it would not be so violent as before, its energies bled into heat.

For a moment I dared to think that we might be safe.

Then I thought about the elevators below us. They might have slowed down as well, or even been flung off the thread completely. Automatic safety systems may have come on-line – but there was no way to know for sure. And if the car below was still ascending at normal speed, it would run into us very soon indeed.

I thought about it for a few moments before speaking, raising my voice above the moans of the injured. 'I'm sorry,' I said. 'But there's something I've just thought of . . .'

There was no time to explain. They'd just have to follow me or take the consequences of staying in the elevator. Not even time to get to the elevator's emergency airlock; it would take at least a minute to cycle all seven – or six now – of us through it. Besides, the further we could get away from the thread, the safer we'd be if there was a collision between the elevators.

There was really only one option.

I retrieved the clockwork gun from my suit pouch, gripping it clumsily in my gloved fingers. There was no way to aim it with any precision, but thankfully, none was called for. I merely pointed the gun in the general direction of the fracture pattern left on the glass by the falling servitor.

Someone tried to stop me, not understanding that what I was doing might save their lives, but I was stronger; my finger pulled the trigger. In the gun, nano-scale clockwork unravelled, unleashing a ferocious pulse of stored molecular-binding energy. A haze of flèchettes ripped from the barrel, shattering the glass, creating a widening network of fractures. The window puckered outward, straining, and then broke into a billion white shards. The storm of air hurled all of us through the ragged opening, into space.

I held onto the gun, clinging to it as if it were the only solid thing in the universe. I looked around frantically, trying to orientate myself relative to the others. The wind had knocked them all in different directions, like the fragments of a starshell, but though our trajectories were different, we were all falling downward.

34

Below was only planet.

My suit spun slowly, and I saw the elevator again, still attached to the thread, climbing away above me as I fell, growing smaller by the second. Then there was an almost subliminal flash of motion as the elevator which had been riding the thread below flashed by, still climbing at normal ascent speed, and an instant later an explosion almost as bright and quick as one of the nuke flashes.

When the flash had gone, there was nothing left at all – not even thread.

FOUR

Sky Haussmann was three when he saw the light.

Years later, in adulthood, that day would be his first clear memory: the earliest that he could clearly anchor to a time and a place and know to be something from the real world, rather than some phantasm which had transgressed the hazy border between a child's reality and its dreams.

He had been banished to the nursery by his parents. He had disobeyed them by visiting the dolphinarium: the dark, dank, forbidden place in the belly of the great ship *Santiago*. But it was Constanza who had really led him astray; she who had taken him through the warren of train tunnels, walkways, ramps and stairwells to reach the place where the dolphins were hidden. Constanza was only two or three years older than Sky, but in his eyes she was almost fully grown; supremely wise in the ways of the adults. Everyone said Constanza was a genius; that one day – perhaps when the Flotilla was nearing the end of its long, slow crossing – she would become the Captain. It was said half in jest but half in seriousness as well. Sky wondered if she would make him her second-in-command when that day came, the two of them sitting together in the control room he had still never visited. It was not such a ridiculous idea: the adults also kept telling him that he was an unusually clever child as well; even Constanza was sometimes surprised at the things he came out with. But for all Constanza's cleverness, Sky would later remind himself, she was not infallible. She had known how to reach the dolphinarium without anyone seeing them, but she had not quite known how to get them back unseen.

It had been worth it, though.

'The grown-ups don't like them,' Constanza had said, when they had reached the side of the tank which held the dolphins. 'They'd rather they didn't exist at all.'

They stood on drainage grilles slick with spilled water. The tank was a high-sided glass enclosure bathed in sickly blue light, reaching away for tens of metres into the darkness of the hold. Sky peered into the gloom. The dolphins were purposeful grey shapes somewhere in the turquoise distance, their outlines constantly breaking up and reforming in the liquid play of light. They looked less like animals than things carved from soap; slippery and not quite real.

Sky had pressed his hand against the glass. 'Why don't they like them?'

Constanza's reply was measured. 'Something's not quite right with them, Sky. These aren't the same dolphins the ship had when it left Mercury. These are the grandchildren, or the great-grandchildren – I'm not sure which. They've never known anything except this tank, and nor have their parents.'

'I've never known anything except this ship.'

'But you're not a dolphin; you weren't expecting oceans to swim in.' Constanza had paused because one of the animals was swimming towards them. It had left its companions at the far end of the tank, huddled around what looked like a set of television screens showing different pictures. Now that it emerged into the volume of clear water immediately beyond the glass, it assumed a presence it had lacked a moment earlier; suddenly it was a large, potentially dangerous thing of muscle and bone, rather than something bordering on translucence. Sky had seen photos of dolphins in the nursery, and there was something not quite right about this creature: a network of surgically fine lines encased its skull, and there were geometric bumps and ridges around its eyes; evidence of hard metal and ceramic things buried just below the dolphin's flesh.

'Hello,' Sky said, tapping the glass.

'That's Sleek,' Constanza said. 'I think so, anyway. Sleek's one of the oldest ones.'

The dolphin looked at him, the sly curve of its jaw making the scrutiny appear both benign and demented. Then it whiplashed around so that it was face-on to him and Sky felt the glass reverberate with unheard vibration. Something formed in the water in front of Sleek, sketched in arcs of transient bubbles. At first the trails of bubbles were random – like an artist's preliminary brushstrokes – but then they became more structured and deliberate, Sleek's head jerking animatedly as if the creature was in the throes of electrocution. The display lasted for only a handful of seconds, but what the dolphin was shaping was unmistakably a face, rendered three-dimensionally. The form lacked any fine details, but Sky knew that it was more than just a suggestion that his subconscious was creating from a few random bubble-trails. It was too symmetric and well-proportioned for that. There was emotion there as well, though it was almost certainly horror or fear.

Sleek, his work done, departed with a contemptuous flick of his tail.

'They hate us as well,' Constanza said. 'But you can't really blame them for that, can you?'

'Why did Sleek do that? How?'

'There are machines in Sleek's melon – that bump between its eyes. They're

37

implanted when they're babies. The melon's what they normally make sound with, but the machines let them focus the sound more precisely, so they can draw with bubbles. And there are little things in the water – micro-organisms – which light up when the sound hits them. The people who made the dolphins wanted to be able to communicate with them.'

'You'd have thought the dolphins would be grateful.'

'Maybe they would be – if they didn't keep having to have operations. And if they had somewhere else to swim other than this horrible place.'

'Yes, but when we reach Journey's End . . .'

Constanza looked at him with sad eyes. 'It'll be too late, Sky. For these ones, anyway. They won't be alive then. We'll even be grown-up; our parents old or dead.'

The dolphin came back with another, slightly smaller companion and the two of them began to draw something in the water. It looked like a man being pulled apart by sharks, but Sky turned away before he could be certain.

Constanza continued, 'And they're too far gone anyway, Sky.'

Sky turned back to the tank. 'I still like them. They're still beautiful. Even Sleek.'

'They're bad, Sky. Psychotic, that's the word my father uses.' She said it with not-quite-convincing hesitation, as if slightly ashamed of her own fluency.

'I don't care. I'll come back and see them again.' He tapped the glass and spoke much louder. 'I'll come back, Sleek. I like you.'

Constanza, though she was only slightly taller than him, patted Sky maternally on the shoulder. 'It won't make any difference.'

'I'll still come.'

The promise, as much to himself as to Constanza, had been sincere. He did want to understand the dolphins, to communicate with them and in some way alleviate their misery. He imagined the bright, wide oceans of Journey's End – Clown, his friend in the nursery, had told him that there would be oceans – and imagined the dolphins suddenly freed from this dark, dismal place. He pictured them swimming with people; creating joyous sound-pictures in the water; the memory of the time aboard the *Santiago* fading like a claustrophobic dream.

'C'mon,' Constanza said. 'We'd better be going, Sky.'

'You'll bring me back, won't you?'

'Of course, if that's what you want.'

And they had left the dolphinarium and commenced the intricate return trip, the two of them working their way through the *Santiago*'s dark interstices; children trying to find their way through an enchanted forest. Once or twice they passed adults, but Constanza's demeanour was so confident that they were never questioned – not until they were well within the small part of the ship which Sky considered familiar territory.

It was there that his father had found them.

Titus Haussmann was a stern but kindly figure amongst the *Santiago*'s living; a man whose authority had been earned through respect rather than fear. He towered over the two of them, but Sky felt no real anger emanate from him; only relief.

'Your mother's been worried sick,' his father said. 'Constanza – I'm deeply disappointed in you. I always had you down as the sensible one.'

'He only wanted to see the dolphins.'

'Oh, the dolphins, was it?' His father sounded surprised, as if this was not quite the answer he had been expecting. 'I thought it was the dead that interested you, Sky – our beloved *momios*.'

True enough, Sky thought – but one thing at a time.

'And now you're sorry,' his father continued. 'Because they weren't what you were expecting, were they? I'm sorry, too. Sleek and the others are sick in the head. The kindest thing we could do would be to put them all to sleep, but they keep being allowed to raise young, and each generation's more . . .'

'Psychotic,' Sky said.

'. . . yes.' His father regarded him strangely. 'More psychotic than the last. Well, now that your vocabulary's showing such tremendous growth, it would be a shame to stifle it, don't you think? A shame to deny you the potential to enlarge it?' He ruffled Sky's hair. 'I'm talking about the nursery, young man. A spell in it, where you can't come into any harm.'

It was not that he hated the nursery, or even especially disliked it. But when he was banished there it could not help but feel like a punishment.

'I want to see my mother.'

'Your mother's outside the ship, Sky, so there's no use running to her for a second opinion. And you know if you did she'd say exactly the same thing. You've disobeyed us and you need to be taught a lesson.' He turned to Constanza, shaking his head. 'As for you, young madam, I think it might be for the best if you and Sky were not to play together for a period of time, don't you think?'

'We don't play,' Constanza said with a scowl. 'We talk, and explore.'

'Yes,' Titus said, with a long-suffering sigh, 'and visit parts of the ship you're expressly not allowed to go to. That, I'm afraid, can't go unpunished.' He softened his voice now, as he always did when he was about to discuss something of genuine importance. 'This ship is our home – our only real home – and we have to feel like we live here. That means feeling safe in the places where it's right to do so – and knowing where it isn't safe to go. Not because there are monsters or anything silly like that, but because there are dangers – adult dangers. Machinery and power systems. Robots and drop shafts. Believe me, I've seen what happens when people go into places they're not meant to go, and it usually isn't very pleasant.'

Sky did not doubt his father for an instant. As head of security aboard a ship which generally enjoyed political and social harmony, Titus Haussmann's duties usually concerned accidents and the very occasional suicide. And although Titus had always spared Sky the more intimate details of how it was possible to die aboard a ship like the *Santiago*, Sky's imagination had done all the rest.

'I'm sorry,' Constanza said.

'Yes – I'm sure you are, but that doesn't change the fact that you took my son into forbidden territory. I'll be speaking to your parents, Constanza, and I don't think they'll be best pleased. Now run along home, and perhaps in a week or two we'll review the situation. Very well?'

She nodded, said nothing, and left along one of the curving corridors which radiated away from the intersection where Titus had cornered them. It was not really far to her parents' domicile – no part of the *Santiago*'s major habitation section was far from any other part – but the ship's designers had cunningly avoided making any route too direct, except for the emergency crawlways and the train lines which reached down the spine. The snaking general-use corridors gave the illusion that the ship was considerably larger than its true size, and two families could live almost next to each other and feel that they lived in entirely different districts.

Titus escorted his son back to their dwelling. Sky was sorry that his mother was outside, for – despite what Titus had said – her punishments were generally a shade more lenient than those his father prescribed. He dared to hope that she was already back aboard ship, having returned from her shift early, the work on the hull completed ahead of schedule, and that she would be waiting for them when they reached the nursery. But there was no sign of her.

'In,' Titus said. 'Clown will take care of you. I'll be back to let you out in two, possibly three hours.'

'I don't want to go in.'

'No – and if you did, it wouldn't be much of a punishment, would it?'

The nursery door opened. Titus propelled his son into the room without stepping across the threshold himself.

'Hello, Sky,' said Clown, who was waiting for him.

There were many toys in the nursery, and some of them were capable of holding limited conversations – even, fleetingly, giving the impression of true intelligence. Sky sensed that these toys were built for children of about his age, designed to mesh with a typical three-year-old's view of the world. In most cases, he had begun to find them simplistic and stupid not long after his second birthday. But Clown was different; not really a toy at all, although not quite a person either. Clown had been with Sky for as long as he remembered, confined to the nursery, but not always present even then. Clown could not touch things, or allow himself to be touched by Sky, and when Clown spoke, his voice did not come from quite the place where Clown stood – or seemed to be standing.

Which was not to say that Clown was a figment of his imagination; without influence. Clown saw everything that happened in the nursery and was punctilious in telling Sky's parents when he had done something that required reprimanding. It was Clown who told his parents he had broken the rocking horse, that it had not been – as he had tried to make them think – the fault of one of the other smart toys. He had hated Clown for that betrayal, but not for long. Even Sky had understood that Clown was, apart from Constanza, the only real friend he had, and that there were some things Clown knew that were beyond even Constanza.

'Hello,' Sky said, mournfully.

'You've been banished here, I see, for visiting the dolphins.' Clown stood alone in the plain white room, the other toys concealed tidily away. 'That wasn't the right thing to do, was it, Sky? I could have shown you dolphins.'

'Not the same ones. Not real ones. And you've shown them to me before.'

'Not like this. Watch!'

And suddenly the two of them were standing up in a boat, out at sea, under a blue sky. All around them the waves were broken by cresting dolphins, their backs like wet pebbles in the sunlight. The illusion of being at sea was marred only by the narrow black windows which ran along one side of the room.

In a story book, Sky had once found a picture of someone else like Clown, dressed in puffed-out, striped clothes with big white buttons, with a comical, permanently smiling face framed by bouffant orange hair under a soft, sagging striped hat. When he touched the picture in the book, the clown moved and did the same kinds of tricks and vaguely amusing things that his own Clown did. Sky remembered, dimly, a time when his response to the Clown's tricks had been to laugh and clap, as if there were nothing more that could be asked of the universe than to provide the antics of a clown.

Now, subtly, even Clown had begun to bore him. He humoured Clown, but their relationship had undergone a profound sea-change which could never be entirely reversed. To Sky, Clown had become something to be understood; something to be dissected and parameterised. Clown, he now recognised, was something like the bubble-drawing the dolphin had made in the water: a projection carved from light rather than sound. They were not really in a boat, either. Under his feet, the room's floor felt as hard and flat as when his father had pushed him inside. Sky did not quite understand how the illusion was created, but it was perfectly realistic, the walls of the nursery nowhere to be seen.

'The dolphins in the tank – Sleek and the others – had machines in them,' Sky said. He might as well learn something while he was prisoner. 'Why?'

'To help them focus their sonar.'

'No. I don't mean what were the machines for. I mean, who had the idea to put them there in the first place?'

'Ah. That would have been the Chimerics.'

'Who were they? Did they come with us?'

'No, to answer your last question, though they very much wanted to.' Clown's voice was slightly high-pitched and quavery – almost womanly – but never anything other than infinitely patient. 'Remember, Sky, that when the Flotilla left Earth's system – left the orbit of Mercury, and flew into interstellar space – the Flotilla was leaving from a system that was still technically engaged in war. Oh, most of the hostilities had ceased by then, but the terms of ceasefire had still not been completely thrashed out, and everyone was still very much on a war footing; ready to return to the fray at a moment's notice. There were many factions who saw the closing stages of the war as their last chance to make a difference. Some of them, by this time, were little more than highly organised brigands. The Chimerics – or more precisely, the Chimeric faction that created the dolphins – were certainly one of those. The Chimerics in general had taken cyborgisation to new extremes, blending themselves and their animals with machines. This faction had pushed those limits even further, to the point where they were shunned even by the mainstream Chimerics.'

Sky listened and followed what Clown was telling him. Clown's judgement of Sky's cognitive skills was adept enough to prevent a lapse into incomprehensibility, while at the same time forcing Sky to concentrate intently on his every word. Sky was aware that not all three-year-olds could have understood what Clown was saying, but that did not concern him in the least.

'And the dolphins?'

'Engineered by them. For what purpose, we can't begin to guess. Perhaps to serve as aquatic infantry, in some planned invasion of Earth's oceans. Or perhaps they were simply an experiment which was never completed, interrupted by the war's decline. Whatever the case, a family of dolphins was captured from the Chimerics by agents of the *Confederacion Sudamericana*.'

That, Sky well knew, was the organisation that had spearheaded the construction of the Flotilla. The *Confederacion* had remained studiously neutral for most of the war, concentrating on ambitions beyond the narrow confines of the solar system. After garnering a handful of allies, they had built and launched humankind's first serious attempt at crossing interstellar space.

'We took Sleek and the others with us?'

'Yes, thinking they'd come in useful at Journey's End. But removing the augmentation that the Chimerics had added was a lot harder than it looked. In the end it was easier to leave it in place. Then when the next generation of dolphins was born, it was found that they couldn't communicate with the adults properly unless they had the augmentation as well. So we copied it and implanted it in the young.'

'But they ended up psychotic.'

Clown registered the tiniest flicker of surprise, his answer not immediately forthcoming. Later Sky would learn that in those frozen moments Clown was seeking advice from one of his parents, or one of the other adults, about how best to respond.

'Yes . . .' Clown said finally. 'But that wasn't necessarily our fault.'

'What, not our fault to keep them down in the hold, with only a few cubic metres to swim around in?'

'Believe me, the conditions we keep them in now are vastly preferable to the Chimerics' experimentation lab.'

'But the dolphins can't be expected to remember that, can they?'

'They're happier, trust me.'

'How can you know?'

'Because I'm Clown.' The mask of his face, ever-smiling, pulled into a more agonised smile. 'Clown always knows.' Sky was about ask Clown exactly what he meant by that when there was a flash of light. It was very bright and sudden, but completely silent, and it had come from the window strip along one wall. When Sky blinked he could still see the after-image of the window: a hard-edged pink rectangle.

'What happened?' he asked, still blinking.

But there was something very wrong with Clown, and indeed, with the entire view. In the instant of the flash, Clown had become misshapen, stretched and malformed in all the wrong directions, painted across the walls, his expression frozen. The boat in which they had seemed to be standing curved away in sickeningly distorted perspective. It was as if the entire scene had been rendered in thick wet pain which someone had begun to stir with a stick.

Clown had never allowed that to happen before.

Worse still, the room's source of illumination – the glowing imagery on the walls – became dark, then black. There was no light save for the faintest milky glow from the high-set window. But even that faded after a while, leaving Sky alone in utter darkness.

'Clown?' Sky said, at first quietly, and then with more insistence.

No answer came. Sky began to feel something odd and unwelcome. It came from deep within him; a welling-up of fear and anxiety that had everything to do with a typical three-year-old's response to the situation and nothing to do with the gloss of adulthood and precosity which normally distanced Sky from other children of his age. He was suddenly a small child, alone in the dark, not understanding what was happening.

He asked for Clown again, but there was desperation in his voice; a realisation that Clown would already have answered him if that were possible. No; Clown was gone; the bright nursery had become dark and – yes – cold, and he could hear nothing; not even the normal background noises of the *Santiago*.

Sky crawled until he met the wall, and then navigated around the room, trying to find the door. But when the door shut, it sealed itself invisibly flush, and now he could not locate even the hair-thin crack which would have betrayed its position. There was no interior handle or control, for – had he not been banished to the room – Clown would normally have opened the door at his request.

Sky groped for an appropriate response and found that, whether he liked it or not, one was happening to him anyway. He was starting to cry; something he could not remember having done since he was much younger.

He cried and cried and – however long that took – finally ran out of tears, his eyes feeling sore when he rubbed them.

He asked for Clown again, and then listened intently, and still there was nothing. He tried screaming, but that did no good either, and eventually his throat became too raw for him to continue.

He had probably been alone only for twenty minutes, but now that time stretched onwards to what was almost certainly an hour, and then perhaps two hours, and then tortured multiples of hours. Under any circumstances, that time would have seemed long, but not understanding his plight – wondering maybe if it were some deeper punishment his father had not told him about – it was almost an eternity. Then even the idea that Titus was inflicting this on him began to seem unlikely, and while his body shivered, his mind began to explore nastier avenues. He imagined that the nursery had somehow become detached from the rest of the ship, and that he was falling away through space, away from the *Santiago* – away from the Flotilla – and that by the time anyone knew, it would be far too late to do anything about it. Or perhaps monsters had invaded the ship from beyond the hull, silently exterminating all aboard it, and he was the only person left aboard that they had not yet found, even though it would only be a matter of time . . .

He heard a scratching from one side of the room.

It was, of course, the adults. They worked the door for some time before persuading it to open, and when it did, a crack of amber light spilled across the floor towards him. His father was the first to enter, accompanied by four or five other grown-ups Sky could not name. They were tall, stooping shapes carrying torches. Their faces were ashen in the torch-light; grave as storybook kings. The air that came into the room was colder than it usually was – it made him shiver even more – and the adults' breath stabbed out in dragonlike exhalations.

'He's safe,' his father said, to one of the other adults.

'Good, Titus,' a man answered. 'Let's get him somewhere secure, then we'll continue working our way downship.'

'Schuyler, come here.' His father was kneeling down, his arms open. 'Come here, my boy. You're safe now. No need to worry. Been crying, haven't you?'

'Clown went away,' Sky managed.

'Clown?' one of the others asked.

His father turned to the man. 'The nursery's main educational program, that's all. It would have been one of the first non-essential processes to be terminated.'

44

'Make Clown come back,' Sky said. 'Please.'

'Later,' his father said. 'Clown's . . . taking a rest, that's all. He'll be back in no time at all. And you, my boy, probably want something to eat or drink, don't you?'

'Where's mother?'

'She's . . .' His father paused. 'She can't be here right now, Schuyler, but she sends her love.'

He watched one of the other men touch his father's arm. 'He'll be safer with the other kids, Titus, in the main crèche.'

'He isn't like one of the other kids,' his father said.

Now they were ushering him out, into the cold. The corridor beyond the nursery plunged into darkness in either direction, away from the little pool of light defined by the adults' torches.

'What happened?' Sky said, realising for the first time that it was not just his own microcosm that had been upset; that whatever had happened had touched the world of the adults as well. He had never seen the ship like this before.

'Something very, very bad,' his father said.

FIVE

I came crashing out of the dream of Sky Haussmann and for a moment thought I was still inside another dream, one whose central feature was a terrifying sense of loss and dislocation.

Then I realised it wasn't a dream at all.

I was wide awake, but it felt as if half my mind was still sound asleep: the part that held memory and identity and any comforting sense of how I had ended up where I now found myself; any threadlike connection to the past. What past? I expected to look back and at some point to encounter sharp details – a name; a hint of who I was – but it was like trying to focus on grey fog.

Yet I could still name things; language was still there. I was lying on a hard bed under a thin brown, knitted blanket. I felt alert and rested – and at the same time completely helpless. I looked around and nothing clicked; there was not the slightest tinge of familiarity on any level. I held my hand in front of my face, studying the ridge-lines of veins on the back of it, and it looked only slightly less strange.

Yet I remembered the details of the dream well enough. It had been dazzlingly vivid; less the way a dream ought to be – incoherent, with shifting perspectives and haphazard logic – than a strictly linear slice of documentary. It was as if I had been there with Sky Haussmann; not seeing things from exactly his point of view, but following him like an obsessive phantom.

Something made me turn my hand over.

There was a neat rust-spot of dried blood in the middle of my palm, and when I examined the sheet beneath me, I saw more freckles of dried blood, where I must have been bleeding before I woke up.

Something almost solidified in the fog; a memory almost assuming definition.

I got out of the bed, naked, and looked around me. I was in a room with roughly shaped walls – not hewn from rock, but formed from something like dried clay, painted over with brilliant white stucco. There was a stool adjacent to the bed and a small cupboard, both made from a type of wood I didn't recognise. There was no ornamentation anywhere except for a small brown vase set into an alcove in one wall.

I stared at the vase in horror.

There was something about it that filled me with terror; terror that I knew instantly to be irrational, but couldn't do anything about. So maybe there is some neurological damage, I heard myself say – *you've still got language, but there's something deeply screwed up somewhere in your limbic system, or whatever part of the brain handles that old mammalian innovation called fear.* But as I found the focus of my fear, I realised it wasn't actually the vase at all.

It was the alcove.

There was something hiding in it: something terrible. And when I realised that, I snapped. My heart was racing. I had to get out of the room; had to get away from the thing that I knew made no sense, but which was still turning my blood to ice. There was an open doorway at one end of the room, leading 'outside' – wherever that was.

I stumbled through it.

My feet touched grass; I was standing on a patch of moist, neatly cut lawn surrounded on two sides by overgrowth and rock. The chalet where I'd woken was behind me, set into a rising slope, with the overgrowth threatening to lap over it. But the slope simply kept on rising; assuming an ever-steepening angle – reaching vertical and then curving over again in a dizzying verdant arc, so that the foliage resembled Chinese spinach glued to the sides of a bowl. It was difficult to judge distance, but the world's ceiling must have been about a kilometre over my head. On the fourth side, the ground dropped away a little before resuming its climb on the opposite side of a toylike valley. It rose and rose and met the ground which climbed behind me.

Beyond the overgrowth and rock on either side of me, I could just make out the distant ends of the world, blurred and blued by the haze of intervening air. At first glance, I seemed to be in a very long cylinder-shaped habitat, but that wasn't the case: the sides met each other at either end, suggesting that the overall shape of the structure was that of a spindle: two cones placed back to back with my chalet somewhere near the point of maximum width.

I racked my memory for knowledge of habitat design and came up with nothing except the nagging sense that there was something out of the ordinary about this place.

There was a hot blue-white filament running the length of the habitat; some kind of enclosed plasma tube which must have been able to be dimmed and shaded to simulate sunset and darkness. The greenery was enlivened and counterpointed by small waterfalls and precipitous rockfaces, artfully arranged like details in a Japanese watercolour. On the far side of the world I saw tiered, ornamental gardens; a quilt of different cultivations like a matrix of pixels. Here and there, dotted like white pebbles, I saw other chalets and the occasional larger hamlet or dwelling. Stone roads meandered around the valley's contours, linking chalets and communities. Those near the endpoints of the two cones were closer to the habitat's spin axis and the illusion of gravity must have been weaker there. I wondered if the need for that had been a driving force in the habitat's design.

Just as I was beginning to seriously wonder where I was, something crept out of the undergrowth, picking its way into the clearing via an elaborate set of articulated metal legs. My hand shaped itself around a nonexistent gun, as if, on some muscular level, it had expected to find one.

The machine came to a halt, ticking to itself. The spider legs supported a green ovoid body, featureless except for a single glowing blue snowflake motif.

I stepped backwards.

'Tanner Mirabel?'

The voice came from the machine, but there was something about it which told me the voice didn't belong to the robot. It sounded human and female, and not entirely sure of itself.

'I don't know.'

'Oh dear. My Castellano isn't all it could be . . .' She had said the latter in Norte, but now she shifted to the language I'd spoken, sounding even more hesitant than before. 'I hope you can understand me. I don't get much practice in Castellano. I'm – um – hoping you recognise your name, Tanner. Tanner Mirabel, I should say. Um, Mister Mirabel, that is. Am I making any sense?'

'Yes,' I said. 'But we can speak Norte if it makes it any easier on you. If you can put up with me being the rusty one.'

'You speak both very well, Tanner. You don't mind if I call you Tanner, do you?'

'I'm afraid you could call me just about anything you liked.'

'Ah. Then there is some amnesia, am I correct in assuming that?'

'I'd say there's more than a little, to be honest.'

I heard a sigh. 'Well, that's what we're here for. That is indeed what we're here for. Not that we wish it upon our clients, of course . . . but if, God forgive, they happen to have it, they've really come to the very best place. Not, of course, that they had much choice, though . . . Oh dear, I'm rambling, aren't I? I always do this. You must feel confused enough without me wittering on. You see we weren't expecting that you'd wake quite so soon. That's why there isn't anyone to meet you, you see.' There was another sigh, but this one was more businesslike; as if she was steeling herself to get to work. 'Now then. You're in no danger, Tanner, but it would be best if you stayed by the house for now, until someone arrives.'

'Why. What's wrong with me?'

'Well, you're completely naked, for a start.'

I nodded. 'And you're not just a robot, are you? Well, I'm sorry. I don't usually do this.'

'There's no need at all to apologise, Tanner. No need at all. It's quite right and proper that you should be a little disorientated. You've been asleep for a great length of time, after all. Physically, you may have suffered no obvious ill effects . . . none at all that I can see, in fact . . .' She paused, then seemed to snap out of whatever reverie she was in. 'But mentally, well . . . it's only to be expected, really. This kind of transient memory loss is really much commoner than they would have us believe.'

'I'm glad you used the word "transient" there.'

'Well, usually.'

I smiled, wondered if that was an attempt at humour or just a crass statement of the statistics.

'Who would "they" be, while we're at it?'

'Well, obviously, the people who brought you here. The Ultras.'

I knelt down and fingered the grass, crushing a blade until it left green pulp on my thumb. I sniffed the residue. If this was a simulation, it was an extraordinarily detailed one. Even battle-planners would have been impressed.

'Ultras?'

'You came here on their ship, Tanner. You were frozen for the journey. Now you have thaw amnesia.'

The phrase caused a fragment of my past to fall lopsidedly into place. Someone had spoken to me of thaw amnesia – either very recently or very long ago. It looked like both possibilities might be correct. The person had been the cyborg crewperson of a starship.

I tried to remember what they had told me, but it was like groping through the same grey fog as before, except this time I did have the sense that there were things within the fog; jagged shards of memory: brittle, petrified trees, reaching out stiff branches to reconnect with the present. Sooner or later I was going to stumble into a major thicket.

But for now all I remembered were reassurances; that I should have no qualms about whatever it was they were about to do to me; that thaw amnesia was a modern myth; very much rarer than I had been led to believe. Which must have been a slight distortion of the facts, at the very least. But then the truth – that shades of amnesia were almost normal – wouldn't have been conducive to good business.

'I don't think I was expecting this,' I said.

'Funnily enough, almost no one ever does. The hard cases are the ones who don't even remember ever dealing with Ultras. You're not that badly off, are you?'

'No,' I admitted. 'And that makes me feel a lot happier, you know.'

'What does?'

'Knowing that there's always some poor bastard worse off than me.'

'Hmm,' she said, with a note of disapproval. 'I'm not sure that's *quite* the attitude one should be having, Tanner. On the other hand, I don't think it's going to be very long before you're as right as rain. Not very long at all. Now, why don't you return to the house? You'll find some clothes there that will fit you. And it's not that we're prudish or anything here at the hospice, but you'll catch your death like that.'

'It wasn't intentional, believe me.'

I wondered what she'd make of my chances for a swift recovery if I told her that I'd had to run out of the house because I was terrified by an architectural feature.

'No, of course it wasn't,' she said. 'But do try the clothes on – and if they aren't to your liking, we can always alter them. I'll be along shortly to see how you're doing.'

'Thank you. Who are you, by the way?'

'Me? Oh, no one in particular, I'm afraid. A very small cog in a blessedly large machine, one might say. Sister Amelia.'

Then I hadn't misheard her when she called the place a hospice. 'And where exactly are we, Sister Amelia?'

'Oh, that's easy. You're in Hospice Idlewild, under the care of the Holy Order of Ice Mendicants. What some people like to call Hotel Amnesia.'

It still didn't mean anything to me. I'd never heard of either Hotel Amnesia or the place's more formal name – let alone the Holy Order of Ice Mendicants.

I walked back into the chalet, the robot following me at a polite distance. I slowed as I approached the door back into the house. It was stupid, but though I'd been able to dismiss my fears almost as soon as I was outside, they now came back with almost the same force. I looked at the alcove. It seemed to me to be imbued with deep evil; as if there were something waiting coiled in there, observing me with malignant intent.

'Just get dressed and get out of here,' I said to myself, aloud and in Castellano. 'When Amelia comes, tell her you need some kind of neurological once-over. She'll understand. This sort of thing must happen all the time.'

I inspected the clothes that were waiting for me in a cupboard. Nothing too fancy, and nothing at all that I recognised. They were simple and had a handmade feel to them: a black V-neck jersey and baggy, pocketless trousers, a pair of soft shoes; adequate for padding round the clearing, but not much else. The clothes fitted me perfectly, but even that made them feel wrong, as if it was not something I was used to.

I rummaged deeper in the cupboard, hoping to find something more personal, but it was empty apart from the clothes. At a loss, I sat on the bed and stared sullenly at the textured stucco of the wall, until my gaze passed over the little alcove. After years of being frozen, my brain chemistry must have been struggling back towards some kind of equilibrium, and in the meantime I was getting a taste of what psychotic fear must feel like. I felt a strong temptation to just curl up and block the world from my senses. What kept me from losing it completely was the quiet knowledge that I had been in worse situations – confronted hazards that were just as terrifying as anything my psychotic mind could imprint on an empty alcove – and that I had survived. It hardly mattered that at the moment I couldn't bring any specific incidents to mind. It was enough to know that they had happened, and that if I failed now, I would be betraying a buried part of me which remained fully sane, and perhaps remembered everything.

I didn't have long to wait before Amelia arrived.

She was out of breath and flushed when she entered the house, as if she'd climbed quickly up from the bottom of the valley or cleft I'd seen after I'd awakened. But she was smiling, as if she had enjoyed the exertion for its own sake. She wore a black wimpled vestment, a chained snowflake hanging from her neck. Dusty boots poked out from beneath the hem of her vestment.

'How are the clothes?' she said, placing her hand atop the robot's ovoid head. It might have been to steady herself, but it also looked like a show of affection towards the machine.

'They fit me very well, thanks.'

'You're quite sure of that? It's no trouble at all to change them, Tanner. You'd just have to whip them off, and well . . . we could have them altered in no time.' She smiled.

'They're fine,' I said, studying her face properly. She was very pale; much more so than anyone I had ever seen before. Her eyes almost lacked pigment; her eyebrows were so fine that they looked like they'd been brushed in by an expert calligrapher.

'Oh, good,' she said, as if not completely convinced. 'Do you remember anything more?'

'I seem to remember where I've come from. Which is a start, I suppose.'

'Just try not to force things. Duscha – Duscha's our neural specialist – she said you'd soon begin to remember, but you shouldn't worry if it takes a little while.'

Amelia sat down on the end of the bed where I'd been asleep only a few minutes ago. I had turned the blanket over to hide the speckles of blood from my palm. For some reason I felt ashamed of what had happened and wanted to do my best to make sure Amelia didn't see the wound in my palm.

'I think it might take more than a little while, to be honest.'

'But you do remember that Ultras brought you here. That's more than a lot of them do, as I said. And you remember where you came from?'

'Sky's Edge, I think.'

'Yes. The 61 Cygni-A system.'

I nodded. 'Except we always called our sun Swan. It's a lot less of a mouthful.'

'Yes; I've heard others say that as well. I really should remember these details, but we get people through from so many different places here. I'm all a muddle at times, honestly, trying to keep track of where's where and what's what.'

'I'd agree with you, except I'm still not sure where we are. I won't be sure until my memory comes back, but I'm not sure I've ever heard of the, whatever you said you were . . .'

'Ice Mendicants.'

'Well, it doesn't ring any kind of a bell.'

'That's understandable. I don't think the Order has any presence in the Sky's Edge system. We exist only where there's substantial traffic in and out of a given system.'

I wanted to ask her which system this happened to be, but I assumed she'd get round to that detail in good time.

'I think you're going to have to tell me a little bit more, Amelia.'

'I don't mind. You'll just have to excuse me if this comes out a bit like a prepared speech. I'm afraid you're not the first one I've had to explain all this to – and you won't be the last, either.'

She told me that as an Order, the Mendicants were about a century and a half old – dating from the middle of the twenty-fourth century. That was around the time that interstellar flight broke out of the exclusive control of governments and superpowers and became almost commonplace. By then the Ultras were beginning to emerge as a separate human faction – not just flying ships, but living their entire lives aboard them, stretched out by the effects of time-dilation beyond anything that constituted a normal human lifespan. They continued to carry fare-paying passengers from system to system, but they were not above cutting corners in the quality of the service they offered. Sometimes they promised to take people somewhere and flew to another system entirely, stranding their passengers years of flight-time away from where they wanted to be. Sometimes their reefersleep technology was so old or poorly maintained that their passengers woke massively aged upon arrival, or with their minds completely erased.

It was into this customer care void that the Ice Mendicants came, establishing chapters in dozens of systems and offering help to those sleepers whose revival had not gone as smoothly as might have been wished. It was not just starship passengers they tended to, for much of their work concerned people who had been asleep in cryocrypts for decades, skipping through economic recessions or periods of political turmoil. Often those people would waken with their savings wiped out, their personal possessions sequestered and their memories damaged.

'Well,' I said, 'I guess now you're going to tell me the catch.'

'There's one thing you need to understand from the outset,' Amelia said. 'There *is* no catch. We care for you until you're well enough to leave. If you want to leave sooner than that, we won't stop you – and if you want to stay longer, we can always use an extra pair of hands in the fields. Once you've left the Hospice, you won't owe us anything or hear from us again, unless you wish it.'

'How do you make something like this pay, in that, case?'

'Oh, we manage. A lot of our clients do make voluntary donations once they're healed – but there's no expectation on our part that they will. Our running costs are remarkably low, and we've never been in hock to anyone for the construction of Idlewild.'

'A habitat like this couldn't have come cheap, Amelia.' Everything cost something; even matter that had been shaped by droves of mindless, breeding robots.

'It was a lot cheaper than you'd think, even if we had to accept some compromises in the basic design.'

'The spindle shape? I wondered about that.'

'I'll show you when you're a bit better. Then you'll understand.' She paused and had the robot dispense some water into a little glass. 'Drink this. You must be parched. I imagine you want to know a little more about yourself. How you got here and where *here* is, for instance.'

I took the glass and drank gratefully. The water had a foreign taste to it, but it wasn't unpleasant.

'I'm not in the Sky's Edge system, obviously. And this must be near one of the main centres of traffic, or you wouldn't have built the place in the first place.'

'Yes. We're in the Yellowstone system – around Epsilon Eridani.' She seemed to observe my reaction. 'You don't seem too surprised.'

'I knew it had to be somewhere like that. What I don't remember is what made me come here.'

'That'll come back. You're fortunate, in a way. Some of our clients are perfectly well, but they're just too poor to afford immigration into the system proper. We allow them to earn a small wage here until they can at least afford the cost of a ship to take them to the Rust Belt. Or we arrange for them to spend a period in indentured servitude for some other organisation – quicker, but usually a lot less pleasant. But you won't have to do either, Tanner. You seem to be a man of reasonable means, judging by the funds you arrived with. And mystery, too. It may not mean very much to you, but you were quite a hero when you left Sky's Edge.'

'I was?'

'Yes. There was an accident, and you were implicated in the saving of more than a few lives.'

'I don't remember, I'm afraid.'

'Not even Nueva Valparaiso? That's where it happened.'

It did, faintly, mean something – like a half-familiar reference stirring memories of a book or play experienced years earlier. But the plot and principal protagonists – not to mention the outcome – remained resolutely unclear. I was staring into fog.

'I'm afraid it's still not there. Tell me how I got here, anyway. What was the name of the ship?'

'The *Orvieto*. She would have left your system about fifteen years ago.'

'I must have had a good reason for wanting to be on her. Was I travelling alone?'

'As near as we can tell, yes. We're still processing her cargo. There were twenty thousand sleepers aboard her, and only a quarter of them have been warmed yet. There's no great hurry, when you think about it. If you're going to spend fifteen years crossing space, a few weeks' delay at either end isn't worth worrying about.'

It was odd, but though I couldn't put my finger on it, I did feel that there was something that needed to be done urgently. The feeling it reminded me of was waking from a dream, the details of which I didn't recall, but which none-theless put me on edge for hours afterwards.

'So tell me what you know about Tanner Mirabel.'

'Nowhere near as much as we'd like. But that in itself shouldn't alarm you. Your world is at war, Tanner – has been for centuries. Records are hardly less confused than our own, and the Ultras aren't particularly interested in who they carry, provided they pay.'

The name felt comfortable, like an old glove. A good combination, too. Tanner was a worker's name; hard and to the point; someone who got things done. Mirabel, by contrast, had faint aristocratic pretensions.

It was a name I could live with.

'Why are your own records confused? Don't tell me you had a war here as well?'

'No,' Amelia said, guardedly. 'No; it was something quite different to that. Something quite different indeed. Why? For a moment you almost sounded pleased.'

'Perhaps I used to be a soldier,' I said.

'Escaping with the spoils of war, after committing some unspeakable atrocity?'

'Do I look like someone capable of atrocities?'

She smiled, but there was a decided lack of humour in her expression. 'You wouldn't credit it, Tanner, but we get all sorts through here. You could be anything or anyone, and looks would have very little to do with it.' Then she opened her mouth slightly. 'Wait. There's no mirror in the house, is there? Have you seen yourself since you woke?'

I shook my head.

'Then follow me. A little walk will do you the power of good.'

We left the chalet and followed an ambling path into the valley, Amelia's robot scooting ahead of us like an excited puppy. She was at ease with the machine, but the robot left me feeling intimidated; the way I would have felt if she had walked around with a poisonous snake. I recalled my reaction when the robot had first appeared: an involuntary reaching for a weapon. Not just a theatrical gesture, but an action which felt well-rehearsed. I could almost feel the heft of the gun I lacked, the precise shape of its grip under my palm, a lattice of ballistics expertise lurking just below consciousness.

I knew guns, and I didn't like robots.

'Tell me more about my arrival,' I said.

'As I said, the ship which brought you here was the *Orvieto*,' Amelia said. She's in-system, of course, since she's still being unloaded. I'll show her to you, if you like.'

'I thought you were going to show me a mirror.'

'Two birds with one stone, Tanner.'

The path descended deeper, winding down into a dark, shadowed cleft overhung with a canopy of tangled greenery. This must have been the small valley I had seen below the chalet.

Amelia was right: it had taken me years to reach this place, so a few days spent regaining my memory was an inconsequential burden. But the last thing I felt was patient. Something had been straining at me ever since I had awakened; the feeling that there was something I had to do; something so urgent that even now, a few hours could make all the difference between success and failure.

'Where are we going?' I asked.

'Somewhere secret. Somewhere I shouldn't really take you, but I can't resist. You won't tell, will you?'

'Now I'm intrigued.'

The shadowed cleft took us to the valley floor; to a point maximally distant from the axis of Hotel Amnesia. We were at the rim where the two conic ends of the habitat were joined to each other. It was here that gravity was highest, and I felt the extra effort required to move around.

Amelia's robot came to a halt ahead of us, pivoting around to present its blank ovoid face to us.

'What's up with it?'

'It won't go any further. Programming won't allow it.' The machine was blocking our path, so Amelia took a step off the trail, wading into knee-high grass. 'It won't want us to pass for our own safety, but on the other hand, it won't actively stop us if we make an effort to go around it. Will you, good boy?'

I stepped gingerly past the robot.

'You said something about me being a hero.'

'You saved five lives when the bridge at Nueva Valparaiso came down. The fall of the bridge was all over the news nets, even here.'

As she spoke, I felt like I was being reminded of something told to me before; that I was always only an instant away from remembering it all myself. The bridge had been severed some way up its length by a nuclear explosion, causing the thread below the cut to fall back to ground while the part above the cut whiplashed lethally. The official explanation was that a rogue missile had been responsible; some aspirant military faction's test firing which had gone badly awry and shimmied through the protective screen of anti-missiles around the bridge, but – though I couldn't easily explain it – I had the insistent feeling that there was more to it than that; that my being on the bridge at the same time was not just ill fortune.

'What exactly happened?'

'The car you were in was above the cut. It came to a halt on the thread, and would have been safe there except that there was another car racing up from below. You realised that and persuaded the people with you that their only hope of surviving was to jump into space.'

'Doesn't sound like much of an alternative, even with suits on.'

'No, it didn't – but you knew they'd still stand a chance of surviving. You were quite a long way above the top atmosphere. You had more than eleven minutes to fall before you hit it.'

'Great. What good is an extra eleven minutes if you're going to die anyway?'

'Another eleven minutes of God-given life, Tanner. And it also happened to be enough time for rescue ships to pick you up. They had to skim the atmosphere to grab you all, but they got everyone in the end – even the man who had already died.'

I shrugged. 'I was probably only thinking of my own self-preservation.'

'Perhaps – but only a real hero would even *admit* to thinking that way. That's why I think you might really be Tanner Mirabel.'

'Hundreds of people must have died anyway,' I said. 'Not much of a heroic effort, was it?'

'You did what you could.'

We continued in silence for a few more minutes, the track becoming increasingly overgrown and sketchy until the ground jogged downwards even more, below the level of the valley floor. The extra energy required to move around was sapping my strength.

I was leading now and for a moment Amelia lingered behind me, as if expecting someone else. Then she caught up with me and moved in front. Above, plants arched over, gradually closing off into a dark, verdant tunnel. We pushed on into what was not quite absolute darkness, Amelia more surefooted than I. When it became very dark she turned on a little penlight and poked its thin beam ahead of her, but I suspected the light was more for my benefit than hers. Something told me that she had come down here often enough to know every triphole in the flooring and how to step past it. Eventually, however, the torch became almost superfluous: there was a milky light ahead of us, periodically dimming then returning perhaps once every minute.

'What is this place?' I asked.

'An old construction tunnel, dating from when Idlewild was built. They filled in most of them, but they must have forgotten this one. I come down here a lot on my own when I need to think.'

'You're showing quite some trust by bringing me down here, then.'

She looked back at me, her face almost lost in the gloom. 'You're not the only one I've brought down here. But I *do* trust you, Tanner. That's the odd thing. And it's got very little to do with your being a hero. You seem like a kind man. There's an aura of calm about you.'

'They say the same thing about psychopaths.'

'Well, thank you for that pearl of wisdom.'

'Sorry. I'll shut up now.'

We walked on in mutual silence for a few more minutes, but before very long the tunnel opened out into a cavelike chamber with an artificially flat floor. I took a cautious step onto its glossy surface, and then looked down. The floor was glass, and things were moving beneath it.

Stars. And worlds.

Once every rotation, a beautiful yellow-brown planet hoved into view, accompanied by a much smaller reddish moon. Now I knew where the periodic light had come from.

'That's Yellowstone,' Amelia said, pointing to the larger world. 'The moon with the big chain of craters on it? That's Marco's Eye, named after Marco Ferris, the man who discovered the chasm on Yellowstone.'

Some impulse made me kneel down to get a better look.

'We're pretty close to Yellowstone, then.'

'Yes. We're at the trailing Lagrange point of the moon and the planet; the gravitational balance point sixty degrees behind Marco's Eye in its orbit. This is where most of the big ships are parked.' She waited a moment. 'Look; here they come now.'

A vast conglomeration of ships came into view: sleek and jewelled as ceremonial daggers. Each ship, sheathed in diamond and ice, was as large as a small city – three or four kilometres long – but rendered tiny by the sheer number and distance of them, like a shoal of brilliant tropical fish. They were clustered around another habitat, smaller ships docked around the habitat's rim like sea-urchin spines. The whole ensemble must have been two or three hundred kilometres away. Already it was passing out of sight as the carousel spun, but there was time enough for Amelia to point out the ship which had brought me here.

'There. That one on the edge of the parking swarm is the *Orvieto*, I think.'

I thought of that ship slamming through the interstellar void, cruising just below light for nearly fifteen years, and for a moment I had a visceral grasp of the immensity of space which I had crossed from Sky's Edge, compressed into a subjective instant of dreamless sleep.

'There's no going back now, is there?' I said. 'Even if one of those ships were going back to Sky's Edge, and even if I had the means to get aboard, I wouldn't be returning home. I'd be a hero from thirty years in the past – probably long forgotten. Someone born after me might have decided to classify me as a war criminal and order my execution the instant I was awakened.'

Amelia nodded slowly. 'Most people never go home again, that's true enough. Even if there isn't a war, too much will have changed. But most people have already resigned themselves to that before they leave.'

'You're saying I didn't?'

'I don't know, Tanner. You do seem different, that's for sure.' Suddenly her tone of voice changed. 'Ah, look! There's one of the sloughed hulls!'

'One of the what?'

But I followed her gaze all the same. What I saw was an empty conic shell, looking as huge as one of the ships in the parking swarm, though it was hard to be sure. She said, 'I don't know much about those ships, Tanner, but I know that they're almost alive, in some ways – capable of altering themselves, improving themselves over time, so that they never end up obsolete. Sometimes the changes are all inside, but sometimes they affect the whole shape of the ship – making it larger, for instance. Or sleeker, so it can go closer to the speed of light. Usually when they do that, it's cheaper for the ship to discard its old diamond armour rather than tear it down and rebuild it piece by piece. They call it sloughing – it's like a lizard shedding its skin.'

'Ah.' I understood. 'And I presume they were prepared to sell that armour at a knock-down price?'

'They didn't even sell it – just left the blessed thing lying in orbit, waiting to be rammed into by something. We took it over, stabilised its spin and lined it with rock tailings from Marco's Eye. We had to wait a long time for another piece that matched, but eventually we had two shells we could join together to make Idlewild.'

'Cheap at the price.'

'Oh, it was still a lot of work. But the design works quite well for us. For a start, it takes a lot less air to fill a habitat of this shape than a cylindrical one of the same length. And as we get older and frailer and less able to take care of our duties near the point where the shells were married together, we can spend more and more time working in the low-gravity highlands, gradually approaching the endpoints – closer to heaven, as we say.'

'Not too close, I hope.'

'Oh, it's not so bad up there.' Amelia smiled. 'The old dears can look down on the rest of us, after all.'

There was a sound from behind us; soft footfalls. I tensed, and once again my hand seemed to twitch in expectation of a weapon. A figure, barely visible, stole into the cave. I saw Amelia tense. For a moment the figure waited, its breathing the only sound. I said nothing, but waited patiently for the world to come around again and throw some light on the stranger.

He spoke. 'Amelia, you know you shouldn't come down here. It's not allowed.'

'Brother Alexei,' she said. 'You should know that I'm not alone.'

The echo of his laughter – false and histrionic – reflected from the cave walls. 'That's a good one, Amelia. I know you're alone. I followed you, don't you see? I saw that there was no one with you.'

'Except there is someone with me. You must have seen me when I held back. I thought you were following us, but I couldn't be sure.'

I said nothing for a moment.

'You were never a very good liar, Amelia.'

'Perhaps not, but right now I'm telling the truth – aren't I, Tanner?'

I spoke just as the light returned, revealing the man. I already knew him to be another Mendicant from the way Amelia had greeted him, but he was dressed differently from Amelia, in a simple hooded black cloak, sewn on its chest with the snowflake motif. His arms were crossed casually beneath the motif and his face bore an expression less of serenity than hunger. He looked the hungry sort, too: pale and cadaverous, his cheekbones and jaw etched with shadow.

'She's telling the truth,' I said.

He took a step closer. 'Let me get a better look at you, slush puppy.' His deepset eyes gleamed in the darkness, inspecting me. 'Been awake long, have you?'

'Just a few hours.' I stood, allowing him to see what I was made of. He was taller than me, but we probably weighed about the same. 'Not long, but long enough to know that I don't like being called slush puppy. What's that – slang amongst Ice Mendicants? You're not as holy as you pretend, are you?'

Alexei smirked. 'What would you know?'

I stepped towards him, my feet pressing against the glass, stars wheeling under them. I thought I had the picture now. 'You like to bother Amelia, don't you? That's how you get your kicks – by following her down here. What do you do when you catch her alone, Alexei?'

'Something divine,' he said.

I could see why she had hesitated now, allowing Alexei to spy on her and conclude that she was alone. On this one occasion she must have wanted him to follow her because she knew I'd be there as well. How long had this been going on – and how long had she had to wait before reviving someone she thought she could trust?

'Be careful,' Amelia said. 'This man is the hero of Nueva Valparaiso, Alexei. He saved lives there. He isn't just some meek tourist.'

'What is he, then?'

'I don't know,' I said, answering for her. But in the same breath I crossed the two metres that spaced me from Alexei, pressing him hard against the cave wall, locking an arm under his chin, applying just enough pressure to make him think I was choking him. The movement felt as effortless and fluid as a yawn.

'Stop . . .' he said. 'Please . . . you're hurting me.'

Something dropped from his hand: a sharp-edged cultivating tool. I kicked it across the floor.

'Silly boy, Alexei. If you're going to arm yourself, don't throw your weapon away.'

'You're choking me!'

'If I was choking you, you wouldn't be able to talk. You'd be unconscious about now.' But I released the pressure anyway, shoving him towards the tunnel. He tripped on something and hit the ground hard. Something rolled from his pocket; another makeshift weapon, I presumed.

'Please . . .'

'Listen to me, Alexei. That was just a warning. Next time we cross paths, you walk away with a broken arm, understand? I don't want you here again.' I picked up the cultivating tool and threw it towards him. 'Get back to your gardening, big boy.'

We watched him get up, mumble something under his breath then scuttle back into the darkness.

'How long has that been going on?'

'A few months.' Her voice was very quiet now. We watched Yellowstone and the swarm of parked ships rotate into view again before she continued, 'What he said – what he implied – never happened. All he's ever done is just scare me. But every time he goes a bit further. He frightens me, Tanner. I'm glad you were with me.'

'It was deliberate, wasn't it? You were hoping he would try something today.'

'Then I was afraid you might kill him. You could have, couldn't you? If you had wanted to.'

Now that she formed the question I had to ask it of myself as well. And I saw that killing him would have been easy for me; simply a technical modification of the restraint I had imposed. It wouldn't have demanded any more effort; would hardly have impinged on the calm I had felt during the whole incident.

'He wouldn't have been worth the effort,' I said, reaching over to pick up the thing which had slipped from his pocket. No weapon, I saw now – or at least nothing with which I was familiar.

It was more like a syringe, containing some fluid which could have been black or dark-red, but was most likely the latter.

'What's this?'

'Something he shouldn't have had in Idlewild. Give it to me, will you? I'll have it destroyed.'

60

I passed the hypodermic device willingly; it was of no use to me. As she pocketed it with something close to revulsion, Amelia said, 'Tanner, he'll be back, when you've left us.'

'We'll worry about that later – and I'm not going anywhere in a hurry, am I? Not with my memory in the state it is.' Trying to lighten the mood, I added, 'You said something about showing me my face, earlier on.'

She answered hesitantly. 'Yes, I did, didn't I?' Then she fished out the little penlight she had used in the tunnel and instructed me to kneel down again, looking into the glass. When Yellowstone and its moon had gone by and the cave had become dark again, she shone the torch on my face. I looked at my reflection in the glass.

There was no shocking sense of unfamiliarity. How could there have been, when I had already traced the outline of my face with my fingers a dozen times since waking? I already sensed that my face would be blandly handsome, and that was the case. It was the face of a moderately successful actor or a motivationally suspect politician. A dark-haired man in his early forties – and, without quite knowing from where I had dredged this fact, I knew that on Sky's Edge, that more or less meant exactly what it said; that I could not be drastically older than I seemed, for our methods of longevity extension lagged centuries behind the rest of humanity.

Another shard of memory clicking into place.

'Thank you,' I said, when I had seen enough for now. 'I think that helped. I don't think my amnesia's going to last forever.'

'It almost never does.'

'Actually, I was being flippant. Are you saying there are people who never get their memories back?'

'Yes,' she said, with unconcealed sadness. 'Mostly, they never function well enough to immigrate.'

'What happens to them, in that case?'

'They stay here. They learn to help us; to cultivate the terraces. Sometimes they even join the Order.'

'Poor souls.'

Amelia stood, beckoning me to follow her. 'Oh, there are worse fates, Tanner. I should know.'

SIX

Ten years old, he moved with his father across the curved, polished floor of the freight bay, their booted feet squeaking on the high-gloss surface, the two of them suspended above their own dark reflections; a man and a boy forever walking up what looked to the eye like an ever-steepening hill, but which always felt perfectly level.

'We're going outside, aren't we?' Sky said.

Titus looked down at his son. 'Why do you assume that?'

'You wouldn't have brought me here otherwise.'

Titus said nothing, but the point could not be denied. Sky had never been in the freight bay before; not even during one of Constanza's illicit trips into the *Santiago*'s forbidden territory. Sky remembered the time she had taken him to see the dolphins, and the punishment that had ensued, and how that punishment had been eclipsed by the ordeal that had followed: the flash of light and the period he had spent trapped alone and cold in the utter darkness of the nursery. It seemed so long ago now, but there were still things about that day that he did not fully understand now; things he had never persuaded his father to speak about. It was more than his father's recalcitrance; more than simply Titus's grief at the death of Sky's mother. The censorship by omission – it was more subtle than a simple refusal to discuss the incident – extended to every adult Sky had spoken to. No one would speak of that day when the whole ship had turned dark and cold, yet to Sky the events were still clearly fixed in his memory.

After what felt like days – and now that he thought about it, it probably *had* been days – the adults had made the main lights come on again. He noticed when the air-circulators began to work – a faint background ambience which he had never really noticed until it had ceased. In all that time, his father told him later, they had been breathing unrecirculated air; slowly turning staler and staler as the hundred and fifty waking humans dumped more and more carbon dioxide back into their atmosphere. In a few more days it would have started causing serious problems, but now the air became fresher and the ship slowly warmed back up to the point where it was possible to move along the corridors without shivering. Various secondary systems that had been unavailable during the blackout were brought hesitantly back online. The trains which ferried equipment and technicians up and down the spine began to run again. The ship's information nets, which had been silent, could now be queried. The food improved, but Sky had hardly noticed that they had been eating emergency rations during the blackout.

Yet still none of the adults would discuss exactly what had happened.

Eventually, when something like normal shipboard life had returned, Sky managed to sneak back into the nursery. The room was lit, but to his surprise everything looked more or less as he had left it: Clown frozen in that strange shape he had assumed after the flash. Sky had crept closer to examine the distorted form of his friend. He could see now that all Clown had ever been was a pattern in the tiny coloured squares that covered the nursery's walls, floor and ceiling. Clown had been a kind of moving picture that only made sense – only looked *right* – when seen from precisely Sky's point of view. Clown had appeared to be physically present in the room – not simply drawn on the wall – because his feet and legs had been drawn on the floor as well, but with a perspective distorted such that it looked perfectly real from where Sky happened to be. The room must have mapped Sky and his direction of gaze. Had he been able to shift his viewpoint fast enough, faster than the room could recompute Clown's image, he would perhaps have seen through that trick of perspective. But Clown was always much faster than Sky. For three years, he had never doubted that Clown was real, even if Clown could never touch or be touched by anything.

His parents had abdicated responsibility to an illusion.

Now, however – in a mood of eager forgiveness – he pushed such thoughts from his mind, awed by the sheer size of the freight bay and the prospect of what lay ahead. What made the place all the larger was the fact that the two of them were quite alone, surrounded only by a puddle of moving light. The rest of the chamber was suggested rather than clearly seen; its dimensions hinted at by the dark, looming shapes of cargo containers and their associated handling machines receding along curved lines into blackness. Parked here and there were various spacecraft; some little more than single-person tugs or broomsticks designed for flying immediately outside the ship, while others were fully pressurised taxi craft, built for crossing to the other Flotilla craft. The taxis could enter an atmosphere in an emergency, but they were not designed to make the return trip to space. The delta-winged landers which would make multiple journeys down to the surface of Journey's End were too large to store inside the *Santiago*; they were attached instead to the outside of the ship and there was almost no way to see them unless you worked on one of the external work crews, as his mother had done before her death.

Titus halted near one of the small shuttles. 'Yes,' he said, 'we're going outside. I think it's time you saw things the way they really are.'

'What things?'

But by way of answer Titus only elevated the cuff of his uniform and spoke quietly into his bracelet. 'Enable excursion vehicle 15.'

There was no hesitation; no querying of his authority. The taxi answered him instantly, lights flicking on across its wedge-shaped hull, its cockpit door craning open on smooth pistons and the pallet on which it was mounted rotating to bring the door closer and align the vehicle with its departure track. Steam started to vent from ports spaced along the vehicle's side and Sky could hear the growing whine of turbines somewhere inside the machine's angular hull. A few seconds ago the thing had been a piece of sleek, dead metal, but now there were awesome energies at its disposal; barely contained.

He hesitated at the door, until his father beckoned that he lead.

'After you, Sky. Go forward and take the seat on the left of the instrument column. Don't touch anything while you're about it.'

Sky hopped into the spacecraft, feeling the floor vibrating beneath his feet. The taxi was considerably more cramped inside than it had looked – the hull was thickly plated and armoured – and he had to duck and dive to reach the forward seats, brushing his head against a gristle-like tangle of internal pipework. He found his seat and fiddled with the blue-steel buckle until he had it tight across his chest. In front of him was a cool turquoise-green display – constantly changing numbers and intricate diagrams – beneath a curved, gold-tinted window. To his left was a control column inset with neat levers and switches and a single black joy-stick.

His father settled into the rightmost seat. The door had closed on them now and suddenly it was quieter, save for the continuous rasp of the taxi's air-circulation. His father touched the green display with his finger, making it change, studying the results with narrow-eyed concentration.

'Word of advice, Sky. Never trust these damned things to tell you that they're safe. Make sure for yourself.'

'You don't trust machines to tell you for yourself?'

'I used to, once.' His father eased the joystick forward and the taxi commenced gliding along its departure track, sliding past the parked ranks of other vehicles. 'But machines aren't infallible. We used to kid ourselves that they were because it was the only way to stay sane in a place like this, where we depend on them for our every breath. Unfortunately, it was never true.'

'What happened to change your mind?'

'You'll see, shortly.'

Sky spoke into his own bracelet – it offered a limited subset of the capabilities of his father's unit – and asked the ship to connect him to Constanza. 'You'll never guess where I'm calling from,' he said when her face had appeared, tiny and bright. 'I'm going outside.'

'With Titus?'

'Yes, my father's here.'

Constanza was thirteen now, although – like Sky – she was often taken to be older. In neither case had the assumption much to do with their looks, for while Constanza at least looked no older than her true age, Sky looked substantially younger than his: small and pale and difficult to imagine being afflicted by adolescence in anything like the near future. But both were still intellectually precocious; Constanza was now working more or less fulltime within Titus's security organisation. As was naturally the case aboard a ship with such a small living crew, her duties generally had little to do with enforcement of rules and much more to do with the overseeing of intricate safety procedures and the studying and simulating of operational scenarios. And while it was demanding work – the *Santiago* was a phenomenally complex thing to understand as a single entity – it was almost certainly work that had never required Constanza to leave the confines of the ship. Since she had begun working for his father, their friendship had become more tenuous – she had responsibilities Sky lacked, and moved in the adult world – but now he was about to do something that could not help but impress her; something that would elevate him in her eyes.

He waited for her answer, but when it came it was not quite what he had been expecting. 'I'm sorry for you, Sky. I know it won't be easy, but you have to see it, I think.'

'What are you talking about?'

'What Titus is about to show you.' She paused. 'I've always known, Sky. Ever since it happened, the day we got back from the dolphins. But it was never something it was right to talk about. When you come back inside, you can talk to me about it, if you want.'

He seethed; the way she spoke was less like a friend than what he imagined a condescending older sister might be like. And now his father compounded it by placing a comforting hand on his forearm. 'She's right, Sky. I wondered if I should forewarn you, then in the end decided not to – but what Constanza has said is true. It won't be pleasant, but the truth seldom is. And I think you're ready for it now.'

'Ready for what?' he said, and then realised the link to Constanza was still open. He addressed her: 'You knew this trip was going ahead, didn't you?'

'She had some idea that I'd be taking you outside,' his father said, before the girl could defend herself. 'That's all. You mustn't – can't – blame her for that. It's a flight outside the ship; everyone in security has to know about it, and – since we're not crossing over to one of the other ships – the reason for it.'

'Which is?'

'To learn what happened to your mother.'

All the while they had been moving, but now they reached the freight bay's sheer metal wall. A circular door in the wall whisked open to admit them, the taxi sliding off its pallet into a long, red-lit chamber not much wider than the machine itself. They waited there for a minute or so while the chamber's air was sucked out, then the taxi moved downwards abruptly, sinking into a shaft. Sky's father took the opportunity to lean over to adjust Sky's belt, and then they were outside the ship – blackness below, and the gentle curve of the hull above their heads. The feeling of vertigo was quite intense, even though there was nothing below to suggest height.

They dropped. It was only for an instant, but it was nauseating enough; like the feeling Sky remembered from the rare times when he had been near the ship's centre, where gravity dwindled almost to zero. Then the taxi's engines kicked in, and something like weight returned. Expertly his father vectored the taxi away from the looming grey bulk of the massive ship, adjusting their course with taps of steering thrust, his fingers as delicate on the controls as a concert pianist's.

'I feel sick,' Sky said.

'Close your eyes. You'll be fine in a moment.'

Despite the disquiet he felt about his mother's death – and the fact that this trip had something to do with it – Sky could not completely suppress a thrill of excitement at the thought of being outside. He released the safety buckle and started clambering all around the taxi to get a better view. His father scolded him gently and told him to get back in his seat, but not with any great conviction. Then he yawed the taxi around and smiled as the great ship they had just left came into sight.

'Well, there she is. Your home for the last ten years, Sky, and the only home I've ever known. I know; there's no need to hide your feelings. She's not exactly beautiful, is she?'

'She's big, though.'

'She'd better be – she's just about all we'll ever have. You're luckier than me, of course. At least you'll see Journey's End.'

Sky nodded, but his father's quiet certainty that *he* would be dead by then could not help but make him feel sad.

He looked back to the ship.

The *Santiago* was two kilometres long; longer than any ship which had ever sailed any of Earth's oceans and easily the equal of any of the largest craft which had plied the solar system in the days before the Flotilla's departure. Her skeleton, in fact, was an old fusion-drive space freighter, retrofitted for a journey into interstellar space. With small variations, the other Flotilla ships had been converted from the same sources.

This far from any star, almost no light fell upon the ship, and she would have been invisible were it not for the light spilling from tiny windows dotted along her length. At the very front was a big sphere encircled by lights. That was the command section, where the bridge was, and where the crew spent most of their time when they were on duty. It was where the navigational and scientific instruments were kept, forever pointed towards the destination star; the one they had nicknamed Swan, but which Sky knew really had the much less poetic name 61 Cygni A: one cool red half of a binary star system located in the random sprinkle of stars which had been given the name Cygnus in antiquity. Only towards the end of the voyage would the ship flip around to bring its tail to bear on Swan, so that it could slow itself down with exhaust thrust from the engines.

Behind the control sphere was a cylinder of the same diameter, which held the freight bay from which they had just come. Beyond that was a long, thin spine, studded with regularly spaced modules like immense dinosaur verte-brae. At the very end of the spine was the propulsion system, the intricate and fearsome engines which had once burned to accelerate the ship up to its present cruising speed, and which would burn again on some immeasurably remote day when Sky was fully grown.

Sky knew all these aspects of the ship; he had seen models and holograms of it many times, but it was something else to be seeing it for himself, from outside, for the first time. Slowly, but with grinding stateliness, the whole ship was rotating on its long axis, spinning to create the illusion of gravity on its curving decks. Sky watched it turn; watched lights hove into view and disappear ten seconds later. He could see the tiny aperture in the cargo cylinder, where the taxi had departed. It looked very small, but not perhaps as small as it should have done, given that this ship was all his world could ever be. Almost. He was young now, and he had only been allowed to explore a small fraction of the *Santiago*, but surely it would not be long before he knew it all intimately.

He noticed something else, too; something that the models and the holos had definitely not got right. *As the ship turned, it looked darker on one side than the other.*

What could that mean?

But almost as soon as the troubling inconsistency had begun to worry him, he had forgotten it; marvelling in the sheer immensity of the ship; the pin-sharp way the details held their clarity across kilometres of vacuum; trying to imagine where his favourite places in the ship mapped into this strange new view. He had never been very far down the spine, that was for certain, and even then only under Constanza's guidance, some daredevil adventure before the adults caught them. No one had really blamed him for that, however. It was natural curiosity to want to see the dead, once their existence was known.

Of course, they were not really dead – just frozen.

The spine was a kilometre long; half the ship's total length. In cross-section it had a hexagonal form, with six long, narrow sides. Along each of those sides were spaced sixteen sleeper modules; each a disk-shaped structure rooted to the spine by umbilical attachments. Ninety-six disks in total, and each of those disks, Sky knew, contained ten triangular compartments, each of which held a single *momio* sleeper and the bulky machines necessary for their care. Nine hundred and sixty frozen passengers, then. Nearly a thousand people in total, all submerged in an icy sleep which would last the entire duration of the voyage to Swan. The sleepers, needless to say, were the most precious commodity that the ship carried; its sole reason for existence. The one hundred and fifty-strong living crew were there only to ensure the wellbeing of the frozen and to keep the ship on course. Again Sky measured his current familarity with the ship against that which he could reasonably hope to attain by the time he was an adult. At the moment he knew fewer than a dozen people, but that was only because his upbringing had been deliberately sheltered. Soon he would know many of the others. His father said that there were one hundred and fifty warm humans on the ship because that was some kind of magic number in sociological terms; the population size towards which village communities tended to converge and which carried with it the best prospects for internal harmony and general wellbeing amongst its members. It was large enough to allow individuals to move in slightly different circles if they wished, but not so large that there were likely to be dangerous internal schisms. In that sense, Old Man Balcazar was the tribal leader and Titus Haussmann, with his deep knowledge of secret lore and his abiding concern for the safety of the population, chief medicine man, or top hunter, perhaps. Either way, Sky was the son of someone in a position of authority, what the adults sometimes called a *caudillo*, meaning big man, and that augured well for his own future. It was open talk amongst his parents and the other adults that Captain Balcazar was an 'old man' now. Old Man Balcazar and his father were professionaly close: Titus always had the Captain's ear and Balcazar routinely consulted Sky's father for advice. This trip outside would have required Balcazar's authorisation, since use of any of the *Santiago's* spacecraft was to be kept to a minimum, the ships themselves irreplaceable.

He felt the taxi decelerate, false gravity easing off again.

'Take a good look,' Titus said.

They were passing the engines: a huge and bewildering tangle of tanks and pipes and flared orifices, like the gaping mouths of trumpets.

'Antimatter,' Titus said, mouthing the word like a quiet oath. 'It's the devil's own stuff, you know. We carry a small amount even in this shuttle, just to initiate fusion reactions, but even that makes me shiver. But when I think about the amount aboard the *Santiago*, the hairs on the back of my neck stand up.'

Titus pointed to the two magnetic storage bottles at the rear of the ship: huge reservoirs for penning macroscopic quantities of pure antilithium. The larger of the two reservoirs was empty now, the fuel it had contained completely consumed during the initial boost phase up to interstellar cruising speed. Though there was no external indication that this was the case, the second bottle still contained its complete load of antimatter, delicately balanced in a vacuum fractionally more perfect than the one through which the great ship flew. There was less antimatter in the smaller bottle, since the ship's mass would be less during deceleration than acceleration, but there was still enough to give anyone nightmares.

No one, at least in Sky's experience, ever joked about antimatter.

'All right,' his father said. 'Now get back in your seat and do your belt up.'

When he was secure Titus gunned the taxi, increasing the thrust to its maximum. The *Santiago* diminished until it was just a thin grey sliver, and then became difficult to see unless one searched the starfields carefully. It was hard to believe, seeing it against apparently fixed stars, that the ship was moving at all. It was, but eight hundredths of lightspeed, though faster than any crewed ship had ever moved before, was still almost zero when set against the vast distances between the stars.

That was why the passengers were frozen, so that they could sleep out the whole thing while three generations of crew lived almost their entire lives tending them. Cocooned in their cryogenic sleeper berths, the passengers were nicknamed mummies by the crew, *momios* in the Castellano which was still used for casual conversation within the ship.

Sky Haussmann was crew. So was everyone he knew.

'Can you see the other ships yet?' asked his father.

Sky searched the forward view for long moments before finding one of the other vessels. It was hard to see, but his eyes must have adapted to the darkness since leaving home. Had he imagined it, even so?

No – there it was again, a tiny, toylike constellation in its own right.

'I see one.' Sky pointed.

His father nodded. 'That's the *Brazilia*, I think. The *Palestine* and the *Baghdad* are out there too, but they're much further away.'

'Can you see it?'

'Not without a little assistance.' Titus's hands moved in the dark across the taxi's control board, painting an overlay of coloured lines over the window, bright against space like chalk on a blackboard. The lines boxed the *Brazilia* and the two more distant ships, but it was only when the *Brazilia* loomed large that he thought he could make out the slivers of the other two vessels. By then the *Brazilia* had revealed itself to be identical to his home ship, down to the disks studding its spine.

He looked around the taxi's window, searching for an intersection of coloured lines that would demark the fourth ship, and found nothing.

'Is the *Islamabad* behind us?' he asked his father.

'No,' his father said, softly. 'It isn't behind us.'

There was a tone in his father's voice which troubled Sky. But in the gloom of the taxi's interior his father's expression was hard to read. Perhaps that was deliberate.

'Where is it, then?'

'It isn't there now.' His father spoke slowly. 'It hasn't been there for some time, Sky. There are only four ships left now. Seven years ago something happened to the *Islamabad*.'

There was a silence in the taxi which stretched endlessly before Sky found the will to reply.

'What?'

'An explosion. An explosion like nothing you can imagine.' His father paused before speaking again. 'Like a million suns shining for the tiniest of instants. Blink, Sky – and think of a thousand people turning to ashes in that blink.'

Sky thought back to the flash he had seen in his nursery when he was three. The flash would have troubled him more if it had not been eclipsed by the way Clown broke down that day. Though he had never quite forgotten it, when he thought back to that incident, it was never the flash that was the more important thing but his companion's betrayal; the stark realisation that Clown had only ever been a mirage of flickering wall pixels. How could the brief, bright flash ever have signified something more upsetting than that?

'Someone made it happen?'

'No, I don't think so. Not intentionally, anyway. They might have been experimenting, though.'

'With their engines?'

'Sometimes I think that was what it probably was.' His father's voice grew hushed; almost conspiratorial. 'Our ships are very old, Sky. I was born aboard our ship, just as you were. My father was a young man, hardly even an adult, when he left Mercury orbit with the first generation of crew. That was a hundred years ago.'

'But the ship isn't wearing out,' Sky said.

'No,' Titus said, nodding emphatically. 'Our ships are nearly as good as the day they were built. The problem is that they aren't getting any better. Back on Earth, there were still people that supported us; wanted to help us on our way. Over the years they had thought long and hard about the designs of our ships, trying to find small ways in which our lives might be improved. They transmitted suggestions to us: improvements in our life-support systems; refinements in our sleeper berths. We lost dozens of sleepers in the first few decades of the voyage, Sky – but with the refinements we were slowly able to stabilise things.'

That was news to him, too: the idea that any of the sleepers had died was not at first easy to accept. After all, being frozen was a kind of death itself. But his father explained that there were all sorts of things that could happen to the frozen which would still prevent them being thawed out properly.

'Recently though . . . in your lifetime, at least – things have become much better. There have only been two die-offs in the last ten years.' Sky would later ask himself what became of those dead; whether they were still being carried along by the ship. The adults cared deeply about the *momios*, like a religious sect entrusted with the care of fabulously rare and delicate icons. 'But there was another kind of refinement,' his father continued.

'The engines?'

'Yes.' He said it with emphatic pride. 'We don't use the engines now, and we won't use them again until we reach our destination – but if there *was* a way to make the engines work better, we could slow down faster when we reach Journey's End. As it is, we'll have to start our slowdown years from Swan – but with better engines we could stay in cruise mode longer. That would get us there quicker. Even a marginal improvement – shaving a few years off the mission – would be worth it, especially if we start losing sleepers again.'

'Will we?'

'We won't know for years to come. But in fifty years we'll be very near our destination, and the equipment which keeps the sleepers frozen will be getting very old. It's one of the few systems we can't keep upgrading and repairing – too intricate, too dangerous. But a saving in flight time would always be a good thing. Mark my words – in fifty years, you'll want to shave every month possible off this voyage.'

'Did the people back home come up with a way to make the engines work better?'

'Yes, exactly that.' His father was pleased that he had guessed that much. 'All the ships in the Flotilla received the transmission, of course, and we were all capable of making the modifications that it suggested. At first, we all hesitated. A great meeting of the Flotilla captains was held. Balcazar and three of the other four thought it was dangerous. They urged caution – pointing out that we could study the design for another forty or fifty years before we had to make a decision. What if Earth discovered an error in their blueprint? News of that mistake could be on its way to us – an urgent message saying "Stop" – or perhaps, a year or two down the line, they would think of something even better, but which it was not now possible to implement. Perhaps if we followed the first suggestion, we would rule out ever being able to follow another.'

Again Sky thought of the cleansing brilliance of that flash. 'So what happened to the *Islamabad*?'

'As I said, we'll never know for sure. The meeting broke up with the Flotilla Captains agreeing not to act until we had further information. A year passed; we kept debating the issue – Captain Khan included – and then it happened.'

'Perhaps it was an accident after all.'

'Perhaps,' his father said doubtfully. 'Perhaps. Afterwards . . . the explosion didn't do any serious damage. Not to us or the others, luckily. Oh, it seemed pretty bad at first. The electromagnetic pulse fried half our systems, and even some of the mission-critical ones didn't come back online immediately. We had no power, except for the auxiliary systems serving the sleepers and our own magnetic containment bottle. But in our part of the ship – up front – we had nothing. No power. Not even enough to run the air-recyclers. That could have killed us, but there was so much air in the corridors we had a few days' grace: enough time to hard-wire repair pathways and lash together replacement parts. Gradually we got things running again. We got hit by debris, of course – the ship wasn't totally destroyed in its own explosion, and some of those shards went through us at half the speed of light. The flash burned our hull shielding pretty badly, too – that's why she's darker on one side than the other.' His father said nothing for a moment, but Sky knew that there was more coming. 'That was how your mother died, Sky. Lucretia was outside the ship when it happened. She was working with a team of techs, inspecting the hull.'

He had known his mother had died that day – known even that she was outside – but he had never been told exactly how it had happened.

'Is that the reason you brought me out here?'

'Almost.'

The taxi banked, executing a wide turn which took it back towards the *Santiago*. Sky felt only a small stab of disappointment. He had dared to imagine that this trip might actually take him to one of the other ships, but such excursions were rare things indeed. Instead – wondering if he should try and force some tears now that the topic of his mother's death had been raised, even though he did not actually feel like crying – he waited patiently for his home ship to enlarge, coming in out of the dark like a strip of friendly coastline on a stormy night.

'Something you should understand,' Titus said, eventually. 'The fact that the *Islamabad's* gone doesn't really threaten the success of the mission. There are four ships left now – say four thousand settlers for Journey's End – but we could still establish a colony even if only one ship arrived safely.'

'You mean we might be the only ship to get there?'

'No,' his father said. 'I mean we might be one of those which never arrives. Understand that, Sky – understand that any one of us is expendable – and you'll be a long way to understanding what makes the Flotilla tick; what decisions might have to be taken fifty years from now, if the worst comes to the worst. Only one ship needs to arrive.'

'But if another ship blew up . . .'

'Agreed, we'd probably not be hurt this time. Since the *Islamabad* went up, we've moved all the ships much further apart. It's safer, but it makes physical travel between them harder. In the long run, that might not be such a good idea. Distance can breed suspicion, and it can make enemies hardly worthy of consideration as human beings. Much easier to consider killing.' Titus's voice had grown cold and remote, almost like that of a stranger, but then he softened his tone. 'Remember that, Sky. We're all in this together, no matter how hard things become in the future.'

'You think things will?'

'I don't know, but they're almost certainly not going to get easier. And by the time that any of this matters – when we get close to the end of the crossing – you'll be my age, in a position of senior responsibility, even if not actually running the ship.'

'You think that could happen?'

Titus smiled. 'I'd say it for certain – if I didn't also know a certain talented young lady by the name of Constanza.'

While they had been speaking, the *Santiago* had grown much larger, but now they were approaching it from a different angle, so that the bulbous sphere of the command section loomed like a miniature grey moon, filigreed by panel lines and the boxy accretions of sensor modules. Sky thought of Constanza, now that his father had mentioned her, and wondered if – perhaps after all – this trip might have impressed her. After all, he *had* been outside, even if it had not been quite the surprise to her that he had originally hoped. And what he had been shown – what he had been told – had really not been so hard to take, had it?

But Titus was not done yet.

'Take a good look,' his father said as the darkened side of the sphere rotated into view. 'This is where your mother's inspection team was working. They were attached to the hull by magnetic harnesses, working very close to the surface. The ship was spinning of course – just like she is now – and if luck had been on their side, your mother's team would have been working on the other side when the *Islamabad* went up. But the rotation had brought them right round into full view when she detonated. They caught the full blast, and they were wearing only lightweight suits at the time.'

He understood now why his father had brought him out here. It was not simply to be told how his mother had died, or to be initiated into the chilling knowledge that one fifth of the Flotilla no longer existed. That was part of it, but the central message was here; on the hull of the ship itself.

Everything else had just been preparation.

When the flash had hit them, their bodies had temporarily shielded the hull from the worst excesses of the radiation. They had burned quickly – there had probably been no pain, he later learned – but in that moment of death they had left negative shadows of themselves; lighter patches against the generally scorched hull. They were seven human shapes, frozen in postures which could not help but look tortured, but which were probably just the natural positions they had been working in when the flash had hit them. They all looked alike in every other respect; there was no way to tell which shadow had been cast by his mother.

'You know which one was her, don't you?' he said.

'Yes,' Titus said. 'Not that I found her, of course – someone else did. But yes, I do know which one belonged to your mother.'

Sky looked at the shadows again, burning their shapes into his brain, knowing that he would never have the courage to come out here again. Later he would learn that there had never been any serious attempt to remove the shadows; that they had been left as a monument not just to the seven dead workers, but to the thousand who had died in that soul-flensing flash. The ship wore them like a scar.

'Well?' Titus said, with the tiniest trace of impatience. 'Do you want to know?'

'No,' Sky said. 'No, I don't want to know, ever.'

SEVEN

The next day Amelia brought my possessions to the chalet and then left me alone while I went through them. But as curious about them as I was, it was difficult to focus on the task. I was troubled by the fact that I'd dreamed about Sky Haussmann again: an unwilling observer to another incident in his life. The first dream about him that I clearly remembered must have happened to me during my revival; now I'd experienced another, and while there seemed to be a large gap in his life between them, they had clearly happened in chronological order. Like instalments.

And my palm had bled again, a hard new encrustation of dried blood over the wound. Spots of blood marred the sheet.

It didn't take a massive leap of imagination to see that the two were connected. From somewhere I remembered that Haussmann had been crucified; that the mark in my palm signified his execution, and that I'd met another man with a similar wound in what seemed simultaneously like the recent and the infinitely remote past. I seemed to remember that the man had suffered the dreams as well, and hadn't been an especially willing recipient of them either.

But maybe the things Amelia had brought me would explain the dreams. Trying to put Haussmann temporarily from mind, I focused on the task at hand. Everything I owned now – apart from any holdings back around Swan – lay in an unassuming briefcase which had come with me on the *Orvieto*.

There was some Sky's Edge currency in large denomination Southlander bills; about half a million Australs. Amelia had told me it amounted to a reasonable fortune on Sky's Edge – based on the information she had, anyway – though it had negligible value here in the Yellowstone system. Why had I brought it with me, then? The answer seemed obvious enough. Even allowing for inflation, the Sky's Edge money would still be worth *something* thirty years after my departure, though perhaps only enough to buy a room for the night.

The fact that I had carried the money with me suggested that I had planned on returning home some day.

So I wasn't emigrating then. I'd come here on business.

To do something.

I had also brought experientials: pencil-sized data sticks crammed with recorded memories. They must have been what I was planning to sell on my revival. Unless you were an Ultra trader specialising in esoteric high-technologies, experientials were about the only way a rich individual could preserve some of their wealth while crossing interstellar space. A market always existed for them, no matter how advanced or primitive the buyer – provided, of course, that they had the basic technology to make use of the experientials. Yellowstone would be no problem in that regard. It had been the wellspring of all major technological and social advances across human space for the last two centuries.

The experientials had been sealed in clear plastic. Without playback equipment, there was no way I could tell what they contained.

What else?

Some money which felt truly unfamiliar to me: strangely textured bank-notes with unfamiliar faces on them and surreal, random denominations.

I had asked Amelia what they were.

'That's local money, Tanner. From Chasm City.' She pointed to a man on one side of each bill. 'That's Lorean Sylveste, I think. Or it could be Marco Ferris. It's ancient history, anyway.'

'The money must have travelled from Yellowstone to Sky's Edge and then back again – it's at least thirty years old. Is it worth anything at all now?'

'Oh, a little. I'm no expert in these matters, of course, but I think this would be enough to get you to Chasm City. Not much more than that, though.'

'And how would I get to Chasm City?'

'It's not difficult, even now. There's a slowboat shuttle which makes the run down to New Vancouver, in orbit around Yellowstone. From there you'd need to buy a place on a behemoth, to get down to the surface. I think what you have should be enough, if you were prepared to abstain from some luxuries.'

'Such as?'

'Well, any guarantee of arriving safely, for a start.'

I smiled. 'I'd better hope my luck's in, then.'

'But you're not planning on leaving us yet, are you Tanner?'

'No,' I answered. 'Not just yet.'

There were two other things in the briefcase: a dark, flat envelope and another, fatter one. Amelia had left me alone by the time I tipped the flatter of the two onto the chalet's bed. The contents spilled out; less in it than I had expected and nothing that seemed like a revelatory message from my past. If anything, the contents were designed to confuse me even more: a dozen passports and laminated ID cards for myself, all valid at the time I had boarded the ship, and all applicable to some part of Sky's Edge and its surrounding space. Some were simply printed; others had computer systems embedded into them.

I suspected that most people could have managed with only one or two such documents, accepting that there were areas they could not legally enter – but from what I gathered from the documents' small print, I would have been able to travel more or less freely, in and out of war zones and militia-controlled states, into the neutral zones and into the low-orbital space around the planet. They were the documents of someone who needed to get around without interference. There were some anomalies, though: what appeared to be trifling inconsistencies in the personal data in each document, places of birth and places I had visited. In some of the documents I was listed as having been a soldier in the Southland Militia, whereas in others I was affiliated to the Northern Coalition as a tactical specialist. Other documents failed to mention any soldiering history at all – listing me only as a personal security consultant or an agent for an import/export firm.

Suddenly the documents stopped being a confusing jumble and cohered into a clear indication of the kind of man I had been. I was someone who needed to be able to slip across borders like a ghost; a man of many guises and pasts – most of them probably fictitious. I sensed that I had been a man who lived dangerously; someone who probably made enemies the way most people made acquaintances. I guessed that it had seldom bothered me much. I was a man who could think about killing a pervert monk without breaking sweat, and then refrain from the act because the monk was not worth the tiny expenditure of energy it would have taken.

But there were three other things in the envelope, tucked at the back so that they had not fallen out at first. I pulled them out carefully, my fingers feeling the gloss surfaces of photographs.

The first picture showed a woman of striking, dark beauty, a nervous smile on her face, backdropped by what looked like the edge of a jungle clearing. The picture had been taken at night. Angling the picture to look past her, I could just see the back of another man examining a gun. It could almost have been me – but then who had taken the picture, and why did I have it with me?

'Gitta,' I said; without any effort I had remembered her name. 'You're Gitta, aren't you?'

The second picture showed a man standing in what might once have been a road, but which was little more than a pot-holed trail, curtained on either side by jungle. The man was walking towards the person taking the picture, a huge black weapon slung over his shoulder. He wore a shirt and a bandolier, and though his build and age were more or less the same as mine, his face was not quite the same. Behind the man, there was what seemed to be a fallen tree blocking the road, except that the tree ended in a bloodied stump, and much of the road was covered in a thick impasto of gore.

'Dieterling,' I said, the name springing from somewhere. 'Miguel Dieterling.'
And knew that he had been a good friend of mine who was dead now.

Then I looked at the third picture. There was no trace of the intimacy of the first about this image, or even the dubious triumph of the second, since the man did not seem to be aware that his picture had been taken. It was a flat-image, taken with a long lens. The man was moving quickly through a mall, the neon lights of stores blurred into hyphens by the panned exposure. The man was slightly blurred too, but sharp enough for recognition. Sharp enough for *acquisition*, I thought.

I remembered his name, too.

I picked up the heavier of the two envelopes and allowed it to empty itself on the bed. The sharp-edged, intricately shaped pieces that fell out of it seemed to invite me to fit them together. I could feel the thing squeezed into my palm, ready to be used. It would be difficult to see; pearly in colour, like opaque glass.

Or diamond.

'This is a blocking move,' I said to Amelia. 'You've immobilised me now. I may be taller and stronger than you, but there's nothing I can do at this point which won't cause me a lot of pain.'

She looked at me expectantly. 'What now?'

'Now you take the weapon from me.' I nodded down towards the little trowel we were using as an ersatz weapon. She removed it from my grip softly with her free hand, then flung it away as if it were poisoned.

'You're letting go too easily.'

'No,' I said. 'With the pressure you're putting on that nerve, it's all I could do not to drop it. It's simple biomechanics, Amelia. I think you'll find Alexei even easier to deal with.'

We were standing in the clearing before the chalet in what passed for late afternoon in Hospice Idlewild, the central filament of the sun turning from white to sullen orange. It was an odd kind of afternoon because the light always stayed overhead, imparting none of the flattering face-on glow and long shadows of a planetary sundown. But we were paying it little attention anyway. For the last two hours I had been showing Amelia some basic self-defence techniques. We had spent the first hour with Amelia trying to attack me, which meant touching any part of my body with the edge of the trowel. In all that time she had not succeeded once, even when I willed myself to let her through my defences. No matter how hard I gritted my teeth and said that this time I was going to let her win, it never happened. But at least it demonstrated something, which was that the right technique would almost always beat a clumsy assailant. She was getting closer, though, and things had improved when we reversed roles for the second hour. Now at least I was able to hold back, moving in slow enough for Amelia to learn the right blocking moves for each situation. She was a very good pupil; achieving in an hour what normally took two days. Her moves were not yet graceful – not yet hardwired into muscle memory – and she telegraphed her intentions, but neither of these defects would count much against an amateur like Brother Alexei.

'You could show me how to kill him, too, couldn't you?' Amelia said, while we took a breather on the grass – or rather, while she caught her breath and I waited.

'Is that what you want?'

'No; of course not. I just want to make him stop.'

I looked across the curve of Idlewild to the tiny, dotlike figures toiling in the cultivation terraces on the far side, hurrying while there was still enough light to work in. 'I don't think he'll come back,' I said. 'Not after what happened in the cave. But if he does, you'll have an edge on him – and I'm damn sure he won't come back after that. I know his type, Amelia. He'll just fixate on an easier target.'

She thought about that for a while, doubtless pitying whoever would have to go through the same thing she had. 'I know it's not the sort of thing we're meant to say, but I hate that man. Can we go through these moves tomorrow again?'

'Of course. In fact, I insist on it. You're still weak – although you're well ahead of the curve.'

'Thanks. Tanner – do you mind if I ask how you know these things?'

I thought back to the documents I had found in the envelope. 'I was a personal security consultant.'

'And?'

I smiled ruefully, wondering how much she knew about the contents of that envelope. 'And some other things.'

'They told me you were a soldier.'

'Yes; I think I was. But then almost everyone alive on Sky's Edge had some connection to the war. It wasn't something you stayed out of easily. The attitude was, if you weren't part of the solution, you were part of the problem. If you didn't sign up for one side, you were considered by default to have sympathies with the other.' That was an over-simplification, of course, since it ignored the fact that the aristocratic rich could buy neutrality off the shelf like a new outfit – but for the average non-wealthy Peninsula citizen, it wasn't so far from the truth.

'You seem to be remembering well now.'

'It's beginning to come back. Having a look at my personal possessions certainly helped.'

She nodded encouragingly and I felt the tiniest stab of remorse at lying to her. The pictures had done very much more than just jog my memory, but for the moment I chose to maintain the illusion of partial amnesia. I just hoped Amelia was not shrewd enough to see through my subterfuge, but I would be careful not to underestimate the Mendicants in any of the moves that lay ahead.

I was, indeed, a soldier. But as I had also inferred from the slew of passports and ID documents in the envelope, soldiering was nowhere near the end of my talents, merely the core around which my other skills orbited. Not everything had come into absolutely sharp focus yet, but I knew a lot more than I had the day before.

I'd been born into a family at the low end of the aristocratic wealth scale: not actively poor but consciously struggling to maintain any façade of wealth. We'd lived in Nueva Iquique, on the south-eastern shore of the Peninsula. It was a fading settlement buffered from the war by a range of treacherous mountains; sleepy and dispassionate even in the war's darkest years. Northerners would often sail down the coast and put into Nueva Iquique without fear of violence, even when we were technically enemies, and inter-marriage between Flotilla lines was not uncommon. I grew up able to read the enemy's hybrid language with almost the same fluency I read ours. To me it seemed strange that our leaders inspired us to hate these people. Even the history books agreed that we'd been united when the ships left Mercury.

But then so much had happened.

As I grew older, I began to see that, while I had nothing against the genes or beliefs of those who were allied within the Northern Coalition, they were still our enemies. They'd committed their share of atrocities, just as we had. While I might not have despised the enemy, I still had a moral duty to bring the war to a conclusion as swiftly as possible by aiding our side in victory. So at the age of twenty-two I signed up for the Southland Militia. I wasn't a natural soldier, but I learned quickly. You had to; especially if you were thrown into live combat only a few weeks after handling your first gun. I turned out to be a proficient marksman. Later, with proper training, I became an exceptional one – and it was my extreme good fortune that my unit happened to need a sniper.

I remembered my first kill – or multiple killing, as it turned out.

We were perched high in jungle-enshrouded hills, looking down at a clearing where NC troops were off-loading supplies from a ground-effect transport. With ruthless calm I lined up the gun, squinting into the sight, aligning the cross-hairs one at a time on each man in the unit. The rifle was loaded with subsonic micro-munitions; completely silent and with a programmed detonation delay of fifteen seconds. Time enough to put a gnat-sized slug in every man in the clearing – watching each reach up idly to scratch his neck at what he imagined was an insect bite. By the time the eighth and last man noticed something wrong, it was much too late to do anything about it.

The squad dropped to the dirt in eerie unison. Later, we descended from the hill and requisitioned the supplies for our own unit, stepping over corpses grotesquely bloated from internal explosions.

That was my first dreamlike taste of death.

Sometimes I wondered what would have happened if the delay had been set to less than fifteen seconds, so that the first man dropped before I'd finished putting slugs in the others. Would I have had the true sniper's nerve – the cold will to carry on regardless? Or would the shock of what I was doing have rammed home so brutally that I would have dropped the gun in revulsion? But I always told myself that there was no point dwelling on what might have happened. All I did know was that after that first series of unreal executions, it was never a problem again.

Almost never.

It was in the nature of a sniper's work that one almost never saw the enemy as anything other than an impersonal stick-figure; too far away to be humanised by either facial details or an expression of pain when the slug found its mark. I almost never needed to send another slug. For a time, I thought I'd found a safe niche where I could psychologically barrier myself from the worst that the war had to offer. I was valued by my unit, protected like a talisman. Although I never once did anything heroic, I became a hero by virtue of my technical skill at aiming a gun. If such a thing were possible in any kind of combat, I was happy. In fact, I *knew* it was possible: I'd seen men and women for whom the war was a capricious and spiteful lover; one who would always hurt them, but to whom – bruised and hungry – they would inevitably return. The greatest lie ever told was the one that said war made us universally miserable; that if the choice was truly ours, we would free ourselves of war forever. Maybe the human condition would have been something nobler if that were the case – but if war did not have a strange and dark allure, why did we always seem so unwilling to abandon it for peace? It went beyond anything as mundane as acclimatisation to the normality of war. I had known men and woman who boasted of sexual arousal after killing an enemy; addicted to the erotic potency of what they had done.

My happiness, though, was simpler: born out of the realisation that I'd found the luckiest of roles. I was doing what I rationalised as morally right, while at the same time being sheltered from the very real risk of death that usually accompanied front-line forces. I assumed it would continue like that; that eventually I would be decorated and that if I didn't stay a sniper until the war's end, it would be only because the army considered my skills too valuable to risk in the front-line. I suppose it was possible I might have been promoted to one of the covert assassination squads – certainly more hazardous – but as far as I could see it, the most likely outcome would be a training role in one of the boot camps, followed by early retirement and the smug assurance that I'd helped expedite the war's conclusion – even if that conclusion.

Of course, it didn't happen like that.

One night our unit got ambushed. We were cut down by guerrillas of an NC Deep Incursion squad, and in minutes I learnt the true meaning of what was euphemistically described as close-quarters combat. No line-of-sight particle-beam weapons now; no delayed-detonation nano-munitions. What close-quarters combat meant was something which would have been infinitely more recognisable to a soldier of a thousand years earlier: the screaming fury of human beings packed so close together that the only effective way to kill each other was with sharpened metal weapons: bayonets and daggers, or with hands around each other's throats; fingers pressed into each other's eye-sockets. The only way to survive was to disengage all higher brain-functions and regress to an animal state of mind.

So I did. And in doing so, I learned a deeper truth about war. She punished those who flirted with her by making them like herself. Once you opened the door to the animal, there was no shutting it.

I never stopped being an expert shot when the situation called for it, but I was never again purely a sniper. I pretended I had lost my edge; that I could no longer be trusted with the most critical kills. It was a plausible enough lie: snipers were insanely superstitious, and many did develop some psychoso-matic block that stopped them functioning. I moved through different units, requesting operational transfers that each time took me closer to the front. I developed a proficiency with weapons that went far beyond mere marksman-ship: a fluidity of ease like a preternaturally skilled musician who could pick up any instrument and make it sing. I volunteered for deep-insertion missions that put me behind enemy lines for weeks at a time, living off carefully measured field-rations (Sky's Edge's biosphere was superficially Earthlike – but down on the level of cell chemistry it was completely incompatible, con-taining almost no native flora which could be safely eaten without either providing zero nourishment or triggering a fatal anaphylactic reaction). During those long episodes of solitude I allowed the animal to emerge again, a feral mindstate of almost limitless patience and tolerance for discomfort.

I became a lone gunman, no longer receiving orders via the usual chain of command, but from mysterious and untraceable sources in the Militia hierarchy. My missions became stranger; their goals less fathomable. My targets shifted from the obvious – mid-ranking NC officers – to the seemingly random, but I never questioned that there was a logic behind the kills; that it was all part of some devious and painstakingly planned scheme. Even when, on more than one occasion, I was required to put slugs in certain targets who wore the same uniform as I did, I assumed they were spies, or potential traitors, or – and this was the least palatable of conclusions – just loyal men who had to die because in some way their living had conflicted with the scheme's inscrutable progress.

I no longer even cared whether my actions served any kind of greater good. Eventually I stopped taking orders and began soliciting them – severing connections with the hierarchy, and taking contracts from whoever would pay me. I stopped being a soldier and became a mercenary.

Which was when I met Cahuella for the first time.

'My name is Sister Duscha,' said the older of the two Mendicants, a thin woman with an unsmiling demeanour. 'You may have heard of me; I'm the Hospice's neurological specialist. And I'm afraid, Tanner Mirabel, that there's something quite seriously wrong with your mind.'

Duscha and Amelia were standing in the chalet's doorway. Only half an hour earlier I'd told Amelia of my intention to leave Idlewild within the day. Now Amelia looked apologetic. 'I'm very sorry, Tanner, but I had to tell her.'

'No need to apologise, Sister,' Duscha said, brushing imperiously past her subordinate. 'Whether he likes it or not, you did precisely the right thing by informing me of his plans. Now then, Tanner Mirabel. Where shall we begin?'

'Wherever you like; I'm still leaving.'

One of the ovoid-headed robots trotted in behind Duscha, clicking across the floor. I made a move to get off the bed, but Duscha placed a firm hand on my thigh. 'No; we'll have none of that nonsense. You're going nowhere for the time being.'

I looked at Amelia. 'What was all that about being able to leave whenever I wanted?'

'Oh, you're free to leave, Tanner . . .' But even as Amelia said it, she didn't sound completely convincing.

'But he won't want to, when he knows the facts,' Duscha said, lowering herself onto the bed. 'Let me explain, shall I? When you were warmed, we made a very thorough medical examination of you, Tanner – focused especially on your brain. We suspected you were amnesiac, but we had to make sure there was no fundamental damage, or any implants that might warrant removal.'

'I don't have any implants.'

'No, you don't. But I'm afraid there is damage – of a sort.'

She clicked her fingers at the robot and had it trot closer to the bed. There was nothing on the bed now, but a minute earlier I had been in the process of assembling the clockwork gun, fitting the pieces together by a process of trial and error until I had the thing half-completed. When I had seen Amelia and Duscha striding across the lawn beyond the chalet, I had pushed the pieces under the pillow. I thought of it brooding there now, difficult to mistake for anything other than a weapon. They might have puzzled over the odd-shaped diamond pieces when they examined my belongings, but I doubted that they'd have realised what the pieces implied. Now there would have been very little doubt.

I said, 'What sort of damage, Sister Duscha?'

'I can show you.'

The robot's ovoid head popped up a screen, filling with a slowly rotating, lilac image of a skull, packed with ghostly structures like intricate clouds of milky ink. I didn't recognise it as my own, of course, but I knew it had to be my skull that they were showing me.

Duscha sketched her fingers over the rotating mass. 'These light spots are the problem, Tanner. Before you woke, I injected you with bromodeoxy-uridine. It's a chemical analogue for thymidine; one of the nucleic acids in DNA. The chemical supplants thymidine in new brain cells; acting as a marker for neurogenesis; the laying down of new brain cells. The light spots show where there's a build-up of the marker – highlighting foci of recent cell growth.'

'I didn't think brains grew new cells.'

'That's a myth we buried five hundred years ago, Tanner – but in a sense you're right; it's still rather a rare process in higher mammals. But what you're seeing in this scan is something a lot more vigorous: concentrated, specialised regions of recent – and continuing – neurogenesis. They're functional neur-ons, organised into intricate structures and connected to your existing neurons. All very deliberate. You'll notice how the light spots are situated near your perceptual centres? I'm afraid it's very characteristic, Tanner – if we didn't already know from your hand.'

'My hand?'

'You have a wound in your palm. It's symptomatic of infection by one of the Haussmann family of indoctrinal viruses.' She paused. 'We picked up the virus in your blood, once we looked for it. The virus inserts itself into your DNA and generates the new neural structures.'

There was little point in bluffing now. 'I'm surprised you recognised it for what it was.'

'We've seen it enough times over the years,' Duscha said. 'It infects a small fraction of every batch of slush . . . every group of sleepers we get from Sky's Edge. At first, of course, we were mystified. We knew something about the Haussmann cults – needless to say, we don't approve of the way they've appropriated the iconography of our own belief system – but it took us a long time to realise there was a viral infection mechanism, and that the people we were seeing were victims rather than cultists.'

'It's a blessed nuisance,' Amelia said. 'But we can help you, Tanner. I take it you've been dreaming about Sky Haussmann?'

I nodded, but said nothing.

'Well, we can flush out the virus,' Duscha said. 'It's a weak strain, and it will run its course with time, but we can speed up the process if you wish.'

'If I wish? I'm surprised you haven't flushed it out already.'

'Goodness, we'd never do that. After all, you might have willingly chosen infection. We'd have no right to remove it in that case.' Duscha patted the robot, which retracted its screen and clicked its way outside again, moving like a delicate metal crab. 'But if you want it removed, we can administer the flushing therapy immediately.'

'How long will it take to work?'

'Five or six days. We like to monitor the progress, naturally – sometimes it needs a little fine-tuning.'

'Then it'll have to work its way out, I'm afraid.'

'On your own head be it,' Duscha said, tutting. She stood up from the bedside and left in a huff, her robot following obediently.

'Tanner, I . . .' Amelia began.

'I don't want to talk about it, all right?'

'I had to tell her.'

'I know, and I'm not angry about that. I just don't want you to try and talk me out of leaving, understand?'

She said nothing, but the point was well made.

Afterwards I spent half an hour with her on some more exercises. We worked almost in silence, giving me plenty of time to think about what Duscha had shown me. I'd remembered Red Hand Vasquez by then and his assurance that he was no longer infectious. He was the most likely source of the virus, but I couldn't rule out having picked it up by sheer bad luck when I was in the bridge, in the vicinity of so many Haussmann cultists.

But Duscha had said it was a mild strain. Maybe she was right. So far, all I had to show for it was the stigma and the two nocturnal dreams I'd had. I wasn't seeing Sky Haussmann in broad daylight, or having waking dreams about him. I didn't feel any lingering obsession with Sky, or any hint of one; no desire to surround myself with paraphernalia relating to his life and times; no sense of religious awe at the mere thought of him. He was just what he'd always been: a figure from history, a man who had done a terrible thing and been terribly punished for it, but who could not be easily forgotten because he'd also given us the gift of a world. There were older historical figures who had mixed reputations, their deeds painted in equally murky shades of grey. I wasn't about to start worshipping Haussmann just because his life was rerunning itself when I slept. I was stronger than that.

'I don't understand why you're in so much of a hurry to leave us,' Amelia said while we took a break, pushing a wet strand of hair away from her brow. 'It took you fifteen years to get here – what's a few more weeks?'

'I guess I'm just not the patient type, Amelia.' She looked at me sceptic-ally, so I tried to offer some justification. 'Look, those fifteen years never happened for me – it seems like only yesterday that I was waiting to board the ship.'

'The point still applies. Your arriving a week or two later will make blessedly little difference.'

But it would, I thought. It would make all the difference in the world – but there was no way Amelia could know the whole truth. All I could do was act as casually as possible when I answered her.

'Actually . . . there is a good reason for me to leave as soon as possible. It won't have shown in your records, but I've remembered that I was travelling with another man who must already have been revived.'

'That's possible, I suppose, if the other man was put aboard the ship earlier than you.'

'That's what I was thinking. In fact, he might not have passed through the Hospice at all, if there were no complications. His name is Reivich.'

She seemed surprised, but not suspiciously so. 'I remember a man with that name. He did come through here. Argent Reivich, wasn't it?'

I smiled. 'Yes; that's him.'

EIGHT

Argent Reivich.

There must have been a time when the name meant nothing to me, but it was hard to believe now. For too long the name – his name; his continued existence – had been the defining fact of my universe. I well remembered when I'd first heard it, however. It was the night at the Reptile House I taught Gitta how to handle a gun. I thought back to that time as I showed Amelia how to defend herself against Brother Alexei.

Cahuella's palace on Sky's Edge was a long, low H-shaped building surrounded by overgrown jungle on all sides. Rising from the roof of the palace was another H-shaped storey, but slightly smaller in all its dimensions, so that it was surrounded on all sides by a flat, walled terrace. From the vantage point of the terrace, the hundred metres or so of cleared land surrounding the Reptile House were not visible at all unless you stood at the wall and looked over the edge. The jungle, rising high and dark, seemed to be on the point of inundating the terrace's wall like a thick green tide. At night the jungle was a black immensity drained of any colour, filled with the alien sounds of a thousand native lifeforms. There was no other human settlement of any kind for hundreds of kilometres in any direction.

The night I taught Gitta was unusually clear, the sky flecked with stars from tree-top to zenith. Sky's Edge had no large moons, and the few bright habitats which orbited the planet were below the horizon, but the terrace was lit by scores of torches, burning in the mouths of golden hamadryad statues set on stone pedestals along the wall. Cahuella had an obsession with hunting. His ambition was to catch himself a near-adult hamadryad, rather than the single immature specimen he'd managed to bag the previous year and which now lived deep below the Reptile House.

I hadn't long been in his employment on that hunting trip, and that was the first time I had seen his wife. Once or twice she had handled one of Cahuella's hunting rifles, but with no sign that she had ever touched a weapon before that trip. Cahuella had asked me to give her a few impromptu shooting lessons while we were in-country, which I had, and while she had improved, it was clear that Gitta was never going to be any kind of expert shot. It hardly mattered; she had no interest in hunting and while she had endured the trip with quiet stoicism, she could not share Cahuella's primal enthusiasm for killing.

Soon even Cahuella realised that he was wasting his time trying to turn Gitta into another hunter. But he still wanted her to know how to use a gun – something smaller now, for the purposes of self-defence.

'Why?' I said. 'You hire people like me so people like Gitta won't have to worry about their own safety.'

We had been alone at the time, down in one of the empty vivarium chambers. 'Because I've got enemies, Tanner. You're good, and the men under you are good as well – but they're not infallible. A single assassin could still break through our defences.'

'Yes,' I said. 'But anyone that good would also be good enough to take out either of you without you even knowing it was about to happen.'

'Someone as good as you, Tanner?'

I thought about the defences I had arranged around and within the Reptile House. 'No,' I answered. 'They'd need to be a hell of a lot better than me, Cahuella.'

'And are there people like that out there?'

'There's always someone better than you. It's just a question of whether anyone's prepared to pay them for their services.'

He rested a hand on one of the empty amphibian cases. 'Then she needs this more than ever. A chance at self-defence is better than none at all.'

I had to concede there was a kind of logic there. 'I'll show her, then . . . if you insist.'

'Why are you so reluctant?'

'Guns are dangerous things.'

Cahuella smiled in the wan yellow light spilling from the tubes set into the empty cases.

'That's the idea, I think.'

We began soon after. Gitta was a perfectly willing student, but nowhere near as quick as Amelia. It was nothing to do with her intelligence; just a fundamental deficit in her motor skills; a basic weakness in hand-to-eye coordination which would never have manifested itself had not Cahuella insisted on this tuition. Which was not to say that she was beyond hope, but what Amelia could have mastered in an hour, it took Gitta all day to just stumble through at the most basic level of competence. Had she been a trainee soldier back in my old unit, I would never have been forced through this rigmarole. It would have been someone else's problem to find a task better suited to her skills – intelligence-gathering, or something.

But Cahuella wanted Gitta to know how to use a gun.

So I followed orders. I had no problem with this. It was up to Cahuella how he used me. And spending time with Gitta was not exactly the most onerous of tasks. Cahuella's wife was a lovely woman: a striking high-cheekboned beauty of Northern ancestry, lithe and lissom, with a dancer's musculature. I had never touched her until this shooting lesson, had hardly had good cause to speak to her, though I had fantasised often enough.

Now, whenever I had to straighten her posture by applying gentle pressure to her arm or her shoulders or the small of her back, I felt my heart race ridiculously. When I spoke, I tried to keep my voice as soft and calm as I felt the situation demanded, but to my ears what came out sounded strained and adolescent. If Gitta noticed anything in my behaviour, she gave no sign of it. Her attention was focused tightly on the lesson at hand.

I had installed a radio-frequency field-generator around this part of the terrace which addressed a processor in the anti-flash goggles Gitta wore. It was standard military training equipment; part of the vast cache of stolen or black-market equipment Cahuella had hoarded over the years. Ghosts would appear in the goggles, mapped into Gitta's field of view as if they were moving around the terrace. Not all of the ghosts would be hostile, but Gitta would have only a fraction of a second to decide for herself who needed shooting.

It was a joke, really. Only a very skilled assassin would stand any chance of getting inside the Reptile House to begin with, and anyone that good would never give Gitta those precious moments to make her mind up.

But Gitta wasn't doing too badly by her fifth lesson. She was at least pointing and firing the gun at the right targets ninety per cent of the time, a margin of error I could live with for now, hoping that I would never have the misfortune to be the one victim in ten who was not planning to kill her.

But she was still not taking down her targets with any kind of efficiency. We were using live projectile ammo since the beam-weapons we had access to were just too bulky and heavy for self-defence. For the sake of safety, I could have arranged matters so that the gun would only fire when either Gitta or myself was out of the line of fire, not to mention any of Cahuella's valuable hamadryad statues. But I felt that the instants when the gun was disabled would have rendered the session too inauthentic to be much use. Instead, I'd loaded the gun with smart ammo, each slug holding a buried processor addressed by the same training field which spoke to Gitta's goggles. The processor controlled tiny spurts of gas which would shove the bullet off-course if the trajectory was deemed dangerous. If the required deflection angle was too sharp, the bullet would self-destruct into a speeding cloud of hot metal vapour – not exactly harmless, but a lot better than a small-calibre slug if it happened to be headed straight for your face.

'How am I doing?' Gitta asked, when we had to reload the gun.

'Your target acquisition's improving. You still need to aim lower – go for the chest rather than the head.'

'Why the chest? My husband said you could kill a man with a single shot to the head, Tanner.'

'I've had more practice than you.'

'But it's true, though – what they say about you? That when you shot someone, you . . .'

I finished it for her. 'Took out specific areas of brain function, yeah. You shouldn't believe everything they tell you, Gitta. I could probably put a slug into one hemisphere rather than the other, but beyond that . . .'

'Still, it isn't a bad reputation to live with.'

'I suppose not, no. But that's all it is.'

'If it was my husband they were saying that about, he'd milk it for all it was worth.' She cast a wary eye back to the upper storey of the house. 'But you always try and play it down. That makes it seem more likely to me, Tanner.'

'I try and play it down because I don't want you to think I'm something I'm not.'

She looked at me. 'I don't think there's any danger of that, Tanner. I think I know exactly who you are. A man with a good conscience who happens to work for someone who doesn't sleep quite so well at night.'

'My conscience isn't exactly pristine, believe me.'

'You should see Cahuella's.' She locked eyes with me for a few moments; I broke it and looked down at the gun. Gitta raised her voice an octave. 'Oh; speak of the devil.'

'Talking about me again?' He was stepping onto the terrace from the upper storey of the building. Something glinted in his hand: a glass of pisco sour. 'Well, I can't blame you for that, can I? So. How are the lessons coming along?'

'I think we're making reasonable progress,' I said.

'Oh, don't believe a word he says,' Gitta said. 'I'm absymal, and Tanner's too polite to say so.'

'Nothing worthwhile's ever easy,' I answered. To Cahuella, I said, 'Gitta can fire a gun now and discriminate between friend and foe most of the time. There isn't anything magical about it, though she's worked hard to achieve what she has and deserves credit. But if you want more than that, it might not be so easy.'

'She can always keep learning. You're the master teacher, after all.' He nodded down at the gun, into which I'd just slipped a fresh clip. 'Hey. Show her that trick you do.'

'Which one would that be?' I said, trying to keep my temper under control. Normally Cahuella knew better than to label my painfully acquired skills as tricks.

Cahuella took a sip of his drink. 'You know the one I mean.'

'Fine; I'll take a guess.'

I reprogrammed the gun so that the bullets would no longer be deflected if they were on hazardous trajectories. If he wanted a trick, he was going to get one – whether it cost him or not.

Normally when I shot a small weapon, I adopted the classic marksman's stance: legs slightly spread for balance, gun's grip held in one hand, supported by the other hand from beneath; arms outstretched at eye-level, locked against recoil if the gun fired slugs rather than energy. Now I held the gun single-handed at waist-height, like an oldtime quick-draw gunfighter with a six-shooter. I was looking down on the gun, not sighting along it. But I had practised this position so thoroughly that I knew exactly where the bullet would go.

I squeezed the trigger and put a slug into one of his hamadryad statues.

Then walked to inspect the damage.

The statue's gold had flowed like butter under the impact of the bullet, but it had flowed with beautiful symmetry around the entrance point, like a yellow lotus. And I had placed the shot with beautiful symmetry as well – mathematically centred on the hamadryad's brow; between the eyes if the creature's eyes had not been situated *inside* its jaw.

'Very good,' Cahuella said. 'I think. Have you any idea what that snake cost?'

'Less than you pay me for my services,' I said, programming the gun back into safe mode before I forgot.

He looked at the ruined statue for a moment before shaking his head, chuckling. 'You're probably right. And I guess you've still got the edge, right, Tanner?' He clicked his fingers at his wife. 'Okay; end of lesson, Gitta. Tanner and I need to talk about something – that's why I came out here.'

'But we've only just begun.'

'There'll be other times. You wouldn't want to learn everything right away, would you?'

No; I thought – I hoped that never happened, because then I would have no reason to be around her. The thought was dangerous – was I seriously thinking about trying something on with her, while Cahuella was no further away than another room in the Reptile House? Crazy too, because until tonight nothing Gitta had done had indicated any kind of reciprocal attraction towards me. But some of the things she'd said had made me wonder. Maybe she was just getting lonely, out here in the jungle.

Dieterling came out behind Cahuella and escorted Gitta back into the building, while another man dismantled the field generator. Cahuella and I walked away towards the wall around the terrace. The air was warm and clammy, with no hint of a breeze. During the day it could be almost unbearably humid; nothing like Nuevo Iquique's balmy coastal climate where I had spent my childhood. Cahuella's tall, broad-shouldered frame was wrapped in a black kimono patterned with interlocked dolphins, his feet bare against the terrace's chevroned tiles. His face was broad, with what always struck me as a touch of petulance around the lips. It was the look of a man who would never accept defeat gracefully. His thick black hair was permanently slicked back from his brow; brilliant grooves like beaten gold in the light from the hamadryad flames. He fingered the damaged statue, then bent down to pick up a few shards of gold from the floor. The shards were leaf-thin, like the foil which illuminators once used to decorate sacred texts. He rubbed them sadly between his fingers, then tried to place the gold back into the statue's wound. The snake was depicted curling around its tree, in its last phase of motility before the arboreal fusion-phase.

'I'm sorry about the damage,' I said. 'But you did ask for a demonstration.'

He shook his head. 'It doesn't matter; I've got dozens of them in the basement. Maybe I'll even leave it as a feature, right?'

'Deterrence?'

'Has to be worth something, hasn't it?' Then his voice lowered. 'Tanner, something's come up. I need you to come with me tonight.'

'Tonight?' It was already late, but then Cahuella tended to keep unusual hours. 'What are you planning – a late-night hunting trip?'

'I'm in the mood, but this is something else entirely. We've got visitors coming in. We need to go and meet them. There's a clearing about twenty klicks up the old jungle road. I want you to drive me there.'

I thought about that carefully before answering. 'What kind of visitors are we talking about here?'

He stroked the hamadryad's pierced head, almost lovingly. 'Not the usual kind.'

Cahuella and I were on our way from the Reptile House within half an hour, driving one of the ground-effect vehicles. It had just been enough time for Cahuella to dress for the trip, donning khaki trousers and shirt, under an elaborately pocketed tan hunting jacket. I nosed the car between the shells of derelict, vine-enshrouded buildings around the Reptile House until I found the old trail, just before it plunged into the forest. In another few months the journey would not have been possible at all – the jungle was slowly healing the wound cut through the heart of it. It would take flame-throwers to scythe it clear again.

The Reptile House and its environs had once been part of a zoological garden, built during one of the hopeful ceasefires. That particular ceasefire had only lasted a decade or so – but at the time it must have seemed that there was a good chance of peace enduring; enough for people to build something as militarily valueless and as civically improving as a zoo. The idea had been to house Terran and native specimens in similar exhibits, emphasising the similarities and differences between Earth and Sky's Edge. But the zoo had never been properly completed, and now the only intact part of it was the Reptile House, which Cahuella had made into his personal residence. It served him well: isolated and easily fortified. He had ambitions to restock its basement vivaria with a private collection of captured animals, prime amongst which would be the pre-adult hamadryad he had yet to catch. The juvenile took up a large volume already; he would need a whole new basement for a large one – not to mention extensive new expertise in the care of a creature with a substantially different biochemistry than its younger phase. Elsewhere, the House was already filled with the skins and teeth and bones of animals he had brought home as dead prizes. He had no love for living things, and the only reason that he wanted live specimens was because it would be obvious to his visitors that greater skill had been required in their capture than if they had been killed in the field.

Branches and vines slapped against the car's bodywork as I gunned it down the track, the howl of the turbines out-screeching every other living thing for miles around.

'Tell me about these visitors,' I said, my throat-mike relaying my words to Cahuella through the headphones which clamped his skull.

'You'll see them soon enough.'

'Did they suggest this clearing as a meeting place?'

'No – that was my idea.'

'And they know which clearing you were talking about?'

'They don't have to.' He nodded upwards. I risked a glance towards the forest canopy, and when the canopy thinned for a moment – revealing sky – I saw something painfully bright loitering above us, like a triangular wedge cut out of the firmament. 'They've been following us ever since we left the House.'

'That's not a native aircraft,' I said.

'It's not an aircraft, Tanner. It's a spaceship.'

We reached the clearing after an hour's drive through thickening forest. Something must have burned the clearing away a few years earlier – a seriously rogue missile, probably. It might even have been intended for the Reptile House; Cahuella had enough enemies to make that a reasonable possibility. Fortunately, most of them had no idea where he lived. Now the clearing was beginning to grow back, but the ground was still level enough to permit a landing.

The spacecraft stopped above us, silent as a bat. It was delta-shaped, and now that it had sunk lower, I saw that the underside was quilted by thousands of glaringly bright heat elements. It was fifty metres wide; half the width of the clearing. I felt the first slap of warmth, and then – at the edge of audibility – the first trace of an almost subsonic humming.

The jungle around us fell into silence.

The deltoid came in lower, three inverted hemispheres puckering gracefully from the apex points. Now it was below the treeline. The heat was making me sweat. I held up my hand to shield my eyes from the sun-bright glare.

Then the glare shut down, dimming to a dull brick-red, and the vehicle dropped the last few metres under its own weight, settling down on the hemispheres which cushioned the impact with muscle-like smoothness. For a few moments, silence, and then a ramp slid down like a tongue from the front. Blue-white glare from the doorway at the top of the ramp threw the surrounding vegetation into stark relief. In my peripheral vision I saw things scurrying and slithering for shadow.

Two spindly, elongated figures stepped into the light at the top of the ramp.

Cahuella stepped ahead of me, towards the ramp.

'You're going aboard that thing?'

He looked back, silhouetted by the light. 'Damn right I am. And I want you with me.'

'I've never dealt with Ultras before.'

'Well, now's your big chance.'

I left the car and followed him. I had a gun with me, but it felt ridiculous just to be holding it. I slipped it into my belt and never touched it again the whole time we were away. The two Ultras at the top of the ramp waited silently, standing in faintly bored postures, one leaning against the doorway's surround. When Cahuella was halfway to the parked ship he knelt down and fingered the ground, brushing aside undergrowth. I glanced down and thought I saw something exposed, like a sheet of battered metal – but before I could pay it any more attention, or wonder what it had been, Cahuella was urging me on.

'C'mon. They're not known for their immense reserves of patience.'

'I didn't even know there was an Ultra ship in orbit,' I said, keeping my voice low.

'Not many people do.' Cahuella started up the ramp. 'They're keeping very dark for now, so they can conduct certain types of business which wouldn't be possible if everyone knew they were here.'

The two Ultras were a man and a women. They were both very thin, their near-skeletal frames encased in looms of exo-support machinery and prosthetics. They were both pale and high-cheekboned, with black lips and eyes that appeared to be outlined in kohl, lending them a doll-like, cadaverous look. Both had elaborate dark hair worked in a viper's nest of stiff locks. The man's arms were smoked glass, inlaid with glowing machines and luminous pulsing feed-lines, while the woman had an oblong hole right through her abdomen.

'Don't let them freak you out,' Cahuella whispered. 'Freaking people out is part of their armoury of business techniques. You can bet the Captain sent down the two weirdest specimens he had, just to put us ill at ease.'

'He did a good job, in that case.'

'Trust me; I've dealt with Ultras. They're pussies, really.'

We ambled up the ramp. The woman, the one leaning against the doorframe, pulled herself upright and studied us with impassively pursed lips. 'You're Cahuella?' she said.

'Yeah, and this is Tanner. Tanner goes with me. That's not open to negotiation.'

She looked me over. 'You're armed.'

'Yes,' I said, only slightly unnerved that she had seen the gun through my clothes. 'You're telling me you're not?'

'We have our means. Step aboard, please.'

'The gun isn't a problem?'

The woman's smirk was the first emotional response she had shown. 'I don't seriously think so, no.'

Once we were aboard they retracted the ramp and closed the door. The ship had a cool medical ambience, all pale pastels and glassy machines. Two other Ultras waited aboard it, reclined in a pair of enormous command couches, nearly buried under readouts and delicate control stalks. The pilot and co-pilot were both naked, purple-skinned beings with impossibly dexterous fingers. They had the same stiff dreadlocks as the other two, but rather more per head.

The woman with a hole in her gut said, 'Take us up nice and easy, Pellegrino. We don't want our guests blacking out on us.'

I mouthed in Cahuella's direction, 'We're going up?'

He nodded back.

'Enjoy it, Tanner. I'm going to. Word is I won't be able to leave the surface before too long – even the Ultras won't want to touch me.'

We were shown to a pair of vacant couches. Almost as soon as we were buckled in, the ship pulled itself aloft. Through transparent patches arranged around the walls I saw the jungle clearing dropping below until it looked like a single footprint, bathed in a smudge of light. There, far off towards one horizon, was a single spot of light which had to be the Reptile House. The rest of the jungle was ocean-black.

'Why did you pick that clearing for our meeting?' asked the Ultra woman.

'You'd have looked pretty stupid parking on top of a tree.'

'That's not what I mean. We could have provided our own landing space with minimal effort. But that clearing was significant, wasn't it?' The woman sounded as if the resolution to this line of enquiry could be of only passing interest to her. 'We scanned it on our approach. There was something buried beneath it; a regularly-sided hollow space. Some kind of chamber, filled with machines.'

'We all have our little secrets,' Cahuella said.

The woman looked at him carefully, then flicked her wrist, dismissing the matter.

Then the ship surged higher, the gee-force crushing me into my seat. I made a stoic effort not to show any kind of discomfort, but there was nothing pleasant about it. The Ultras all looked cool as ice, softly mouthing technical jargon at each other; airspeed and ascent vectors. The two who had met us had plugged themselves into their seats with thick silver umbilicals which presumably assisted their breathing and circulation during the ascent phase. We shrugged off the planet's atmosphere and kept climbing. By then we were over dayside. Sky's Edge looked blue-green and fragile; deceptively serene, just as it must have looked the day the *Santiago* first made orbit. From here there was no sign of war at all, until I saw the featherlike black trails of burning oilfields near the horizon.

It was the first time I had ever seen such a view. I'd never been in space before now.

'On finals for the *Orvieto*,' reported the pilot called Pellegrino.

Their main ship came up fast. It was as dark and massive as a sleeping volcano; a chiselled cone four kilometres long. A lighthugger; that was what Ultras called their ships – sleek engines of night, capable of slicing through the void at only the tiniest of fractions below the speed of light. It was hard not to be impressed. The mechanisms which made that ship fly were more advanced than almost anything I would ever have experienced on Sky's Edge; more advanced than almost anything I could imagine.

To the Ultras our planet must have seemed like some kind of experiment in social engineering: a time-capsule imperfectly preserving technologies and ideologies which were three or four centuries out of date. That was not all our own fault, of course. When the Flotilla had left Mercury at the end of the twenty-first century, the technologies on board had been cutting-edge. But the ships took a century and a half to crawl across space to Swan's system – during which time technology stampeded back around Sol, but remained locked in stasis aboard the Flotilla.

By the time we landed, other worlds had developed near-light space travel, making our entire journey look like some pathetic, puritanical gesture of self-inflicted punishment.

Eventually the fast ships arrived at Sky's Edge, their data caches pregnant with the technological templates that could have leap-frogged us into the present, had we wished.

But by then we were at war.

We knew what *could* be achieved, but we lacked the time or resources to duplicate what had been achieved elsewhere, or the planetary finances to buy off-the-shelf miracles from passing traders. The only occasions when we bought any new technologies was when they had some direct military application, and even then it almost bankrupted us. Instead, we fought centuries-long wars with infantry, tanks, jet fighters, chemical bombs and crude nuclear devices; only very rarely graduating to such giddy heights as particle-weapons or nanotech-inspired gadgetry.

No wonder the Ultras had treated us with such ill-concealed contempt. We were savages compared to them, and the hardest thing of all was the fact that we knew it to be true.

We docked inside the *Orvieto*.

Inside, it was like a much larger version of the shuttle, all twisting pastel passages reeking of antiseptic purity. The Ultras had arranged gravity by spinning parts of their ship within the outer hull; it was slightly heavier than on Sky's Edge, but the effort was no worse than walking around with a heavy backpack. The lighthugger was also a ramliner: a passenger-carrying vessel outfitted with thousands of reefersleep berths in her belly. Some people were already being brought aboard; wide-awake aristocrats complaining loudly about the way they were being treated. The Ultras seemed not to care. The aristocrats must have paid well for the privilege of riding the *Orvieto* to wherever its next destination was, but to the Ultras they were still savages – just marginally cleaner and richer ones.

We were shown to the Captain.

He sat on an enormous powered throne, suspended on an articulated boom so that he could move throughout the bridge's vast three-dimensional space. Other senior crew were riding similar seats, but they carefully steered away from us when we entered, moving towards displays set into the walls which showed intricate schematics. Cahuella and I stood on a low-railed extensible catwalk which jutted halfway into the bridge.

'Mister . . . Cahuella,' said the man in the throne, by way of greeting. 'Welcome aboard my vessel. I am Captain Orcagna.'

Captain Orcagna was only slightly less impressive than his ship. He was dressed from neck to foot in glossy black leather, his feet in knee-length black boots with pointed toes. His hands, which he steepled beneath his chin, were gloved in black. His head was perched above the high collar of his black tunic like an egg. Unlike his crew he was completely bald, utterly hairless. His unlined, characterless face could almost have belonged to a child – or a corpse. His voice was high, almost feminine.

'And you are?' he said, nodding in my direction.

'Tanner Mirabel,' Cahuella said, before I had a chance to speak. 'My personal security specialist. Where I go, Tanner goes. That's not . . .'

'. . . open to negotiation. Yes, I gathered.' Absently, Orcagna glanced at something in mid-air, which only he could see. 'Tanner Mirabel . . . yes. A soldier once, I see – until you moved into Cahuella's employment. Confide in me: are you a man entirely without ethics, Mirabel, or are you only gravely ignorant of the kind of man you work for?'

Again, Cahuella answered. 'It's not his job to lose sleep, Orcagna.'

'But would he anyway, if he knew?' Orcagna looked at me again, but there was nothing much to be read into his expression. We might even have been talking to a puppet driven by a disembodied intelligence running on the ship's computer net. 'Tell me, Mirabel . . . are you aware that the man you work for is regarded as a war criminal in some quarters?'

'Only by hypocrites happy to buy weapons from him, as long as he doesn't sell to anyone else.'

'A level killing field is so much better than the alternative,' Cahuella said. It was one of his favourite sayings.

'But you don't just sell weapons,' Orcagna said. Once again he seemed to be viewing something hidden from us. 'You steal and kill for them. Documentary evidence implicates you in at least thirty murders on Sky's Edge, all connected with the arms black market. On three occasions you were responsible for the redistribution of weapons which had been decommissioned under peace agreements. Indirectly, you can be shown to have prolonged – even reignited – four or five local territorial disputes which had been close to negotiated settlement. Tens of thousands of lives have been lost through your actions.' Cahuella started to protest at that point, but Orcagna was having none of it. 'You are a man driven utterly by profit; completely devoid of morals or any fundamental sense of right and wrong. You are a man enthralled by the reptilian . . . perhaps because in reptiles you see your own reflected self, and at heart you are infinitely vain.' Orcagna stroked his chin, and then allowed a faint smile. 'In short, therefore, you are a man much like myself . . . someone with whom I believe I can do business.' His gaze snapped to me again. 'But tell me, Mirabel – why do you work for him? I've seen nothing in your history to suggest that you have much in common with your employer.'

'He pays me.'

'That's all?'

'He's never asked me to do anything I wouldn't do. I'm his security specialist. I protect him and those around him. I've taken bullets for him. Laser impacts. Sometimes I set up deals and meet potential new suppliers. That's dangerous work, too. But what happens to the guns after they've changed hands is no concern of mine.'

'Mm.' He touched his little finger to the corner of his mouth. 'Perhaps it should be.'

I turned to Cahuella. 'Is there a point to this meeting?'

'Yes, as always,' Orcagna snapped. 'Trade, of course, you tiresome man. Why else do you think I would risk contaminating my ship with planetary dirt?'

So it was a business meeting after all.

'What are you selling?' I asked.

'Oh, the usual – weaponry. That's all your master ever wants from us. It's the usual local attitude. Time and again, my trading associates have offered your planet access to the longevity techniques commonplace on other worlds, but on each occasion the offer has been declined in favour of sordid military goods . . .'

'That's because what you ask for the longevity tech would bankrupt half the Peninsula,' Cahuella said. 'It'd put quite a dent in my assets, too.'

'Not as big a dent as death,' Orcagna mused. 'Still; it's your funeral. Something I have to say, though: whatever we give you, look after it, will you? It would be quite unfortunate if it were to fall into the wrong hands again.'

Cahuella sighed. 'It's not my fault if terrorists rob my clients.'

The incident he was talking about had happened a month earlier. Amongst those who knew something about the transactional web of black market commerce on Sky's Edge, it was something of a talking point even now. I had set up the deal with a legitimate, treaty-abiding military faction. The exchange had been conducted through an elaborate series of fronts, with the ultimate source of the arms – Cahuella – discreetly concealed. I had handled the swap, too, conducted in a clearing similar to the one where the Ultras had met us – and that was where my involvement ended. But someone had tipped off one of the less-legitimate factions about the arms transfer, and they had ambushed the first faction on their way home from the deal.

Cahuella called the new faction terrorists, but that was to place too great a distinction between them and their legitimate victims. In a war in which the rules of engagement and the definitions of criminality changed by the week, what distinguished a legitimate faction from a less-legitimate one was often only the quality of the former's legal advice. Alliances were always shifting, past actions constantly being rewritten to cast a revisionist light on the participants. It was true that Cahuella was regarded as a war criminal now by many observers. In a century, they might be fêting him as a hero . . . me his trusty man-at-arms.

Stranger things had happened.

But it would be very hard to see the outcome of that terrorist ambush in anything but a negative light. Within a week of the ambush, they had used the same stolen weapons to murder most of an aristocratic family in Nueva Santiago.

'I don't remember the family's name.'

'Reivich, or something,' Cahuella said. 'But listen. Those terrorists were animals, agreed. If I could, I'd skin them for wallpaper and make furniture out their bones. But that doesn't mean I'm overflowing with sympathy for Reivich's clan. They were rich enough to get off-world. The whole planet's a shithole. They want somewhere safe to live, there's a whole galaxy out there.'

'We have some intelligence that might interest you,' said Orcagna. 'The youngest surviving son – Argent Reivich - has sworn vengeance against you.'

'Sworn vengeance. What is this, a morality play?' Cahuella held out a hand in front of him. 'Hey, look. I'm trembling.'

'It doesn't mean anything,' I said. 'If I had thought it was worth bothering you about, you'd already have known. That's another thing you pay me for: so you don't have to worry about every crank with a grudge against us.'

'But we don't think the fellow is, as you say, a crank.' Orcagna examined his black-gloved fingers, pulling each sequentially until there was a tiny pop. 'Our intelligence suggests that the gentleman has recovered weapons from the same militia which murdered his family. Heavy-particle armaments – suitable for a full-scale assault against a fortified stronghold. We've detected signatures from these devices, indicating that they are still operational.' The Ultra paused, then added, almost casually, 'It may amuse you to know that the signatures are moving south, down the Peninsula, towards the Reptile House.'

'Give the positions to me,' I said. 'I'll meet the kid and find out what he wants. It's possible he just wants to negotiate more arms – he may not have fingered you as the supplier.'

'Yeah,' Cahuella said. 'And I deal in fine wines. Forget it, Tanner. You think I need someone like you to handle a louse like Reivich? You don't send a pro against an amateur.' To Orcagna, he said, 'He's up country, you say? How far, what kind of territory?'

'That information can, of course, be provided.'

'Fucking bloodsucker.' For a moment his face was blank, then he smiled and pointed at the Ultra. 'I like you, I really like you. You're a fucking leech. Name your price, then. I don't need to know exactly where he is. Give me a positional fix accurate to – oh – a few kilometres. Otherwise it just wouldn't be fun, would it?'

'What the hell are you thinking of?' The words had jumped out of my mouth before I had time to censor them. 'Reivich may be inexperienced, but that doesn't mean he isn't dangerous – especially if he has the kind of weapons the militia used against his family.'

'So it'll be sporting, then. A real safari. Maybe we'll catch us a hamadryad while we're at it.'

'You like sport,' Orcagna said, knowingly.

I understood it, then. If Cahuella had not had this audience, he would never have acted like this. If we'd been back in the Reptile House, alone, he would have done the logical thing: ordered me or one of the men under me to take Reivich out with no more ceremony than flushing a toilet. It would have been beneath him to waste his time with someone like Reivich. But in front of the Ultras he could not be seen to show any weakness. He had to play the hunter.

When all was over; when our ambush against Reivich had failed, and when Gitta had been murdered, Cahuella with her, and Dieterling and myself injured, one thing became clearer than anything I had ever known in my life.

It was my fault.

I had allowed Gitta to die through my ineptitude. I had allowed Cahuella to die at the same time. The two deaths were horribly wedded. And Reivich, his hands bloodied with the wife of the man he had really sworn vengeance against, had walked away unharmed, valiant. He must have thought Cahuella would survive, too – his wounds couldn't have seemed as life-threatening as mine. Had Cahuella survived, Reivich would have inflicted maximum pain on him over the maximum span of time; a victory far less trivial than simply killing the man. In Reivich's plan, Cahuella would have had the rest of his life to miss Gitta. The pain of that loss would have been beyond words. I think she was the only living creature in the universe he was capable of loving.

But Reivich had taken her from me instead.

I thought of the way Cahuella had laughed at Reivich swearing vengeance. There had always been a fine line between the absurd and the chivalric. But that was exactly what I did: swearing that I would dedicate the rest of my life to killing Reivich; avenging Gitta. If someone had told me then that I would have to die before bringing death to Reivich, I think I would have quietly accepted that as part of the bargain.

In Nueva Valparaiso he had slipped through my fingers. At that point I'd been forced to take the gravest of decisions – whether to abandon Reivich or continue chasing him beyond the system entirely.

In hindsight, it hadn't been too difficult.

'I don't remember there being any particular problems with Mister Reivich,' Amelia said. 'He had some transient amnesia, but it wasn't as severe a case as yours – it only lasted a few hours and then he began to piece himself back together. Duscha wanted him to stay and have his implants attended to, but he was in quite a hurry to leave.'

'Really?' I did my best to sound surprised.

'Yes. God only knows what we did to offend him.'

'I'm sure it wasn't anything.' I wondered what it was about his implants that needed fixing, but decided the question could wait. 'I suppose there's a good chance he's already on Yellowstone, or nearly there. I wouldn't want to be too late following him down. I can't let him have all the fun, can I?'

She eyed me judiciously. 'You were friends with him, Tanner?'

'Well, sort of.'

'Travelling companions, then?'

'I suppose that about sums it up, yes.'

'I see.' Her face was serenely impassive, but I could imagine what she was thinking: that Reivich had never mentioned travelling with anyone else, and that if our friendship had existed at all, it must have been lopsided.

'Actually, I was rather hoping he'd have waited for me.'

'Well, he probably didn't want to burden the infirmary with someone who had no need of its ministrations. Either that, or there was some amnesia after all. We can try and contact him, of course. It won't be simple, but we do our best to keep tabs on those we revive – just in case there are complications.'

And, I thought, because some of them repay the Idlewild hospitality, when they are rich and secure on Yellowstone, and they see the Mendicants as a means of gaining influence over newcomers.

But I only said, 'No, that's kind but not at all necessary. Best if I meet him in person, I think.'

She regarded me carefully before answering. 'You'll be wanting his address on the surface, then.'

I nodded. 'I appreciate there are matters of confidentiality to be considered, but . . .'

'He'll be in Chasm City,' Amelia said, as if the utterance itself was a heresy; as if the place was the vilest pit of degradation imaginable. 'That's our largest settlement; the oldest one.'

'Yes; I've already heard of Chasm City. Can you narrow it down slightly?' I did my best not to sound sarcastic. 'A district would help.'

'I can't really help you very much – he didn't tell us exactly where he was going. But you could start in the Canopy, I suppose.'

'The Canopy?'

'I've never been there. But they say you can't miss it.'

I discharged myself the day after.

I wasn't under any illusion that I was totally well, but I knew that if I waited any longer the chances of my picking up Reivich's trail again would dwindle to zero. And while some parts of my memory had still not come back into absolutely sharp focus, there was enough there to function with; enough to let me get on with the job in hand.

I went back into the chalet to gather my things – the documents, the clothes they had given me and the pieces of the diamond gun – and once again found my attention drawn to the alcove in the wall which had so disturbed me upon waking. I'd managed to sleep in the chalet since then, and while I wouldn't have described my dreams as restful, the images and thoughts that had raced through them were of Sky Haussmann. The blood on my sheets each morning testified to that. But when I woke, there was still something about the alcove that chilled me, and which was as irrational as ever. I thought of what Duscha had told me about the indoctrinal virus, and wondered if there was anything in my infection which could cause such a baseless phobia – the virally generated structures linking to the wrong brain centres, perhaps. But at the same time I wondered if the two things might not be connected at all.

Afterwards, Amelia met me and walked with me up the long, meandering trail which led to heaven, climbing higher and higher towards one of the habitat's conic end-points. The gradient was so mild that walking was barely an effort, but there was a feeling of euphoric relief as my weight diminished and each step seemed to send me a little higher and further.

When we had walked in silence for ten or fifteen minutes, I said, 'Is it true what you hinted at earlier, Amelia? That you were once one of us?'

'A passenger, you mean? Yes, but I was just a child when it happened – I barely knew how to speak. The ship which brought us in had been damaged, and they'd lost most of the identifying records for their sleepers. They'd been picking up passengers in more than one system, too, so there was no real way to tell where I'd ever come from.'

'You mean you don't know what world you were born on?'

'Oh, I can make a few guesses – not that it interests me greatly these days.'

The path steepened momentarily, and Amelia suddenly bounded ahead of me to take the rise. 'This is my world now, Tanner. It's a blessedly small place, but it isn't a bad one, I think. Who else can say that they've seen all their world has to offer?'

'That must make it very boring.'

'Not at all. Things always change.' She pointed across the curve of the habitat. 'That waterfall wasn't always there. Oh, and there was a little hamlet down there once, where we've made a lake now. It's like that all the time. We keep having to change these paths to stop erosion – every year it's like I have to remember the place anew. We have seasons, and years when our crops don't grow as well as in other years. Some years we get a glut, too, God willing. And there's always something to explore. We get new people coming through all the time, of course – and some of them do join the Order.' She lowered her voice. 'Thankfully, they're not all like Brother Alexei.'

'There's always one bad apple.'

'I know. And I shouldn't say this . . . but after what you've taught me, I'm almost hoping Alexei tries it on again.'

I understood how she must have felt. 'I doubt that he will, but I wouldn't want to be in his shoes if he does.'

'I'll be gentle with him, don't worry.'

There was an uncomfortable silence, during which we scaled the last slope towards the end of the cone. My weight had probably dropped to a tenth of what it had been in the chalet, but walking was still possible – it just felt like the ground was receding beneath each footfall. Ahead, discreetly veiled by a copse of trees which had grown haphazardly in the low gravity, was an armoured door leading out of the chamber.

'You're serious about leaving, aren't you?' Amelia said.

'The sooner I get to Chasm City the better.'

'It won't be all that you're expecting, Tanner. I wish you'd stay with us a little longer, just so that we could bring you up to speed . . .' She trailed off, evidently realising that I was not going to be persuaded.

'Don't worry about me; I'll catch up on my history.' I smiled at her; hating myself at the same time for the way I had been forced to lie to her, but knowing there was no other way. 'Thank you for your kindness, Amelia.'

'It was my pleasure, Tanner.'

'Actually . . .' I looked around to see if anyone was observing us, but we were alone. 'There's something I'd be happy if you were to accept from me.' I reached into the pocket of my trousers and pulled out the fully assembled clockwork gun. 'It's probably best if you don't ask why I was carrying this, Amelia. It won't do me much good to carry it any further, I think.'

'I don't think I should take that from you, Tanner.'

I pushed it into her palm. 'Then confiscate it.'

'I should, I suppose. Does it work?'

I nodded; there was no need to go into details. 'It will do you some good if you ever get into real trouble.'

She slipped the gun away. 'I'm confiscating it, that's all.'

'I understand.'

She reached out and shook my hand. 'God go with you, Tanner. I hope you find your friend.'

I turned away before she could see my face.

NINE

I stepped through the armoured door.

Beyond lay a corridor walled in burnished steel, eradicating any lingering impression that Idlewild was a place, rather than an engineered human construct spinning in vacuum. Instead of the distant simmer of bonsai waterfalls, I heard the drone of circulation fans and power generators, The air had a medicinal smell it had lacked a moment earlier.

'Mister Mirabel? We heard you were leaving. This way, please.'

The first of the two Mendicants who waited for me gestured that I should follow him along the corridor. We walked along it with springy steps. At the end was an elevator which carried us the short vertical distance to the true axis of rotation of Idlewild, followed by the considerably longer horizontal distance to the true endpoint of the discarded hull which formed this half of the structure. We rode the elevator in silence, which was fine by me. I imagined the Mendicants had long since exhausted every possible conversation with the revived; that there was no answer I could give them to any question which they would not have heard a hundred times previously. But what if they had asked me what my business was, and what if I had answered truthfully?

'My business? I'm planning to kill someone, actually.'

It would have been worth it, I think, just to see their faces.

But they probably would have assumed I was just some delusional case who was discharging myself too soon.

Soon the elevator was threading its way along the inside of a glass-walled tube that ran along the outside of Idlewild. There was almost no gravity now, so we had to station ourselves by hooking limbs into padded staples sewn onto the elevator's walling. The Mendicants did this with ease, quietly amused by my fumbling attempts to anchor myself.

The view beyond was worth it, though.

More clearly now, I could see the parking swarm Amelia had shown me two days earlier – the vast shoal of starships, each tiny barbed sliver a vessel almost as large as Idlewild, yet made to seem tiny by the size of the swarm itself. Now and then violet light edged the whole swarm for an instant, as one of the ships fired its hull thrusters to adjust its lazy orbit around the other ships; a matter of etiquette, sly positioning or an urgent collision-avoidance manoeuvre. There was something heartbreakingly beautiful about the lights of distant ships, I thought. It was something that touched both on human achievement and the vastness against which those achievements seemed so frail. It was the same thing whether the lights belonged to a caravel battling the swell on a stormy horizon or a diamond-hulled starship which had just sliced its way through interstellar space.

Between the swarm and Idlewild, I could see one or two brighter smudges which must have been the exhaust flames of shuttles in transit, or new starships arriving or departing. Closer, Idlewild's hub – the tapering end of the cone – was a tangle of random docking ports, servicing bays, quarantine and medical areas. There were a dozen or so ships here, most of them tethered to the Hospice, but the majority looked like small servicing vessels – the kinds of craft the Mendicants would use if they needed to jet around the outside of their world to conduct repairs. There were only two large ships, both of which would have been minnows in comparison to one of the lighthuggers in the parking swarm.

The first was a sleek, shark-shaped ship which must have been designed for atmospheric travel. The black, light-sucking hull was offset with silver markings: Harpies and Nereids. I recognised it immediately as the shuttle which had taken me from the top of the Nueva Valparaiso bridge to the *Orvieto*, after we had been rescued. The shuttle was attached to Idlewild by a transparent umbilical, down which I could see a slow, steady stream of sleepers passing. They were still cold; still in reefersleep caskets, which were being pushed along by some kind of peristaltic compression wave of the umbilical. It looked uncomfortably as if the shuttle were laying eggs.

'They're still unloading?' I said.

'A few more bays of the sleeper hold to clear, and then she's done,' said the first Mendicant.

'I bet it depresses you, seeing all those slush puppies coming through.'

'Not at all,' the second one said, without much enthusiasm. 'It's God's will, whatever happens.'

The second large ship – the one to which our elevator was headed – was very different from the shuttle. At first glance it looked just like a random pile of floating junk which had somehow agreed to drift together. It looked barely capable of keeping itself in one piece while stationary, let alone moving.

'I'm going down in that thing?'

'The good ship *Strelnikov*,' said the first Mendicant. 'Cheer up. It's a lot safer than it looks.'

'Or is it lot less safe than it looks?' asked the other one. 'I always forget, Brother.'

'Me too. Why don't I check.'

He reached into his tunic for something. I don't know what I was expecting, but it wasn't the wooden cosh that he came out with. It looked to have been formed from the handle of a gardening tool, equipped with a leather strap at the narrow end and a few interesting scratches and stains at the other. The other Mendicant held me from behind while his friend gave me a few bruises to be going away with, concentrating his efforts on my face. There wasn't much I could do about it – they had the advantage on me in zero gravity, and they were built more like wrestlers than monks. I don't think the one with the kosh actually broke anything, but when he was done, my face felt like a large, overripe fruit. I could hardly see out of one eye and my mouth was swimming with blood and little chips of shattered enamel.

'What was all that about?' I asked, my voice moronically slurred.

'A leaving present from Brother Alexei,' said the first Mendicant. 'Nothing too serious, Mister Mirabel. Just a reminder not to interfere in our business ever again.'

I spat out a crimson sphere of blood, observing the way it retained its globular shape as it crossed from one side of the elevator to the other.

'You won't be getting a donation,' I said.

They debated whether to rough me up some more, then decided that it would be best if I didn't run the risk of any neurological damage. Maybe they were a little scared of Sister Duscha. I tried to show some gratitude, but my heart just wasn't in it.

I got a good close look at the *Strelnikov* as the elevator approached it, and the view hadn't got much better. The thing was roughly brick-shaped, about two hundred metres from end to end. Dozens of control, habitation and propulsion modules had been lashed together to make her, embedded in an intestinal explosion of snaking fuel lines and gizzard-like tanks. Here and there were what looked like the remains of hull plating; a few ragged-edged plates like the last traces of flesh on a maggot-ridden corpse. Parts of the ship appeared to have been glued back on, covered in cauls of glistening epoxy; other parts were still being welded back in place by repair teams deep inside the ship's ill-defined surface. Gases were venting steadily from six or seven places, but no one seemed particularly bothered by that.

I told myself that the ship could have looked a lot worse and it still wouldn't have mattered. The route down to the Glitter Band – the conglomeration of habitats in low orbit around Yellowstone – was a typical workhorse run. There were a dozen similar operations around Sky's Edge. There was no need for any hefty acceleration at any point in the journey, which meant that, with modest maintainence, ships could ply the same routes for centuries on end, toiling up and down the gravity well until some final, fatal systems failure turned them into macabre pieces of drifting space sculpture. There were few essential overheads, so while such routes would always have a couple of prestigious operators running luxurious shuttles on high-burn trajectories, there would also be a series of steadily more ramshackle operations, each cutting more costs than the last. At the very bottom of the heap would be chemical-rocket or ion-drive scows making painfully slow transfers between different orbits – and while the slowboat I had been assigned wasn't quite that bad, it was most definitely not at the luxury end of the scale.

But, slow as the ship was, it still represented the fastest route down to the Glitter Band. The high-burn shuttles made that run more swiftly, but no high-burners came anywhere near Idlewild. It didn't take an economics theorist to understand why: most of Idlewild's clients barely had the funds to cover their own revival, let alone an expensive shortcut to Chasm City. I'd first have had to travel to the parking swarm, and then negotiate a slot on a high-burner, with no guarantee that one was available until a later flight. Amelia had advised against that, saying that there were not nearly so many high-burners operating as before – before *what*, I didn't have a chance to ask – and that the time-saving compared to getting straight on the slow shuttle would have been marginal at best.

Eventually the elevator reached the connecting passage to the *Strelnikov*, and my Mendicant friends bade me farewell. They were all smiles now, as if the bruises on my face were just another psychosomatic manifestation of the Haussmann virus and nothing they were responsible for.

'Best of luck, Mister Mirabel.' The Mendicant with the cosh gave me a cheery wave.

'Thanks. I'll send a postcard. Or maybe I'll come back and let you know how I got on.'

'That would be nice.'

I spat out a final coagulating globule. 'Don't count on it.'

A few other prospective immigrants were being manhandled aboard ahead of me, mumbling drowsily in unfamiliar languages. Inside, we were shunted through a disorientating maze of narrow crawlways until we reached a hub somewhere deep in the *Strelnikov*'s bowels. There we were assigned accommodation cubicles for the journey down to the Glitter Band.

By the time I got to mine I was weary and aching; feeling like an animal that had come off second best in a fight and had crawled back to its den to lick its wounds. I was glad of the privacy of the cubicle. It wasn't fragrantly clean, but it wasn't filthy either: just some yellowing hybrid of the two. There was no artificial gravity on the *Strelnikov* – for which I was grateful; it wouldn't have been prudent to spin her or accelerate her too hard – so the cubicle came outfitted with a zero-gee bunk bed and various nourishment and sanitary facilities designed with the same lack of gravity in mind. There was a general network console which looked like it should have been lovingly preserved in a museum of cybernetics, and there were stained and faded warning notices stuck to every available surface appertaining to what could and couldn't be done in the ship, and how to get out of it as quickly as possible if something went wrong. Periodically, a thick-accented voice came over a Tannoy system with announcements concerning delays to the departure, but eventually the voice said that we had cast off from Idlewild, engaged drive and were on our way down. The departure had been so soft I hadn't noticed it.

I picked at the shards of tooth in my mouth, mapped the painful extremities of the bruises the Mendicants had given me, and gradually fell asleep.

TEN

On the day that the passenger was to awake – and nothing would ever be the same after that – Sky and his two closest associates were riding a service train along the *Santiago*'s spine, rumbling down one of the narrow access tunnels which threaded the ship from nose to tail. The train moved at a few lumbering kilometres per hour, stopping now and then to allow its crew to offload stores, or to wait for another train to clear the tunnel section ahead. As usual Sky's companions were passing the time with tall stories and boasts, while Sky played devil's advocate, unable to share fully in their fun but more than willing to ruin it if he saw an opportunity.

'Viglietti told me something yesterday,' Norquinco said, raising his voice to be heard above the roar of the train's passage. 'He said he didn't believe it himself, but he knew other people that did. It was about the Flotilla, actually.'

'Astonish us,' Sky said.

'Simple question: how many ships were there originally, before the *Islamabad* went up?'

'Five, of course,' Gomez said.

'Ah, but what if that's wrong? What if there were six, originally? One blew up – we know that – but what if the other one's still out there?'

'Wouldn't we have seen it?'

'Not if it's dead; just a haunted husk of a ship trailing behind us.'

'Very convenient,' Sky said. 'It wouldn't happen to have a name by any chance, would it?'

'As a matter of fact . . .'

'I knew it.'

'They say it's called the *Caleuche*.'

Sky sighed, knowing it was going to be one of *those* journeys again. There had been a time – many years ago, now – when the three of them had viewed the ship's train network as a source of amusement and carefully controlled danger; a place for hazardous games and make-believe; ghost stories and challenges. There were disused tunnels branching off from the main routes, leading, so it was rumoured, to hidden cargo bays or secret caches of stowaway sleepers, smuggled aboard by rival governments at the last moment. There were places where he and his friends had dared each other to ride on the outsides of the trains, grazing their backs against the speeding walls of the tunnels. Older now, he looked back on those games with wry bewilderment, half proud that they had taken those risks, half horrified that they had come so close to what would obviously have been gruesome death.

It was a lifetime ago. They were serious now; doing their bit for the ship. Everyone had to pull their weight in these lean new times, and Sky and his companions were regularly assigned the work of escorting supplies to and from the workers in the spine and the engine section. Usually they had to help unload the stuff and manhandle it through crawlways and down access shafts to wherever it was needed, so the work was far from the soft option it might have appeared. Sky seldom finished a shift without some fresh cuts and bruises, and all the effort had given him a set of muscles he had never expected to gain.

They were an unlikely trio. Gomez was working his way towards a job in the engine section, in the hallowed priesthood of the propulsion team. Now and then he would get to ride the train all the way there and even talk with some of the whispering engine techs, trying to impress them with his knowledge of containment physics and the other arcana of antimatter propulsion theory. Sky had watched some of those exchanges and had observed the way Gomez's questions and replies were not always swatted ruthlessly down by the techs. Sometimes they were even moderately impressed, implying that Gomez would one day be allowed to graduate to their soft-spoken priesthood.

Norquinco was a different creature entirely. He had a capacity to become completely and obsessively lost in a problem; overwhelmingly able to be fascinated by *anything*, provided it was sufficiently complex and layered. He was an assiduous keeper of lists, deeply enamoured of serial numbers and classifications. His favourite realm of study, unsurprisingly, was the hideous complexity of the *Santiago*'s nervous system; the computer networks which veined the ship and which had been altered, rerouted and written over like a palimpsest countless times since the launch; most recently after the blackout. Most sane adults quailed at attempting to understand more than a tiny sub-set of that complexity, but Norquinco was actually drawn to the entirety, perversely thrilled by something that most people saw as bordering on the pathological.

Because of that, he frightened people. The techs who worked on the network problems had well-trodden solution pathways for most glitches, and the last thing they needed was someone showing them how to do things fractionally more efficiently. Jokingly, they said it would put them out of work – but that was just a polite way of saying that Norquinco made them uneasy. So he rode with Sky and Gomez, out of harm's way.

'The *Caleuche*,' Sky said, repeating the name. 'And I suppose there's some significance in that name?'

'Enough,' Norquinco said, reading Sky's expression of deep contempt. 'The island where my ancestors came from had a lot of ghost stories. The *Caleuche* was one of them.' Norquinco was speaking earnestly now, all trace of his usual nervousness gone.

'And I suppose you're going to enlighten us about her.'

'She was a ghost ship.'

'Funny, I'd never have guessed.'

Gomez thumped him. 'Look, shut up and let Norquinco get on with it, all right?'

Norquinco nodded. 'They used to hear her; sending accordion music out across the sea at night. Sometimes she would even put into port, or take sailors from other ships. The dead aboard her were having a party that never stopped. Her crew were wizards; *brujos*. They cloaked the *Caleuche* in a cloud that followed her around everywhere. Now and then people saw her, but they could never get close to her. She would sink under the waves, or turn into a rock.'

'Ah,' Sky said, 'so this ship which people couldn't see very clearly – because it was covered in a cloud – also had the ability to turn into an old rock when they got closer? That's remarkable, Norquinco; proof of magic if ever I heard it.'

'I'm not saying there was ever an actual ghost ship,' Norquinco said testily. 'Then. But now, who knows? Perhaps the myth concerned one that was yet to come.'

'It gets better, it really does.'

'Listen,' Gomez said. 'Forget the *Caleuche*; forget the ghost ship bollocks. Norquinco's right – in a sense. It could have happened, couldn't it? There could easily have been a sixth ship, and the knowledge of it might have become confused with time.'

'If you say so. You could also argue that the whole thing was a tissue of lies made up by the terminally bored crew of a generation ship to minutely enrich the mythic fabric of their lives. If you so wished.' Sky paused as the train swerved into a different tunnel, rattling against its induction rails, gravity rising as it moved a little closer to the skin.

'Ah, I know what your problem is,' Norquinco said, with half a smile. 'It's your old man, isn't it? You don't want to believe any of this because of who your father is. You can't stand the idea of him not knowing about something so significant.'

'Maybe he does know, has that ever occurred to you?'

'So you admit the ship could be real.'

'No, actually . . .'

But Gomez interrupted him, obviously warming to the subject. 'As a matter of fact, I don't find it hard to believe that there was once a sixth ship. Launching six rather than five wouldn't have been much more effort, would it? After that – after the ships had got up to cruising speed – there could have been some disaster . . . some tragic event, deliberate or otherwise, which left the sixth ship essentially dead. Coasting, but derelict, with its crew all killed, probably its *momios* as well. There must have been enough residual power to keep the remaining antimatter in containment, of course, but that wouldn't have taken much.'

'What,' Sky said, 'and we just forgot about it?'

'If the other ships had also played a part in the destruction of the sixth, it wouldn't have been difficult to edit the data records of the entire Flotilla to remove any reference to the crime itself, or even the fact the victim had ever existed. That generation of crew could have sworn not to pass on the knowledge of the crime to their descendants, our parents.'

Gomez nodded enthusiastically. 'So by now all we'd have been left is with a few rumours; half-forgotten truths mixed up in myth.'

'Exactly what we *do* have,' Norquinco said.

Sky shook his head, knowing it was futile to argue any further.

The train came to a halt in one of the loading bays which serviced this part of the spine. The three of them got out carefully, crunching their sticky-soled shoes onto the flooring for traction. There was scarcely any feeling of gravity now since they were so close to the axis of rotation. Objects still fell towards the floor, but with a certain reluctance, and it was easy to hurt your head against the ceiling if you took too ambitious a stride.

There were many such bays, each servicing a cluster of *momios*. There were six sleeper modules attached around this part of the spine, each of which held ten individual cryogenic berths. The trains reached no closer, and almost all equipment and supplies had to be manhandled from this point, via laddered shafts and winding crawlways. There were freight elevators and handler robots, but neither was used very often. Robots in particular needed diligent programming and maintenance, and even the simplest task had to be spelled out to them as if they were particularly slow-witted children. Usually, it was quicker just to do it yourself. That was why there were so many techs, usually leaning against the pallets looking bored, smoking homemade cigarettes or tapping styluses against clipboards, doing their best to look semi-occupied despite the fact that nothing was actually happening. The techs generally wore blue overalls flashed with section decals, but the overalls were usually ripped or amended in some fashion, exposing crudely tattooed skin. Sky knew all of them by face, of course – on a ship with only one hundred and fifty warm human beings, it was difficult not to. But he had only a vague idea what their names were, and next to none about the kinds of lives the techs lived when they were not working. Off-duty techs tended to keep to their own parts of the

Santiago, and they tended to socialise amongst themselves, even to the extent of producing their offspring. They spoke their own patois, drenched in carefully guarded jargon.

But something was slightly different now.

No one was lazing around or trying to look busy. In fact, there were hardly any techs in the room at all, and the few that were here looked edgy, as if waiting for an alarm to go off.

'What's the matter?' Sky said.

But the man who stepped gingerly from behind the nearest tower of equipment pallets was not a tech. He brushed his hand across the chrome shoulder of a crouched handler robot as if looking for support, sweat blistering on his forehead.

'Dad?' Sky said. 'What are you doing here?'

'I could ask you the same question, unless this is one of your chores.'

'Of course it is. I told you we work the trains now and then, didn't I?'

Titus looked distracted. 'Yes . . . yes, you did. I forgot. Sky, help these men unload the goods, and then get you and your friends away from here, will you?'

Sky looked at his father. 'I don't understand.'

'Just do it, will you?' Then Titus Haussmann turned to the nearest tech, a heavily bearded fellow with grotesquely muscled forearms folded across his chest like hams. 'The same goes for you and your men, Xavier. Get all non-essential people out of here, all the way back up the spine. As a matter of fact I want the engine section evacuated while we're at it.' He flipped up his sleeve and whispered orders into his bracelet. Recommendation, more accurately, Sky thought, but Old Man Balcazar would never fail to abide by Titus Haussmann's advice. Then he turned to Sky again, blinking to see his son still present. 'Didn't I just tell you to get on with it, son? I wasn't kidding.'

Norquinco and Gomez took their leave, accompanying a couple of techs to the waiting train, flipping open one of its freight covers and beginning the knuckle-grazing work of unloading supplies. They passed the boxes from hand to hand, out of the bay altogether, where they would presumably be lowered down the levels to the sleeper berths themselves.

'Dad, what is it?' Sky said.

He thought his father was going to reprimand him, but Titus simply shook his head. 'I don't know. Not yet. But there's something not right with one of our passengers – something that has me a little worried.'

'What do you mean, not right?'

'One of the bastard *momios* is waking up.' He mopped his forehead. 'That's not supposed to happen. I've been down there, into the berth, and I still don't understand it. But it has me worried. That's why I want this area cleared.'

This was a marvel indeed, Sky thought. None of the passengers had ever awakened, even though a few of them had certainly died. But his father seemed less than overjoyed at the situation. Gravely concerned, more accurately.

'Why is it a problem, Dad?'

'Because they're not meant to wake up, that's why. If it happens at all, it must mean it was planned from day one. Before we ever left the solar system.'

'But why clear the area?'

'Because of something my father told *me*, Sky. Now do what I just told you and get that train unloaded and then get the hell away from here, will you?'

At that moment another train slid into the bay from the opposite direction, nosing up against the one Sky had arrived upon. Four of Titus's security people emerged from it, three men and a woman, and began buckling on plastic armour that had been too bulky to wear during the journey. This was practically the entire operational militia for the ship, its police force and army, and even these people were not fulltime security officers. The squad moved forward to another part of the train and unracked guns: gloss-white weapons which they handled with nervous care. His father had always told him that there were no guns aboard ship, but never very convincingly.

There were, in fact, many aspects of shipboard security about which Sky wanted to know more. His father's small, tight, highly efficient organisation fascinated him. But Sky had never been allowed to work with his father. The explanation which Titus gave for this was plausible enough: he could not claim impartiality or fairness if his son were to be given a role in the organisation, no matter how apt Sky might have been – but that did not make it any less bitter a pill to swallow. Consequently the tasks Sky was assigned were always as far away from anything remotely security-related as Titus could ensure. Nothing would or could change while Titus remained head of security, and both of them understood that.

Sky went to join his friends, helping them off-load the supplies. They were getting through the job quickly, without any of the carefully honed dawdling that usually accompanied the process. His friends were unnerved; whatever was going on here was out of the ordinary and Titus Haussmann was not a man to pretend there was a crisis where none existed.

Sky kept one eye on the security squad.

They settled fabric headsets over their shaven skulls, tapping microphones and checking communication frequencies. Then they pulled armoured helmets from the train and pushed their heads into them, adjusting drop-down overlay monocles which covered one eye. A slim black line ran from each helmet to the sight attached to the top of each gun, so that the guns could be discharged without the guard having to look in the direction of fire. They probably had infra-red or sonar overlays as well. That would be useful down in the gloomy sub-levels.

When they had stopped fiddling with their equipment, the squad moved over to his father, who briefed them quickly and quietly, with the absolute minimum of fuss. Sky watched his father's lips move; his expression one of complete calm now that he was in the presence of his own squad. Occasionally he made a taut, precise hand gesture or shook his head. He might as well have been telling them all a nursery rhyme. Even the sweat on his forehead seemed to have dried up.

Then Titus Haussmann left the squad, and went back over to the train they had arrived on and pulled his own gun from it. No armour or helmet; just the weapon. It was the same gloss-white as the others. There was a sickle-shaped magazine beneath it and a skeletal stock. His father handled it with quiet respect rather than easy familiarity: the way a man might handle a venomous snake that had just been milked.

All for a single sleepless passenger?

'Dad . . .' Sky said, leaving his duty again. 'What is it? What is it really?'

'Nothing you need worry about,' his father said.

Titus took three of the squad with him and left the fourth behind, standing guard in the freight bay. The detachment disappeared down one of the access shafts which led to the berths, the clatter of their progress growing quieter, but never quite silencing. When he was certain that his father was out of earshot, Sky moved over to the guard who had been stationed in the bay.

'What's going on, Constanza?'

She flipped up the monocle. 'What makes you think I'm about to tell you, if your father didn't?'

'I don't know. A wild shot in the dark along the lines of us both having been friends at one point, I suppose.'

He had known it was her the instant the train had arrived; given the apparent severity of the situation it had been certain that she would be amongst the squad.

'I'm sorry,' Constanza said. 'It's just that we're all a tiny bit edgy, understand?'

'Of course.' He studied her face, as beautiful and fierce as ever, wondering how it would feel to trace the line of her jaw. 'I heard it was about one of the passengers waking up too early. Is that true?'

'More or less,' she said, as if through gritted teeth.

'And for that you need more firepower than I've ever seen before on the ship? More than I ever knew existed?'

'Your father determines how we handle individual incidents, not me.'

'But he must have said something. What is it about this one passenger?'

'Look, I don't know, all right? Just that whatever it is, it isn't supposed to happen. The *momios* aren't meant to wake up early. That just isn't possible, unless someone programmed their sleeper berth to make it happen. And no one would have done that unless they had a good reason.'

'I still don't understand why anyone would want to wake up *early*.'

'To sabotage the mission, of course.' She lowered her voice now, and clicked her fingernails against the gun, edgily. 'A single sleeper placed aboard not as a passenger, but as a time-bomb. A volunteer on a suicide mission, say – a criminal, or someone else with nothing to lose. Someone angry enough to want to kill us all. It wasn't easy to get a slot on the Flotilla when she left Sol, remember. The *Confederacion* made as many enemies as friends when it built the fleet. It wouldn't be difficult to find someone willing to die, if it allowed them to punish us.'

'It would be difficult to do, though.'

'Only if you forgot to bribe the right people.'

'I suppose you're right. When you say time-bomb you're not talking literally, are you?'

'No – but now that you mention it, it isn't such an absurd idea. What if they – whoever they were – managed to plant a saboteur aboard every ship? Maybe the one aboard the *Islamabad* was just the first to wake. And they wouldn't have had any warning.'

'Maybe a warning wouldn't have helped them much, in that case.'

She clenched her teeth. 'I guess we're about to find out. On the other hand, it could just be a malfunctioning sleeper berth.'

That was when the first gunshots were heard.

Whatever was happening was taking place tens of metres beneath the loading bay, but the shots still sounded fearsomely loud. There were shouts as well. He thought he heard his father, but it was difficult to tell: the acoustics lent a metallic quality to the voices, rendering the words indistinct and blurring the differences in timbre.

'Shit,' Constanza said. For a moment she froze, then she was making for the access well. She turned and flashed wild eyes at him. 'You stay here, Sky.'

'I'm coming with you. That's my father down there.'

The shots had ceased, but there was still a lot of noise, voices mainly, raised to the point of hysteria, and what sounded like things being thrown around. Constanza checked her gun again and then stowed it over a shoulder. She walked towards the access well, preparing to lever herself into its laddered, echoing depths.

'Constanza . . .'

He grabbed her gun and wrestled it from her shoulder before she had time to act. Constanza turned round in fury, but he was already easing past her, not exactly pointing the gun at her, but not exactly pointing it away from her either. He had no idea how to use it, but he must have looked sufficiently purposeful. Constanza backed off now, her eyes flicking to the gun. It was still tethered to her helmet by the black flex, which was now stretched to its limit.

'Give me the head-gear,' Sky said, nodding towards her.

'You'll be in deep shit for this,' she said.

'What, going after my father when he's in danger? I don't think so. A mild reprimand at the very worst, I think.' He nodded again. 'The helmet, Constanza.'

She grimaced and pulled the helmet from her head. Sky settled it over his own, not bothering to ask her for the fabric underlayer. The helmet was a little small for him, but there was no time to adjust it now. He flipped down the monocle, gratified when it lit up with the view that the gun was seeing. The image was all shades of grey-green, overlaid by cross-hairs, range-finder numerics and weapons-status summaries. None of that meant anything to him, but when he looked at Constanza he saw her nose stand out as a white smudge of heat. Infra-red; that was all he needed to know.

He lowered himself into the shaft, aware that Constanza was following him at a discreet distance.

There were no shouts now, but there were still voices. They were quiet, but there was nothing calm about them. He could hear his father quite distinctly now; there was something not quite right about the way he was talking.

He reached the nexus which connected the sleeper berths of this node. They radiated out in ten directions, but only one of the connecting doors was open. That was where the voices were coming from. He pointed the gun ahead of him and moved towards the berth, down the normally dark, pipe-lined corridor which led to it. Now the corridor shone in sickly shades of grey-green. He was scared, he realised. Fear had always been there, but it was only now that he had the gun and had climbed down that he had time to pay attention to it. Fear was a nearly unfamiliar thing to him, but not completely so. He remembered his first real taste of it, alone in the nursery, betrayed and deserted. Now he watched his own shadow trace phantom shapes along the wall, and for a fleeting moment wished that Clown were with him now to offer guidance and friendship. The idea of returning to the nursery was suddenly very tempting. It was a world unsullied by rumours of ghost ships or sabotage, of present and real hardships.

He crept round a dogleg in the corridor and there was the berth ahead of him: the large, machine-filled support chamber for a single sleeper. It was like a dedicated burial room in a church, reeking of antiquity and reverence. The room had been cold until recently and much of it was still olive-green or black in his vision.

From behind he heard Constanza speak. 'Give me the gun, Sky, and no one will know you took it.'

'I'll give it back when the danger's passed.'

'We don't even know what the danger is yet. Perhaps someone's gun just went off by accident.'

'And the sleeper berth just happened to be malfunctioning, as well? Yeah, right.'

He entered the sleeper berth and took in the tableau that greeted him. The three security guards were there, as was his father – blobs of pale-green shading to white.

'Constanza,' one of them said. 'I thought you were supposed to cover . . . shit. It isn't you, is it?'

'No. It's me. Sky Haussmann.' He flipped up the monocle, the room gloomier than it had been a moment ago.

'And where's Constanza?'

'I took her helmet and gun, entirely against her wishes.' He looked behind him, hoping that Constanza had heard this attempt at exonerating her. 'She did put up a fight, believe me.'

The berth was one of ten in a ring, each fed by its own corridor from the node. The room had probably been entered only one or two times since the Flotilla's launch. The sleeper support systems were as delicate and complex as the antimatter engines; just as likely to go horribly wrong if tampered with by anything other than expert hands. Like buried pharaohs, the sleepers had not expected their places of slumber to be violated until they reached what passed for the afterlife – arrival around 61 Cygni-A. It felt a little wrong just to be here at all.

But not half as wrong as it felt to see his father.

Titus Haussmann was lying on the floor, his upper body cradled by one of the security guards. His chest was covered in a dark, cloying fluid that Sky knew was blood. There were canyonlike gashes in his uniform, in which the blood was pooling thickly, gurgling disgustingly with each laboured breath.

'Dad . . .' Sky said.

'It's all right,' one of the guards answered. 'There's a medical team on their way.'

Which, Sky thought – given the general state of medical expertise aboard the *Santiago* – was about as useful as saying there were priests coming. Or undertakers.

He looked at the sleeper casket; the long, plinth-like, machine-encrusted cryo-coffin which filled much of the room. The upper half of it was cracked wide open, huge jagged fractures like shattered glass. Sharp bits of it formed a haphazard glass mosaic on the floor. It was exactly as if something inside the casket had forced its way out.

And there was something inside it.

The passenger was dead, or nearly dead; that much was obvious. At first glance the man looked normal enough apart from the bullet wounds: a naked human being invaded by monitoring wires, blood-shunts and catheters. He was younger than most of them, Sky thought – excellent fanatic fodder, in other words. But with his bald head and masklike lack of facial muscle tone, the man could have passed for a thousand other sleepers.

Except that his forearm had come off.

It was lying on the floor, in fact – a limp, glove-like thing, ending in flaps of ragged skin. But there was no bone or meat showing from the end, and very little blood had leaked from the severed limb. The stump was wrong as well. The man's skin and bone stopped a few inches below his elbow, and then it was all tapering metal prosthesis: a complex, blood-lathered, glittering obscenity which ended not in steel fingers but in a vicious assemblage of blades.

Sky imagined how it must have happened.

The man had woken inside his casket, probably following a plan laid down before the Flotilla had left Mercury. He must have intended to wake up unobserved, smash his way to freedom and then set about inflicting stealthy harm on the ship, in precisely the way that might have happened on the *Islamabad*, if Constanza's theory was correct. A lone man could certainly do great damage, if he was not obliged to allow for his own survival.

But his revival had not gone unnoticed. He must have been in the process of waking when the secuity team had entered the berth. Perhaps Sky's father had been leaning over the casket, examining it, when the man had cracked it open with his forearm weapon. It would have been very easy for him to stab Titus then, even if the other squad members were doing their best to put magazine-loads of bullets into him. Drugged with pain-nullifying revival chemicals, he had probably barely noticed the shots eating into him.

They had stopped him, maybe even killed him, but not before he had inflicted extreme harm on Titus. Sky knelt down next to his father. Titus's eyes were still open, but they seemed not quite to focus.

'Dad? It's me. Sky. Try and hang on, will you? The medics are coming. It'll be all right.'

One of the guards touched his shoulder. 'He's strong, Sky. He had to go in first, you know. That was his way.'

'Is his way, you mean.'

'Of course. He'll pull through.'

Sky started to say something, the words assembling in his head, but suddenly the passenger was moving; at first with dreamlike slowness then with terrifying speed. For a yawning instant it was not something he was prepared to believe; the man's injuries were simply too severe for him to be capable of movement, let alone movement that was swift and violent.

The passenger rolled from the casket, the movement lithe and animal-like, and then the man was standing, and with one elegant scythe-like sweep of his arm he cut one of the guards open across the throat, the guard collapsing to his knees with blood fountaining from the wound. The passenger paused, holding his weapon-arm in front of him, and then the complex cluster of knives whirred and clicked, one blade retracting while another slotted into place, gleaming with pure-blue surgical brilliance. The passenger studied this process with what looked like quiet fascination.

He stepped forward, towards Sky.

Sky still had Constanza's gun, but the fear was so intense that he could not even hold the weapon up to threaten the passenger. The passenger looked at him, the muscles beneath the flesh rippling strangely, as if dozens of orchestrated maggots were crawling over the bones of his skull. The rippling halted, and for a moment the face staring back at Sky was a crude approxima-tion of his own. Then the rippling resumed and the face was no longer one Sky recognised.

The man smiled, and pushed his clean new blade into Sky's chest. There was a curious lack of pain, and the immediate effect was only as if the man had thumped him hard across the ribs. He fell back, winded, out of the passenger's way.

Behind, the two uninjured guards had their guns levelled and ready to fire.

Sky, slumped down, attempted to draw his next breath. The pain was exquisite, and he felt none of the relief that the inhalation should have brought. The passenger's knife had almost certainly punctured a lung, he decided, and the blow might well have shattered a rib in the process. But the blade appeared to have missed his heart, and he could still move his legs, so it had probably not damaged his spine.

Another moment elapsed and he wondered why the guards had yet to open fire. He could see the passenger's back; they must have had a clear target.

Constanza, of course. She was just beyond the passenger, and if they shot at him their rounds had a high likelihood of passing right through his body and ripping through her. She could retreat, but with the connecting doors to the other berths sealed – and no chance of opening them in a hurry – the only way to go was up the ladder. And the passenger would be immediately behind her. Ordinarily, having just one arm would have hindered anyone's ascent of a ladder, but the normal physiological rules did not seem to apply here.

'Sky . . .' she said. 'Sky. You've got my gun. You've got a clearer line of fire than the other two. Shoot now.'

Still lying down, still struggling for breath – he could hear his lung wound gurgling like a baby – he raised the gun and aimed it in the vague direction of the passenger, who was walking calmly towards Constanza.

'Do it now, Sky.'

'I can't.'

'Do it. It's a question of Flotilla safety.'

'I can't.'

'Do it!'

His hand trembling, barely able to hold the gun now, let alone aim it with any precision, he directed the muzzle in the approximate direction of the passenger's back, then closed his eyes – though by then he was fighting a black tide of unconsciousness anyway – and squeezed the trigger.

The burst of fire was short and sharp, like a loud, deep burp. Combined with the sound of the gun's discharge was a metallic roar: the sound of bullets ramming not into flesh but into the corridor's armoured cladding.

The passenger halted, as if about to turn around and return for something it had forgotten, and then fell down.

Constanza, beyond, was still standing.

She advanced forward, then kicked the passenger, eliciting no visible response. Sky allowed the gun to slip from his fingers, but by then the other two guards were level with him and their weapons were trained on the passenger.

Sky struggled for the breath to speak. 'Dead?'

'I don't know,' Constanza said. 'Not going anywhere in a hurry, anyway. Are you all right?'

'Can't breathe.'

She nodded. 'You'll live. You should have shot him when I said, you know.'

'Did.'

'No, you didn't. You fired indiscriminately and got a lucky break with a ricochet. You could have ended up killing all of us.'

'Didn't.'

She stooped down and retrieved the gun. 'Mine, I think.'

By then the medical team had arrived, clambering down the ladder. There had been no time to brief them, of course, and for a moment they dithered, unsure who to treat first. A respected and high-ranking member of the crew was severely injured before them; two other crew members had wounds that might also be life-threatening. But there was also an injured passenger, a member of that even higher elite they had spent their entire lives serving. The fact that the *momio* was not quite what he seemed did not immediately register with them.

One of the medics found Sky and after an initial check-up placed a breather mask over his face, flooding his ailing respiratory system with pure oxygen. He felt some of that black tide lap away.

'Help Titus,' Sky said, indicating his father. 'But do what you can for the passenger as well.'

'Are you certain?' the medic said, who by then must have grasped something of what had gone on.

Sky pressed the mask to his face again before answering, his mind racing ahead to what he could do to the passenger; the labyrinthine ways in which he might inflict pain on the killer.

'Yes. I'm more than certain.'

ELEVEN

I woke up shivering; trying to extricate myself from the coils of the Haussmann dream. The dream's after-image was disturbingly vivid; I could still feel myself there with Sky, watching his wounded father being taken away. I examined my hand in the dim light of the sleeping cubicle, the blood at the centre of my right palm black and cloying like a spot of tar.

Sister Duscha had told me this was a mild strain, but I was obviously nowhere near getting over it on my own. There was no way I could have delayed chasing Reivich, but Duscha's suggestion that I spend another week or so in Idlewild having the virus flushed out by professionals suddenly seemed infinitely preferable to weathering it on my own. And while the strain might have been weak compared to some, there was no guarantee that it had reached its worst.

Now I felt a familiar and not very welcome feeling: nausea. I wasn't at all used to zero-gravity, and the Mendicants hadn't given me drugs to make the trip any more bearable. I thought about it for a few minutes, debating whether it was worth leaving my cubicle, or whether I should just lie low and accept the discomfort until we reached the Glitter Band. Eventually my stomach won and I decided to make my way to the ship's communal core. One of the instruction labels in the cabin told me I'd be able to buy something to kill the worst of the sickness.

Just getting to the commons was more adventure than I really needed. It was a wide, furnished and pressurised sphere somewhere near the front of the ship, where food, drugs and entertainment were available, but it was only accessible through a warren of claustrophobic one-way crawlways which snaked around and through the engine components. The instructions in my cubicle advised against tardiness during crawls through certain parts of the ship, leaving the reader to draw their own conclusions about the state of the internal nuclear shielding in those areas.

On my way there I thought about the dream.

There was something about it that bothered me, and I kept asking myself whether what had happened in it meshed with what I already knew about Sky Haussmann. I was no expert on the man (I hadn't been, anyway) but there were certain basic facts about him which it was difficult to avoid if you had been brought up on Sky's Edge. We all knew about the way he had become frightened of the dark after the blackout aboard the *Santiago*, when the other ship blew up, and we all knew about the way his mother had died in the same incident. Lucretia had been a good woman, by all accounts, well loved across the Flotilla. Titus, Sky's father, was a man who was respected and feared but never truly hated. They called him the *caudillo*: the strong man. Everyone agreed that while Sky might have had an unusual upbringing, his parents could not really be blamed for the crimes that followed.

We all knew that Sky had not had many friends, but nonetheless we remembered the names of Norquinco and Gomez, and how they had been complicit – if not truly equal partners – in what had happened later. And we all knew that Titus had been gravely injured by a saboteur placed amongst the passengers. He had died a few months later, when the saboteur broke out of his restraints in the ship's infirmary and murdered him while he was recuperating nearby.

But now I was puzzled. The dream had veered into an area which was unfamiliar to me. I didn't remember anyone ever mentioning the rumour of another ship, a sinister ghost vessel trailing the Flotilla like the fabled *Caleuche*. Even the *Caleuche*'s name failed to ring any bells. What was happening? Was the indoctrinal virus just sufficiently detailed in its knowledge of Sky's life that it was revealing my own prior ignorance of events, or had I been infected with an undocumented strain, one that contained hidden curlicues of story missing from most of the others? And were those embellishments historically accurate (but simply not well known), or sheer fiction: addendums put in there by bored cultists trying to spice up their own religion?

There was no way to know – yet. But it seemed I was going to have to sleep through further instalments of Haussmann's life whether I liked it or not. Although I couldn't say I exactly welcomed the dreams – or the way they seemed to smother any I might have been planning to have myself – at least now I would admit to some mild curiosity as to how they played out.

I crawled onwards, forcing the dreams from my mind, and concentrated instead on the place to which the *Strelnikov* was ultimately headed.

The Glitter Band.

I had heard of it, even on Sky's Edge. Who hadn't? It was one of a few dozen places that were famous enough to be known about in other solar systems; places that had a certain allure even across light years. On scores of settled worlds, the Glitter Band was shorthand for a place of limitless bounty and luxury and personal freedom. It was everything that Chasm City was, but without the inescapable crush of gravity. It was where people jokingly talked of going when they made their fortunes, or married into the family with the right connections. There was nowhere in our own system that had anything like the same glamour. To many people the place might as well have been mythical, for all the likelihood of them ever getting there.

But the Glitter Band was real.

It was the string of ten thousand elegant, wealthy habitats which orbited Yellowstone: a beautiful concatenation of arcologies and carousels and cylinder-cities, like a halo of stardust thrown around the world. Although Chasm City was the ultimate repository for the system's wealth, the city had a reputation for conservatism, rooted in its three-hundred-year history and immense sense of self-importance. The Glitter Band, by contrast, was constantly being reinvented, habitats shuffling in and out of formation, being dismantled and made anew. Subcultures blossomed like a thousand flowers before their proponents decided to try something else instead. Where art in Chasm City verged on the staid, almost anything was encouraged in the Glitter Band. One artist's masterworks existed only in the tiniest instants when they could be sculpted out of quark-gluon plasma and held stable, their existence implied only by a subtle chain of inference. Another used shaped fission charges to create nuclear fireballs which assumed the brief likenesses of celebrities. Wild social experiments took place: voluntary tyrannies, in which thousands of people willingly submitted themselves to the control of dictatorial states so that they could be freed from having to make any moral choices in their own lives. There were whole habitats where people had had their higher brain functions disengaged, so that they could live like sheep under the care of machines. In others, they'd had their minds implanted into monkeys or dolphins: lost in intricate arboreal power struggles or sorrowful sonar fantasies. Elsewhere, groups of scientists who'd had their minds reshaped by Pattern Jugglers plunged deep into the metastructure of spacetime, concocting elaborate experiments which tinkered with the very fundamentals of existence. One day, it was said, they'd discover a technique for faster-than-light propulsion, passing the secret to their allies who would install the necessary gadgetry in their habitats. The first anyone else would know about it would be when half the Glitter Band suddenly winked out of existence.

The Glitter Band, in short, was a place where a reasonably curious human being could easily squander half a lifetime. But I didn't think Reivich would spend much time there before making his way down to Yellowstone's surface. He would want to lose himself in Chasm City as quickly as possible.

Either way, I wouldn't be far behind him.

Still fighting nausea, I crawled into the commons and looked around at the dozen or so fellow passengers in the sphere. Although everyone was at liberty to float at whatever angle they liked (at the moment the slowboat's engines were off), everyone had anchored themselves the same way up. I found a vacant wall strap, fed my elbow into it and surveyed my fellow slush puppies with what I knew would appear only casual interest. They were clustered into twos and threes, talking quietly while a spherical servitor moved through the air, impelled by tiny fans. The servitor moved from group to group, offering services which it dispensed from a compendium of hatches around its body. It reminded me of a hunter-seeker drone, silently selecting its next target.

'You needn't look so nervous, friend,' someone said, in thick, slurred Russish. 'It's just *robot*.'

I was losing my edge. I'd been unaware of anyone sidling up to me. Languidly, I turned to look at the man who had spoken. I was confronted by a wall of meat blocking half the commons. His pink, raw-looking face was triangular, anchored to his torso by a neck thicker than my thigh. His hairline began only a centimetre or so above his eyebrows: long black hair laquered back over the roughly hewn boulder that was his scalp. His wide, downcurved mouth was framed by a thick black moustache and a beard that was no more than a razor-thin line of hair tracing the enormous width of his jaw. He had his arms crossed in front of his chest like a Cossack dancer, hypertrophied muscles bulging through the fabric of his coat. It was a long quilted coat sewn with rough patches of stiff, glistening fabric which caught the light and refracted it back in a million spectral glints. His eyes stared through me rather than at me, and seemed not to be focused on quite the same thing, as if one were glass.

Trouble, I thought.

'Nobody's nervous,' I said.

'Hey, talkative guy.' The man anchored himself to the wall next to me. 'I just make conversation, *da*?'

'That's good. Now go and make it somewhere else.'

'Why you so unfriendly? You not like Vadim, friend?'

'I was prepared to give you the benefit of the doubt,' I said, answering him in Norte, even though I could more or less get by in Russish. 'But on balance . . . no, I don't think I do. And until we're better acquainted, I'm not your friend. Now go away and let me think.'

'I think about it.'

The servitor lingered near us. Oblivious to the increasing tension between us, its dumb processor soldiered on, addressing us as a pair of fellow travellers, asking what services we might require. Before the huge man could say anything, or even move, I told the servitor to supply me with a scopolamine-dextrose shot. It was the oldest and cheapest anti-nausea drug in the book. Like all the passengers I had established a shipboard credit account for the duration of the journey, although I was only half-certain I had the funds to cover the scop-dex. But the servitor obliged, a hatch popping open to reveal a disposable hypodermic.

126

I took the hypo, rolled up my sleeve and slammed the needle into a vein, just as if I was readying myself for a possible biological warfare attack.

'Hey, you do that like *pro*. No hesitation.' The man spoke with what sounded like genuine admiration, shifting to slow, slurred Norte. 'What are you, doctor?'

I rolled my sleeve over the upwelling mark where the needle had gone in.

'Not quite. I work with sick people, though.'

'Yes?'

I nodded. 'I'd be happy to give you a demonstration.'

'I am not sick.'

'Trust me, that's never been a problem in the past.'

I wondered if he was getting the message just yet; that I was not his ideal choice for a conversation partner for the next day. I popped the used hypo back into the servitor, the scop-dex already beginning to blast my nausea into a fog of merely mild unpleasantness. There were almost certainly more effective treatments for space sickness – anti-agonists – but even if they had been available, I doubted that I had the funds to cover them.

'Tough guy,' the man said, nodding, an articulation for which his neck was not really engineered. 'I like it. But how tough you really?'

'I don't think it's any of your business, but you're welcome to try me.'

The servitor loitered near us for a few more moments before deciding to float to the next cluster. A few other people had just drifted into the commons, looking around with sickly expressions. It was ironic that after crossing so many light-years between stars, this little slowboat transfer was for many of us our first conscious taste of space travel.

He eyed me. I could almost hear the little gears working away in his skull, grinding laboriously. No doubt most of the people he approached were more easily intimidated than I was.

'Like I say, I am Vadim. Everyone calls me that. Just Vadim. I'm quite *character* – part of what you might call local colour. And you are?'

'Tanner,' I said. 'Tanner Mirabel.'

He nodded slowly, wisely, as if my name meant something to him.

'That real name?'

'Yes.'

It was my real name, but I lost nothing by using it. There was no way Reivich could have learned my name yet, even though it was clear that he knew *someone* was following him. Cahuella kept a very tight lid on his operation, sheltering the identities of his employees. The best he could have managed was to weasel out of the Mendicants a list of everyone else who had been on the *Orvieto* – but that would still not have told him who amongst those people was the man who intended to kill him.

Vadim tried to inject a tone of comradely interest into his voice. 'Where you come from, Meera-Bell?'

'You don't need to know,' I said. 'And please, Vadim – I was serious just now. I don't want to talk to you, local colour or not.'

'But I have business proposition, Meera-Bell. One you should hear, I think.' He continued to stare through me with one eye. The other gazed obliquely past my shoulder, unfocused.

'I'm not interested in business, Vadim.'

'I think you should be.' He had lowered his voice now. 'It is dangerous place where we are headed, Meera-Bell. Dangerous, dangerous place. Especially for newcomers.'

'What's so dangerous about the Glitter Band?'

He smiled, then cancelled the smile. 'Glitter Band . . . yes. That is really quite interesting. I am sure you'll find it at odds with . . . expectations.' He paused, caressing his stubbled chin with one hand. 'And we have not even mentioned Chasm City, *nyet?*'

'Danger's a relative term, Vadim. I don't know what it means here, but where I come from, it implies more than just the ever-present hazard of committing a social gaffe. Trust me, I think I can handle the Glitter Band. And Chasm City, for that matter.'

'You think you know about danger? I do not think you have first idea what you are walking into, Meera-Bell. I think you are very ignorant man.' He paused, toying with the rough fabric patches of his quilted coat, refraction patterns racing away under the pressure of his fingertips. 'Which is why I am talking to you now, understand? I am being *good Samaritan* to you.'

I could see where this was heading. 'You're going to offer me protection, aren't you?'

Vadim winced. 'Such crude term. Please, do not say it again. I would much rather we talk about benefits of *mutual security agreement*, Meera-Bell.'

I nodded. 'Let me speculate here, Vadim. You really are local, aren't you? You haven't come off a ship at all. My guess is you're pretty much a permanent fixture on this slowboat – am I right?'

He grinned, quickly and nervously. 'Let us just say I know my way around ship better than average recently defrosted slush puppy. And let us just say I have influential associates in neighbourhood of Yellowstone. Associates with muscle. People who can take care of newcomer, make sure he – or she – does not get into any trouble.'

'And if this newcomer were to decline your services, what would happen then? Would these self-same associates just possibly become the source of the same trouble?'

'Now you are being very cynical man.'

Now it was my turn to grin. 'You know what, Vadim? I think you're just a slimy little con-artist. This network of associates of yours doesn't really exist, does it? Your influence extends about as far as the hull of this ship – and even then, it isn't exactly all-pervasive, is it?'

He unfolded his colossal arms and then refolded them. 'Watch your step, Meera-Bell – I am warning you.'

'No, I'm warning you, Vadim. I could have killed you already if I thought you were any more than an irritant. Go away and try your routine on someone else.' I nodded around the commons. 'There are plenty of candidates. Better still, why don't you crawl back to your smelly little cabin and work on your technique a bit? I really think you need to come up with something more convincing than the threat of violence in the Glitter Band, you know. Maybe if you were to offer fashion advice?'

'You really do not know, do you, Meera-Bell?'

'Know what?'

He looked at me pityingly, and for the tiniest of instants I wondered if I had fatally misjudged the situation. But then Vadim shook his head, unhooked himself from the commons wall and propelled himself across the sphere, his coat flapping behind him like a mirage. The slowboat had ramped up its thrust again now, so his trajectory was a lazy arc, bringing him expertly close to another solitary traveller who had just arrived: a short, overweight, balding man who looked pasty-faced and dejected.

I watched Vadim shake hands with the man, beginning to run through the same spiel he had tried out on me.

I almost wished him better luck.

The other passengers were an equal mixture of male and female, with an egalitarian blend of genetic types. I felt sure that two or three people were from Sky's Edge, aristocrats by the look of them, but no one I was interested in. Bored, I tried to listen in on their conversation, but the acoustics of the commons blurred their words into a mush, from which only the occasional word emerged when one or other of the party raised their voice. I could still tell they were speaking Norte. Very few people on Sky's Edge spoke Norte with great fluency, but almost everyone understood it to some extent: it was the only language which spanned all the factions, and was therefore used for diplomatic overtures and trade with external parties. In the south we spoke Castellano, the principle language of the *Santiago*, with of course some contamination from the other languages spoken in the Flotilla. In the north they spoke a shifting Creole of Hebrew, Farsi, Urdu, Punjabi and the old ancestor tongue of Norte called English, but mainly Portuguese and Arabic. Aristocrats tended to have better grasp of Norte than the average citizen; fluency in it was a badge of sophistication. I had to speak it well for professional reasons – which is why I also spoke most of the northern tongues, as well as having a passable ability in Russish and Canasian.

Russish and Norte would almost certainly be understood in the Glitter Band and Chasm City, even if the mediation was done by machines, but the default tongue of the Demarchists who had refounded Yellowstone was Canasian, a slippery amalgam of Québecois French and Cantonese. It was said that no one without a head full of linguistics processors ever really achieved genuine fluency in Canasian – the language was just too fundamentally strange, too much at odds with the hardwired constraints of human deep grammar.

I would have been worried, had the Demarchists not been such consummate traders. For more than two centuries Yellowstone had been the hub of the burgeoning interstellar trade network, feeding innovation out to nascent colonies, drinking it back in like a vampire when those colonies reached a basic level of technological maturity. It would be a commercial necessity for the Stoners to cope with dozens of other languages.

Of course, there would be dangers ahead. In that sense Vadim was entirely correct, but the dangers were not the kind to which he alluded. They would be subtle, arising from my own unfamiliarity with the nuances of a culture at least two centuries beyond my own. The outcome was less likely to be my own injury than the abject failure of my mission. That was enough of a danger to make me wary. But I did not need to buy a spurious assurance of protection from thugs like Vadim – whether he had his contacts or not.

Something caught my eye. It was Vadim again, and this time he was causing more of a commotion.

He was wrestling with the man who had just come into the commons, the two of them grappling with each other while remaining anchored to the commons wall. The other man looked like he was holding his own against Vadim, but there was something in Vadim's movements – something languid to the point of boredom – which told me that Vadim was only letting the man think that he had the edge. The other passengers were doing a good job of ignoring the scuffle; grateful, perhaps, that the thug had selected someone else for his attention.

Abruptly, Vadim's mood changed.

In an instant he had the newcomer pinned to the wall, in obvious pain, Vadim pushing his brow hard against the man's terrified face. The man started to say something, but Vadim had his hand against the man's mouth before more than a mumble emerged. Then what emerged was the man's last meal, streaming vilely between Vadim's fingers. Vadim recoiled in disgust and pushed himself away from the man. Then he secured himself with his clean arm and drove his fist into the man's stomach, just below the ribcage. The man coughed hoarsely, his eyes bloodshot; he tried to catch his breath before Vadim delivered another blow.

But Vadim was done with him. He paused only to wipe his arm against the fabric walling of the commons, then unhooked himself, ready to kick off towards one of the exits.

I calculated my arc and kicked off first, savouring an instant of breezy freefall before I impacted with the wall a metre from Vadim and his victim. For a moment Vadim looked at me in shock.

'Meera-Bell . . . I thought we concluded negotiations?'

I smiled.

'I just reopened them, Vadim.'

I had myself nicely anchored. With the same casual ease with which Vadim had struck the man, I struck Vadim, in more or less the same place. Vadim folded in on himself like a soggy origami figure, emitting a soft moan.

By now the rest of the people were less interested in minding their own business.

I addressed them. 'I don't know if any of you have been approached by this man yet, but I don't think he's the professional he'd like you to think. If you've bought protection from him, you've almost certainly wasted your money.'

Vadim managed a sentence. 'You're dead man, Meera-Bell.'

'Then I've very little to fear.' I looked at the other man. He had regained some of his colour now, wiping his sleeve across his mouth. 'Are you all right? I didn't see how the fight started.'

The man spoke Norte, but with a thick accent which it took me a moment to penetrate. He was a small man, with the compact build of a bulldog. The bulldog look didn't stop at his physique, either. He had a pugnacious, permanently argumentative face, a flat nose and a scalp bristling sparsely with extremely short hairs.

He unrumpled his clothes. 'Yes . . . I'm quite all right, thank you. The oaf started threatening me verbally, then started actually hurting me. At that point I was hoping someone would do something, but it was like I'd suddenly become part of the décor.'

'Yes, I noticed.' I looked around at the other passengers disparagingly. 'You fought back, though.'

'Fat lot of good it did me.'

'I'm afraid Vadim here doesn't look the type to recognise a valiant gesture when he sees one. Are you sure you're all right?'

'I think so. A little nausea, that's all.'

'Wait.'

I snapped my fingers at the servitor, hovering in cybernetic indecision some metres away. When it came closer I tried to buy another shot of scop-dex, but I had exhausted my shipboard funds.

'Thank you,' the man said, setting his jaw. 'But I think I've sufficient funds in my own account.' He spoke to the machine in Canasian, too quickly and softly for me to follow, and a fresh hypo popped out for use.

I turned to Vadim while the other man fumbled the hypo into a vein. 'Vadim; I'm going to be generous and let you leave now. But I don't want to see you in this room again.'

He looked at me with his lips curled, flecks of vomit glued to his face like snowflakes.

'Is not over between you and me, Meera-Bell.'

He unhooked himself, paused and looked around at the other passengers, obviously trying to regain some margin of dignity before he departed. It was a pretty wasted effort, since I had something else planned for him.

Vadim tensed, ready to kick off.

'Wait,' I said. 'You don't think I'm going to let you leave before you pay back whatever you've stolen, do you?'

He hesitated, looking back at me. 'I have not stolen anything from you.' Then to the other man. 'Or you, Mister Quirrenbach . . .'

'Is that true?' I asked the man he'd just addressed.

Quirrenbach hesitated too, glancing at Vadim before answering. 'Yes . . . yes. He hasn't stolen anything from me. I didn't speak to him until now.'

I raised my voice. 'What about the rest of you? Did this bastard con you out of anything?'

Silence. It was more or less what I had expected. No one was going to be the first to admit that they had been duped by a small-time rat like Vadim, now that they had seen how pitiful he could become.

'See,' Vadim said, 'there isn't anyone, Meera-Bell.'

'Maybe not here,' I said. I reached out with my free hand and snagged the fabric of his coat. The rough quilted patches were as cool and dry as snakeskin. 'But what about all the other passengers on the slowboat? Chances are you've already fleeced a few of them since we left Idlewild.'

'So what if I did?' he said, almost whispering. 'It is none of your concern, is it?' Now his tone was changing by the second. He was squirming before me, shifting into something infinitely more pliant than when he had first entered the commons. 'What do you want to stay out of this? What is it worth to you to back out and leave me alone?'

I had to laugh. 'Are you actually trying to buy me off?'

'It's always worth try.'

Something inside me snapped. I dragged Vadim back, slamming him against the wall so hard that he was winded again, and began to pummel him. The enveloping red haze of my anger washed over me like a warm, welcoming fog. I felt ribs shatter under my fists. Vadim tried to fight back, but I was faster, stronger, my fury more righteous.

'Stop!' said a voice, sounding like it came from halfway to infinity. 'Stop it; he's had enough!'

It was Quirrenbach, pulling me away from Vadim. A couple of other passengers had arced over to the scene of violence, studying the work I had inflicted on Vadim with horrified fascination. His face was a single ugly bruise, his mouth weeping shiny scarlet seeds of blood. I must have looked about the same when the Mendicants had finished with me.

'You want me to be lenient with him?' I said.

'You've already gone beyond leniency,' Quirrenbach said. 'I don't think you need to kill him. What if he's telling the truth and he really does have friends?'

'He's nothing,' I said. 'He doesn't have any more influence than you or I. Even if he did . . . this is the Glitter Band we're headed to, not some lawless frontier settlement.'

Quirrenbach gave me the oddest of looks. 'You're serious, aren't you? You really think we're headed to the Glitter Band.'

'We're not?'

'The Glitter Band doesn't exist,' Quirrenbach said. 'It hasn't existed for years. We're heading for something else entirely.'

From out of the bruise which was Vadim's face came something unexpected: a gurgle which might have been him clearing his mouth of blood. Or it might just have been a chuckle of vindication.

TWELVE

'What did you mean by that?'

'By what, Tanner?'

'That little throwaway remark about the Glitter Band not existing. Are you planning on just leaving it hanging there enigmatically?'

Quirrenbach and I were working our way through the bowels of the *Strelnikov* to Vadim's hideaway, my progress made all the harder because I had my suitcase with me. We were alone; I'd locked Vadim in my quarters once he had revealed the location of his berth. I assumed that if we searched his quarters we'd find whatever he had stolen from the other passengers. I had already helped myself to his coat and had no immediate plans to return it to him.

'Let's just say there have been some changes, Tanner.' Quirrenbach was wriggling awkwardly behind me, like a dog chasing something down a hole.

'I didn't hear about anything.'

'You wouldn't have. The changes happened recently, when you were on your way here. Occupational hazard of interstellar travel, I'm afraid.'

'One of several,' I said, thinking of my bruised face. 'Well, what kind of changes?'

'Rather drastic ones, I'm afraid.' He paused, his breathing coming in hard, sawlike rasps. 'Look, I'm sorry to shatter all your perceptions in one go, but you'd better start dealing with the fact that Yellowstone isn't anything like the world it used to be. And that, Tanner, is something of an understatement.'

I thought back to what Amelia had said about where I would find Reivich. 'Is Chasm City still there?'

'Yes . . . yes. Nothing *that* drastic. It's still there; still inhabited; still reasonably prosperous by the standards of this system.'

'A statement you're about to qualify, I suspect.' I looked ahead and saw that the crawlway was widening out into a cylindrical corridor with oval doors spaced along one side. It was still dark and claustrophobic, the whole experience feeling unpleasantly familiar.

'Regrettably . . . yes,' Quirrenbach said. 'The city's become very different. It's almost unrecognisable, and I gather much the same goes for the Glitter Band. There used to be ten thousand habitats in it, thrown around Yellowstone like – and here I'm going to indulge in some shameless mixing of metaphors – a garland of fabulously rare and artfully cut gems, each burning with its own hard radiance.' Quirrenbach stopped and wheezed for a moment before continuing, 'Now there are perhaps a hundred or so which still hold enough pressure to support life. The rest are derelict, vacuum-filled husks, silent and dead as driftwood, attended by vast and lethal shoals of orbital debris. They call it the Rust Belt.'

When that had sunk in, I said, 'What was it? A war? Did someone insult someone else's taste in habitat design?'

'No, it wasn't any war. Though it might have been better if it had been. You can always claw back from a war, after all. They're not as bad as they're cracked up to be, wars . . .'

'Quirrenbach . . .' My patience was wearing thin.

'It was a plague,' he said hastily. 'A very bad one, but a plague nonetheless. But before you start asking deep questions, remember that I know scarcely any more details than you do – I only just arrived here as well, you realise.'

'You're a lot better informed than I am.' I passed two doors and arrived at a third, comparing the number with the key Vadim had given me. 'How did a plague manage to do so much damage?'

'It wasn't *just* a plague. I mean, not in the usual sense. It was more . . . fecund, I suppose. Imaginative. Artistic. Quite deviously so, at times. Um, have we arrived?'

'I think this is his cabin, yes.'

'Careful, Tanner. There might be traps or something.'

'I doubt it; Vadim didn't look like the kind to indulge in any kind of longterm planning. You need a developed frontal cortex for that.'

I slipped Vadim's pass into the lock, gratified when the door opened. Feeble, muck-encrusted lights stammered on as I pushed through, revealing a cylindrical berth three or four times as large as the place I'd been assigned. Quirrenbach followed me and stationed himself at one of end of the cabin, like a man not quite ready to descend into a sewer.

I couldn't blame him for not wanting to come much further in.

The place had the smell of months of accumulated bodily emissions, a greasy film of dead skin cells glued to every yellowing plastic surface. Pornographic holograms on the walls had come alive at our arrival, twelve naked women contorting themselves into anatomically unlikely postures. They'd begun talking as well; a dozen subtly different contraltos offering an enthusiastic appraisal of Vadim's sexual prowess. I thought of him bound and gagged back in my quarters, oblivious to this flattery. The women never stopped talking, but after a while their gestures and imprecations became repetitive enough to ignore.

'I think, on balance, this is probably the right room,' Quirrenbach said.

I nodded. 'Not going to win any awards, is it?'

'Oh, I don't know – some of the stains are quite interestingly arranged. It's just a pity he went in for the smeared-excrement look – it's just so last century.' He pulled aside a little sliding hatch at his end – touching it only with the very tips of his fingers – revealing a grubby, micrometeorite-crazed porthole. 'Still, he had a room with a view. Not entirely sure it was worth it, though.'

I looked at the view myself for a few moments. We could see part of the ship's hull, strobed now and again in stuttering flashes of bright violet. Even though we were underway, the *Strelnikov* had a squad of workers outside the whole time welding things back together.

'Well, let's not spend any longer here than strictly necessary. I'll search this end; you start at yours, and we'll see if we turn up anything useful.'

'Good idea,' Quirrenbach said.

I began my search; the room – panelled wall-to-wall with recessed lockers – must once have been a storage compartment. There was too much to go through methodically, but I filled my briefcase and the deep pockets of Vadim's coat with anything that looked even remotely valuable. I scooped up handfuls of jewellery, data-monocles, miniature holo-cameras and translator brooches; exactly the kinds of thing I'd have expected Vadim to steal from the *Strelnikov*'s slightly more wealthy passengers. I had to hunt to find a watch – space travellers tended not to take them when they were crossing between systems. In the end I found one that had been calibrated for Yellowstone time, its face a series of concentric dials, around which tiny emerald planets ticked to mark the time.

I slipped it on my wrist, the watch pleasantly hefty.

'You can't just steal his possessions,' Quirrenbach said meekly.

'Vadim's welcome to file a complaint.'

'That's not the point. What you're doing isn't any better than . . .'

'Look,' I said, 'do you seriously imagine he bought any of this stuff? It's all stolen; probably from passengers who aren't aboard any more.'

'Nonetheless, some of it might have been stolen recently. We should be making every effort to return these goods to their rightful owners. Don't you agree with me?'

'On some distant theoretical level, just possibly.' I continued my search. 'But there's no way we'll ever know who those owners were. I didn't notice anybody coming forward in the commons. Anyway – what does it matter to you?'

'It's called retaining the vestigial trace of a conscience, Tanner.'

'After that thug nearly killed you?'

136

'The principle still applies.'

'Well – if you think it'll help you sleep at night – you're very welcome to leave me alone while I search his belongings. Come to think of it, did I actually ask you to follow me here?'

'Not as such, no . . .' His face contorted in an agony of indecision as he glanced through the contents of one opened drawer, pulling out a sock which he studied sadly for some moments. 'Damn you, Tanner. I hope you're right about his lack of influence.'

'Oh, I don't think we need worry ourselves about that.'

'You're quite certain?'

'I've a reasonable grasp of lowlife, believe me.'

'Yes, well . . . I suppose you could be right. For the sake of argument.' Slowly at first, but with increasing enthusiasm, Quirrenbach started trousering Vadim's booty indiscriminately, wads of Stoner currency, mainly. I reached over and pocketed two bundles of cash before Quirrenbach made it all vanish.

'Thanks. They'll do nicely.'

'I was about to pass some to you.'

'Of course you were.' I flicked through the notes. 'Is this stuff still worth anything?'

'Yes,' he said, thoughtfully. 'In the Canopy, anyway. I've no idea what passes for currency in the Mulch, but I doubt that it can hurt, can it?'

I helped myself to some more. 'Better safe than sorry, that's my philosophy.'

I continued searching – digging through more of the same junk and jewellery – until I found what looked like an experiential playback device. It was slimmer and sleeker than anything I'd ever seen on Sky's Edge, cleverly engineered so that in its collapsed form it was no larger than a Bible.

I found a vacant pocket and slipped the unit home, along with a cache of experientials which I assumed might have some value in their own right.

'This plague we were talking about . . .' I said.

'Yes?'

'I don't understand how it did so much damage.'

'That's because it wasn't a biological one – I mean, not in the way we'd usually understand such things.' He paused and stopped what he was doing. 'Machines, that's what it went for. Made almost all machines above a certain complexity level stop working, or start working in ways they were never meant to.'

I shrugged. 'That doesn't sound that bad.'

'Not if the machines are merely robots and environmental systems, like the ones in this ship. But this was Yellowstone. Most of the machines were microscopic devices inside human beings, already intimately linked to mind and flesh. What happened to the Glitter Band was just symptomatic of something far more horrific happening on the human scale, in the same way that – say – the lights going out all over Europe in the late fourteenth century was indicative of the arrival of the Black Death.'

'I'll need to know more.'

'Then query the system in your room. Or Vadim's, for that matter.'

'Or you could just tell me now.'

He shook his head. 'No, Tanner. Because I know very little more than you. Remember, we both came in at the same time. On different ships, yes – but we were both crossing interstellar space when this happened. I've had little more time to adjust to it than you've had.'

Quietly and calmly, I said, 'Where was it you came from?'

'Grand Teton.'

His world was another of the original Amerikano colonies, like Yellowstone, Yosemite, Glacier and two or three others I couldn't remember. They'd all been settled by robots four centuries ago; self-replicating machines carrying the templates necessary to construct living humans upon their arrival. None of those colonies had been successful, all of them failing after one or two subsequent generations. A few rare lineages might still be able to trace themselves back to the original Amerikano settlers, but the majority of people living on those worlds were descended from later colonisation waves, arriving by lighthugger. Most were Demarchist states, like Yellowstone.

Sky's Edge, of course, was another case entirely. It was the only world that had ever been settled by generation ship.

There were some mistakes you didn't make twice.

'I hear Grand Teton's one of the nicer places to live,' I said.

'Yes. And I suppose you're wondering what brought me here.'

'No, actually. Not really my business.'

He slowed in his rummaging through Vadim's loot. I could see that my lack of curiosity was not something to which he was accustomed. I continued my investigations, silently counting the seconds before he broke his silence.

'I'm an artist,' Quirrenbach said. 'Actually, a composer. I'm working on a symphony cycle; my life's work. That's what brings me here.'

'Music?'

'Yes, music – though that contemptible little word barely encapsulates what I have in mind. My next symphony will be a work inspired by nothing less than Chasm City.' He smiled. 'It was going to be a glorious, uplifting piece, celebrating the city in all its *Belle Epoque* splendour; a composition teeming with vitality and energy. Now, I think, it will have to be a darker piece entirely; Shostakovichian in its solemnity; a work weighed down by the crushing realisation that history's wheel has finally turned and crushed our mortal dreams to dust. A plague symphony.'

'And that's what you've come all this way for? To scribble down a few notes?'

'To scribble down a few notes, yes. And why not? Someone, after all, has to do it.'

'But it'll take you decades to get back home.'

'A fact that has, surprisingly, impinged on my consciousness before you so kindly pointed it out. But my journey here is a mere prelude, occupying a span of time that will become inconsequential when set against the several centuries that I confidently expect to elapse before the work nears completion. I myself will probably age the better part of a century in that time – the equivalent of two or three whole working lives of any of the great composers. I shall be visiting dozens of systems, of course – and adding others to my itinerary as they become significant. There will almost certainly be more wars, more plagues, more dark ages. And times of miracle and wonder, of course. All of which will be grist to the mill of my great work. And when it is polished, and when I am not utterly disgusted and disillusioned with it, I will very probably find myself in my twilight years. I simply won't have time to keep abreast of the latest longevity techniques, you see; not while I'm pouring my energies into my work. I'll just have to take whatever's easily available and hope I live to finish my magnum opus. Then, when I have tidied up the work, and achieved some form of reconciliation between the crude scribblings I have set down now and the undoubtedly masterful and fluid work I will be producing at the end of my life, I will take a ship back to Grand Teton – assuming it still exists – where I will announce the great work's premier. The premier itself won't be for another fifty or so years afterwards, depending on the extent of human space at that time. That will give time for word to reach even the most distant colonies, and for people to begin converging on Grand Teton for the performance. I will sleep while the venue is constructed – I already have something suitably lavish in mind – and an orchestra worthy of the event is assembled, or bred, or cloned – whichever the case may be. And when that fifty years is done, I will rise from slumber, step into the limelight, conduct my work and, in what little time remains to me, bask in a fame the like of which no living composer has ever or will ever know. The names of the great composers will be reduced to mere footnote entries; barely flickering embryo stars set against the gemlike brilliance of my own stellar conflagration. My name will ring down the centuries like a single undying chord.'

There was a long silence before I responded.

'Well, you've got to have something to aim for, I suppose.'

'I suppose you must think me monstrously vain.'

'I don't think the thought ever crossed my mind, Quirrenbach.' While I was speaking I touched something at the back of one of the drawers. I'd been hoping to locate a weapon of some sort – something with a little more punch than the clockwork gun – but Vadim appeared to have managed without one. Still, I felt I had something. 'This is interesting.'

'What have you found?'

I pulled out a matte-black metal box the size of a cigar case, opening it to reveal six scarlet vials tucked into pouches. Set into the same case was something like an ornate steel hypodermic, with a gunlike handle, marked with a delicately painted bas-relief cobra.

'I don't know. Any thoughts?'

'Not exactly, no . . .' He examined the cache of vials with what looked like genuine curiosity. 'But I'll tell you one thing. It doesn't look legal, whatever it is.'

'More or less what I was thinking.'

As I reached to take back the cache, Quirrenbach said, 'Why are you so interested in it?'

I remembered the syringe which had slipped from the pocket of the monk in Amelia's cave. There was no way to tell for sure, but the substance I had seen in that syringe – admittedly in the dim light of the cave – looked much like the chemical in Vadim's cache. I remembered, too, what Amelia had told me when I had asked her about the syringe: that it was something the monk should not have had in Idlewild. Some kind of narcotic, then – and perhaps prohibited not just in the Mendicant hospice but across the whole system.

'I'm assuming this might open some doors for me.'

'It might open a lot more than that,' Quirrenbach said. 'The very gates of hell, for a start. I've remembered something. Something I heard up in the parking swarm. Concerning some very nasty substances doing the rounds.' He nodded at the row of scarlet vials. 'One of which is something they call Dream Fuel.'

'And this might be it?'

'I don't know, but it's exactly the kind of thing I would expect our dear friend Vadim to be trading in.'

'Where would he have got it from?'

'I didn't say I was an expert, Tanner. All I know is that it has some unpleasant side-effects and whatever authorities there are in this system don't exactly encourage its use – or the possession of it, for that matter.'

'It must have some uses, though.'

'Yes – but exactly what they do with it, I don't know. That device is a wedding gun, incidentally.'

He must have seen the blank look on my face.

'It was a local custom for a husband and wife to exchange, in some fashion, actual neural material cultured from each other's brains. They used that thing – the wedding gun – to implant the stuff into each other.'

'They don't do that anymore?'

'Not since the plague, I think.' He looked rueful. 'Actually, come to think of it, there are lots of things they don't do since the plague.'

When Quirrenbach had gone with his gains – back to ponder the next instalment in his symphony cycle, I hoped – I crossed over to Vadim's network console. For the first time since departure I had weight again, as the *Strelnikov* executed a thrust burn, minutely adjusting its fall towards the Rust Belt. From somewhere else I heard low, saurian moans of structural protest, and couldn't help wondering if I'd picked the one voyage which would end with the ship's hull finally giving up the ghost. Presently, however, the groans and creaks subsided into the ship's normal sonic background and I was able to concentrate on the matter at hand.

The console looked ancient, like something children would have laughed at in a museum. There was a flat screen surrounded by controls embossed with finger-worn icons, above an alphanumeric keyboard. I didn't know what the state of the art around Yellowstone was, but this wasn't even it by Sky's Edge standards.

It would have to do.

I found the key which turned the console on, the screen stammering through a series of warm-up messages and adverts before displaying a complex tree of options. Shipboard data services. Realtime networks – the web of data streams within a light-second or so of the *Strelnikov*, so that normal conversations were possible. Deep system networks, with typical timelags ranging from seconds to tens of hours, depending on the complexity of the enquiry. There was no explicit possibility to access networks with response times longer than that, which made sense: any enquiry sent out to the system's Kuiper Belt habitats would have returned a reply long after the sender had left the slowboat at journey's end.

I entered the option for the deep system networks, waiting a few seconds while the screen busied itself with more advertising material. A tree of sub-menus appeared. News of arriving and departing starships, including an entry for the *Orvieto*. The Yellowstone system was still a busy interstellar hub, which also made a kind of sense. If the plague had struck in the last decade or so, many ships would have already been on their way here. It would take decades for news of the plague to spread out into the main volume of human-settled space.

I skimmed through the options.

The deep system networks carried comms traffic to and from the habitats in orbit around the system's gas giants: typically mining stations and outposts for the more reclusive factions. There were Conjoiner nests, Skyjack enclaves and semi-automated military or experimental facilities. I searched in vain for any reference to the plague. Occasionally there was talk of containment procedures, or crisis management, but for the most part it looked as if the plague – or its consequences – had become so fundamental an aspect of life that there was seldom any need to refer to the thing itself.

The local networks told me a little more. Once or twice, at least, I found references to the crisis by name, and learned that they had given it a specific and chilling name: the *Melding Plague*. But most of the messages assumed total familiarity with the basic facts of the plague itself. There were references to

Hermetics, and the Canopy, and the Mulch, and sometimes to something called the Game, but none of these terms were elaborated upon.

I had heard of the Canopy, though. That was where Amelia had said I'd stand a good chance of finding Reivich. It was a district of Chasm City.

But had she told me less than I had imagined?

I put the console into send mode and composed a query concerning the plague; a request for general information for newcomers. I couldn't believe I was the first to want this information before being plunged into the thick of the Rust Belt, but it was also entirely possible that no one would bother replying to me, or that no kind of automated handling system was functioning now.

I sent my query, then stared at the console for a few seconds. The screen stared back at me, unchanging.

Nothing came.

Disappointed and still no closer to the truth, I went to the pockets of the coat I had taken from Vadim and pulled out the neatly stowed playback kit. The device almost assembled itself, the slim black parts sliding home with the pleasing precision of rifle components. The result was a skeletal black helmet, nubbed with field-generators and input ports, ornamented with luminous green and red cobras. A pair of stereoscopic eyepieces folded down from the helmet's front, their rims formed from material that automatically conformed to the skin around the eye. A pair of earplugs functioned similarly, and there were even noseplugs for olfactory input.

I hefted the helmet, then placed it on my head.

The helmet gripped my scalp firmly, like a torture vice. The little eyepieces moved into position, glueing themselves around my sockets. Inside each was a high-resolution imaging system which was currently showing exactly the view I'd have seen had I not been wearing the helmet, except for a slight and probably deliberate graininess. To do much better I would have needed neural implants and a more sophisticated playback system, something that could interrogate and adjust brain signals with the finesse of a military trawl.

I opened my briefcase.

Inside, I found the cache of experientials I'd carried from Sky's Edge, still wrapped in clear plastic. I removed the plastic and examined the six pen-like sticks, but there was nothing written on them to give any clue as to what they contained. Were they simply commodities to be traded, or did the sticks contain messages to me from my pre-amnesiac self?

There was a port in the brow of the helmet into which one inserted the metallic tip of the experiential, so that it stuck out like a thin horn. I took the first of my six and pushed it home.

A menu popped into existence ahead of me, giving options for entering the simulation at various points and with various artistic settings. I accepted the defaults and plunged into the experiential at random, making my choices with hand gestures. The helmet generated a low-level electric field which my body modified, enabling the system to read any large-scale movements.

Vadim's room greyed out smoothly, a hiss of white-noise in my ears. The noise faded to near-silence, quieter than it had ever been aboard the slow-boat. The grey lightened, shapes and colours emerging like phantoms out of fog.

I was in a jungle clearing, shooting enemy soldiers.

I was stripped to the waist, over-muscled, even for a soldier, paint daubed across my chest, with an old model of particle-beam rifle gripped in one hand, while my other hand held a smaller, slug-firing machine-gun. I'd handled similar weapons myself and I knew that it was physically impossible to fire either singlehandedly, let alone held out nearly at arm's length. Both weapons chugged away as I doused them at an unending stream of enemy soldiers, who seemed perfectly willing to run screaming towards me from the bush, even though any one of them could have picked me off from cover with a single well-aimed shot. I was screaming as well. Maybe it was the effort of having to hold both those guns.

It was laughable, but I didn't doubt that there'd be a market for something like it. There was a market for that kind of thing on Sky's Edge, after all – and we already had a real war.

I tried the next one.

This time I was sitting inside a skeletally framed single-seat wheeler, racing it across a mud flat with a dozen or so other wheelers trying to sneak past me on either side. I'd entered this one with the experiential set to interactive, so I was able to steer the wheeler and throttle its turbine up and down. I played it for a few minutes, keeping ahead of the pack, until I badly misjudged the angle of a sandbank and lost control. Another car slammed into mine and there was an instant of painless carnage before I was back at the starting line again, gunning my engine. Difficult to tell how this one would sell. They might lap it up as a unique Sky's Edge product, or they might find the whole thing irredeemably quaint.

I continued through the remaining four experientials, but the results were just as disappointing. Two of them were fictionalised episodes from my planet's past: one a melodrama about Sky Haussmann's life aboard the *Santiago* – really the last thing I needed – while the other was a love story set during the time of Sky's imprisonment, trial and execution, but in which Sky was only very a minor background character. The other two experientials were adventures, both of which involved snake-hunting, though whoever had scripted them had only a passing knowledge of hamadryad biology.

I'd expected more: some kind of specific message from my past. Although I remembered a great deal more now than I'd done upon first waking in Idlewild, there were still aspects of my past that were unclear; things that refused to snap into focus. I could have lived with these absences if I'd been stalking Reivich in familiar territory, but even my knowledge of the city ahead of me was inaccurate.

I turned to the cache of experientials I had taken from Vadim. They were all blank except for a tiny silver motif near the top of each. I wasn't going to learn anything about myself, but I'd at least learn a little more about what passed for entertainment in Chasm City. I slipped one of them in.

It was a mistake.

I was expecting pornography, or mindless violence – something from the extremes of human experience, but still recognisable as such. What I got was so strange that at first it was difficult to articulate what I was experiencing and I began to wonder if there was some compatibility problem between the experientials and the helmet, so that the wrong parts of my brain were being stimulated. But they'd all come from the same source: Vadim's room.

This was how it was meant to be.

It was dark, dank, squalid, and there was a feeling of terrible, crushing claustrophobia – an emotion so intense that it was like my skull was slowly squeezing my brain. My body was all wrong: elongated and limbless, pale and soft and infinitely vulnerable. I couldn't guess how that sensation was engendered, unless the device was stimulating some ancient part of the brain which remembered what it was like to ooze or swim rather than walk. And yet I was not actually alone, and nor was the darkness as absolute as it had originally seemed. My body occupied a warm, humid hollow inside a space which had been cored out with labyrinthine black tunnels and chambers. And there were others with me; other pale, elongated presences. I couldn't see them – they must have been in adjacent chambers – but I could taste their proximity, ingest the souplike chemical flow of their emotions and thoughts. And in some sense they were me as well, detached avatars of myself. They moved and quivered at my bidding, and I sensed what they sensed.

The claustrophobia was total and crushing, but it was also reassuring. Beyond the hard, rocklike volume in which we were caged was an absolute void from which my thoughts flinched. That emptiness was worse than the claustrophia, and what made it worse still was the fact that it was not truly empty; that the void held terrible, silent, infinitely patient enemies.

Who were coming closer.

I felt a convulsion of fear so absolute that I screamed and removed the helmet. For a moment I floated in Vadim's cabin, breathing hard, wondering just what I'd experienced. The feeling of immense claustrophobia, combined with even worse agoraphobia, took long seconds to abate, like the after-chime of an awful bell.

My hands trembling – although I was beginning to regain some control – I removed the experiential and examined it more closely, this time paying proper attention to the little motif near the top of the stick.

It looked a lot like a maggot.

I watched our approach to the Rust Belt through the observation window in Vadim's cabin.

I knew something of what lay ahead now. Shortly after I'd tried the disturbing experiential – while I was still reeling from its effects, in fact – the console had chimed, announcing the arrival of a response to my earlier query. I was surprised; in my experience such things usually happened instantaneously or not at all, and the delay served only to emphasise how disrupted the system's data networks must have been.

The message, it turned out, was a standard-issue document, rather than a personally composed reply. An automated mechanism must have decided that it would answer most of my questions; an assumption that turned out to be reasonably accurate.

I started reading.

Dear Newcomer

Welcome to the Epsilon Eridani system.

Despite all that has happened, we hope your stay here will be a pleasant one. For your information we have compiled this note to explain some of the key events in our recent history. It is intended that this information will ease your transition into a culture which may be markedly different from the one you were expecting to find when you embarked at your point of origin. It is important that you realise that others have come before you . . .

The document was long, but I quickly read the thing in its entirety, then reread it carefully, picking out the salient points which might assist me in the hunt for Reivich. I'd already been forewarned about the scale of the plague's effects, so the document's revelations were perhaps not as shocking to me as they would have been to someone freshly defrosted. But it was still chilling to see it anatomised in such a coolly detached manner, and it was easy to imagine how unsettling it must have been to someone who had come to Yellowstone in search of riches rather than blood. The Mendicants had clearly elected not to spring this news on their slush puppies too quickly, and doubtless if I'd stayed in Idlewild a little longer they would have begun to break it to me gently. But perhaps the document was right: there were some truths it was best to deal with as quickly as possible, no matter how repugnant that truth might have been.

I wondered how long it would take me to adjust to it, or if I'd be one of the unfortunate few who never quite made the transition.

Perhaps, I thought, they were actually the sane ones.

Through the window the larger Rust Belt habitats had begun to assume definite shapes, rather than just being indistinct orbiting flecks. I tried to imagine what it would have looked like seven years ago, in the last days before the plague.

There'd been ten thousand habitats in the Glitter Band, each as opulent and faceted as a chandelier, each distinguished from its neighbours by some wild architectural flourish that had far less to do with the practicalities of structural design than it had with aesthetics and prestige. They'd circled Yellowstone in low orbit, almost nose-to-tail, each vast and stately construct maintaining polite distance from those ahead and behind it with tiny puffs of correcting thrust. A constant flow of commerce had shuffled between the habitats along narrow traffic lanes, so that from a distance the habitats themselves looked as if they were entwined in tinsel-like filaments of light. Depending on the ever-shifting spectrum of allegiances and feuds, the habitats either communicated with each other via looms of quantum-encrypted laser light, or maintained sullen silences. Such silences were not at all unusual, for there were profound rivalries even amongst the constituents of what was technically the very model of a unified Demarchist society.

Amongst ten thousand habitats, there was every human specialisation imaginable: every expertise, every ideology, every perversion. The Demarchists permitted everything, even experimentation in political models which chafed against their underlying paradigm of absolute non-hierarchical democracy. Provided those experiments remained experiments, they were tolerated; even actively encouraged. Only the development and stockpiling of armaments was forbidden, unless they were to be used artistically. And it was here in the Glitter Band that the system's most illustrious clan, the Sylveste family, had performed much of the work that had brought them eventual fame. Calvin Sylveste had attempted the first neural downloads since the Transenlight-enment in the Band. Dan Sylveste had collated all known information on the Shrouders here; work that eventually led to his own fateful expedition to Lascaille's Shroud.

But that was the deep past now. History had turned the glory of the Glitter Band into . . . *this*.

When the Melding Plague had hit, the Glitter Band had stayed intact for far longer than Chasm City, for most of the Band's habitats already had effective quarantine protocols. Some were so secretive and self-sufficient that no one had entered them in decades anyway.

But they were not, ultimately, immune.

It took only one habitat to fall to the plague. Within days most of the people aboard died, and most of their habitat's self-replicating systems began to go haywire in ways that seemed nastily purposeful. The habitat's ecosystem collapsed fatally. Uncontrolled, the habitat drifted out of its orbital slot like a chunk of calved iceberg. Ordinarily the chances of a collision would have been small . . . but the Glitter Band was already congested to within a hairsbreadth of disaster.

The first rule of collisions between two orbital bodies was that they were very rare indeed . . . *until* one happened. Then the shards of the destroyed bodies would splinter off in different directions, significantly increasing the likelihood of another impact. It would not be such a long wait until the next collision. And when it happened again, the number of shards increased once more . . . such that the next collision was a practical certainty . . .

Within weeks, most of the habitats in the Glitter Band had been fatally holed by collisional debris . . . and even when those impact fragments were not in themselves sufficient to kill all aboard, they also tended to be contaminated by traces of the plague originating from the first habitat to fall. They became orbiting hulks, as dark and dead as driftwood. By the end of the year, barely two hundred habitats had remained intact: principally the oldest and sturdiest structures, sheathed in rock and ice against radiation storms. With batteries of anti-collision lasers emplaced around their skins, they had managed to fend off most of the large chunks.

That was six years ago. In the intervening time, Quirrenbach told me, the Rust Belt had been stabilised, with most of the debris mopped up and conglomerated into hazardous lumps which had been sent spinning into the boiling face of Epsilon Eridani. Now at least the Belt was not growing any more fragmented. The hulks, for the most part, were kept in check by periodic nudges from robot tugs. Only a handful had been successfully repressurised and settled, although there were predictable rumours of all manner of sinister factions squatting furtively amongst the ruins.

This much I had learned from the nets. Seeing the ruins for the first time was something else entirely. Yellowstone was an ochre immensity blocking half the sky, now tangibly a world like the one I'd left, rather than a pale two-dimensional disk against the stars. As the *Strelnikov* swooped towards the habitat where it would dock, the silhouettes of other, ravaged ones crossed the face of Yellowstone. They were gnarled, gutted, pocked and cratered with the evidence of titanic collisions. I tried to hold in my head the numbers of dead the Rust Belt represented: although many of the habitats had been in the process of being evacuated when they were struck, it couldn't have been easy to remove a million people at such short notice.

Our habitat was shaped like a fat cigar, spun about its long axis for gravity in the same manner as Idlewild. Sister Amelia had told me that the place where we were headed was called Carousel New Vancouver. It was carapaced in ice, mostly dirty-grey in hue, but occasionally patched with acres of bright new ice to repair what I assumed were recent impact points. It was spinning silently, throwing off a dozen lazy coils of steam from its skin like the arms of a spiral galaxy. A huge spacecraft was attached to the rim, shaped like a manta-ray and with scores of tiny windows around the edges of its wings. But the *Strelnikov* arced in towards one tip of the cigar, a triad of jaws opening to admit it. We nosed into a chamber walled in a maze of intestinal pipes and fuel tanks. I saw a few other shuttles clamped in parking bays: two sleek atmosphere cutters like bottle-green arrowheads and a couple of vessels which looked like cousins to the slowboat, all blunt angularity and exposed engine components. Space-suited figures were swarming around all the ships, carrying umbilical lines and repair kits. A few robots were toiling away on hull-repair tasks, but for the most part the work was being done by humans or bio-engineered animals.

I couldn't help remembering my earlier fears about this system. I'd expected to be entering a culture several centuries ahead of my own in nearly every respect, a peasant stumbling through kaleidoscopic wonders. Instead, I was looking at a scene which could easily have belonged to my own world's past . . . even something out of the era of the Flotilla's launch.

We docked with a bump. I gathered my belongings – including the things I had appropriated from Vadim – and set about worming my way upship to the exit.

'Goodbye, I suppose,' Quirrenbach said, amongst the general throng of people waiting to filter through into New Vancouver.

'Yes.' If he was expecting any other kind of response, he was out of luck.

'I – um – went back to check on Vadim.'

'A piece of dirt like that can take care of himself, you know. We probably should have thrown him out the airlock while we had the chance.' I forced a smile. 'Still, as he said, he was part of the local colour. I'd hate to deprive anyone of a unique cultural experience.'

'Are you staying here long? In NV, I mean?'

It took me a moment to realise he was talking about New Vancouver.

'No.'

'Taking the first behemoth down to the surface, then?'

'Very probably.' I looked over his shoulder to where the crowd was pushing through the exit. Through another window I could see a part of the *Strelnikov*'s hull plating which had broken loose during the docking sequence and was now being nudged and epoxied back into place.

'Yes; get down as quickly as possible, that's my intention as well.' Quirrenbach patted the briefcase he clutched to his chest like a tabard. 'The sooner I can get to work on my plague symphony the better, I think.'

'I'm sure it'll be a resounding success.'

'Thanks. And you? If I'm not being too nosy? Any particular plans for when you get down there?'

'One or two, yes.'

Doubtless he would have kept grilling me – getting nowhere – but there was a release of pressure in the jam of people ahead of us, opening up a little gap through which I inserted myself. In a few moments I was out of Quirrenbach's conversational range.

Inside, New Vancouver was nothing like Hospice Idlewild. There was no artificial sun, no single air-filled volume. Instead, the entire structure was a densely packed honeycomb of much smaller enclosed spaces, squeezed together like components in an antique radio. I didn't think there was any hope of Reivich still being in the habitat. There were at least three departures to Chasm City per day, and I was fairly sure he'd have been on the first available flight down.

Still, I stayed vigilant.

Amelia's estimate had been unerringly accurate: the Stoner funds I had brought with me would just cover my trip to Chasm City. I had already spent half on the *Strelnikov*; what remained was just enough to pay for the descent. True, I had harvested some money from Vadim, but when I examined the cash properly it only amounted to about as much as the change left from my own funds. His victims, newcomers obviously, had not carried much local cash with them.

I checked the time.

Vadim's watch had concentric dials for both local twenty-six-hour Yellowstone time and twenty-four-hour system time. I had a couple of hours before my flight down. I planned to kill the time walking around NV, looking for local information sources, but I quickly found that large areas of the habitat were not accessible to anyone who had arrived via anything as lowly as the *Strelnikov*. People who had come in via high-burn shuttles were segregated from scum like us by armoured glass walls. I found somewhere to sit down and drink a cup of bad coffee (the one universal commodity, it seemed) and watched the two immiscible streams of humanity flow past. The place where I was sitting was a dingy thoroughfare, seats and tables jostling for space with metre-thick industrial pipes which ran from floor to ceiling like hamadryad trees. Smaller pipes branched off the main arteries, curving through the air like rusty intestines. They throbbed unnervingly, as if titanic pressures were only just being contained by thin metal and crumbling rivets. Some effort had been made to gentrify the surroundings by weaving foliage around the pipes, but the attempt had been distinctly halfhearted.

Not everyone shuffling through this area looked poor, but almost everyone looked as if they wished they were elsewhere. I recognised a few faces from the slowboat, and perhaps one or two from Hospice Idlewild, but I had certainly not seen the majority of the people before. I doubted that all of them were from beyond the Epsilon Eridani system; it was just as likely that NV was a gateway for in-system travellers. I even saw some Ultras, strutting around flaunting their chimeric modifications, but there were just as many on the other side of the glass.

I remembered dealing with their kind: Captain Orcagna's crew aboard the *Orvieto*; the woman with the hole in her gut who had been sent to meet us. Thinking of the way Reivich had known about our ambush, I wondered if – ultimately – we hadn't all been betrayed by Orcagna. Perhaps Orcagna had even arranged my revival amnesia, to slow me down in my hunt.

Or perhaps I was just being paranoid.

Beyond the glass, I saw something even stranger than the black-clad, cyborg wraiths who crewed the lighthuggers: things like upright boxes, gliding with sinister grace amongst the crowds. The other people seemed oblivious to the boxes – almost unaware of them, except that they stepped carefully aside as the boxes moved amongst them. I sipped my coffee and noticed that some of the boxes had clumsy mechanical arms attached to their fronts – but most did not – and that almost all of the boxes had dark windows set into their fronts.

'They're palanquins, I think.'

I sighed, recognising the voice of Quirrenbach, who was easing himself into the seat next to me.

'Good. Finished your symphony yet?'

He did a good job of pretending not to hear me. 'I heard about them, those palanquins. The people inside them are called hermetics. They're the ones who've still got implants and don't want to get rid of them. The boxes are like little travelling microcosms. Do you think it's really that dangerous still?'

I put down my coffee cup testily. 'What would I know?'

'Sorry, Tanner . . . just trying to make conversation.' He glared at the vacant seats around me. 'It's not like you were overburdened with companionship, is it?'

'Maybe I wasn't desperate for any.'

'Oh, come on.' He snapped his fingers, bringing the grimy, coffee-dispensing servitor over to our table. 'We're both in this together, Tanner. I promise I won't follow you around once we get to Chasm City, but until then, would it really hurt to be a little civil to me? You never know, I might even be able to help you. I may not know much about this place, but I do appear to know fractionally more than you.'

'Fractionally's the word.'

He got himself a coffee from the machine and offered me a refill. I declined, but with what I hoped was grudging politeness.

'God, this is foul,' he said, after a trial sip.

'At least we're in agreement on something.' I made a stab at humour. 'I think I know what's in those pipes now, anyway.'

'Those pipes?' Quirrenbach looked around us. 'Oh, I see. No; those are steam pipes, Tanner. Very important, too.'

'Steam?'

'They use their own ice to keep NV from over-heating. Someone on the *Strelnikov* told me: they pump the ice down from the outer skin as kind of slush, then run it all around the habitat, through all the gaps between the main habitation areas – we're in one of those gaps now – and then the slush soaks up all the excess heat and gradually melts and then boils, until you've got pipes full of superheated steam. Then they blast the steam back into space.'

I thought of the geysers I had seen on the surface of NV on the approach.

'That's pretty wasteful.'

'They didn't always use ice. They used to have huge radiators, like moths' wings, a hundred kilometres across. But they lost them when the Glitter Band broke up. Bringing in the ice was an emergency measure. Now they've got to have a steady supply or this whole habitat becomes one big meat oven. They get it from Marco's Eye, the moon. There're craters near the poles in perpetual shadow. They could've used methane ice from Yellowstone, too, but there's no way to get it here cheaply enough.'

'You know a lot.'

He beamed, patting the briefcase in his lap. 'Details, Tanner. Details. You can't write a symphony about a place unless you know it intimately. I've already got plans for my first movement, you know. Very sombre at first, desolate woodwind, shading into something with stronger rhythmic impetus.' He sketched a finger through the air as if tracing the topography of an invisible landscape. '*Adagio – allegro energico.* That'll be the destruction of the Glitter Band. You know, I almost think it deserves a whole symphony in its own right . . . what do you think?'

'I don't know, Quirrenbach. Music's not really my forte.'

'You're an educated man though, aren't you? You speak with economy, but there's no little thought behind your words. Who was it who said that a wise man speaks when he has something to say, but a fool speaks because he must?'

'I don't know, but he probably wasn't a great conversationalist.'

I looked at my watch – it felt like my own now – wishing the green gems would instantly whirl into the relative positions which would signify departure time for the surface. They hadn't visibly shifted since the last time I looked.

'What did you used to do on Sky's Edge, Tanner?'

'I was a soldier.'

'Ah, but that's nothing really unusual, is it?'

Out of boredom – and the knowledge that nothing would be lost by doing so – I elaborated upon my answer. 'The war worked its way into our lives. It was nothing you could hide from. Even where I was born.'

'Which was?'

'Nueva Iquique. It was a sleepy coastal town a long way from the main centres of battle. But everyone knew someone who had been killed by the other side. Everyone had some theoretical reason for hating them.'

'Did *you* hate the enemy?'

'Not really. The propaganda was designed to make you hate them . . . but if you stopped and thought about it, it was obvious they would be telling their own people much the same lies about us. Of course, some of it was probably true. Equally, one didn't need much imagination to suspect that we'd committed some atrocities of our own.'

'Did the war really go all the way back to what happened on the Flotilla?'

'Ultimately, yes.'

'Then it was less about ideology than territory, isn't that true?'

'I don't know, or care. It all happened a long time ago, Quirrenbach.'

'Do you know much about Sky Haussmann? I hear that there are people on your planet who still worship him.'

'I know a thing or two about Sky Haussmann, yes.'

Quirrenbach looked interested. I could almost hear the mental note-taking for a new symphony. 'Part of your common cultural upbringing, you mean?'

'Not entirely, no.' Knowing that I would lose nothing by showing him, I allowed Quirrenbach to see the wound in the centre of my palm. 'It's a mark. It means the Church of Sky got to me. They infected me with an indoctrinal virus. It makes me dream about Sky Haussmann even when I don't particularly want to. I didn't ask for it and it'll take a while to work its way out of my system, but until then I have to live with the bastard. I get a dose of Sky every time I close my eyes.'

'That's awful,' he said, doing a poor job of not sounding fascinated. 'But I presume once you're awake, you're reasonably . . .'

'Sane? Yes, totally.'

'I want to know more about him,' Quirrenbach said. 'You don't mind talking, do you?'

Near us, one of the elephantine pipes began leaking steam in a shrill, scalding exhalation.

'I don't think we'll be together much longer.'

He looked crestfallen. 'Really?'

'I'm sorry, Quirrenbach . . . I work best alone, you know.' I groped for a way to make my rejection sound less negative. 'And you'll need time alone, too, to work on your symphonies . . .'

'Yes, yes – later. But for now? There's a lot we have to deal with, Tanner. I'm still worried by the plague. Do you really think it's risky here?'

'Well, they say there are still traces of it around. Do you have implants, Quirrenbach?' He looked blank, so I continued, 'Sister Amelia – the woman who looked after me in the Hospice – told me that they sometimes removed implants from immigrants, but I didn't understand what she meant at the time.'

'Damn,' he said. 'I should have had them removed in the parking swarm, I knew it. But I hesitated – didn't like the looks of anyone who was prepared to do it. And now I'll have to find some blood-spattered butcher in Chasm City to do it.'

'I'm sure there'll be plenty of people willing to help with that. I'd need to speak to the same people myself, as it happens.'

The stocky little man scratched at the stubble across his scalp. 'Oh, you too? Then it really does make sense for us to travel together, doesn't it.'

I was about to answer – to try and wheedle my way out of his company – when an arm locked itself around my throat.

I was pulled backwards, out of my seat, hitting the ground painfully. The breath exited my lungs like a flock of startled birds. I floundered on the edge of consciousness, too winded to move, although every instinct screamed that moving might be my best course of action.

But Vadim was already leaning over me, his knee pressed across my ribcage.

'You didn't expect to see Vadim again, did you Meera-Bell? I think you are sorry you did not kill Vadim now.'

'I haven't . . .' I tried to complete the sentence, but there was no air left in my lungs. Vadim examined his fingernails, doing a good impression of boredom. My peripheral vision was turning dark, but I could see Quirrenbach standing to one side with his arms pinned behind him, another figure holding him hostage. Beyond that, an indifferent blur of passers-by. No one was paying the slightest attention to Vadim's ambush.

He released the pressure on me. I caught my breath.

'You have not what?' Vadim said. 'Go on, say it. I am all ears.'

'You owe me a debt of gratitude that I didn't kill you, Vadim. And you know it, too. But scum like you aren't worth the bother.'

He feigned a smile and reapplied the weight on my chest. I was beginning to have my doubts about Vadim. Now that I saw he had an accomplice – the man pinning down Quirrenbach – his story about a wider network of associates began to look a little more likely.

'Scum, is it? I see you were not above *cleaning* my watch, nasty little thief that you are.' He fiddled with the strap on my wrist, wriggling the watch off with a grin of triumph. Vadim held it up to one of his eyes, for all the world like a horologist studying some fabulous movement. 'No scratches, I hope . . .'

'You're welcome to it. It wasn't really me.'

Vadim slipped the watch back over his hand, turning his wrist this way and that to inspect his reclaimed prize. 'Good. Anything else you would like to declare?'

'Something, yes.'

Because I had not tried to push him off me with my other arm, he had ignored it completely. I had not even removed my hand from the pocket in which I had slipped it as I fell back from the chair. Vadim might have contacts, but he was still no more of a professional than when we had tussled on the slowboat.

Now I removed my arm. The movement was quick, fluid, like a striking hamadryad. It was nothing Vadim was prepared for.

In my fist I held one of his black experientials. He played his part perfectly – his gaze shifting minutely as my arm came up, just enough to bring his nearest eye into my reach. The eye was opened in surprise; an easy target, almost as if Vadim was complicit in what I was about to do to him.

153

I pushed the experiential into his eye.

I remembered wondering if his one good eye had in fact been glass, but as the experiential's white haft sunk in, I saw that it had only *seemed* glassy.

Vadim fell back off me and started screaming, blood jetting from his eye like a dying red sliver of sunset. He was flailing around insanely, not wanting to reach up and confront the foreign thing parked in his eye-socket.

'Shit!' the other man said, while I scrambled to my feet. Quirrenbach wrestled with him for an instant, and then he was free, and running.

Moaning, Vadim was bent double over our table. The other man was holding him, whispering frantically in his ear. He appeared to be saying it was time the both of them left.

I had a message of my own for him.

'I know it hurts like hell, but there's something you need to know, Vadim. I could have driven that thing straight into your brain. It wouldn't have been any harder for me. You know what that means, don't you?'

Eyeless now, his face a mask of blood, he still managed to turn towards me.

'. . . what?'

'It means that's another one you owe me, Vadim.'

Then I carefully removed the watch from his wrist and replaced it on my own.

THIRTEEN

If there was any kind of law enforcement operating in New Vancouver's plumbing-filled interstices, it was subtle to the point of invisibility. Vadim and his accomplice stumbled away from the scene unquestioned. I lingered, almost honour-bound to explain myself – but nothing happened. The table where Quirrenbach and I had been sipping coffee only minutes earlier was in a deplorable state now, but what was I supposed to do? Leave a tip for the cleaning servitor that would doubtless amble round shortly, so dim-witted that it would probably clean up the pools of blood, aqueous and vitreous humours with the same mindless efficiency as it tackled the coffee stains?

No one stopped me leaving.

I slipped into a washroom to slap some cold water on my face and clean the blood from my fist. Inside, I forced slow and deliberate calm. The room was empty, furnished with a long row of lavatories, the doors of which were marked with complicated diagrams to show how they were meant to be used.

I poked and prodded my chest until I'd satisfied myself that nothing was more than bruised, then completed the rest of my walk to the departure area. The behemoth – the manta-shaped spacecraft – was attached like a lamprey to the rotating skin of the habitat. Up close, the thing looked a lot less smooth and aerodynamic than it had from a distance. The hull was pitted and scarred, with streaks of sooty black discoloration.

Two streams of humanity were being fed aboard the ship from opposing sides. My stream was a shuffling, dun-coloured slurry of despondency: people trudging down the spiralling access tunnel as if to the gallows. The other stream looked only slightly more enthusiastic, but through the transparent connecting tube I saw people attended by servitors, bizarrely enhanced pets, even people shaped towards animal forms themselves. The palanquins of hermetics glided amongst them: dark, upright boxes like metronomes.

There was a commotion behind me; someone pushing past.

'Tanner!' he said, in a hoarse stage-whisper. 'You made it too! When you disappeared, I was worried that more of Vadim's thugs had found you!'

'He's pushing in,' I heard someone mutter behind me. 'Did you see that? I've a good mind to . . .'

I turned back, locking eyes with the person I instinctively knew had been speaking. 'He's with me. If you've got a problem with it, you deal with me. Otherwise, shut up and stand in line.'

Quirrenbach slipped in to the line next to me. 'Thanks . . .'

'All right. Just keep your voice down, and don't mention Vadim again.'

'So you think he really might have friends all over the place?'

'I don't know. But I could do without any kind of trouble for a while.'

'I can imagine, especially after . . .' He blanched. 'I don't even want to think about what happened back there.'

'Then don't. With any luck, you'll never have to.'

The line pushed forward, completing the final spiral into the top of the behemoth. Inside it was vast and tastefully lit, like the lobby of a particularly grand hotel. The walkway made several more loops before it reached the floor. People were wandering around with drinks in their hands, their luggage scooting ahead of them or being handled by monkeys. Sloping windows arced away in either direction, roughly defining the edge of one of the manta's wings. The interior of the behemoth must have been almost completely hollow, but I couldn't see more than a tenth of it from where I was standing.

Scattered here and there were clusters of seats – sometimes grouped for conversation, sometimes surrounding a dribbling fountain or a clump of exotic foliage. Now and then the rectilinear shape of a palanquin slid across the floor like a chess piece.

I moved towards an unoccupied pair of seats overlooking one of the window panels. I was tired enough to want to doze quietly, but I didn't dare close my eyes. What if there hadn't been an earlier behemoth departure and Reivich was somewhere inside the spacecraft even now?

'Preoccupied, Tanner?' said Quirrenbach, sliding into the seat next to mine. 'You have that look about you.'

'Are you sure this is the best place to get a good view?'

'Excellent point, Tanner; excellent point. But if I'm not sitting next to you, how am I going to hear about Sky?' He began to fiddle with his briefcase. 'Now there's plenty of time for you to tell me all the rest.'

'You nearly get killed, and all you can think about is that madman?'

'You don't understand. I'm thinking now – what about a symphony for Sky?' Then he pointed a finger at me, like a gun. 'No. Not a symphony: a mass; a vast choral work, epic in its scope . . . studiedly archaic in structure . . . consecutive fifths and false relations, with a brooding Sanctus . . . a threnody for lost innocence; an anthem to the crime and the glory of Schuyler Haussmann . . .'

'There isn't any glory, Quirrenbach. Only crime.'

'I won't know until you tell me the rest, will I?'

There was a series of thumps and shudders as the behemoth was unplugged from its connecting point on the habitat. Through the windows I could see the habitat falling away very quickly, accompanied by a moment of dizziness. But almost before the moment had begun to register physically, the habitat came swooping past again, its skin rushing by the great windows. Then only space. I looked around, but people were still walking unaffected around the lobby.

'Shouldn't we be in free-fall?'

'Not in a behemoth,' Quirrenbach said. 'The instant she detached from NV, she fell away on a tangent to the habitat's surface, like a sling-shot. But that only lasted for an instant before she ramped up her thrusters to one-gee. Then she had to curve slightly to avoid ramming into the habitat on the way past. That's the only really tricky part of the journey, I understand – the only time where there's really any likelihood of your drinks going for a ride. But the pilot seemed to know what it was doing.'

'It?'

'They use genetically engineered cetaceans to fly these things, I think. Whales or porpoises, wired permanently into the behemoth's nervous system. But don't worry. They've never killed anyone. It'll feel as smooth as this most of the way down. She just lowers herself down into the atmosphere, very gently and slowly. A behemoth's like a huge rigid airship, once it gets into any kind of air density. By the time she gets near the surface, she's got so much positive buoyancy that she actually has to use her thrusters to hold herself *down*. It's a lot like swimming, I think.' Quirrenbach clicked his fingers at a servitor which was passing. 'Drinks, I think. What can I offer you, Tanner?'

I looked out the window: Yellowstone's horizon was rising vertically, so that the planet looked like a sheer yellow wall.

'I don't know. What do they drink around here?'

Yellowstone's horizon tilted slowly back towards horizontal as the behemoth cancelled out the orbital velocity it had matched with the carousel. The process was smooth and uneventful, but it must have been planned meticulously so that when we finally came to a halt relative to the planet we were hovering precisely over Chasm City, rather than thousands of kilometres away.

By then, although we were thousands of kilometres above the surface, Yellowstone's gravity was still almost as strong as it would have been on the ground. We might as well have been sitting atop a very tall mountain; one that protruded beyond the atmosphere. Slowly, however – with the unhurried calm which had characterised the whole journey so far – the behemoth began to descend.

Quirrenbach and I watched the view in silence.

Yellowstone was a heavier sibling to Sol's Titan; a fully-fledged world rather than a moon. Chaotic and poisonous chemistries of nitrogen, methane and ammonia produced an atmosphere daubed with every imaginable shade of yellow; ochre, orange, tan, whorled into beautiful cyclonic spirals, curlicued and filigreed as if by the most delicate brushwork. Over most of its surface Yellowstone was exquisitely cold, lashed by ferocious winds, flash floods and electrical storms. The planet's orbit around Epsilon Eridani had been disturbed in the distant past by a close encounter with Tangerine Dream, the system's massive gas giant, and even though that event must have taken place hundreds of millions years ago, Yellowstone's crust was still relaxing from the tectonic stress of the encounter, bleeding energy back to the surface. There was some speculation that Marco's Eye – the planet's solitary moon – had even been captured from the gas giant; a history that would explain the odd cratering on one side of the moon.

Yellowstone was not a hospitable place, but humans had come nonetheless. I tried to imagine what it must have been like at the height of the *Belle Epoque*; descending into Yellowstone's atmosphere and knowing that beneath those golden cloud layers lay cities as fabulous as dream, Chasm City the mightiest of them all. The glory had lasted more than two hundred years . . . and even in its terminal years, there had been nothing to suggest it was not capable of lasting centuries more. There'd been no decadent decline; no failure of nerve. But then the plague had come. All those hues of yellow became hues of sickness; hues of vomit and bile and infection; the world's febrile skies masking the diseased cities strewn across its surface like chancres.

Still, I thought, sipping the drink Quirrenbach had bought me, it had been good while it lasted.

The behemoth didn't cut its way into the atmosphere; it *submerged* itself, descending so slowly that there was barely any friction on its hull. The sky above stopped being pure black and began to assume faint hints of purple and then ochre. Now and then our weight fluctuated – presumably as the behemoth hit a pressure cell which it couldn't quite squeeze past – but never by more than ten or fifteen per cent.

'It's still beautiful,' he said. 'Don't you think?'

He was right. We could see the surface occasionally now, when some chaotic squall or shift in the underlying atmospheric chemistry opened a temporary rent in the yellow cloud layers. Shimmering lakes of frozen ammonia; psychotic badlands of wind-carved geology; broken spires and mile-high arches like the half-buried bones of titanic animals. There were forms of single-celled organism down there, I knew – staining the surface in great, lustrous purple and emerald monolayers or veining deep rock strata – but they existed in such glacial time that it was hard to think of them as living at all. Here and there were small domed outposts, but nothing one would think of as cities. Yellowstone had only a handful of settlements even a tenth the size of

Chasm City now; nothing equalling it. Even the second largest city, Ferrisville, was a township compared to the capital.

'Nice place to visit,' I said, not needing to complete the old saying.

'Yes . . . you're probably right,' Quirrenbach said. 'Once I've soaked up enough of the ambience to fuel my composition, and earned enough to pay for a hop out of here . . . I doubt very much that I will linger.'

'How are you going to make money?'

'There's always work for composers. All you need to do is find some rich benefactor who fancies sponsoring a great work of art. They feel like they're achieving some small measure of immortality themselves.'

'And what if they're already immortal, or postmortal, or whatever it is they call themselves?'

'Even the postmortal can't be certain they aren't going to die at some point, so the instinct to leave a dent on history is still strong. Besides which, there are many people in Chasm City who used to be postmortal, but who now have to deal with the imminent prospect of death, the way some of us always have.'

'My heart bleeds.'

'Quite . . . well, let us just say that for a good many people death is now back on the agenda in a way it hasn't been for several centuries.'

'Even so, what if there aren't any rich benefactors amongst them?'

'Oh, there are. You've seen those palanquins. There are still rich people in Chasm City, even though there isn't much of what you'd call an economic infrastructure. But you can be sure there are pockets of wealth and influence, and I'm willing to wager that a few people are wealthier and more influential than they were before.'

'That's always the way with disasters,' I said.

'What?'

'They're never bad news for everyone. Something nasty always rises to the top.'

As we descended further I thought about cover stories and camouflage. I hadn't given much thought to either, but – weapons and logistics aside – that was the way I usually operated, preferring to adapt to my surroundings as I found them, rather than to plan things in advance. But what about Reivich? He couldn't have known about the plague, which meant that any plans he'd formulated would have been in disarray as soon as he learned what had happened. But there was a vital difference: Reivich was an aristocrat, and they had webs of influence which reached between worlds, often based on familial ties which reached back centuries. It was possible – likely, even – that Reivich had connections amongst Chasm City's élite.

Those connections would have been useful to him even if he hadn't managed to contact them before his arrival. But they'd have been even more useful if he'd been able to signal them while he was on his way here, forewarning them. A lighthugger moved at nearly the speed of light, but it had to speed up and slow down at either end of its journey. A radio signal from Sky's Edge – sent just before the *Orvieto*'s departure – would have reached Yellowstone a year or two in advance of the ship itself, giving his allies that much time to prepare for his arrival.

Or perhaps he had no allies. Or they existed, but the message had never got through, lost in the confusion that was the system's communications net and condemned to bounce endlessly between malfunctioning network nodes. Or perhaps there just hadn't been time to arrange for a message to be sent at all, or it hadn't crossed his mind.

I'd have liked to have drawn comfort from any of those possibilities, but the one thing I never counted on was having luck on my side.

It was generally simpler that way.

I looked out the window again, seeing Chasm City for the first time as the clouds parted, and thought: *he's down there, somewhere . . . waiting and knowing.* But even then the city was too large to take in, and I felt a crushing sense of the enormity of the task that lay ahead of me. Give up now, I thought; it's impossible. You'll never find him.

But then I remembered Gitta.

The city nestled within a wide, jagged crater wall, sixty kilometres from side to side, and nearly two kilometres high at its tallest point. When the first explorers arrived here, they had sought shelter from Yellowstone's winds within the crater, building flimsy, air-filled structures that would have survived five minutes in the true badlands. But they'd also been lured by the chasm itself: the deep, sheer-sided, mist-enshrouded gully at the geometric centre of the crater.

The chasm belched perpetual warm gas, one of the outlets for the tectonic energy pumped into the core during the encounter with the gas giant. The gas was still poisonous, but much richer in free oxygen, water vapour and other trace gases than any comparable outgassing anywhere on Yellowstone's surface. The gas still needed to be filtered through machinery before it could be breathed, but that process was much simpler than it would have been elsewhere, and the scalding heat could be used to drive immense steam turbines, supplying as much energy as any burgeoning colony could use. The city had sprawled across the entire level surface of the crater, surrounding the chasm at its heart and spilling some way into its depths. Structures were perched on perilous ledges hundreds of metres below the chasm's lip, connected by elevators and walkways.

Most of the city, however, lay under a vast toroidal dome, encircling the chasm. Quirrenbach told me the locals called it the Mosquito Net. Technically, it was actually eighteen individual domes, but because they were merged it was hard to tell where one ended and another began. The surface hadn't been cleaned in seven years and was now stained in filthy, near-opaque shades of brown and yellow. It was largely accidental that some areas of the dome remained clean enough to reveal the city beneath them. From the behemoth, it looked almost normal: a phenomenal mass of immensely tall buildings compressed into festering urban density, like a glimpse into the innards of a fantastically complex machine. But there was something queasily wrong about those buildings; something sick about their shapes, contorted into forms no sane architect would have chosen. Above ground, they branched and rebranched, merging into a single bronchial mass. Except for a sprinkling of lights at their upper and lower extremities – strewn through the bronchial mass like lanterns – the buildings were dark and dead-looking.

'Well, you know what this means,' I said.

'What?'

'They weren't kidding. It wasn't a hoax.'

'No,' Quirrenbach said. 'They most certainly weren't. I also foolishly allowed myself to entertain that possibility; thinking that even after what had become of the Rust Belt, even after the evidence I had seen with my own eyes, the city itself might be intact, a reclusive hermit hoarding its riches away from the curious.'

'But there's still a city,' I said. 'There are still people down there; still some kind of society.'

'Just not quite the one we were expecting.'

We skimmed low over the dome. The structure was a sagging geodesic drapery of latticed metal and structural diamond stretching for kilometres, as far into the brown caul of the atmosphere as it was possible to see. Tiny teams of suited repair workers were dotted across the dome like ants, their labours revealed by the intermittent sparks of welding torches. Here and there I saw gouts of grey vapour streaming from cracks in the dome, internal air freezing as it hit Yellowstone's atmosphere, high above the crater's thermal trap. The buildings below reached almost to the underside of the dome itself, groping up like arthritic fingers. Black strands stretched between those painfully swollen and crooked digits; for all the world like the last tracery of gloves which had rotted almost away. Lights were clumped near the tips of those fingers, reaching in long meandering filaments along the thickest webs which bridged them. Now that we were closer I saw that there was a finer tracery altogether, the buildings enveloped in a convoluted tangle of fine dark filaments as if delirious spiders had tried to fashion webs between them. What they had produced was an incoherent mass of dangling threads, lights moving through it along drunken trajectories.

I remembered what the welcome message aboard the *Strelnikov* had told me about the Melding Plague. The transformations had been extraordinarily rapid – so rapid, in fact, that the shifting buildings had killed a great many people in ways far cruder than the plague itself would have done. The buildings had been engineered to repair themselves and reshape themselves according to architectural whims imposed by democratic will – the populace having only to wish a building to alter its shape in sufficient numbers for the building to obey – but the changes wrought by the plague had been uncontrolled and sudden, more like a series of abrupt seismic shifts. That was the hidden danger of a city so Utopian in its fluidity that it could be reshaped time and again, frozen and melted and refrozen like an ice-sculpture. No one had told the city that there were people living within it, who might be crushed once it began to shape itself. Many of the dead were still down there, entombed in the monstrous structures which now filled the city.

Then Chasm City was no longer beneath us, but the toothed edge of the crater wall; the behemoth slicing expertly through a notch in the rim which looked only just wide enough to accommodate it.

Ahead I could see a huddle of armoured structures near one edge of a butterscotch-coloured lake. The behemoth lowered itself towards the lake, the scream of its thrusters audible now as it fought to hold itself at this altitude against its natural tendency to float upwards.

'Disembarkation time,' Quirrenbach said. He got up from his seat, indicating a general flow of people across the lobby.

'Where are they all going?'

'To the drop capsules.'

I followed him across the lobby, where a dozen sets of spiral stairs led to the disembarkation level, a whole deck below. People were waiting by glass airlocks to board teardrop-shaped capsules, dozens of them which were slowly being pushed forward along guideways. At the front, the capsules slid down a short ramp which was jutting from the behemoth's belly, before falling the rest of the distance – two or three hundred metres – and splashing into the lake.

'You mean this thing doesn't actually land?'

'Good heavens, no.' Quirrenbach smiled at me. 'They wouldn't risk landing. Not these days.'

Our drop capsule slid from the behemoth's belly. There were four of us in it: Quirrenbach, myself and two other passengers. The other two were engaged in an animated conversation about a local celebrity called Voronoff, but they spoke Norte with such a strong local accent that I could only follow about one word in three. They were completely unfazed by the experience of dropping from the behemoth; even when we plunged deep into the lake and appeared in some danger of not bobbing to the surface. But then we did, and because the drop capsule's skin was glassy, I could see other capsules bobbing around us.

Two giant machines strode across the lake to receive us. They were tripods, rising high above us on skeletal, pistonned mechanical legs. With cranelike appendages they began to collect the floating capsules and deposit each in a collecting net stowed beneath the body of each tripod. I could see a driver perched at the top of each machine, tiny inside a pressurised cabin, working levers furiously.

The machines walked to the lake's edge and emptied their catches onto a moving belt which fed into one of the buildings I'd seen from the behemoth.

Inside, we were passed into a pressurised reception chamber where the pods were removed from the belt and opened by bored-looking workers. Empty pods were shuttling around to an embarkation area similar to the one aboard the behemoth, where passengers waited with luggage. I presumed they'd be carried out to the middle of the lake by the tripods, which would then loft each pod high enough up for the behemoth to grab it.

Quirrenbach and I left our pod and followed the flow of passengers from the reception chamber through a warren of cold, dim tunnels. The air tasted stale, as if each breath had already been through a few lungs before it reached my own. But it was breathable, and the gravity not noticeably heavier than in the Rust Belt habitat.

'I don't know quite what I was expecting,' I said. 'But this wasn't it. No welcoming signs; no visible security; nothing. It makes me wonder what the immigration and customs section will be like.'

'You don't have to wonder,' Quirrenbach said. 'You've just left it.'

I thought about the diamond gun I'd given Amelia, secure in the knowledge that there was no way I would be able to take it with me to Chasm City.

'That was it?'

'Think about it. You'd find it exceedingly difficult to bring anything into Chasm City which wasn't already there. There's no point checking for weapons – they've got enough of them already, so what difference would one more make? They'd be far more likely to confiscate whatever you had and offer you part-exchange on an upgrade. And there's no point screening for diseases. Too complicated, and you're far more likely to catch something than bring something into the city. A few nice foreign germs might actually do us some good.'

'Us?'

'Them. Slip of the tongue.'

We passed into a well-lit area with wide windows overlooking the lake. The behemoth was being loaded with capsules, the dorsal surface of the manta-like machine still bright with the thrusters it had to burn to hold this position. Each pod was sterilised by being passed through a ring of purple flame before being accepted into the behemoth's belly. Maybe the city didn't care what came into it, but the outside universe certainly seemed to care what left it.

'I suppose you have some idea how we get to the city from here?'

'There's really only one way, I gather, and that's the Chasm City Zephyr.'

Quirrenbach and I brushed past a palanquin, moving slowly down the next connecting tunnel. The upright box was patterned in bas-relief black, showing

163

scenes from the city's vainglorious past. I risked a glance back as we overtook the slow-moving machine and my gaze met the fearful eyes of the hermetic sitting within: face pale behind thick green glass.

There were walking servitors carrying luggage, but there was something primitive about them. They were not sleek intelligence machines, but clunking, error-prone robots with about as much sentience as a dog. There were no genuinely clever machines left now, outside of the orbital enclaves where such things were still possible. But even the crude servitors that remained were obviously valued: signs of residual wealth.

And then there were the wealthy themselves, those travelling without the sanctuary of palanquins. I presumed none of these people had implants of any great complexity; certainly nothing that might be susceptible to plague spore. They moved nervously, in hurried packs, surrounding themselves with servitors.

Ahead the tunnel widened into an underground cavern, dimly lit by hundreds of flickering lamps burning in sconces. There was a steady warm breeze blowing through it, carrying a stench of machine oil.

And something enormous and bestial waited in the cavern.

It rode four sets of double rails arranged around it at intervals of ninety degrees: one set below the machine, one above and one on either side. The rails themselves were supported by a framework of skeletal braces, though at either end of the cavern they vanished into circular tunnels where they were anchored to the walls themselves. I couldn't help but think of the trains in the *Santiago* which had featured in one of Sky's dreams, braced within a similar set of rails – even though those rails had only been guidance ways for induction fields.

This wasn't like that.

The train itself was constructed with a four-way symmetry. At the centre was a cylindrical core tipped with a bullet-shaped prow and a single Cyclopean headlight. Jutting from this core were four separate double rows of enormous iron wheels, each of which contained twelve axles and was locked onto one of the pairs of rail lines. Three pairs of huge cylinders were interspersed along each set of twelve main wheels, each connected to four sets of wheels by a bewildering arrangement of gleaming pistons and thigh-thick greased articulated cranks. A mass of pipe-runs snaked all around the machine; whatever symmetry or elegance of design it might have had was ruined by what appeared to be randomly placed exhaust outlets, all of which were belching steam up towards the cavern's ceiling. The machine hissed like a dragon whose patience was wearing fatally thin. It seemed worryingly alive.

Behind was a string of passenger cars built around the same four-fold symmetry, engaging with the same rails.

'That's the . . . ?'

'. . . Chasm City Zephyr,' Quirrenbach said. 'Quite a beast, isn't she?'

'You're telling me that thing actually goes somewhere?'

'It wouldn't make much sense if it didn't.' I gave him a look so he continued, 'I heard that they used to have magnetic levitation trains running into Chasm City and out to the other colonies. They had vacuum tunnels for them. But they must have stopped working properly after the plague.'

'And they thought replacing them with this was a good idea?'

'They didn't have much choice. I don't think anyone needs to get anywhere very quickly nowadays, so it doesn't matter that the trains can't run at the supersonic speeds they used to attain. A couple of hundred kilometres per hour is more than sufficient, even for journeys out to the other settlements.'

Quirrenbach started walking towards the back of the train where ramps led up to the passenger cars.

'Why steam?'

'Because there aren't any fossil fuels on Yellowstone. Some nuclear generators still work, but, by and large, the chasm itself is about the only useful energy source around here. That's why a lot of the city runs on steam pressure these days.'

'I still don't buy it, Quirrenbach. You don't jump back six hundred years just because you can't use nanotechnology any more.'

'Maybe you do. After the plague hit, it affected a lot more than you'd think. Almost all manufacturing had been done by nano for centuries. Materials production; shaping – it all suddenly got a lot cruder. Even things which didn't use nano themselves had been *built* by nano; designed with incredibly fine tolerances. None of that stuff could be duplicated any more. It wasn't just a question of making do with things which were slightly less sophisticated. They had to go right back before they reached any kind of plateau from which they could begin rebuilding. That meant working with crudely forged metals and metalworking techniques. And remember that a lot of the data relating to these things had been lost as well. They were fumbling around in the blind. It was like someone from the twenty-first century trying to work out how to make a mediaeval sword without knowing anything about metallurgy. Knowing that something was primitive didn't necessarily mean it was any easier to rediscover.'

Quirrenbach paused to catch his breath, standing beneath a clattering destination board. It showed departures to Chasm City, Ferrisville, Loreanville, New Europa and beyond, but only about one train a day was leaving to anywhere other than Chasm City.

'So they did the best they could,' Quirrenbach said. 'Some technology had survived the plague, of course. That's why you'll still see relics, even here – servitors, vehicles – but they tend to be owned by the rich. They've got all the nuclear generators, and the few antimatter power-plants left in the city. Down in the Mulch it'll be a different story, I think. It'll be dangerous, too.'

While he talked I looked at the destination board. It would have made my job a lot easier if Reivich had taken a train to one of the smaller settlements, where he would have been both conspicuous and trapped, but I thought the chances were good that he'd have taken the first train to Chasm City.

Quirrenbach and I paid our fares and boarded the train. The carriages strung behind the locomotive looked much older than the rest of it, and therefore much more modern, salvaged from the old levitating train and mounted on wheels. The doors irised shut, and then the whole procession clanked into motion, creeping forward at a walking pace and then gathering speed laboriously. There was an intermittent squeal of slipping wheels, and then the ride became smoother, steam billowing past us. The train threaded its way through one of the narrow-bored tunnels faced with an enormous irising door, and then we passed through a further series of pressure locks, until we must have been moving through near-vacuum.

The ride became ghostly quiet.

The passenger compartment was as cramped as a prison transport, and the passengers seemed subdued to the point of somnolence, like drugged prisoners being carried to a detention centre. Screens had dropped down from the ceiling and were now cycling through adverts, but they referred to products and services which were very unlikely to have survived the plague. Near one end I could see a huddle of palanquins, grouped together like a collection of coffins in an undertaker's backroom.

'The first thing we've got to do is get these implants out,' Quirrenbach said, leaning conspiratorially towards me. 'I can't bear the idea of the things still sitting in my head now.'

'We should be able to find someone who'll do it quickly,' I said.

'And safely, too – the one's not much good without the other.'

I smiled. 'I think it's probably a little late to worry about *safely*, don't you?'

Quirrenbach pursed his lips.

The screen next to us was showing an advert for a particularly sleek-looking flying machine, something like one of our volantors, except it seemed to have been made out of insect parts. But then the screen flashed with static and a geisha-like woman appeared on it instead.

'Welcome aboard the Chasm City Zephyr.' The woman's face resembled a china doll with painted lips and rosy cheeks. She wore an absurdly elaborate silver outfit which curved up behind her head. 'We are currently transiting the Trans-Caldera Tunnel and will be arriving at Grand Central Station in eight minutes. We hope you will enjoy your journey with us and that your time in Chasm City will be both pleasant and prosperous. In the meantime, in anticipation of our arrival, we invite you to share some of our city's highlights.'

'This'll be interesting,' Quirrenbach said.

The windows of the train carriage flickered and became holographic displays, no longer showing the rushing walls, but an impressive vista of the city,

166

just as if the train had tunnelled through seven years of history. The train was threading between dreamlike structures, rising vertiginously on either side like mountains sculpted out of solid opal or obsidian. Below us was a series of stepped levels, landscaped with beautiful gardens and lakes, entwined with walkways and civic transit tubes. They dwindled into a haze of blue depth, riven by plunging abysses full of neon light, immense tiered plazas and rockfaces. The air was thick with a constant swarm of colourful aerial vehicles, some of which were shaped like exotic dragonflies or hummingbirds. Passenger dirigibles nosed indolently through the swarms; scores of tiny revellers peered over the railed edges of their gondolas. Above them, the largest buildings loomed like geometric clouds. The sky was a pure electric blue woven with the fine, regular matrix of the dome.

And all around the city marched into terrible distance, wonder upon wonder receding as far as the eye could see. It was only sixty kilometres, but it could have been infinity. There appeared to be enough marvels in Chasm City to last a lifetime. Even a modern one.

But no one had told the simulation about the plague. I had to remind myself that we were still rushing through the tunnel under the crater wall; that in fact we had yet to arrive in the city itself.

'I can see why they called it a *Belle Epoque*,' I said.

Quirrenbach nodded. 'They had it all. And you know the worst of it? They damn well knew it. Unlike any other golden age in history . . . they *knew* they were living through it.'

'It must have made them pretty insufferable.'

'Well, they certainly paid for it.'

It was round about then that we burst into what passed for daylight in Chasm City. The train must have crossed under the crater rim and passed through the boundary of the dome. It was racing through a suspended tube just like the one which had been suggested by the hologram, but this tube was covered in dirt which only gave way fleetingly; just enough to show that we were passing through what looked like a series of densely packed slums. The holographic recording was still playing, so that the old city was superimposed on the new one like a faint ghost. Ahead, the tube curved round and vanished into a tiered cylindrical building from which other tubes radiated, threading out across the city. The train was slowing as we approached the tiered building.

Grand Central Station, Chasm City.

As we entered the building, the holographic mirage faded, taking with it the last faint memory of the *Belle Epoque*. Yet for all its glory, only Quirrenbach and I seemed to have taken much notice of the hologram. The other passengers stood silent, scrutinising the scorched and littered floor.

'Still think you can make it here?' I asked Quirrenbach. 'After what you've seen now?'

He gave the question a lot of thought before answering.

'Who's to say I won't? Maybe there are more opportunities now than ever before. Maybe it's just a question of adaptation. One thing's for sure, though.'

'What's that?'

'Whatever music I write here, it isn't going to cheer anyone up.'

Grand Central Station was as humid as deep Peninsula jungle, just as starved of light as the forest floor. Sweltering, I removed Vadim's coat and bundled it under one arm.

'We've got to get these implants out,' Quirrenbach said yet again, tugging at my sleeve.

'Don't worry,' I said. 'It hadn't slipped my mind.'

The roof was supported by fluted pillars which rose up like hamadryad trees before thrusting their fingers through the roof into the brown gloom beyond. In between these pillars was a densely packed bazaar: a motley city of tents and stalls, through which passed only the narrowest and most twisting of passageways. Stalls had been built or piled above each other, so that some of the passageways became backbreakingly low, lamplit tunnels through which people were forced to stoop like hunchbacks. There were several dozen vendors and many hundreds of people, very few of whom were accompanied by servitors. There were exotic pets on leashes; genetically enhanced servants; caged birds and snakes. A few hermetics had made the error of trying to force their way through the bazaar rather than finding a route around it, and now their palanquins were mired, harried by traders and tricksters.

'Well?' I said. 'Do we risk it, or find a way around?'

Quirrenbach clutched his briefcase closer to his chest. 'Much against my better judgement, I think we should risk it. I have a hunch – merely a hunch, mind – that we may be pointed towards the services we both so urgently require.'

'It might be a mistake.'

'And it probably won't be the first of the day, either. I'm somewhat on the ravenous side, anyway. There's bound to be something edible around here – and it might not be immediately toxic.'

We pushed our way into the bazaar. Quirrenbach and I had taken barely a dozen steps before we had attracted a mob of optimistic kids and surly beggars.

'Do I have affluent and gullible written in conspicuous neon letters on my forehead?' Quirrenbach said.

'It's our clothes,' I said, pushing another urchin back into the throng. 'I recognised yours as being Mendicant-made, and I wasn't even paying you much attention.'

'I don't see why that should make much difference.'

'Because it means we're from outside,' I said. 'Beyond the system. Who else would be wearing Mendicant clothing? That automatically guarantees a certain prosperity, or at least the possibility of it.'

Quirrenbach clutched his luggage to his chest with renewed protectiveness. We pushed our way deeper into the bazaar until we found a stall selling something which looked edible. In Hospice Idlewild they'd treated my gut flora for Yellowstone compatibility, but it had been a fairly broad-spectrum treatment, not guaranteed to be any use against anything *specific*. Now was my chance to test exactly how non-specific it had been.

What we bought were hot, greasy pastries filled with some unidentifiable, semi-cooked meat. It was heavily spiced, probably to disguise the meat's underlying rancidity. But I had eaten less appetising rations on Sky's Edge and found it more or less palatable. Quirrenbach wolfed down his, then bought another, and finished that one off with equal recklessness.

'Hey, you,' said a voice. 'Implants, out?'

A kid tugged the hem of Quirrenbach's Mendicant jacket, dragging him deeper into the bazaar. The kid's clothes would be graduating to raghood in a week or two, but were now lingering on the edge of dilapidation.

'Implants, out,' the kid said again. 'You new here, you no need implants, misters. Madame Dominika, she get them out, good price, fast, not much blood or pain. You too, big guy.'

The kid had hooked his fingers around my belt and was dragging me as well.

'It's, um, not necessary,' Quirrenbach said, pointlessly.

'You new here, got Mendicant suits, need implants out now, before they go wacko. You know what that mean, misters? Big scream, head explode, brain everywhere, get real mess on clothes . . . you not want that, I think.'

'No, thank you very much.'

Another kid had appeared, tugging at Quirrenbach's other sleeve. 'Hey, mister, don't listen to Tom – come and see Doctor Jackal! He only kill one in twenty! Lowest mortality rate in Grand Central! Don't go wacko; see the Jackal!'

'Yeah, and get free permanent brain damage,' said Dominika's kid. 'Don't listen; ev'ryone know Dominika best in Chasm City!'

I said, 'Why are you hesitating? Isn't this exactly what you were hoping to find?'

'Yes!' Quirrenbach hissed. 'But not like this! Not in some filthy damned tent! I was anticipating a reasonably sterile and well-equipped clinic. In fact I know there are better places we can use, Tanner, just trust me on this . . .'

I shrugged, allowing Tom to haul me along. 'Maybe a tent is as good as it gets, Quirrenbach.'

'No! It can't be. There must be . . .' He looked at me helplessly, willing me to take control and drag him away, but I simply smiled and nodded towards the tent: a blue and white box with a slightly cambered roof, guylines attached to iron pins driven into the floor.

'In you go,' I said, inviting Quirrenbach to step ahead of me. We were in an ante-room to the tent's main chamber, just us and the kid. Tom, I saw now, had a kind of elfin beauty; gender indeterminate beneath tattered clothes, the face was framed by curtains of lank black hair. The kid's name could have been Thomas or Thomasina, but I decided it was probably the former. Tom swayed in time to sitar music emanating from a little malachite box which rested on a table set with perfumed candles.

'This isn't too bad,' I said. 'I mean, there's no actual blood anywhere. No actual brain tissue lying around.'

'No,' Quirrenbach said, suddenly making a decision. 'Not here; not how. I'm leaving, Tanner. You can stay or follow me; it's entirely up to you.'

I spoke to him as quietly as I could manage: 'What Tom says is true. You need to have your implants out now, if the Mendicants didn't already do it for you.'

He reached up and rasped a hand across his scalp stubble. 'Maybe they were just trying to scare up business with those stories.'

'Perhaps – but do you really want to take that risk? The hardware's just going to be sitting in your head like a timebomb. Might as well have it out. You can always have it put back in again, after all.'

'By a woman in a tent who calls herself Madame Dominika? I'd rather take my chances with a rusty penknife and a mirror.'

'Whatever. Just so long as you do it before you go wacko.'

The kid was already dragging Quirrenbach through the partition into the room beyond. 'Talking of money, Tanner – neither of us are exactly flush. We don't know we can afford Dominika's services, do we?'

'That's a very good point.' I grabbed Tom by the collar, hauling him gently back into the ante-room. 'My friend and I need to sell some goods in a hurry, unless your Madame Dominika is given to charity.' When that remark had no effect on Tom, I opened my suitcase and showed him some of what was inside. 'Sell, for cash. Where?'

That seemed to work. 'Green and silver tent, 'cross market. Say Dominika sent you, you no get major sting.'

'Hey, wait a minute.' Quirrenbach was halfway through the gash now. I could see into the main room, where a phenomenally bulky woman sat behind a long couch, consulting her fingernails, medical equipment suspended over the couch on articulated booms, metal glinting in candlelight.

'What?'

'Why should I be the guinea pig? I thought you said you needed to have your implants removed as well.'

'You're right. And I'll be back shortly. I just need to convert some of my possessions into cash. Tom said I could do it in the bazaar.'

His face turned from incomprehension to fury.

'But you can't go now! I thought we were in this together! Travelling companions! Don't betray a friendship almost before it's begun, Tanner . . .'

'Hey, calm down. I'm not betraying anything. By the time she's finished with you, I'll have got enough cash together.' I clicked a finger towards the fat woman. 'Dominika!'

Languidly, she turned to face me, her lips forming a silent interrogative.

'How long will it take with him?'

'One hour,' she answered. 'Dominika real quick.'

I nodded. 'That's more than enough time, Quirrenbach. Just sit back and let her do her job.'

He looked into Dominika's face and seemed to calm slightly.

'Really? You will be back?'

'Of course. I'm not stepping into the city with implants still in my head. What do you think I am, insane? But I do need money.'

'What are you planning to sell?'

'Some of my own goods. Some of the stuff I lifted from our mutual friend Vadim. There's got to be a market for that kind of thing or he wouldn't have been hoarding it.'

Dominika was trying to pull him onto her couch, but Quirrenbach was still managing to stay on his feet. I remembered how he had impulsively changed his mind when we began looting Vadim's quarters – at first resisting the theft, then throwing himself enthusiastically into the process. I saw a similar sea-change now.

'Dammit,' he murmured, shaking his head. He looked at me curiously, then cracked open his own case, riffling through sheet music until he reached a set of compartments below it. He fished out some of the experientials he had taken from Vadim. 'I'm no good at bartering anyway. Take these and get a good price on them, Tanner. I'm assuming they'll cover the cost of this.'

'You trust me to do that?'

He looked at me through squinted eyes. 'Just get a good price.'

I took the items and placed them amongst my own.

Behind him, the bulky woman hovered across the room like an unmoored dirigible, her feet skimming inches from the ground. She was cradled in a black metal harness, attached to one wall by a complexly-jointed pneumatic arm, hissing steam as it articulated and flexed. Rolls of fat disguised the indeterminate region where her head and torso merged. Her hands were spread out as if she was drying recently painted fingernails. Each fingertip vanished into – or possibly *became* – a kind of thimble. Each thimble was tipped with something medical and specialised.

'No; him first,' she said, extending a little finger in my direction, its thimble adorned with what looked like a tiny sterile harpoon.

'Thank you, Dominika,' I said. 'But you'd best attend to Quirrenbach first.'

'You come back?'

'Yes – once I've acquired some finance.'

I smiled and left the tent, hearing the sound of drills whining up to speed.

FOURTEEN

The man who looked through my belongings had a whirring and clicking eyeglass strapped to his head. His hairless scalp was quilted with fine scars, like a broken vase that had been inexpertly mended. He examined everything I showed him with tweezers, holding the items up to his eyeglass in the manner of an aged lepidopterist. Next to him, smoking a handmade cigarette, was a youth wearing the same kind of helmet I'd taken from Vadim.

'I can use *some* of this shit,' the man with the eyeglass said. 'Probably. You say it's all real, huh? All factual?'

'The military episodes were trawled from soldiers' memories after the combat situations in question, as part of the normal intelligence gathering process.'

'Yeah? And how'd they fall into your hands?'

Without waiting for an answer, he reached under the table, pulled out a little tin sealed with an elastic band and counted out a few dozen bills of the local currency. As I had noticed before, the bills seemed to have been printed in strange denominations – thirteens, fours, twenty-sevens, threes.

'It's none of your damned business where I got them from,' I said.

'No, but that doesn't stop me asking.' He pursed his lips. 'Anything else, now that you're wasting my time?'

I allowed him to examine the experientials I'd taken from Quirrenbach, watching as his lip curled first into contempt and then disgust.

'Well?'

'Now you're insulting me, and I don't like it.'

'If the items are worthless,' I said, 'just tell me and I'll leave.'

'The items aren't worthless,' he said, after examining them again. 'Fact is, they're exactly the kind of the thing I might have bought, a month or two ago. Grand Teton's popular. People can't get enough of those slime-tower formations.'

'So what's the problem?'

'This shit has already hit the market, that's what. These experientials are already out there, depreciating. These must be – what? Third or fourth generation bootlegs? Real cheap-ass crap.'

He still tore off a few more bills, but nowhere near as much as he'd paid for my own experientials.

'Anything else up your sleeve?'

I shrugged. 'Depends what you're after, doesn't it.'

'Use your imagination.' He passed one of the military experientials to his sidekick. The youth's chin was fuzzed by the first tentative wisps of a beard. He ejected the experiential he was running at the time and slipped mine in instead, without once lifting the goggles from his eyes. 'Anything black. Matte-black. You know what I mean, don't you?'

'I've a reasonably good idea.'

'Then either cough up or get out of the premises.' Next to him, the youth started convulsing in his seat. 'Hey, what *is* that shit?'

'Does that helmet have enough spatial resolution to stimulate the pleasure and pain centres?' I said.

'What if it does?' He leaned over and slapped the convulsing youth hard on the head, knocking the playback helmet flying. Drooling, still convulsing, the youth subsided into his seat, his eyes glazed over.

'Then he probably shouldn't have accessed it at random,' I said. 'My guess is he just hit an NC interrogation session. Have you ever *had* your fingers removed?'

The eyeglass man chuckled. 'Nasty. Very nasty. But there's a market for that kind of shit – just like there is for the black stuff.'

Now was as good a time as any to see what the quality of Vadim's merchandise was like. I handed over one of the black experientials, one of those embossed with a tiny silver maggot motif. 'Is this what you mean?'

He looked sceptical at first, until he had examined the experiential more closely. To the trained eye, there were presumably all manner of subliminal indicators to distinguish the genuine article from sub-standard fakes.

'It's a good quality bootleg if it's a bootleg, which means it's worth *something* whatever's on it. Hey, shit-for-brains. Try this.' He knelt down, picked up the battered playback helmet and jammed it onto the youth's head, then prepared to insert the experiential. The youth was just beginning to perk up when he saw the experiential, at which point he pawed the air, trying to stop the man pressing it into the helmet.

'Get that maggot shit away from me . . .'

'Hey,' the man said. 'I was just going to give you a flash, dickface.' He tucked the experiential away in his coat.

'Why don't you try it yourself?' I said.

'Same damn reason he doesn't want that shit anywhere near his skull. It's not nice.'

'Nor's an NC interrogation session.'

'That's a trip to the cake shop by comparison. That's just *pain*.' He patted his breast pocket delicately. 'What's on this could be about nine million times less pleasant.'

'You mean it's not always the same?'

'Of course not, or there wouldn't be an element of risk. And the way these ones work, it's never exactly the same trip twice. Sometimes it's just maggots, sometimes you *are* the maggots . . . sometimes it's much, much worse . . .' Suddenly he looked cheerful. 'But, hey, there's a market for it, so who am I to argue?'

'Why would people want to experience something like that?' I asked.

He grinned at the youth. 'Hey, what is this, fucking philosophy hour? How am I supposed to know? This is human nature we're talking about here; it's already deeply fucking perverted.'

'Tell me about it,' I said.

At the centre of the concourse, rising above the bazaar like a minaret, was an ornately encrusted tower surmounted by a four-faced clock set to Chasm City time. The clock had recently struck the seventeenth hour of the twenty-six in Yellowstone's day, animated spacesuited figurines emerging beneath the dial to enact what might have been a complex quasi-religious ritual. I checked the time on Vadim's watch – my own watch, I forced myself to think, since I had now liberated it twice – and found that the two were in passable agreement. If Dominika's estimate had been accurate, she would still be busy with Quirrenbach.

The hermetics had passed through now, along with most of the obviously rich, but there were still many people who wore the slightly stunned look of the recently impoverished. Perhaps they had been only moderately wealthy seven years ago; not sufficently well-connected to barrier themselves against the plague. I doubted that there had been anyone truly poor in Chasm City back then, but there were always degrees of affluence. For all the heat, the people wore heavy, dark clothes, often ballasted with jewellery. The women were often gloved and hatted, perspiring under wide-brimmed fedoras, veils or chadors. The men wore heavy greatcoats with upturned collars, faces shadowed under Panama hats or shapeless berets. Many had little glass boxes around their necks, containing what looked like religious relics, but which were actually implants, extracted from their hosts and now carried as symbols of former wealth. Though there was a spectrum of apparent ages, I saw no one who looked genuinely old. Perhaps the old were too infirm to risk a trip to the bazaar, but I also recalled what Orcagna had said about the state of longevity treatments on other worlds. It was entirely possible that some of the people I saw here were two or three centuries old; burdened with memories which reached back to Marco Ferris and the Amerikano era. They must have lived through great strangenesses . . . but I doubted that any of them had witnessed anything stranger than the recent transfiguration of their city, or the collapse of a society whose longevity and opulence must have seemed unassailable. No wonder so many of the people I saw looked so sad, as if knowing that – no matter how things might improve from day to day – the old times would *never* come again. Seeing that all-pervasive melancholia, it was impossible not to feel some empathy.

I started navigating my way back to Dominika's tent, then wondered why I was bothering.

There were questions I wanted to ask Dominika, but they could equally well be directed to one of her rivals. I might need to talk to them all eventually. The only thing that connected me to Dominika was Quirrenbach . . . and even if I had begun to tolerate his presence, I'd known all along that I would have to ditch him eventually. I could walk away now, leave the terminus completely, and the chances were that we'd never meet again.

I pushed through until I reached the far side of the bazaar.

Where the furthest wall should have been was only an opening through which the lower levels of the city could be seen, behind a perpetual screen of dirty rain sluicing from the side of the terminus. A haphazard line of rickshaws waited: upright boxes balanced between two wide wheels. Some of the rickshaws were powered, coupled behind steam-engines or chugging methane-powered motors. Their drivers lounged indolently, awaiting fares. Others were propelled by pedal-power, and several looked to have been converted from old palanquins. Behind the row of rickshaws there were other, sleeker vehicles: a pair of flying machines much like the volantors I knew from Sky's Edge, crouched down on skids, and a trio of craft which looked like helicopters with their rotors folded for stowage. A squad of workers eased a palanquin into one of them, tipping it at an undignified angle to get it through the entrance door. I wondered if I was witnessing a kidnapping or a taxi pick-up.

Although I might have been able to afford one of the volantors, the rickshaws looked the most immediately promising. At the very least I could get a flavour of this part of the city, even if I had no specific destination in mind.

I started walking, cutting through the crowds, my gaze fixed resolutely ahead.

Then, when not quite halfway there, I stopped, turned around and returned to Dominika's.

'Is Mister Quirrenbach finished yet?' I asked Tom. Tom had been shimmying to the sitar music, apparently surprised to find someone entering Dominika's tent without being coerced.

'Mister, he no ready – ten minutes. You got money?'

I had no idea how much Quirrenbach's excisions were going to cost him, but I figured the money he had recovered on the Grand Teton experientials might just cover it. I separated the bills from my own, laying them down on the table.

'No enough, mister. Madame Dominika, she want one more.'

Grudgingly I unpeeled one of my own lower-denomination bills and added it to Quirrenbach's pile. 'That'd better be good,' I said. 'Mister Quirrenbach's a friend of mine, so if I find out you're going to ask him for more money when he comes out, I'll be back.'

'Is good, mister. Is good.'

I watched as the kid scurried through the partition into the room beyond, briefly glimpsing the hovering form of Dominika and the long couch on which she did her business. Quirrenbach was prone on it, stripped to the waist, with his head enfolded in a loom of delicate-looking probes. His hair had been shaved completely. Dominika was making odd gestures with her fingers, like a puppeteer working invisibly fine strings. In sympathy, the little probes were dancing around Quirrenbach's cranium. There was no blood, nor even any obvious puncture marks on his skin.

Maybe Dominika was better than she looked.

'Okay,' I said when Tom re-emerged. 'I have a favour to ask of you, and it's worth one of these.' I showed him the smallest denomination I had. 'And don't say I'm insulting you, because you don't know what it is I'm about to ask.'

'Say it, big guy.'

I gestured towards the rickshaws. 'Do those things cover the whole city?'

'Most of Mulch.'

'Mulch is the district we're in?' No answer was forthcoming, so I just left the tent with him following me.

'I need to get from here – wherever here is – to a specific district of the city. I don't know how far it is, but I don't want to be cheated. I'm sure you can arrange that for me, can't you? Especially as I know where you live.'

'Get good price, you no worry.' Then a thought must have trickled through his skull. 'No wait for friend?'

'No – I'm afraid I have business elsewhere, as does Mister Quirrenbach. We won't be meeting again for a while.'

I sincerely hoped it was the truth.

Some kind of hairy primate provided the motive power for most of the rickshaws, a human gene splice resetting the necessary homeoboxes so that his legs grew longer and straighter than the simian norm. In unintelligibly rapid Canasian, Tom negotiated with another kid. They could almost have been interchangeable, except that the new kid had shorter hair and might have been a year older. Tom introduced him to me as Juan; something in their relationship suggested they were old business partners. Juan shook my hand and escorted me to the nearest vehicle. Edgily now, I glanced back, hoping Quirrenbach was still out cold. I didn't want to have to justify myself to him if he came round soon enough to have Tom tell him I was about to get a ride out of the terminus. There were some pills that could not be sugared, and being dumped by someone you imagined was your newfound travelling companion was one of them.

Still, perhaps he could work the agony of rejection into one of his forth-coming *Meisterwerks*.

'Where to, mister?'

It was Juan speaking now, with the same accent as Tom. It was some kind of post-plague argot, I guessed; a pidgin of Russish, Canasian, Norte and a dozen other languages known here during the *Belle Epoque*. 'Take me to the Canopy,' I said. 'You know where that is, don't you?'

'Sure,' he said. 'I know where Canopy is, just like I know where Mulch is. You think I'm idiot, like Tom?'

'You can take me there, then.'

'No, mister. I *no* can take you there.'

I began to unpeel another bill, before realising that our communicational difficulties stemmed from something more basic than insufficient funds, and that the problem was almost certainly on my side.

'Is the Canopy a district of the city?'

This was met by a long-suffering nod. 'You new here, huh?'

'Yes, I'm new. So why don't you do me a favour and explain just why taking me to the Canopy is beyond your means?'

The bill I had half unpeeled vanished from my grip, and then Juan offered me the rear seat of the rickshaw as if it were a throne finished in plush velvet. 'I show you, man. But I no take you there, you understand? For that you need more than rickshaw.'

He hopped in next to me, then leant forward and whispered something in the driver's ear. The primate began to pedal, grunting in what was probably profound indignation at the outcome to which his genetic heritage had been shaped.

The bio-engineering of animals, I later learned, had been one of the few boom industries since the plague, exploiting a niche that had opened up once machines of any great sophistication began to fail.

Like Quirrenbach had said not long ago, nothing that happened was ever completely bad for everyone.

So it was with the plague.

The missing wall provided an entrance and exit point for the volantors (and, I presumed, the other flying craft), but rickshaws entered and left the parking area by means of a sloping, concrete-lined tunnel. The dank walls and ceiling dripped thick mucosal fluids. It was at least cooler, and the noise of the terminus quickly faded, replaced only by the soft creaking of the cogs and chains which transmitted the ape's cycling motion to the wheels.

'You new here,' Juan said. 'Not from Ferrisville, or even Rust Belt. Not even from rest of system.'

Was I so obtrusively ignorant that even a kid could see it?

'I guess you don't get many tourists these days.'

'Not since bad time, no.'

'What was it like to live through?'

'I dunno mister; I just two.'

Of course. It *was* seven years ago. From a child's perspective, that really was most of a lifetime ago. Juan, and Tom, and the other street children would barely be able to remember what life was like in Chasm City prior to the plague. Those few years of limitless wealth and possibility would be blurred with the soft-focus simplicity of infancy. All they knew, all they truly remembered, was the city as it now was: vast and dark and again filled with possibility – except now it was the possibility that lay in danger and crime and lawlessness; a city for thieves and beggars and those who could live by their wits rather than their credit ratings.

It was just a shock to find myself in one.

We passed other rickshaws returning to the concourse, slick sides glossy with rain. Only a few of them carried passengers, hunched sullenly down in raincoats, looking as if they would rather have been anywhere else in the universe than Chasm City. I could relate to that. I was tired, I was hot, sweat pooling under my clothes, and my skin itched and crawled for want of a wash. I was acutely conscious of my own body odour.

What the hell was I doing here?

I had a chased a man across more than fifteen light-years, into a city which had become a sick perversion of itself. The man I was chasing was not even truly bad – even I could see that. I hated Reivich for what he had done, but he had acted much as I would have done in the same circumstances. He was an aristocrat, not a man of arms, but in another life – if the history of our planet had followed another course – he and I might even have been friends. Certainly I had respect for him now, even if it was a respect born out of the way he had acted completely beyond my expectations when he destroyed the bridge at Nueva Valparaiso. Such casual brutality was to be admired. Any man that I misjudged that badly had my respect.

And yet, for all that, I knew I'd have no qualms about killing him.

'I think,' Juan said, 'you need history lesson, mister.'

What I had managed to learn aboard the *Strelnikov* had not been very much, but it was all the history I felt that I had an appetite for right now. 'If you're thinking I don't know about the plague . . .'

The tunnel was growing lighter ahead. Not much, but enough to indicate that we were about to enter the city proper. The light which suffused it had the same caramel-brown texture I'd seen from the behemoth: the colour of already murky light filtered through yet more murk.

'Plague hit, make building go wacko,' said Juan.

'That much they told me.'

'They no tell you enough, mister.' His syntax was rudimentary, but I suspected it was an improvement on anything the rickshaw driver was capable of. 'Them building change, real fast.' He made expansive hand gestures. 'Many folk get die, get squashed or end up in wall.'

'That doesn't sound too nice.'

'I show you people in wall, mister. You no make joke no more. You shit own pants.' We swerved to avoid another rickshaw, scraping against us. 'But listen – them building, they change fastest up at top, right?'

'I don't follow.'

'Them building like tree. Got big lot of root, stick in ground, right?'

'Constructional feedlines, is that it? Leeching raw materials from the bedrock for repair and regrowth?'

'Yeah. What I say. Like big tree. But like big tree in other way, too. Always grow up top. Unnerstan'?' More hand gestures, as if he were shaping the outline of a mushroom cloud.

Perhaps I did understand. 'You're saying the growth systems were concentrated in the upper parts of the structures?'

'Yeah.'

I nodded. 'Of course. Those structures were designed to dismantle themselves as well as grow higher. Either way, you'd always want to add or remove material from the top. So the nerve centre of the self-replicating machinery would always rise with the structure. The lower levels would need fewer systems; just the bare minimum to keep them ticking over and for repairing damage and wear, and for periodic redesigns.'

It was hard to tell if Juan's smile was one of congratulation – that I had worked this out for myself – or sympathy that it had taken me as long as it had.

'Plague get to top first, carried by root. Start making top of building go wacko first. Lower down, stay same as before. By time plague got there, people cut root, starve building. No change any more.'

'But by then the upper parts had already changed beyond recognition.' I shook my head. 'It must have been a terrible time.'

'No shit, mister.'

We plunged into daylight, and I finally understood what Juan meant.

FIFTEEN

We were at the lowest level of Chasm City, far below the rim of the caldera. The street on which we ran crossed a black lake on pontoons. Rain was falling softly from the sky – from the dome, in fact, many kilometres above our heads. All around us, vast buildings rose from the flood, sides slab-sided and immense. They were all I could see in any direction, until – forestlike – they merged into a distant, detailless wall, like a bank of smog. They were encrusted – at least for the first six or seven storeys – in a barnacle-like accretion of ramshackle dwellings and markets, lashed together and interlinked with flimsy walkways and rope-ladders. Fires burned in the slums, and the air was even more pungent than in the concourse. But it was fractionally cooler, and because there was a constant breeze, it felt less stifling.

'What's this place called?' I said.

'This Mulch,' said Juan. 'Everything down here, street level, this Mulch.'

I understood then that the Mulch was less a district of the city than a stratification. It included perhaps the first six or seven storeys which rose above the flooded parts. It was a carpet of slum from which the great forest of the city rose.

Looking up, craning my neck to peer around the rickshaw's roof, I saw the slab-sided structures ram skywards, perspective forcing them together at least a kilometre above my head. For most of that height, their geometries must have been much as their architects had intended: rectilinear, with parallel rows of windows, now dark, the edifices marred only by the occasional haphazard extrusion or limpetlike excrescence. Up higher, though, the picture changed sickeningly. Although no two buildings had mutated in quite the same manner, there was something common to their shape-changing, a kind of uniform pathology which a surgeon might have recognised and diagnosed as stemming from the same cause. Some of the buildings split in two halfway up their length, while others bulged with unseemly obesity. Some sprouted tiny avatars of themselves, like the elbowed towers and oubliettes of fairytale castles. Higher, these structural growths bifurcated and bifurcated again, interpenetrating and linking like bronchioli, or some weird variant of brain coral, until what they formed was a kind of horizontal raft of fused branches, suspended a kilometre or two from the ground. I had seen it before, of course, from the sky, but the meaning of it – and its sheer, city-spanning scale – was only now apparent from this vantage point.

Canopy.

'Now you see why I no take you there, mister.'

'I'm beginning to. It covers the whole city, right?'

Juan nodded. 'Just like Mulch, only higher.'

The one thing that had not been really obvious from the behemoth was that the Canopy's dense entanglement of madly deformed buildings was confined to a relatively shallow vertical stratum; the Canopy was a kind of suspended ecology and below it was another world – another city – entirely. The complexity of it was obvious now. There were whole communities floating within it; sealed structures embedded in the Canopy like birds' nests, each as large as a palace. Fine as gossamer, a mass of weblike strands filled the spaces between the larger branches, dangling down almost to street level. It was difficult to tell if they had come with the mutations, or had been some intentional human addition.

The effect was as if the Canopy had been cobwebbed by monstrous insects, invisible spiders larger than houses.

'Who lives there?' I knew it wasn't a completely stupid question, since I had already seen lights burning in the branches; evidence that, no matter how distorted the geometries of those sick dead husks of buildings, they had been claimed for human habitation.

'No one you wanna know, mister.' Juan chewed on his statement before adding, 'Or no one who wanna know you. That no insult, either.'

'None taken, but please answer my question.'

Juan was a long time responding, during which time our rickshaw continued to navigate the roots of the giant structures, wheels jumping over water-filled cracks in the road. The rain hadn't stopped of course, but when I pushed my head beyond the awning, what I felt was warm and soft; hardly a hardship at all. I wondered if it ever ended, or whether the pattern of condensation on the dome was diurnal; if it were all happening according to some schedule. I had the impression, though, that very little that happened in Chasm City was under anyone's direct control.

'Them rich people,' the kid said. 'Real rich – not small-time rich like Madame Dominika.' He knuckled his bony head. 'Don't need Dominika, either.'

'You mean there are enclaves in the Canopy where the plague never reached?'

'No, plague reach everywhere. But in Canopy, them clean it out, after building stop changing. Some rich, they stay in orbit. Some never leave CC, or come down after shit hit fan. Some get deported.'

'Why would anyone come here after the plague, if they didn't have to? Even if parts of the Canopy are safe from residual traces of the Melding Plague, I can't see why anyone would choose to live there rather than stay in the remaining habitats of the Rust Belt.'

'Them get deported no have big choice,' said the kid.

'No; I can understand that. But why would anyone else come here?'

'Because them think thing got to get better, and them wanna be here when it happen. Plenty way to make money, when thing get better – but only few people gonna get serious rich. Plenty way to make money now, too – less p'lice here than upside.'

'You're saying there are no rules here, are there? Nothing that can't be bought? I'd imagine that must have been tempting, after the strictures of Demarchy.'

'Mister, you talk funny.'

My next question was obvious. 'How do I get there? To the Canopy, I mean?'

'You not already there, you don't.'

'You're saying I'm not rich enough, is that it?'

'Rich not enough,' the kid said. 'Need connection. Gotta be tight with Canopy, or you ain't nobody.'

'Assuming I was, how would I get there? Are there routes through the buildings, old access shafts not sealed by the plague?' I figured this was the kind of street knowledge the kid would know backwards.

'You no wanna take inside route, mister. Plenty dangerous. Special when hunt coming down.'

'Hunt?'

'This place no good at night, mister.'

I looked around at the gloom. 'How would you ever be able to tell? No; don't answer that. Just tell me how I'd get up there.' I waited for an answer, and when it showed no sign of arriving I decided to recast my question. 'Do Canopy people ever come down to the Mulch?'

'Sometime. Special during hunt.'

Progress, I thought, even though it was like pulling a tooth. 'And how do they get here? I've seen what look like flying vehicles, what we used to call volantors, but I can't imagine anyone could fly through the Canopy without hitting some of those webs.'

'We call them volantor too. Only rich got 'em – difficult to fix, keep flying. No good in some part of city, either. Most Canopy kid, they come down in cable-car now.'

'Cable-car?'

For a moment a look of helpfulness crossed his face, and I realised he was desperately trying to please me. It was just that my enquiries were

so far outside of his usual parameters that it was causing him physical
pain.

'Those web, those cable? Hang between building?'

'Can you show me a cable-car? I'd like to see one.'

'It not safe, mister.'

'Well, nor am I.'

I sugared the question with another bill, then settled back into the seat as we
sped on through the soft interior rain, through the Mulch.

Eventually Juan slowed and turned round to me. 'There. Cable-car. Them
often come down here. Want we go closer?'

At first I wasn't sure what he meant. Parked diagonally across the shattered
roadbed was one of the sleek private vehicles I'd seen in and around the concourse. One door was folded open from the side, like the wing of a gull, with
two greatcoated individuals standing in the rain next to it, faces lost under
wide-brimmed hats.

I looked at them, wondering what I was going to do next.

'Hey mister, I already ask you, you want we go closer?'

One of the two people by the cable-car lit a cigarette and for a moment I saw
the fire chase the shadows from his face – it was aristocratic, with a nobility I
had not seen since arriving on the planet. His eyes were concealed behind
complex goggles which emphasised the exaggerated sharpness of his cheekbones. His friend was a woman, her slender gloved hand holding a pair of
toylike binoculars to her eyes. Pivoting on her knifelike heels, she scanned the
street, until her gaze swept over me. I watched her flinch as it happened,
though she tried to control it.

'They nervous,' Juan breathed. 'Mostly, Mulch and Canopy keep far apart.'

'Any particular reason?'

'Yeah, one good one.' Now he was whispering so quietly I could barely
hear him above the relentless hiss of the rain. 'Mulch get too close, Mulch
vanish.'

'Vanish?'

He drew his finger across his throat, but discreetly. 'Canopy like games,
mister. They bored. Immortal people, they all bored. So they play games.
Trouble is, not everyone get asked they wanna take part.'

'Like the hunt you mentioned?'

He nodded. 'But no talk it now.'

'All right. Stop here then, Juan, if you'd be so good.'

The rickshaw lost what little forward momentum it had had, the primate
showing agitation in every ridge of his back muscles. I observed the reactions
on the faces of the two Canopy dwellers – trying to look cool, and almost
achieving it.

I stepped out of the rickshaw, my feet squelching as they made acquaintance with the sodden roadbed. 'Mister,' said Juan. 'You be careful now. I ain't earned a fare home yet.'

'Don't go anywhere,' I said, then thought better of it. 'Listen, if this makes you nervous, leave and return in five minutes.'

This obviously struck him as excellent advice. The woman with the binoculars returned them to her exuberantly patterned greatcoat, while the goggled man reached up and made what was obviously a delicate readjustment of his optics. I walked calmly in their direction, paying more attention to their vehicle. It was a glossy black lozenge, resting on three retractable wheels. Through a tinted forward window I glimpsed upholstered seats facing complicated manual controls. What appeared to be three rotor blades were furled on the roof. But as I examined the mounting more closely, I saw that this wasn't any kind of helicopter. The blades were not attached to the body of the vehicle by a rotating axle, but vanished into three circular holes in a domelike hump which rose seamlessly from the hull itself. And, now that I looked closer, I saw that the blades were not really blades at all, but telescopic arms, each tipped with a scythelike hook.

That was all the time I had for sightseeing.

'Don't come any closer,' the woman said. She backed up her words, spoken in flawless Canasian, by flourishing a tiny weapon, little larger than a brooch.

'He's unarmed,' the man said, loud enough for me to hear, intentionally, it seemed.

'I don't mean you any harm.' I spread my arms – slowly. 'These are Mendicant clothes. I've just arrived on the planet. I wanted to know about reaching the Canopy.'

'The Canopy?' the man said, as if this was vastly amusing.

'That's what they all want,' the woman said. The weapon had not budged, and her grip on it was so steady that I wondered if it contained tiny gyroscopes, or some kind of biofeedback device which acted on the muscles in her wrist. 'Why should we talk to you?'

'Because I'm harmless – unarmed, as your partner observed – and curious, and it might amuse you.'

'You've no idea what amuses us.'

'No, I probably don't, but, as I said – I'm curious. I'm a man of means—' the remark sounded ridiculous as soon I had spoken it, but I soldiered on '—and I've had the misfortune to arrive in the Mulch with no contacts in the Canopy.'

'You speak Canasian reasonably well,' the man observed, lowering his hand from his goggles. 'Most Mulch can barely manage an insult in anything other than their native tongue.' He threw away what remained of his cigarette.

'But with an accent,' the woman said. 'I don't place it – it's offworld, but nothing I'm familiar with.'

'I'm from Sky's Edge. You may have met people from other parts of the planet who speak differently. It's been settled long enough for linguistic drift.'

'So had Yellowstone,' said the man, feigning no real interest in this line of debate. 'But most of us still live in Chasm City. Here, the only linguistic drift is vertical.' He laughed, as if the remark were more than just a statement of fact.

I wiped rain from my eyes, warm and viscous. 'The driver said the only way to reach the Canopy was by cable-car.'

'An accurate statement, but that doesn't mean we can help you.' The man removed his hat, revealing long blond hair tied back.

His companion added, 'We have no reason to trust you. A *Mulch* could have stolen Mendicant clothes and learnt a few words of Canasian. No sane person would arrive here without already establishing ties with Canopy.'

I took a calculated risk. 'I've got some Dream Fuel. Does that interest you?'

'Oh yes, and how in hell's name did a Mulch get hold of Dream Fuel?'

'It's a long story.' But I reached into Vadim's coat and removed the cache of Dream Fuel vials. 'You'll have to take my word that is the genuine article, of course.'

'I'm not in the habit of taking anyone's word on anything,' the man said. 'Pass me one of those vials.'

Another calculated risk. The man might run off with the one, but that would still leave me with the others.

'I'll throw you one. How does that sound?'

The man took a few steps towards me. 'Do it, then.'

I tossed him the vial. He caught it deftly and then vanished into the vehicle. The woman remained outside, still covering me with the little gun. A few moments passed, then the man emerged from the vehicle again, not bothering to don his hat. He held up the vial. 'This . . . seems to be the genuine article.'

'What did you do?'

'Shone a light through it, of course.' He looked at me as if I was stupid. 'Dream Fuel has a unique absorption spectrum.'

'Good. Now that you know it's real, throw the vial back to me and we'll negotiate terms.'

The man made a throwing gesture, but pulled at the last moment, holding the vial in front of him tauntingly. 'No . . . let's not be hasty, shall we? You have more of these, you say? Dream Fuel's in short supply these days. At least the good stuff. You must have stumbled on quite a haul.' He paused. 'I've done you a favour, which we'll think of as fair payment for this vial. I've asked that another cable-car meet you here shortly. You'd better not have been lying about your means.' He removed his goggles, revealing iron-grey eyes of extraordinary cruelty.

'I'm grateful,' I said. 'But what would it matter if I had been lying?'

'That's an odd question.' The woman made her weapon vanish, like a well-rehearsed conjuring trick. Perhaps it had sprung back into a sleeve-holster.

'I told you, I'm curious.'

'There is no law here,' she said. 'A kind of law, in the Canopy – but only that which suits us; that which conveniences us, like the playground law of children. But we're not in the Canopy now. Down here, anything goes. And we have very little patience with those who deceive us.'

'That's all right,' I said. 'I'm not a patient man myself.'

They both climbed into their vehicle, momentarily leaving the doors splayed open. 'Perhaps we'll see you in the Canopy,' the man said, and then smiled at me. It was not the kind of smile one relished. It was the kind of smile I had seen on snakes in the vivaria at the Reptile House.

The doors clammed down and their vehicle came to life with a subliminal hum.

The three telescopic arms on the roof of the cable-car swung outwards and upwards, and then continued extending outwards at blinding speed, doubling, tripling, quadrupling their length. They were reaching skywards. I looked up, shielding my eyes against the perpetual embalming rain. The rickshaw driver had pointed out that the cables spanning the gnarled structures of the Canopy occasionally draped down to the level of the Mulch, like hanging vines, but I hadn't paid enough attention to his remark. Now I saw the significance of it as one of the car's arms snagged the lowest line with its hooked claw. The other two arms extended even further, out to perhaps ten times their original length, until they found their own draping lines and made purchase.

And then – smoothly, as if it were lifting on thrusters – the cable-car pulled itself aloft, accelerating all the time. The nearest arm released its grip on the cable, contracted and jerked, stabbing upwards with the speed of a chameleon's tongue, until it had locked around another cable. And while that happened, the car rose further still, and then another arm switched cables, and another, until the car was hundreds of metres above me and dwindling. Still the motion was eerily smooth, even though the vehicle always seemed to be on the point of missing its purchase altogether and plummeting back towards the Mulch.

'Hey, mister. You still here.'

At some point during the vehicle's ascent, the rickshaw had returned. I had expected the driver to do what seemed sensible and return to the concourse, more or less in profit. But Juan had kept his word, and would probably have been insulted if I registered any surprise.

'Did you honestly think I wouldn't be?'

'When Canopy come down, you never know. Hey, why you stand in rain?'

'Because I'm not returning with you.' He had barely had time to register disapointment – although the expression which had begun to form on his face suggested that I'd cast grave aspersions on his entire lineage -- when I offered him a generous cancellation fee. 'It's more than you'd have earned carrying me.'

He looked at the two seven-Ferris bills, glumly. 'Mister, you no wanna stay here. This nowhere; not good part of Mulch.'

'I don't doubt it,' I said, coming to terms with the idea that even somewhere as misbegotten and miserable as the Mulch had its good and bad neighbourhoods. Then I said, 'The Canopy people said they'd send down a cable-car for me. It's possible they were lying, of course, but I imagine I'll find out sooner or later. And if they weren't, I'm just going to have to find my way up the inside of one of these buildings.'

'This not good, mister. Canopy, they never do favour.'

I decided not to mention the Dream Fuel. 'They were probably not willing to rule out the possibility I was who I claimed. What if I was as powerful as I said I was? They wouldn't want to make an enemy of me.'

Juan shrugged, as if my point was a faint theoretical possibility, but no more than that. 'Mister, I go now. No hurry stay here, you not coming.'

'That's all right,' I said. 'I understand. And I'm sorry I asked you to wait.'

That was the end of our relationship, Juan shaking his head but accepting that there was no way to persuade me otherwise. And then he went, the rickshaw clattering away into the distance, leaving me alone in the rain – genuinely alone, this time. The kid was not just around the corner, and I had lost – or more accurately got rid of – the closest thing I had yet found in Chasm City to an ally. It was an odd feeling, but I knew that what I had done was necessary.

I waited.

Time passed, perhaps half an hour, long enough for me to become aware of the city darkening. As Epsilon Eridani sunk beneath the horizon, its light, already turned sepia by the dome, became the colour of ancient blood. What light reached me now had to pass through the tangle of intervening buildings, an ordeal which seemed to sap it of any real enthusiasm for the task of illumination. The towers around me grew dark, until they really did look like enormous trees, and the tangled limbs of the Canopy, lit up with habitation, were like branches hung with lanterns and fairy-lights. It was both nightmarish and beautiful.

Finally one of those dangling lights detached itself like a falling star leaving the firmament, growing in intensity as it neared me. As my eyes readjusted to the night, I saw that the light was a descending cable-car, and that it was headed for the place where I stood.

Oblivious to the rain, I watched transfixed as the vehicle slowed and lowered itself almost to street level, the tensioning and detensioning cables singing above me. The vehicle's single headlight panned across the rainswept road, heightening every crack in the surface, and then swept towards me.

Not far from my feet, something made the puddled water jump comically upwards.

And then I heard a gunshot.

I did what any ex-soldier would do under those circumstances: not stop to consider the situation, or determine the type and calibre of weapon being used against me, or the location of the shooter – or even pause to establish that I was really the target, and not just a hapless intercessionary.

I ran, very quickly, towards the shadowed base of the nearest building. I resisted the perfectly sensible flight reflex which told me to throw my suitcase away, knowing that without it, I would quickly sink into the anonymity of the Mulch. If I lost it, I might as well offer myself up to be shot.

The gunfire chased me.

I could tell from the way each shot landed a metre or so behind my heels that the person shooting at me was not lacking in skill. It would not have taxed them to kill me – they would have needed only to advance their line of fire fractionally, and I recognised that their marksmanship was more than sufficient. Instead, it suited them to play with me. They were in no hurry to execute me with a shot in the back, though it could have been achieved at any point.

I reached the building, my feet submerged in water. The structure was slab-sided; no little indentations or crannies in which I could secrete myself. The gunfire halted, but the ellipse of the spotlight remained steady, the shaft of harsh blue light making curtains of the rain between me and the cable-car.

A figure emerged from the darkness, clad in a greatcoat. At first I thought it was either the man or the woman I had spoken to earlier, but when the man emerged into the spotlight, I realised I hadn't seen his face before. He was bald, with a jaw of almost cartoon squareness, and one of his eyes was lost behind a pulsing monocle.

'Stand perfectly still,' he said, 'and you won't be harmed.' And his coat flapped apart to reveal a weapon, bulkier than the toy gun which the Canopy woman had carried, somehow more serious in intent. The gun consisted of a handled black rectangle, tipped with a quartet of dark nozzles. His knuckles were white around the grip, his forefinger caressing the trigger.

He fired from hip-height; something buzzed out of the gun towards me, like a laser beam. It connected with the side of the building with a fizzle of sparks. I started running, but his aim was surer the second time. I felt a stabbing pain in my thigh, and then suddenly I was no longer running. Suddenly I was doing nothing except screaming.

And then even screaming became too hard.

The medics had done very well, but no one could be expected to work miracles. The monitoring machines crowding around his father's bed attested to that, voicing a slow and solemn liturgy of biological decline.

It was six months since the sleeper had awakened and injured Sky's father, and it was to everyone's credit that they had kept Titus Haussmann and his assailant alive until now. But with medical supplies and expertise stretched to breaking point, there had never really been any realistic prospect of nursing both of them back to health.

The recent series of disputes between the ships had certainly not assisted matters. The troubles had intensified a few weeks after the sleeper had awoken, when a spy had been discovered aboard the *Brazilia*. The security organisation had traced the agent back to the *Baghdad*, but the *Baghdad*'s administration had declared that the spy had never been born on their ship at all and had probably originated on the *Santiago* or the *Palestine* all along. Other individuals had been fingered as possible agents, and there had been cries of wrongful imprisonment and violations of Flotilla law. Normal relations had chilled to a frosty four-way standoff, and now there was almost no trade between the ships; no human traffic except for despondent diplomatic missions which always ended in failure and recrimination.

Against this backdrop, the requests for more medical supplies and knowledge to help nurse Sky's father had been shrugged aside. It was not, they said, as if the other ships did not have crises of their own. And as head of security, Titus was not beyond suspicion of having instigated the spying incident in the first place.

Sorry, they had said. *We'd like to help, we really would . . .*

Now his father struggled to speak.

'Schuyler . . .' he said, his lips like a rip in parchment. 'Schuyler? Is that you?'

'I'm here, Dad. I never went away.' He sat down on the bedside stool and studied the grey, grimacing shell that bore so little resemblance to the father he had known before the stabbing. This was not the Titus Haussmann who had been feared and loved in equal measure across the ship, and grudgingly respected throughout the Flotilla. This was not the man who had rescued him from the nursery during the blackout, nor the man who had taken his hand and escorted him to the taxi and out beyond the ship for the very first time, showing him the wonder and terror of his infinitely lonely home. This was not the *caudillo* who had gone into the berth ahead of his team, knowing full well that he might be walking into extreme danger. This was a faint impression of that man, like a rubbing taken off a statue. The features were there, and the proportions were accurate, but there was no depth. Rather than solidity, there was just a paper-thin layer.

'Sky, about the prisoner.' His father struggled to raise his head from the pillow. 'Is he still alive?'

'Just barely,' Sky said. He had forced his way into the security team after his father had been injured. 'Frankly, I don't expect him to last much longer. His wounds were a lot worse than yours.'

'But you managed to talk to him, anyway?'

'We've got this and that out of him, yes.' Sky sighed inwardly. He had told his father this much already, but either Titus was losing his memory or he wanted to hear it again.

'What exactly did he tell you?'

'Nothing we couldn't have guessed for ourselves. We're still not clear who put him aboard the ship, but it was almost certainly one of the factions they expected to cause some sort of trouble.'

His father raised a finger. 'That weapon of his; the machinery built into his arm . . .'

'Not as unusual as you'd think. There were apparently a lot of his kind around towards the end of the war. We were lucky they didn't build a nuclear device into his arm – although that would have been a lot harder to hide, of course.'

'Had he ever been human?'

'We'll probably never know. Some of his kind were engineered in labs. Others were adapted from prisoners or volunteers. They had brain surgery and psycho-conditioning so that they could be used as weapons of war by any interested power. They were like robots, except they were constructed largely of flesh and blood and had a limited capacity to empathise with other people, where and when it suited their operational needs. They could blend in quite convincingly, crack jokes and share in smalltalk, until they reached their target, at which point they'd flip back into mindless killer mode. Some of them had weapons grafted into them for specific jobs.'

'There was a lot of metal in that forearm.'

'Yes.' Sky saw the point his father was making. 'Too much for him to have made his way aboard without someone turning a blind eye. Which only proves that there was a conspiracy, which we as good as knew anyway.'

'We found the only one, though.'

'Yes.' In the days after the attack, the other sleeping passengers had all been scanned for buried weaponry – the process had been difficult and dangerous – but nothing had been found. 'Which shows how confident they must have been.'

'Sky . . . did he say anything about why he did it, or why they made him do it?'

Sky raised an eyebrow. This line of questioning, admittedly, was new. His father had concentrated only on specifics before.

'Well, he did mention something.'

'Go on.'

'It didn't seem to make an awful lot of sense to me.'

'Perhaps not, but I'd still like to hear it.'

'He talked about a faction which had discovered something. He wouldn't say who or what they were, or where they were based.'

His father's voice was very weak now, but he still managed to ask, 'And what exactly was it that they had discovered?'

'Something ridiculous.'

'Tell me what it was, Sky.' His father paused. Sensing his thirst, Sky had the room's robot administer a glass of water to the cracked gash of his lips.

190

'He said there had been a breakthrough just before the Flotilla left the solar system – a scientific technique, in fact, which had been perfected towards the end of the war.'

'And this was?'

'Human immortality.' Sky said the words carefully, as if they were imbued with magic potency and ought not be uttered casually. 'He said that the faction had combined various procedures and lines of research pursued during the century, bringing them together to create a viable therapeutic treatment. They succeeded where others had failed, or had their work suppressed for political reasons. What they came up with was complicated, and it wasn't simply a pill you took once and then forgot about.'

'Go on,' Titus said.

'It was a whole phalanx of different techniques, some of them genetic, some of them chemical, some of them dependent on invisibly small machines. The whole thing was fantastically delicate and difficult to administer, and the treament needed to be applied regularly – but it was something that was capable of working, if done properly.'

'And what did you think?'

'I thought it was absurd, of course. Oh, I don't deny that something like that might have been possible – but if there'd been that kind of breakthrough, wouldn't everyone have known about it?'

'Not necessarily. It was the end of a war, after all. The ordinary lines of communication were broken.'

'Then you're saying the faction might really have existed?'

'Yes, I believe it did.' His father paused, gathering his energies. 'In fact, I know it did. I suspect most of what the Chimeric told you was true. The technique wasn't magic – there were some diseases it couldn't beat – but it was much better than anything evolution had given us. At best it would extend your lifespan to about one hundred and eighty years; two hundred in exteme cases – those were extrapolations, of course – but that didn't matter; all that did was that you'd get a chance at staying alive until something better came along.'

He slumped back into his pillow, exhausted.

'Who knew?'

His father smiled. 'Who else? The wealthy. Those whom the war had been kind to. Those in the right places, or those who knew the right people.'

The next question was obvious and chilling. The Flotilla had been launched while the war was still in its end stages. Many of those who had obtained sleeper berths, in fact, had been seeking to escape what they saw as a ruined and dangerous system just waiting to slip into another fullscale bloodbath. But competition for those spaces had been immense, and although they had supposedly been allocated on the basis of merit, there must have means for those with sufficient influence to get aboard. If Sky had ever doubted that, the presence of the saboteur proved it. Someone, somewhere, had pulled strings to get the Chimeric aboard.

'All right. What about the sleepers? How many of them knew about the immortality breakthrough?'

'All of them, Sky.'

He looked at his father lying there, wondering how close to death the man really was. He should have recovered from the stab wounds – the damage had not really been that great – but complications had set in: trivial infections which nonetheless lingered and spread. Once, the Flotilla's medicine could have saved him, could have got him up on his feet in a matter of days with no more than a little discomfort. But now there was essentially nothing that could be done except to assist his own healing processes. And they were slowly losing the battle.

He thought of what Titus Haussmann had just said. 'How many of them actually had the treatment, then?'

'The same answer.'

'All of them?' He shook his head, almost not believing it. 'All the sleepers we carry?'

'Yes. With a few unimportant exceptions – those who chose not to undergo it, on ethical or medical grounds, for instance. But most of them did take the cure, shortly before coming aboard.' His father paused again. 'It's the single biggest secret of my life, Sky. I've always known this – ever since my father told me, anyway. I didn't find it any easier to take, believe me.'

'How could you keep a secret like that?'

His father managed the faintest of shrugs. 'It was part of my job.'

'Don't say that. It doesn't excuse you. They betrayed us, didn't they?'

'That depends. Admittedly, they didn't bestow their secret on the crew. But that was a form of kindness, I think.'

'Why do you say that?'

'Imagine if we'd been immortal. We'd have had to endure a century and a half of imprisonment aboard this thing. It would have driven us slowly mad. That was what they feared. Better to let the crew live out a normal lifespan, and then have another generation take over the reins.'

'You call that kindness?'

'Why not? Most of us don't know any better, Sky. Oh, we serve the sleepers, but because we know that not all of them will wake up safely when we reach Journey's End, it isn't easy to feel too envious. And we have ourselves to look after, too. We run the ship for the sleepers, but also for ourselves.'

'Yes. Very equitable. Knowing that they kept the secret of immortality from us does alter the relationship a smidgeon, you have to admit.'

'Perhaps. That's why I was always so careful to keep the secret from anyone else.'

'But you just told me.'

'You wanted to know if there was any truth to the saboteur's story, didn't you? Well, now you know.' His father's face grew momentarily serene, as if a great burden had been lifted from him. Sky thought for an instant that his father had slipped away from him, but shortly afterwards his eyes moved and he licked his lips to speak again. It was still an immense effort to talk at all. 'And there was another reason, too . . . this is very hard, Sky. I'm not sure I'm doing the right thing by telling you.'

'Why not let me be the judge of that.'

'Very well. You may as well hear it now. I almost told you on countless other occasions, but never quite had the courage of my convictions. A little knowledge is a dangerous thing, as they say.'

'What little knowledge would that be, exactly?'

'About your own status.' He asked for more water before speaking again. Sky thought of the water in that glass; the molecules which were slipping between his father's lips. Every drop of water on the ship was ultimately recycled, to be drunk again and again. In interstellar space there could be no wastage. At some point, months or years from now, Sky would drink some of the same water that was now bringing relief to his father.

'My status?'

'I'm afraid you're not my son.' He looked at him hard, as if waiting for Sky to crack under the revelation. 'There, I've said it. No going back now. You'll have to hear the rest of it.'

Maybe he was losing it faster than the machines had indicated, Sky thought. Slipping swiftly down into the lightless trench of dementia, his bloodstream poisoned, his brain grasping for oxygen.

'I am your son.'

'No. No; you're not. I should know, Sky. I pulled you out of that sleeper berth.'

'What are you talking about?'

'You were one of them – one of our *momios*; one of our sleepers.'

Sky nodded, accepting this truth instantly. On some level he knew that the normal reaction would have been disbelief, perhaps even anger, but he felt none of that; only a deep and calming sense of rightness.

'How old was I?'

'Barely a child, only a few days old when you were frozen. There were only a few others as young as you.'

He listened to his father – *not* his father – as he explained that Lucretia Haussmann – the woman Sky thought of as his mother – had given birth to a baby aboard the ship, but that the child, a boy, had died within hours. Distraught, Titus had kept the truth from Lucretia for hours, then days, stretching his ingenuity to the limit while she was kept as sedated as possible. Titus feared the truth would kill her if she found out; maybe not physically, but he worried that it would crush her spirit. She was one of the most loved women on the ship. Her loss would affect them all: a poison that might sour the general mood of the crew. They were a tiny community, after all. They all knew each other. The loss of a child would be a dreadful thing to bear.

So Titus conceived a terrible plan, one he would regret almost as soon as he had brought it to fruition. But by then it was much too late.

He stole a child from the sleepers. Children, it turned out, were far more tolerant of revival than adults – it was something to do with the ratio of body volume to surface – and there had been no serious problems in warming the selected child. He had picked one of the young ones, one that would pass as his dead son. He did not have to be too meticulous. Lucretia had not seen her own baby long enough to tell that any deception had taken place.

He put the dead child in its place, cooled the berth down again and then asked for forgiveness. By the time the dead child was discovered, he would be long dead himself. It would be a dreadful thing for the parents to wake to, but at least they would also be waking to a new world, with time enough to try for another child. It would not be the same for them as it would have been for Lucretia. And if it was . . . well, without this crime, things might deteriorate on the ship to the point where it never reached its destination. That was an extreme case, but it was not beyond the bounds of possibility. He had to believe that. Had to believe that in some way what he had done was for the greater good of them all.

A crime of love.

Of course, Titus could have accomplished none of this without help, but only a handful of his closest friends had ever known the truth, and they had all been good associates who had never again spoken of the matter. They were all dead now, Titus said.

That was why it was so necessary that he tell Sky now.

'You understand?' Titus asked. 'When I always told you you were precious . . . ? That was the literal truth. You were the only immortal amongst us. That was why I raised you in isolation at first; why you spent so much time alone, in the nursery, away from the other children. Partly I wanted to shield you from infections – you were no less vulnerable than the other children, and you're no less vulnerable now, as an adult. Mainly it was so that I could know for myself. I had to study your developmental curve. It's slower for those who have had the treatment, Sky, and it keeps on flattening as you get older. You're twenty now, but you could pass for a tall young man barely into his teens. By the time you're thirty or forty, people will speak of you as someone with uncommonly youthful looks. But they won't begin to guess the truth – not until you're much, much older.'

'I'm immortal?'

'Yes. It changes everything, doesn't it.'

Sky Haussmann rather had to admit that it did.

*

194

Later, when his father had fallen into one of the abyssal dreamless sleeps that was like an inevitable foreshadowing of his death, Sky visited the saboteur. The Chimeric prisoner lay on exactly the same kind of bed as his father, attended by machines, but there the similarities ended. The machines were observing the man, but he was strong enough not to need their direct assistance. Too strong, in fact – even after they had dug a magazine-load of slugs out of him. He was attached to the bed with plastic bonds, a broad hoop across his waist and legs, two smaller hoops anchoring his upper arms. He could move one forearm enough to touch his face, while the other arm, of course, had ended only in the weapon he had used to stab Titus. Even the weapon was gone now, the cyborg's forearm ending in a neatly sewn stump. They had searched him for other kinds of weapon, but he carried no other concealed devices, except for the implants his masters had used to shape him to their goals.

In a way, the faction that had sent the infiltrator had been spectacularly unimaginative, Sky thought. They had placed too much emphasis on him being able to sabotage the ship, when a nice, easily transferred virus would have been just as effective. It might not have directly harmed the sleepers, but their chances of making it anywhere without a living crew would have been vanishingly small.

Which was not to say that the Chimeric might not still have its uses.

It was strange, infinitely so, to know that one was suddenly immortal. Sky did not concern himself with trifling matters of definition. It was true enough that he was not invulnerable, but with care and forethought he could minimise the risks to himself.

He took a step back from the killer's bed. They thought they had the better of the saboteur, but one could never be entirely sure. Even though the monitors said the man was in a sleep at least as deep as his father's, it paid not to take chances. They were engineered to deceive, these things. They could do inhuman tricks with their heartrate and neural activity. That one unbound forearm could have grabbed Sky by the throat and squeezed him until he died, or pulled him so close that the man could have eaten his face off.

Sky found a medical kit on the wall. He flipped it open, studied the neatly racked implements inside and then pulled out a scalpel, glistening with blue sterility in the room's subdued lighting. He turned it this way and that, admiring the way the blade vanished as he turned it edge on.

It was a fine weapon, he thought; a thing of excellence.

With it he moved towards the saboteur.

SIXTEEN

'He's coming round,' a voice said, crystallising my sluggish thoughts towards consciousness.

One of the things you learnt as a soldier – at least on Sky's Edge – was that not everyone who shot you necessarily wanted to kill you. At least not immediately. There were reasons for this, not all of them to do with the usual mechanics of hostage-taking. Memories could be trawled from captured soldiers without the crudities of torture – all it required was the kind of neural-imaging technology which Ultras could supply, at a price, and for there to be something worth learning in the first place. Intelligence, in other words – the kind of operational knowledge which soldiers must know if they are to have any value at all.

But it had never happened to me. I had been shot at, and hit, but on all the occasions when it happened, no one had been intending that I live, for even the relatively short length of time that it would take to winnow my memories. I had never been captured by the enemy, and so had never had the dubious pleasure of waking to find myself in anything other than safe hands.

Now, though, I was learning exactly how it felt.

'Mister Mirabel? Are you awake?' Someone wiped something soft and cold across my face. I opened my eyes and squinted against light, which was painfully bright after my period of unconsciousness.

'Where am I?'

'Somewhere safe.'

I looked around blearily. I was in a chair at the high end of a long sloping room. On either side of me the fluted metal walls angled downwards, as if I were descending an escalator down a gently angled tunnel. The walls were punctured by oval windows, but I couldn't see much except darkness ribboned with long chains of tangled fairy-lights. I was high above the surface of the city, then almost certainly in some part of the Canopy. The floor consisted of a series of horizontal surfaces which descended towards the low end of the room, which must have been fifteen metres away and two or three metres below me. They looked like they'd been added on afterwards, as if the room's slope was not quite intentional.

I wasn't alone, of course.

The square-jawed man with the monocle was standing next to me, one hand toying with his chin, as if he needed to keep reminding himself of its magnificent rectilinearity. In his other hand was a limp flannel, the means by which I had been so gently assisted towards consciousness.

'I've got to hand it to you,' the man said. 'I miscalculated the dose in that stun beam. It would have killed some people, and I expected you to be out cold for a good few hours more.' Then he placed a hand on my shoulder. 'But you're fine, I think. A pretty strong fellow. You'll have to accept my apologies – it won't happen again, I assure you.'

'You'd better not do it again,' said the woman who had just stepped into my field of vision. I recognised her, of course – and her companion, who hoved into view on my right, pushing a cigarette to his lips. 'You're getting sloppy, Waverly. This man must have thought you were planning to kill him.'

'That wasn't the idea?' I said, finding that I sounded nowhere near as slurred as I had been expecting.

Waverly shook his head gravely. 'Not at all. I was doing my best to save your life, Mister Mirabel.'

'You've got a pretty funny way of going about it.'

'I had to act quickly. You were about to be ambushed by a group of pigs. Do you know about pigs, Mister Mirabel? You probably don't want to. They're one of the less salubrious immigrant groups we've had to deal with since the fall of the Glitter Band. They had arranged a tripwire across the roadway connected to a crossbow. Normally they don't stalk anyone until later in the evening, but they must have been hungry tonight.'

'What did you shoot me with?'

'Like I said, a stun beam. Quite a humane weapon, really. The laser beam is only a precursor – it establishes an ionised path through the air, down which a paralysing electrical flux can be discharged.'

'It's still painful.'

'I know, I know.' He raised his hands defensively. 'I've taken a few hits myself. I'm afraid I had it calibrated to stun a pig, rather than a human. But perhaps it was for the best. You'd have resisted me if I hadn't put you under so comprehensively, I suspect.'

'Why did you save me, anyway?'

He looked put out. 'It was the decent thing to do, I'd have thought.'

Now the woman spoke. 'At first I misjudged you, Mister Mirabel. You put me on edge and I didn't trust you completely.'

'All I did was ask for some advice.'

'I know – the fault's all mine. But we're all so nervous these days. After we'd left, I felt bad about it and told Waverly to keep an eye on you. Which is what he did.'

'*An* eye, yes, Sybilline,' Waverly said.

'And where would here happen to be?' I said.

'Show him, Waverly. He must want to stretch his legs by now.'

I'd half expected to have been secured to the chair, but I was free to move. Waverly offered me a supporting arm while I tested the usefulness of my legs. The muscle in the leg where the beam had touched still felt like jelly, but it was just about able to support me. I stepped past the woman, descending the series of level surfaces until I'd reached the lowest part of the room. At that end there was a pair of double doors which opened onto the night air. Waverly led me out onto a sloping balcony, bounded by a metal railing. Warm air slapped against my face.

I looked back. The balcony surrounded the building where I had awoken, rising up on either side of it. But the building wasn't really a building.

It was the gondola of an airship, tipped up at an angle. Above us, the craft's gasbag was a dark mass pinned between branches of the Canopy. The airship must have been trapped here when the plague hit, caught like a balloon in a tree. The gasbag was so impermeable that it was still fully inflated, seven years after the plague. But it was crimped and distorted by the pressure of the branches which had formed around it, and I couldn't help wondering how strong it really was – and what would happen to the gondola if the bag was punctured.

'It must have happened really fast,' I said, having visions of the airship trying to steer itself out of the path of the malforming building.

'Not that quickly,' Waverly said, as if I'd said something deeply foolish. 'This was a sightseeing airship – there were dozens of them, back in the old days. When the trouble came, no one was much interested in sightseeing anymore. They left the airship moored here while the building grew around it, but it still took a day or so for the branches to trap it completely.'

'And now you live in it?'

'Well, not exactly. It isn't all that safe, really. That's why we don't have to worry too much about anyone else paying us any attention.'

Behind, the door swung open again and the woman emerged. 'An unorthodox place to wake you, I admit.' She joined Waverly next to the railing, leaning bravely over the edge. It must have been an easy kilometre to the ground. 'But it does have its uses, discretion being one of them. Now then, Mister Mirabel. I expect you are in need of some good food and hospitality – am I right?'

I nodded, thinking that if I stayed with these people, they might provide a means for me to enter the Canopy proper. That was the rational argument for agreeing. The other part was born out of sheer relief and gratitude and the fact that I was as tired and hungry as she probably imagined.

'I don't want to impose.'

'Nonsense. I did you a great disservice in the Mulch, and then Waverly rather compounded the error with his ham-fisted stun setting – didn't you, Waverly? Well, we'll say no more of it – provided you do us the honour of providing you with a little food and rest.' The woman took something black out of a pocket, folding it open and elongating an aerial before speaking into it. 'Darling? We're ready now. We'll meet at the high end of the gondola.'

She snapped the telephone shut and pushed it back into her pocket.

We walked around the side of the gondola, using the railing to haul our way up the slope without slipping. At the highest point the railing had been cut away so that there was nothing between me and the ground except a lot of air. Waverly and Sybilline – if that was her name – could have easily pushed me over the edge had either of them meant me any harm, especially in my generally disorientated state. More than that, they'd had plenty of opportunities to do it before I woke up.

'Here he comes,' Waverly said, pointing under the sagging curve of the gasbag. I watched a cable-car descend into view. It looked a lot like the one I'd first seen Sybilline in, but I wasn't pretending to be an expert just yet. The car's arms grasped threads entangled around the gasbag, tugging the blimp out of shape, but managing not to puncture it. The car came close, its door opening and a ramp extending out to bridge the gap to the gondola.

'After you, Tanner,' Sybilline said.

I crossed the bridge. It was only a step of a metre or so, but there was no protection on either side and it took an effort of nerve to make the crossing. Sybilline and Waverly followed me blithely. Living in the Canopy must have given everyone an inhuman head for heights.

There were four seats in the rear compartment and a windowed partition between us and the driver. Before the window was closed, I saw that the driver was the high-cheekboned, grey-eyed man who had been with Sybilline earlier.

'Where are you taking me?' I said.

'To eat? Where else?' Sybilline placed a hand on my forearm, trustingly. 'The best place in the city, Tanner. Certainly the place with the best view.'

A night-time flight across Chasm City. With only the lights to trace the geometry of the city, it was almost possible to pretend that the plague hadn't happened. The shapes of the buildings were lost in the darkness, except where the upper branches were picked out by tentacles and star-streams of glowing windows, or the neon scribbles of advertisements whose meaning I couldn't fathom, spelt in the cryptic ideograms of Canasian. Now and then we would pass one of the older buildings that hadn't been affected by the plague, standing stiff and regular amongst the changed ones. More often than not those buildings were still damaged, even if they hadn't been caused to physically mutate. Other adjacent structures had thrust limbs through their neighbours, or undermined their foundations. Some had wrapped themselves around other buildings like strangler vines. There had been fires, explosions and riots during the days of the plague, and very little had emerged from those times completely unscathed.

'You see that one?' Sybilline said, drawing my attention to a pyramid-shape which was more or less intact. It was a very low structure, almost lost in the Mulch, but it was picked out by searchlights arcing down from above. 'That's the Monument to the Eighty. I assume you know the story?'

'Not in any detail.'

'It was a long time ago. This man tried to scan people into computers, but the technology wasn't mature. They were killed by the scanning process, which was bad enough, but then the simulations started to go wrong. There were eighty of them, including the man himself. When it was all over, when most of them had failed, their families had that monument built. But it's seen better days now.'

'Like the whole city,' Waverly said.

We continued across town. Travelling by cable-car took a little getting used to, as my stomach was discovering. When the car was passing through a place where there were many threads, the ride was almost as smooth and level as a volantor. But as soon as the threads started to thin out – as the car traversed the parts of the Canopy where there were no major branches, for instance – the trajectory became a lot less crowlike and a lot more gibbonlike: wide, stomach-churning arcs punctuated by jolts of upwards thrust. It should have felt very natural, given that the human brain was supposed to have evolved for exactly this kind of arboreal living.

But that was a few too many million years ago for me.

Eventually the cable-car's sickening arcs took us down towards ground level. I remembered Quirrenbach telling me the locals referred to the city's great merged dome as the Mosquito Net, and here it reached down until it touched the ground near the chasm's rim. In this inner perimeter region the vertical stratification of the city was less pronounced. There was an intermingling of Canopy and Mulch, an indeterminate zone where the Mulch reached up to brush the underneath of the dome, and places where the Canopy forced itself underground, into armoured plazas where the wealthy could walk unmolested.

It was into one of those enclaves that Sybilline's driver took us, dropping the cable-car's undercarriage and steering the craft onto a landing deck where other cars were parked. The edge of the dome was a sloping stained-brown wall leaning over us like a breaking wave. Through the parts which were still more or less transparent, the huge wide maw of the chasm was visible; the city on the other side of it only a distant forest of twinkling lights.

'I've called ahead and booked us a table at the stalk,' said the man with the iron-grey eyes, stepping out of the car's driving compartment. 'Word is Voronoff's going to be eating there tonight, so the place is pretty packed.'

200

'I'm pleased,' Sybilline said. 'You can always rely on Voronoff to add a little gloss to the evening.' Casually she opened a compartment in the side of the car and pulled out a black purse, opening it to reveal little vials of Dream Fuel and one of the ornate wedding-guns I'd seen aboard the *Strelnikov*.

She tugged down her collar and pressed the gun against her neck, gritting her teeth as she shunted a cubic centimetre of the dark red fluid into her bloodstream. Then she passed the gun to her partner, who injected himself before returning the baroquely ornamented instrument to Sybilline.

'Tanner?' she said. 'Do you want a spike?'

'I'll pass,' I said.

'Fine.' She folded the kit away in the compartment as if what had taken place was of no particular consequence.

We left the car and walked across the landing deck to a sloping ramp which led down into a brightly lit plaza. It was a lot less squalid than any part of the city I'd seen so far: clean, cool and packed with wealthy-looking people, palanquins, servitors and bio-engineered animals. Music pulsed from the walls, which were tuned to show city scenes from before the plague. A strange, spindly robot made its way down the thoroughfare, towering over people on its bladelike legs. It was made entirely out of sharp, gleaming surfaces, like a collection of enchanted swords.

'That's one of Sequard's automata,' said the man with the iron-grey eyes. 'He used work in the Glitter Band, one of the leading figures in the Gluonist Movement. Now he makes these things. They're very dangerous, so watch out.'

We stepped gingerly around the machine, avoiding the slow arcs of its lethal limbs. 'I don't think I caught your name,' I said to the man.

He looked at me oddly, as if I'd just asked him his shoe-size.

'Fischetti.'

We made our way down the thoroughfare, bypassing another automaton much like the first one, except this robot had distinct red stains on some of its limbs. Then we passed over a series of ornamental ponds where plump gold and silver koi were mouthing near the surface. I tried to work out where we were. We'd landed near the chasm and had been walking all the time towards it, but it had appeared much closer to begin with.

Finally the thoroughfare widened out into a huge domed chamber, large enough for the hundred or so dining tables it must have contained. The place was nearly full. I even saw a few palanquins parked around one table which had been neatly set out for diners, but I couldn't see how they were going to eat. A series of steps led down to the chamber's glass floor, and then we were escorted to a vacant table at the edge of the room, next to one of the huge windows set into the chamber's midnight blue dome. An astonishingly intricate chandelier hung from the dome's apex.

'Like I said, best view in Chasm City,' Sybillene said.

I could see where we were now. The restaurant was at one end of a stalk which emerged from the side of the chasm, fifty or sixty metres from the top. The stalk must have been a kilometre long, as thin and brittle-looking as a sliver of blown glass. It was supported at the chasm end by a bracket of filigreed crystal; the effect of which was to make the rest of it look even more perilous.

Sybilline passed me a menu. 'Choose what you like, Tanner – or let me choose for you, if you aren't familiar with our cuisine. I won't let you leave here without a good meal.'

I looked at the prices, wondering if my eye was adding a zero or two to each figure. 'I can't pay for this.'

'No one's asking you to. This is one we all owe you.'

I made some choices, consulted with Sybilline and then sat back and waited for the food. I felt out of place, of course – but then again, I *was* hungry, and by staying with these people I'd learn a lot more about Canopy life. Luckily I wasn't required to make smalltalk. Sybilline and Fischetti were talking about other people, occasionally spotting someone across the room who they pointed out discreetly. Waverly butted in now and again with an observation, but at no point was my opinion solicited except out of occasional politeness.

I looked around the room, sizing up the clientèle. Even the people who had reshaped their bodies and faces looked beautiful, like charismatic actors wearing animal costumes. Sometimes it was just the colour of their skin that they had changed, but in others their whole physiology had been shifted towards some lean animal ideal. I saw a man with elaborate striped spines radiating from his forehead, sitting next to a woman whose enlarged eyes were periodically veiled behind irridescent lids patterned like moth's wings. There was an otherwise normal-looking man whose mouth opened to reveal a forked black tongue which he stuck out at every opportunity, as if tasting the air. There was a slender, nearly-naked woman covered in black and white stripes. She caught my eye for an instant and I suspect she would have held her gaze had I not looked away.

Instead I looked down into the steaming depths of the chasm beneath us, my sense of vertigo slowly abating. Though it was night-time, there was a ghostly reflected glow of the city all around us. We were a kilometre out from one wall, but the chasm was easily fifteen or twenty kilometres wide, the other side appearing just as distant as it had from the landing deck. The walls were mostly sheer, except for occasional narrow natural ledges where rock had fallen away from the sides. Sometimes there were buildings set into the ledges, connected to the higher levels by elevator tubes or enclosed walkways. There was no sign of the bottom of the chasm; the walls rose from a placid white cloud layer which hid the lower depths completely. Pipes stretched down into the mist, reaching towards the atmospheric processing machinery which I knew to be down there. The hidden machines supplied Chasm City with power, air and water, and were robust enough to have continued functioning even after the plague had hit.

I could see luminous things flying down in the depths, tiny bright triangles of colour. 'Gliders,' Sybilline said, watching my gaze. 'It's an old sport. I used to do it, but the thermals are insane near the walls. And the amount of breathing gear you have to wear . . .' She shook her head. 'The worst thing is the mist, though. You get a speed buzz from flying just above the mist level, but as soon as you drop into it, you lose all sense of direction. If you're lucky, you head upwards and you make clear air before you run into the wall. If you're not, you think down is up and you head into higher and higher pressure until you cook yourself alive. Or you get to add some interesting new coloration to the side of the chasm.'

'Radar doesn't work in the mist?'

'It does – but that wouldn't make it any fun, would it?'

The food came. I ate cautiously, not wanting to make an exhibition of myself. It was good, too. Sybilline said the best food was still grown in orbit and shipped down by behemoth. That explained the extra zeroes after almost every item.

'Look,' Waverly said, when we were on the final course. 'That's Voronoff, isn't it?'

He was pointing discreetly across the room to where a man had just stood up from one of the tables.

'Yes,' Fischetti said, with a smile of self-congratulation. 'I knew he'd be here somewhere.'

I looked at the man they were talking about. He was probably one of the least ostentatious people in the room, a small, immaculate-looking man with neatly curled black hair and the pleasingly neutral face of a mime artist.

'Who is he?' I said. 'I've heard of him, but I'm not sure where.'

'Voronoff's a celebrity,' Sybilline said. She was touching my arm again, divulging another confidence. 'He's a hero to some of us. He's one of the oldest post-mortals. He's done everything; mastered every game.'

'He's some kind of game player?'

'More than that,' Waverly said. 'He's into every extreme situation you can imagine. He makes the rules; the rest of us just follow.'

'I hear he's got something planned for tonight,' said Fischetti.

Sybilline clapped her hands together. 'A mist jump?'

'I think our luck could be in. Why else would he come here to eat? He must be bored shitless of the view.'

Voronoff was walking away from his table, accompanied by a man and a women who had been sitting with him. Everyone in the room was watching them now, sensing that something was about to happen. Even the palanquins had turned.

I watched the three of them leave the room, but the air of anticipation remained. After a few minutes I understood why: Voronoff and the others had appeared on a ring-shaped balcony around the outside of the restaurant, encircling its dome. They were wearing protective clothes and masks, their faces almost hidden.

'Are they going to fly gliders?' I said.

'No,' Sybilline answered. 'That's entirely passé as far as Voronoff's concerned. A mist jump's something much, much more dangerous.'

Now they were fitting glowing harnesses around their waists. I strained to get a better view. Each harness was attached to a coiled line of rope, the other end of which was anchored to the side of the dome. By now half the diners had crowded over to this side of the restaurant for a better view.

'You see that coil?' Sybilline said. 'It's up to each jumper to calculate the length and elasticity of their line. Then they have to time the moment that they jump, based on their knowledge of the thermals in the chasm. See how they're paying close attention to what the gliders are doing, down below?'

That was when the woman jumped over the edge. She must have decided that the moment was right for her leap.

Through the floor I watched her drop, dwindling to a tiny human speck as she fell towards the mist. The coil was almost invisibly thin as she dragged it behind her.

'What's the idea?' I said.

'It's supposed to be pretty exciting,' Fischetti said. 'But the real trick is to fall enough to enter the mist; to disappear completely from view. But you don't want to fall too much. And even if you calculate the right length of line, you can still get creamed by thermals.'

'She's misjudged,' Sybilline said. 'Oh, silly girl. She's getting sucked closer and closer to that outcrop.'

I watched the glowing dot of the falling woman ram against the side of the chasm. There was a moment of stunned silence in the restaurant, as if the unspeakable had happened. I was expecting the silence to be broken by a cries of horror and pity. Instead there was a polite round of applause and some muted sounds of commiseration.

'I could have told her that was going to happen,' Sybilline said.

'Who was she?' Fischetti said.

'I don't know, Olivia something or other.' Sybilline picked up the menu again and began scanning the desserts.

'Careful, you'll miss the next one. I think it's going to be Voronoff . . . yes!' Fischetti hammered the table as his hero stepped off the balcony and dropped gracefully towards the mist. 'See how cool he was? That's class, that is.'

Voronoff fell like an expert swimmer, his line as straight and true as if he were plunging through vacuum. It was all a matter of timing, I could see: he'd waited for the exact moment when the thermals would behave the way he wanted, working with him rather than against him. As he fell deeper it was almost as if they were nudging him helpfully away from the chasm walls. A screen in the middle of the room was relaying a side-on image of Voronoff, captured by what must have been a flying camera chasing him down the chasm. Other diners were following his trajectory with opera glasses, telescopic monocles and elegant lorgnette binoculars.

'Is there a point to this?' I said.

'Risk,' Sybilline said. 'And the thrill of doing something new and dangerous. If there's one thing the plague's given us, it's that: the opportunity to test ourselves; to stare death in the face. Biological immortality won't help you much if you've just hit a rockface at two hundred kilometres per hour.'

'Why do they do it, though? Doesn't potential immortality make your lives all the more precious?'

'Yes, but that doesn't mean we still don't need to be reminded of death now and then. What's the point of beating an old enemy if you deny yourself the thrill of ever remembering what it was like in the first place? Victory loses its meaning without the memory of what you've vanquished.'

'But you could die.'

She looked up from the menu. 'All the more reason not to cock up your timing, then.'

Voronoff was nearing the end of his fall. I could barely see him now.

'He's picking up tension now,' Fischetti said. 'Beginning to slow down. See how beautifully he's timed it?'

The line was stretched almost to its limit, now starting to arrest Voronoff's fall. But his timing was as good as his admirers had evidently been expecting. He disappeared for three or four seconds, vanishing into the whiteness before the coil began to contract, hauling him back upwards towards us.

'Textbook,' Sybillene said.

There was more applause, but in contrast to before, this time it was wildly enthusiastic. People began to hammer their cutlery in appreciation of Voronoff's fall. 'You know what?' Waverly said. 'Now that he's mastered mist-jumping, he'll get bored and try something else even more insanely dangerous. You mark my words.'

'There goes the other one,' Sybillene said, as the last jumper stepped from the balcony. 'Timing looks good – better than the woman's, anyway. You'd have thought he'd have the decency to let Voronoff come back up first, wouldn't you?'

'How will he get back up?' I said.

'He'll haul himself up. There's some kind of motorised winch in his harness.'

I watched the last jumper plummet into the depths. To my untrained eye the jump looked at least as good as Voronoff's – the thermals didn't seem to be steering the man towards the sides, and his posture as he dropped looked amazingly balletic. The crowd had quietened down now and were watching the fall intently.

'Well, he's no amateur,' Fischetti said.

'He just copied Voronoff's timing,' Sybillene said. 'I was watching the way the vortex affected the gliders.'

'You can't blame him for that. You don't get marks for originality, you know.'

He dropped further still, his harness a glowing green dot receding towards the mist. 'Wait,' Waverly said, pointing to the uncoiling line on the balcony. 'He should have run out of line by now, shouldn't he?'

'Voronoff had by this point,' Sybillene agreed.

'Silly fool's given himself too much,' Fischetti said. He took a sip from his wine glass and studied the depths with renewed interest. 'It's reached the limit now, but it's much too late.'

He was right. By the time the glowing green dot reached the level of the mist, it was falling almost as quickly as ever. The screen showed a last side-on view of him vanishing into the whiteness, and then there was only the taut filament of his line. Seconds passed – first the three or four that Voronoff had taken before emerging, and then ten . . . and then twenty. By thirty seconds people were beginning to get a little uncomfortable. Obviously they had seen this sort of thing happen before and had some idea of what to expect.

Nearly a minute passed before the man emerged.

I'd already been told what happened to glider pilots who went too deep, but I hadn't imagined it could be that bad. But the man had gone very far into the mist. The pressure and temperature had been too much for the flimsy protection of his suit. He had died: boiled alive within a few seconds. The camera lingered on his corpse, lovingly mapping the horror of what had happened to him. I felt revolted and looked away from the image. I'd seen some bad things during my years as a soldier, but never while sitting at a table digesting a large and luxurious meal.

Sybilline shrugged. 'Well, he should have used a shorter line.'

Afterwards we walked back across the stalk to the landing deck where Sybilline's cable-car was still waiting.

'Well, Tanner, where can we take you?' she said.

I wasn't exactly enjoying their company, I had to admit. It had begun badly and though I was grateful for the sight-seeing trip to the stalk, the cold way they had responded to the deaths of the mist-jumpers had left me wondering whether I wouldn't have been better off with the pigs they had mentioned.

But I couldn't throw away a chance like this. 'I take it you're heading back to the Canopy at some point?'

She looked pleased. 'If you want to come with us, it's absolutely no problem. In fact, I insist on it.'

206

'Well, don't feel any obligation. You've been generous enough as it is. But if it won't inconvenience you . . .'

'Not at all. Get in the car.'

The vehicle opened before me, Fischetti getting in the driver's compartment and the rest of us in the back. We lofted; the cable-car's motion began to feel familiar, if not actually comfortable. The ground dropped away quickly; we reached the interstices of the Canopy and settled into a semi-regular rhythm as the car picked its route along one of the main cable ways.

That was when I started to think I really should have taken my chances with the pigs.

'Well, Tanner – did you enjoy your meal?' Sybilline asked.

'Like you said, it's a hell of a view.'

'Good. You needed the energy. Or at least you *will* need it.' Deftly, she reached into a compartment set into the car's plush and pulled out a nasty little gun. 'Well, to state the obvious, this is a weapon and I'm pointing it at you.'

'Ten out of ten for observation.' I looked at the gun. It appeared to be made out of jade and was embossed with red demons. It had a small, dark maw and she was holding it very steadily.

'The point being,' Sybilline continued, 'that you shouldn't think of doing anything untoward.'

'If you wanted to kill me, you could have done it dozens of times already.'

'Yes. But there's just one flaw in your thinking. We *do* want to kill you. Just not in any old manner.'

I should have felt immediate fear as soon as she pulled out the gun, but there'd been a delay of a few seconds while my mind assimilated the situation and decided it was probably just as bad as it appeared.

'What are you going to do to me?'

Sybilline nodded at Waverly. 'Can you do it here?'

'I've got the tools, but I'd far rather do it back at the airship.' Waverly nodded at her. 'You can keep that gun pointed until then, can't you?'

I asked what they were going to do to me again, but all of a sudden no one seemed very interested in what I had to say. I'd walked into big trouble, that much was obvious. Waverly's story of shooting me to protect me from the pigs hadn't ever sounded more than halfway convincing, but who had I been to argue? I'd kept telling myself that if they had wanted me dead . . .

Nice line. But like Sybilline had said, there was a certain flaw in my thinking . . .

It didn't take very long to reach the trapped airship. As we swung up towards it I had an excellent view of the imprisoned craft, suspended precariously high above the city. There were no Canopy lights anywhere near it, no signs of habitation in the branches that supported it. I remembered what they had said about it being nice and discreet.

We landed. By then Waverly had found a gun as well, and when I stepped onto the connecting ramp which led to the gondola, Fischetti was covering me with a third. About the only thing I could have done was jump over the side.

But I wasn't that desperate. Not yet.

Inside the gondola, I was escorted back to the chair where I had woken up only a couple of hours earlier. This time Waverly strapped me into the seat.

'Well, get on with it,' Sybilline said, standing with her hip to one side with the gun held in one hand like a chic cigarette holder. 'It isn't brain surgery, you know.'

She laughed.

Waverly spent the next few minutes circumnavigating my chair, emitting odd grunts which might have indicated distaste. Now and then he touched my scalp, examining it with gentle fingers. Then, seemingly satisfied, he retrieved some equipment from somewhere behind me. Whatever it was looked medical.

'What are you going to do?' I asked, trying again to get a response out of them. 'You won't get far by torturing me, if that's what you've got in mind.'

'You think I'm going to torture you?' Waverly had one of the medical devices in his hand now, an intricate probe-like thing fashioned from chrome and inset with blinking status lights. 'It would amuse me, I admit. I'm a colossal sadist. But aside from my own self-gratification, it would serve no purpose. We've trawled your memories, so we know all that you'd tell us under pain.'

'You're bluffing.'

'No, we're not. Did we have to ask you your name? No, we didn't. But we knew you were called Tanner Mirabel, didn't we?'

'You know I'm telling the truth, in that case. I have nothing to offer you.'

He leant closer to me, his lens clicking and whirring as it absorbed visual data across an unguessable spread of the spectrum. 'We don't really know what to know, Mister Mirabel. Assuming that's really your name. It's all so very foggy in there, you see. Confused memory traces – whole swathes of your past which we just can't access. You'll understand that this does not put us in the best possible frame of mind to trust you. I mean, you accept that this is a reasonable response, don't you?'

'I've only just been revived.'

'Ah, yes – and the Ice Mendicants normally do such a marvellous job, don't they? But in your case not even their artistry could restore the whole.'

'Are you working for Reivich?'

'I doubt it. I've never heard of him.' He glanced at Sybilline, as if seeking her opinion on the matter. She did her best to mask it, but I saw the way she pulled the facial equivalent of a shrug; a momentary widening of the eyes as if to say that she hadn't heard of Reivich either.

It looked genuine, too.

'All right,' Waverly said. 'I think I can do this nice and cleanly. It helps that there aren't any other implants in his head to get in the way.'

'Just do it,' Sybilline said. 'We haven't got all damned night.'

He held the surgical device against the side of my skull, so that I could feel its cold pressure against my skin. I heard a click as he pulled a trigger—

SEVENTEEN

The head of security stood before his prisoner, studying him as a sculptor might study a roughly hewn work in progress; satisfied with the effort that had already taken place, but acutely aware of all the labour that lay ahead. Much remained to be done, but he promised himself that there would be no errors.

Sky Haussmann and the saboteur were almost alone. The torture room was in a distant and largely forgotten annex of the ship, accessible only by one of the train routes which everyone else assumed was disused. Sky had outfitted the room and its surrounding chambers himself, equipping it with pressure and heat by tapping into the ship's lymphatic system of supply lines. In principle, a detailed audit of power/air consumption might have revealed the room's existence, but, as a possible security issue, the matter would only have been referred to Sky himself. It had never happened; he doubted that it ever would.

The prisoner was splayed before him on one wall, anchored there and surrounded by machines. Neural lines plunged into the man's skull, interfacing with the control implants buried in his brain. Those implants were exceedingly crude, even by Chimeric standards, but they did their job. They were mainly webbed into the regions of the temporal lobe associated with deep religious experience. Epileptics had long reported feelings of divinity when intense electrical activity flickered across those regions; all the implants did was subject the saboteur to mild and controllable versions of the same religious impulses. It was probably how his old masters had controlled him, and how he had been able to give himself up so selflessly to their suicidal cause.

Now Sky controlled him via the same devotional channels.

'Do you know, no one ever mentions you these days,' Sky said.

The saboteur offered him bloodshot crescent eyes beneath heavy lids. 'What?'

'It's as if the rest of the ship has decided to quietly forget that you ever existed. How exactly does it feel, to have been erased from the public record?'

'You remember me.'

'Yes.' Sky nodded towards the pale aerodynamic shape which floated at the other end of the room, cased in armoured green glass. 'And so does he. But that's not saying much, is it? To be remembered only by your tormentors?'

'It's better than nothing.'

'They suspect, of course.' He thought of Constanza, the only serious thorn in his side. 'Or at least they used to, when they gave the matter any thought. After all, you did kill my father. I'd be perfectly within my moral rights to torture you, wouldn't I?'

'I didn't kill . . .'

'Oh, but you did.' Sky smiled. He was standing at the lashed-up control panel which allowed him to talk to the saboteur's implants, idly fingering the chunky black knobs and glass-panelled analogue dials. He had built the machine himself, scavenging its components from across the ship, and had given it the name God-Box. That was what it was, ultimately: an instrument for placing God inside the killer's head. In the early days he had used it solely to inflict pain, but – once he had smashed the infiltrator's personality – he had begun to reconstruct it towards his own ideal, via controlled doses of neural ecstasy. At the moment only the tiniest trace of current was dribbling into the man's temporal lobe, and in this null state his feelings towards Sky bordered on agnosticism rather than awe.

'I don't remember what I did,' the man said.

'No, I don't suppose you do. Shall I remind you?'

The saboteur shook his head. 'Perhaps I did kill your father. But someone must have given me the means to do so. Someone must have cut my restraints and left that knife by my bed.'

'It was a scalpel, an infinitely finer thing.'

'You'd know, of course.'

Sky turned one of the black knobs a couple of notches higher, watching as the analogue dials quivered. 'Why would I have given you the means to kill my own father? I'd have had to be insane.'

'He was dying anyway. You hated him for what he had done to you.'

'And how would you know?'

'You told me, Sky.'

That, of course, was entirely possible. It was amusing to push the man to the desperate, bowel-loosening edge of total fear, and to then relent. He could do that with the machine if he wished, or just by unwrapping some surgical tools and showing them to the prisoner.

'He didn't do anything to me to make me hate him.'

'No? That's not what you said before. You were the son of immortals, after all. If Titus hadn't meddled – hadn't stolen you from them – you'd still be sleeping with the other passengers.' In his subtly archaic accent he continued, 'Instead you'll spend years of your life in this miserable place, growing older, risking death each day, never knowing for sure if you'll make it to Journey's

End. What if Titus was wrong, too? What if you aren't immortal? It'll be years before you can be certain.'

Sky turned the knob higher. 'Do you think I look my age?'

'No . . .' He watched the saboteur's lower lip tremble with the first unmistakable signs of ecstasy. 'But that could just be good genes.'

'I'll take my chances.' He pushed the current higher. 'I could have tortured you, you know.'

'Ahh . . . I know. Oh God, I know.'

'But I chose not to. Are you feeling a reasonably intense religious experience now?'

'Yes. I feel I'm in the presence of something . . . something . . . ahhh. Jesus. I can't talk now.' The man's face rippled in an inhuman manner. There were twenty additional facial muscles anchored to his skull, capable of dramatically altering his appearance when the need arose. Sky assumed that he had transformed his face to slip aboard the ship in place of the man who should have had his sleeper berth. Now he mirrored Sky, the artificial muscles twitching involuntarily to this new configuration. 'It's too beautiful.'

'Are you seeing bright lights yet?'

'I can't talk.'

Sky turned the knob up another few notches, until it was near the end of its range. The analogue dials were nearly all full-over. But not quite, and because they were logarithmically calibrated, that last twitch could mean the difference between a feeling of intense spirituality and a full-on vision of heaven and hell. He had never taken the prisoner to that plateau yet, and he was not entirely sure he wanted to risk it.

He stepped away from the machine and approached the saboteur. Behind him Sleek quivered in his tank, waves of anticipation running up and down the dolphin's body. The man was drooling, losing basic muscular control. His face had melted now, the muscles sagging hopelessly. Sky took the man's head in his hands and forced him to look at his own face. He could almost feel a tingling in his fingers from the current worming into the man's skull. For a moment they locked eyes, pupil to pupil, but it was too much for the saboteur. It must be like seeing God, he thought; not necessarily the most pleasant of experiences even if it was drenched in awe.

'Listen to me,' he whispered. 'No; don't try to speak. Just listen. I could have killed you, but I didn't. I chose to spare you. I *chose* to show mercy. Do you know what that makes me? Merciful. I want you to remember that, but I also want you to remember something else. I can be jealous as well, and vengeful.'

Just then Sky's bracelet chimed. It was the one he had inherited from his father upon assuming command of security. He swore softly, allowed the prisoner's head to loll, and then took the call. He was careful to keep his back to the prisoner.

'Haussmann? Are you there?'

212

It was Old Man Balcazar. Sky smiled and did his best to look and sound crisply professional.

'It's me, Captain. How may I help?'

'Something's come up, Haussmann. Something important. I need you to escort me.'

With his free hand Sky began to turn down the gain on the machine, then stopped before he dropped it too low. With the current off, the prisoner might regain the ability to speak. He kept the juice on while he spoke.

'Escort you, sir? To somewhere else in the ship?'

'No, Haussmann. Off ship. We're going over to the *Palestine*. I want you to come with me. Not too much to ask, is it?'

'I'll be in the taxi hangar in thirty minutes, sir.'

'You'll be there in fifteen, Haussmann, and you'll have a taxi prepped and ready for departure.' The Captain inserted a phlegmatic pause. 'Balcazar out.'

Sky stood staring at the bracelet for a few moments after the Captain's image had blanked, wondering what was afoot. With the four remaining ships locked in what was essentially a cold war, the kind of trip of which Balcazar spoke was extremely rare, usually planned days in advance with meticulous attention to detail. A full security escort would normally accompany any senior crew making the crossing to another ship, Sky himself staying behind to co-ordinate things. But this time Balcazar had given him only a few minutes' warning, and there had been no rumour of anything pending before the Captain's call.

Fifteen minutes – of which he had squandered at least one already. He snapped down the cuff of his tunic and started to leave the room. He was almost gone when he remembered that the prisoner was still plugged into the God-Box, his mind still bathed in electrical ecstasy.

Sleek quivered again.

Sky returned to the machine and adjusted the settings, so that the dolphin had control of the electrical current stimulation. Sleek's quivering became maniacal, the creature's body thrashing against the tight constraints of the tank, enveloping his body in a manic froth of bubbles. The implants in the dolphin's skull were able to talk to the machine now; able to make the prisoner scream in agony or gasp in the heights of joy.

With Sleek, though, it was generally the former.

He heard the old man wheezing and creaking his way across the floor of the hangar long before he saw him. The Captain's two medical aides, Valdivia and Rengo, kept a discreet distance behind their charge, slightly crouched as they walked, monitoring his life-signs on handheld readouts, their expressions of concern so profound that it looked like the old man had only minutes of life left in him. But Sky was a long way from feeling any concern over the Captain's imminent demise: they had been wearing those expressions for years, and what they constituted was only a glaze of carefully maintained professionalism. Valdivia and Rengo had to give everyone the impression that the Captain was almost on his deathbed, or else they would be forced to apply their not overly-honed medical skills elsewhere.

Which was not to say that Balcazar was exactly in the prime of life, either. The old man was sustained by a chest-girdling medical device, across which his dress tunic was tightly buttoned, giving him the plump-breasted look of a well-fed rooster. The effect was exacerbated by his comb of stiff grey hair and the suspicious gleam of his dark, widely-set eyes. Balcazar was easily the oldest of the crew, his Captaincy dating back to long before Titus's time, and while it was perfectly clear that he had once had a mind like a steel trap, steering his crew through innumerable minor crises with icy skill, it was equally clear that those days were long since over; that the trap was now a rusted travesty of itself. Privately they said that his mind was nearly gone, while publicly they spoke of his infirmity and the need to hand over the reins to the younger generation; to replace him with a young or middle-aged Captain now who would be merely senior when the Flotilla arrived at its destination. Wait too long, they said, and his replacement would not have time to acquire the necessary skills before those undoubtedly difficult days were upon them.

There had been votes of censure and no confidence, and talk of forced retirement on medical grounds – nothing actually mutinous, of course – but the old bastard had stood his ground. Yet his position had never been weaker than now. His staunchest allies had themselves begun to die out. Titus Haussmann, who Sky could still not quite stop thinking of as his father, had been amongst them. Losing Titus had been a major blow for the Captain, who had long relied on the man for tactical advice and soundings regarding the true feelings of the crew. It was almost as if the Captain could not adjust to the loss of his confidant and was perfectly happy to let Sky assume Titus's role. Speedy promotion to head of security had been only part of it. When the Captain occasionally called him Titus rather than Sky, he had at first assumed the slip was an innocent mistake, but on reflection it signified something much more problematic. The Captain, as they said, was losing his marbles; events were becoming jumbled in his head, the recent past slipping in and out of clarity. It was no way to run a ship.

Something, Sky had resolved, would have to be done about it.

'We'll be accompanying him, of course,' the first of the aides whispered. The man, Valdivia, looked enough like the other one for him and Rengo to have been brothers. They both had close-cropped white hair and worry lines corrugated into their foreheads.

'Impossible,' Sky said. 'There's only a two-seat shuttle available.' He indicated the nearest craft, parked on its transport pallet. Other, larger ships were parked around the two-seater, but all had components missing or access panels folded open. It was part of the general deterioration of services;

throughout the ship, things that had been meant to last the mission were failing prematurely. The problem would not have been so severe if parts and expertise could have been swapped between the Flotilla vessels, but that was unthinkable in the current diplomatic climate.

'How long would it take to patch together one of those larger ones?' Valdivia said.

'Half a day at the earliest,' Sky said.

Balcazar must have heard part of that, because he murmured, 'There won't be any damned delay, Haussmann.'

'You see?'

Rengo sprang forward. 'Then, Captain, may I?'

It was a ritual they had gone through many times before. With a long-suffering sigh, Balcazar allowed the medic to undo his side-buttoned tunic, revealing the gleaming expanse of the medical tabard. The machine whirred and wheezed like a piece of clapped-out air purification equipment. There were dozens of windows set into it, some showing readouts or dials, others pulsing fluid lines. Rengo extended a probe from his handheld device and plugged it into various apertures, nodding or shaking his head slowly as numbers and graphs flowed across the device's screen.

'Something amiss?' Sky said.

'As soon as he gets back, I want him down in medical for a complete overhaul,' Rengo said.

'Pulse is a bit on the thready side,' Valdivia said.

'It'll hold. I'll up his relaxant.' Rengo punched controls on his handset. 'He'll be a bit drowsy on the way over, Sky. Just don't let the bastards on the other ship get him worked up, all right? Bring him back here on medical grounds if there's any sign of tension.'

'I'll be sure to.' Sky helped the already dozy Captain towards the two-seat shuttle. It was a lie that the larger ships were not ready, of course, but of those present only Sky had the technical knowledge to catch himself out.

Departure was uneventful. They cleared the access tunnel, unlatched and curved away from the *Santiago*, stabs of thrust pushing the shuttle towards their destination, the *Palestine*. The Captain sat before him, his reflection in the cockpit window resembling the formal portrait of some octagenarian despot from another century. Sky had expected him to nod off, but he seemed awake enough. He had the habit of delivering portentous utterances every few minutes, interspersed between fusillades of coughs.

'Khan was a reckless bloody fool, you know . . . should never have been left in command after the upheavals of '15 . . . if I'd damn well had my way, beggar would have been frozen for the rest of the trip, or thrown into space . . . losing his mass would have given them just the kind of decelerational edge they were looking for in the first place . . .'

'Really, sir?'

'Not literally, you damn fool! What would a man weigh, one ten millionth of the mass of one our ships? What kind of bloody edge would that have been?'

'Not much of one, sir.'

'I don't damn well think so, no. The trouble with you, Titus, is you take everything I say too damn literally . . . like a bloody amanuensis hanging off my every word, quill poised above parchment . . .'

'I'm not Titus, sir. Titus was my father.'

'What?' For a moment Balcazar glared at him, his eyes yellow with suspicion. 'Oh, never mind, damn you!'

But this was actually one of Balcazar's better days. There had been no outright lapses into surrealism. He could be very much worse: as poetically oblique as any sphinx, when the mood seized him. Perhaps there had once been a context in which even his maddest statement might have meant something, but to Sky they sounded only like premature deathbed ramblings. That was no problem of his. Balcazar seldom invited any kind of riposte when he was in soliloquy mode. If Sky had really back-answered him – or even dared to question some minute, trifling detail in Balcazar's stream-of-consciousness – the shock of it would probably have given him multiple organ failure, even with the relaxant Rengo had administered.

How utterly convenient that would have been, Sky thought.

After a few minutes, he said, 'I suppose you can tell me what this is all about now, sir.'

'Of course, Titus. Of course.'

And as placidly as if they were two old friends catching up on lost times over a couple of pisco sours, the Captain told him that they were heading to a conclave of senior Flotilla crew. It was to be the first in many years, precipitated by the unexpected arrival of another update from Sol system. A message from home, in other words, containing elaborate technical blueprints. It was the kind of exterior event which was still sufficient to push the Flotilla towards some kind of unity, even in the midst of the cold war. It was the same kind of gift which might have annihilated the *Islamabad*, when Sky was very young. Even now, no one was entirely sure whether Khan had chosen to sip from that poisoned chalice, or whether the accident had just happened then out of a sense of malign cosmic caprice. Now there was a promise of another squeeze in engine efficiency, if only they would make certain trifling changes to the magnetic confinement topology; all very safe, the message said – tested endlessly back home, with mock-ups of the Flotilla's engines; the potential for error was really negligible provided certain basic precautions were taken . . .

But at the same time, another message had arrived.

Don't do it, said the other message. *They're trying to trick you.*

It hardly mattered that the other message offered no plausible reason why such trickery might be attempted. The doubt that it brought was enough to lend this conclave an entirely new *frisson* of tension.

216

Eventually they were within visual range of the *Palestine*, where the conclave would be held. A whole swarm of shuttle taxis was converging on her from the other three ships, carrying senior ships' officers. The choice of the meeting place had been arrived at in haste, but that did not mean the process had been devoid of difficulty. Yet the *Palestine* was the obvious choice. In any war, Sky thought, cold or otherwise, it was always to the mutual benefit of all participants to agree on a neutral ground, whether it be for negotiation, exchange of spies or – if all else failed – early demonstration of new weapons – and the *Palestine* was the ship that had assumed that role.

'Do you think this is really a trick, sir?' Sky asked, when Balcazar had finished one of his coughing sessions. 'I mean, why would they do that?'

'Why would they bloody do what?'

'Try and kill us, sir, by transmitting erroneous technical data? There'd be no gain for them back home. It's a wonder they even bother sending us anything.'

'Precisely.' Balcazar spat the word, as if its obviousness was beneath contempt. 'There'd be no gain in sending us something useful, either – and it would be a lot more work than sending us something dangerous. Can't you see that, you little fool? God help all of us if one of your generation ever assumes command . . .' He trailed off.

Sky waited for him to finish coughing, then wheezing. 'But there must still be a motivation . . .'

'Pure malice.'

He was treading very thin ice now, but he soldiered on. 'The malice could just as easily lie in the message warning us not to implement the change.'

'Oh, and you're willing to risk four thousand lives to put that little bit of schoolboy speculation to the test, are you?'

'It's not my job to take such a decision, sir. I'm just saying I don't envy you the responsibility.'

'And what would you know about responsibility anyway, you insolent little prick?'

Little now, Sky thought. But one day . . . perhaps one day not too far from this one, all that might change. Thinking it best not to reply, he flew the taxi on in silence, broken only by the old man's cardiovascular labours.

But he thought deeply. It was something that Balcazar had said; that remark about it being better to bury the dead in space, rather than carry them to the destination world. It made a kind of sense, when he thought about it.

Every kilogramme that the ship carried was another kilogramme that had to be decelerated down from interstellar cruise speed. The ships massed close on a million tonnes – ten million times the mass of a man, as Balcazar had said. The simple laws of Newtonian physics told Sky that decreasing the mass of a ship by that amount would bring a proportional increase in the rate at which the ship could decelerate, assuming the same engine efficiency.

An improvement of one part in ten million was hardly spectacular . . . but who said you had to make do with the mass of just one man?

Sky thought about all the dead passengers the *Santiago* was carrying: the sleepers who were medically beyond any kind of revival. Only human sentimentality would argue that they needed to be brought to Journey's End. And for that matter, the huge and heavy machinery that supported them could be ditched as well. He thought about it some more, and began to think that it would not be impossible to shave off tonnes from the ship's mass. Put like that, it almost sounded compelling. The improvement would still be much less than one part in a thousand. Still – who was say more sleepers would not be lost in the years to come? A thousand things could go wrong.

It was a risky business, being frozen.

'Maybe we should all just wait and see, Titus,' the Captain said, jolting him from his thoughts. 'That wouldn't be such a bad approach to take, would it?'

'Wait and see, sir?'

'Yes.' There was a cold clarity to the Captain now, but Sky knew that it could go as easily as it came. 'Wait and see what they do about it, I mean. They'll have received the message as well, you realise. They'll have debated what to do about it as well, of course – but they won't have been able to talk it over with any of us.'

The Captain sounded lucid enough, but Sky was having trouble following him. Doing his best to conceal the fact, he said, 'It's a long time since you've mentioned them, isn't it?'

'Of course. One doesn't go around blabbing, Titus – you of all people would know that. Loose lips sink ships, that sort of thing. Or get them discovered.'

'Discovered, sir?'

'Well, we know damn well that our friends on the other three don't even seem to know about them. We've had spies penetrate right to the highest echelons on the other ships, and there's been no word about them at all.'

'Could we know for sure, though, sir?'

'Oh, I think so, Titus.'

'You do, sir?'

'Of course. You keep your ear to the ground on the *Santiago*, don't you? You know that the crew are at least familiar with the rumour of the sixth ship, even if most of them don't give it any credence.'

Sky masked his surprise as well as he was able. 'The sixth ship's just a myth to most of them, sir.'

'And that's the way we'll keep it. We, on the other hand, know better.'

Sky thought to himself: *so it's real. After all this time, the damned thing really exists. At the very least in Balcazar's mind.* But the Captain also seemed to be talking as if Titus had been in on the secret himself. Since the sixth ship constituted a possible security issue – no matter how little might have been known about that – it was entirely possible that he had been. And Titus had died before he could pass that particular item of knowledge to his successor.

Sky thought of Norquinco, his friend from the time when he had ridden the trains. He remembered well how Norquinco had been utterly convinced of the reality of the sixth ship. Gomez, too, had needed little convincing. It had been a year or so since he had spoken to either, but Sky imagined the two of them here now, nodding silently, enjoying the way he was forced to calmly accept this truth; this thing that he had so vehemently argued against. He had hardly given the matter any thought since that conversation on the train, but now he racked his brains, trying to remember what Norquino had told them.

'Most of the crew who buy into the rumour at all,' he said, 'assume that the sixth ship is dead; just drifting behind us.'

'Which only shows that there's a grain of truth underlying the rumour. She's dark, of course – no lights, no strong evidence of human presence at all – but all of that could be subterfuge. Her crew could still be alive, running her quietly. We can't guess their pyschology, of course, and we still don't know what really happened.'

'It would be good to know. Especially now.' Sky paused and took what he knew to be a major risk. 'Given the current gravity of the situation, with this technical message from back home, is there anything else I need to know about the sixth ship – anything which might help us make the right choice?'

To his relief, the Captain shook his head without rancour.

'You've seen all that I have, Titus. We really don't know anything more. I'm afraid those rumours encapsulate as much knowledge as we really have.'

'An expedition would settle the matter.'

'As you never tire of telling me. But consider the risks: yes, she's just within range of one our shuttles. About half a light-second behind us the last time we took an accurate radar fix, although she must have been a lot closer once. It would be simpler still if we could refuel when we got there. But what if they don't want visitors? They've maintained the illusion of non-existence for more than a generation. They might not be willing to give that up without a fight.'

'Unless they're dead. Some of the crew think we attacked them, and then erased them from the historical record.'

The Captain shrugged. 'Perhaps that's what happened. If you could erase a crime like that, you would, wouldn't you? Some of them might have survived, though, and chosen to lie low, so they can spring a surprise on us later in the voyage.'

'You think this message from back home might be enough to make them break their cover?'

'Perhaps. If it encourages them to fiddle with their antimatter engine, and the message really is a trap . . .'

'They'll light up half the sky.'

The Captain chuckled, a wet cruel sound, and that seemed to be the cue for him to doze off properly. The rest of the journey passed without incident, but Sky's mind was racing anyway, trying to digest what he had learned. Every time he said the words they were like a casual slap against his cheek; punishment for his own presumption in doubting Norquinco and the other believers. *The sixth ship existed. The sixth damned ship existed* . . .

And that, potentially, could change anything.

EIGHTEEN

They took me down to the Mulch again. I woke up in the cable-car as it was descending through night, rain hammering against the craft's windows. For a moment I thought I was with Captain Balcazar, escorting him across space to the meeting aboard the other Flotilla ship. The dreams seemed to be getting more insistent, pushing me ever deeper into Sky's thoughts, so that they were harder to shake off when I came around. But it was just me and Waverly in the cable-car's compartment.

I wasn't sure it was an improvement.

'How does it feel? I did a good job, I think.'

He was sitting opposite me with a gun. I remembered him pushing the probe against my head. I reached up to touch my scalp. Above my right ear was a shaven patch, still scabbed with blood, and the feeling of something hard encysted beneath the skin.

It hurt like hell.

'I think you need some practice.'

'Story of my life. You're a strange one, though. What's with all the blood coming out of your hand? Is that some medical condition I should know about?'

'Why? Would it make any difference?'

He debated the point with himself for a few moments. 'No, probably not. If you can run, you're fit enough.'

'Fit enough for what?' I touched the scab again. 'What have you put inside me?'

'Well, let me explain.'

I hadn't expected him to be so talkative, but I began to understand why it might make sense for me to know some of the facts. It must have stemmed less from any concern for my wellbeing than the need to have me primed in the right way. From previous games, it had become clear that the hunted made the whole affair more entertaining if they knew exactly what was at stake, and what their own chances were.

'Basically,' he said urbanely, 'it's a hunt. We call it the Game. It doesn't exist, not officially; not even within the relatively lawless environs of Canopy. They know about it, and speak about it, but always with discretion.'

'Who?' I said, for the sake of saying something.

'Postmortals, immortals, whatever you want to call them. They don't all play it, or even want to play it, but they all know someone who *has* played it, or has connections with the network which makes the Game possible in the first place.'

'This been going on long?'

'Only in the last seven years. Perhaps one might think of it as a barbaric counterpoint to the gentility which pervaded Yellowstone before the fall.'

'Barbaric?'

'Oh, exquisitely so. That's why we adore it. There's nothing intricate or subtle about the Game, methodologically or psychologically. It needs to be capable of being organised at very short notice, anywhere in the city. There are rules, naturally, but you don't need a trip to the Pattern Jugglers to understand them.'

'Tell me about these rules, Waverly.'

'Oh, they're nothing that need concern you, Mirabel. All you need do is run.'

'And then?'

'Die. And die well.' He spoke kindly, like an indulgent uncle. 'That's all we ask of you.'

'Why do you do it?'

'To take another's life is a special kind of thrill, Mirabel. To do it while being immortal elevates the act to an entirely different level of sublimity.' He paused, as if marshalling his thoughts. 'We don't really grasp the nature of death, even in these difficult times. But by taking a life – especially the life of someone who wasn't immortal, and who therefore already had an acute awareness of death – we can obtain some vicarious sense of what it means.'

'Then the people you hunt are never immortal?'

'Not generally, no. We usually select from the Mulch, picking someone reasonably healthy. We want them to give us a good chase for our money, of course, so we're not above feeding them first.'

He told me more; that the Game was financed by a clandestine network of subscribers. Mostly Canopy, their numbers were rumoured to be augmented by pleasure-seekers from some of the more libertarian carousels still inhabited in the Rust Belt, or some of the other settlements on Yellowstone, like Lorean-ville. Nobody in the network knew more than a handful of other subscribers, and their true identities were camouflaged by an elaborate system of deceits and masques, so that no one could be exposed in the open chambers of Canopy life, which still affected a kind of decadent civility. Hunts were organised at short notice, with small numbers of subscribers alerted at any one time, convening in disused parts of the Canopy. On the same night – or no more than a day before – a victim would be extracted from the Mulch and prepared.

The implants were a recent refinement.

They allowed the progress of the hunt to be shared amongst a larger pool of subscribers, boosting the potential revenue enormously. Other subscribers would help with ground coverage, risking the Mulch to bring video images of the hunt back to the Canopy, with cachets to those who obtained the most spectacular footage. Simple rules of play – which were more strictly enforced than any actual laws which still prevailed in the city – determined the accepted parameters within which the hunt could take place, the permitted tracking devices and weapons, what constituted a fair kill.

'There's just one problem,' I said. 'I'm not from the Mulch. I don't know my way around your city. I'm not sure you're going to get your money's worth.'

'Oh, we'll manage. You'll have an adequate headstart on the hunters. And to be frank, your not being local is actually something of an advantage to us. The locals know far too many shortcuts and hidey-holes.'

'Pretty unsporting of them. Waverly, there's something I want you to know.'

'Yes?'

'I'm going to come back and kill you.'

He laughed. 'Sorry, Mirabel, but I've heard it all before.'

The cable-car landed, the door opened and he invited me to step out.

I started running as the cable-car damped its lights and climbed above me, heading back to the Canopy. Even as it ascended, a dark mote against the milky strands of aerial light, more cars were descending, like fireflies. They were not headed straight for me – that wouldn't have been sporting – but they were certainly headed for my general part of the Mulch.

The Game had started.

I kept running.

If the area of the Mulch where the rickshaw kid had left me was a bad one, then this was something else: a territory so depopulated that it could not even be termed dangerous in the same sense – unless you happened to be the unwilling participant in a night's hunt. There were no fires burning in the lower levels, and the encrustations around the structures had a look of deserted neglect: half-collapsed and inaccessible. The surface roads were even more dilapidated than those I had travelled earlier, cracked and twisted like strips of toffee, apt to end abruptly in mid-span as they crossed a flooded abyss, or simply to plunge into the flood itself. It was dark, and I had to constantly watch my footing.

Waverly had done me a kind of favour, dimming the interior lights as we dropped, so that my eyes had at least accustomed themselves to the darkness, but I didn't feel an overwhelming rush of gratitude.

I ran, glancing over my shoulder to watch the cable-cars as they sank lower, dropping behind the closest structures. The vehicles were close enough now that I could see their occupants. For some reason, I'd assumed that only the man and the woman would be chasing me, but obviously this wasn't the case. Maybe – in the way these things were handled in the network – it was just their turn to find a victim, and I had strolled blithely into their plans.

Was this how I was going to die, I thought? I'd nearly died dozens of times in the war; dozens more times while working for Cahuella. Reivich had tried to kill me at least twice, and had nearly succeeded on both occasions. But if I hadn't managed to have survived any of those earlier brushes with death, I would at least have admitted some grudging respect for my adversaries, a sense that I had chosen to do battle with them, and thereby accepted whatever fate had in mind for me.

But I hadn't chosen anything like this.

Seek shelter, I thought. There were buildings all around me, even if it wasn't immediately clear how to get inside any of them. My movements would be limited once I was inside, but if I stayed outside there would be plenty of opportunities for the chasers to get a clear shot at me. And I clung to the idea – unsupported by any evidence – that the implanted transmitter might not function so well if I was concealed. I also had a suspicion that close combat was not the kind of endgame my pursuers really wanted; that they would rather shoot me from a distance, crossing open ground. If so, I was more than happy to disappoint them, even if it only bought me minutes.

Up to my knees in water, I waded as quickly as I could to the unlit side of the nearest building, a fluted structure which climbed for seven or eight hundred metres above my head before turning mutant, fanning out into the Canopy. Unlike some of the other structures I had seen, this one had suffered considerable damage at street level, punctured and holed like a lightning-struck tree. Some of the apertures were only niches, but others must reach deeper, into the structure's dead heart, from where I might be able to access higher levels.

Light scythed across the ruined exterior, harsh and blue. Crouching into the flood so that my chest was fully submerged and the stench almost unbearable, I waited for the searchlight to complete its business. I could hear voices now, raised like a pack of jackals in musk. Man-shaped patches of utter blackness flitted between the closest buildings, beckoning each other, arms laden with those instruments of murder permitted by the Game.

A few desultory shots rained against the building, dislodging shards of calcified masonry into the flood. Another patch of light began sweeping the side, grazing only inches above my head. My breathing, laboured as it was by the pressure of the filthy water, was like a barking weapon itself.

I sucked in air and lowered myself into the flood.

I could see nothing, of course, but that was hardly a handicap. Relying on touch, I skirted my fingers against the building's side until I found a place where the wall curved abruptly in. I heard more shots, transmitted through the water, and more splashes. I wanted to vomit. But then I remembered the smile of the man who had arranged for my capture and realised I wanted *him* to die first; Fischetti and then Sybilline. Then I'd kill Waverly while I was at it, and piece by piece I'd dismantle the entire apparatus of the Game.

In that same moment I realised that I hated them more than I hated Reivich.

But he'd get his, too.

Still kneeling beneath the waterline, I closed my fists around the edges of the aperture and thrust myself into the building's interior. I could not have been beneath water for more than a few seconds, but I slammed upward with so much anger and relief that I almost screamed as air rushed into my mouth. But apart from gasping, I made as little noise as possible.

I found a relatively dry ledge and hauled myself from the murk. And there, for long moments, I just lay, until my breathing settled down and enough oxygen reached my brain for it to resume the business of thinking, rather than simply keeping me alive.

I heard voices and shots outside, louder now. And sporadically, blue light stabbed through rents in the building, making my eyes sting.

When the darkness resumed, I looked up and saw something.

It was faint – fainter, in fact, than I had imagined any visible object could possibly be. I had read that the human retina was in principle capable of detecting only two or three photons at at time, if conditions of sufficient sensitivity were reached. I had also heard – and met – soldiers who claimed extraordinary night vision; soldiers who spent every hour in darkness, for fear of losing their acclimatisation.

I'd never been one of them.

What I was looking at was a staircase, or the ruined skeleton of what had once been a staircase. A spiral thing, ribbed by cross-members, which reached a landing and then climbed higher towards an irregular gash of pale light, against which it was silhouetted.

'He's inside. Thermal trace in the water.'

That was Sybilline's voice, or someone who sounded very much like her, with the same tone of arrogant surety. Now a man spoke, knowingly, 'That's unusual for a Mulch. They don't like the insides, usually. Too many ghost stories.'

'It isn't just ghost stories. There are pigs down here. We should be careful, too.'

'How are we going to get in? I'm not going in that water, no matter what the bloodmoney is.'

'I have structural maps of this one. There's another route on the other side. Better hurry, though. Skamelson's team are only a block down-trace, and they've got better sniffers.'

I heaved myself from the ledge and moved towards the lower end of the ruined staircase. I hit it too soon, judging the distance poorly. But it was growing clearer all the time. I could see that it climbed ten or fifteen metres above me before vanishing through a sagging, doughlike ceiling which more resembled a stomach diaphragm than anything architectural.

What I could not tell, for all my visual acuity, was how near my chasers were, or how structurally sound the staircase was going to be. If it collapsed while I was climbing, I would fall into the flood, but the water would be too shallow for the drop to be endured without some kind of injury.

Still, I climbed, using the ghostly banister where it existed, heaving myself across gaps in the treads, or where there were no treads at all. The staircase creaked, but I just kept on – even when the tread on which I'd just placed my weight shattered and dropped into the water.

Below me, light filled the chamber, and then black-clad figures emerged through a hole in one wall, trudging through the water. I could see them quite clearly: Fischetti and Sybilline, both masked and carrying enough firepower for a small war. I paused on the landing I'd reached. There was darkness on either side of me, but even as I looked at it details began to emerge from the blackness like solidifying phantoms. I thought about going left or right rather than higher, knowing that I'd have to make the decision quickly and that I didn't want to get trapped in a dead-end.

Then something else emerged from the darkness. It was crouched, and at first I thought it was a dog. But it was much too large for that, and its flat face looked a lot more like a pig. The thing began to stand up on its legs as far as the low ceiling would allow. It was roughly human in build, but instead of fingers on each hand it had a set of five elongated trotters, both sets of which were gripping a vicious-looking crossbow. It was clothed in what looked like patches of leather and crudely fashioned metal, like mediaeval armour. Its flesh was pale and hairless and its face was somewhere between human and pig, with just enough attributes of each to make the composite deeply disturbing. Its eyes were two small black absences and its mouth was curved in a permanent gluttonous smile. Behind it I could see another couple of pigs approaching in the same four-footed manner. The way their back legs were articulated seemed to make walking awkward at best.

I screamed and kicked out, my foot connecting squarely with the pig's face. The thing fell backwards with a snort of anger, dropping the crossbow. But the others were armed as well, both holding long curved knives. I grabbed the fallen crossbow and hoped that the thing would work when I fired it.

'Get back. Get the hell away from me.'

The pig I'd kicked started up on its hindquarters again. It moved its jaw as if trying to speak, but all that came out was a series of snuffles. Then it reached out towards me, its trotters clasping the air in front of my face.

I fired the crossbow; the bolt thudded into the pig's leg.

It squealed and fell back, clutching the end of the bolt where it protruded. I watched blood trickle out, almost luminously bright. The other two pigs moved towards me, but I shuffled backwards with the crossbow still in my hands. I pulled a fresh bolt from the cache in the bow's stock and fumbled it into place, winching back the mechanism. The pigs raised their knives, but hesitated to come closer. Then they snorted angrily and began to drag the wounded one back into the darkness. I froze for an instant, then resumed my ascent, hoping to reach the gap before either the pigs or the hunters got to me.

I almost made it.

Sybilline saw me first, shrieking in either delight or fury. She raised a hand and her little gun appeared in it, springing from the sleeve-holster I had guessed she was wearing. Almost simultaneously, a flash of muzzle-fire whitened the chamber, the pain of its brilliance lancing into my eyes.

Her first shot shattered the staircase below me, the entire structure crashing down like a spiral snowstorm. She had to duck to avoid the debris, and then she got off another shot. I was halfway through the ceiling, halfway into whatever lay beyond, reaching out with my hands for some kind of purchase. Then I felt her shot gnaw into my thigh, soft at first, and then causing pain to blossom like a flower opening at dawn.

I dropped the crossbow. It tumbled down the flight of stairs onto the landing, where I saw a pig snatch it from the darkness with a snort of triumph.

Fischetti raised his own weapon, got off another shot, and that took care of what remained of the staircase. If his aim had been any better – or if I had been any slower – his shot might also have taken care of my leg.

But instead, holding the agony at bay, I slithered onto the ceiling and lay very still. I had no idea what kind of weapon the woman had used; whether my wound had been caused by a projectile or a pulse of light or plasma, nor could I know how severe was the wound. I was probably bleeding, but my clothes were so sodden, and the surface on which I was lying was so damp, that I couldn't tell where blood ended and rain began. And for a moment that was unimportant. I'd escaped them, if only for the time it would take them to find a way up to this level of the building. They had blueprints of the structure, so it would not take long, then, if a route existed at all.

'Get up, if you're able.'

The voice was calm and unfamiliar, and it came not from below, but from a little above me.

'Come now; there isn't much time. Ah, wait. I don't expect you can see me. Is this better?'

And suddenly it was all I could do to screw my eyes shut against the sudden glare. A woman stood over me, dressed like the other Canopy players in all the sombre shades of black: dark, extravagantly heeled boots which reached to her thighs, jet-black greatcoat which skirted the ground and rose behind her neck to encircle her head, which was itself englobed in a helmet which was more black openwork than anything solid, like a gauze, with goggles like the faceted eyes of insects covering half her face. What I could see of her face, in all this, was so pale it was literally white, like a sketch that had never been tinted. A diagonal black tattoo traced each cheekbone, tapering towards her lips, which were the darkest red imaginable, like cochineal.

In one hand she held a huge rifle, its scorched energy-discharge muzzle pointed at my head. But it did not appear that she was aiming the rifle at me.

Her other hand, gloved in black, was reaching out to me.

'I said you'd better move, Mirabel. Unless you're planning to die here.'

She knew the building, or at least this part of it. We didn't have far to go. That was good, because locomotion was no longer my strong point. I could just about move along if I allowed one wall to take most of my weight, freeing the injured leg, but it was neither rapid nor elegant, and I knew I would not be able to sustain it for more than a few dozen metres before blood loss or shock or fatigue took their debt.

She took me up one flight – intact, this time – and then we emerged into the night air. It was a measure of how squalid the last few minutes had been that the air hit my lungs as something cooling and fresh and clean. But I felt myself on the verge of unconsciousness, and still had no real idea what was happening. Even when she showed me a small cable-car, parked in a kind of rubble-strewn cave in the building's side, I could not quite adjust my perceptions to accept that I was being rescued.

'Why are you doing this?' I asked.

'Because the Game stinks,' she said, pausing to mouth a subvocal command at the vehicle, causing it to jerk to life and slink towards us, retracted grapples finding purchase points amongst the dangling debris which covered the cave's ceiling. 'The Gamers think they have the tacit support of the entire Canopy, but they don't. Maybe once, when it wasn't quite so barbaric – but not now.'

I fell into the vehicle's interior, sprawling across the rear seat. Now I could see that my Mendicant trousers were covered in blood, like rust. But the bleeding seemed to have stopped, and while I felt light-headed, it hadn't got any worse in the last few minutes.

While she lowered herself into the pilot's seat and brought the controls on line, I said, 'There was a time when this wasn't barbaric?'

'Once, yes – immediately after the plague.' Her gloved hands took hold of a pair of matched brass joysticks and pushed them forward and I felt the cable-car glide out of the cave with rapid whisking sounds of its arms. 'The victims used to be criminals; Mulch they caught invading the Canopy or committing crimes against their own sort; murderers or rapists or looters.'

'That makes it all right, then.'

'I'm not condoning it. Not at all. But at least there was some kind of moral equilibrium. These people were scum. And they were chased by scum.'

'And now?'

'You're talkative, Mirabel. Most people who've taken a shot like that don't want to do anything except scream.' As she spoke, we left the cave, and for a moment I felt sickening free-fall as the cable-car dropped, before finding a nearby cable and correcting its descent. Then we were rising. 'In answer to your question,' she said, 'there started to be a problem finding suitable victims. So the organisers began to get a little less – how shall I put it? Discriminatory?'

'I understand,' I said. 'I understand, because all I did was wander into the wrong part of the Mulch by mistake. Who are you, by the way? And where are you taking me?'

She reached up one hand and removed the gauzy helmet and faceted goggles, so that, when she turned around to face me, I could see her properly. 'I'm Taryn,' she said. 'But my friends in the sabotage movement call me Zebra.'

I realised I'd seen her earlier that night, amongst the clientèle at the stalk. She had seemed beautiful and exotic then, but she was even more so now. Perhaps it helped that I was lying down in pain having just been shot, fevered with the adrenalin which came from unexpected survival. Beautiful and very strange – and, in the right light, perhaps barely human at all. Her skin was either chalk-white or hard-edged black. The stripes covered her forehead and cheekbones, and from what I remembered seeing in the stalk, a large fraction of the rest of her. Black stripes curved from the edges of her eyes, like flamboyant mascara applied with maniacal precision. Her hair was a stiff black crest which probably ran all the way down her back.

'I don't think I've met anyone like you before, Zebra.'

'It's nothing,' she said. 'Some of my friends think I'm rather conservative; rather unadventurous. You're not Mulch, are you, Mister Mirabel?'

'You know my name, what else do you know about me?'

'Not as much as I'd like to.' She took her hand from the controls, having set the machine into some kind of auto-pilot mode, allowing it to pick its own trajectory through the interstices of the Canopy.

'Shouldn't you be driving this thing?'

'It's safe, Tanner, believe me. The control system of a cable-car is quite intelligent – almost as smart as the machines we had before the plague. But it's best not to spend too much time down in the Mulch with a machine like this.'

'About my earlier question . . .'

'We know you arrived in the city wearing Ice Mendicant clothes and that someone called Tanner Mirabel is known to the Mendicants.' I was about to ask Zebra how she knew this much, but she was already continuing, 'What we don't know is whether or not this is all a carefully constructed identity to suit some other purpose. Why did you allow yourself to be captured, Tanner?'

'I was curious,' I said, feeling like a repetitious refrain in a third-rate symphony – maybe one of Quirrenbach's early efforts. 'I didn't know much about the social stratification in Yellowstone. I wanted to reach the Canopy, and I didn't know how to go about it without threatening anyone.'

'That's understandable. There isn't any way.'

'How did you find any of this out?'

'Through Waverly.' She looked at me carefully, squinting deep black eyes, causing the stripes on one side of her face to bunch together. 'I don't know if he introduced himself, but Waverly was the man who shot you with the stun beam.'

'You know him?'

She nodded. 'He's one of ours – or at least, he has sympathies with us, and we have means of ensuring his compliance. He likes to indulge certain tastes.'

'He told me he was a sadist, but I thought it was part of the banter.'

'It wasn't, believe me.'

I winced as a wave of pain raced up my leg. 'How do you know my name?'

'Waverly passed it to us. Before that, we'd never even heard of Tanner Mirabel. But once we had a name, we could backtrack and confirm your movements. He didn't get much, though. Either he was lying – which I don't rule out; it's not like I particularly trust the one-eyed bastard – or else your memories really are confused.'

'I had revival amnesia. That's why I spent time with the Mendicants.'

'Waverly seemed to think it went deeper than that. That you might have had something to hide. Is that possible, Tanner? If I'm going to help you, it might help if I trusted you.'

'I'm who you think I am,' I said, which seemed to be all I could manage just then. The odd thing was, I wasn't quite sure I believed myself.

Something strange happened then: a hard, sharp discontinuity in my thoughts. I was still conscious; still aware of myself sitting in Zebra's cable-car; still aware that we were moving through Chasm City at night and that she had rescued me from Sybilline's little hunting party. I was conscious of the pain in my leg – even though it had abated to a dull throb of highly concentrated discomfort by then.

And yet a chunk of Sky Haussmann's life had just revealed itself to me.

The previous episodes had come during unconsciousness, like orchestrated dreams, but this one had exploded, fully-formed, into my mind. The effect was disturbing and disconcerting, interrupting the normal flow of my thoughts like an EMP burst playing momentary havoc with a computer system.

The episode, mercifully, was not a long one. Sky was still with Balcazar (Christ, I thought – I was even remembering the names of the supporting characters); still ferrying him across space to the meeting – the conclave – aboard the other ship, the *Palestine*.

What had happened last time? That was it – Balcazar had told Sky about the sixth ship being real; the ghost ship.

The one Norquinco had called the *Caleuche*.

By the time he had turned the revelation over in his head, examining it from every angle, they were almost there. The *Palestine* loomed huge, looking very much like the *Santiago* – all the ships of the Flotilla were built to more or less the same design – but without quite the same degree of discoloration around her rotating hull. She had been much further away from the *Islamabad* when she went up, the flash of energy weakened by the inverse square law of radiative propagation until it was barely a warm breeze, rather than the killing flux which had burned the shadow of his mother onto the skin of his own ship. They had their problems, of course. There had been viral outbreaks, psychoses, putches, and as many sleepers had died aboard that ship as aboard the *Santiago*. He thought of her burdened with her own dead; cold corpses strung along her spine like rotten fruit.

A harsh voice said, 'Diplomatic flight TG5, transfer command to *Palestine* docking network.'

Sky did as he was asked; there was a jolt as the larger ship hijacked the shuttle's avionics and slotted it onto an approach course, with what felt like minimal concern for the comfort of its human occupants. Projected onto the cockpit window, the approach corridor floated in space, edged in skeletal orange neon. The stellar backdrop began to cartwheel; they were moving in the same rotational frame as the *Palestine* now, sliding towards an open parking bay. Suited figures in unfamiliar uniforms floated there to greet them, aiming weapons with something that was not quite diplomatic cordiality.

He turned to Balcazar as the taxi found a berth. 'Sir? We're nearly there.'

'What, oh? Damn you, Titus . . . I was sleeping!'

Sky wondered how his father had felt about the old man. He wondered if Titus had ever considered killing the Captain.

It would not, he thought, present insurmountable difficulties.

NINETEEN

'Tanner? Snap out of it. I don't want you falling unconscious on me.'

We were approaching a building now – if you could call it that. It looked more like an enchanted tree, huge and gnarled branches pocked with haphazard windows, and cable-car landing decks set amongst the limbs. Cableway threads reached through the interstices of the major branches, and Zebra guided us in fearlessly, as if she had navigated this approach thousands of times. I looked down, through vertiginous layers of branches, the firelights of the Mulch twinkling sickeningly far below.

Zebra's apartment in the Canopy was near the middle of the city, on the edge of the chasm, near the inner dome boundary which surrounded the great belching hole in Yellowstone's crust. We had travelled some way around the chasm and from the landing deck I could see the tiny, jewelled sliver of the stalk projecting out for one horizontal kilometre, far below us and around the great curve of the chasm's edge. I looked down into the chasm but I couldn't see any sign of the luminous gliders, or any other mist-jumpers taking the great fall.

'Do you live here alone?' I asked when she had led me into her rooms, striking what I hoped was the right note of polite curiosity.

'Now I do, yes.' The answer was quick, almost glib. But she continued speaking. 'I used to share this place with my sister, Mavra.'

'And Mavra left?'

'Mavra got killed.' She left that remark hanging there long enough to have its effect. 'She got too close to the wrong people.'

'I'm sorry,' I said, fishing for something to say. 'Were these people hunters, like Sybilline?'

'Not exactly, no. She was curious about something she shouldn't have been, and she asked the wrong kinds of questions of the wrong people, but it wasn't directly to do with the hunt.'

'What, then?'

'Why are you so interested in knowing?'

'I'm not exactly an angel, Zebra, but I don't like the idea of someone dying just because they were curious.'

'Then you'd better be careful you don't ask the wrong kinds of question yourself.'

'About what, exactly?'

She sighed, obviously wishing our conversation had never taken this tack. 'There's a substance . . .'

'Dream Fuel?'

'You've encountered it, then?'

'I've seen it being used, but that's about the extent of my knowledge. Sybilline used it in my presence, but I didn't notice any change in her behaviour before or afterwards. What is it, exactly?'

'It's complicated, Tanner. Mavra had only pieced together a few parts of the story before they got her.'

'It's a drug of some sort, obviously.'

'It's a lot more than a drug. Look, can we talk about something else? It hasn't been easy for me to deal with her being gone, and this is just opening up old wounds.'

I nodded, willing to let it lie for now. 'You were close, weren't you?'

'Yes,' she said, as if I'd picked up on some profound secret in their relationship. 'And Mavra loved it here. She said it had the best view anywhere in the city, apart from the stalk. But when she was around we could never have afforded to eat in that place.'

'You haven't done too badly. If you like heights.'

'You don't, Tanner?'

'I guess it takes some getting used to.'

Her apartment, ensconced in one of the major branches, was a complex of intestinally twisted rooms and corridors; more like an animal's sett than anything a human would choose for use. The rooms were in one of the narrower branches, suspended two kilometres above the Mulch, with lower levels of the Canopy hanging below, linked to ours by vertical threads, strands and hollowed-out trunks.

She led me into what might have been her living room.

It was like entering an internal organ in some huge, walk-through model of the human anatomy. The walls, floor and ceiling were all softly rounded into each other. Level surfaces had been created by cutting into the fabric of the building, but they had to be stepped on different levels, connected by ramps and stairs. The surfaces of the walls and ceiling were rigid, but uneasily organic in nature; veined or patterned with irregular platelets. In one wall was what looked like a piece of expensive, *in-situ* sculpture: a tableau of three roughly hewn people who had been depicted forcing their way out of the wall, clawing to escape from it like swimmers trying to outswim the wall of a tsunami wave.

Most of their bodies were hidden; all you could see was half a face or the end of a limb, but the effect was forceful enough.

'You have pretty unique taste in art, Zebra,' I said. 'I think that would give me nightmares.'

'It's not art, Tanner.'

'Those were real people?'

'Still are, by some definitions. Not alive, but not exactly dead either. More like fossils, but with the fossil structure so intricate that you can almost map neurons. I'm not the only one with them, and no one really wants to cut them away in case someone thinks of a way to get them back the way they were. So we live with them. No one used to want to share a room with them, once, but now I hear it's quite the chic thing to have a few of them in your apartment. There's even a man in the Canopy who makes fake ones, for the truly desperate.'

'But these are real?'

'Credit me with some taste, Tanner. Now, I think you need to sit down for a moment. No; stay where you are.'

She snapped her fingers at her couch.

The larger items of Zebra's furniture were autonomous, responding to our presence like nervous pets. The couch perambulated from its station, neatly stepping down to our level. In contrast to the Mulch, where nothing much more advanced than steam power could be relied upon, there were obviously still machines of reasonable sophistication in the Canopy. Zebra's rooms were full of them; not just furniture, but servitors ranging from mice-sized drones to large ceiling-tracked units, as well as fist-sized fliers. You had only to reach for something and it would scuttle helpfully closer to your hand. The machines must have been crude compared to what had existed before the plague, but I still felt like I'd wandered into a room animated by poltergeists.

'That's right; sit down,' Zebra said, easing my transition onto her couch. 'And just lie still. I'll be back in a moment.'

'Believe me, I'm not going anywhere in a hurry.'

She disappeared from the room, and I lolled in and out of consciousness, for all that I was unwilling to surrender myself to sleep so easily. No more Sky dreams. When Zebra returned she had removed her coat, and she carried two glasses of something hot and herbal. I let it run down my throat, and while I couldn't say it actively improved the way I felt, it was an improvement on the gallons of Mulch rainwater which I had already consumed.

Zebra had not returned alone: gliding behind her had come one of her larger ceiling-tracked servitors, a multi-limbed white cylinder with an ovoid glowing green face alive with flickering medical readouts. The machine descended until it could bring its sensors into play on my leg, chirruping and projecting status graphics as it diagnosed the severity of the wound.

'Well? Do I live or die?'

'You're lucky,' Zebra said. 'The gun she used against you? It was a low-yield laser; a duelling weapon. It's not designed to do any real harm unless it touches vital organs, and the beam's finely collimated, so the surrounding tissue damage is pretty minimal.'

'You could have fooled me.'

'Well, I never said it wouldn't hurt like hell. But you'll live, Tanner.'

'Nonetheless,' I said, grimacing as the machine probed the entry wound with minimal gentleness, 'I don't think I'll be able to walk on it.'

'You won't have to. At least not until tomorrow. The machine can heal you while you sleep.'

'I'm not sure I feel like sleeping.'

'Why – have you got a problem with it?'

'It might surprise you, but yes, actually I have.' She looked at me blankly, so I decided there was no harm in telling her about the indoctrinal virus. 'They could have cleaned it out in Hospice Idlewild, but I didn't want to wait. So now I get a quick trip into Sky Haussmann's head every time I fall asleep.' I showed her the scab of blood in the middle of my palm.

'A man with a wound, come to our mean streets to right some wrongs?'

'I've come to finish some business, that's all. But you'll understand the idea of sleeping doesn't exactly fill me with overwhelming enthusiasm. Sky Haussmann's head isn't a pleasant place to spend any great length of time.'

'I don't know much about him. It would be ancient history even if it wasn't another planet as well.'

'It doesn't feel like ancient history to me. It feels like he's slowly worming his way into me, like a voice that keeps getting louder and louder in my head. I met a man who had the virus before I did – in fact, he probably gave it to me. He was pretty far gone. He had to surround himself with Sky Haussmann iconography or he started shaking.'

'That doesn't have to happen here,' Zebra said. 'Has the indoctrinal virus been around for a few years?'

'It depends on the strain, but the viruses themselves are an old invention.'

'Then you might be in luck. If the virus showed up in Yellowstone's medical databases before the plague hit, the servitor will know about it. It might even be able to synthesise a cure.'

'The Mendicants thought it would take a few days to take effect.'

'They were probably being over-cautious. A day, perhaps two – that should be all the time it takes to flush it out. *If* the robot knows about it.' Zebra patted the white machine. 'But it will do its best. Now will you think about sleeping?'

I had to find Reivich, I told myself. That meant not wasting any time at my disposal; not a single hour. I had already wasted half a night since arriving in Chasm City. But it would take more than another couple of hours to track him down, I knew. Days, perhaps. I would only last that time if I allowed my recent injuries some time to heal. It would be sweet irony if I dropped dead of fatigue just as I was about to kill Reivich. For him, anyway. I wouldn't be laughing.

'I'll think about it,' I said.

The odd thing was, after all that I had told Zebra, this time I didn't dream about Sky Haussmann at all.

I dreamt about Gitta.

She'd always been there in my thoughts, ever since waking in Idlewild. Just thinking about her beauty – and the fact that she was dead – was like a mental whiplash; a crack of pain against which my senses never seemed to dull. I could hear the way she spoke; smell her as if she were standing next to me, listening intently while I gave her one of the lessons Cahuella had insisted upon. I don't think there had been a minute since I'd arrived around Yellowstone when Gitta had left me completely. When I saw another woman's face, I measured her against Gitta – even if that measurement took place on a barely conscious level. I knew with a heartfelt certainty that she was dead, and although I could not absolve myself of all responsibility for her death, it was Reivich that had really killed her.

And yet, I had given very little thought to the events leading up to her death, and almost none to her death itself.

Now they came crashing in.

I didn't dream it like this, of course. The episodes from Sky Haussmann's life might have played through my head in a neatly linear fashion – even if some of the events in those episodes contradicted what I thought I knew about him – but my own dreams were as disorganised and illogical as anyone's. So while I dreamed about the journey up the Peninsula, and the ambush that had ended with Gitta's death, it wasn't with the clarity of the Haussmann episodes. But afterwards, when I woke, it was as if the act of dreaming had unlocked a whole raft of memories which I had barely realised were missing. In the morning, I was able to think in detail about all that had happened.

The last thing I'd remembered in any depth was when Cahuella and I had been taken aboard the Ultra ship, where Captain Orcagna had warned us against Reivich's planned attack on the Reptile House. Reivich, the captain said, was moving south down through the jungle. They were tracking him via the emissions from the heavy armaments his party was carrying.

It was good that Cahuella had completed his dealings with the Ultras as soon as he had. He had taken a significant risk in visiting the orbiting ship even then, but only a week afterwards it would have been nearly impossible. The bounty on him had increased enough that some of the neutral observer factions had declared that they would intercept any vessel known to be carrying Cahuella, shooting it down if arrest was not an option. If less had been at stake, the Ultras might have ignored that kind of threat, but now they had made their presence officially known and were engaged in sensitive trade negotiations with those selfsame factions. Cahuella was effectively confined to the surface – and a steadily diminishing area of it at that.

But Orcagna had stayed true to his word. He was still feeding us information on Reivich's position as he moved south towards the Reptile House, at the fuzzy accuracy which Cahuella had requested.

Our plan was simple enough. There were very few routes through the jungle north of the Reptile House, and Reivich had already committed himself to one of the major trails. There was a point on the trail where the jungle had encroached badly, and it was there that we would lay our ambush.

'We'll make an expedition of it,' Cahuella had said, as he and I pored over a map table in the basement of the Reptile House. 'That's prime hamadryad country, Tanner. We've never been there before – never had the opportunity. Now Reivich is giving it to us on a plate.'

'You've already got a hamadryad.'

'A juve.' He said it contemptuously, as if the animal were almost not worth having. I had to smile, remembering how triumphant he'd been at its capture. To capture any size of hamadryad alive was quite an achievement, but now he had set his sights higher. He was the classic hunter, incapable of being sated. There was always a bigger kill out there to taunt him, and he always deluded himself that after *that* one there would be yet another, as yet undreamt of.

He stabbed the map again. 'I want an adult. A near-adult, I should say.'

'No one's ever caught a near-adult hamadryad alive.'

'Then I'll have to be the first, won't I?'

'Leave it,' I said. 'We've enough of a hunt on our hands with Reivich. We can always use this trip to scope the terrain and go back in a few months with a full hunting expedition. We don't even have a vehicle that could carry a dead near-adult, let alone a live one.'

'I've been thinking about it,' he said. 'And doing some preliminary work on the problem. C'mon, let me show you something, Tanner.'

I had a horrible sinking feeling.

We walked through connecting corridors into another part of the Reptile House's basement levels. Down in the basement vivaria there were hundreds of large display cases, equipped with humidifiers and temperature control for the comfort of reptilian guests. Most of the creatures that would have filled these exhibits moved in conditions of low light, along the forest floor. The cases would have held realistic habitats for them, stocked with exactly the right kinds of flora. The largest was a series of stepped rockpools into which a pair of boa constrictors would have been introduced, but the embryos had been damaged years earlier.

By any strict definition, there were no creatures on Sky's Edge that were exactly reptilian. Reptiles, even on Earth, were only one possible evolutionary outcome from a vast range of possibilities.

The largest invertebrates on Earth had been squid, but on Sky's Edge, invertebrate forms had invaded land as well. No one really knew why life had gone down this road, but the best guess was that some catastrophic event had made the oceans shrink to perhaps half their previous area, exposing vast new areas of dry ground. Life on the ocean fringes had been given a huge incentive to adapt to land. The backbone had just never been invented, and through slow, fumbling, mindless ingenuity, evolution had managed to do without it. Life on Sky's Edge was genuinely spineless. The largest animals – the hamadryads – maintained structural rigidity through the pressure of circulatory fluids alone, pumped by hundreds of hearts spread throughout the creature's volume.

But they were cold-blooded, regulating their body temperatures by their surroundings. There had never been a winter on Sky's Edge; nothing to select for mammal-like creatures. It was that cold-bloodedness which was most evocative of the reptilian. It meant that Sky's Edge animals moved slowly, feeding infrequently, and lived to great ages. The largest of them, the hamadryads, did not even die in any familiar sense. They simply changed.

The connecting corridor opened out into the largest of the basement chambers, where we kept the juvenile. Originally this area had been intended for a family of crocodiles, but they were on ice for now. The entire display area which they had been assigned was just barely large enough for the young hamadryad. Fortunately, it had not grown perceptibly bigger in its time in captivity, but we would certainly have to build a huge new chamber if Cahuella was serious about bagging a near-adult.

It was some months since I had seen the juvenile. Frankly, it did not interest me greatly. Eventually it dawned on one that the creature did not actually do very much. Its appetite was negligible once it had fed. Typically, it would curl up and enter a state not far from death. Hamadryads had no real predators so they could afford to digest their food and conserve energy in peace.

Now we overlooked the deep white-walled pit which had been originally intended for the crocs. Rodriguez, one of my men, was leaning over the side, sweeping the bottom with a ten-metre-long broom. That was how far below us the floor was, surrounded by sheer walls in white ceramic. Sometimes Rodriguez had to go into the pit to fix something, a task I never greatly envied him, even when the juvenile was on the other side of a barrier. There were just some places in life where it was best not to be, and a snake pit was one of them. Rodriguez grinned at me beneath his moustache, hauling the broom out and racking it on the wall behind him, along with an array of similarly long-handled tools: claws, anaesthetic harpoons, electrical prods and such like.

'How was your trip to Santiago?' I said. He had been down there on business for us, exploring new lines of trade.

'Glad to be back, Tanner. The place is full of aristocratic arseholes. They talk about indicting the likes of us for war crimes and at the same time they hope the war never ends because it adds some colour to their miserable rich lives.'

'Some of us they already have indicted,' Cahuella said.

Rodriguez picked leaves from the broom's bristles. 'Yeah, I heard. Still, this year's war criminal is next year's saviour of the people, right? Besides – we all know guns don't kill people, do they?'

'No, it's the small metal projectiles that generally do the killing,' Cahuella said, smiling. He fingered the cattle-prod lovingly, perhaps remembering the time he had used it to shepherd the juvenile into its transport cage. 'How is my baby, anyway?'

'I'm a little worried about that skin infection. Do these things moult?'

'I don't think anyone knows. We'll probably be the first to find out if they do.' Cahuella leaned over the wall – it was waist height – and looked down into the pit. It looked unfinished. Here and there were a few sparse attempts at vegetation, but we had quickly discovered that the hamadryad behaviour appeared to have very little to do with its surroundings. It breathed and smelled prey and occasionally ate. Otherwise it just lay coiled like the hawser of a vast maritime ship.

Even Cahuella had become bored with it after a while – after all, it was just a juvenile: he would be dead long before it grew to anything near its adult size.

The hamadryad wasn't visible. I leaned over the edge, but it was obviously nowhere in the pit itself. There was an alcove, cool and dark, set into the wall beneath us; that was where the thing could usually be found when it was sleeping.

'She's asleep,' Rodriguez said.

'Yeah,' I said. 'Come back in a month and maybe it'll have moved.'

'No,' Cahuella said. 'Take a look at this.'

There was a white metal box set on our side of the wall; I hadn't noticed it before. He flipped open a lid on the box and removed something like a walkie-talkie: a control pad with an aerial and a matrix of controls set into it.

'You're not serious, are you?'

Cahuella stood with his legs slightly apart, the control unit in one hand. With his other hand he jabbed hesitantly at the matrix of buttons, as if not quite certain of the sequence he should be entering. But whatever he did had some effect: I heard the unmistakable dry slithering of the uncoiling snake below us. It was a sound like a sheet of tarpaulin being dragged over concrete.

'What's happening?'

'Have a guess.' He was enjoying himself, leaning over the edge and watching the creature emerge from its hideaway.

The hamadryad might well have been a juvenile, but it was still as large as any I wanted to be this close to. The snakelike body was twelve metres long, as thick as my torso for most of that length. It moved like a snake, of course: there was really only one way for a long, limbless predator to move, especially one that weighed more than a tonne. The body was textureless, almost bloodlessly pale, for the creature was adjusting its skin coloration to match the white walls of the chamber. They had no predators, but they were masters of ambush.

The head was eyeless. No one was exactly sure how the snakes managed that trick of camouflaging themselves when they were blind, but there must have been optical organs distributed around the skin, purely to serve the coloration function and not wired into the higher nervous system at all. Not that they were truly blind, either, for the hamadryad did have a set of eyes, with remarkable acuity, spaced apart for binocular vision. But the eyes were set inside the upper roof of its jaw, analogous to the heat sensors in the mouth of a venomous snake. It was only when the animal opened its mouth to strike that it saw anything of the world. By then a host of other senses – infrared and smell, mainly – would have ensured that it had locked onto likely prey. The jaw-mounted eyes were only there to guide the final moments of the attack. It sounded deeply alien, but I had heard of a mutation in frogs which caused the eyes to grow inside the mouth, with no serious impact on the frog's well-being. It was also the case that terrestrial snakes functioned almost as well blind as sighted.

Now it stopped. It had emerged fully from the alcove, lightly coiled around itself.

'Well?' I said. 'That's a nice trick. Are you going to tell me how it's done?'

'Mind control,' Cahuella said. 'Doctor Vicuna and I drugged it and did a little neural experimentation.'

'The ghoul's been here again?'

Vicuna was the resident veterinarian. He was also an ex-interrogation specialist with a past that was rumoured to harbour a number of war crimes involving medical experiments on prisoners.

'The ghoul is an expert in methods of neural regimentation. It was Vicuna who mapped the major control nodes of the hamadryad's rather rudimentary central nervous system. Vicuna who developed the simple electrical-stimulation implants which we emplaced at strategic positions throughout what I rather charitably refer to as the creature's brain.'

He told me they had experimented with these implants until they could coax a simple series of behaviour patterns out of the snake. There was nothing too subtle about it, either – the snake's behaviour patterns were simple to begin with. A hamadryad, no matter how large it grew, was basically a hunting machine with a few quite simple subroutines. It was the same with the crocodiles, until we put them on ice. They were dangerous, but easy to work with once you understood how their minds worked. The same stimulus always gave the same result with crocs. The hamadryad's routines were different – honed to life on Sky's Edge – but not much more complex.

'All I did was hit the node that tells the snake it's time to wake up and find some food,' Cahuella said. 'It doesn't really need to feed, of course – we fed it a live goat a week ago – but its little brain doesn't remember that.'

'I'm impressed.' I was, but I was also uncomfortable. 'What else can you get it to do?'

'This is a good one. Watch.'

240

He jabbed at a control and the hamadryad moved with whiplash speed towards the wall. The jaws opened at the last instant, the blunt head smacking into the ceramic tiles with tooth-shattering force.

The snake, stunned, retreated into a coil.

'Let me guess. You just made it think it had seen something worth eating.'

'It's child's play,' Rodriguez said, smiling at the demonstration. Evidently he had seen something of it before.

'Look,' Cahuella said. 'I can even make it go back to its hole.'

I watched the snake gather itself and neatly insert itself into the alcove again, until the last of its thigh-thick coils had slipped from view.

'Any point to this?'

'Yeah, of course.' His look at me was one of acute disappointment, that I had not grasped this sooner. 'A brain of a near-adult hamadryad isn't any more complicated than this one. If we can catch ourselves a big one, we can drug it while we're still out in the jungle. We know what tranquillisers work on snake biochemistry from our work on the juvenile. Once the thing's out cold, Vicuna can climb up and implant the same hardware, rigged to another control unit like this one. Then all we've got to do is point the snake towards the Reptile House and tell it there's food in front of its nose. It'll slither all the way home.'

'Through a few hundred kilometres of jungle?'

'What's to stop it? If the thing starts showing signs of malnutrition, we feed it. Otherwise, we just let the bastard slither – isn't that right, Rodriguez?'

'He's right, Tanner. We can follow it in our vehicles; protect it from any other hunters who might want to take a pot at it.'

Cahuella nodded. 'And when it gets here we park it in a new snakepit and tell it to curl up and sleep for a while.'

I smiled, reaching for an obvious technical objection – and came back empty-handed. It sounded insane, but when I tried to pick a hole in any single aspect of it, Cahuella's plan was difficult to fault. We knew enough about the behaviour of near-adults to at least have a good idea where to begin hunting one, and we could increase our tranquilliser dosages accordingly, multiplying by the ratio of body volumes. We would also have to scale up our needles – they would need to be more like harpoons now, but again, that was within our capabilities. Somewhere in his cache of weapons, Cahuella was bound to have harpoon guns.

'We'll still need to dig a new pit,' I said.

'Get your men working on it. They can have it ready by the time we get back.'

'Reivich is just a detail in all this, isn't he? Even if Reivich turned back tomorrow, you'd still find an excuse to go up there and look for your adult.'

Cahuella sealed the control box away and leaned with his back to the wall, studying me critically. 'No. What do you think I am, some kind of obsessive? If it meant that much to me, we'd have been up there already. I'm just saying it'd be stupid to waste an opportunity like this.'

'Two birds with one stone?'

'Two snakes,' he said, with careful emphasis on the last word. 'One literally, one metaphorically.'

'You don't really think of Reivich as a snake, do you? In my book he's just a scared rich kid doing what he thinks is right.'

'What do you care what I think?'

'I think we need to be clear about what's driving him. That way we understand him and can predict his actions.'

'What does it matter? We know where the kid's going to be. We set the ambush and that's that.'

Beneath us, the snake rearranged itself. 'Do you hate him?'

'Reivich? No. I pity him. Sometimes I even think I might sympathise with him. If he was going up against anyone else because they'd killed his family – which, incidentally, I did not do – I might even wish him the best of luck.'

'Is he worth all this?'

'You got an alternative in mind, Tanner?'

'We could deter him. Hit first and take out a few of his men, just to demoralise him. Maybe even that wouldn't be necessary. We could just set some kind of physical barrier – start a forest fire, or something. The monsoons won't arrive for a few weeks. There must be a dozen other things we could do. The kid doesn't necessarily have to die.'

'No; that's where you're wrong. No one goes up against me and lives. I don't give a shit if they've just buried their whole family and their fucking pet dog. It's a point I'm making, understand? If we don't make it now, we'll have to make it over and again in the future, every time some aristocrat cocksucker starts feeling lucky.'

I sighed, seeing that this was not an argument I was going to win. I had known it would come to this: that Cahuella would not be talked out of his hunting expedition. But I had felt some show of disagreement was necessary. I was senior enough in his employment that I was almost obliged to question his orders. It was part of what he paid me for: to play his conscience in the moments when he searched for his own and found only an abscessive hole where one had been.

'But it doesn't have to be personal,' I said. 'We can take out Reivich cleanly, without turning it into some kind of recriminatory bloodbath. You thought you were joking when you said I went for specific areas of brain function when I shot people in the head. But you weren't. I can do that, if it suits the situation.' I thought of the soldiers on my own side I had been forced to assassinate; innocent men and women whose deaths served some inscrutable higher plan. Though it was no kind of absolution from the evil that I had perpetrated, I had always tried to take them out as quickly and painlessly as my expertise allowed. I felt – then – that Reivich deserved something of the same kindness.

242

Now, in Chasm City, I felt something else entirely.

'Don't worry, Tanner. We'll make it nice and quick on him. A real clinical job.'

'Good. I'll be hand-picking my own team, of course . . . is Vicuna coming with us?'

'Of course.'

'Then we'll need two tents. I'm not eating from the same table as the ghoul, no matter what tricks he's learned to do with snakes.'

'There'll be more than two tents, Tanner. Dieterling'll be with us, of course – he knows snakes better than anyone – and I'm taking Gitta as well.'

'There's something I want you to understand,' I said. 'Just going up into the jungle carries some risk. The instant Gitta leaves the Reptile House, she's automatically in greater danger than if she remained. We know some of our enemies keep a close watch on our movements, and we know there are things in the jungle that are best avoided.' I paused. 'I'm not abdicating responsibility, but I want you to know I can't guarantee anyone's safety on this expedition. All I can do is my best – but my best might not be good enough.'

He patted me on the shoulder. 'I'm sure your best will suffice, Tanner. You've never let me down before.'

'There's always a first time,' I said.

Our small hunting convoy consisted of three armoured ground-effect vehicles. Cahuella, Gitta and I rode in the lead vehicle, along with Dieterling. He had his hands on the joystick, guiding us expertly along the overgrown trail. He knew the terrain and was also an expert on hamadryads. It hurt me to think he was dead as well now.

Behind, Vicuna and three other security people rode in the second vehicle: Letelier, Orsono and Schmidt; all with expertise in deep-country work. The third vehicle carried heavy weapons – amongst them the ghoul's harpoon guns – together with ammunition, medical supplies, food and water rations and our deflated bubbletents. It was driven by one of Cahuella's old trustees, while Rodriguez rode shot-gun in the rear, sweeping the path in case anyone tried to attack us from behind.

On the dashboard was a map of the Peninsula divided into grid sections, with our current position marked by a pulsing blue dot. Several hundred kilometres to the north, but on what would eventually become the same track as us, was a red pulse which moved a little south each day. That was Reivich's squad; thinking they were moving covertly, but betrayed by the signatures of their weapons which Orcagna was tracking. They made about fifty or sixty kilometres a day, which was about as good a rate as anyone was capable of maintaining through the jungle. Our plan was to set up camp a day's travel south of Reivich.

In the meantime, we were passing through the lower extent of the hamadryad range. You could see the excitement in Cahuella's eyes as he peered deep into the jungle for a hint of large, slow movement. Near-adults moved so ponderously – and were so invulnerable to any kind of natural predation – that they had never evolved any flight response. The only thing that made a hamadryad move was hunger or the migratory imperative of their breeding cycle. Vicuna said they did not even have what we would think of as a survival instinct. They had no more need of one than a glacier did.

'There's a ham tree,' Dieterling said, towards the end of the day. 'Newly fused, by the look of it.' He pointed off to one side, into what looked like impenetrable gloom. My eyesight was good, but Dieterling's was apparently superhuman.

'God . . .' Gitta said, slipping a pair of camouflaged image-amplifier goggles to her eyes. 'It's huge.'

'They're not small animals,' her husband said. He was looking in the same direction as Dieterling, his eyes squinting intently at something. 'You're right. That tree must have had – what, eight or nine fusions?'

'At the very least,' Dieterling said. 'The most recent fusion might still be in its transition state.'

'Still warm, you mean?' Cahuella said.

I could see the way his mind was working. Where there was a tree with recent growth layers, there might be near-adult hamadryads as well.

We decided to set up camp in the next clearing, a couple of hundred metres further down the trail. The drivers needed a rest after a day pushing through the trail, and the vehicles tended to accumulate minor damage which had to be put right before the next stage. We were in no haste to reach our ambush point and Cahuella liked to spend a few hours each night hunting around the camp's perimeter before retiring.

I used a monofilament scythe to widen the clearing, then helped with the inflation of the bubbletents.

'I'm going into the jungle,' Cahuella said, tapping me on the shoulder. He wore his hunting jacket, a rifle slung over one shoulder. 'I'll be back in an hour or so.'

'Go easy with any near-adults you find,' I said, only half joking.

'This is just a fishing trip, Tanner.'

I reached over to the card table I had set up outside the tent, with some of our equipment on it. 'Here. Don't forget these, especially if you're going to wander far.' I held up the image-amp goggles.

He hesitated, then reached out and took the goggles, slipping them into a shirt pocket. 'Thanks.'

He stepped away from the pool of light around the tents, unhitching the gun as he went. I finished the first tent, the one where Gitta and Cahuella were sleeping, and then went to find her to tell her it was ready. She was sitting in the cab of the vehicle, an expensive compad propped on her lap. She was thumbing through something indolently, skimming pages of what looked like poetry.

'Your tent's done,' I said.

She closed the compad with something like relief and allowed me to lead her towards the tent's opening. I had already checked the clearing for any lurking unpleasantnesses – the smaller, venomous cousins of hamadryads which we called dropwinders – but the place was safe. Still, Gitta moved hesitantly, afraid of putting her foot down on anything other than a brightly lit spot of ground, despite my reassurances.

'You look like you're enjoying yourself,' I said.

'Is that sarcasm, Tanner? Do you expect me to enjoy this?'

'I told him it would be better for all of us if you stayed at the Reptile House.'

I unzipped the opening. Within was a pantry-sized airlock which kept the tent from deflating whenever someone came or went. We set up the three tents at the apexes of a triangle, linked together by pressurised corridors a few strides long. The tiny generator which fed the tents the air which kept them inflated was small and silent. Gitta stepped within and then said, 'Is that what you think, Tanner – that this is no place for a woman? I thought attitudes like that died before they ever launched the Flotilla.'

'No . . .' I said, trying not to sound overly defensive. 'That's not what I think at all.' I moved to seal the outer door between us, so that she could enter the tent in her own privacy.

But she put a hand up and held mine from the zip. 'What is it you think, then?'

'I think what's going to happen here won't be very pleasant.'

'An ambush, you mean? Funny; I'd never have guessed that for myself.'

I said something foolish. 'Gitta, you have to realise, there are things you don't know about Cahuella. Or me, for that matter. Things about the work we do. Things we have done. I think you will soon have a better idea about some of those things.'

'Why are you telling me this?'

'I think you should be ready for it, that's all.' I looked over my shoulder, towards the jungle where her husband had vanished. 'I should get to work on the other tents, Gitta . . .'

When she answered her voice had an odd quality to it. 'Yes, of course.' She was looking at me intently. Perhaps it was the way the light played on it, but her face seemed extraordinarily beautiful to me then; like something painted by Gaugin. I think it was in that instant that my intention to betray Cahuella crystallised. The thought of it must have always been there, but it had taken that instant of searing beauty to bring it to light. If the shadows had fallen slightly differently across her face, I wondered, would I still have made that decision?

'Tanner, you're wrong, you know.'

'About what?'

'Cahuella. I know a lot more about him than you think. A lot more than anyone here thinks they do. I know he's a violent man, and I know he's done terrible things. Evil things. Things you wouldn't even believe.'

'You'd be surprised,' I said.

'No; that's precisely the point, I wouldn't be. I'm not talking about the violent little deeds he's committed since you've known him. They're barely worthy of consideration compared to the things he did before. And unless you're aware of those things, you really don't know him at all.'

'If he's so bad, why do you stay with him?'

'Because he isn't the evil man he used to be.'

Something flashed between the trees; a stammer of blue-white light, followed a moment later by the report of a laser-rifle. Something dropped through foliage to the ground. I imagined Cahuella stepping forward until he had found his kill; probably a small snake.

'Some people would say that an evil man never really changes, Gitta.'

'Then they'd be wrong. It's only our deeds that make us evil, Tanner; they're what define us, nothing else, not our intentions or feelings. But what are a few bad deeds compared to a life, especially the kinds of lives we can live now?'

'Only some of us,' I said.

'Cahuella's older than you think, Tanner. And the evil things he did were a long, long time ago, when he was much younger. They were what led me to him, eventually.' She paused, glancing towards the trees, but before I could ask her what she had meant by that, she was already speaking again. 'But the man I found wasn't an evil one. He was cruel, violent, dangerous, but he was also capable of giving love; of accepting love from another human being. He saw beauty in things; recognised evil in others. He wasn't the man I'd expected to find, but someone better. Not perfect – not by a long stretch – but not a monster; not at all. I found that I couldn't hate him as easily as I'd hoped.'

'You expected to hate him?'

'I expected to do a lot more than that. I expected to kill him, or bring him to justice. Instead . . .' Gitta paused again. There was another crack of blue light from the forest: the deadfall of another animal. 'I found myself asking a question; one I'd never thought of before. How long would you have to live as a good man – doing good – before the sum of your good actions cancelled out something terrible you'd once done? Could any human life be long enough?'

'I don't know,' I answered, truthfully. 'But I do know one thing. Cahuella may be better than he used to be, but he still not anyone's idea of citizen of the month, is he? If you define the way he is now as a man doing good, I'd hate to think what he was like before.'

'You would, yes,' Gitta said. 'And I don't think you could handle it, either.'

I bade her goodnight and returned to preparing the other tents.

TWENTY

In the midmorning, while the others struck camp, five of us walked back on foot until we had reached the point in the track where we had seen the hamadryad tree. From there it was an uncomfortable but short scramble through overgrowth until we reached the flared base. I led the party, sweeping the monofilament scythe ahead of me in an arc which cleared most of the vegetation.

'It's even bigger than it looked from the trail,' Cahuella said. He was rosy-cheeked and jovial this morning, for his hunting last night had been successful, as we had discovered by the carcasses hung up outside the clearing. 'How old do you think it is?'

'It definitely predates the landing,' said Dieterling. 'Four hundred years old, perhaps. We'd need to cut it to know better.' He began to stroll around the tree's circumference, tapping the bark lightly with the back of his knuckles.

With us were Gitta and Rodriguez. They looked up towards the tree's upper reaches, craning their necks and squinting against the sunlight which filtered through the jungle canopy.

'I don't like it,' Gitta said. 'What if . . .'

He had appeared out of earshot, but Dieterling answered her. 'The chances of another snake coming by here are pretty damn minimal. Especially as this one seems to have fused very recently.'

'Are you sure?' Cahuella said.

'Check it out for yourself.'

He was nearly round the back of the tree. We crunched through the overgrowth until we reached him.

The hamadryad trees were a mystery to the first explorers, in those dream-like years before the war began. They had swept through this part of the Peninsula at haste, eyes wide for the wonders of a new world, searching for marvels, knowing that everything would be studied in greater detail in the future. They were like children ripping open presents, scarcely glancing at the contents of each wrapper before beginning to unpeel another gift. There was just too much to be seen.

If they had been methodical, they would have discovered the trees and decided that they were worthy of immediate further study, rather than simply consigning them to the growing list of planetary anomalies. Had they done so, they would only have needed to place a few trees under study for a few years before the secret would have been revealed to them. But it was many decades into the war before the proper nature of the trees was established.

They were rare, but distributed across a large area of the Peninsula. It was that very rarity which had made them the focus of early attention, for the trees were conspicuously different to the other forest species. Each rose to the height of the canopy and no higher – forty or fifty metres above the forest floor, depending on the surrounding growth. Each was shaped like a spiral candlestick, thickening towards the base. Near the top, the trees flared into a wide, flattened structure like a dark green mushroom, tens of metres across. It was these mushrooms which had made the hamadryad trees so obvious to the first explorers, overflying the jungle in one of the *Santiago*'s shuttles.

Now and then they found a clearing near a tree and set down to investigate on foot. The biologists amongst them had struggled to find an explanation for the trees' shapes, or the strange differentiation in cell types which occurred around the tree's perimeter and along radial lines through it. What was clear was that the wood at the heart of the trees was dead growth, with the living matter existing in a relatively thin layer around the husk.

The spiral candlestick analogy was accurate up to a point, but a better description, I felt, was of an enormously tall and thin helter-skelter, like the dilapidated old one I remembered from an abandoned fairground in Nueva Iquique, its pastel blue paint peeling away a little more with each summer. The tree's underlying shape was more or less a tapering cylindrical trunk, but wrapped around this, ascending to the summit, was a helical structure whose spirals did not quite lie in contact with each other. The helix was smooth, patterned in geometric brown and green shapes which shimmered like beaten metal. In the gaps where the underlying trunk was visible, there was often evidence for a similar structure which had been worn down or absorbed into the tree, and perhaps levels of structure behind that too, though only a skilled botanist really had the eye to read those subtleties of tree growth.

Dieterling had indentified the major spiral around this tree. At the base, just where it looked as if the spiral ought to plunge into the ground like a root, it terminated in a hollow opening.

He pointed it out to me. 'It's hollow almost all the way to the top, bro.'

'Meaning what?' Rodriguez said. He knew how to handle the juvenile, but he was no expert on the creatures' biological cycle.

'Meaning it's already hatched,' Cahuella said. 'The juveniles from this one have already left home.'

'They eat their way out of their mother,' I said. We still had no idea whether there were distinct hamadryad sexes, so it was entirely possible that they had eaten their way out of their father as well – or neither. When the war was over, probing hamadryad biology would fuel a thousand academic careers.

'How big would they have been?' Gitta asked.

'As big as our own juve,' I said, kicking the maw at the base of the spiral. 'Maybe a touch smaller. But nothing you'd want to meet without some heavy firepower.'

'I thought they moved too slowly to pose us any threat.'

'That's the near-adults,' Dieterling said. 'And even then, you wouldn't necessarily be able to out-run it – not through overgrowth like this.'

'Would it want to eat us – I mean, would it even recognise us as something to be eaten?'

'Probably not,' Dieterling said. 'Which might not be much consolation as it slithers over you.'

'Ease off it,' Cahuella said, putting a hand round Gitta. 'They're like any wild animal – only dangerous if you don't know what the fuck you're doing. And we do know, don't we?'

Something crashed through the overgrowth behind us. Startled, we all turned around, half expecting to see the eyeless head of a near-adult bearing down on us like a slow-moving freight train, crunching through the jungle which impeded its implacable slithering progress about as efficiently as fog.

Instead, what we saw was Doctor Vicuna.

The doctor had shown no inclination to follow us when we had left camp, and I wondered what had made him change his mind. Not that I was in any way glad of the ghoul's company.

'What is it, Doctor?'

'I became bored, Cahuella.' The doctor high-stepped through what remained of the overgrowth I had scythed. His clothes, as usual, were impeccable, even as ours picked up cuts and stains from the time in the field. He wore a knee-length dun field jacket, unzipped at the front. Around his neck dangled a pair of dainty image-amp goggles. His hair was kiss-curled, lending him the sordid air of a malnourished cherub. 'Ah – and this is the tree!'

I stepped out of his path, my hand sweating around the haft of the monofilament scythe, imagining what it would do to the ghoul if I were to accidentally extend the cutting arc and flick it through him. Whatever pain he suffered in the process, I thought, could not be measured against the cumulative dose he had inflicted in his career.

'Quite a specimen, isn't it,' Cahuella said.

'The most recent fusion probably only happened a few weeks ago,' Dieterling said, as comfortable with the ghoul as his master. 'Take a look at the cell-type gradient here.'

The doctor ambled forward to see what Dieterling was talking about.

Dieterling had unpacked a slim grey device from the waist pocket of his hunting jacket. Of Ultra manufacture, it was the size of an unopened Bible, set with a screen and a few cryptically marked controls. Dieterling pressed one side of the device to the helix and thumbed one of the buttons. In shades of pale blue, vastly magnified cells appeared on the screen. They were hazy cylindrical shapes, packed together haphazardly like body bags in a morgue.

'These are essentially epithelial cells,' Dieterling said, sketching a finger across the image. 'Note the soft, lipid structure of the cell membrane – very characteristic.'

'Of what?' Gitta said.

'Of an *animal*. If I took a sample of your liver lining, it wouldn't look too dissimilar to this.'

He moved the device to another part of the helix, a little closer to the trunk. 'Now look. Totally different cells – arranged much more regularly, with geometric boundaries locked together for structural rigidity. See how the cell membrane is surrounded by an additional layer? That's basically cellulose.' He touched another control and the cells became glassy, filled with phantom shapes. 'See those podlike organelles? Nascent chloroplasts. And those labyrinthine structures are part of the endoplasmic reticulum. All these things are defining characteristics of plant cells.'

Gitta tapped the bark where Dieterling had made the first scan. 'So the tree is more like an animal here, and more like a plant – here?'

'It's a morphological gradient, of course. The cells in the trunk are pure plant cells – a cylinder of xylem around a core of old growth. When the snake first attaches itself to the tree, wrapping around it, it's still an animal. But where the snake comes into contact with the tree, its own cells begin to change. We don't know what makes that happen – whether the triggering cue comes from something in the snake's own lymphatic system, or whether the tree itself supplies the chemical signal to begin fusion.' Dieterling indicated where the helix merged seamlessly with the trunk. 'This process of cellular unification would have taken a few days. When it was over, the snake was inseparably attached to the tree – had, in fact, become part of the tree itself. But most of the snake was still an animal at that point.'

'What happens to its brain?' Gitta asked.

'It doesn't need one anymore. Doesn't even need anything we'd exactly recognise as a nervous system, to be frank.'

'You haven't answered my question.'

Dieterling smiled at her. 'The mother's brain is the first thing that the juveniles eat.'

'They eat their mother?' Gitta said, horrified.

The snakes merged with their host trees, becoming plants themselves. It only happened when the snakes were in their near-adult phase, large enough to spiral around the tree all the way from the ground to the canopy. By then young hamadryads were already developing in what passed for the creature's womb.

The host tree had almost certainly already seen several fusions. Perhaps the original, true tree had long since rotted away, and what remained were only the locked spirals of dead hamadryads. It was likely, however, that the last snake to attach itself to the tree was still technically alive, having spread its photosynthetic cowl wide from the top of the tree, drinking sunlight. No one knew how long the snakes could have lived in that final brainless plant-phase. What was known was that another near-adult would arrive sooner or later and claim the tree for itself. It would slither up the tree and force its head through the cowl of its predecessor, then spread its own cowl over the old. Deprived of sunlight, the shadowed cowl would wither away quickly. The newcomer would fuse with the tree, becoming mostly plant. What little animal tissue remaining was there only to supply the young with food, born within a few months of the fusion. Some chemical trigger would cause them to eat their way out of the womb, digesting their mother as they went. Once they had eaten her brain, they would chew their way down the spiral length of her body, until they emerged at ground-level as fully formed, rapacious juvenile hamadryads.

'You think it's vile,' Cahuella said, reading Gitta's thoughts expertly. 'But there are life-cycles amongst terrestrial animals which are just as unpleasant, if not more so. The Australian social spider turns to mush as her spiderlings mature. You have to admit it has a kind of Darwinian purity to it. Evolution doesn't greatly care about what happens to creatures once they've passed on their genetic heritage. Normally adult animals have to stick around long enough to raise their young and safeguard them from predators, but hamadryads aren't constrained by those factors. Even juveniles are nastier than any other indigenous animals, which means there's nothing to protect them against. And they don't need to learn anything they don't already have hardwired into them. There's almost no selection pressure to prevent the adults from dying the instant they've given birth. It makes perfect sense for the juveniles to gorge themselves on their mothers.'

It was my turn to smile. 'You almost sound like you admire it.'

'I do. The purity of it – who couldn't admire that?'

I am not sure quite what happened then. I was looking at Cahuella, with half an eye on Gitta, when Vicuna did something. But the first flash of movement seemed to have come not from Vicuna but from my own man Rodriguez.

Vicuna had reached into his jacket and pulled out a gun.

'Rodriguez,' he said. 'Step away from the tree.'

I had no idea what was happening, but I saw now that Rodriguez's own hand was buried in his pocket, as if he had been on the point of reaching for something. Vicuna waggled the end of his gun emphatically.

'I said step away.'

'Doctor,' I said, 'would you mind explaining why you are threatening one of my men?'

'Gladly, Mirabel. After I've dealt with him.'

Rodriguez looked at me, eyes wide in what looked like confusion. 'Tanner, I don't know what he's on about. I was just going for my rations pack . . .'

I looked at Rodriguez, then at the ghoul.

'Well, doctor?'

'He has no rations pack in that pocket. He was reaching for a weapon.'

It made no sense. Rodriguez was already armed – he had a hunting rifle slung over one shoulder, just like Cahuella.

The two of them faced each other, frozen.

I needed to make a decision. I nodded at Cahuella. 'Let me handle this. Get yourself and Gitta away from here; away from any possible line of fire. I'll meet you back at the camp.'

'Yes!' Vicuna hissed. 'Get away from here, before Rodriguez kills you.'

Cahuella took his wife and stepped hesitantly away from the tableau. 'Are you serious, doctor?'

'He seems adequately serious to me,' Dieterling murmured. He was already edging away himself.

'Well?' I said, towards the ghoul.

Vicuna's hand was trembling. He was no gunman – but no kind of marksmanship would have been necessary to take out Rodriguez at the distance that spaced them. He spoke slowly and with forced calm. 'Rodriguez is an imposter, Tanner. I received a message from the Reptile House while you were here.'

Rodriguez shook his head. 'I don't need to listen to this!'

I realised that it was entirely possible that he had received some kind of message from the Reptile House. Normally I snapped on a comms bracelet before I left camp, but I had forgotten it in my haste this morning. Someone calling from the House would only have been able to get as far as the camp.

I turned to Rodriguez. 'Then take your hand slowly out of your pocket.'

'Don't tell me you believe the bastard!'

'I don't know what I believe. But if you're telling the truth, all you've got in there is a rations pack.'

'Tanner, this is—'

I raised my voice. 'Just do it, damn you!'

'Careful,' Vicuna hissed.

Rodriguez drew his hand from the pocket with majesterial slowness, glancing to myself and then Vicuna all the while. What came out, gripped between thumb and forefinger, was slim and black. The way he held it, in the perpetual gloom of the forest floor, it was almost possible to believe it was a rations pack. For a moment I did.

Until I saw that it was a gun, small and elegant and vicious; engineered for assassination.

Vicuna fired. Perhaps I had underestimated the skill that it would take to seriously incapacitate someone even when they stood so close, for the doctor's slug only hit Rodriguez in the shoulder of his other arm, causing him to stagger back and grunt, but no more than that. Rodriguez's gun flashed and the doctor fell backwards into the mulch.

On the edge of the clearing, Cahuella shrugged off his rifle and was on the point of bringing it to bear.

'No!' I started to shout, willing my master to save himself by getting as far away as possible from Rodriguez, but – as I belatedly realised – Cahuella was not the kind to walk away from a fight, even one in which his own life might be contested.

Gitta screamed for her husband to follow her.

Rodriguez levelled the gun towards Cahuella and fired . . .

And missed, his slug slicing through the bark of a nearby tree.

I tried to find some sense in what was happening, but there was no time. Vicuna appeared to have been correct. Everything that Rodriguez had done in the last few moments was consistent with the ghoul's statement . . . which meant that Rodriguez was – what?

An imposter?

'This is for Argent Reivich,' Rodriguez said, drawing his aim again.

This time, I knew, he would not miss.

I raised the monofilament scythe, thumbed the invisibly fine cutting thread to its maximum, piezo-electrically maintained length: a hyper-rigid mono-molecular line extending fifteen metres ahead of me.

Rodriguez, out of the corner of his eye, caught what I was about to do, and made the one mistake which marked him as an amateur, rather than a professional assassin.

He hesitated.

I swung the scythe through him.

As the realisation of what had happened dawned on him – there could have been no immediate pain, for the cut was surgically clean – he dropped the gun. There was a terrible frozen moment, one in which I wondered if I had not made a mistake as grave as his hesitation, and that I had somehow failed to extend the scythe's invisible line as far as I had imagined.

But there had been no mistake.

Rodriguez toppled to the ground, twice.

'He's dead,' Dieterling said, when we were back in the one tent in the camp which had not been deflated. Three hours had passed since the incident by the tree, and now Dieterling was leaning over the body of Doctor Vicuna. 'If only I had understood how these tools of his worked . . .' Dieterling had spread a pile of the ghoul's advanced surgical toys next to him, but their subtle secrets had refused to yield to him. The normal medical supplies had not been sufficient to save him from Rodriguez's shot, but we had hoped that the doctor's own magic – gleaned at considerable expense from Ultra traders – would have been powerful enough. Perhaps, in the right hands, it would have been – but the one man who could have used those tools profitably had been the one who most needed them.

'You did your best,' I said, a hand on Dieterling's shoulder.

Cahuella looked down at the body of Vicuna with unconcealed fury. 'Typical of that bastard to die on us before we could use him properly. How the hell are any of us going to be able to put those implants into a snake?'

'Maybe catching the snake isn't our absolute top priority now,' I said.

'You think I don't know that, Tanner?'

'Then try acting like it.' He glared at me for my insubordination, but I continued anyway, 'I didn't like Vicuna, but he risked his life for you.'

'And whose fucking fault was it that Rodriguez was an imposter? I thought you screened your recruits, Mirabel.'

'I did screen him,' I said.

'Meaning what?'

'The man I killed couldn't have been Rodriguez. Vicuna seemed to agree with me, too.'

Cahuella looked at me as if I was something he had found stuck to the bottom of his shoe, then stormed out, leaving me alone with Dieterling.

'Well?' he said. 'I hope you have some idea what happened out there, Tanner.' He pulled a sheet over the dead Vicuna, then began to gather up the neatly glistening surgical tools.

'I don't. Not yet. It *was* Rodriguez . . . at least it looked like him.'

'Try calling the Reptile House again.'

He was right; it was an hour since I had last tried, and I had not been able to get a call through then. As always, the girdle of comsats around Sky's Edge was patchy and subject to constant military interference, elements mysteriously breaking down and coming back online for the nefarious purposes of other factions.

This time, however, the link worked.

'Tanner? You're all OK?'

'More or less.' I would elaborate on our loss later; for now I need to know what Doctor Vicuna had been told. 'What was the warning you relayed to us about Rodriguez?'

The man I was dealing with was called Southey; someone I had known for years. But I had never seen him look as disconcerted as he did now. 'Tanner, I hope to God . . . we got a warning ourselves, from one of Cahuella's allies. A tip-off about Rodriguez.'

'Go on.'

'Rodriguez is dead! They found his body in Nueva Santiago. He'd been murdered, then dumped.'

'You're sure it was him?'

'We have his DNA on file. Our contact in Santiago ran an analysis on the body – it was a one-to-one match.'

'Then the Rodriguez who came back from Santiago must have been someone else, is that what you're saying?'

'Yes. Not a clone, we think, but an assassin. He would have been surgically modified to look like Rodriguez; even his voice and smell must have been altered.'

I thought about that for a few moments before replying, 'There's no one on Sky's Edge with the skill to do something like that. Especially not in the few days that Rodriguez was away from the Reptile House.'

'No, I agree. But the Ultras could have done it.'

That much I knew, Orcagna having practically rubbed our faces in his superior science. 'It would have to be more than just cosmetic,' I said.

'What do you mean?'

'Rodriguez – the imposter – still behaved like himself. He knew things only Rodriguez really knew. I know – I talked to him often in the last few days.' Now that I considered those conversations, there had at times been something evasive about Rodriguez, but obviously nothing serious enough to rouse my suspicions at the time. There had been much that he had been perfectly willing to discuss.

'So they used his memories as well.'

'You think they trawled Rodriguez?'

Southey nodded. 'It must have been done by experts, because there was no sign that it was the trawl itself that killed him. But again, they were Ultras.'

'And you think they have the means to implant the memories into their assassin?'

'I've heard of such things,' Southey said. 'Tiny machines which swarm through the subject's mind, laying down new neural connections. Eidetic imprinting, they call it. The NCs tried it for training purposes, but they never got it to work really well. But if Ultras were involved . . .'

'It would have been child's play. It wasn't just that the man had access to Rodriguez's memories, though – it went deeper than that. Like he had almost become Rodriguez in the process.'

'Maybe that's why he was so convincing. Those new memory structures would have been fragile, though – the assassin's own personality would have begun to emerge sooner or later. But by then Rodriguez would have gained your confidence.'

Southey was right: it was only in the last day or so that Rodriguez had seemed more than usually evasive. Was that the point when the assassin's buried mind began to shine through the veil of camouflaging memories?

'He gained it pretty well,' I said. 'If it wasn't for Vicuna warning us . . .' I told him about what had happened around the tree.

'Bring the bodies back,' Southey said. 'I want to see how well they really disguised their man – whether it was cosmetic, or whether they tried to change his DNA as well.'

'You think they went to that much trouble?'

'That's the point, Tanner. If they went to the right kind of people, it wouldn't have been much trouble at all.'

'To the best of my knowledge, there's only one group of Ultras in orbit around the planet at the moment.'

'Yes. I'm fairly sure that Orcagna's people must have been involved in this. You met them, didn't you? Did you think they could be trusted?'

'They were Ultras,' I said, as if that were answer enough. 'I couldn't read them like one of Cahuella's usual contacts. That doesn't mean they'd automatically betray us, though.'

'What would they have to gain by *not* betraying us?'

That, I realised, was the one question I had never really asked. I had made the error of treating Orcagna like any other of Cahuella's business contacts – someone who would not want to exclude dealing with Cahuella again in the future. But what if Orcagna's crew had no intention of returning to Sky's Edge for decades, even centuries? They could burn all their bridges with impunity.

'Orcagna might not have known that the assassin was aimed at us,' I said. 'Someone affiliated to Reivich just presented them with a man who needed his appearance changed; another man who needed his memories transferred into the first . . .'

'And you think it didn't even occur to Orcagna to ask questions?'

'I don't know,' I said, even my own argument sounding weak.

Southey sighed. I knew what he was thinking. It was what I was thinking myself. 'Tanner, I think we need to play it very carefully from here on in.'

'At least one good thing's come out of it,' I said. 'Now that the doctor's dead, Cahuella's had to abandon his snake quest. He just hasn't realised it yet.'

Southey forced a thin smile. 'We've already dug half the new pit.'

'I wouldn't worry about finishing the rest by the time we get back.' I paused and checked the map again, the blinking dot which represented Reivich's progress. 'We'll camp again tonight, about sixty klicks north of here. Tomorrow we'll be on our way home.'

'Tonight's the night?'

With Rodriguez and the doctor dead, we would be undermanned when it came to the ambush. But there would be still be enough of us to make victory a near-mathematical certainty.

'Tomorrow morning. Reivich should enter our trap two hours before noon, if he maintains his progress.'

'Good luck, Tanner.'

I nodded and closed the connection with the Reptile House. Outside, I found Cahuella and told him what I had learned from Southey. Cahuella had calmed down a little since our last conversation, while his men worked around us packing up the rest of the camp. He was strapping a black leather bandolier from waist to shoulder, with numerous little leather pockets for cartridges, clips, ammo-cells and other paraphernalia.

'They can do that kind of shit as well? Memory transfer?'

'I'm not sure how permanent it would have been, but – yes – I'm reasonably sure they could have trawled Rodriguez so that Reivich's man had enough of his knowledge not to arouse our suspicions. You're less surprised that they could change his shape so convincingly?'

He seemed unwilling to answer me immediately. 'I know they can . . . change things, Tanner.'

There were times when I felt I knew Cahuella as well as anyone; that at times we were as close as brothers. I knew him to be capable of a cruelty more imaginative and instinctive than anything I could devise. I had to work at being cruel, like a hard-working musician who lacked the easy, virtuoso flair of the true-born genius. But we saw things similarly, judged people with the same jaundiced eye and were both possessed of an innate skill with weapons. Yet there were times, like now, that it was if Cahuella and I had never met; that there were infinite secrets he would never share with me. I thought back to what Gitta had told me the night before; her implication that what I knew about him was only the tip of the iceberg.

An hour later and we were on our way, with the two bodies – Vicuna and the bipartite Rodriguez – in refrigerated coffins, stowed in the last vehicle. The hard-shelled coffins had doubled as rations stores until now. Predictably enough, the hunting trip no longer felt like much of a holiday. I had never seen it like that, of course, but Cahuella certainly had, and I could read the tension in the muscles of his neck as he strained to look forward along the trail. Reivich had been a step ahead of us.

Later, when we stopped to fix a turbine, he said, 'I'm sorry I blamed you back there, Tanner.'

'I'd have done the same.'

'That's not the point, is it? I trust you like a brother. I did and I still do. You saved us all when you killed Rodriguez.'

Something green and leathery flapped over the road. 'I prefer not to think of that imposter as Rodriguez. Rodriguez was a good man.'

'Of course . . . it was just verbal shorthand. You – um – don't think there are likely to be any more of them, do you?'

I had given the matter some thought. 'We can't rule it out, but I don't think it's very likely. Rodriguez had come back from a trip, whereas everyone else on the expedition hasn't left the Reptile House for weeks – apart from you and me, of course, when we visited Orcagna. I think we can remove ourselves from suspicion. Vicuna might have been a possibility, but he's neatly removed himself as well.'

'All right. One other thing.' He paused, casting a wary eye over his men as they hammered at something under an engine cowling with what looked like less than professional care. 'You don't think that might have actually been Reivich, do you?'

'Disguised as Rodriguez?'

Cahuella nodded. 'He did say he was going to get me.'

'Yes . . . but my guess is he's with the main party. That's what Orcagna told us. The imposter might even have planned to lie low with us, not compromising his cover until the rest of the party came through.'

'It could have been him, though.'

'I don't think so; not unless the Ultras are even cleverer than we thought. Reivich and Rodriguez were nowhere near the same size. I can believe they altered his face, but I can't see them having the time to change his entire skeleton and musculature – not in a few days. Then they'd still have to adjust his body-image so he didn't keep bumping into ceilings. No; their assassin must have been a man of similar build to Rodriguez.'

'It's possible he got a warning through to Reivich, though?'

'Possible, yes – but if he did, Reivich isn't acting on it. The weapons traces are still moving at the normal rate towards us.'

'Then – essentially – nothing's changed, right?'

'Essentially nothing,' I said, but we both knew that neither of us felt it.

Shortly afterwards his men made the turbine sing again and we were on our way. I had always taken the security of the expedition seriously, but now I had redoubled my efforts and rethought all my arrangements. No one was leaving camp unless they were armed, and no one was to leave alone – except, of course, for Cahuella himself, who would still insist on his nocturnal prowls.

The camp we set tonight would form the basis of our ambush, so I was determined to spend more than the usual amount of time searching for the best place to pitch the bubbletents. The camp had to be nearly invisible from the road, but close enough that we could mount an attack on Reivich's group. I did not want us to become too separated from our munitions stores, which meant placing the tents no more than fifty or sixty metres into the trees. Before nightfall, we could scythe out strategic lines of fire through the wood and arrange fall-back routes for ourselves in case Reivich's men laid down a heavy suppressing fire. If time allowed we would set deadfalls or mines along other, more obvious paths.

I was drawing a map in my mind, crisscrossing it with intersecting lines of death, when the snake began to cross our path.

My attention had wandered slightly from the route ahead, so it was Cahuella shouting 'Stop!' which first alerted me that something was happening.

Turbines cut; our vehicles bellied down.

Two or three hundred metres down the trail, just where the trail began to curve out of sight, the hamadryad had poked its head out of the curtain of greenery which marked the edge of the jungle. The head was a pale, sickly green, under the olive folds of its photosensitive cowl, retracted like a cobra's hood. It was crossing from right to left; towards the sea.

'Near-adult,' Dieterling said, as if what we were looking at was a bug stuck to the windshield.

The head was nearly as big as one of our vehicles. Behind it came the first few metres of the creature's snakelike body. The patterning was the same as I had seen on the helical structure wrapped around the hamadryad tree, very snakelike.

'How big do you think it is?' I asked.

'Thirty, thirty-five metres. Not the biggest I've ever seen – that has to be a sixty-metre snake I saw back in '71 – but this isn't any juvenile. If it can find a tree which reaches the canopy and isn't much higher than its length, it'll probably begin fusion.'

The head had reached the other side of the road. It moved slowly, creeping past us.

'Take us closer,' Cahuella said.

'Wait,' I said. 'Are you sure? We're safe here. It'll pass soon. I know they don't have any deeply wired defensive instincts, but it might still decide we look like something worth eating. Are you sure you want to risk that?'

'Take us closer.'

I fired up the turbine, gunning it to the minimum number of revs sufficient to give us lift, and crept the vehicle forward. Hamadryads were thought to have no sense of sound, but seismic vibrations were another thing entirely. I wondered whether the air-cushion of our car, drumming against the ground, sounded exactly like part of the snake's diet coming closer.

The snake had arced itself so that the length of two-metre-thick body spanning the road was always elevated. It continued to move slowly and smoothly, betraying absolutely no sign that it had even registered our presence. Perhaps Dieterling was right. Perhaps all the snake was interested in was finding a nice tall tree to curl itself around, so that it could give up this tedious business of having a brain and having to move around.

We were fifty metres from it now.

'Stop,' Cahuella said again.

This time I obeyed unquestioningly. I turned to look at him, but he was already hopping out of the car. We could hear the snake now: a constant low rumble as it pushed itself through foliage. It was not an animal sound at all. What it sounded like was the continuous crunching progress of a tank.

Cahuella reappeared at the side of the vehicle. He had gone round the back to where the weapons were stored and had drawn out his crossbow.

'Oh, no . . .' I started to say, but it was too late.

He was already racking a tranquilliser dart into the bow, coded for use against a thirty-metre adult. The weapon, on the face of it, seemed like an affectation, but it made a kind of sense. A huge quantity of tranquilliser would have to be delivered to an adult to dope it as we had the juvenile. Our normal hunting rifles were just not up to the job. A crossbow, on the other hand, could fire a much larger dart – and the apparent drawbacks of limited range and accuracy were hardly relevant when one was dealing with a deaf and blind thirty-metre snake which took a minute to move its body length.

'Shut up, Tanner,' Cahuella said. 'I didn't come out here to see one of these bastards and turn away from it.'

'Vicuna's dead. That means we have no one to implant those control electrodes.'

It was as if I had not spoken. He set off down the trail, the crossbow in one hand, the muscles in his muscular back defined against the sweat-sodden shirt he wore under his bandolier.

'Tanner,' Gitta said. 'Stop him, before he gets hurt.'

'He's not in any real danger . . .' I started to say.

But it was a lie, and I knew it. He might have been safer than if he had been this close to a juvenile, but the behaviour of near-adults was only poorly understood. Swearing, I opened the door on my side, jogged round to the back of the vehicle and unracked a laser-rifle for myself. I checked the ammo-cell's charge, then loped after him. Hearing my footfalls against the dirt, Cahuella looked back irritatedly.

'Mirabel! Get the hell back into the car! I don't want anyone ruining this kill for me!'

'I'll keep my distance,' I called.

The hamadryad's head had vanished into the other side of the forest, leaving an arc of body spanning the road with the elegant bowstring curve of a bridge. The sound, now that I came closer, was immense. I could hear branches snapping along the snake's length, and a relentless susurration of dry skin against bark.

And another noise – identical in timbre, but coming from another direction completely. For a moment my brain sluggishly refused to reach the obvious conclusion, trying to work out how the acoustic properties of the jungle could echo the hamadryad's progress so effectively. I was still wondering about it when the second snake burst through the treeline to my right. It moved as slowly as the first, but it was very much closer, which made the thing's half-metre per second progress seem a lot swifter. It was smaller than the first one we had seen, but still monstrous by any standards. And I remembered an uncomfortable fact about hamadryad biology. The smaller they were, the faster they were capable of moving . . .

But the snake brought its hooded, deltoid head to a stop, metres from me and metres above my own. Eyeless, it seemed to float against the sky like a malign, thick-tailed kite.

In all my years of soldiering, I had never been paralysed by fear. I knew that it happened to some people, but I wondered how it was possible and what kind of people they had really been. Now, belatedly, I was coming to an intimate understanding of just how it could happen. The flight reflex was not completely decoupled from volition: part of me knew that to run could be just as hazardous as to remain fixed to the spot, motionless. Snakes were blind until they located a target, but their infra-red and olfactory sensitivity was acute. There was no doubt that it knew I was standing beneath it, or else it would not have stopped.

I had no idea what to do.

Shoot it, I thought . . . but the laser-rifle was, in hindsight, not the best weapon I could have selected. A few pencil-thin holes right through its body were not going to massively impede this creature. No point aiming for specific areas of brain function, either: it hardly had a brain to begin with, even before giving birth to the young that would eat that tiny knot of neurones. The laser was a pulse-weapon, the beam too transient to be used as a blade. I would have been better off with the scythe I had used against the imposter . . .

'Tanner. Stay still. It has a lock on you.'

Out of the corner of my eye – I didn't dare move my head – I saw Cahuella, approaching in a near-crouch. He had the crossbow against his shoulder, squinting along the weapon's long haft.

'That won't do much more than piss it off,' I said, in not much more than a hiss.

Cahuella answered in a stage whisper, 'Yeah. Big time. The dose was for the first one. This one's no more than fifteen metres . . . that's twelve per cent of the body volume, which means the dose'll be eight times too strong . . .' He paused and halted. 'Or thereabouts.'

He was within range now.

Above me, the head swayed from side to side, tasting the wind. Perhaps, following the other, larger, adult, it was impatient to be moving on. But it could not let this possibility of prey pass without investigation. Perhaps it had not eaten in months. Dieterling had said that they always had one last meal before fusion. Maybe this one was too small to be ready to bind with a tree, but there was no reason to assume it was not hungry.

Moving my hands as slowly and smoothly as I dared, I slipped off the rifle's safety-catch, feeling the subliminal shiver as the discharge cells powered up, accompanied by a faint rising whine.

The head bowed toward me, drawn by the rifle.

'This weapon is now ready for use,' the rifle said brightly.

The snake lunged, its wide mouth opening, the two attack-phase eyes gleaming at me from the mouth's red roof, triangulating.

I fired, straight into the mouth.

The head smashed into the dirt next to me, its lunge confused by the laser pulses. Angered, the snake reared up, its mouth wide, emitting a terrible roar and a smell like a field of butchered corpses. I had squeezed off ten rapid pulses, a stroboscopic volley which had punched ten black craters into the roof of the mouth. I could see the exit wounds peppering the back of the head, each finger-wide. I'd blinded it.

But it had enough memory to remember roughly where I was. I stumbled back as the head daggered down again – and then there was a glint of bright metal cleaving the air, and the thunk of Cahuella's crossbow.

His dart had buried itself in the neck of the snake, instantly discharging its payload of tranquilliser.

'Tanner! Get the fuck away!'

He reached into his bandolier and extracted another dart, then cranked back the bow and slipped the second dart into place. A moment later it joined the other in the snake's neck. That was, if he had done his sums correctly, and the darts were both coded for large adults, something like sixteen times the dose necessary to put this specimen to sleep.

I was out of harm's way now, but I kept firing. And now I realised that we had another problem . . .

'Cahuella . . .' I said.

He must have seen that I was looking beyond rather than at him, for he stopped and looked over his shoulder, frozen in the action of reaching for another dart.

The other snake had curved round in a loop, and now its head was emerging from the left side of the trail, only twenty metres from Cahuella.

'The distress call . . .' he said.

Until now we had not even known they *had* any calls. But he was right: my wounding the smaller snake had drawn the interest of the first, and now Cahuella was trapped between two hamadryads.

But then the smaller snake began to die.

There was nothing sudden about it. It was more like an airship going down, as the head sunk towards the ground, no longer capable of being carried by the neck, which was itself sagging inexorably lower.

Something touched me on the shoulder.

'Stand aside, bro,' said Dieterling.

It seemed like an age since I had left the car, but it could only have been half a minute. Dieterling could never have been far behind me, yet for most of that time Cahuella and I felt completely alone.

I looked at what Dieterling was carrying, comparing it to the weapon I had imagined suitable for the task at hand.

'Nice one,' I said.

'The right tools for the job, that's all.'

262

He brushed past me, shouldering the matte-black bazooka he had retrieved from the weapons rack. There was a bas-relief Scorpion down the side of it and a huge semi-circular magazine jutting asymmetrically from one side. A targeting screen whirred into place in front of his eyes, churning with scrolling data and bullseye overlays. Dieterling brushed it aside, glanced behind to make sure I was out of range of the recoil blast, and squeezed the trigger.

The first thing he did was blow a hole through the first snake, like a tunnel. Through this he walked, his boots squelching through the unspeakable red carpet.

Cahuella pumped the last dart into the larger snake, but by then he was limited to doses calibrated for much smaller animals. It appeared not to notice that it had even been shot. They had, I knew, few pain receptors anywhere along their bodies.

Dieterling reached him, his boots red to the knee. The adult was coming closer, its head no more than ten metres from both of them.

The two men shook hands and exchanged weapons.

Dieterling turned his back on Cahuella and began to walk calmly back towards me. He carried the crossbow in the crook of his arm, for it was useless now.

Cahuella hefted the bazooka and began to inflict grievous harm on the snake.

It was not pretty. He had the bazooka set to rapid fire, mini-rockets streaking from its muzzle twice a second. What he did to the snake was more akin to pruning back a plant snip by snip. First he took the head off, so that the truncated neck hung in the air, red-rimmed. But the creature kept on moving. Losing its brain was obviously not really much of a handicap to it. The slithering roar of its progress had not abated at all.

So Cahuella kept shooting.

He stood his ground, feet apart, squeezing rocket after rocket into the wound, blood and gore plastering the trees on either side of him. Still the snake kept coming, but now there was less and less of it to come, the body tapering towards the tail. When only ten metres were left, the body finally flopped to the ground, twitching. Cahuella put a last rocket in it for good measure and then turned round and walked back towards me with the same laconic stroll Dieterling had used.

When he got close to me I saw that his shirt was filmed in red now, his face slick with a fine film of rouge. He handed me the bazooka. I safed it, but it was hardly necessary: the last shot he had fired, I saw, had been the last in the magazine.

Back at the vehicle, I opened the case which held replacement magazines and slotted a fresh one onto the bazooka, then racked it with the other weapons. Cahuella was looking at me, as if expecting me to say something to him. But what could I say? I could hardly compliment him on his hunting expertise. Apart from the nerve it took, and the physical strength to hold the bazooka, a child could have killed the snake in exactly the same manner.

Instead, I looked to the two brutally butchered animals which lay across our path, practically unrecognisable for what they had been.

'I don't think Vicuna could have helped us very much,' I said.

He looked at me, then shook his head, as much in disgust at my own mistake – that I had forced him to save my own life and lose his chance to capture his prey – as acknowledging the truth of what I said.

'Just drive, Tanner,' he said.

That night we established the ambush camp.

Orcagna's trace showed that Reivich's party was thirty kilometres north of our position and moving south at the same steady rate he had maintained for days. They did not appear to be resting overnight as we did, but as their average rate was somewhat slower than what we were managing, they were not covering much more ground in a day. Between us and them was a river that would need to be forded, but if Reivich made no serious mistakes – or decided against pattern to stop for the night – he would still be five kilometres up the road by dawn.

We set up the bubbletents, this time shrouding each in an outer skin of chameleoflage fabric. We were deep in hamadryad country now, so I took care to sweep the area with deep-look thermal and acoustic sensors. They would pick up the crunching movement of any moderately large adults. Juveniles were another thing entirely, but at least juveniles would not crush our entire camp. Dieterling examined the trees in the area and confirmed that none of them had released juveniles any time recently.

'So worry about the dozen other local predators,' he said, meeting Cahuella and I outside one of the bubbletents.

'Maybe it's seasonal,' Cahuella said. 'The time when they give birth, I mean. That could influence our next hunting trip. We should plan it properly.'

I looked at him with a jaundiced eye. 'You still want to use Vicuna's toys?'

'It'd be a tribute to the good doctor, wouldn't it? It's what he would have wanted.'

'Maybe.' I thought back to the two snakes which had crossed our path. 'I also know we almost got ourselves killed back there.'

He shrugged. 'The textbooks say they don't travel in pairs.'

'So you did your homework. It didn't help, did it?'

'We got out of it. No thanks to you, either, Tanner . . .' He looked at me hard, then nodded at Dieterling. 'At least *he* knew what kind of weapon was needed.'

'A bazooka?' I said. 'Yes. It worked, didn't it? But I don't call that sport.'

'It wasn't sport by then,' Cahuella said. His mood shifted capriciously and he placed a hand on my shoulder. 'Still, you did your best with that laser. And we learned valuable lessons that will stand us in good stead when we come back next season.'

He was deadly serious, I saw. He really wanted that near-adult. 'Fine,' I said, wriggling free of his hand. 'But next time I'll let Dieterling run the whole expedition. I'll stay back at the Reptile House and do the job you pay me for.'

'I'm paying you to be here,' Cahuella said.

'Yes. To take down Reivich. But hunting giant snakes doesn't figure in my terms of employment, the last time I checked.'

He sighed. 'Reivich is still our priority, Tanner.'

'Really?'

'Of course. Everything else is just . . . scenery.' He nodded and vanished into his bubbletent.

Dieterling opened his mouth. 'Listen, bro . . .'

'I know. You don't have to apologise. You were right to pick the bazooka, and I made a mistake.'

Dieterling nodded and then went to the weapons rack to select another rifle. He sighted along it and then slung it over his shoulder on its strap.

'What are you doing?'

'I'm going to check the area again.'

I noticed that he was not carrying any image-amp goggles. 'It's getting dark now, Miguel . . .' I nodded to my own pair, resting on a table next to the map which showed Reivich's progress.

But Miguel Dieterling just smiled and turned away.

Later, much later, after I had set up about half the deadfalls and ambushes (I would rig the others at sunrise; if I did it now there would be too much of a danger of tripping them ourselves), Cahuella invited me into his tent.

'Yes?' I said, expecting another order.

Cahuella indicated a chessboard, bathed in the insipid green light of the bubbletent's glowlamps.

'I need an opponent.'

The chessboard was set up on a folding card table, with folding, canvas-backed seats stationed either side of it. I shrugged. I played chess, and even played it well, but the game held few enticements for me. I approached the game like any other duty, knowing I could not allow myself to win.

Cahuella leant over the chessboard. He wore fatigues crossed by webbing; various daggers and throwing implements were attached to his belt, with the dolphin pendant hanging under his neck. When his hands moved across the board, I thought of an oldtime general positioning little penanted tanks and infantrymen on a vast sand-table. All the while, his face remained placid and imperturbable, the green radiance of the glowlamps reflected oddly in his eyes, as if some part of that radiance came from within. And all the while Gitta sat next to us, occasionally pouring her husband another thimble of pisco; seldom speaking.

I played a difficult game – difficult, because of the tactical contortions I forced myself through. I was a superior chess player to Cahuella, but he wasn't very fond of losing. On the other hand, he was shrewd enough to guess if an opponent was not giving the game his all, so I had to satisfy his ego on both fronts. I played hard, forcing Cahuella into a corner, but incorporated a weakness into my position – something exceedingly subtle, but also potentially fatal. Then, just when it looked like I would put him in check, I arranged for my weakness to reveal itself, like the sudden opening of a hairline fracture. Sometimes, though, he failed to spot my weaknesses, and there was nothing to do but let him lose. The best I could do under those circumstances was contrive to make the margin of my own victory as narrow as possible.

'You've beaten me again, Tanner . . .'

'You played well, though. You have to allow me the occasional victory.'

Gitta appeared at her husband's side and poured another centimetre of pisco into his glass.

'Tanner always plays well,' she said, eyeing me. 'That's why he's a worthy opponent for you.'

I shrugged. 'I do my best.'

Cahuella brushed the pieces from the table, as if in a tantrum, but his voice remained placid. 'Another game?'

'Why not,' I said, knowing with weary certainty that this time I *had* to fail.

We finished the chess game. Cahuella and I finished a few drops of pisco, then reviewed our plan for the ambush, even though we had already been through it dozens of times and there was nothing we had left uncovered. But it was the kind of ritual we had to endure. Afterwards, we made one final check on the weapons, and then Cahuella took his and spoke quietly in my ear.

'I'm stepping outside for a moment, Tanner. I want some final practice. I'd rather not be disturbed until I'm done.'

'Reivich might see the flashes.'

'There's bad weather coming in,' Cahuella said. 'He'll just assume it's lightning.'

I nodded, insisted that I check the settings on the gun for him, then let him slip out into the night. Torchless, with the little miniature laser strapped diagonally across his back, he was quickly lost from sight. It was a dark night and I hoped he knew his way through the part of the jungle immediately surrounding the clearing. Like Dieterling, he was confident of his ability to see well enough in the dark.

A few minutes passed before I heard the pulse of his weapon: regular discharges every few seconds, followed by longer pauses which suggested he was checking his fire pattern or selecting new targets. Each pulse strobed the tree-tops with a sharp flash of light, disturbing wildlife from the canopy; black shadows which cut across the stars. Then I saw that something else – equally black, but far vaster – was obstructing a whole swathe of stars towards the west. It was a storm, as Cahuella had predicted, creeping in from the ocean, ready to engulf the Peninsula in monsoon. As if acknowledging my diagnosis, the night's previously calm and warm air began to stir, a breeze toying with the tops of the trees. I returned to the tent, found a torch and began to follow the path Cahuella had taken, guided by the intermittent pulses of his gun, like a lighthouse beacon. The undergrowth became treacherous and it took me several minutes to find my way to the patch of ground – a small clearing – where he stood shooting. I doused my torch across his body, announcing my arrival.

Still squeezing off pulses, he said, 'I told you not to disturb me, Tanner.'

'I know, but there's a storm coming in. I was worried you wouldn't notice until it began to rain, and then you might have trouble finding your way back to the camp.'

'I'm the one who told you there was a storm coming,' he said, not turning to face me, still engrossed in his target practice. I could barely see what he was shooting at; his laser pulses knifed into a void of darkness devoid of detail. But I noticed that the pulses followed each other very precisely, even after he adjusted his stance, or unshouldered the rifle to slip in another ammo-cell.

'It's late, anyway. We should get some sleep. If Reivich is delayed it could be a long day tomorrow, and we'll need to be sharp for it.'

'You're right, of course,' he said, after due consideration. 'I just want to make sure I can maim the bastard, if I choose.'

'Maim him? I thought we were setting him up for a clean kill.'

'What would be the point of that?'

I stepped toward him. 'Killing him's one thing. You can bet he wants to kill you, so there's a kind of sense to it. But he hasn't done anything to earn that kind of hatred, has he?'

He sighted along the gun and squeezed off a pulse. 'Who said he has to, Tanner?'

Then he snapped the gun's stock and sight into their stowage modes, slipping the gun on to his back, where it looked like a piece of frail rigging lashed to the side of a whale.

We walked in silence to the camp, the storm rising overhead like a cliff of obsidian, pregnant with lightning. The first drops of rain were falling through the treetops when we reached the camp. We checked the guns were protected from the elements, triggered our perimeter infringement detectors and then sealed ourselves into the tents. The rain began to drum against the fabric, like impatient fingers on a tabletop, and thunder roared somewhere to the south. But we were ready, and returned to our bunks to snatch what sleep we could before we had to rise to catch our man.

'Sleep well tonight,' Cahuella said, his head peering through the gash in my tent. 'For tomorrow we fight.'

It was still dark. The storm was still raging. I woke and listened to the rain's fusillade against the fabric of the bubbletent.

Something had troubled me enough to bring me from sleep. It happened, sometimes. My mind would work away at a problem, which had seemed clear-cut in daylight, until it found a catch. It was how I had filled in some of the more subtle security loopholes at the Reptile House; imagining myself as an intruder and then devising a way to penetrate some screen that I had imagined until then to be absolutely foolproof. That was what it felt like when I woke: that something unobvious had suddenly been revealed to me. And that I had been making a terrible error of assumption. But for a moment I could not quite recall the details of the dream; what had been vouchsafed to me by own diligent subconscious processes.

And then I realised that we were being attacked.

'No . . .' I started to say.

But it was much too late for that.

One of the most pragmatic truths about war, and the way it affected us, was that many of the clichés were not very far removed from reality. War was about yawning chasms of inactivity, punctuated by brief, screaming inter-ludes of action. And in those brief, screaming interludes, events happened both quickly and with dreamlike slowness, every instant burned into memory. That was how it was, especially during something as compressed and violent as an ambush.

There was no warning. Perhaps something had reached down into my dreams and alerted me, so that it was both the ambush and the realisation of my error that brought me from sleep, but by the time I awoke I had no conscious memory of what it was. A sound, perhaps, as they disabled the perimeter warning system – or maybe nothing more than a foot crunching through undergrowth, or the alarm call of a startled animal.

It made no difference.

There were three of them against the eight of us, and yet they cut us down with merciless ease. The three were dressed in chameleoflage armour, shape-shifting, texture-shifting, colour-shifting garments which enveloped them from head to foot: full-body suits like that were more advanced than the kinds the average militia had access to; technology which could only be bought through the Ultras. That had to be it, then – Reivich was also dealing with the lighthugger crew. And maybe he had paid them to deceive Cahuella, supplying false positional information. There was another possibility, too, which was what my sleeping mind had come up with.

Perhaps there were two Reivich parties, one moving south thirty kilometres north of here, with the heavy armaments which Orcagna was monitoring. I had assumed that was the only party. But what if there had been a second squad, moving ahead of them? Perhaps they had ligher armaments which could not be traced by the Ultras. The element of surprise would more than compensate for the deficiency in fire-power.

It had, too.

Their weapons were no more advanced or lethal than our own, but they used them with pinpoint accuracy, gunning down first the guards stationed outside the camp, before the guards had had a chance to aim their own weapons. But I was barely aware of this part of the attack; still struggling out of sleep, thinking at first that the light pulses and cracks of energy-discharge outside were only the dying spasms of the storm as it passed into the deep Peninsula. Then I heard the screams, and I began to realise what was happening.

By then, of course, it was far too late to do anything about it.

TWENTY-ONE

Finally, I woke. For a long time, lying in the golden morning light which streamed into Zebra's room, I replayed the dreams in my head, until at last I could put them to rest and start examining my injured leg.

Overnight the healer had worked wonders, utilising a medical science well in advance of anything we'd had on Sky's Edge. The wound was now little more than a whitish star of new flesh, and what damage remained was mainly psychological – the refusal of my brain to accept that my leg was now fully capable of performing its intended role. I rose from the couch and took a few awkward, experimental steps, finally making my way over to the nearest window, navigating the stepped levels of the broken floor, furniture helpfully shuffling aside to ease my passage.

In the light of day, or what passed for day in Chasm City, the great hole at the city's heart looked even closer, even more vertiginous. It was not difficult to imagine how it had lured the first explorers who had come to Yellowstone, whether birthed from robot wombs or riding the first, risky starships that had come afterwards. The blotch of warm atmosphere spilling from the chasm was visible from space when other atmospheric conditions were favourable.

Whether they had crossed land in crawlers or come skimming down through cloud layers, that first sight of the chasm could never have been anything but heart-stopping. Something had injured the planet, thousands of centuries earlier, and this great open wound had still not healed. Some, it was said, had made the descent into the depths, equipped only with fragile pressure suits, and had found treasures upon which empires might be founded. If so, they had been careful to keep those treasures to themselves. But it had not stopped others coming, other chancers and adventurers; around them had accreted the first hints of what would eventually become this city.

There was no universally accepted theory to explain the hole, although the surrounding caldera – in which Chasm City lay, sheltered from winds, and the predation of flash-floods and the encroachment of methane-ammonia glaciers – hinted at something fairly catastrophic, and recent, too, on the geologic timescale – recent enough not to have been erased by the processes of weathering and tectonic reshaping. Yellowstone had probably had a close encounter with its gas giant neighbour which had injected energy into the planet's core, and the chasm was one of the means by which that energy was slowly being bled back towards space, but something must have opened this escape route in the first place. There were theories about tiny black holes slamming into the crust, or fragments of quark matter, but no one really knew what had happened. There were also rumours and fairytales: of alien digs beneath the crust, evidence that the chasm had in some sense been artefactual, if not necessarily deliberate. Perhaps those aliens had come here for the same reason that humans had, to tap the chasm for its energy and chemical resources. I could see very clearly the tentacular pipes which the city extended over the maw towards the bottom, reaching down like grasping fingers.

'Don't pretend you're not impressed,' Zebra said. 'There are people who'd kill for a view like this. Come to think of it, I probably know people who *have* killed for a view like this.'

'That doesn't really surprise me.'

Zebra had entered the room silently. At first glace she appeared to be naked, but then I saw that she was fully clothed, but in a gown of such translucence that it might as well have been made of smoke.

She carried my Mendicant clothes in her arms, washed and neatly folded.

I could see now that she was very thin. Beneath the blue-grey film of her gown black stripes covered her entire body, following the curves of her form, shadowing her genital region. The stripes simultaneously suppressed and emphasised the curves and angles of her body, so that she metamorphosed with each step she took towards me. Her hair ran in a stiff furrow down to the small of her back, ending above the striped swell of her buttocks. When she walked, she glided, like a ballet dancer, her small hooflike feet more for the purpose of anchoring her to the ground than supporting her weight. I could see now that had she chosen to play the Game, she would have made a hunter of considerable skill. She had, after all, hunted me – if only for the purposes of ruining her enemies' entertainment.

'On the planet where I come from,' I said, 'this would be considered provocative.'

'Well, this isn't Sky's Edge,' she said, placing my clothes on the couch. 'It's not even Yellowstone. In the Canopy, we do more or less what we please.' She ran the palms of her hands down her hips.

'Excuse me if this sounds rude, but were you born this way?'

'Not remotely. I haven't always been female, for what it's worth, and I doubt that I'll stay this way for the rest of my life. I certainly won't always be known as Zebra. Who'd choose to be pinned down by one body, one identity?'

'I don't know,' I said, carefully, 'but on Sky's Edge it was beyond most people's means to modify themselves in any way at all.'

'Yes. I gather you were all too busy killing each other.'

'That's a fairly reductive summary of our history, but I don't suppose it's too far from the truth. How much do you know about it, anyway?' Not for the first time since she had entered the room, I was reminded of the troubling dream of Cahuella's camp, and how Gitta had looked at me in the dream. Gitta and Zebra did not have a great deal in common, but in my confused state of waking, I found it easy to transfer some of Gitta's attributes onto Zebra: her lithe build, her high cheekbones and dark hair. It was not that I did not find Zebra alluring in her own right. But she was stranger than any creature – human or otherwise – that I'd ever shared a room with.

'I know enough,' Zebra said. 'Some of us here are quite interested in it, in a perverse way. We find it amusing and quaint and horrifying at the same time.'

I nodded at the people caught in the wall, the tableau that I'd imagined was a piece of artwork.

'I find what happened here fairly horrifying.'

'Oh, it was. But we lived through it, and those of us who survived never really knew the plague at its most ferocious.' She was standing close to me now, and I felt myself aroused by her for the first time. 'Compared to the plague, war seems very alien. Our enemy was our city, our own bodies.'

I took one of her hands and held it in my own, pressing it against my chest. 'Who are you, Zebra? And why do you really want to help me?'

'I thought we went through that last night.'

'I know, but . . .' There was no real conviction in my voice. 'They're still after me, aren't they? The hunt won't have ended just because you brought me to the Canopy.'

'You're safe while you stay here. My rooms are electronically shielded, so they won't be able to get a fix on your implant. Besides, the Canopy itself is out of bounds for the Game. The players don't want to draw too much attention to themselves.'

'So I have to stay here for the rest of my life?'

'No, Tanner. Just another two days and then you're safe.' She removed her hand from mine and used it to caress the side of my head, finding the bulge where the implant lay. 'The thing Waverly put inside your head is wired to stop transmitting after fifty-two hours. That's how they prefer to play.'

'Fifty-two hours? One of the little rules Waverly mentioned?'

Zebra nodded. 'They experimented with different durations, of course.'

It was too long. My Reivich trail was cold enough as it was, but if I waited another two days, I wouldn't stand a chance.

'Why do they play?' I said, wondering whether her answer would accord with what Juan, the rickshaw kid, had told me.

'They're bored,' Zebra said. 'Many of us here are postmortal. Even now, even with the plague, death is still only a remote worry for most of us. Maybe not as remote as it was seven years ago, but still not the animating force it must be to a mortal like yourself. That small, almost silent voice urging you to do something today because tomorrow might be too late . . . it just isn't there for most of us. For two hundred years Yellowstone's society hardly changed. Why create a great work of art tomorrow when you can plan an even better one for fifty years hence?'

'I understand,' I said. 'Some of it, anyway. But it should be different now. Didn't the plague make most of you mortal again? I thought it screwed around with your therapies; interfered with the machines in your cells?'

'Yes, it did. The medichines had to be instructed to dismantle themselves, turning to harmless dust, or they killed you. It didn't stop there, either. Even genetic techniques were difficult to implement, because they relied so heavily on medichines to mediate the DNA rescripting procedures. About the only people who didn't have a problem were the ones who'd inherited extreme-longevity genes from their parents, but they were never a majority.'

'Not everyone else had to abandon immortality, though.'

'No, of course not . . .' She paused, as if to collect her thoughts. 'The hermetics, you'll have seen them – well, they still have all the machines inside them, constantly correcting cell damage. But the price they pay for it is they can't move freely in the city. Once they leave their palanquins they have to restrict themselves to a few environments guaranteed to be free of residual plague spore, and even then there's a small risk.'

I looked at Zebra, trying to judge her. 'But you're not a hermetic. Are you no longer immortal?'

'No, Tanner . . . it's nowhere near as simple as that.'

'Then what?'

'After the plague, some of us found a new technique. It enabled us to keep the machines inside ourselves – most of them, anyway – and still walk unprotected in the city. It's a kind of medication; a drug. It does many things, and no one know how it works, but it seems to barrier our machines against the plague, or weaken the efficacy of any plague spore which enter our bodies.'

'This medication . . . what is it like?'

'You don't want to know, Tanner.'

'Suppose I were interested in immortality as well?'

'Are you?'

'It's a hypothetical viewpoint, that's all.'

'I thought so.' Zebra nodded sagely. 'Where you come from, immortality's something of a pointless luxury, isn't it?'

'For those not descended from the *momios*, yes.'

'*Momios*?'

'That was what we called the sleepers on the *Santiago* – they were immortal. The crew weren't.'

'We? You talk as if you were actually there.'

'Slip of the tongue. The point is, there's not much point being immortal if you're not going to survive more than ten years without getting shot or blown up in a skirmish. Besides, the price the Ultras are charging, nobody could afford it even if they wanted it.'

'And would you have wanted it, Tanner Mirabel?' Then she kissed me, and pulled back to lock eyes with me, much as Gitta had in my dream. 'I intend to make love to you, Tanner. Do you find that shocking? You shouldn't. You're an attractive man. You're different. You don't play our games – don't even understand them – though I imagine you'd play them reasonably well if you wished. I don't know what to make of you.'

'I have the same problem,' I said. 'My past is a foreign country.'

'Nice line, except it isn't remotely original.'

'Sorry.'

'But in a way, it's true, isn't it? Waverly told me that when he ran a trawl on you he didn't come up with anything clear-cut. He said it was like trying to put together a broken vase. No; that's not quite what he said, either. He said it was almost like trying to put together two, or even three, broken vases, and not knowing which piece belonged where.'

'Revival amnesia,' I said.

'Well, perhaps. The confusion looked a little more profound than that, Waverly said . . . but let's not talk about him.'

'Fine. But you still haven't told me about this medication.'

'Why are you so interested?'

'Because I think I might have already encountered it. It's Dream Fuel, isn't it? It's what your sister was investigating when she was killed for her troubles.'

She took her time answering. 'That coat . . . it's not yours, is it?'

'No, I obtained it from a benefactor. What has that got to do with anything?'

'It made me think you might be trying to trick me. But you really don't know much about Dream Fuel, do you?'

'Until a couple of days ago I'd never heard of it.'

'Then there's something you should probably know,' Zebra said. 'I injected you with a small quantity of Fuel last night.'

'What?'

'It wasn't much, I assure you. I probably should have asked you, but you were injured and tired and I knew there was very little risk.' Then she showed me the small bronze wedding-gun she had used, one full vial of Fuel in her cache. 'Fuel protects those of us who still have machines inside our bodies, but it also has general healing properties. That's why I gave it to you. I'll need to get some more.'

'Will that be easy?'

She gave me a half-smile and then shook her head. 'Not as easy as it used to be. Unless you happen to have a hotline to Gideon.'

I was about to ask her what she had meant by the remark about the coat, but now she had distracted me. I didn't think I had heard that name before.

'Gideon?'

'He's a crime lord. No one knows much about him, what he looks like, where he lives. Except he's got absolute control of Dream Fuel distribution across the city and the people who work for him are very serious about their work.'

'And now they're limiting the supply? Just when everyone's become addicted to it? Maybe I should have a word with Gideon.'

'Don't get any more involved than you have to, Tanner. Gideon is extremely bad news.'

'You sound as if you're speaking from experience.'

'I am.' Zebra walked to the window and ran a hand over the glass. 'I told you about Mavra already, Tanner. My sister, the one who used to love this view?' I nodded, remembering the conversation we'd had shortly after arriving here. 'I also told you she was dead. Well, Gideon's people were the people my sister got involved with.'

'They killed her?'

'I'll never know for sure, but that's what I think. Mavra believed they were strangling us, withholding the one substance the city needs. Dream Fuel's dangerous stuff, Tanner – there isn't enough of it to go around, and yet for most of us it's the most precious substance imaginable. It's not just the kind of thing people kill for; it's the kind of thing people fight wars for.'

'So she wanted to persuade Gideon to open up the supply?'

'Nothing so naïve; Mavra was nothing if not a pragmatist. She knew Gideon wasn't going to let it go that easily. But if she could find out how the stuff was being manufactured – even what the stuff was – she could pass on that knowledge to other people so that they could synthesise it for themselves. At the very least she'd have broken the monopoly.'

'I admire her for trying. She must have known it might get her killed.'

'Yes. She was like that. She wouldn't give up a hunt.' Zebra paused. 'I always promised her that if anything happened, I'd . . .'

'Pick up where she left off?'

'Something like that.'

'Maybe it isn't too late. When all this blows over . . .' I touched my head. 'Maybe I'll help you find Gideon.'

'Why would you do that?'

'You helped me, Zebra. It would be the least I could do.' And, I thought, because Marva sounded a lot like me. Perhaps she had come close to finding what she was looking for. If so, those who remembered her – and I counted myself as one now – owed it to her to carry on her work. There was something else, too.

Something about Gideon, and who he reminded me of – sitting, spiderlike,

275

at the dark centre of a web of absolute control, imagining himself invulnerable. I thought again of Cahuella, and what had passed through my mind in sleep. 'The Dream Fuel you gave me. Is that why I had such strange dreams?'

'It does that, sometimes. Especially if it's your first dose. It's working its way through your brain, tinkering with neural connections. That's why they call it Dream Fuel. But that's only half of it.'

'Does that make me immortal now?'

Zebra let the smoke-coloured gown fall away from her and I pulled her to me, looking into her face.

'For today, yes.'

I woke before Zebra, dressing in the Mendicant clothes which she had washed, and quietly paced her rooms until I found the things I was looking for. My hand lingered over the huge weapon she had rescued me with, which she had just left lying in the annex to her apartment as casually as a walking stick. The plasma-rifle would have been a useful piece of artillery on Sky's Edge; using it inside a city seemed almost obscene. On the other hand, so did dying.

I hefted the weapon. I hadn't ever handled anything exactly like it, but the controls were placed intuitively and the readouts showed familiar status variables. It was a very delicate weapon and I didn't rate its chances of surviving very long if it came into contact with a trace of the plague. But that was no reason to leave it lying around, almost inviting me to steal it.

'Careless, Zebra,' I said. 'Very careless indeed.'

I thought back to the night before; how the main thing on her mind must have been tending to my injury. It was perhaps understandable that she had dumped the gun at the door and then forgotten to do anything about it, but it was still negligent. I put the gun down again, quietly.

She was still asleep when I went back into the room. I had to move carefully, trying to avoid causing the furniture to move any more than necessary in case the faint noise and motion woke her up. I found her greatcoat and rummaged through the pockets.

Currency – plenty of it.

And a set of fully charged ammo-cells for the plasma-rifle. I stuffed the money and the cells into the pockets of the coat I'd stolen from Vadim – the one Zebra had found so interesting – and then dithered about whether to leave a note or not. In the end I found a pen and paper – after the plague, old-fashioned writing materials must have come back into vogue – scrawling something to the effect that I was grateful for what she had done, but I was not the kind of man who could wait two days knowing I was being hunted, even though she had offered a kind of sanctuary.

On my way out I picked up the plasma-rifle.

Her cable-car was parked where she had left it, in a niche adjacent to her complex of rooms. Again, she had been hasty – the vehicle was powered, and its control panel was still aglow and awaiting instructions.

I had watched her work the controls and judged that the action of driving was semi-automatic – the driver did not have to choose which cables to employ, just used the joysticks and throttle controls to point the vehicle in a particular direction and set the speed. The cable-car's internal processors did the rest, selecting the cables which allowed the desired route to be achieved or approximated with something approaching optimal efficiency. If the driver tried to point the car into a part of the Canopy where there were no cables, the car would presumably reject the command, or pick a roundabout route which achieved the same ends.

Still maybe there was more skill to operating a cable-car than I'd imagined, because the ride began sickeningly, like a small boat pitching in a squall. Yet somehow I managed to keep the vehicle moving forward, descending through the latticelike enclosure of the Canopy, even though I had no idea where I was going. I had a destination in mind – a very specific one, in fact – but the night's activity had completely erased my sense of direction, and I had no idea where Zebra's apartment lay, except that it was near the chasm. At least now it was daytime, with the morning sun climbing up the side of the Mosquito Net, and I could see far across the city, beginning to recognise certain characteristically deformed buildings that I must have seen yesterday, from other angles and elevations. There was a building which looked uncannily like a human hand, grasping from the sky, its fingers elongating into tendrils which quickly merged with others, from adjacent structures. Here was another, which resembled an oak tree, and others which expanded into a froth of shattered bubbles, like the face of someone stricken by an awful pestilence.

I pushed the car downwards, the Canopy rising above me like an oddly textured cloud deck, into the unoccupied hinterland which separated Canopy from Mulch. The ride became rougher, now – fewer purchase points for the cable-car, and longer, sickening slides as it descended down single strands.

By now, I imagined Zebra would have noticed my absence. A few moments would suffice for her to verify the loss of her weapon, currency and car – but then what would she do? If the Game was pervasive in Canopy society, then Zebra and her allies could hardly report my theft. Zebra would have to explain what I had been doing in her place, and then Waverly would be implicated, and the two of them would be revealed as saboteurs.

The Mulch rose into view below me, all twisted roads and floods and barnacled slums. There were fires sending smoke trails into the air and lights there now; at least I had hit an inhabited district. I could even see people outside, and rickshaws and animals, and if I had opened the car's door, I imagined I would have smelled whatever it was they were cooking or burning in those fires.

The car lurched and began to fall.

There'd had been sickening moments before, but this one seemed to last longer. And now an alarm was shrieking in the cockpit. Then something like normal motion resumed again, although it was noticeably bumpier and the vehicle's rate of descent was swifter than seemed prudent. What had happened? Had the cable snapped, or had the car simply run out of handholds for an instant, plummeting before it found another line?

Finally I looked at the console and I saw a pulsing schematic of the cable-car, with a red box flashing around the area of damage.

One of the arms was gone.

TWENTY-TWO

Someone was attacking me.

Trusting the vehicle to find its own way down as quickly and as safely as possible, I retrieved Zebra's plasma-rifle, steadying myself as the pitch rocked and swayed, my concentration not aided by the shrill insistence of the alarm. I moved back onto the rear bay, past the passenger seat where I'd lain the previous evening. Bracing myself, I knelt and opened the side door, watching it gull open. Then I leaned across and opened its counterpart on the other side, and pushed myself out as far as I could, into the wind, the ground still several hundred metres below me. I risked a quick glance up at the arm assembly, observing the cauterised stump where one of the arms had been shot clean off with some kind of beam weapon.

Then I looked up and back along my route of descent. Two other cable-cars were following me, about two hundred metres higher up and the same distance behind me. A black figure was leaning from the closest car, shouldering something which – even as I watched – flashed a light too intense for words. A line of pink ionised-air slammed past me like a piston, ozone hitting my nose almost before the thunderclap of the collapsing vacuum-tunnel sheared open by the beam weapon.

I looked down. We had lost another hundred metres, but it was still too high for my tastes. I wondered how the vehicle would manage with only one arm.

I flicked on Zebra's rifle, praying that the weapon was not equipped with a user-recognition facility. If it was, she'd disabled it. Sensing that I was bringing the weapon to shoulder level, the sight adjusted itself to bring its retinal-projection systems into line my eyes. I felt the weapon shiver as gyroscopes and accumulators came online, making it seem as if some magic energy coursed through it. Reserve ammo-cells weighing down my pockets like lead ballast, I waited for the retinal aiming system to adjust to my eyes so I could get off a shot. For a moment the system was confused, perhaps because it was configured for Zebra's own peculiarly dark and equine eyes and was having trouble adjusting to my own. The retinal graphics kept springing up, almost focusing – and then crashing in a morass of indecipherable error symbols.

Another line of pink air ripped past me, then another, gouging a silver scratch in the side of the cable-car. The stench of hot metal and plastic filled the cabin for an instant.

'Shit,' I said. The retinal system was down, but it wasn't as if my target was halfway to the horizon, or that I was trying for pinpoint precision. I just wanted to shoot the bastards out of the sky, and if the act ended up being rather messy and involving more than the usual amount of collateral damage, so be it.

I squeezed off a shot, feeling the beam-recoil nudge my shoulder.

My own beam-trail knifed backward, just missing the closest car. That was good. I had intended to just miss, on my first shot. I drew some return fire, throwing myself back into the cabin while the shot lanced past. Now I was forcing my opponent to spread his fire, forcing him to choose between disabling my vehicle and taking me out. I leaned out, shouldered the weapon in one quick fluid movement, something almost beneath conscious thought, and this time I wasn't planning on missing.

I fired.

Because I was aiming for the front of the closest vehicle, I had an easier, more vulnerable target than my opponent. I watched the lead cable-car blow apart in a grey cloud of fused innards. The driver must have died instantly, I assumed, but the gunner had fallen out of the car during the first instant of the explosion. I watched the black-clad figure plummet towards the Mulch, weapon dropping alongside, and then heard nothing as the person hit the ground amidst a confusion of stalls and lashed-together dwelling places.

Something felt wrong. I could feel it coming; unravelling into mind. Another Haussmann episode. I fought it; tried desperately to anchor myself to the present, but it was already as if a second, faint layer of reality was trying to settle over me.

'Go to hell,' I said.

The other car loitered, continuing its descent for a moment, then turning around with a quick and elegant exchange of cable-arms. I watched it rise to the Canopy, and then – for the first time since I had become aware of the attack – realised that the siren was still shrieking in the cabin. Except that now it had gained a new level of urgency.

I placed the weapon down, then navigated the bucking car to the control chair. I could feel the Haussmann episode clawing its way to the front of my head, like a seizure on the point of happening.

The ground was coming up too fast. We were almost dropping, I realised – probably just skimming down a single strand of cable. People, rickshaws and animals were fleeing the area below, although with no real agreement on where it was I was likely to touch down. I got into the chair and worked the controls, largely randomly, hoping that there was something I could do which would level off the rate of descent. And then the ground was so close I could read the expressions on the Mulch people below and none of them looked overjoyed at my arrival.

And then I hit the Mulch.

The conclave room was deep inside the *Palestine*; sealed from the rest of the ship by massive bulkhead doors which had been decorated in ornate metal scrollwork, festooning like alloy vines. Inside was a massive rectangular table surrounded by twenty high-backed seats, less than a dozen of which were occupied. The matter of the messages from home was one of utmost security, and it was considered normal that the other vessels had sent only two or three delegates apiece. They sat around the table now, their stiffly suited figures reflected in the table's polished mahogany surface, so dark and mirrorlike that it resembled a slab of perfectly still moonlit water. Rising from the centre of the table was a projection apparatus which was cycling through the technical schematics contained in the first message, skeletal graphics of dazzling complexity flashing into existence.

Sky sat next to Balcazar, listening to the faint labours of the old man's medical tabard.

'. . . and this modification would appear to give us more elaborate control of the confinement bottle topology than we yet have,' said the *Palestine*'s senior propulsion theorist, freezing one of the schematics. 'Coupled with the other things we've seen, it should give us a steeper deceleration profile . . . not to mention the ability to throttle back the flow without experiencing magnetic blow-back. That would let us turn off an anti-matter engine while there's still fuel in the reservoir – and restart it later – something we can't do with the current design.'

'Could we make those mods, even if we trusted them?' asked Omdurman, the *Baghdad*'s commanding officer. He wore a glossily black tunic flashed with grey and white sigils of rank. Coupled with the paleness of his skin and the deep black of his hair and beard, he was a study in monochrome.

'In principle, yes.' Beneath a sheen of perspiration, the propulsion tech's face was impassive. 'But I'll be honest with you. We'd be making large-scale alterations within centimetres of the confinement bottle, which has to keep functioning perfectly the whole time we're working. We can't shunt the anti-matter somewhere else until we're done. One wrong move and you won't need so many seats at the next conclave.'

'Damn the next conclave,' murmured Balcazar.

Sky sighed and dug a finger between the damp edge of his collar and the skin of his neck. It was unpleasantly warm in the conclave room, almost soporifically so. Nothing felt right on this ship. There was an aura of strangeness aboard the *Palestine* that Sky had not been expecting; one that was heightened all the more by the things that were not strange at all. The ship's layout and design had been instantly familiar, so that as soon as the Captain and he were escorted from their shuttle, he felt he knew exactly where he was. Though they were diplomatic visitors rather than prisoners, they were under constant armed guard, but had that supervision been lax enough for him to vanish into the ship, he was certain he would have been able to find his way to any part of it unaided and perhaps even unseen, exploiting his own knowledge of the *Santiago*'s blind spots and short-cuts, all of which were probably replicated on the *Palestine*. But in nearly every respect other than basic topology, the ship was subtly different, as if he had awakened into a world almost but not quite correct in the most mundane of details. The décor was different, signs and markings in unfamiliar script and language, with slogans and murals painted where the *Santiago* had blank walling. The crew wore different uniforms, flashed with sigils of rank he could not quite interpret, and when they spoke amongst themselves he understood almost nothing they said. They had different equipment and they saluted each other aggressively at every opportunity. Their body language was like a tune being played slightly offkey. The internal temperature felt warmer than on his own ship, and more humid – and there was a constant smell, as of cooking, wherever they went. It was not actually unpleasant, but it served to reinforce the feelings of foreign-ness he felt. It might have been his imagination, too, but even the gravity felt heavier, his footsteps hammering hard against the flooring. Perhaps they had upped their spin rate slightly so that when they arrived at Journey's End they would have an advantage over the other colonists. Perhaps they had done it just to make everyone uncomfortable during the conclave, and turned up the heating while they were at it. Or perhaps he *was* imagining it.

The conclave itself had been tense, but not quite tense enough that he feared – if that was the word – for the Captain's health. Balcazar had become more alert by then, almost fully lucid, for the relaxant that Rengo had administered had been designed to wear off by the time of their arrival. Some of the other senior crew members, Sky observed, were almost as infirm as his own Captain; supported by their own bio-medical rigs and fussed over by their own aides. It was quite an idiosyncratic collection of wheezing ironmongery; almost as if the machines had decided to meet and had dragged their fleshly hosts along for the ride.

They had talked mainly about the messages from home, of course. Everyone agreed that the two messages had been genuine in origin, if not necessarily guaranteed to be truthful, and that they were probably not a complex hoax perpetrated by one of the ships against the rest of the Flotilla. Each frequency component in either radio message had been subjected to a specific delay relative to its neighbour, due to the clouds of interstellar electrons lying between Sol and the Flotilla. That smearing would have been very difficult to fake convincingly, even if a transmitter could have been dropped sufficiently far behind the ships to send the message. There was never any mention of the sixth ship, and the Captain never alluded to anything connected to it. Perhaps it was truly the case that the existence of the sixth ship was only known about on the *Santiago*. A secret worth keeping, in other words.

'Of course,' said the propulsion theorist, 'it could all be a trick.'

'But why would anyone want to send us harmful information?' asked Zamudio, the commander of the host ship. 'Whatever happens to us won't make any difference to anyone back home, so why try and hurt us?'

'The same argument applies to any beneficial data,' said Omdurman. 'There's no reason for them to send that either. Except common human decency.'

'Damn human decency . . . damn it to hell,' Balcazar said.

Sky spoke up at that point, raising his voice above that of the Captain. 'I can think of arguments either way, actually.' They looked at him patiently, as one might humour a child attempting to tell a joke. Hardly anyone in the room must have known who he was, beyond the fact that he was supposedly Titus Haussmann's son. It suited him perfectly well: being underestimated was a highly satisfactory state of affairs.

He continued, 'The organisation that launched the Flotilla might still exist in some shape and form back home, perhaps clandestinely. They'd still have an interest in helping us on our way, if only to ensure that their earlier efforts weren't wasted. We might still be the only interstellar expedition underway; don't forget that. We might still be the only hope anyone has of reaching another star.'

Omdurman stroked his bearded chin. 'I suppose that's possible. We're like a great mosque being built: a project that will take hundreds of years and which no one will see in its entirety . . .'

'Damn them . . . damn them all.'

Omdurman faltered, but pretended not to have heard. '. . . yet those who know they'll die before the end is reached can still feel some satisfaction at having contributed something to the whole, even if it's only the tiniest chip in the least significant pattern. The trouble is we know precious little about what's really happened back home.'

Zamudio smiled. 'And even if they did send more thorough news updates, we still wouldn't know how much to trust them.'

'Back to square one, in other words,' said Armesto, from the *Brazilia*. He was the youngest of the Captains; not much older than Sky. Sky studied him carefully, taking the outline of a possible enemy; one that might not assume definition until years or decades hence.

'Equally, I can think of reasons they might want to kill us,' Sky said. He turned to Balcazar. 'With your permisssion, of course?'

The Captain's head jolted up, as if he had been on the point of sleep.

'Go head, Titus, dear boy.'

'Suppose we're not the only game in town.' Sky leaned forward, his elbows hard against the mahogany. 'It's a century since we left home. There may be faster ships on the drawing board now; maybe even on their way. Maybe there are factions that want to stop us reaching Swan so they can claim it for themselves. Granted, they could always fight us for it, but we're four large ships and we do have nuclear armaments.' The devices he was talking about had been put aboard for landscape engineering when they reached Journey's End – blasting mountain passes, or scooping out natural harbours – but they were perfectly capable of being used as weapons. 'We wouldn't be a pushover. From their point of view, it would be a lot simpler to persuade us to destroy ourselves.'

'So what you're saying is, there are equally strong reasons for trusting the message as not trusting it?'

'Yes. And the same argument applies to the second one; the one warning us from adopting the modifications.'

The propulsion theorist coughed. 'He's right. All we can do is assess the technical content of the message for ourselves.'

'That won't be easy.'

'Then we take a massive risk.'

So it had gone on; arguments for and against trusting the messages bounced around fruitlessly. There had been suggestions that one or other party was withholding valuable knowledge – true enough, Sky thought – but no fingers had been pointed directly and the conclave had ended in a mood of unease rather than outright hostility. All the ships had agreed to continue sharing their interpretation of the messages, together with the establishment of a special pan-Flotilla expert group to examine the technical feasability of the suggested modifications. It was agreed that no ship would act unilaterally, and there would be no attempt to implement the modifications without the express agreement of all other parties. It was even suggested that any ship that wanted to go it alone was welcome to do so, but they would have to pull away from the main body of the Flotilla, increasing their separation to four times the current distance.

'That's an insane proposal,' said Zamudio. He was a tall, handsome man, much older than he seemed, who had been blinded by the flash from the *Islamabad*. A camera was strapped to one of his shoulders like a seadog's parrot, tracking this way and that, seemingly of its own volition. 'When we launched this expedition we did it in a spirit of camaraderie, not as a race to be the first to claim the prize.'

Armesto squared his jaw. 'Then why are you so unwilling to share those supplies you've hoarded with the rest of us?'

'We aren't hoarding supplies,' Omdurman said with little discernible conviction. 'Any more than you've been withholding spare parts for our sleeper berths, as a matter of fact.'

284

Zamudio's camera snapped onto him. 'Why, that's a ridiculous . . .' He trailed off before speaking again. 'No one's denying that there are differences in the qualities of life on the ships. Far from it. It was always part of the plan that it should be like that. From the outset it was always intended that the ships should organise their own affairs independently of one another, if for no other reason than to ensure that not everyone made the same unforeseeable mistakes. Does that mean we all end up with the same basic standard of living aboard each ship? No; of course not. Something would be very wrong if it did. It's inevitable that there should be subtly differing mortality rates amongst the crew; a simple reflection of the differing emphasis placed upon medical science by the ship regimes.' He had their attention now, so he lowered his voice, gazing into the middle distance while his camera eye snapped from face to face. 'Yes, sleeper berth fatalities will vary from ship to ship. Sabotage? I don't think so, comforting as that thought might be.'

'Comforting?' someone said, as if they had misheard him.

'Yes, exactly that. There's nothing more comforting than paranoid con-spiracy-mongering, especially where it hides a deeper problem. Forget talk of saboteurs; think instead of poor operational procedures; inadequate technical understanding . . . I could go on.'

'Enough damned prattling,' Balcazar said, in a flash of lucidity. 'This isn't what we came to discuss. If anyone wants to act on the damned message, let them. I'll be more than interested in observing the results.'

But it seemed unlikely that anyone would be the first to make that move. As the Captain had implied, the natural impulse would surely be to let someone else make the first mistake. Another conclave would take place in three months, after the messages had been reviewed in greater detail. The general shipwide populace would be informed of the existence of the messages some-time after that. The accusations that had been thrown around in the conclave room were quietly forgotten. Cautiously, there was talk that the whole issue, far from heightening inter-ship tensions, might lead to a modest thawing in relations.

Now Sky sat with Balcazar in the homegoing shuttle.

'Not long until we get back to the *Santiago*, sir. Why don't you try and get some rest?'

'Damn you, Titus . . . if I wanted rest I'd . . .' But Balcazar had fallen asleep before he managed to complete the end of the sentence.

The home ship was an outlined speck on the taxi's head-up display. Sometimes it seemed to Sky that the ships of the Flotilla were like the tiny islands of a small archipelago, spaced by stretches of water which nearly ensured that each island was over the horizon from its nearest neighbour. It was always night in the archipelago, too, and the fires of the islands were practically too faint to be seen except when one was close anyway. It took a leap of faith to steer away from one of those islands into the darkness, relying on the navigational systems of the taxi not to take them into oceanic waters. Mulling modes of assassination, as was his wont, Sky thought of sabotaging a taxi's autopilot. It would have to be done just before someone he wanted to kill embarked on what they thought would be a journey to one of the other ships. It would be a simple enough matter to confuse the taxi to the point where it headed in the wrong direction entirely, sliding into blackness. Combine that with a fuel loss or life-support failure, and the possibilities were enticing indeed.

But not for him. He always accompanied Balcazar, so that particular mode was of limited value.

His mind returned to the conclave. The other Flotilla Captains had done their best not show that they noticed Balcazar's lapses of concentration and – at times – outright sanity, but Sky had seen the way they exchanged concerned glances across the polished mahogany gulf of the conference table, just when they imagined Sky to be looking elsewhere. It obviously troubled them immensely that one amongst their number was palpably losing his mind. Who was to say that Balcazar's strain of madness did not lie in wait for all them, once they reached his age? Sky, of course, did not once acknowledge that there was anything of concern in his Captain's state of health. That would have been the gravest of disloyalties. No; what Sky had done was to maintain a poker-faced semblance of obedient solemnity in the presence of his Captain, nodding dutifully at every deranged utterance from his master, never once letting slip that he considered Balcazar as thoroughly mad as any of the other Captains feared was the case.

A loyal servant, in other words.

A reminding ping from the taxi's console. The *Santiago* was looming large now, though it was still hard to see with the cabin's interior lights on. Balcazar was snoring and drooling at the same time, a silvery stream of saliva adorning one of his epaulettes like a subtle new indication of rank.

'Kill him,' Clown said. 'Go on; kill him. There's still time.'

Clown was not really present in the taxi – Sky knew that – but he was here in some sense, his high, quavery voice seeming to come not from within Sky's skull, but from some distance behind it.

'I don't want to kill him,' Sky said, adding a silent 'yet' for his own benefit.

'You know you do really. He's in the way. He's always been in the way. He's a sick old man. You would really be doing him a favour by killing him now.' Clown's voice softened. 'Look at him. He's sleeping like a little baby. I expect he's having a happy dream about his boyhood.'

'You can't know that.'

'I'm Clown. Clown knows everything.'

A soft metallic voice on the console warned Sky that they were about to enter the prohibited sphere around his own ship. The taxi would shortly be seized by the automated traffic vectoring system and guided to its berth.

286

'I've never killed anyone before,' Sky said.

'But you've often thought of it, haven't you?'

There was no point arguing with that. Sky fantasised about killing people all the time. He thought of ways to do it to his enemies – people who had slighted him, or whom he suspected of speaking about him behind his back. Some people, it seemed to him, should be killed for no other reason than that they were weak or trustful. Aboard a ship like the *Santiago*, there was every opportunity to commit murder, but very little chance of doing it in a way which would avoid detection. Nonetheless Sky's fertile imagination had brooded on this problem long enough to have thought up a dozen plausible strategies for reducing the numbers of his enemies.

But until Clown had spoken to him now, it had been enough to entertain the fantasies. Playing those gruesome little deaths over and over in his mind, slowly embroidering them, had been sufficient reward for him. Clown was right though: what was the point of drafting elaborate blueprints in painstaking detail if one at some point did not begin the business of building?

He looked at Balcazar again. So peaceful, as Clown had said.

So peaceful.

And so vulnerable.

TWENTY-THREE

It could have been worse.

I could have hit the ground without hitting the Mulch first, without first punching through two layers of festering, skeletally framed dwellings and stalls. When the car came to a stop, it was pitched nose-down in semi-darkness; faint lights and fires burned around me. I could hear raised voices, but they sounded more excited and angry than hurt, and I dared to hope that no one had been crushed by my arrival. After a few seconds I eased myself from the seat, quickly appraising my condition. I found nothing obviously broken, although everything that could have been broken was at least bruised. Then I climbed back up the length of the car, hearing the voices approach, and agitated scrabbling sounds which might have curious children picking through the wreckage, or the noises of disturbed rats. I grabbed the weapon, checking I still had the currency I had taken from Zebra, then left the vehicle, stepping onto a precarious bamboo platform which had been neatly punctured by the car's nose.

'Can you hear me?' I called, into the darkness, certain someone could. 'I'm not your enemy. I'm not from the Canopy. These are Mendicant clothes; I'm an offworlder. I need your help very urgently. The Canopy people are trying to kill me.'

I said it in Norte. It would carry a lot more conviction than if I'd spoken Canasian, the language of the Chasm City aristocracy.

'Put down the weapon, then, and start explaining how you came by it.' It was a man's voice, accented differently from the Canopy dwellers I had met. His words were imprecise, as if there was something wrong with his palette. He spoke Norte, too, but it sounded faltering, or perhaps over-precise, without the ritual elisions which come from true familiarity. He continued, 'You arrived in a cable-car, as well. That will also require explanation.'

I could see the man now, standing on the edge of the bamboo platform. But he wasn't a man at all.

I was looking at a pig.

He was small and pale-skinned, and he stood on his hind legs with the same awkward ease that I remembered from the other pigs. Goggles occluded his eyes, held in place by strands of leather tied around the back of his head. He wore a red poncho. In one trotter-fingered hand he held a cleaver with the kind of casual dexterity which suggested he used it professionally, and had long since ceased to be intimidated by its sharpness.

I didn't put down the weapon; not immediately.

'My name is Tanner Mirabel,' I said. 'I arrived from Sky's Edge yesterday. I was looking for someone and wandered into the wrong part of the Mulch by mistake. I was captured by a man called Waverly and forced to take part in the Game.'

'And you managed to escape, with a gun like that and a cable-car? Quite a trick for a newcomer, Tanner Mirabel.' He spoke my name as if it were an oath.

'I'm wearing Mendicant clothes,' I said. 'And as you'll have noticed, my accent is that of someone from Sky's Edge. I speak a little Canasian, if that's easier for you.'

'Norte is fine. We pigs aren't as stupid as you all like to think.' He paused. 'Your accent got you that gun? Quite an accent, in that case.'

'People helped me,' I said. I was about to mention Zebra by name, then thought better of it. 'Not everyone in the Canopy agrees with the Game.'

'That's true,' the man said. 'But they're still Canopy, and they still piss on us.'

'He could have been helped,' another voice said, a woman's this time. Looking into the gloom, I saw a taller, female-looking pig approach the man, carefully picking her way through the detritus of my arrival, her expression unrevealing, as if she did this every day. She reached out and took his elbow. 'I've heard of such people. Sabs, they call themselves. Saboteurs. What does he look like, Lorant?'

The first pig – Lorant – snatched off the goggles and offered them to the woman. She was strangely pretty, human hair framing her snouted, doll-like face in greasy curtains. She pushed the goggles to her eyes for a moment, nodding. 'He doesn't look Canopy. He's human, for a start – as their God intended. Except for his eyes, although maybe that's a trick of the light.'

'It's no trick,' Lorant said. 'He can see us without goggles. I noticed that when you arrived. His gaze locked onto you.' He retrieved the goggles from the female pig and said, in my direction, 'Perhaps some of what you have told us is true, Tanner Mirabel. Not all of it though, I'd wager.'

You would not lose your bet, I thought, almost mouthing the words. 'I don't intend you any harm,' I said, and then made a grand show of placing the weapon down on the bamboo, reasonably sure I could reach for it if the pig made a move towards me with the cleaver. 'I'm in a lot of trouble and the

Canopy people will return to finish me off before very long. I'm not sure I haven't made enemies of the saboteurs as well, since I stole from them.' I gambled that admitting theft from the Canopy would not harm me in Lorant's eyes, but might actually do my cause some good. 'There's something else, too. I don't know anything about people like you – good or otherwise.'

'But you know that we're pigs.'

'It's hard to miss, isn't it?'

'Like our kitchen. You didn't miss that either, did you?'

'I'll pay for it,' I said. 'I have currency, as well.' I reached into the voluminous pockets of Vadim's coat, dredging a wad from the depths. 'This isn't much,' I said. 'But it might cover some of your costs.'

'Except this isn't our property,' Lorant said, studying my outstretched hand. He would have to step forward if he wished to accept it, and at the moment neither of us was prepared to commit to that level of trust. 'The man who owns this kitchen is away visiting his brother's shrine in the Monument to the Eighty. He won't be back until sundown. He's not a man disposed to leniency or forgiveness. And then I will have to trouble him with news of the damage you have done, and he will naturally turn his anger on me.'

I offered him half of another wad, cutting deep into the reserves I had taken from Zebra. 'Maybe this will ease your troubles, Lorant. That's another ninety or hundred Ferris marks. Anything more, I might begin to suspect you were fleecing me.'

He might have smiled at that point; I could not be sure. 'I can't shelter you, Tanner Mirabel. Too dangerous.'

'What he means,' the other pig said, 'is that there will be an implant in your head. The Canopy people will know where you are, even now. And if you have angered them, that puts all of us in danger.'

'I know about the implant,' I said. 'And that's what I need you to help me with.'

'Help you get it out?'

'No,' I said. 'I know someone who can do that for me. Her name is Madame Dominika. But I've no idea how to get to her. Could you take me there?'

'Do you have any idea where that would be?'

'Grand Central Station,' I said.

The pig looked around the wreckage of the kitchen. 'Well, I don't suppose I am going to be doing a great deal of cooking today, Tanner Mirabel.'

They were refugees from the Rust Belt.

Before that, they'd been refugees from somewhere else – the cold, cometary fringes of another solar system. But the cook and his wife – I couldn't think of them as just pigs any more – had no real idea how the first of their kind had ever got there, just theories and myths. The one that sounded the most likely was that they were distant, abandoned descendants of a centuries-old programme in genetic engineering. Pigs' organs had once been used for human transplant surgery – there were more similarities than differences between the two species – and it seemed likely that the pigs had been an experiment to make the animal donors even more humanlike by blending human genes into their own DNA. Perhaps it had gone much further than anyone had intended, so that a spectrum of genes had accidentally transferred intelligence to the pigs. Or perhaps that had been the idea all along, with the pigs an aborted attempt at producing a servile race with none of the nasty drawbacks of machines.

At some point, the pigs must have been abandoned; left out in deep space to fend for themselves. Perhaps it was just too much bother to systematically hunt them down and kill them, or perhaps the pigs themselves had broken free of the labs and established their own secretive colonies. By then, Lorant said, they were more than one species anyway, each having a different mix of human and pig genes, and there were groups of pigs which lacked the ability to form words, even though they had all the right neural mechanisms in place. I remembered the pigs I'd met before being rescued by Zebra; how the first of them had made grunting sounds at me which had almost seemed like an attempt at language. Perhaps the attempt had been a lot closer than I'd imagined.

'I met some of your kind,' I said. 'Yesterday.'

'You can call us pigs, you know. We aren't bothered. It's what we are.'

'Well, these pigs appeared to be trying to kill me.'

I told Lorant what had happened, sketching in the broad details without explaining exactly what I had been doing trying to get to the Canopy in the first place. He listened intently as I spoke, then began to shake his head, slowly and sadly.

'I don't think they really wanted *you*, Tanner Mirabel. I think they probably wanted the people coming after you. They would have recognised that you were being chased. They were probably trying to persuade you to come with them, to shelter.'

I thought back to what had happened, and though I wasn't totally convinced, I did begin to wonder if things had really happened the way Lorant said.

'I shot one of them,' I said. 'Not fatally, but the leg would have needed surgery.'

'Well, don't feel too bad about it. They probably weren't little angels, you know. We get a lot of problems around here with gangs of young pigs, raising hell and causing damage.'

I surveyed the damage I had caused. 'I suppose the last thing you needed was me.'

'It can all be mended, I dare say. But I think I will help you on your way before you do any more damage, Tanner Mirabel.'

I smiled. 'That would probably be for the best, Lorant.'

After they had come down from the Rust Belt, Lorant and his wife had found themselves in the employment of a man who must have been amongst the richer individuals in the Mulch. They had their own ground-vehicle: a methane-driven tricycle with enormous balloon-wheels. The superstructure of the vehicle was a mish-mash of plastic and metal and bamboo, shrouded by rain sheets and parasols; it looked to be on the point of falling to pieces if I so much as breathed in its general direction.

'You don't have to look so disgusted,' Lorant's wife said. 'It goes. And I don't think you're exactly in a position to complain.'

'Never a truer word was said.'

But it worked, tolerably, and the balloon-wheels did a passable job of smoothing out the imperfections in the roadbed. Once Lorant had agreed to my terms, I managed to persuade him to detour to the place where the wreckage of the other cable-car had come down. By the time we got there a large crowd had assembled, and I then had to persuade Lorant to wait while I pushed through to the middle. There, in what remained of the front of the cable-car, I found Waverly, dead, his chest impaled on a piece of Mulch bamboo, just like one of the deadfalls I had rigged for Reivich. His face was a mass of blood, and might have been unrecognisable except for the blood-filled crater where his monocle had been. It must have been surgically attached.

'Who did this?'

'Harvested,' said a stooped woman next to me, spitting the word through the gaps in her tooth. 'That's good optics, that is. Get a good price for that, they will.'

I resisted any burning curiosity to find out who 'they' were.

I walked back to Lorant's tricycle, feeling that in some way part of my own conscience had been ripped out, no less brutally than Waverly's eyepiece.

'Well,' Lorant said, while I climbed back into the tricycle. 'What is it you took from him?'

'You think I went back for a trophy?'

He shrugged, as if the matter were of no importance. But as we moved off, I had to ask myself just why I had gone back, if it was not for the reason he had thought.

The journey to Grand Central Station took an hour, though it seemed to me that much of this time was spent doubling back on our route to avoid areas of the Mulch which were either feared or impassable. It was possible that we only travelled three or four kilometres from the place where I had been attacked by Waverly's people. Nonetheless, none of the landmarks I had made out from Zebra's apartment were visible here – or if they were, I was seeing them from unrecognisable angles. My earlier sense of having found my feet – the sense that I had begun to assemble a mental map of the city – evaporated like a ridiculous dream. It would happen eventually, of course, if I spent enough time working on it. But not today; not tomorrow, and maybe not for weeks to come. And I didn't plan on staying that long.

When we finally arrived at Grand Central Station, it was as if less than a heartbeat had elapsed since I was last there, desperately trying to detach myself from Quirrenbach. It was much earlier in the day now – not even noon, as far as I could tell by the angle of the sun on the Net – but no sense of that penetrated the station's gloomy interior. I thanked Lorant for bringing me this far, and asked him if he would allow me to buy him a meal in addition to what I had already paid him, but he declined, refusing to get out of the driving seat of his trike. With goggles and fedora on and his clothes drawn up tightly around his face, he looked completely human, but I guess the illusion would have been harder to sustain indoors. Pigs, it appeared, were not universally loved and there were whole swathes of the Mulch which were out of bounds to them.

We shook hands – and trotters – anyway, and then he drove away into the Mulch.

TWENTY-FOUR

My first port of call was the broker's tent, where I sold Zebra's weapon at what was probably an extortionate mark-down on its true value. I could hardly complain; I was less interested in cash than in in losing the weapon before it could be traced to me. The broker asked if it was hot, but I could see there was no real interest in his eyes. The rifle was far too cumbersome and conspicuous for an operation like the Reivich job. The only place you could walk into with a piece of hardware like that and not raise eyebrows would be a convention of heavy-artillery fetishists.

Madame Dominika, I was gratified to see, was still open for business. This time I didn't need to be dragged there, but walked in willingly, my coat pockets swinging with the ammo-cells I had forgotten to sell.

'She no open for business,' said Tom, the kid who had originally hassled Quirrenbach and myself.

I palmed a few notes and slapped them on the table before Tom's goggle-eyed face. 'She is now,' I said, and pushed on through to the tent's inner chamber.

It was dark, but it took only a second or two for the room's interior to snap into view, as if someone had turned on a very faint grey lantern. Dominika was sleeping on her operating couch, her generous anatomy shrouded in a garment which might have begun life as a parachute.

'Wake up,' I said, not too loudly. 'You've got a customer.'

Her eyes opened slowly, like cracks in swelling pastry. 'What is this, you got no respect?' The words came out quickly, but she sounded too lethargic to register real alarm. 'You ain't come barging in here.'

'My money seemed to cut some ice with your assistant.' I dredged up another note and flashed it in front of her face. 'How does this look to you?'

'I don't know, I can't see nothing. What wrong with your eyes? Why they like that?'

'There's nothing wrong with my eyes,' I said, and then wondered how convincing I sounded to her. After all, Lorant had said something similar. And it was a long time since I had experienced any difficulty seeing in the dark.

I extinguished that line of thought – unsettling as it was – and kept up the pressure on Dominika. 'I need you to do a job for me, and to answer a few questions. That's not asking too much, is it?'

She propelled her bulk from the couch, fitting her lower reaches into the steam-powered harness which waited by her side. I heard a hiss of leaking pressure as it took her bulk. Then Dominika moved away from the bed with all the grace of a barge.

'What kind job, what kind questions.'

'There's an implant I need removing. Then I need to ask some questions about a friend of mine.'

'Maybe I ask you questions about friend too.' I had no idea what she meant by that, but before I could ask, she had turned on the tent's interior light, exposing her waiting instruments, clustered around the couch which I now saw was spattered with faint rusty scabs of dried blood of varying vintage and hue. 'But that cost too. Show me implant.' I did, and after examining it for a few moments, her sharp thimbled fingers digging into the side of my head, she seemed satisfied. 'Like Game implant, but you still alive.'

Evidently that meant it could not possibly be a Game implant, and for a moment there was no faulting her logic. After all, how many of the hunted ever stood a chance of making it back to Madame Dominika and having the trace removed from their skulls?

'Can you remove it?'

'If neural connections shallow, no problem.' Saying this, she guided me to the couch and swung a viewing device in front of her eyes, chewing her lower lip as she peered into my skull. 'No. Neural connections shallow; barely reach cortex. Good news for you. But look like Game implant. How it get there? Mendicants?' Then she shook her head, the rolls of flesh around her neck oscillating like counterweights. 'No, not Mendicants, unless you lie to me yesterday, when you say you no have implants. And this insertion wound new. Not even day old.'

'Just get the damned thing out,' I said. 'Or else I walk out of here with the money I've already given the kid.'

'That you can do, but you no find better than Dominika. That not threat, that promise.'

'Then do it,' I said.

'First you ask question,' she said, levitating around the couch to prep her other instruments, swapping her thimbles with impressive dexterity. She carried a pouch of them somewhere down in the infolded complexity of her waist, finding those she wanted by touch alone, without cutting or pricking her fingers in the process.

'I have a friend called Reivich,' I said. 'He arrived a day or two ahead of me and we've lost touch. Revival amnesia, the Mendicants said. They could tell me he was in the Canopy, but no more than that.'

'And?'

'I think there was a good chance he sought your services.' Or could not avoid them, I thought. 'He would have had implants that needed removing, like Mister Quirrenbach, the other gentleman I travelled with.' Then I described Reivich to her, aiming for the kind of vaguely correct level of recall which would imply friendship rather than an assassin's physiometric target profile. 'It's very important that we get in contact, and so far I haven't succeeded.'

'What make you think I know this man?'

'I don't know – how much do you think it would take? Another hundred? Would that jog your memory?'

'Dominika's memory, it not so fast this time of morning.'

'Two hundred then. Now is Mister Reivich springing to mind?' I watched as a look of theatrical recollection appeared on her face. I had to hand it to her, she did it with style. 'Oh, good. I'm so glad.' If only she knew exactly how much.

'Mister Reivich, he special case.'

Of course he was. An aristocrat like Reivich, even on Sky's Edge, would have had almost as much ironmongery floating around in his body as a *Belle Epoque* high-roller; maybe more than some top-level Demarchists. And, like Quirren-bach, he would not even have heard of the Melding Plague until he arrived around Yellowstone. No time either to seek out the few remaining orbital clinics capable of doing the extraction work. He would have been in a hurry to get down to the surface and lose himself in Chasm City.

Dominika would have been his first and last chance at salvation.

'I know he was a special case,' I said. 'And that's why I know you'd have a means to contact him.'

'Why I want contact him?'

I sighed, realising that this was going to be hard work, or expensive, or both. 'Supposing you removed something from him, and he seemed healthy, and then a day later you discovered that there was something anomalous with the implant you'd removed – that perhaps it had plague traces. You'd be obliged to contact him then, wouldn't you?'

Her expression hadn't changed during all this, so I decided a little harmless flattery ought to be brought into play.

'It's what any self-respecting surgeon would do. I know not everyone around here would bother chasing up a client like that, but as you've just said, no one's better than Madame Dominika.'

She grunted acknowledgement. 'Client information, confidential,' Domin-ika added, but we both knew what *that* meant.

A few minutes later, I was a few dozen notes lighter, but I also had an address in the Canopy; something called Escher Heights. I had no idea how specific it was – whether it referred to a single apartment, or a single building, or simply some predefined region of the tangle.

'Now you close eyes,' she said, pushing a blunt thimbled fingertip against my forehead. 'And Dominika work her magic.'

She adminstered a local anaesthetic before getting to work. It didn't take her long, and I felt no real discomfort as she removed the hunt implant. She might as well have been excising a cyst. I wondered why Waverly had not thought to include an anti-tamper system in the implant, but perhaps that had been considered just a tiny bit too unsporting. In any case – in so far as I understood things, based on what I had gleaned from Waverly and Zebra – in the normal rules of play the implant's telemetry was not meant to be accessed by the people actually doing the hunting. They were allowed to chase the prey using whatever forensic techniques they liked, but homing in on a buried neural transmitter was just too easy. The implant was purely for spectators, and for the people like Waverly who monitored the progress of the game.

Idly, as my mind free-associated on Dominika's couch, I thought of the refinements I might have introduced if it had been up to me. For a start, I would have made the implant very much harder to remove, putting in the deep neural connections Dominika had worried about, and then an anti-tamper system; something which would fry the brain of the subject if anyone tried removing the implant ahead of time. I would also make sure that the hunters carried their own implants, equally difficult to remove. I'd arrange for the two types of implant – hunter and hunted – to emit some kind of coded signal which each recognised. And when the parties approached each other within some predefined radius – say a city block, or less – I would arrange for both implants to inform their wearers of the proximity of the other, via the deep neural connections I had already sewn. I would cut the voyeurs out of the loop completely; let them track the game in their own fashion. Make the whole thing more private, and limit the number of hunters to a nice round number, like one. That way the whole thing would become infinitely more personal. And why limit the hunt to a mere fifty hours? In a city the size of this one, it struck me that the hunt could easily last tens of days, or longer, provided the target was allowed sufficient time to run and hide in the maze of the Mulch. For that matter, I saw no reason to limit the arena of play to the Mulch alone, or even to Chasm City. Why not every settlement on the planet, if they wanted a real challenge?

Of course, there was no way they'd go for it. What they wanted was a quick kill; a night's blooding, with as little expense, danger and personal involvement as possible.

'Okay,' Dominika said, pressing a sterilised pad against the side of my head. 'You done now, Mister Mirabel.' She held the implant between two fingers, glinting like a tiny grey jewel. 'And if this not hunt implant, then Dominika skinniest woman in Chasm City.'

'You never know,' I said, 'miracles do happen.'

'Not to Dominika.' Then she helped me from the couch. I felt a little light-headed, but when I fingered the head wound it felt tiny and there was no sign of infection or scarring. 'You no curious?' she asked, as I shrugged myself back into Vadim's coat, anxious for the anonymity it afforded despite the heat and humidity.

'No curious – I mean not curious – about what?'

'I say I ask you questions about friend.'

'Reivich? We've already covered that.'

She began packing away her thimbles. 'No. Mister Quirrenbach. Other friend, the one you with yesterday.'

'Actually, Mister Quirrenbach and I were more acquaintances than friends. What was it anyway?'

'He pay me not to tell you this, good money. So I say nothing. But you rich man now, Mister Mirabel. You make Mister Quirrenbach seem poor. You get Dominika's drift?'

'You're saying Quirrenbach bribed you into secrecy, but if I top his bribe I can bribe you out of it?'

'You smart cookie, Mister Mirabel. Dominika's operations, they no give you brain damage.'

'Enthralled to hear it.' With a long-suffering sigh I reached into my pockets again and asked her to tell me what it was Quirrenbach had not wanted me to know. I was unsure exactly what it was I was expecting – very little, perhaps, since my mind had not really had time to dwell on the idea that Quirrenbach had ever had something to hide.

'He come in with you,' Dominika said. 'Dressed like you, Mendicant clothes. Ask for implants out.'

'Tell me something I don't know.'

Dominika smiled then, a salacious smile, and I knew that whatever it was she was about to inflict on me, she was going to enjoy it.

'He no *have* implants, Mister Mirabel.'

'What do you mean? I saw him on your couch. You were operating on him. You'd shaved his hair.'

'He tell me make it look good. Dominika, she no ask questions. Just do what client says. Client always right. 'Specially when client pay good, like Mister Quirrenbach. Client say fake surgery. Shave hair, go through motion. But I never open his head. No need. I scan him anyway – nothing in there. Him already clean.'

'Then why the hell would—'

And then suddenly it all made sense. Quirrenbach did not need to have his implants removed because – if he had ever had any to start with – they had been removed years earlier, during the plague. Quirrenbach was not from Grand Teton at all. He was not even from outside the system. He was local talent, and he had been recruited to follow me down and find out what was making me tick.

He had been working for Reivich.

Reivich had reached Chasm City ahead of me, travelling down while I was still having my memories reassembled by the Ice Mendicants. A few days' lead was not much, but it had obviously been sufficient time to recruit some help. Quirrenbach might have been his first point of contact. And then Quirrenbach had returned to orbit and mingled with the immigrants who had just arrived from beyond the system. His mission would have been simple enough. Investigate the people revived from the *Orvieto* and find someone who might just possibly be a hired killer.

I thought back to how it had all happened.

First I had been accosted by Vadim in the commons of the *Strelnikov*. I had shrugged off Vadim, but a few minutes later I had seem him beating up Quirrenbach. I had crossed the commons sphere, forcing Vadim to give up on Quirrenbach, and then I had beaten up Vadim myself. I remembered well how it had been Quirrenbach who urged me not to kill him.

At the time, I put it down to forgiveness on his part.

Afterwards Quirrenbach and I had then crawled to Vadim's quarters. I remembered again how Quirrenbach had at first seemed uneasy as we rifled through his belongings – Quirrenbach questioning the morality of what I was doing. I had argued with him, and then Quirrenbach had been forced to go along with the theft.

All along, I hadn't seen the obvious: that Quirrenbach and Vadim were working together.

Quirrenbach had needed a way to get close to me without rousing my suspicions; a way to find out more about me. The two of them had set me up; Vadim undoubtedly hurting Quirrenbach in the commons, but only because they needed that realism. They must have known I would be unable to resist intervening, especially after my earlier brush with Vadim. Later, when we had been attacked in the carousel, I remembered how I had seen Quirrenbach standing to one side, restrained by the other man, while I took the brunt of Vadim's punishment.

I should have seen it then.

Quirrenbach had latched onto me, which implied that he was very good at his job; that he had singled me out amongst all the passengers on the ship – but it was not necessarily like that. Reivich might have employed half a dozen other agents to tail other passengers, all using different strategems to get close to their targets. The difference was, the others were all shadowing the wrong person, and Quirrenbach – by luck or intuition or deduction – had hit the bullseye. But there was no way he could have known for sure. In all the conversations we had had, I had still been careful enough not to give away anything which would have established my identity as Cahuella's security man.

I tried to put myself in Quirrenbach's position.

It must have been very tempting for him and Vadim to kill me. But they could not do that; not until they had become totally *certain* that I was the real assassin. If they had killed me then, they would never know for sure that they had got the man they were after – and that doubt would always shadow them.

So Quirrenbach had probably been planning to tail me for as long as it took; as long as it took to establish a pattern; that I was after a man called Reivich for some purpose unspecified. Visiting Dominika's was an essential part of his disguise. He must not have realised that as a soldier I would lack implants and would therefore not require the good Madame's talents. But he had taken it calmly – trusting me with his belongings while he was under the knife. Nice touch, Quirrenbach, I thought. The goods had served to reinforce his story.

Except again, in hindsight, I should have realised. The broker had complained that Quirrenbach's experientials were bootlegged; that they were copies of originals he had handled weeks earlier. And yet Quirrenbach said he had only just arrived. If I checked the manifests of lighthuggers arriving in the last week, would I even find that a ship had come in from Grand Teton? Perhaps, or perhaps not. It depended on how fastidious Quirrenbach had been in the manufacturing of his cover. I doubted that it went very deep, since he would have had only a day or two to manufacture the whole thing from scratch.

All things considered, he hadn't done an entirely bad job.

It was sometime after noon, when I had finished with Dominika, that the next Haussmann episode happened. I was standing with my back against the wall of Grand Central Station, idly watching a skilled puppeteer entertain a small group of children. The puppeteer worked above a miniature booth, operating a tiny model of Marco Ferris, making the delicately jointed, spacesuited figurine descend a rockface formed from a heap of crumbled masonry. Ferris was supposed to be climbing into the chasm, because there was a pile of jewels at the base of the slope guarded by a fierce, nine-headed alien monster. The children clapped and screamed as the puppeteer made the monster lunge at Ferris.

That was when my thoughts stalled and the episode inserted itself, fully-formed.

Afterwards – when I'd had time to digest what had been revealed to me – I thought about the one that had come before it. The Haussmann episodes had begun innocently enough, reiterating Sky's life according to the facts as I knew them. But they'd begun to diverge, at first in small details and then with increasing obviousness. The references to the sixth ship didn't belong in any orthodox history that I'd ever heard of, and nor did the fact that Sky had kept alive the assassin who had murdered, or been given the means to murder, his father. But those were minor aspects of the story compared with the idea that Sky had actually murdered Captain Balcazar. Balcazar was just a footnote in our history; one of Sky's predecessors – but no one had ever intimated that Sky had actually *killed* him.

Clenching my fist, blood raining against the floor of the concourse, I began to wonder what I'd really been infected with.

'There wasn't anything I could do about it. He was sleeping there, not making a sound – I never suspected anything was wrong.'

The two medics examining Balcazar had come aboard the instant the ship was secure, after Sky had raised the alarm about the old man. Valdivia and Rengo had closed the airlock behind them so that they had space to work. Sky watched them intently. They both looked weary and sallow, with bags under their eyes from overwork.

'He didn't cry out, gasp for air, anything like that?' said Rengo.

'No,' Sky said. 'Not a peep.' He made a show of looking distraught, but was careful not to overdo it. After all, with Balcazar out of the way, the path to the Captaincy was suddenly much clearer than it had been before, as if a complicated maze had suddenly revealed itself to have a very simple route to its heart. He knew that; they knew it too – and it would have been even more suspicious if he had not tempered his grief with the merest hint of pleasure at his considerable good fortune.

'I'll bet those bastards on the *Palestine* poisoned him,' Valdivia said. 'I always was against him going over, you know.'

'It was certainly a stressful meeting,' Sky said.

'That was probably all it took,' Rengo said, scratching at the raw pink skin under his eye. 'There's no need to blame it on the others. He just couldn't take the stress.'

'There's nothing I could have done, then?'

The other medic was examining the prosthetic web across Balcazar's chest, strapped on beneath the side-buttoned tunic which the men had now opened. Valdivia prodded the device doubtfully. 'This should have given off an alarm. You didn't hear one, I take it?'

'As I said, not a peep.'

'Damn thing must have broken down again. Listen, Sky,' Valdivia said. 'If a word of this gets out, we're absolutely done for. That damn web was always breaking down, but the way Rengo and I have been over-stretched recently . . .' He blew out air and shook his head in disbelief at the hours he had been working. 'Well, I'm not saying we didn't repair it, but obviously we couldn't spend all our time nursing Balcazar to the exclusion of everyone else. I know they've got gear on the *Brazilia* better than this clapped-out rubbish, but what good does it do us?'

'Very little,' Sky said, nodding keenly. 'Other people would have died if you had devoted too much attention to the old man. I understand perfectly.'

'I hope you do, Sky – because there's going to be one hell of a shitstorm once news of his death leaks out.' Valdivia looked at the Captain again, but if he was hoping for a miraculous recovery, there was no sign of it. 'We're going to come under examination for the quality of our medical support. You're going to be grilled about the way you handled the trip over to the *Palestine*. Ramirez and those other council bastards are going to try and say we screwed up. They're going to try and say you were negligent. Trust me; I've seen it all before.'

'We all know it wasn't our fault,' Sky said. He looked down at the Captain, the snail-trail of dried saliva still adorning his epaulette. 'He was a good man; he served us well, long after he should have retired. But he was old.'

'Yes, and he would have died in a year or so, no matter what happened. But try explaining *that* to the ship.'

'We'll just have to watch our backs, then.'

'Sky . . . you won't say a word, will you? About what we've told you?'

Someone was banging on the airlock, trying to get into the taxi. Sky ignored the commotion. 'What do you want me to say, exactly?'

The medic drew in a breath. 'You have to say the web gave you a warning. It doesn't matter that you didn't act on it. You couldn't have – you didn't have the resources or the expertise, and you were a long way from the ship.'

Sky nodded, as if all this was perfectly reasonably and exactly what he would have suggested. 'Just so long as I never imply that the prosthetic web never actually worked in the first place?'

The two medics glanced at each other. 'Yes,' said the first. 'That's exactly it. No one will blame you, Sky. They'll see that you did everything you could have done.'

The Captain, now that Sky thought about it, looked very peaceful now. His eyes were shut – one of the medics had fingered down his eyelids to give the man some semblance of dignity in death. It was, as Clown had said, entirely possible to imagine that the man was dreaming of his boyhood. Never mind that the man's childhood, aboard the ship, had been every bit as sterile and claustrophobic as Sky's own.

The knocking on the airlock had not stopped. 'I'd better let that fellow in,' Sky said.

'Sky . . .' the first medic said imploringly.

He put a hand on the man's forearm. 'Don't worry about it.'

Sky composed himself and palmed the door control. Behind, there were at least twenty people all wanting to be first into the cabin. They were all trying to get a look at the dead Captain, professing concern while secretly hoping this was not another false alarm. Balcazar had been in the distasteful habit of almost dying for several years now.

'Dear God,' said one of them, a woman from Propulsion Concepts. 'It's true, isn't it . . . what in heaven's name happened?'

One of the medics started to speak, but Sky was faster. 'His prosthetic web malfunctioned,' he said.

'What?'

'You heard me. I was watching Balcazar the whole time. He was fine until his web started making an alarm sound. I opened his tunic and looked at the diagnostic readout. It said he was having a coronary.'

'No . . .' one of the medics said, but he might as well have been addressing an empty room.

'And you're sure he wasn't having one?' the woman said.

'Hardly. He was talking to me at the time, quite lucidly. No sign of discomfort, just annoyance. Then the web told me it was going to attempt defibrillation. Needless to say, he became quite agitated at that point.'

'And what happened then?'

'I started to try and remove the web, but with all the lines running into him, I realised it was going to be impossible in the seconds I had before the defib began. I had no choice but to get away from Balcazar. I might have been killed myself had I been touching him.'

'He's lying!' the medic said.

'Ignore him,' Sky said placidly. 'He's bound to say that, isn't he? I'm not saying this was deliberate . . .' He allowed the word to linger, so that it would at least have time to settle in people's imaginations before he moved on. 'I'm not saying this was deliberate, just a terrible mistake due to overwork. Look at the two of them. These two men are close to nervous exhaustion. It's no wonder they started making mistakes. We shouldn't blame them too much for that.'

There. When the conversation was replayed in people's memories, what would stick out would not be Sky trying to weasel out of accepting the blame himself, but Sky being magnanimous in victory; even compassionate. They would see that and applaud, while at the same time conceding that some blame should still be apportioned to the sleepwalking medics. They would see no harm in that, Sky thought. A great and respected old man had died under regrettable circumstances. It was only right and proper that there should be some recrimination.

He had covered himself well.

An autopsy would establish that the Captain had indeed died from heart failure, although neither the autopsy nor the memory readout from the prosthetic web would ever quite elucidate the precise chronology of his death.

'You did very well,' Clown said.

True; but Clown deserved some credit as well. It was Clown who had told him to unbutton the tunic when Balcazar was asleep, and Clown who had shown him how to access the web's private functions so that he could program it to deliver the defibrillating pulse even though the Captain was as well as he had ever been lately. Clown had been clever, even if on some level Sky knew that this knowledge had always been his. But Clown had dredged it from his memory, and for that he was thankful.

'I think we make a good team,' Sky said, under his breath.

Sky watched the bodies of the men tumble into space.

Valdivia and Rengo had died by the simplest means of execution available aboard a spacecraft: asphyxiation in an airlock, followed by ejection into the vacuum. The trial into the old man's death had taken up two years of shiptime; grindingly slow as appeals were lodged, discrepancies found in Sky's account. But the appeals had failed and Sky had managed to explain the discrepancies to almost everyone's satisfaction. Now a retinue of senior ship's officers crowded around the adjacent portholes, straining for a glimpse into the darkness. They had already heard the dying men thumping on the door of the airlock as the air was sucked from the chamber.

Yes, it was a harsh punishment, he reflected – more so, given the already overstretched medical expertise aboard the ship. But such crimes could not be taken lightly. It hardly mattered that these men had not *meant* to kill Balcazar with their negligence – although that lack of intention itself was open to doubt. No; aboard a ship negligence was itself scarcely less a crime than mutiny. It would have been negligent, too, not to make examples of these men.

'You murdered them,' Constanza said, quietly enough so that only he heard it. 'You may have convinced the others, but not me. I know you too well for that, Sky.'

'You don't know me at all,' he said, his voice a hiss.

'Oh, but I do. I've known you since you were a child.' She smiled exaggeratedly, as if the two of them were sharing an amusing piece of smalltalk. 'You were never normal, Sky. You were always more interested in twisted things like Sleek than real people. Or monsters like the infiltrator. You've kept him alive, haven't you?'

'Kept who alive?' he said, his expression as strained as Constanza's.

'The infiltrator.' She looked at him with narrow, suspicious eyes. 'If it even happened that way. Where is he, anyway? There are a hundred places you could hide something like that aboard the *Santiago*. One day I'll find out, you know, put an end to whatever sadistic little experiment you're running. The same way I'll eventually prove that you framed Valdivia and Rengo. You'll get your punishment.'

Sky smiled, thinking of the torture chamber where he kept Sleek and the Chimeric. The dolphin was several degrees less sane than he had ever been: an engine of pure hate that existed only to inflict pain on the Chimeric. Sky had conditioned Sleek to blame the Chimeric for his confinement, and now the dolphin had assumed the role of Devil against the God that Sky had become in the Chimeric's eyes. It had been much easier to shape the Chimeric that way, giving him a figure to fear and despise as well as one to revere. Slowly but surely, the Chimeric was approaching the ideal Sky had always had in mind. By the time the Chimeric was needed – and that would not be for years to come – the work would be done.

'I don't know what you mean,' he said.

A hand rested on his shoulder. It was Ramirez, the leader of the executive council, the shipwide body with the power to elect someone to the vacant Captaincy. Ramirez, they were saying, was very likely to be Balcazar's successor.

'Monopolising him again, Constanza?' the man said.

'We were just going over old times,' she answered. 'Nothing that can't wait, I assure you.'

'He did us proud, don't you think, Constanza? Other men might have been tempted to give those fellows the benefit of the doubt, but not our Sky.'

'Not him, no,' Constanza said, before turning away.

'There's no room for doubt in the Flotilla,' Sky said, watching the two bodies dwindle. He nodded to the Captain, lying in state in his own cooled casket. 'If there's one lesson that dear old man taught me, it's never to give any house room to uncertainty.'

'That dear old man?' Ramirez sounded amused. 'Balcazar, you mean?'

'He was like a father to me. We'll never see his like again. If he were alive, these men would be lucky to get away with anything as painless as asphyxiation. Balcazar would have seen a painful death as the only valid form of deterrence.' Sky looked at him intently. 'You do agree, don't you, sir?'

'I . . . wouldn't pretend to know.' Ramirez seemed slightly taken aback, but he blinked and continued speaking, 'I had no great insights into Balcazar's mind, Haussmann. Word is, he wasn't at his very sharpest towards the end. But I suppose you'd know all about that, having been his favourite.' Again that hand on his shoulder. 'And that means something to some of us. We trusted Balcazar's judgement, just as he trusted Titus, your father. I'll be frank: your name has been bandied about . . . what would you think to . . .'

'The Captaincy?' No sense in beating about the bush. 'It's a bit premature, isn't it? Besides – someone with your own excellent record and depth of experience . . .'

'A year ago, I might have agreed. I will probably take over, yes – but I'm not a young man, and I doubt that it'll be very long before questions are being asked about my likely successor.'

'You have years ahead of you, sir.'

'Oh, I may live to see Journey's End, but I'll be in no position to oversee the difficult early years of the settlement. Even you will no longer be a young man when that happens, Haussmann . . . but you will be much younger than some of us. Importantly, I see you have nerve as well as vision . . .' Ramirez glanced at Sky oddly. 'Something's troubling you, isn't it?'

Sky was watching the dots of the executed men dissolve into darkness, like two tiny spots of cream dropped into the blackest coffee imaginable. The ship was not under thust, of course – it had been drifting for Sky's entire life – which meant that the men were taking an eternity to fall away.

'Nothing, sir. I was just thinking. Now that those two men have been ejected, and we don't have to carry them with us any more, we'll be able to decelerate just that little bit harder when it comes time to initiate the slow-down burn. That means we can stay in cruise-mode a little longer, at our current speed. It means we'll reach our destination sooner. Which means those men have, in some small, barely sufficient way, paid us back for their crimes.'

'You do come out with the oddest things, Haussmann.' Ramirez tapped him on the nose and leaned closer. There had never been any danger of the other officers overhearing the conversation, but now he was whispering. 'Word of advice. I wasn't joking when I said your name had been bandied about – but you aren't the only candidate, and one wrong word from you could have a disastrous effect on your chances. Am I making myself clear?'

'Crystal, sir.'

'Good. Then watch your step, keep your head about you at all times, and you may be in with a chance.'

Sky nodded. He imagined that Ramirez expected him to feel grateful for this titbit of confidentiality, but what Sky actually felt – and did his level best to hide – was unmitigated contempt. As if the wishes of Ramirez and his cronies in any way influenced him! As if they actually had any say in whether he became Captain or not. The poor, blind fools.

'He's nothing,' Sky breathed. 'But I've got to let him feel he is useful to us.'

'Of course,' Clown said, for Clown had never been far away. 'It's what I would do.'

TWENTY-FIVE

After the episode had happened, I walked around the concourse until I found a tent where I could rent the use of a telephone for a few minutes. Everyone relied on phones now that the city's original elegantly swift data networks had stopped working. It was something of a comedown for a society whose machines had once elevated the art of communication into an effortless form of near-telepathy, but the phones had become a minor fashion accessory in their own right. The poor didn't have them and so the rich flaunted them, the larger and more conspicuous the better. The phone I rented looked like a crude, military-hardened walkie-talkie: a bulky black handheld unit with a popup two-d screen and a matrix of scuffed push-buttons marked with Canasian characters.

I asked the man renting the phone what I needed to do to reach both an orbital number and someone in the Canopy. He gave me a long and involved explanation about both, the details of which I struggled to hold in my head. The orbital number was easier since I already knew it – engraved onto the Mendicant business card which Sister Amelia had left me – but I had to get through four or five temperamental network layers before I reached it.

The Mendicants conducted their business in an interesting manner. They maintained ties with many of their clients long after they had left Hospice Idlewild. Some of those clients, on ascending to positions of power in the system, returned favours to the Mendicants – donations which allowed them to keep their habitat solvent. But it went beyond that. The Mendicants relied on their clients returning to them for additional services – information and the something which could only be described as the politest kind of espionage, so it was always in their interests to be in easy reach.

I had to walk out of the station, into the rain, before the phone was able to hook into any of the city's surviving data systems. Even then it took many seconds of stuttering attempts before an informational route was established to the Hospice, and once our conversation began it was punctuated by significant timelags and dropouts as data packets ricocheted around near-Yellowstone space, occasionally arcing off on parabolas which never returned.

'Brother Alexei of the Ice Mendicants, how may I serve God through you?'

The face which had appeared on the screen was gaunt and lantern-jawed, the man's eyes gleaming with calm benevolence, like an owl. One of the eyes, I noticed, was surrounded by a deep purple bruise.

'Well, well,' I said. 'Brother Alexei. How nice. What happened? Fell on your trowel?'

'I'm not sure I follow you, friend.'

'Well, I'll jog your memory for you. My name is Tanner Mirabel. I came through the Hospice a few days ago, from the *Orvieto*.'

'I'm . . . not sure I recall you, brother.'

'Funny. Don't you remember how we exchanged vows in the cave?'

He gritted his teeth, all the while maintaining that benevolent half-smile. 'No . . . sorry. Drawing a blank there. But please continue.'

He was wearing an Ice Mendicant smock, hands clasped across his stomach. Behind him, I was afforded a view of climbing stepped vineyards which rose up and up until they curved overhead, bathed in the mirrored light of the habitat's sunscreens. Little chalets and rest places dotted the steps, blocks of cool white amidst the overwhelmingly florid green, like icebergs on a briny sea.

'I need to speak to Sister Amelia,' I said. 'She was very kind to me during our stay and she dealt with my personal affairs. I seem to remember you and she are acquainted?'

The look of placidity did not diminish. 'Sister Amelia is one of our kindest souls. It does not surprise me that you wish to show your gratitude. But I am afraid she is indisposed in the cryocrypts. Perhaps I can – in my own way – at least be of service, even if my own ministerings can not even begin to approximate the degree of devotion tended you by the divine Sister Amelia?'

'Have you hurt her, Alexei?'

'God forgive you.'

'Cut the pious act. I'll break your spine if you've hurt her. You realise that, don't you? I should have done it while I had the chance.'

He chewed on that for a few moments before responding, 'No, Tanner . . . I haven't hurt her. Does that satisfy you?'

'Then get me Amelia.'

'Why is it so urgent that you speak to her, and not me?'

'I know from the conversations we had that Sister Amelia dealt with a lot of newcomers coming through the Hospice, and I'd like to know if she ever remembered dealing with a Mister . . .' I started saying Quirrenbach, then bit my tongue.

'Sorry, didn't quite catch the name.'

'Never mind. Just put me through to Amelia.'

He hesitated, then asked me to repeat my own name again.

'Tanner,' I said, gritting my teeth.

It was like we had only just been introduced. 'Just a moment of your – um – patience, brother.' The look was still in place, but his voice had an edge of strain to it now. He lifted one sleeve of his frock, exposing a bronze bracelet into which he spoke, very softly and possibly in a tongue specific only to the Mendicants. I watched an image appear on the bracelet, but it was far too small for me to identify anything other than a pink blur which might have been a human face, and which might also have been Sister Amelia. There was a pause of five or six seconds before Alexei lowered the sleeve of his smock.

'Well?'

'I cannot reach her immediately, brother. She is tending to the slush . . . to the sick, and one would be sorely inadvised to interrupt her when she is so engaged. But I have been informed that she has been seeking you as much as you seek her.'

'Seeking me?'

'If you would care to leave a message where Amelia may reach you . . .'

I killed the connection to the Hospice before Alexei had completed his sentence. I imagined him standing in the vineyard, staring glumly down at whichever deadened screen he had been addressing, his words trailing off. He had failed. He had failed to trace me, as must have been his intention. Reivich's people, it appeared, had also reached and infiltrated the Mendicants. They had been waiting for me to resume contact, hoping that by some indiscretion I would reveal my location.

It had almost worked.

It took me a few minutes to find Zebra's number, remembering that she had called herself Taryn before revealing the name used by her contacts in the sabotage movement. I had no idea if Taryn was a common first name in Chasm City, but for once luck was on my side – there were less than a dozen people with that as first name. There was no need to phone them all, since the phone showed me a map of the city and only one number was anywhere near the chasm. The connection was much swifter than the one to the Hospice, but it was far from instantaneous, and still plagued by episodes of static, as if the signal had to worm along a continent-spanning telegraphic cable, rather than jump through a few kilometres of smog-laden air.

'Tanner, where are you? Why did you leave?'

'I . . .' I paused, on the verge of telling her I was near Grand Central Station, if that was not adequately obvious from the view behind me. 'No, I'd better not. I think I trust you, Zebra, but you're too close to the Game. It's better if you don't know.'

'You think I'd betray you?'

'No, although I wouldn't blame you if you did. But I can't risk anyone finding out via you.'

'Who's left to find out? You did a fairly comprehensive job on Waverly, I hear.' Her striped face filled the screen, monochrome skin tone offset by the bloodshot pink of her eyes.

'He played the Game from both sides. He must have known it would get him killed sooner or later.'

'He may have been a sadist, but he was one of us.'

'What was I supposed to do – smile nicely and ask them to desist?' A warm squall of harder rain lashed out of the sky, and I moved under the ledged side of a building for protection, cupping my hand over the phone, Zebra's image dancing like a reflection in water. 'I had nothing personal against Waverly, in case you wondered. Nothing that a warm bullet wouldn't have fixed.'

'You didn't use a bullet, from what I heard.'

'He put me in a position where killing him was my only option. And I did it efficiently, in case you were wondering.' I spared her the details of what I had found when I caught up with Waverly on the ground; it would not change anything to know he had been harvested by the Mulch.

'You're quite capable of looking after yourself, aren't you? I began to wonder when I found you in that building. Mostly, they don't even make it that far. Certainly not if they've been shot. Who are you, Tanner Mirabel?'

'Someone trying to survive,' I said. 'I'm sorry about what I took from you. You took care of me, and I'm grateful, and if I can find a way of repaying you for that and the things I took, I will.'

'You didn't have to go anywhere,' Zebra said. 'I said I'd offer you sanctuary until the Game was over.'

'I'm afraid I had business I had to attend to.' It was a mistake; the last thing Zebra needed to know about was the business with Reivich, but now I had invited her to speculate about just what it would take to bring a man out of hiding.

'The odd thing is,' she said, 'I almost believe you when you say you'll pay me back. I don't know why, but I think you're a man of your word, Tanner.'

'You're right,' I said. 'And I think one day it'll be the death of me.'

'What's that meant to mean?'

'Never mind. Is there a hunt tonight, Zebra? I thought you might know, if anyone would.'

'There is,' she said, after consideration. 'But I don't see how it concerns you, Tanner. Haven't you learnt your lesson yet? You're lucky to be alive.'

I smiled. 'I guess I'm just not sick enough of Chasm City yet.'

I returned the rented phone to its owner and considered my options. Zebra's face and the timbre of her voice lurked behind every conscious thought. Why had I called her? There had been no reason for it, except to apologise, and even *that* was pointless; a gesture more aimed at ameliorating my conscience than aiding the woman from whom I had stolen. I had been well aware how much my betrayal would hurt her, and well aware that I was not going to be able to pay her back at any point in the foreseeable future. Yet something had made me make that call, and when I tried to pare away my superficial motives to find what really lay below them, all I found was a mélange of emotions and impulses: her smell; the sound of her laugh, the curve of her hips and the way the stripes on her back had contorted and released when she rolled aside from me after our lovemaking. I did not like what I found, so I slammed the lid on those thoughts just as if I had opened a box of vipers . . .

I walked back into the crowds of the bazaar, letting their noise oppress my thoughts into submission, concentrating instead on the now. I still had money; I was still a rich man by Mulch standards, no matter how little influence it counted for in the Canopy. Asking around and comparing prices, I found a room for rent, a few blocks across the Mulch, in what was apparently one of the less rundown districts.

The room was shabby, even by Mulch standards. It was one cubic corner element in a teetering eight-storeyed encrustation of structures lashed around the footslopes of a major structure. On the other hand, it also looked very old and established, having gained its own parasitic layer of encrustations in the form of ladders, staircases, horizontal landings, drainage conduits, trellises and animal cages, so while the complex might not be the safest in the Mulch, it had obviously endured for some years and was unlikely to choose my arrival as a sign to start collapsing. I accessed my room via a series of ladder and landing traverses, my feet padding over rents in the wattlelike bamboo flooring, street level dizzyingly far below. The room was lit by gas lamps, although I noticed that other parts of the complex were furnished with electricity, served by constantly droning methane-powered generators somewhere below, machines which were locked in furious competition with the local street musicians, criers, muezzins, vendors and animals. But I soon stopped noticing the sounds, and when I drew the room's blinds, it became tolerably dark.

The room contained no furniture except a bed, but that was all that I needed.

I sat down on it and thought about all that had happened. I felt myself free of any Haussmann episodes for the time being and that allowed me to look back on those that I had experienced so far, with something bordering on cool, clinical detachment.

There was something *wrong* about them.

I'd come to kill Reivich and yet – almost accidentally – I was getting glimpses of something larger, something I didn't like the shape of. It wasn't just the Haussmann episodes, although they were a large part of it. Certainly they had begun normally enough. I hadn't exactly welcomed them, but given that I already knew roughly what form they were going to take, I thought I could ride them out.

But it wasn't happening like that.

The dreams – episodes now, since they had begun to invade daylight – were revealing a deeper history: additional crimes which no one even suspected Sky had committed. There was the question of the infiltrator's continued existence; the sixth ship – the fabled *Caleuche* – and the fact that Titus Haussmann had believed Sky to be one of the immortals. But Sky Haussman was dead, wasn't he? Hadn't I seen his crucified body in Nueva Valparaiso? Even if that body had been faked, it was a matter of public record that, in the dark days following the landing, he had been captured, imprisoned, tried, sentenced and executed, all in full view of the people.

So why did I have my doubts that he was really dead?

It's just the indoctrinal virus screwing with your head, I told myself.

But Sky wasn't the only thing troubling me as I fell asleep.

I was overlooking a rectangular room, as if the chamber were a dungeon or baiting pit, and I was standing on some balconied observation gallery. The room was blindingly white, walled and floored in shiny ceramic tiles, but strewn with large glossy green ferns and artfully arranged tree branches, creating a tableau of jungle vegetation. And there was a man on the floor.

I thought I recognised the chamber.

The man was curled up in a foetal position, naked, as if he had just been placed there and been allowed to wake. His skin was pallid and was covered in a sheen of sweat, like sugar glazing. Gradually he raised his head and opened his eyes, looking around, and tried slowly rising to his feet – tried, and then stumbled into another permutation of the huddle in which he had begun. He could not stand because one of his legs ended in a clean, bloodless stump just below the ankle, like the sewn-up end of a sausage. He tried again, and this time managed to reach a wall, hopping to get there, before balance deserted him. There was a look of inexpressible terror on his face. The man started shouting, and then his shouts became more frantic.

I watched him shiver. And then something moved on the other side of the room, in a dark alcove situated in one of the white walls. Whatever it was moved slowly and silently, but the man was aware of its presence, and now his shouts became shrieks, like the squealing of a pig being slaughtered. The thing emerged from the alcove on the other side of the room, dropping in a bundle of dark coils, thick as a human thigh. It still moved languidly, hooded head rising to test the air, and yet more of it struggled from the alcove. By now the man's screams were punctuated by sharp silences as he drew breath, a contrast which only served to heighten the dread in the sounds he made. And I felt nothing, except a kind of expectancy, my heart tight in my chest, as the hamadryad moved towards the man, and there was nowhere he could run to.

312

I woke, sweating.

A while later I hit the streets. I had slept for most of the afternoon, and while I did not exactly feel refreshed – my mind, certainly, was in a worse state of turmoil than it had been before – I was at least not so crippled with tiredness. I moved through lazy Mulch traffic: pedestrians, rickshaws, steam and methane-driven contraptions; the occasional palanquin, volantor or cable-car passing through, though never lingering for very long. I noticed that I attracted less attention than when I had first entered the city. Unshaven, my eyes sunk into tired sockets, I was looking more like I belonged in the Mulch.

The late afternoon vendors were setting up stalls, some of them already hanging lanterns in preparation for the coming dusk. A misshapen, maggot-like methane-filled dirigible navigated ponderously overhead, someone lashed to a gondola beneath it calling out slogans through a megaphone. Broken neon images flickered over a projection screen hanging beneath the gondola. I heard what sounded like a muezzin call across the Mulch, calling the faithful to prayer, or whatever observance they practised here. And then I saw a man with pendulous, jewel-studded ears whose mobile stall was hung with small wicker baskets holding snakes of every size and colour imaginable. When I watched him open a cage and prod one of the darker snakes, its coils shifting uneasily, I thought of the ceramic-white room in my dream which I now recognised as the pit where Cahuella kept the juvenile, and shivered, and wondered what any of it meant.

Later, I bought a gun.

Unlike the weapon I had stolen from Zebra, and then pawned, it was neither cumbersome nor conspicuous. It was a small pistol which I could comfortably slip into one of the pockets of the greatcoat. It was manufactured off-world. The gun fired ice-slugs: bullets of pure water-ice accelerated to supersonic speed by a captive jacket which was driven down the barrel by a sequenced ripple of magnetic fields. Ice-slugs did as much damage as metal or ceramic bullets, but when they shattered into the body, their fragments melted away invisibly. The main advantage in such a weapon was that it could be charged from any supply of reasonably pure water, although it worked best with the carefully pre-frozen cache of slugs in the weapon's manufacturer-supplied cryo-clip. It was also nearly impossible to trace the owner of such a gun if a crime had been committed, making it an ideal assassination tool. It didn't matter that the slugs had no autonomous target-seeking capacity, or that they would not penetrate some kinds of armour. Something as absurdly powerful as Zebra's rifle would make sense as an instrument of assassination only if I got an opportunity to kill Reivich from halfway across the city, which was very unlikely. It was never going to be the kind of kill where you sat in a window squinting through the telescopic sight of a high-powered rifle, waiting until the target intersected the crosshairs, his image wavering through kilometres of heat-haze. It was always going to be the kind where you walked into the same room and did it with a single bullet at close range, close enough to see the whites of his fear-dilated eyes.

Evening fell over the Mulch. Apart from the streets in the area immediately around the bazaars, pedestrian traffic thinned out and the shadows cast by the towering roots of the Canopy began to assume an air of sullen menace.

I got to work.

The kid driving the rickshaw might have been the same one who had originally taken me into the Mulch, or his virtually interchangeable brother. He had the same aversion to my planned destination as well – unwilling to ferry me where I wanted to go until I sweetened the proposition with the promise of a generous tip. Even then he was reluctant, but we set off anyway, navigating through the darkening glade of the city at a pace which suggested he was more than eager to complete the journey and return home. Some of his nervousness rubbed off on me, because I found my hand wandering into the pocket of my coat to feel the comforting cold mass of the gun, reassuring as any talisman.

'What you want, Mister? Ev'ryone know this no good part of Mulch, you better stay out of it, you smart.'

'That's what people keep telling me,' I said. 'So I suppose you'd better assume that I'm not as intelligent as I seem.'

'I no say that, Mister. You pay plenty fine; you plenty smart feller. I just give you good advice, is all.'

'Thanks, but my advice to you is to just drive and keep your eye on the road. Let me worry about the rest.'

It was a conversation killer, but I wasn't in much of a mood for idle banter. Instead I watched the darkening trunks of the buildings creep past, their deformities beginning to assume a weird normality, a strange sense that this was how all cities were meant to look, ultimately.

There were parts of the Mulch relatively uncovered by Canopy, and parts where the density of the overlying structures could not have been any higher, so that the Mosquito Net itself was completely blocked out and when the sun was at its zenith, none of its light permeated to the ground. These were supposedly the worst areas of the Mulch: areas of permanent night where crime was the only law which mattered, and where the inhabitants played games which were no less bloody and cruel than those favoured by the people who lived overhead. I could not persuade the rickshaw kid to take me into the heart of the slum zone, so I settled for being dropped on the perimeter, pocketed hand wrapped around the slug-gun.

I trudged through the ankle-deep rainwater for several minutes until I reached the side of a building which I recognised from the description Zebra had given me, and then crouched in a niche which offered some protection from the rain. Then I waited, and waited, while the last meagre traces of

314

daylight vanished from the scene and all the shadows merged conspiratorially into one great city-hugging pall of gloomy grey.

And then waited, and waited again.

Night fell across Chasm City, the Canopy lighting up above me, the arms of the linked structures dimpled with light like the glowing tentacles of phosphorescent sea-creatures. I watched cable-cars move through the tangle, their motion like pebbles skipping waves as they swung from line to line. An hour passed and I readjusted my position dozens of times, never finding one that was comfortable for more than a few minutes, before cramps began to set in. I'd take out the gun and sight along it, and I allowed myself the luxury of wasting a slug, shooting at the side of the building across from me, anticipating the recoil and getting a feel for the weapon's accuracy or lack thereof. No one disturbed me, and I doubt that there was anyone close enough to hear the gun's high-pitched shots.

Finally, however, they came.

TWENTY-SIX

I watched the car drop down two or three blocks away: sleek and black as polished coal, with five telescopic arms retracting on the roof. The side door cracked open and four people spilled out of it, cradling weapons which made my own little gun look like a bad joke. Zebra had told me there was a hunt going down tonight, though that was nothing unusual; hunts were the norm rather than the exception. But she had also – after considerable persuasion – revealed the likely site for the bloody revelry. There was a lot riding on it, the failure to kill me having ruined a perfectly good night's entertainment for the paying voyeurs who followed each chase.

'I'll tell you where it is,' she had said. 'Only on the grounds that you use that information to keep away from it. Is that understood? I saved you once, Tanner Mirabel, but then you betrayed my trust. That hurt. It doesn't particularly dispose me towards helping you a second time.'

'You know what I'll do with that information, Zebra.'

'Yes, I suppose I do. At least you haven't lied to me, I'll give you that. You really are a man of your word, aren't you?'

'I'm not all that you think I am, Zebra.' I felt I owed her that, if she had not already worked that part out for herself.

She had told me the sector that had been cleared for the chase. The subject, she said, had already been acquired and equipped with an implant – sometimes they made several raids on a given night, and kept the victims asleep until a gaming slot arose.

'Does anyone ever escape, Zebra?'

'You did, Tanner.'

'No, I mean, really escape, without being helped by the sabs. Does that happen?'

'Sometimes,' she said. 'Sometimes – maybe more often than you'd think. Not because the hunted manage to outwit the chasers, but because the organisers occasionally allow it. Otherwise, it would get boring, wouldn't it?'

'Boring?'

'There'd be no element of chance. The Canopy would always win.'

'That certainly wouldn't do,' I said.

I watched them creep through the rain now, guns swept ahead of them, their masked faces darting from side to side, examining every nook and cranny. The target must have been dropped in this zone a few minutes before, quietly, perhaps not even fully awake, like the naked man in the white-walled room, slowly coming to his senses to realise that he was sharing his confines with something unspeakable.

There were two women and two men, and as they came closer I saw that their masks were a combination of theatrical decoration and practicality. The two women both wore cat masks: long tapering feline eyeslits packed with specialised lenses. Their gloves were clawed, and when their black, high-backed cloaks parted, I saw that their clothes were patterned in tiger stripes and leopard spots. Then I realised that they were not clothes at all, but furred synthetic skin, and that those clawed gloves were not gloves but unsheathed hands. One of the women grinned, flashing jewelled fangs, sharing a cruel joke with her friends. The men were not so ostentatiously transformed, their animal personae derived solely from their costumes. The nearest man had a bear's head, his own face peering from under the bear's upper jaw. His companion's face sported two ugly, faceted insect eyes which constantly caught and refracted the light of the suspended Canopy.

I waited until they were twenty metres from my place of hiding, then made my move, sprinting across their path in a low, crablike crouch, convinced that none of them would get their weapons onto me in time. I was right, although they were better than I had thought they would be, scything the water behind my heels, but not quite reaching me until I had found shelter on the other side of the street.

'It's not him,' I heard one of them say, probably one of the women. 'He's not meant to be here!'

'Whoever it was needs a good shooting, that's all I know. Fan out; we'll get the little shit.'

'I'm telling you, it isn't him! He should be three blocks south – and even if it was him, why would he leave shelter?'

'We were about to find him, that's why.'

'He was too fast. Mulch aren't usually so fast.'

'So you've got a challenge. You complaining?'

I risked a view around the edge of my protective niche. A bolt of lightning had chosen that moment to strike; they were framed for me in complete clarity.

'I just saw him!' I heard the other woman shout, and now I heard the whine of an energy-discharge, followed by a burst of projectile weapons fire farting across the night.

'There's something funny with his eyes,' the first woman said. 'They were glowing in his face!'

'Now you're getting spooked, Chanterelle.' It was the voice of one of the men, maybe the ursine one, very close now. I still held the mental image of them in my mind, burned into my memory, but I ran the image forward in my head, allowing them to walk to where I now knew they would be, like actors following stage instructions. Then I moved from my cover, squeezing off three shots, three precise squeaks from the gun, barely having to re-aim, since the view I saw agreed so well with the image in my head. I shot low, dropping three of the four with shots to the thigh, deliberately aiming wide with the last one, and then swung myself back behind the wall.

You don't take a thigh shot and keep standing. Maybe it was my imagination, but I think I heard three separate splashes as they impacted with the water. It was rather hard to tell, since the other thing you seldom do after you've taken a thigh shot is remain silent. The wound I had taken the night before had been reasonably painless by comparison, executed with precision, by a duelling beam-weapon with a very narrow spread. Even so, I hadn't exactly enjoyed the experience.

My gamble was that the three on the ground were essentially out of play, unable to aim their weapons even if they hadn't dropped them out of reach. They might try to fire a few pot-shots in my general direction, but – like the woman who had shot me in the leg – they were not using the kinds of weapon which forgave inaccuracy. As for the fourth, she figured in my plans, which was why she wasn't currently emptying her soul into a puddle of warm rain.

I stepped out of cover, making sure my gun was conspicuous – no mean feat, given its size, and I began to wish I also had Zebra's huge club of a rifle for moral support.

'S . . . stop,' the woman who was standing said. 'Stop, or I'll drop you.'

She was twelve to fifteen metres from me, her weapon still trained in roughly my direction: Miss Leopardskin with the spotted cat's-eye mask, only now her saunter had lost most of its cattiness.

'Put down the toy,' I said. 'Or I put it down for you.'

If she'd stopped to contemplate the wounds I'd inflicted on her whimpering friends, it might have occurred to her that I was a more than averagely good shot and therefore capable of doing exactly what I said. But evidently she wasn't the contemplative type, because what she did was to minutely raise the angle of her gun, and I watched her supporting forearm tense as if in anticipation of the recoil from the shot.

So I fired first, and her gun went spinning out of her hand with a chime of ricocheting ice-slugs. She made a little canine yelp, hastily examining her hand to check that she still had all her fingers.

I was insulted. Who did she think I was, some kind of amateur?

*

'Good,' I said. 'You've dropped it. How wise; it'll save me putting a slug through your brachial nerve. Now step away from your piss-poor excuses for friends and start walking back towards the vehicle.'

'They're hurt, you bastard.'

'Look on the bright side. They could be dead.' And they would be too, I thought, if they didn't reach help in the reasonably imminent future. The water around them was already assuming an ominous cherry-coloured complexion, in what little light there remained. 'Do what I told you,' I said. 'Walk towards the cable-car and we'll take it from there. You can call for help once we're airborne. Of course, if they're very lucky, someone from the Mulch may get to them first.'

'You piece of shit,' she said. 'Whoever you are.'

Dodging my gun between the woman and her moaning friends, I trudged between the bodies, examining them out of the corner of my eye. 'Hope none of them have implants,' I said. 'Because I hear the Mulch people like to harvest, and I'm not sure they're too particular about going through paperwork first.'

'You piece of shit.'

'Why are you so upset with me, just because I had the nerve to fight back?'

'You're not the target,' she said. 'I don't know who you are, but you're not the target.'

'Who are you, incidentally?' I tried the remember the one name I had heard the hunting quartet use. 'Chanterelle? Is that your name? Very aristocratic. I bet your family was high in the Demarchy before the *Belle Epoque* went belly-up.'

'Don't imagine you understand anything about me or my life.'

'As if I wanted to.' I leant down and retrieved one of the rifles, inspecting its readout cartouches to ascertain that it was still functional. I felt edgy, even though I had the situation essentially under control. I had the feeling – indefinable, but present nonetheless – that another of their number had lurked behind the main party, was even now scoping me out through the sight of something high-powered and unsportingly accurate. But I tried not to let it show. 'I'm afraid you were set up, Chanterelle. Here. Look at the side of my head. Can you see it? There's a wound there, for an implant. But it never functioned properly.' I took a risk, assuming that Waverly would have done the work on the real victim before he died, or would have been replaced at short notice by an equally surly understudy. 'You were tricked. The man was working for saboteurs. He wanted to lead you into a trap. So the implant was modified, so that the positional trace was no longer accurate.' I grinned cockily, though I had no idea whether such a thing was possible. 'You thought I was blocks from here, so you weren't expecting an ambush. You also weren't expecting me to be armed, but – hey – some days you get the bear.' Then I glanced down at her ursine friend. 'No, sorry – my mistake. Today *I* got the bear, didn't I?'

319

The man thrashed in the water, his palms clenched around his thigh. He started to say something, but I kicked him quiet.

Chanterelle had almost reached the black wedge of the cable-car. A large part of my gamble depended on the vehicle being empty, but it was only now that I felt reasonably sure that the risk had payed off and there was no one hiding inside.

'Get in,' I said. 'And don't try any funny tricks; I'm not known for my massive sense of humour.'

The car was sumptuously laid out, with four plush maroon seats, a glittering control panel and a well-appointed drinks cabinet ensconced in one wall, along with a rack of gleaming weapons and trophies. Keeping the gun aimed at the back of her neck, I had Chanterelle take us aloft.

'I presume you have a destination in mind,' she said.

'Yes, but for now I just want you to find a nice altitude and loiter. You can give me a tour of the city, if you like. It's a wonderful night for it.'

'You're right,' Chanterelle said. 'You're not known for your sense of humour. In fact you're about as hilarious as the Melding Plague.' But after delivering this *bon mot* she grudgingly laid in a course and let the car do its swinging thing before turning around slowly to face me. 'Who are you, really, and what do you want with me?'

'I'm who I said I was – someone brought into your little game to add some well-needed equality.'

Her hand moved quickly to the side of my head – evidence of either bravery or considerable stupidity, given the proximity of my gun to her skull, and my demonstrated eagerness to use it.

She rubbed the place where Dominika had excised the hunt implant.

'It's not there,' Chanterelle said. 'If it ever was.'

'Then Waverly lied to me as well.' I observed her face for an anomalous reaction, but my use of the man's name did not seem to strike her as unreasonable. 'He never put the device in at all.'

'Then who were we following?'

'How am I supposed to know? You don't use the implants to track your prey, do you? Or is that some new refinement I wasn't aware of?' As I spoke, the car made one of its intermittent sickening swoops, leaping between cables which were just a shade too far apart for comfort.

Chanterelle did not even flinch.

'Do you mind if I call for help for my friends?'

'Be my guest,' I said.

She sounded more nervous making the call than at any point since we had met. Instead Chanterelle spun a story about going down into the Mulch to film a documentary she was making, and how she and her friends had been waylaid by a gang of vicious juvenile pigs. She said this with such conviction that I almost believed it myself.

'I'm not going to harm you,' I said, wondering how plausible I sounded. 'I just want some information from you – information of a very general nature, which it won't hurt you to provide – and then I want you to take me somewhere in the Canopy.'

'I don't trust you.'

'Of course you don't. I know I wouldn't. And I'm not asking you to. I'm not putting you in a situation in which your trust of me is even remotely relevant. I'm just pointing a gun to your head and giving you orders.' I licked my lips, thirsty and dry. 'You either do what I say or you get to redecorate the interior of this car with your cranium. It's not the hardest choice in the world, is it?'

'What do you want to know?'

'Tell me about the Game, Chanterelle. I've heard Waverly's side of it, and what he said sounded very reasonable, but I want to be sure I'm getting the whole picture. You're capable of that, aren't you?'

As it was, Chanterelle was eloquent. Part of this I put down to the natural helpfulness which befalls anyone with a gun at their head. But a lot more of it, I thought, stemmed from the fact that Chanterelle rather liked the sound of her own voice. And I could not really fault her for that. It was a very nice voice and it came out of a very comely head.

Her family line was Sammartini, which I learned was one of the major clans in the pre-plague power-structure, a lineage which extended right back to the Amerikano era. Families who could trace their descents that far back were highly regarded; the closest thing to Royalty in the rarefield heights of *Belle Epoque* society.

Her family had connections with the most famous clan of all, the Sylvestes. I remembered Sybilline telling me about Calvin, the man who had resurrected the forgotten and discredited technologies of neural-scanning which enabled the living to be translated – fatally, as it happened – into immortal computer simulations of themselves.

Of course, it hadn't really bothered the Transmigrants that their bodies were destroyed in the course of the scanning. But when the simulations themselves started to fail, no one was quite so happy. There had been seventy-nine volunteers in the first wave of Transmigrants – eighty if you counted Calvin himself – and the majority of those simulations had stopped running long before the plague began to attack the logical substrates on which they were being computed. To commemorate the dead, they had built a vast and dejected Monument to the Eighty in the centre of the city, where shrines of the departed were tended by those relatives who remained corporeal. It was still there, after the plague had come.

The family of Chanterelle Sammartini were amongst the commemorated. 'But we were lucky,' she said, almost chattily. 'The Sammartini scans were amongst the five per cent which never failed, and because my grandmother and father already had children, our lineage persisted corporeally.'

I tried to get my head around this. Her family had bifurcated – one thread of it propagating in simulation, the other in what we laughingly called actuality. And to Chanterelle Sammartini this was no more or less usual than as if she had relatives who lived overseas, or in another part of the system. 'Because there was no stigma,' she said, 'our family sponsored further research, picking up where Calvin left off. Our ties with House Sylveste had always been close, and we had access to most of his research data. We made breakthroughs very quickly. Nonlethal modes of scanning.' Her tone of voice changed, querulously. 'Why do you want to know this? If you're not Mulch, you must be Canopy. In which case you already *know* what I'm telling you.'

'Why do you assume I'm not Mulch?'

'You're clever, or at least not irredeemably stupid. That isn't a compliment, incidentally. It's simply an observation.'

Evidently the idea that I might be from beyond the system was so outside Chanterelle's accepted norms that it did not even enter her head.

'Why don't you just entertain me. Have you been scanned, Chanterelle?'

Now she really looked at me as if I was stupid. 'Of course.'

'Interactive scans – what do you call them?'

'Alpha-level simulations.'

'So there's a simulation of you running right now, somewhere in the city?'

'In orbit, idiot. The technology which facilitates the scans would never have survived the plague if it hadn't been quarantined.'

'Of course, silly me.'

'I go up six or seven times a year for a refresh. It's like a little holiday, visiting Refuge. That's a habitat high above the Rust Belt, safe from any plague spore. And then I have the scan and my last two or three months of experience are assimilated by the simulation of me which is already running. I don't think of her as a copy of me any more. She's more like an older and wiser sister who knows everything which has ever happened to me – as if she's been looking over my shoulder my whole life.'

'It must be very reassuring,' I said, 'to know that even if you die, you won't really be dying at all; just dispensing with one mode of existence. Except none of you even die physically, do you?'

'That might have been true before the plague. It isn't now.'

I thought back to what Zebra had said. 'What about you? You're not a hermetic, obviously. Were you one of the immortals who were born with genes for extreme longevity?'

'Mine weren't the worst you could inherit, if that's what you mean.'

'But not the best, either,' I said. 'Which means you were probably still reliant on machines in your blood and cells to keep correcting nature's little mistakes. Am I right?'

'It doesn't take a massive deductive leap.'

'And those machines? What happened to them after the plague?' I looked down as we passed over a suspended railway line, one of the quadrilaterally symmetric steam locomotives sliding through the night with a string of carriages behind it, bound for some remote district of the city. 'Did you have them self-destruct, before plague spore reached them? I gather that's what most of your kind had to do.'

'What business is it of yours?'

'I'm just wondering whether you're a Dream Fuel user, that's all.'

But Chanterelle did not answer me directly. 'I was born in 2339. I'm one hundred and seventy-eight standard years old. I've seen wonders you can't even imagine, terrors that would make you shrivel. I've played at being God, explored the parameters of that game, and then moved beyond it, like a child discarding a simplistic plaything. I've seen this city shift and change a thousand times, becoming ever more beautiful – ever more radiant – with each transformation, and I've seen it change into something vile and dark and poisonous, and I'll still be here when it claws its way back to the light, whether that's a century or a thousand years from now. Do you think I would discard immortality that easily, or confine myself to a ridiculous metal box like some cowering child?' Behind her cat's-eye mask, her own vertically pupilled eyes flared ecstatically. 'God, no. I've drunk from that fire, and it's a thirst you never quench. Can you grasp the thrill that it is to walk in the Mulch, amidst so much strangeness, unprotected, knowing that the machines are still inside me? It's a savage thrill; like firewalking or swimming with sharks.'

'Is that why you play the Game as well? Because it's another savage thrill?'

'What do you think?'

'I think you used to be more bored than you remember. That's why you play, isn't it? That's what I gathered from Waverly. By the time the plague hit, you and your friends had exhausted every legal experience society could offer you, every experience that could possibly be staged or simulated, every game or adventure or intellectual challenge.' I looked at her, daring her to contradict me. 'But it was never enough, was it? You were never testing your own mortality. Never confronting it. You could leave the system, of course – plenty of danger and excitement and potential glory out there – but if you did that, you'd be leaving behind the support system of your friends; the culture in which you grew up.'

'There's more to it than that,' Chanterelle said, seemingly willing to volunteer information when she thought I was misjudging her and her kind. 'Some of us *did* leave the system. But those that did knew what they were throwing away. They could never be scanned again. Their simulations could never be updated. Eventually they would diverge so far from the living copy that there would be no compatibility.'

I nodded. 'So they needed something much closer to home. Something like the Game. A way to test themselves – to push themselves to the edge, and invoke a little danger, but in a controlled manner.'

'And it was good. When the plague came, and we could do what we chose, we began to remember what it felt like to live.'

'Except that you had to kill to do it.'

There was not even a flinch. 'No one who hadn't earned it.'

She believed it, too.

As we continued our flight across the city I asked more questions, trying to discover how much Chanterelle knew about Dream Fuel. I'd made a vow to Zebra that I'd help her avenge her sister's death, and that meant finding out as much as possible about the substance and its supplier, the mysterious Gideon. Chanterelle was clearly a Dream Fuel user, but it quickly became apparent that she didn't know anything more about the drug than any of the other people I'd spoken to.

'Let me get a few things straight in my head,' I said. 'Was there any mention of Dream Fuel before the plague?'

'No,' Chanterelle said. 'I mean, it's sometimes difficult to remember what it was like before, but I'm sure Dream Fuel only emerged in the last seven years.'

'Then whatever it is might just have some connection with the plague, don't you think?'

'I don't follow.'

'Look, whatever Dream Fuel is, it protects you against the plague, allows you to walk in the Mulch with all those machines floating inside you. That suggests to me that there might be an intimate relationship between the two; that Fuel recognises the plague and can neutralise it without harming the host. That can't be accidental.'

Chanterelle shrugged. 'Then someone must have engineered it.'

'Which would make it another kind of nanomachinery, wouldn't it?' I shook my head. 'Sorry, but I don't believe anyone could have engineered something that useful; not here and now.'

'You can't guess at the kind of resources Gideon has.'

'No, I can't. But you can tell me what you know about him, and we can work from there.'

'Why are you so interested?'

'A promise I made to someone.'

'Then I'll have to disappoint you. I don't know anything about Gideon, and I don't know anyone who does. You'd need to talk to someone closer to the line of supply, I think.'

'You don't even know where he operates from, where his production labs are?'

'Somewhere in the city, that's all.'

'You're sure of that? The first time I encountered Dream Fuel was . . .' I trailed off, not wanting to tell her too much about how I'd been revived in Hospice Idlewild. 'Not on Yellowstone.'

'I can't know for sure, but I've heard that it isn't manufactured in the Canopy.'

'Which leaves the Mulch?'

'I suppose so.' She squinted, the vertical pupils of her eyes becoming thin slivers. 'Who are you, anyway?'

'Now that,' I said, 'would take rather too long to explain. But I'm sure you've guessed the essentials.'

She nodded at the controls. 'We can't circle for ever.'

'Then take us to the Canopy. Somewhere public, not too far from Escher Heights.'

'What?'

I showed Chanterelle the place name Dominika had given me, hoping that my ignorance of the nature of the address – whether it constituted a domicile or a whole district – was not too obvious.

'I'm not sure I know that place.'

'My, but my finger is growing tense. Rack your memory, Chanterelle. Failing that, there has to be map somewhere in this thing. Why don't you look it up?'

Grudgingly she did as I asked. I hadn't known about the existence of a map of the Canopy, but I figured such a thing had to exist, even if it was buried deep in the processor of the cable-car.

'I remember it now,' she said. The map glowing on the console looked like an enlargement of the synaptic connections in part of the human brain, labelled in eye-hurting Canasian script. 'But I don't know that district too well. The plague took on strange forms there. It's different – not like the rest of the Canopy, and some of us don't like it.'

'No one's asking you to. Just take me there.'

It was a half-hour's travel through the interstices, skirting the chasm in a long undulating arc. It was visible only as an absence, a circular black occlusion in the luminous sprawl of the Canopy. It was ringed in the lights of the undomed peripheral structures, like phosphorescent lures around the jaw of some monstrous benthic predator. The occasional ledged structure was visible deeper into the maw, down for a depth of a kilometre, and the city's enormous taplines extended even deeper, sucking air, power and moisture, but they were hardly visible at all. Even at night, a constant dark exhalation rose from the maw.

'There it is,' Chanterelle said, eventually. 'Escher Heights.'

'I understand now,' I said.

'What?'

'Why you don't like it.'

For several square kilometres, with a vertical extent of several hundred metres, the forestlike tangle of the Canopy transmuted into something very different: a jumbled agglomeration of freakish crystalline shapes, like something magnified from a geology textbook, or a photomicrograph of a fantastically adapted virus. The colours were glorious, pinks and greens and blues picked out by the lanterns of dug-out rooms and tunnels and public spaces threading the crystals. Great layered sheets of greyish-gold, like muscovite, rose in tiers above the topmost layer of the Canopy. Brittle turquoise encrustations of tourmaline curled into spires; there were pinkish rods of quartz the size of mansions. Crystals threaded and interpenetrated one another, their complex geometries folding around each other in ways no mind could ever have purposefully intended. It almost *hurt* to look at Escher Heights.

'It's insane,' I said.

'Hollow, mostly,' Chanterelle said. 'Otherwise it could never hang so high. The parts which broke away were absorbed into the Mulch years ago.' I looked down, under the looming, luminous crystalline mass, and saw what she meant: blocky, overly-geometric concentrations of Mulch, like a carpet of lichen, covering the shards of the fallen city.

'Can you find somewhere public nearby where we can land?'

'I'm doing it,' Chanterelle said. 'Although I don't know what good it will do. You can hardly walk into a plaza with a gun at my head.'

'Maybe people will assume we're a living exhibit and leave us alone.'

'Is that as far as your plan goes?' She sounded disappointed in me.

'No, actually. It goes a bit further than that. This coat, for instance, has very capacious pockets. I know I can conceal the gun in one without any difficulty, and I can keep it pointed at you without it looking as if I'm just exceptionally pleased to see you.'

'You're serious, aren't you? You're going to walk through the plaza with a gun at my back.'

'It would look a little silly if I pointed it at your front. One of us would have to walk backwards, and that wouldn't do. We might bump into one of your friends.'

TWENTY-SEVEN

We landed with the absolute minimum of ceremony.

Chanterelle's cable-car had come to rest on a ledge of flat metal buttressed out from the side of Escher Heights, large enough to accommodate about a dozen other vehicles. Most of them were cable-cars, but there were a couple of stubby-winged volantors. Like all the other flying machines I had seen in the city, they had the sleek, hyper-adapted look which told me they had been built before the plague. It must have been difficult, flying them through the warped thicket the city had become, but perhaps the owners just enjoyed the challenge of flying through the tangle. Perhaps it was even a kind of high-risk sport.

People were coming and going from their vehicles, some of which were private and some of which carried the insignia of taxi firms. Other people were just standing around the edge of the landing pad, peering at the rest of the city through pedestal-mounted telescopes. Everyone, without exception, was out-landishly dressed, in billowing capes or overcoats, offset with studiedly bizarre headgear, patterned in a riot of colours and textures which made even the surrounding architecture look a little on the restrained side. People wore masks or hid behind shimmering veils or elegant fans and parasols. There were bioengineered pets on leashes, creatures which conformed to no known taxonomy, like cats with lizard crests. And some of the pets were not even as strange as their owners. There were people who had become centaurs; fully quadrupedal. There were people who, while still basically conforming to the standard-issue human shape, had twisted and stretched it so far that they looked like avant garde statues. One woman had elongated her skull to such an extent that it resembled the horned beak of an exotic bird. Another man had transformed himself into one of the ancient mythic prototypes of an extraterrestrial, his body preposterously thin and elongated, his dark slitted eyes like almonds.

Chanterelle told me these kind of changes could be affected in days; weeks

327

at the most. It was possible that someone who was sufficiently determined could reshape their body image a dozen times in a year; with the same frequency with which I thought about cutting my hair.

And I expected to find Reivich in such a place?

'If I were you,' Chanterelle said, 'I wouldn't stand around staring all day. I take it you don't want people to realise you aren't from around here?'

I felt the ice-slug gun in my pocket and hoped that she saw my arm tense as I found it. 'Just walk on. When I want advice I'll ask for it.' Chanterelle continued wordlessly, but after a few steps I began to feel guilty at snapping at her so strongly. 'I'm sorry; I realise you were trying to help.'

'It's in my interests,' the woman said, out of the corner of her mouth, as if sharing an anecdote. 'I don't want you attracting so much attention that someone makes a move on you and I end up getting caught in the crossfire.'

'Thanks for the concern.'

'It's self-preservation. How could I feel concerned for you when you've just hurt my friends and I don't even know your name?'

'Your friends will be okay,' I said. 'This time tomorrow they won't even be limping, unless they choose to keep their injuries for show. And they'll have a very good story to tell in hunt circles.'

'What about your name, then?'

'Call me Tanner,' I said, and forced her on.

A warm, moist wind blew across us as we crossed the pad towards the arched entrance which led back into Escher Heights. A few palanquins darted ahead of us like moving tombstones. At least it had decided not to rain. Perhaps rain was less frequent in this part of the city, or perhaps we were sufficiently high to escape the worst of it. My clothes were still wet from standing in the Mulch, but in this respect Chanterelle looked no better than I.

The arch led into a brightly lit enclosure cool with perfumed air, the ceiling strung with lanterns and banners and slowly spinning circulators. The corridor followed a gentle curve to the right, crossing ornamental pools via stone bridges. For the second time since arriving in the city I saw koi gaping up at me.

'What's the big deal with the fish?' I asked.

'You shouldn't talk about them like that. They mean a lot to us.'

'But they're just koi.'

'Yes, and it was just koi that gave us immortality. Or the first steps towards it, anyway. They live a long time, koi. Even in the wild, they don't really die of old age. They just get larger and larger until their hearts can't cope. But it's not the same as dying of old age.'

I heard Chanterelle murmur something which might have been 'koi be blessed' as she crossed the bridge, and allowed my own lips to echo the sentiment. I didn't want to be seen or doing anything unusual.

The walls were crystalline, an endlessly repeating motif of bustling octagons, but at intermittent distances they had been hollowed out to admit little boutiques and parlours, offering services in florid scrawls of neon or pulsing holographic light. Canopy people were shopping or strolling, most of them couples who at least looked young, although there were very few children present, and those I saw might well have been neotenous adults in their latest body image, or even androform pets programmed with a few childlike phrases.

Chanterelle led me into a much larger chamber, a huge vaulted hall of crystalline magnificence, into which several malls and plazas converged on multiple levels. Chandeliers the size of re-entry capsules hung from the ceiling. The paths tangled around each other, meandering past koi ponds and ornamental waterfalls, encircling pagodas and teahouses. The centre of the atrium was given over to a huge glass tank, encased in smoked filigreed metal. There was something in the tank, but there were too many people packed around the perimeter, jostling parasols and fans and leashed pets, for me to see what it was.

'I'm going to sit down at that table,' I said, waiting until Chanterelle acknowledged me. 'You're going to walk over to that teahouse and order a cup of tea for me and something for yourself. Then you're going to walk back to the table and you're going to look like you're enjoying it.'

'You're going to keep that gun on me the whole time?'

'Look on it as a compliment. I just can't keep my eyes off you.'

'You're hilarious, Tanner.'

I smiled and eased myself into the chair, suddenly conscious of the Mulch filth in which I was caked, and the fact that, surrounded by the gaudily dressed canopy strollers, I looked like an undertaker at a carnival.

I half expected Chanterelle not to return with the tea. Did she really think I would shoot her here, in the back? Did she also imagine I had the skill to be able to aim the gun from my pocket, and not run the risk of hitting someone else? She should have just strolled away from me, and that would have been the end of our acquaintance. And – like her friends – she would have a very good story to tell, even if the night's hunting had not gone quite as planned. I would not have blamed her. I tried to summon up some dislike for her, but nothing much welled up. I could see things from Zebra's side clearly enough, but what Chanterelle had said also made sense to me. She believed the people they hunted were bad people who ought to die for what they had done. Chanterelle was wrong about the victims, but how was she to know? From her point of view – denied the exquisite viewpoint which I had experienced thanks to Waverly – Chanterelle's actions were almost laudable. Wasn't she doing the Mulch a favour by culling its sickest?

It was enough that I allowed this notion into my head, even if I stopped short of preparing a bed for it.

Sky Haussmann would have been very proud of me.

*

'Don't look so grateful, Tanner.'

Chanterelle had returned with the tea.

'Why did you come back?'

She placed the two cups on the ironwork top of the table, then lowered herself into the seat opposite me, as sinuously as any cat. I wondered if Chanterelle's nervous system had been adjusted to give her that edge of felinity, or whether it just came from a lot of practice. 'I suppose,' she said, 'I wasn't quite bored with you yet. Quite the opposite, perhaps. Intrigued. And now that we're somewhere public, I don't find you half as threatening.'

I sipped the tea. It was almost tasteless, the oral equivalent of an exquisitely pale watercolour.

'There must be more to it than that.'

'You kept your word about my friends. And you could have killed them, I think. But instead you did them a favour. You showed them what pain is really like – real pain; not the soft-edged approximation you get from experientials – and, like you said, you gave them something to brag about afterwards. I'm right, aren't I? You could have killed them just as easily, and it would not have made any difference to your plans.'

'What makes you think I have plans?'

'The way you ask questions. I also think that, whatever it is you need to do, you don't have long to do it.'

'Can I ask another question?'

Chanterelle nodded, and used the moment to remove the cat's-eye mask from her face. Her eyes were leonine, inset with a vertical pupil, but other than that her face was rather human, broad and open, with high cheekbones, framed by a halo of auburn curls which tumbled to her neckline.

'What is it, Tanner?'

'Just before I shot your friends, one of them said something. It might have been you, but I don't remember so well.'

'Go on. What was it?'

'That there was something wrong with my eyes.'

'That was me,' Chanterelle said, uneasily.

So I had not been imagining it. 'What did you say? What was it you saw?'

Her voice lowered now, as if she was conscious of how strange the whole conversation had become.

'It was like they were glowing, like there were two glowing dots in your face.' She spoke quickly, nervously. 'I assumed you must have been wearing some kind of mask, and that you discarded it before you emerged again. But you weren't, were you?'

'No. No, I wasn't. But I wish I was.'

She looked into my eyes, the vertical slits of her own eyes narrowing as she focused intently. 'Whatever it was, it isn't there now. Are you telling me you don't know why that happened?'

'I guess,' I said, finishing the watery tea with no great enthusiasm, 'it will have to remain one of life's little mysteries.'

'What kind of an answer is that?'

'The best I'm capable of giving at this moment in time. And if that sounds like the kind of thing someone who was a little scared of what the truth might hold might say, maybe you're not entirely wrong.' I reached under the coat and scratched my chest, my skin itching beneath the sweat-sodden Mendicant clothes. 'I'd rather drop the subject for now.'

'Sorry I raised it,' Chanterelle said, heavy with irony. 'Well, what happens now, Tanner? You've already told me you were surprised that I came back. That suggests to me that my presence isn't vital to you, or you'd have done something about it. Does it mean we go our separate ways now?'

'You almost sound disappointed.' I wondered if Chanterelle was aware that my hand had not been on the hilt of the gun for several minutes now, and that the weapon had barely entered my thoughts during that time. 'Am I that fascinating to you, or are you just more bored than I imagined?'

'A bit of both, probably. But you *are* fascinating, Tanner. Worse than that, you're a puzzle I've only half solved.'

'Half already? You'd better slow down. I'm not as unfathomable as you think. Scratch the surface and you might be surprised at how little lies beneath. I'm just—'

What was I going to tell her – just a soldier, just a man keeping his word? Just a fool who did not even know when it was time to break it?

I stood up, conspicuously removing my hand from the gun pocket. 'I could use your help, Chanterelle, that's all. But there's not much more to me than meets the eye. If you want to show me something of this place, I'd be grateful. But you can walk away now.'

'Do you have any money, Tanner?'

'A little. Nothing that would amount to much here, I'm afraid.'

'Show me what you have.'

I pulled out a fistful of greasy Ferris notes, laying them in their sad entirety on the table. 'What does that buy me, another cup of tea if I'm lucky?'

'I don't know. It's enough to buy you another set of clothes, which I think you could use if you want to blend in at least approximately.'

'Do I look that out of place?'

'You look so out of place, Tanner, you might be in serious danger of starting a fashion. But somehow I don't think that's quite what you had in mind.'

'Not really, no.'

'I don't know Escher Heights well enough to recommend the best, but I saw some boutiques on the way in which should be able to outfit you.'

'I'd like to look at that tank first, if you don't mind.'

'Oh, I know what *that* is. That's Methuselah. I'd forgotten they kept him here.'

I knew the name, vaguely, and I had the impression it had already been half-remembered once this evening. But Chanterelle was leading me away. 'We can come back later, when you don't stand out so much.'

I sighed and put up my hands in surrender. 'You can show me the rest of Escher Heights as well.'

'Why not. The night's still young, after all.'

Chanterelle made some calls while we walked to a nearby boutique, chasing up her friends and establishing that they were all alive and safe in the Canopy, but she did not leave a message for any of them, and then never mentioned them again. That, I supposed, was how it went: many of the people I saw in Escher Heights would be cognisant of the Game, and might even follow it avidly, but none would admit it to themselves, beyond the private parlours where the sport's existence was acknowledged and celebrated.

The boutique was staffed by two gloss-black bipedal servitors, far more sophisticated than any I had seen in the city so far. They kept oozing insincere compliments, even when I knew that I looked like a gorilla which had accidentally broken into a theatrical suppliers. With Chanterelle's guidance, I settled on a combination which wouldn't offend or bankrupt me. The trousers and jacket were of similar cut to the Mendicant clothes I now gratefully discarded, but were cut from fabrics which were wildly ostentatious by comparison, all dancing metallic threads in coruscant golds and silvers. I felt conspicuous, but when we left the boutique – Vadim's coat billowing raffishly behind me – people gave me no more than a fleeting glance, rather than the studied suspicion I'd elicited before.

'So,' Chanterelle said, 'are you going to tell me where you're from?'

'What have you worked out for yourself?'

'Well, you're not from around here. Not from Yellowstone; almost certainly not from the Rust Belt; probably not from any other enclave in the system.'

'I'm from Sky's Edge,' I said. 'I came in on the *Orvieto*. Actually, I assumed you'd have figured out that much from my Mendicant clothes.'

'I did, except the coat confused me.'

'This old thing? It was donated to me by an old friend in the Rust Belt.'

'Sorry, but no one donates a coat like that.' Chanterelle fingered one of the lustrous, rough-cut patches which had been quilted over it. 'You have no idea what this signifies, have you?'

'All right; I stole it. From someone who had stolen it himself, I expect. A man who had worse coming to him.'

'That's fractionally more plausible. But when I first saw it, it made me wonder. And then when you mentioned Dream Fuel . . .' She had lowered her voice to speak the last two words, barely breathing them.

'Sorry, you've lost me completely. What does Dream Fuel have to do with a coat like this?'

But even as I said it I remembered how Zebra had hinted at the same connection. 'More than you seem to realise, Tanner. You asked questions about Dream Fuel which made you look like an outsider, and yet you were wearing the kind of coat which said you were part of the distribution system; a supplier.'

'You weren't telling me everything you knew about Dream Fuel then, were you?'

'Almost everything. But the coat made me wonder if you were trying to trick me, so I was careful what I said.'

'So now tell me what else you know. How big is the supply? I've seen people inject themselves with a few cubic centimetres at a time, with maybe a hundred or so ccs in reserve. I'm guessing use of Dream Fuel's restricted to a relatively small number of people; probably you and your élite, risk-taking friends and not many others. A few thousand regular users across the city, at the very maximum?'

'Probably not far off the mark.'

'Which would imply a regular supply, across the city, of – what? A few hundred ccs per user per year? Maybe a million ccs per year across the whole city? That isn't much, really – a cubic metre or so of Dream Fuel.'

'I don't know.' Chanterelle looked uncomfortable discussing what was obviously an addiction. 'That seems about right. All I know is the stuff's harder to get hold of than it used to be a year or two ago. Most of us have had to ration our use; three or four spikes a week at the most.'

'And no one else has tried manufacturing it?'

'Yes, of course. There's always someone trying to sell fake Dream Fuel. But it's not just a question of quality. It's either Fuel or it isn't.'

I nodded, but I didn't really understand. 'It's obviously a seller's market. Gideon must be the only person who has access to the right manufacturing process, or whatever it is. You postmortals need it badly; without it you're dead meat. That means Gideon can keep the price as high as he likes, within reason. What I don't see is why he'd restrict the supply.'

'He's raised the price, don't you worry.'

'Which might simply be because he can't sell as much of it as he used to, because there's a bottleneck in the manufacturing chain; maybe a problem with getting the raw materials or something.' Chanterelle shrugged, so I continued, 'All right, then. Explain what the coat means, will you?'

'The man who donated you that coat was a supplier, Tanner. That's what those patches on your coat mean. Its original owner must have had a connection to Gideon.'

I thought back to when Quirrenbach and I had searched Vadim's cabin, reminding myself now that Quirrenbach and Vadim had been secret accomplices. 'He had Dream Fuel,' I said. 'But this was up in the Rust Belt. He can't have been that close to the supply.'

No, I added to myself, but what about his friend? Perhaps Vadim and

Quirrenbach had worked together in more ways than one: Quirrenbach was the real supplier and Vadim merely his distributor in the Rust Belt.

I already wanted to speak to Quirrenbach again. Now I'd have more than one thing to ask him about.

'Maybe your friend wasn't that close to the supply,' Chanterelle said. 'But whatever the case, there's something you need to understand. All the stories you hear about Gideon? About people vanishing because they ask the wrong questions?'

'Yes?' I asked.

'They're all true.'

Afterwards I let Chanterelle take me to the palanquin races. I thought there might be a chance that Reivich would show his face at an event like that, but although I searched the crowds of spectators, I never saw anyone who might have been him.

The circuit was a complicated, looping track that wormed its way through many levels, doubling under and over itself. Now and then it even extended beyond the building, suspended far above the Mulch. There were chicanes and obstacles and traps, and the parts which looped out into the night were not barriered, so there was nothing to stop a palanquin going over the edge if the occupant took the corner too sharply. There were ten or eleven palaquins per race, each travelling box elaborately ornamented, and there were stringent rules about what was and wasn't permitted. Chanterelle said these rules were taken only semi-seriously, and it wasn't unusual for someone to equip their palanquin with weapons to use against the other racers – projecting rams, for instance, to shove an opponent over the edge on one of the aerial bends.

The races had begun as a bet between two bored, palanquin-riding immortals, she said. But now almost anyone could take part. Half the palanquins were being ridden by people who had nothing to fear from the plague. Major fortunes were lost and won – but mainly lost – in the course of a night's racing.

I suppose it was better than hunting.

'Listen,' Chanterelle said as we were leaving the races. 'What do you know about the Mixmasters?'

'Not too much,' I said, giving as little away as possible. The name was vaguely familiar, but no more than that. 'Why do you ask?'

'You really don't know, do you? That settles it, Tanner; you really aren't from around here, as if there was any doubt.'

The Mixmasters predated the Melding Plague and were one of the system's comparatively few old social orders which had weathered the blight more or less intact. Like the Mendicants, they were a self-supporting guild, and like the Mendicants, they concerned themselves with God. But there the difference ended. The Mendicants – no matter what their other agendas happened to be – were there to serve and glorify their deity. The Mixmasters, on the other hand, wanted to *become* God.

And – by some definitions – they'd long ago succeeded.

When the Amerikanos settled Yellowstone, the better part of four centuries ago, they brought with them all the genetic expertise of their culture: genomic sequences, linkage and function maps for literally millions of Terran species, including all the higher primates and mammals. They knew genetics intimately. It was how they had arrived on Yellowstone in the first place, sending their fertilised eggs via frail robot envoys; machines which, upon arriving, fabricated artificial wombs and brought those eggs to term. They hadn't lasted, of course – but they had left their legacy. DNA sequences allowed later descendants to merge Amerikano blood with their own, enriching the biodiversity of the resettlers, who came by ship rather than seed-carrying robot.

But the Amerikanos left more than that. They also left vast files of expertise, knowledge which had not so much been lost as allowed to grow stale, so that subtle relationships and dependencies were no longer appreciated. It was the Mixmasters who appropriated this wisdom. They became the guardians of all biological and genetic expertise, and they expanded that sphere of brilliance via trade with Ultras, who occasionally offered snippets of foreign genetic information, alien genomes or manipulative techniques pioneered in other systems. But, for all this, the Mixmasters had seldom been at the hub of Yellowstone power. The system, after all, was in thrall to the Sylveste clan, that powerful old-line family which advocated transcendence via cybernetic modes of consciousness-expansion.

The Mixmasters had made a living, of course, since not everyone subscribed utterly to the Sylveste doctrine, and also because the gross failures of the Eighty had soured many on the idea of transmigration. But their work had been discreet: correcting genetic abnormalities in newborns; ironing out inherited defects in supposedly pure clan lines. It was work which became more invisible the more adeptly it was done, like an exceedingly efficient assassination, in which the crime did not appear to have happened at all, and in which no one remembered who the victim was in the first place. The Mixmasters worked like the restorers of damaged art, trying to bring as little of their own vision to the matter as possible. And yet the power of transformation they held was awesome. But it was held in check, because society could not tolerate two massively transforming pressures operating at once, and on some level the Mixmasters knew this. To unleash their art would have been to rip Yellowstone culture to shreds.

But then the plague had come. Society had indeed been ripped to shreds, but like an asteroid blasted with a too-small demolition charge, the pieces had not gained sufficient escape velocity to fly apart completely. Yellowstone society had crashed back into existence – fragmented, jumbled and liable to crumble at any instant, but it was society nonetheless. And a society in which the ideologies of cybernetics were, momentarily, a kind of heresy.

The Mixmasters had slipped effortlessly into the power vacuum.

'They maintain parlours throughout the Canopy,' Chanterelle said. 'Places were you can get your heritage read, check out your clan affiliations, or look over the brochures for makeovers.' She indicated her eyes. 'Anything you weren't born with, or weren't meant to inherit. Can be transplants – although that's reasonably rare, unless you're after something outrageous like a set of Pegasus wings. More likely it's going to be genetic. The Mixmasters rewire your DNA so that the changes happen naturally – or as close to naturally as makes no difference.'

'How would that happen?'

'It's simple. When you cut yourself, does the wound heal over in fur, or scales? Of course not – there's a knowledge of your body's architecture buried deep in your DNA. All the Mixmasters do is edit that knowledge, very selectively, so that your body carries on doing its job of maintenance against injury and wear and tear, but with the *wrong* local blueprint. You end up growing something that was never meant to be expressed in your phenotype.' Chanterelle paused. 'Like I said, there are parlours throughout the Canopy where they ply their trade. If you're curious about your eyes, perhaps we should stop by.'

'What have my eyes got to do with it?'

'Don't you think there's something wrong with them?'

'I don't know,' I said, trying hard not to sound sullen. 'But maybe you're right. Maybe the Mixmasters can tell me something. Are they confidential?'

'As confidential as anyone around here.'

'Great. That really reassures me.'

The nearest parlour was one of the holographically fronted booths we had already passed on our way in, overlooking a tranquil pool filled with gape-mouthed koi. Inside, it made Dominika's tent seem spacious. The male attendant wore a relatively sober tunic in ash-grey, offset only by the sigil of the Mixmasters below his shoulder: a pair of outstretched hands spanned by a cat's cradle of DNA. He was sitting behind a floating console shaped like a boomerang, above which various molecular projections were rotating and pulsing, their bright primary colours evoking nursery toys. His gauntleted hands were dancing above the molecules, orchestrating complex cascades of fission and recombination. I was certain that he had noticed us immediately we entered the booth, but he made no show of it and continued his manipulations for another minute or so before deigning to acknowledge our presence.

'I presume I may be of assistance.'

Chanterelle took the lead. 'My friend wants his eyes examined.'

'Does he now.' The Mixmaster canted aside his console, producing an eyepiece from his tunic. He leaned closer to me, nose wrinkling in what was probably justified distaste at my smell. He squinted through the eyepiece, scrutinising both my eyes, so that the vast lens seemed to fill half the room. 'What about his eyes?' he asked, bored.

On the way to the booth we'd rehearsed a story. 'I was a fool,' I said. 'I wanted eyes like my partner's. But I couldn't afford Mixmaster services. I was in orbit and—'

'What were you doing in orbit if you couldn't afford *our* prices?'

'Getting myself scanned, of course. It doesn't come cheap; not if you want a good provider who'll keep you properly backed up.'

'Oh.' It was an effective end to that line of enquiry. The Mixmasters were ideologically opposed to the whole idea of neural scanning, arguing that the soul could only be maintained biologically, not by capturing it in some machine.

The attendant shook his head, as if I had betrayed some solemn promise.

'Then you were indeed foolish. But you know that already. What happened?'

'There were Black Geneticists in the carousel; bloodcutters, offering much the same services as the Mixmasters, but at a much lower cost. Since the work I sought didn't involve large-scale anatomical reconstruction, I thought the risk was worth it.'

'And of course now you come crawling to us.'

I offered him my best apologetic grin, placating myself by imagining the several interesting and painful ways in which I could have killed him, there and then, without breaking into a sweat.

'It's several weeks since I returned from the carousel,' I said. 'And nothing's happened to my eyes. They still look the same. I want to know if the bloodcutters did anything other than fleece me.'

'It'll cost you. I've a good mind to charge you extra just because you were stupid enough to go to bloodcutters.' Then, barely perceptibly, his tone softened. 'Still, perhaps you've already learnt your lesson. I suppose it depends on whether I find any changes.'

I did not particularly enjoy much of what followed. I had to lie on a couch, more intricate and antiseptic than the one in Dominika's, then wait while the Mixmaster immobilised my head using a padded frame. A machine lowered down above my eyes, extending a hair-fine filament which quivered slightly, like a whisker. The probe wandered over my eyes, mapping them with stuttering pulses of blue laser light. Then – very quickly, so that it felt more like a single sting of cold – the whisker dropped into my eye, snatched tissue, retracted, moved to another site and re-entered, perhaps a dozen times, on each occasion sampling a different depth of the interior. But it all happened so swiftly that before my blink reflex had initiated, the machine had done its work and moved to the other eye.

'That's enough,' the Mixmaster said. 'Should be able to tell what the bloodcutters did to you, if they did anything – and why it isn't taking. A few weeks, you said?'

I nodded.

'Perhaps it's too soon to rule out success.' I had the feeling he was talking to himself more than us. 'Some of their therapies are actually rather sophisticated, but only those which they've stolen in their entirety from us. Of course they cut all the safety margins and use outdated sequences.'

He lowered himself into his seat again, folding down the console, which immediately threw up a display too cryptic to make any sense to me: all shifting histograms and complex boxes full of scrolling alphanumerics. A huge eyeball popped into reality, half a metre in diameter, like a disembodied sketch from one of da Vinci's notebooks. The Mixmaster made sweeping movements with his gauntlets and chunks of the eyeball detached like slices of cake, exposing deeper strata.

'There are changes,' he said, after kneading his chin for several minutes and burrowing deeper into the hovering eye. 'Profound genetic changes – but there are none of the usual signatures of Mixmaster work.'

'Signatures?'

'Copyright information, encoded into redundant base pairs. The bloodcutters probably didn't steal their sequences from us in this case, or else there'd be residual traces of Mixmaster design.' He shook his head emphatically. 'No; this work never originated on Yellowstone. It's fairly sophisticated, but . . .'

I pulled myself from the couch, wiping a tear of irritation from my cheek. 'But what?'

'It's almost certainly not what you asked for.'

Well, I knew that much had to be the case, since I had never asked for anything in the first place. But I made appropriate noises of surprise and annoyance, knowing the Mixmaster would enjoy my shock at having been duped by the bloodcutters.

'I know the kind of homeobox mutations you need for a cat's-eye pupil, and I'm not seeing major changes in any of the right chromosomal regions. But I am seeing changes elsewhere, in the parts which oughtn't to have been edited at all.'

'Can you be more specific?'

'Not immediately, no. It doesn't help that the sequences are fragmentary in most chains. The specific DNA changes are normally inserted by a retrovirus, one which would be engineered by us – or bloodcutters – and programmed to effect the right mutations for the desired transformation. In your case,' he continued, 'the virus doesn't seem to have copied itself very efficiently. There are very few intact strands where the changes are expressed fully. It's inefficient, and it might explain why the changes haven't begun to affect the gross

338

structure of your eye. But it's also nothing I've seen before. If this is really bloodcutter work, it might mean that they're using techniques we don't know anything about.'

'This isn't good, is it?'

'At least when they stole their techniques from us, there was some guarantee they'd work, or wouldn't be actively dangerous.' He shrugged. 'Now, I'm afraid, there's no such guarantee. I imagine you're already beginning to regret that visit. But it's rather too late for regrets.'

'Thanks for your sympathy. I presume if you can map these changes, you can also undo them?'

'That'll be much harder than making them in the first place. But it could be done, at a cost.'

'You don't surprise me.'

'Will you be requiring our services, then?'

I moved towards the door, letting Chanterelle walk ahead of me. 'I'll be sure to let you know, believe me.'

I was unsure how she *expected* me to act after the examination, whether she imagined that the Mixmaster's enquiries would jog my memory, and that I would suddenly realise just what it was that was wrong with my eyes and how they had ended up like that? Maybe she had. And – just maybe – so had I, clinging to the idea that the nature of my eyes was something I had temporarily forgotten, a long-delayed aspect of the revival amnesia.

But nothing like that happened.

I was none the wiser, but even more unsettled, because I knew that something was really happening, and I could no longer dismiss how my eyes seemed to glow in my face. There had to be more to it than that. Since arriving in Chasm City, I had been growing steadily more aware of a faculty I had never known before: I could see in the dark, when other people needed image-intensifying goggles or infrared overlays. I had noticed it for the first time – without really consciously recognising it – when I had entered the ruined building and looked upwards to see the staircase which had led me to safety, and to Zebra. There should not have been enough light for me to see what I had seen, but of course I had more than my share of other things to worry about. Later, after the cable-car had crashed into Lorant's kitchen, the same thing had happened. I had crawled from the wrecked vehicle and seen the pig and his wife long before they saw me – even though I was the only one not looking through night-goggles. And again, too doped on adrenalin to reflect on the matter, I'd let it pass, although by then it was not quite so easy to put out of mind.

Now, though, I knew that there was some deep genetic shift taking place in my eyes, and that nothing which had happened before had been my imagination. Perhaps the changes were already complete, irrespective of the degree of genetic fragmentation which the Mixmaster had observed.

'Whatever he told you,' Chanterelle said, 'it wasn't what you wanted to hear, was it?'

'He didn't tell me anything. You were there; you heard every word he said.'

'I thought maybe some of it would make sense to you.'

'That was my hope, but none of it did.'

We ambled back to the open area where the teahouse was, my mind running like an unchecked flywheel. Someone had tampered with my eyes on the genetic level, reprogramming them to grow in an alien manner. Could it have been initiated by the Haussmann virus? Perhaps – but what did seeing in the dark have to do with Sky? Sky hated the dark; feared it totally.

But he couldn't see in it.

The change could not have happened since I had arrived on Yellowstone, unless Dominika had done it when I was having the implant removed. I had been conscious, but sufficiently disorientated that she might have been able to do it. But that didn't fit. I had experienced the night-vision before that.

What about Waverly?

It was possible, especially from the chronological aspect. I'd been unconscious in the Canopy while Waverly installed the implant. That would have allowed only a few hours between administration of the genetic treatment and the onset of physical changes in the eye. Given that the changes could be thought of as a kind of controlled growth, it seemed nowhere near long enough, but maybe it was, given that only a relatively small area of cells was affected, rather than a major organ or large region of the anatomy. And suddenly I saw that it was at least possible from the point of view of motivation. Waverly had been working for both sides, and he had tipped off Zebra about me, giving me a sporting chance of making it alive through the game. Was it also possible that he had opted to give me another advantage, that of night-vision?

It was possible, yes. It was even comforting.

But nothing I was ready to believe in.

'You wanted to look at Methuselah,' Chanterelle said, pointing towards the large metal-framed tank I had seen earlier. 'Well, now's your chance.'

'Methuselah?'

'You'll see.'

I pushed my way through the throng of people rimming the tank. Actually, it was not necessary to do much pushing. People tended to get out of my way before I even made eye contact, pulling the same look of nasal insult that I had seen on the face of the Mixmaster. I sympathised with them.

'Methuselah's a fish,' Chanterelle said, joining me against the smoky-green glass. 'A very big and very old one. The oldest, actually.'

'How old?'

'No one knows, except that he's at least as old as the Amerikano era. That makes him comfortably older than any organism alive on this planet, with the possible exception of a few bacterial cultures.'

The huge and bloated koi, unspeakably ancient, filled the tank like a basking sea-cow. His eye, as large as a plate, observed us with a complete lack of sentience; as if we were looking into a slightly tarnished mirror. Whitish cataracts spanned the eye like chains of islands on a slate-grey sea. His scales were pale and almost entirely colourless, and the distended bulk of his body was marred by odd protrusions and lacunae of diseased flesh. His gills opened and closed with a slowness that suggested it was only the stirring of the currents in the tank that animated the fish.

'How come Methuselah didn't die like the other koi?'

'Maybe they remade his heart for him, or gave him other hearts, or a mechanical one. Or maybe he just doesn't need to use it very much. I understand it's very cold in there. The water's nearly freezing, so they put something in his blood to keep it liquid. His metabolism is about as slow as it can get without stopping altogether.' Chanterelle touched the glass, her fingers leaving a frosty imprint against the chill. 'He's worshipped, though. The old venerate him. They think that by communing with him – by touching his glass – they ensure their own longevity.'

'What about you, Chanterelle?'

She nodded. 'I did once, Tanner. But like everything, it's just a phase you grow out of.'

I gazed into that mirrorlike eye again, wondering what Methuselah had seen in all his years, and whether any of that data had percolated down to whatever passed for memory in a bloated old fish. I had read somewhere that goldfish had exceptionally short spans of recall; that they were incapable of remembering something for more than a few seconds.

I was sick of eyes for one day; even the unknowing, uncomprehending eyes of an immortal and venerated koi. So my gaze wandered momentarily down, beneath the sagging curve of Methuselah's jaw, to the wavering bottle-green gloom which was the other side of the tank, where a dozen or so faces were crowded against the glass.

And saw Reivich.

It was impossible, but there he was; standing almost exactly opposite me on the other side of the tank, his face registering supreme calm, as if lost in the contemplation of the ancient animal between us. Methuselah stirred a fin – a movement indescribably languid – and the current caused the face of Reivich to swirl and distort. When the water calmed, I dared to imagine that what I would see would be only one of the locals who possessed the same set of genes for bland aristocratic handsomeness.

But when the water settled, I was still looking at Reivich.

He hadn't seen me; though we were standing opposite each other, his gaze hadn't yet intersected mine. I averted mine, while still holding him in peripheral vision, then reached in my pocket for the ice-slug gun, almost shocked to find that it was still there. I flicked off the safety.

Reivich still stood there, unreacting.

He was very close. Despite what I had said to Chanterelle earlier in the evening, I felt reasonably sure I could put a slug through him now, without removing the gun from the concealment of my coat. If I fired three slugs I could even allow for the distortion caused by the intervening water; bracketing my angle of fire. Would the slugs leave the gun with sufficient muzzle velocity to pass through two sheets of armoured glass and the water in between them? I couldn't guess, and maybe it was academic anyway. From the angle at which I'd need to fire to take out Reivich, there was something else in the way.

I couldn't simply kill Methuselah . . . could I?

Of course I could. It was just a question of pulling the trigger and putting the giant koi out of whatever extremely simplistic mental state it was currently in, certainly nothing sophisticated enough to be termed misery, I was sure. It would be a crime no more heinous than damaging some prized work of art.

The unseeing silver bowl of Methuselah's eye drew my gaze.

There was no way I could do it.

'Damn,' I said.

'What is it?' Chanterelle said, almost blocking me as I pulled away from the side of the glass, reversing into the press of jostlers behind me, rubbernecking to get a glimpse of the fabled fish.

'Someone I just saw. On the other side of Methuselah.' I had the gun half out of the pocket now; it would only take an inadvertent glimpse for someone to see what I was about to do.

'Tanner, are you insane?'

'Very probably several kinds of insane,' I said. 'But I'm afraid it doesn't change anything. I'm perfectly happy with my current delusional system.' And then – approximating a leisured stroll – I started to walk around to the other side of the tank, the perspiration from my palm dampening the metal of the gun. I eased it fractionally from my pocket, hoping that the gesture looked casual, like someone extracting a cigar case, but freezing before the action was complete, as if something else had snared their attention.

I turned the corner.

Reivich was gone.

TWENTY-EIGHT

'You were going to kill someone,' Chanterelle said as her cable-car brachiated home, swinging through the lantern-bedecked brain coral growth of the Canopy with the Mulch hung below, dark except for a dappling of scattered fires.

'What?'

'You had your gun half out of your pocket like you meant to use it. Not the way you showed it to me – not as a threat – but like you weren't going to say a word before you squeezed the trigger. Like you were just going to walk up, put a bullet through someone and walk away.'

'There'd be little point lying, would there?'

'You have to start talking to me, Tanner. You have to start telling me something. You said I wouldn't like the truth because it would complicate things. Well, trust me – this is complicated enough. Are you ready to let some of that mask slip, or are we going to carry on this game?'

I was still playing the whole incident over in my head. The face had been that of Argent Reivich, and he had been standing only a few metres from me, in a public place.

Was it possible he had actually seen me all along, and was much cleverer than I had realised? If he'd recognised me, he could have left the area in the opposite direction while I walked around Methuselah. I'd been too fixated on the idea of him still standing up against the glass to pay enough attention to the people who had just left. So it was possible, yes. But in accepting that Reivich had been aware of my presence all along, I opened myself up to a far more unsettling set of questions. Why had he stayed there, if he had already seen me? And how had we met each other so easily? I hadn't even been looking for him at that point; I was just getting the feel of the area before I began the real work of tightening the net. As if that was not enough, now that I reviewed the few moments which separated my discovery of Reivich from the moment when I realised he had left, I became aware that something else had happened. I had seen something or someone, but my mind had suppressed it, concentrating my attention on the imminent kill.

I had seen another face in the glass – another face that I knew, standing very close to Reivich.

She had erased the surface markings, but the underlying bone structure was reasonably intact, and her expression very familiar.

I had seen Zebra.

'I'm still waiting,' Chanterelle said. 'There's only so much of that meaningful frown I can take, you know.'

'I'm sorry. It's just—' I found myself grinning. 'I almost think you might like me for who I am.'

'Don't push your luck, Tanner. Only a couple of hours ago you were pointing a gun at me. Most relationships that start like that tend to go downhill.'

'Ordinarily, I'd agree. But you also happened to be pointing a gun at me, and your gun was considerably larger than mine.'

'Hmm, maybe.' She sounded far from convinced. 'But if we're going to take it any further – and make of that what you will – you'd better start elaborating on that dark and mysterious past of yours. Even if there are things you don't really want me to know.'

'Oh, there are plenty of those, believe me.'

'Then get them out into the open. By the time we get back to my place, I want to know why that man was going to die. And if I were you, I'd seriously try and persuade me that he deserves it – whoever it was. Otherwise you might begin to slip in my estimation.'

The car pitched and swayed, but I no longer found the motion really sickening.

'He deserves to die,' I said. 'But I can't say he's a bad man. If I'd been in his place, I'd have done exactly what he did.' Except done it professionally, I thought, and not left anyone alive afterwards.

'Mm, bad start, Tanner. But please continue.'

I thought about giving Chanterelle the sanitised version of my story – before realising that there *was* no sanitised version. So I explained about about my soldiering days, and how I had fallen into Cahuella's orbit. I told her that Cahuella was a man of both power and cruelty, but not genuinely evil since he was also a man of trust and loyalty. It was not hard to respect him and to want to earn his respect in return. I suppose there was something very primitive about the relationship between Cahuella and me: he was a man who desired excellence in everything around him – in his surroundings; in the accoutrements he collected; in the way he chose his sexual partners, like Gitta. He also desired excellence in his employees. I considered myself a fine soldier, bodyguard, liege, man-at-arms, assassin; whatever label suited. But only in Cahuella could I measure my excellence against any kind of absolute.

'A bad man, but not a monster?' Chanterelle said. 'And that was enough reason for you to work for him?'

'He also paid pretty well,' I said.

'Mercenary bastard.'

'There was something else, too. I was valuable to him because I had experience. He wasn't willing to risk losing that wisdom by placing me in situations of undue danger. So a lot of the work I did for him was purely advisory – I hardly ever had to carry a weapon. We had real bodyguards for that; younger, fitter, stupider versions of myself.'

'And how did the man you saw in Escher Heights come into it?'

'The man's name is Argent Reivich,' I said. 'He used to live on Sky's Edge. The family name's rather well-established there.'

'It's also an old name in the Canopy.'

'I'm not surprised. If Reivich already had connections here, that would explain why he managed to infiltrate the Canopy so quickly, when I was still getting soaked down in the Mulch.'

'You're getting ahead of yourself. What brought Reivich here? And you, for that matter?'

I told her how Cahuella's weapons had fallen into the wrong hands, and how those wrong hands had used them against Reivich's family. How Reivich had traced the arms back to my employer, and his determination to exact revenge.

'That's rather honourable of him, don't you think?'

'I have no quarrel with Reivich about that,' I said. 'But if I'd done it, I'd have made sure everyone died. That was his one mistake; the one I can't forgive him for.'

'You can't forgive him for leaving you alive?'

'It wasn't an act of mercy, Chanterelle. Quite the opposite. The bastard wanted me to suffer for failing Cahuella.'

'Sorry, but the logic's just a little too tortuous for me.'

'He killed Cahuella's wife – the woman I should have been protecting. Then he left Cahuella, Dieterling and me alive. Dieterling was lucky – he looked dead. But Reivich deliberately left Cahuella and me alive. He wanted Cahuella to punish me for letting Gitta die.'

'Did he?'

'Did he what?'

She sounded like she was about to lose patience with me. 'Did Cahuella do anything to you afterwards?'

The question seemed simple enough to answer. No, obviously, he hadn't – because *Cahuella had died afterwards*. His injuries had eventually killed him, even though they hadn't appeared particularly life-threatening at the time.

So why did I find it difficult to answer Chanterelle? Why did my tongue stumble on the obvious, and something else come to mind? Something that made me doubt that Cahuella *had* died?

Finally I said, 'It never came to that. But I had to live with my shame. I guess that was a kind of punishment in its own right.'

'But it didn't have to have happened that way; not from Reivich's perspective.'

We were passing through a part of the Canopy now that resembled a solid map of the alveoli in a lung: endlessly branching globules, bridged by dark filaments of what might have been coagulated blood.

'How could it have been otherwise?' I said.

'Maybe Reivich spared you because with you it wasn't personal. He knew that you were just an employee and that his argument wasn't with you but with Cahuella.'

'Nice idea.'

'And just possibly the right one. Has it occurred to you that you don't have to kill this man at all, and that you might owe him your life?'

I was beginning to tire of this particular line of debate.

'No, it hadn't – for the pure and simple reason that it's completely irrelevant. I don't care what Reivich thought of me when he decided to let me live – whether it was intended as a punishment or an act of mercy. It doesn't matter at all. What matters is that he did kill Gitta, and that I swore to Cahuella that I'd avenge her death.'

'Avenge her death.' She smiled humourlessly. 'It's all so conveniently mediaeval, isn't it? Feudal honour and bonds of trust. Oaths of fealty and vengeance. Have you checked the calendar recently, Tanner?'

'Don't even pretend to understand any of this, Chanterelle.'

She shook her head vehemently. 'If I did, I'd start worrying about my sanity. What in hell's name have you come here for – to satisfy some ridiculous promise, an eye for an eye?'

'Now you put it like that, I don't see it as being particularly laughable.'

'No, it's not remotely laughable, Tanner. It's tragic.'

'To you, maybe.'

'To anyone with an angstrom of detachment. Do you realise how much time will have passed by the time you get back to Sky's Edge?'

'Don't treat me like a child, Chanterelle.'

'Answer my damned question.'

I sighed, wondering how I had let things get so far out of control. Had our friendship just been an anomaly; an excursion away from the natural state of things?

'At least three decades,' I replied, as if the time I was expressing was of no consequence at all, like a matter of weeks. 'And before you ask, I'm well aware of how much could change in that time. But not the important things. They've already changed, and much as I wish they would, they won't change back. Gitta's dead. Dieterling's dead. Mirabel's dead.'

'What?'

346

'I said Cahuella's dead.'

'No, you didn't. You said Mirabel's dead.'

I watched the city slide by outside, my mind buzzing, wondering what kind of state my head must be in for a slip of the tongue like that. That wasn't the kind of mistake you could easily ascribe to fatigue. The Haussmann virus was clearly having a worse effect on me than I'd dared assume: it had gone beyond simply infecting my waking hours with shards of Sky's life and times and was beginning to interfere with my most basic assumptions about my own identity, undermining my perception of self. And yet . . . even that was a comforting assumption. The Mendicants had told me their therapy would burn out the virus before too long . . . yet the Sky episodes were becoming more insistent. And why would the Haussmann virus bother making me confuse events that had happened in my *own* past, rather than Sky's? Why did it care if I confused Mirabel with myself?

No. Not Mirabel. *Cahuella*.

Disturbed – not wanting to remember the dream I'd had, of the time when I'd been looking down on the man in the white room with the missing foot – I tried to recapture the thread of the conversation.

'All I'm saying is . . .'

'What?'

'All I'm saying is, that when I get back, I'm not expecting to find what I left. But it won't be any worse. The people who mattered to me were already dead.'

The Haussmann virus was really screwing me up.

I was starting to see Sky as myself and Tanner Mirabel was increasingly becoming . . . what? A detached third person, not really me at all?

I remembered my confusion at Zebra's, after I had been playing the chess game over in my mind, time and time again. How sometimes I appeared to win and sometimes I appeared to lose.

But it had always been the same game.

That must have been the start of it. The slip of the tongue just meant that the process had taken a step beyond my dreams, just like the Haussmann virus.

Disturbed, I tried to recapture the thread of the conversation.

'All I'm saying is, when I get back, I'm not expecting to find what I left. But it won't be any worse. The people who mattered to me were dead before I left.'

'I think it's about satisfaction,' she said. 'Like in the old experientials, where the nobleman throws down his glove and says he demands satisfaction. That's how you function. I thought it was absurd at first, when I used to indulge in those experientials. I thought it was too comical to even be part of history. But I was wrong. It wasn't just part of history. It was still alive and well, reincarnated in Tanner Mirabel.' She had replaced her cat's-eye mask now, an act which served to focus attention onto the sneer of her mouth, a mouth I suddenly wanted to kiss, even though I knew the moment – if it had ever existed – was gone for ever. 'Tanner demands satisfaction. And he's going to go to any lengths to get it. No matter how absurd. No matter how stupid or pointless, or how much of a prick he ends up making himself look.'

'Please don't insult me, Chanterelle. Not for what I believe in.'

'It's got nothing to do with belief, you pompous oaf. It's just stupid male pride.' Her eyes narrowed to slits and her voice took on a new vindictiveness which I still managed to find attractive, from some quiet retreat where I observed our argument like a neutral spectator. 'Tell me one thing, Tanner. One little thing which in all of this you haven't explained.'

'Only the best for you, little rich girl.'

'Oh, very incisive. Don't give up the day job for the cut and thrust of debate, Tanner – your rapier wit might be too much for all of us.'

'You were about to ask me a question.'

'It's about this boss of yours – Cahuella. He felt this urge to hunt for Reivich himself, when he learnt that Reivich was moving south towards the – what did you call it? The Reptile House?'

'Go on,' I said, testily.

'So why didn't Cahuella feel he had to end the job? Surely the fact that Reivich killed Gitta would have made it even more of a personal thing for Cahuella. Even more a case of – dare I say it – demanding satisfaction?'

'Get on with it.'

'I'm wondering why I'm talking to you, and not Cahuella. Why didn't Cahuella come here?'

I found it hard to answer, at least not to my own satisfaction. Cahuella had been a hard man, but he had never been a soldier. There were skills which I had learnt on a level below recall, which Cahuella simply lacked – and would have taken half a lifetime to gain. He knew weapons, but he did not really know war. His understanding of tactics and strategy was strictly theoretical – he played the game well, and understood the subtleties buried in its rules – but he had never been thrown into the dirt by the concussion of a shell, or seen a part of himself lying beyond reach on the ground, quivering like a beached jellyfish. Experiences like that did not necessarily improve one – but they certainly changed one. But would any of those deficits have handicapped him? This was not war, after all. And I had hardly come well-equipped for it myself. It was a sobering thought, but I found it hard to entirely dismiss the idea that Cahuella might have already succeeded by now.

So why had I come here, rather than him?

'He would have found it difficult to get off the planet,' I said. 'He was a war criminal. His freedom of movement was restricted.'

'He'd have found a way round it,' Chanterelle said.

The troubling thing was, I thought she was right. And it was the last thing in the world I wanted to think about.

'It's been nice knowing you, Tanner. I think.'

'Chanterelle, don't—'

As the door of the cable-car sealed us from each other, I saw her shake her head, expressionless behind that mask of cattish indifference. Her cable-car lofted, hauling itself away with a series of whisking noises, underpinned by the musical creaking as the cables stressed and released like catgut.

At least she had resisted the temptation to dump me in the Mulch.

But she had dumped me in a part of the Canopy I had no knowledge of. What exactly had I been expecting? I suppose, somewhere at the back of my mind was the thought that we might have ended up sharing a bed by the end of the evening. Given that we had commenced our affair by pointing weapons at each other and trading threats, it would certainly have been an unantici-pated coda. She was beautiful enough as well – less exotic than Zebra; perhaps less sure of herself – a trait which undoubtedly brought out the protector in me. She would have laughed in my face at that – stupid male pride – and of course she would have been correct. But so what. I liked her, and if I needed justification for that attraction, it hardly mattered how irrational it was.

'Damn you, Chanterelle,' I said, without very much conviction.

She had left me on a landing ledge, similar to the touchdown point outside Escher Heights, but significantly less busy – Chanterelle's car had been the only one here, and now that was gone. A muted rain was descending, like a constant moist exhalation from some great dragon poised over the Canopy.

I walked to the edge, feeling Sky come down with the rain.

TWENTY-NINE

He was doing his rounds of the sleepers.

Sky and Norquinco were far along one of the train tunnels that stretched along the ship's spine, their feet clanging against catwalked flooring. Occasionally strings of robot freight pods clattered past along the track, ferrying supplies to and from the small band of technicians who lived at the far end of the ship, studying the engines night and day like worshipping acolytes. Here came one now, its orange hazard lights flashing as it rumbled towards them. The train almost filled the corridor. Sky and Norquinco stepped into a recess while the shipment went past. Sky noticed Norquinco slipping something into a shirt pocket, a piece of paper covered with what looked like a series of numbers partially crossed-out.

'Come on,' Sky said. 'I want to make it to node three before the next shipment comes along.'

'No problem,' the other man said. 'The next one isn't due for . . . seventeen minutes.'

Sky looked at him oddly. 'You know that?'

'Of course. They do run to a timetable, Sky.'

'Of course; I knew that. I just couldn't see why anyone in their right mind would actually *memorise* the times.'

They walked on in silence to the next node. This far from the main living areas, the ship was uncommonly quiet, with hardly any sound of air-pumps or any of the other chugging systems of life-support. The sleepers, for all that they needed constant cybernetic supervision, drew very little power from the ship's grid. The *momios'* refrigeration systems did not have to work hard, for the sleepers had been deliberately situated close to naked space; slumbering only metres from the absolute chill of interstellar vacuum. Sky wore a thermal suit, his breath blasting out in white gouts with each exhalation. Periodically he lifted the hood over his head until he felt warm again. Norquinco, by contrast, kept his hood permanently up.

350

It was a long time since he'd had any contact with Norquinco. They had barely spoken since Balcazar's death, after which Sky had spent time establishing himself in a position of considerable seniority within the crew. From head of security he had moved to overall third-in-command, and now second-in-command, with only Ramirez standing between him and absolute control of the *Santiago*. Constanza was still problematic, of course, even though he had relegated her to a minor role in security – but he would not allow her to upset his plans. In the new régime, Captain was an extremely precarious position. A state of cold war existed between all the ships; internal shipboard politics were a web of paranoia in which errors of judgement were punished mercilessly. It would take only one carefully engineered scandal to oust Ramirez; murdering him would begin to look just a little too suspicious. Sky had something in mind; a scandal that would remove Ramirez and provide a convenient cover for his own plans.

They reached the node and descended to one of the six sleeper modules situated at that point on the spine. Each module held ten berths, and accessing each berth was itself an awkward process, so it wasn't possible to visit more than a small fraction of the *momios* in a single day. Yet throughout his climb to second-in-command, Sky had never allowed himself to spend too much time away from the sleepers.

The task of visiting them all, checking on their progress, had, however, become easier with each year. Now and then one of the sleeper berths failed, ensuring that the *momio* could never be revived. Sky had mapped the dead laboriously, noting clusters which might signify some rogue support system. But by and large the deaths were distributed randomly along the spine. It was all that could be expected from such ancient machinery, both delicate and highly experimental at the time the Flotilla had departed. Messages from back home suggested that they had made great improvements in cryonics technology – advances which would have made these sleeper caskets look scarcely more civilised than Egyptian sarcophagi. But that didn't help anyone on the Flotilla. It was far too risky to try to improve the existing berths.

Sky and Norquinco crawled through the hull until they reached the first sleeper module. They emerged into one of the ten berths spaced around its circumference. Sensing them, pressure had flooded into the chamber, lights warmed and status displays came alive, but it remained deathly cold.

'This one's dead, Sky . . .'

'I know.' Norquinco had not visited many of the sleepers before; this was the first time Sky had felt it necessary to have him along. 'I marked this one down as a failure on one of my earlier inspections.'

The casket's warning icons were pulsing all the shades of hell, to no avail. The glass cover remained hermetic, and Sky had to peer close to satisfy himself that the sleeper really was dead, and not about to become the victim of malfunctioning readouts. But there was no arguing with the mummified form he

351

glimpsed within. He glanced at the sleeper's nameplate, checked it against his list and was satisfied that his judgement before had been wise.

Sky left the chamber, Norquinco following him, and they moved along to the next.

Similar story. Another dead passenger, killed by a similar error. No point even thinking about keeping this one thawed. There was unlikely to be a single intact cell anywhere in her body.

'What a waste,' Norquinco said.

'I don't know,' Sky said. 'Maybe some good can come of these deaths. Norquinco, I've brought you here for a reason. I want you to listen carefully and be very certain that nothing I say goes beyond these walls. Understand?'

'I wondered why you wanted to meet me again. It's been a few years, Sky.'

Sky nodded. 'Yes, and there've been a lot of changes. I've kept my eye on you, though. I've watched you find a niche for your skills, and I've seen how good you are at your job. The same goes for Gomez – but I've already spoken to him.'

'What is this all about, Sky?'

'Two things, really. I'll come to the most urgent in a moment. First of all I want to ask you about something technical. What do you know about these modules?'

'What I need to know, no more and no less. There are ninety-six of them spaced along the spine, ten sleepers to each.'

'Yes. And a lot of those sleepers are dead now.'

'I don't follow, Sky.'

'They're dead mass. Not just the sleepers, but all the useless machinery which is no longer being used to support them. Add it up and it's a sizable fraction of the ship's total mass.'

'I still don't follow.'

Sky sighed, wondering why nothing was ever as clear to other people as it was to him. 'We don't need that mass any more. Right now it doesn't hurt us, but as soon as we start slowing down, it'll prevent us braking as fast as we'd like. Shall I spell it out? That means if we want to come to a stop around 61 Cygni-A, we have to start slowing down sooner than we'd otherwise need to. On the other hand, if we could detach the modules we don't need *now*, we'd be able to slow down harder and faster. That would give us a lead on the other ships. We could reach the planet months ahead of anyone else; time to pick the best landing sites and establish surface settlements.'

Norquinco thought about it. 'That won't be easy, Sky. There are, um, safeguards. The modules aren't meant to be detached until we reach orbit around Journey's End.'

'I'm well aware of that. That's why I'm asking you.'

'Ah. I, um, see.'

'Those safeguards must be electronic. That means they can eventually be

352

bypassed, given time. You still have years in which to do it – I won't want to detach the modules until the absolute last moment before we begin slowing down.'

'Why wait until then?'

'You still don't get it, do you? This is cold war, Norquinco. We have to keep the element of surprise.' He stared hard at the man, knowing that if he decided he could not trust Norquinco, he would soon have to kill him. But he was gambling that the problem itself would entice Norquinco.

'Yes,' he said. 'I mean, yes, technically, I could hack those safeguards. It would be difficult – monumentally difficult – but I could do it. And it *would* take years. Perhaps a decade. To do the work covertly, it would have to be carried out under the camouflage of the six-monthly total system audits . . . that's the only time when those deep-layer functions are even glimpsed, let alone accessed.' His mind was racing ahead now, Sky saw. 'And I'm not even on the squad that runs those audits.'

'Why not? You're clever enough, aren't you?'

'They say I'm not a "team player". If they were all like me, those audits wouldn't take half as long as they do.'

'I can see how they'd have difficulty adjusting to your ethos,' Sky said. 'That's the problem with genius, Norquinco. It's seldom appreciated.'

Norquinco nodded, foolishly imagining that their relationship had finally traversed that hazy line between mutual usefulness and genuine friendship. 'A prophet is without honour, et cetera. You're right, Sky.'

'I know,' Sky said. 'I'm always right.'

He opened his computer slate, shuffling through layers of data until he found the abstracted map of the sleepers. It looked like a strange species of cactus rendered in neon: a spiny, many-branched plant. The living were marked with red icons; the dead with black. For years now, Sky had been segregating the living from the dead, until several sleeper modules were filled only with dead *momios*. It was very tricky work because it required moving the living while they were still frozen, uncoupling their caskets and transporting them by train from one part of the spine to another while they were kept cool on reserve power. Sometimes you ended up with another dead *momio*.

It was all part of the plan. When the time came, and with Norquinco's assistance, Sky would be ready.

But there was another matter he wanted to talk to Norquinco about.

'You said there was something else, Sky.'

'Yes. There is. Do you remember, Norquinco, when we were much younger? Before my father died? You and I and Gomez spoke about something. We called it the sixth ship, but you had another name for it.'

Norquinco looked at him suspiciously, as if certain that there must be a trap. 'You mean the, um, *Caleuche*?'

Sky nodded. 'Yes, exactly that. Remind me – what was the story behind that name again?'

Norquinco filled in more details about the myth than Sky remembered from the first time. It was as if Norquinco had done some research of his own.

But when he had finished, having told Sky about the dolphin that accompanied the ghost ship, he said, 'It doesn't exist, Sky. It was just a story we liked to tell each other.'

'No. That's what I thought, but it was real. *Is* real, in fact.' Sky looked at him carefully, studying the effect his words had on Norquinco. 'My father told me. Security have always known that it exists. They know a thing or two about it, too. It's about half a light second behind us, and it's about the same size and shape as the *Santiago*. It's another Flotilla ship, Norquinco.'

'Why have you waited until now to tell me, Sky?'

'Because until now I haven't had the means to do anything about it. Now, though . . . I do have the means. I want to go there, Norquinco – take a small expedition to her. But it has to be conducted in absolute secrecy. The strategic value of that ship is beyond imagining. There'll be supplies on her. Components. Machines. Drugs. Everything we've had to make do without for decades. More than that, though, she'll have antimatter on her, and she'll probably have a functioning propulsion system. That's why I want Gomez along. But I'll need you as well. I don't expect to find anyone alive on her, but we'll have to get into her; warm her systems and bypass her security.'

Norquinco looked at him wonderingly. 'I can do that, Sky.'

'Good. I knew you wouldn't let me down.'

He told Norquinco that they would leave for the ghost ship as soon as he could arrange to take a shuttle without anyone suspecting his real intention – a problem that in itself would require some careful planning. They would be gone for several days, too, and no one must notice that either. But the risk, he thought, would be worth it. That ship was sitting behind them like a lure, inviting them to plunder the riches that lay aboard her. Only Sky even knew for sure that the ghost ship existed.

'You know,' Clown murmured, with him again, 'it would be a crime to ignore it.'

When Sky had left me – the episode, as usual, had occupied only an instant of actual time – I reached into my pocket for the gun, wondering as I did about the phallic significance of that gesture. Then I shrugged and did the only thing which seemed reasonable, which was to walk towards the light, and the entrance which fed back into the particular neighbourhood of the Canopy where I had been deposited.

I entered the plaza-like interior, trying to put a cocky swagger into my stride, as if by feedback it might make me feel more confident. The place was just as bustling as Escher Heights, even though it was now well beyond midnight. But the architecture was like nothing I had seen. It had been hinted at in the place where Waverly worked me over, and the geometries which passed for domestic in Zebra's rooms. But here, that curvilinear juxtaposition of mismatched topologies, stomachlike tubes and doughy walls and ceilings had been pushed to a mind-wrenching extreme.

I wandered around for an hour, studying the faces and occasionally sitting down near a koi pond (they were ubiquitous), just letting recent events jostle around in my mind. I kept hoping that one of the patterns would strike me as being somehow more truthful than the rest, and that I'd then know what was happening, and what my own part in it all was. But the patterns were halfhearted and incomplete, shards missing and troubling asymmetries spoiling their veracity. Maybe a more intelligent man than I might have seen something, but I was too tired to search for any artfully concealed subtleties. All I knew was the surface events. I'd been sent here to kill a man and, despite all the odds, I had found myself standing only a few metres from him, before I was even properly searching for him. I ought to have felt elated, even though I had failed to put the moment to proper use. But what I felt instead was a queasy sense of wrongness, as if I had drawn four aces in the first hand of a poker game.

The kind of luck which felt like the prelude to ill fortune.

I reached into my pocket, feeling the wad of money I still had. There was less than I'd begun the night with – the clothes and the consultation with the Mixmaster hadn't come cheap – but I wasn't out of cash just yet. I retraced my steps back towards the ledge where Chanterelle had left me, debating what to do next; knowing only that I wanted to speak to Zebra again.

As I prepared to leave the plaza, a swarm of brightly attired socialites emerged from the night, attended by pets, servitors and floatcams, looking for all the world like a procession of mediaeval saints served by cherubim and seraphim. A pair of baroquely ornamented bronze palanquins followed, both no larger than a child's coffin, with a more austere model trailing some distance behind: a hard-edged grey box with a tiny grilled window set into the front. It had no manipulators and I could hear its motors labouring, leaving a greasy trail behind it.

I had a plan, but not much of one. I'd mingle with the party and try and find out if any of them knew Zebra. From there, I could work out a way of getting to her, even if meant forcing one of them to take me there by cable-car.

The party halted, and I watched as a man with a head like a crescent moon removed a cachet of Dream Fuel vials from a pocket. He did it carefully, trying to make sure general passers-by wouldn't see what he had, but not attempting to hide the Fuel from the rest of the party.

I melted into the shadows, satisfied that no one had noticed me until then.

The other members of the party clustered around the man and I saw the gleam of wedding-guns and less ceremonial syringes, both men and women in the party tugging down collars to plunge steel into skin. The two child-sized palanquins remained with the group, but the plainer one was circling the party, and I saw one or two of the people in the group eye it nervously, even as they waited to spike themselves with Fuel.

The grey palanquin wasn't part of the group.

I'd just come to that conclusion when it halted, the front of the palanquin wheezing open, belching vapour from its hinges, and a man almost stumbling out. Someone in the party screamed and pointed at him, and in an instant the party as a whole had fallen back; even the miniature palanquins raced away from the man.

There was something terribly wrong with him.

Down one half of his naked body he was deceptively normal; as cruelly handsome and young as any in the party he'd approached. But the other half of him was submerged in a glistening growth that locked him rigid, countless branching filaments of silver-grey piercing his flesh, radiating outwards for tens of centimetres until they became only an indistinct grey haze. As he shuffled forward, the haze of filaments made a constant, barely audible tinkling noise as tiny shards detached themselves like seeds.

The man tried to speak, but what came out of his lopsided mouth was only an appalling moan.

'Burn him!' someone in the party shouted. 'For God's sake, burn him!'

'The brigade are on their way already,' someone else said.

The man with the moon-shaped head stepped a little closer to the plague victim, brandishing a single, nearly-exhausted vial.

'Is this what you want?'

The plague victim moaned something, still stumbling closer. He must have risked it, I thought, retaining his implants while not taking the proper precautions to protect himself. Perhaps he'd chosen a cheap palanquin that lacked the hermetic security of a more expensive model. Or perhaps he'd only taken to the device after the plague had reached him, hoping that the spread would be slower if he were barriered from further exposure.

'Here. Take this and leave us all alone, quickly. The brigade won't take long to get here.'

The moon-faced man threw him the vial; the plague victim lunged forward to try and grab it with his good arm. He missed, and the vial shattered on the ground, leaking its reserve of Fuel.

But the plague victim fell forwards anyway; hitting the ground so that his face almost touched the small scarlet puddle. The impact raised a grey cloud of shattered extrusions from his body, but I couldn't tell if the moan he emitted at that point was pleasure or pain. With his good arm, he clawed a few drops of Fuel towards his mouth, while the party looked on with horror and fascination, maintaining their distance but capturing the incident on camera. The spectacle had attracted a few other people by then, and they all studied the man as if his contortions and moans were simply a bizarre piece of performance art.

'He's an extreme case,' someone said. 'I've never seen that degree of asymmetry. Do you think we're far enough away from him?'

'You'll find out eventually.'

The man was still thrashing stiffly on the ground when the brigade arrived from inside the plaza. They couldn't have had far to travel. It was a detachment of armoured technicians, propelling a cumbersome machine which resembled an extremely large, open-fronted palanquin, marked with bas-relief biohazard symbols. Oblivious to their presence, the plague victim kept clawing at the Fuel even as they pushed the humming machine over him and lowered a door over its front. The technicians moved with clinical speed, communicating with precise hand gestures and whispers as their machine thumped and hummed. The party watched wordlessly; no sign now of the Dream Fuel or the devices they'd been using to administer it. Then the technicians propelled their machine backwards, leaving only polished ground behind, one of them sweeping the area with something that looked like a cross between a broom and a mine-detector. After a few sweeps he gave a thumbs-up signal to his colleagues and followed them back into the plaza, behind the still-humming machine.

The party lingered, but the incident had obviously taken the shine off their immediate plans for the night. Before very long they'd all vanished into a pair of private cable-cars, and I'd had no chance to insinuate myself.

But I noticed something on the ground, near where the moon-faced man had been standing. At first I thought it was another vial of Dream Fuel, but as I moved closer – before anyone else saw it – I realised that it was an experiential. It had probably fallen out of his pocket when he retrieved his cachet of Fuel.

I knelt down and picked it up. It was slim and black, and the only marking on it was a tiny silver maggot near the top.

With Vadim, I'd found a similar set of experientials at the same time that I'd found his supply of Dream Fuel.

'Tanner Mirabel?'

The voice held only the slightest hint of curiosity.

I looked around, because the voice had come from behind me. The man who'd spoken was dressed in a dark coat, making the minimum necessary concession to Canopy fashion. His face was unsmiling and grey, like an undertaker on a bad day. There was also a martial tautness to his posture, evidenced in the way the muscles in his neck were rigidly defined.

Not a man to be trifled with, whoever he was.

He spoke softly, hardly moving his lips now that he had my complete attention. 'I am a professional security specialist,' he said. 'I am armed with a neurotoxic weapon which can kill you in under three seconds, silently, and

357

without drawing the slightest attention to myself. You would not even have time to blink in my direction.'

'Well, enough pleasantries,' I said.

'You recognise that I am a professional,' the man said, nodding to emphasise his words. 'Like you, I have been trained to kill in the most efficient manner possible. I hope that gives us some common ground and that we can now discuss matters reasonably.'

'I don't know who you are or what you want.'

'You don't have to know who I am. Even if I told you, I'd be forced to lie, and what would be the point of that?'

'Fair point.'

'Good. In which case, my name's Pransky. As for the other matter, that's easier. I'm here to escort you to someone who wants to meet you.'

'What if I don't *want* to be escorted?'

'That's entirely your choice.' He still spoke calmly and quietly, like a young monk reciting his Breviary. 'But you will have to satisfy yourself that you can absorb a dose of tetrodotoxin of sufficient potency to kill twenty people. Of course, it's entirely possible that your membrane biochemistry is unlike that of any other living human being – or advanced vertebrate, for that matter.' He smiled, flashing a row of brilliant white teeth. 'But you'll have to be the judge of that, I'm afraid.'

'I probably wouldn't want to run that risk.'

'Sensible fellow.'

Pransky beckoned with an open palm that I should walk on, past the kidney-shaped koi-pond which was the focal point of this annex of the building.

'Before you get too cocky,' I said, standing my ground, 'you might like to know that I'm also armed.'

'I do know,' he said. 'I could tell you the specification of your weapon now, if you wanted me to. I could also tell you the probability of one of your ice-slugs managing to kill me before I inject you with the toxin, and I don't think you'd be very impressed by the odds. Failing that, I could tell you that your gun is currently in your right pocket and your hand isn't, which does rather limit its usefulness. Shall we proceed?'

I started moving. 'You're working for Reivich, aren't you?'

For the first time something in his face told me he wasn't in total control of the situation. 'Never heard of him,' he said, irritated. And I allowed myself a smile. It wasn't much of a victory, but it was better than nothing. Of course, Pransky could have been lying. But had he wanted to, I was sure he could have concealed it more effectively. But I'd caught him off guard.

Inside the plaza, there was a vacant silver palanquin waiting for me. Pransky waited until no one was paying us any attention, then had the palanquin clam open, revealing a plush red seat.

'You'll never guess what I'm about to ask,' Pransky said.

I got into the machine, easing myself into the seat. After the door had closed I experimented with some of the controls set into the interior, but none of them did anything. Then, in deathly silence, the palanquin started moving. I looked through the little green window and watched the plaza glide by, Pransky walking slightly ahead of me.

Then I started feeling drowsy.

Zebra looked me over, a long and cool appraisal such as I might have expended on a new rifle. Her expression was difficult to judge. All the theories I'd concocted had depended on her either looking very pleased or very annoyed to be reacquainted with me.

Instead she just looked worried.

'What the hell's going on?' I said. 'If you don't mind my asking.'

She stood legs akimbo, shaking her head slowly as she answered me, 'You've got one hell of a nerve to ask me what I'm doing, after all you did to me.'

'Right now I'd say we're even.'

'Where'd you find him, and what was he doing?' she asked Pransky.

'Hanging around,' the man said. 'Attracting too much attention.'

'I was trying to get to you,' I said to Zebra.

Pransky gestured towards one of the markedly utilitarian chairs which served for furniture in the room to which I had been brought. 'Have a seat, Mirabel. You're not going anywhere in a hurry.'

'I'm surprised you were in any rush to meet me again,' Zebra said. 'After all, you didn't exactly overstay your welcome last time.'

My gaze tracked over Pransky, trying to place him in this and figure out how much he knew.

'I left a note,' I said, plaintively. 'And I called you back to apologise.'

'And the fact that you thought I might know where a Game was going down was sheer coincidence.'

I shrugged, exploring the parameter space of discomforts offered by the stiffly unyielding seat. 'Who else was I going to call?'

'You piece of shit, Mirabel. I don't know why I'm doing this, you know. You don't deserve it at all.'

Zebra still looked like Zebra, unless you focused on the specifics. She had muted her skin-tone now, so that the stripes were little more than rushlike grey blades folded around the contours of her face, delineations that vanished altogether in a certain light. The frill of rigid black hair had become a blonde bob, trimmed in a blunt fringe across her forehead. Her clothes were unostentatious and she wore a coat of similar cut to my own, one which reached past her stiletto-booted ankles and trailed into a pool of dark fabric around her feet. The only thing it lacked was the matrix of rough patches which adorned Vadim's original.

'I never pretended to deserve anything,' I said. 'Although I do think the one thing I might deserve is an explanation. Can we take it as read that you and I almost met earlier this evening, except that there was a substantial bulk of fish between us, name of Methuselah?'

'I was standing behind you,' Zebra said. 'If you saw me, you saw my reflection. It's not my fault you didn't turn around.'

'You could have said something.'

'You were hardly excessively loquacious yourself, Tanner.'

'All right; can we start at the beginning?' I looked at Pransky, soliciting his permission as much as Zebra's. 'How about I tell you what I think, and we take it from there?'

'Sounds eminently reasonable to me,' said the little security expert.

I drew in a deep breath, aware that I was comitting myself further than at any point since my arrival. But here, now, it had to be done. 'You're working for Reivich,' I said. 'Both of you.'

Pransky looked at Zebra. 'He mentioned that name earlier. I don't know who he means.'

'It's all right,' Zebra said. 'I do.'

I nodded, feeling a paradoxical sense of relief, resignation, I supposed. It didn't greatly comfort me to find out that Zebra was working for the man I had been sent to assassinate – most especially now that she had captured me. But there was also a defeatist pleasure in seeing one particular mystery cleared up.

'Reivich must have contacted you as soon as he got here,' I said. 'You're – what – some kind of freelancer? A security specialist in your own right, like Pransky here? It would make sense. You knew how to handle a weapon, and you were a step ahead of Waverly's people when they were hunting me down. The whole hunt sabotage story was just a screen. For all I know you play it every night with the best of them. There. How am I doing?'

'It's fascinating stuff,' Zebra said. 'Please continue.'

'You were detailed by Reivich to find me. He had a suspicion someone had been sent from Sky's Edge, so it was just a matter of putting your ears to the ground and listening. The musician was part of the operation as well – the front man who trailed me down from the Mendicant habitat.'

'Who's the musician?' Pransky said. 'First Reivich, now the musician. Do these people actually exist?'

'Shut up,' Zebra said. 'And let Tanner continue.'

'The musician was good,' I said. 'But I'm not sure whether I gave him enough to go on; whether I allowed him to establish beyond any doubt that I was the man he wanted, and not just some innocent immigrant.' I looked towards Zebra for confirmation, but since none was forthcoming, I continued, 'Maybe all the musician could tell Reivich was that I was still a possibility. So you kept tabs on me. Somehow you had contacts in the hunt movement – maybe connections with a group of genuine saboteurs, for all I know. And via Waverly, you found out I'd been recuited as a victim.'

'What is he talking about?' Pransky said.

'The truth, unfortunately,' Zebra said, dispensing a withering look towards the security specialist, who was probably her subordinate, her understudy or dogsbody. 'At least regarding the hunt. Tanner wandered into the wrong part of the Mulch and got himself captured. He put up a good fight, too, but they might have killed him if I hadn't made it in time.'

'She had to save me,' I said. 'There wasn't anything noble about it, though. Zebra only wanted information. If I died, no one would be able to establish whether or not I'd *really* been the man sent to kill Reivich. That would put Reivich in an uncomfortable situation; he wouldn't be able to relax for the rest of his life. There'd always be the danger that the real assassin was closing in. A lot of sleepless nights. That's how it went, wasn't it Zebra?'

'It might,' she said. 'If I happened to be colluding in your own delusions.'

'Then why did you save me, if it wasn't to keep me alive and find out if I was really the man?'

'For the same reasons I told you. Because I hate the hunt, and I wanted to help you live.' She shook her head, almost apologetically. 'Sorry, Tanner. Much as I'd love to help you with your particular paranoid construct, it doesn't go any deeper than that. I'm who I said I was, and I acted for the reasons I said. And I'd be grateful if you restricted discussion of the sabs to an absolute minimum, even in Pransky's esteemed company.'

'But you just told me – him – you know who Reivich is.'

'I do, now. But I didn't then. Shall we continue? Maybe you ought to hear my side of things.'

'I can't wait.'

Zebra inhaled, looking interestedly around the doughlike acreage of the ceiling before her gaze snapped back to me. I had a feeling what she was about to say was not unrehearsed.

'I rescued you from Waverly's hunt clique,' Zebra said. 'Don't fool yourself into imagining that you might have made it out alive yourself, Tanner. You're good – that's obvious – but no one's *that* good.'

'Maybe you just don't know me well enough.'

'I'm not sure I want to. May I continue?'

'I'm all ears.'

'You stole things from me. Not just clothes and money, but a weapon you shouldn't have known how to use. I won't even mention the cable-car. You could have stayed where you were until the implant stopped transmitting, but for some reason you thought you'd be safer on your own.'

I shrugged. 'I'm still alive, aren't I?'

'For the moment,' Zebra conceded. 'But Waverly isn't, and he was one of the few allies we had at the core of the movement. I know you killed him, Tanner – the trail you left was so hot you might as well have sprinkled plutonium wherever you went.' She strolled around the room, the stiletto heels of her boots clicking against the floor like a pair of matched metronomes. 'That was unfortunate, you know.'

'Waverly just got in the way. It's not like the sadistic bastard was on my Christmas list.'

'Why didn't you wait?'

'I had other business to attend to.'

'Reivich, right? I expect you're dying to know where I got that name from, and how I know what it means to you.'

'I think you were in the process of telling me.'

'After you ditched my car,' Zebra said. 'You showed up in Grand Central Station. It's where you called me from.'

'Go on.'

'I was curious, Tanner. By then I already *knew* Waverly was dead, and that didn't make sense. You should have been the dead man – even with the gun you stole from me. So I began to wonder just who it was I'd been sheltering. I had to find out.' She stopped pacing; the clicking of her heels abated. 'It wasn't difficult. You were inordinately interested in finding out where the night's Game was going to happen. So I told you. If you were there, I thought I'd be there myself.'

I thought back to what seemed like hundreds of hours earlier, but was in fact only the evening of the long night in which I was still immersed. 'You were there, when I caught Chanterelle?'

'It wasn't what I was expecting.'

Of course not – how could it have been? I said, 'Then what about Reivich? How does he come into it?'

'Via a mutual acquaintance of ours by the name of Dominika.' Zebra smiled, knowing she had surprised me with that.

'You went to Dominika?'

'It made sense. I had Pransky tail you to Escher Heights while I went to the bazaar and talked to the old woman. I knew you'd had the device removed, you see. And since you'd been at the bazaar earlier in the day, Dominika was bound to know who'd done the operation, if it wasn't her. Which of course it was, which simplified matters enormously.'

'Is there anyone in Chasm City she hasn't deceived?'

'Possibly, somewhere, but only as an extreme theoretical possibility. Actually, Dominika is a rather pure expression of our city's driving paradigm, which is that there is nothing and no one who can't be bought, given the right price.'

'What did she tell you?'

'Only that you are a very interesting man, Tanner, and that you had a particular interest in locating a gentleman named Argent Reivich. A man who happened to have arrived in Escher Heights only a few days earlier. Now, isn't that a coincidence, given that Pransky just happens to have followed you to that part of the Canopy?'

362

The svelte little security man felt it was his time to take over the narrative. 'I tailed you for most of the night, Tanner. You really began to hit it off with Chanterelle Sammartini, didn't you? Who'd have thought it – you and her.' He shook his head, as if some basic physical law of the universe had been violated. 'But you wandered around like old friends. I even saw you at the palanquin races.'

'How tiresomely romantic,' Zebra drawled, without interrupting Pransky's flow.

'I called Taryn and had her meet me,' the man said. 'Then we followed the two of you – discreetly, of course. You visited a boutique and came out looking a new man – or at least not quite your old self. Then you went to the Mix-master. Now he was a tougher nut to crack. He wouldn't tell me what you wanted in there and I'm awfully keen to find out.'

'Just a check-up,' I said.

'Well, maybe.' Pransky knitted together his long and elegant fingers and then made knuckle-popping sounds. 'Perhaps it doesn't matter. It's certainly hard to see how it could relate to what happened next.'

I tried to sound interested. 'Which was?'

'That you nearly killed someone,' Zebra said, silencing her associate with a soundless cuff of the air. 'I saw you, Tanner. I was on the point of approaching you and asking you what you were doing and then suddenly you were taking a gun out of your pocket. I couldn't see your face, but I'd been following you long enough to know it was you. I watched you move with the gun in your hand; smoothly and calmly, as if this was all you'd ever been born to do.' She paused. 'And then you put the gun away, and no one else had been paying enough attention to you to notice what you'd done. I watched you look around, but it was obvious that whoever it was you'd seen was gone – if he'd ever been there. It was Reivich, wasn't it?'

'You seem to know so much, you tell me.'

'I think you came here to kill him,' Zebra said. 'Why, I don't know. Reivich is an old family in the Canopy, but they don't have as many enemies as some. Yet it makes sense. That would explain why you were so desperate to get into the Canopy that you'd wander into a hunt. And why you were so reluctant to stay in the safety of my home. It was because you were scared of losing Reivich's trail. Tell me I'm right, Tanner.'

'Would there be any point denying it?'

'Not a great deal, no, but you're welcome to try.'

She was right. Just as I had unburdened myself to Chanterelle earlier in the night, I did the same for Zebra. But it felt less intimate. Perhaps it was the fact that Pransky was standing there absorbing it all. Or the feeling that the two of them actually knew more about me than they had said, and that very little of what I was telling them was news. I told them that Reivich was someone from my homeworld, not a genuinely bad man, but one who had done something

363

very bad out of foolishness or weakness, and had to be punished for that with no less severity than if he had been born a snarling knife-twisting psychopath.

When I had finished – when Zebra and Pransky had grilled me to exhaustion, examining every facet of my story as if looking for a flaw they knew must be present – there was one last question, and it was mine.

'Why have you brought me here, Zebra?'

Hands on hips, her elbows jutting from the black enclosure of her coat, she said, 'Why do you think?'

'Curiosity, I suppose. But that's not enough.'

'You're in danger, Tanner. I'm doing you a favour.'

'I've been in danger since I came here. That's nothing new to me.'

'I mean real danger,' Pransky said. 'You're in too deep. You've attracted too much attention.'

'He's right,' Zebra said. 'Dominika was the weak link. She may have alerted half the city by now. Reivich almost certainly knows you're here, and he probably knows you nearly killed him tonight.'

'That's what I don't understand,' I said. 'If he's already been warned of my presence, why the hell was he making himself such an easy target? If I'd been a fraction faster I'd have killed him.'

'Maybe the meeting was a coincidence,' Pransky said.

Zebra looked at him scornfully. 'In a city this big? No; Tanner's right. That meeting happened because Reivich arranged for it to happen. And there's something else, too. Look at me, Tanner. Notice anything different?'

'You changed your appearance.'

'Yes. And it isn't the hardest thing to do, believe me. Reivich could have done the same – nothing drastic; just enough to ensure that he wasn't immediately recognisable in a public place. A few hours under the knife at most. Even a halfway competent bloodcutter could have done it.'

'Then that doesn't make any sense,' I said. 'It's like he was taunting me. Like he *wanted* me to kill him.'

'Maybe he did,' Zebra said.

There had been moments when I thought I might never see the outside of that room; that it was where Pransky and Zebra had brought me to die.

Pransky was clearly a professional, and Zebra was no stranger to death herself, given her affiliation with the sabotage movement.

Yet they didn't kill me.

We took a cable-car to Zebra's place, Pransky going off on some other errand. 'Who is he?' I asked, once we were alone. 'Some kind of hired help?'

'Private intelligence,' Zebra said, discarding her coat in a black puddle. 'It's all the rage these days. There are rivalries in the Canopy – feuds and quiet wars, sometimes between families, and sometimes within.'

'You thought he could help trace me.'

'Seems I wasn't wrong.'

'I still don't know why, Zebra.' Once again I looked beyond the room, towards the maw of the chasm which was like the rim of a volcano around which a city festered, on the eve of its own destruction. There was some dawn-light on the horizon. 'Unless you think you can use me in some way – in which case I'm afraid you're wrong. I'm not interested in any Canopy power games you might be involved in. I'm only here to do one thing.'

'To kill a seemingly innocent man.'

'It's a cruel universe. Do you mind if I sit down?' I helped myself to a seat before she had answered me, the mobile furniture shuffling into place beneath me like an obsequious servant. 'I'm still a soldier at heart and it's my job not to question these things. The instant I start doing that is the instant I stop doing my job properly.'

Zebra, all angularity and knifelike edges, folded herself into the sumptuous-ness of the seat opposite me, retracting her knees beneath her chin.

'Someone's after you, Tanner. That's why I had to find you. It's dangerous for you to stay here. You have to get out of the city.'

'It's nothing I didn't expect. Reivich will have hired all the help he can get his hands on.'

'Local help?'

It was an odd question. 'Yes, I suppose. You wouldn't hire someone who didn't already know the city.'

'Whoever's after you isn't *local*, Tanner.'

I tensed in the seat, causing its buried musculature to generate massaging ripples. 'What do you know?'

'Not very much, except that Dominika said someone had been trying to find you. A man and a woman. They acted like they'd never been here before. Like offworlders. And they were very interested in finding you.'

'A man already did,' I said, thinking of Quirrenbach. 'He followed me down from orbit, posing as an offworlder. I lost him in Dominika's. It's possible he returned with reinforcements.' Vadim, perhaps. But it would be quite a trick to mistake Vadim for a woman.

'Is he dangerous?'

'Anyone who lies for a living is dangerous.'

Zebra summoned one of her ceiling-tracked servitors, having the machine bring us a tray laden with carafes of varying size and colour. Zebra poured me a goblet of wine and I let it wash away some of the accumulated taste of the city, dull some of the roaring in my mind.

'I'm very tired,' I said. 'You offered me sanctuary here a day ago, Zebra. Can I accept that offer now, if only until daybreak?'

She looked at me over the smoked rim of her glass. It was already daybreak, but she knew what I meant. 'After all you've done, you think I'll keep an offer like that open?'

'I'm an optimist,' I said, with what I hoped was the appropriate tone of utter resignation.

Then I took another sip of wine and began to realise how exhausted I really was.

THIRTY

The expedition to the ghost ship almost never left the *Santiago*. Sky and his two associates, Norquinco and Gomez, had made it as far as the cargo bay when Constanza appeared out of the shadows.

She looked much older now, Sky thought, prematurely aged compared to himself. It was hard to believe that the two of them had once been near-equals; children exploring the same dark and labyrinthine wonderland. Now the shadows etched themselves unflatteringly into her face, emphasising the wrinkles and folds of her habitual expression.

'Do you mind if I ask where you're planning to go?' Constanza said, standing between them and the shuttle that they had gone to great trouble to make ready. 'I'm not aware that anyone was supposed to be leaving the *Santiago*.'

'I'm afraid you weren't in the loop on this one,' Sky said.

'I'm still a member of security, you supercilious little worm. How does that put me outside the loop?'

Sky glanced at the others, willing them to let him do the talking. 'I'll be blunt, then. It's a matter that exceeds even the usual security channels. I can't be specific, but the nature of this mission is both delicate and diplomatic.'

'Then why isn't Ramirez with you?'

'It's a high-risk mission; a possible trap. If I'm caught, Ramirez loses his second-in-command, but the routine functioning of the *Santiago* won't be greatly affected. And if it is a genuine attempt to improve relations, the other ship can't complain that we aren't sending a senior officer.'

'Captain Ramirez would still know about this, though?'

'I should imagine so. He authorised it.'

'We'll just check then, shall we?' She elevated her cuff, ready to speak to the Captain.

Sky allowed himself an instant of indecision before acting, weighing the outcome of two equally hazardous strategies. Ramirez did genuinely think there was a diplomatic operation in progress; an excuse that would enable Sky to leave the *Santiago* for a couple of days without too many questions being asked. It had taken years to lay the groundwork for that deception, faking messages from the *Palestine*, doctoring the real messages as they came in. But Ramirez was a clever man, and his suspicions might be raised if Constanza started showing too much interest in the validity of the mission.

So he rushed her, knocking her to the hard, polished floor of the bay. Her head whacked against the ground and she went deathly still.

'Have you killed her?' Norquinco said.

'I don't know,' Sky said, kneeling down.

Constanza was still alive.

They dragged her unconscious body across the cargo bay and arranged it artfully next to a pile of smashed freight pallets. It looked as if she had been exploring the bay on her own and had been knocked out when a tower of pallets had toppled over, catching her on the head.

'She won't remember the encounter,' Sky said. 'And if she doesn't come round of her own accord before we're back, I'll find her myself.'

'She'll still have her suspicions,' Gomez said.

'That won't be a problem. I've set up evidence trails which'll make it look like Ramirez and Constanza were complicit in authorising – ordering – this expedition.' He looked at Norquinco, who had actually done much of the work of which he spoke, but the other man's expression was impassive.

They left before there was any chance of Constanza coming round. Normally Sky would have fired up the shuttle's engines as soon as he was free of the docking bay, but that would have made their leaving all the more obvious. Instead, he gave the shuttle a small kick of thrust while it was hidden behind the *Santiago* – just enough to push it up to one hundred metres per second relative to the Flotilla – and then turned the engines off. With the cabin lights dimmed and maintaining strict comms silence, they fell backwards away from the mother ship.

Sky watched the hull slide by like a grey cliff. He had taken measures to conceal his own absence from the *Santiago* – and in the current atmosphere of paranoia very few people would ask awkward questions anyway – but there was no way that the departure of a small ship could ever be completely concealed from the other vessels. But Sky knew from experience that their radar scans were focused on detecting missiles moving between ships, rather than something falling slowly behind. In fact, now that the race was on to strip mass from all the ships, it was common for surplus equipment to be discarded. Junk was usually sent drifting forward, so that the Flotilla would never run into it while decelerating, but that was a minor detail.

'We'll drift for twenty-four hours,' Sky said. 'That'll put us nine thousand kilometres behind the last ship in the Flotilla. Then we can turn on engines and radar and make a dash to the *Caleuche*. Even if they notice our thrust flame, we'll still get there ahead of any other shuttle they send after us.'

'What if they do send something?' Gomez said. 'We might still only have a few hours of grace. Maybe a day at best.'

'Then we'd better use our time wisely. A few hours will be enough to get aboard and establish what happened to her. A few hours more will give us the time we need to find any intact supplies she's carrying – medical equipment, sleeper berth parts, you name it. We can fit enough aboard the shuttle to make a difference. If we find too much to bring back, we'll hold her until the *Santiago* can dispatch a larger fleet of shuttles.'

'You're talking as if we'd go to war over her.'

Sky Haussmann answered, 'Maybe she'd be worth it, Gomez.'

'Or maybe she was cleaned out years ago by one of the other ships. Considered that, haven't you?'

'Yes. And I'd regard that as reasonable grounds for war as well.'

Norquinco, who had barely spoken since the departure, was examining a bewilderingly complex general schematic of one of the Flotilla ships. It was the kind of thing he could get lost in for hours, his eyes glazed, ignoring sleep and food until he had solved some problem to his satisfaction. Sky envied him that singleminded devotion to one task, while flinching from the idea of ever allowing himself to become that obsessive. Norquinco's value to him was highly specific: a tool that could be applied to certain well-defined problems with predictable results. Give Norquinco something complicated and arcane and he was in his element. Coming up with a plausible model for what the *Caleuche*'s internal data networks might be like was exactly that kind of problem. It could never be more than an educated guess, but there was no one Sky would rather have had doing the guessing.

He replayed what little they knew about the ghost ship. What was clear enough was that the *Caleuche* must once have been an acknowledged part of the Flotilla, built and launched with the other ships from Mercury orbit. Her construction and launch could never have been kept secret, even if she must have once had some more prosaic name than that of the mythical ghost ship. She would have accelerated up to cruising speed with the other five ships, and for a time – many years, perhaps – she would have travelled with them.

But something had happened during those early decades of the crossing to Swan. As political and social upheavals racked the home system, the Flotilla had become steadily more isolated. The home system had become months and then years of light-travel time away, until true communication became difficult. Technical updates had continued to arrive from home, and the Flotilla had continued to send reports back, but the intervals between these transmissions had become longer and longer, the messages increasingly desultory. Even when messages from home did arrive, they were often accompanied by contradictory ones; evidence of squabbling factions with different agendas, not all of which involved the Flotilla arriving safely at Journey's End. Now and then a general news report was picked up, and the ships of the Flotilla even learned the unsettling truth that there were factions back home who were denying that they had ever existed. By and large these attempts to rewrite history were not taken seriously, but it was disconcerting to hear that they had gained even a toehold.

Too much time and distance, Sky thought, the words playing in his head like a mantra. So much boiled down to that, in the end.

And what it also meant was that the ships of the Flotilla became less and less accountable to any other parties save themselves; that it became easier to collectively suppress the truth of whatever had happened to the *Caleuche*.

Sky's grandfather – or rather, Titus Haussmann's father – must have known exactly what had happened. He had imparted some of that truth to Titus, but perhaps not all of it, and it might also have been the case that by the time Titus's father had died even he had not been entirely sure what had really happened. All they could do now was speculate. There were, in Sky's opinion, two likely scenarios. In the first, there had been some dispute between the ships which had culminated in an attack on the *Caleuche*. It could even have extended to the use of the landscaping nuclear weapons: though Titus had spoken of the radar echo of the ghost ship fitting the profile of one of the Flotilla vessels, there might still have been crippling damage to her. Afterwards, the other ships might have been so shamed by their actions that they had chosen to blank them from the historical record. One generation would have to live with the shame, but not the one that followed.

The other idea, and the one Sky favoured, was less dramatic but perhaps even more shaming. What if something had gone terribly wrong with the *Caleuche* – a plague aboard her, say – and the other ships had chosen to offer no assistance? Worse things had happened in history, and who could blame the others for fearing contamination themselves?

Shameful, perhaps. But also perfectly understandable.

What it also meant was that they would have to be very careful. He would assume nothing except that every situation was potentially lethal. Equally, he would accept the risks involved because the prize was so great. He thought of the antimatter which she had to be carrying, still dormant in her penning reservoir, waiting for the day when it should have been used to slow her down. That day might still come, but not in the way her designers had ever anticipated.

Or, for that matter, any of the other ships.

Within a few hours they had escaped the main body of the Flotilla. Once a radar beam from the *Brazilia* lingered over them, like the fingers of a blind person probing an unfamiliar object. The moment was tense, and while they were being scrutinised Sky wondered if this had not, after all, been a fatal misjudgement. But the beam moved on and never returned. If the *Brazilia* had assumed anything it must have accepted that the radar echo signified only a chunk of receding debris; some useless, irrepairable machine jettisoned into the void.

After that they were alone.

It was tempting to fire up the thrusters, but Sky kept his nerve and maintained the drift for the twenty-four hours he had promised. No transmissions came from the *Santiago*, satisfying him that their absence had not yet become problematic. Had it not been for the company of Norquinco and Gomez, he would have been more alone now – further from human company – than at any point in his life. How terrifying this isolation would once have been to the small boy who had been so terrified of the dark when he had been trapped in the nursery. Almost unthinkable, to have willingly drifted this far from home.

Now, though, it was for a purpose.

He waited until the exact second, then turned on the engines again. The flame burned a deep lilac: clean and pure against the stars. He was careful to avoid shining the thrust beam directly back towards the Flotilla, but there was no way he could hide it completely. It hardly mattered; they had the edge now, and whatever the other ships chose to do, Sky would reach the *Caleuche* first. It would give him, he thought, a small foretaste of what the greater victory would be like, when he brought the *Santiago* to Journey's End ahead of the others. It was as well to remember that everything he did now was only part of that larger plan.

But there was a difference, of course. Journey's End was definitely out there; definitely a world which he knew to be real. He still had only Titus's word that the *Caleuche* existed at all.

Sky turned on the long-range phased-array radar and – much like the *Brazilia* had done – extended a hand gropingly into the darkness.

If it was out there, he would find it.

'Can't you just leave him alone?' Zebra said.

'No. Even if I was ready to forgive him – which I'm not – I still have to know why he taunted me the way he did; what he was hoping to get out of it.'

We were in Zebra's apartment. It was late morning; the cloud cover over the city was sparse, the sun was high and the place looked melancholy rather than Satanic; even the more warped buildings assumed a certain dignity, like patients who'd learned to live with gross deformity.

Which did nothing to make me feel any less disturbed; convinced more than ever that there was something fundamentally wrong with my memories. The Haussmann episodes hadn't stopped, yet the bleeding from my hand had become much less severe than it had been at the start of the infection cycle. It was almost as if the indoctrinal virus had catalysed the unlocking of memories which were already present; memories at stark odds with the official version of events on the *Santiago*. The virus might have been close to burning itself out, but the other Haussmann memories were coming on more strongly than ever, my association with Sky becoming more complete. Originally it had been like watching a play; now it was like playing him; hearing his thoughts; feeling the acrid taste of his hatred.

But that wasn't all of it. The dream I'd had the afternoon before, of looking down on the injured man in the white enclosure, had troubled me more than I could easily explain at the time, but now, having had time to think about it, I thought I knew why.

The injured man could only have been me.

And yet my viewpoint had been that of Cahuella, looking down into the hamadryad pit at the Reptile House. I could have put that down to tiredness, but it hadn't been the only time I'd seen the world through his eyes. In the last few days there'd been odd snatches of memory and dream where I'd been more intimate with Gitta than I thought had ever been the case; instants when I felt I could bring to mind every hidden curve and pore of her body; instants when I imagined tracing my hand across the hollow of her back or the swell of her buttocks; instants when I thought I knew the taste of her. But there was something else about Gitta, too – something my thoughts couldn't or wouldn't home in on; something too painful.

All I knew was that it had something to do with the way she'd died.

'Listen,' Zebra said, refilling my coffee cup, 'could it just be that Reivich has a death wish?'

I tried to focus on the here and now. 'I could have satisfied that for him on Sky's Edge.'

'Well, a specific type of death wish, then. Something that has to be satisfied here.'

She looked lovely, her fading stripes permitting the natural geometry of her face to show more clearly, like a statue deprived of gaudy paint. But sitting face to face with each other over breakfast was as close as we had come since Pransky had brought us together. We hadn't shared a bed, and it was not just because I'd been inhumanly tired. Zebra hadn't invited it, and nothing in the way she behaved or dressed had suggested that our relationship had ever been anything other than coolly professional. It was as if in changing her exterior markings she had also shed an entire mode of behaviour. I felt no real loss, not just because I was still fatigued and incapable of focusing my thoughts on anything as simple and devoid of conspiracy as physical intimacy, but also because I sensed her earlier actions had somehow been part of an act.

I tried to feel betrayal, but nothing came. It wasn't as if I'd been honest with Zebra myself, after all.

'Actually,' I said, looking at Zebra's face again, and thinking how easily she'd changed herself, 'there is another possibility.'

'Which is?'

'That the man I saw wasn't Reivich at all.' And then I put down the empty coffee cup and stood up.

'Where are you going?'

'Out.'

We cabled to Escher Heights.

The car nudged down, its retractable legs kissing the rain-slick ground of the ledge. There was more traffic now than when I had last visited the place – it was daytime, after all – and the costumes and anatomies of the strollers were fractionally less ostentatious, as if I was seeing a different cross-section of Canopy society, the more reserved citizens who eschewed nights of delirious pleasure-fulfilment. But they were still extreme by any standards I had defined before arriving here, and while there was no one whose proportions deviated radically from the basic adult human norm, within that boundary every possible permutation was on display. Once you got beyond the obvious cases of outlandish skin pigmentation and body hair, it was not always possible to tell what was hereditary and what was the work of Mixmasters or their shadier kin.

'I hope there's a point to this excursion,' Zebra said as we disembarked. 'In case you've forgotten, there are two people following you. You say they might be working for Reivich, but don't forget Waverly had his friends as well.'

'Would Waverly's friends be arriving from offworld?'

'Probably not. Unless they were just posing as offworlders, like Quirrenbach.' She closed the door of the car behind her and the vehicle immediately took itself off on some other errand. 'He might have come back with reinforcements. It would make sense for him to try and pick up the trail in Dominika's, if that's where you lost Quirrenbach in the first place. Wouldn't it?'

'It would make perfect sense,' I said, hoping that I had kept the edge from my voice.

We walked to the rim of the landing ledge, to one of the pedestal-mounted telescopes. The railing which encircled the ledge was chest-high, but the telescopes all had little plinths at their bases, which meant that one was standing further from the ground, the drop all the more vertiginous. I cupped the end of the telescope to my eyes and panned around an arc of the city, struggling with the focus wheel until I realised that nothing would ever be in focus when there was so much murk in the air. Compressed by perspective, the tangle of the Canopy looked ever more complex and vegetative, like a cross-section through densely veined tissue. Reivich was out there, I knew, somewhere in that tangle; a single corpuscle caught in the pulmonary flow of the city.

'See anything?' Zebra asked.

'Nothing yet.'

'You sound tense, Tanner.'

'Wouldn't you be tense, in my position?' I slammed the scope round on its pedestal. 'I've been sent here to kill someone who probably doesn't deserve it, and my only justification for it is some absurd adherence to a code of honour no one here understands or even respects. The man I've been sent to kill might be taunting me. Two other people might be trying to kill me. I've got one or two problems with my memories. And on top of that one of the people I thought I could trust has been lying to me all along.'

'I don't follow,' Zebra said, but it was obvious from the tone of her voice that she did; more than sufficiently. She did not necessarily understand, but she did follow.

'You aren't who you say you are, Zebra.'

The wind whipped at us, almost snatching her answer away. 'What?'

'You're working for Reivich, aren't you?'

She shook her head angrily, almost laughing at the ludicrousness of the assertion, but she overdid it. I was not the world's best liar, but neither was Zebra. The two of us should have started a self-help group.

'You're mad, Tanner. I always thought you were a little on the edge, but now I know. You're over it. Way over.'

'The night you found me,' I said, 'you were working for him even then, from the very first moment we met. The sabotage story was a cover – a pretty good one, I have to say, but a cover nonetheless.' I stepped down from the plinth, suddenly feeling vulnerable, as if a particularly strong gust might cast me over for the long fall down to the Mulch. 'Maybe I really was kidnapped by Game-players. But you already had your eye on me before then. I'd assumed I'd shaken the tail Reivich put on me – Quirrenbach – but there must have been someone else, keeping more distance so they weren't so obvious. But you lost me until Waverly put the hunt implant in my skull. Then you had a way of tracking me again. How am I doing so far?'

'Insane, Tanner.' But there was no conviction in her words.

'Do you want to know how I realised? Apart from all the little details which just didn't add up?'

'Astonish me.'

'You shouldn't have mentioned Quirrenbach. I *never* said his name. In fact, I was very careful not to, just in case you made a slip and it came out. Seems my luck was in.'

'You bastard.' She said it sweetly, so that – to anyone watching us from a distance – it might have been a term of affection, the kind lovers give themselves. 'You sly bastard, Tanner.'

I smiled. 'You could have used an excuse if you'd wanted. You could have said that Dominika mentioned his name when you asked who I'd been travelling with. I was half expecting you to do that, and I'm not quite sure I know how I'd have reacted. But it's all moot now, isn't it? Now we know just who you are.'

'What were the little details, out of curiosity?'

'Professional pride?'

'Something like that.'

'You made it far too easy for me, Zebra. You left your vehicle active so I could steal it. You left your weapon where I could find it, and enough money to make a difference. You wanted me to do it, didn't you? You wanted me to steal those things, because then you'd know for sure who I was. That I'd come to kill Reivich.'

She shrugged. 'Is that all?'

'Not really, no.' I drew Vadim's coat tighter around myself. 'It didn't escape my attention that we made love the first time we met, despite the fact that you barely knew me. It was good too, for what it's worth.'

'Oh, don't flatter me. Or yourself, for that matter.'

'But the second time, although you seemed relieved, I wouldn't say you were particularly happy to see me. And I didn't feel anything sexual pass between us at all. At least not from you. It took me a while to work out why, but I think I understand now. The first time you needed intimacy, because you were hoping it would lead me into saying something incriminating. So you invited me to sleep with you.'

'There's such a thing as free will, Tanner. You didn't have to go along with me, unless you want to admit your brain is ruled by your dick. And I didn't get the impression you regretted any of that.'

'Probably because I didn't. I'd have been too tired if you had made any overtures the second time – but that was never on the cards, was it? You knew all you needed to by then. And the first time was strictly professional. You slept with me for information.'

'Which I didn't get.'

'No, but that hardly mattered. You got it later, when I skipped with your gun and car.'

'It's a real sob story, isn't it?'

'Not from where I'm standing.' I glanced over the edge. 'From where I'm standing it's a story that might just end with you taking a very long fall, Zebra. You know I've come a long way to kill Reivich. Did it occur to you that I might not have too many qualms about killing anyone who tries to stop me?'

'There's a gun in your pocket. Use it if it'll make you feel any better.'

I reached for the gun to check it was still there, then kept my hand in my pocket. 'I could kill you now.'

To her credit, she managed not to flinch. 'Without taking your hand out of your pocket?'

'You're welcome to try me.' It felt like a charade; like a scripted piece we had fallen into rehearsing. It also felt like we had no choice but to follow the script to its conclusion, whatever that happened to be.

'Do you really think you could hit me like that?'

'It wouldn't be the first time I've killed someone firing from this angle.' But,

I thought, it would be the first time I had meant to do it. After all, I had not intended to kill Gitta. I was also unsure I really wanted to kill Zebra.

Had not meant to kill Gitta . . .

I'd been trying not to think about it, but like a maze with only one exit, my thoughts always meandered back to that one moment. Now, after long repression, they welled up and exploded like a gang of rowdy gatecrashers. I had not remembered it before now. Gitta had died, yes, but I had comfortably avoided thinking too closely about the manner of her death. She had died in the attack – so what else was there to think about? Nothing.

Except the simple fact that I had killed her.

This is what I remembered.

Gitta awoke first. She was the first to hear the attackers as they swept past the cordon, concealed in the strobe-lighting of the electrical storm. Her yelps of fear woke me, her naked body tensing against me. I saw three of them: three silhouetted shapes cast against the fabric of the tent, like grotesqueries in a shadow theatre. When each pulse of lightning flashed, they were somewhere else – sometimes one of them, sometimes two, sometimes all three. I could hear screaming – recognising in the timbre of each exclamation one of our own people. The screams were very short and concentrated, like trumpet blasts.

Ionisation-trails scythed through the tent and the force of the storm reached through the gashes like a creature of rain and wind. I cupped my hand across Gitta's mouth and felt under my pillow for the gun I had placed there before retiring, satisfied when my hand detected its cool presence and found its contoured grip.

I slipped from the bunk. No more than a second or two had passed since I had first become consciously aware of the attack.

'Tanner?' I called, hardly able to hear my own voice against the storm's threnody. 'Tanner, where the hell are you?'

I left Gitta under the thin caul of a blanket, shivering despite the heat and humidity.

'Tanner?'

My night-vision began to come online, the interior details of the ruined tent creeping into greyish clarity. It was a good modification; worth what it had cost to obtain from the Ultras. Dieterling had persuaded me to have it, after having the same mod himself. The gene splice led to a layer of reflective material – an organic substance called tapetum – being laid down behind my retinae. The tapetum reflected light back, maximising absorption. It even shifted the wavelength of the reflected light, fluorescing at the optimum sensivity of the retinae. The Ultras had said the only drawback of the splice – if you could call it a drawback – would be that my eyes would seem to flash back at anyone who shone a bright light in my face.

376

Eyeshine, they called it.

But I rather liked the idea of that. Long before anyone saw my eyeshine, I would have already seen them.

The splice went deeper than that, of course. They had packed my retinae with gene-tinkered rods with a photon-detection efficiency close to optimal, thanks to modified forms of the basic photosensitive chromoprotein pigments; a simple matter of tweaking a few genes on the X chromosome. I had a gene normally inherited only by women which allowed me to differentiate nuances of the colour red I had never imagined before. I even had a cluster of snake-derived cells, pits spaced around the rim of my corneas, which were capable of registering near infrared and ultraviolet, and which had grown neuronal connections back into my optic centre so that I processed the information as a visual overlay on my normal field of view, the way snakes do. But I had yet to activate the snake vision. Like all my faculties, it could be activated and suppressed by tailored retroviruses, triggering brief, controlled cancers which erected or dismantled the necessary cellular structures in a matter of days. I needed time, though, to learn the proper use of each faculty. First, enhanced night-vision. Then, later, colours beyond normal sight.

I pushed through the partition which divided the tent, into Tanner's part, where our chess table was still set up; still displaying the checkmate I had won against him, as I always did.

Tanner – naked but for a pair of khaki shorts – was kneeling down at the side of his bunk, like a man tying his shoes or examining a blister on his foot.

'Tanner?'

He looked up toward me, his hands engulfed in something black. A moan drifted from his mouth, and as my vision sharpened I saw why. He had very little foot below the ankle, and what remained looked more like charcoal than human flesh, just as liable to shatter into black shards at the merest touch.

Now I recognised the stink of incinerated human meat.

He stopped moaning, quite suddenly, as if a subroutine in his mind had judged the gesture inessential to his immediate survival, cancelling the pain. And then he spoke, with ridiculous calm and accuracy.

'I'm hurt, quite badly, as you can probably see. I don't think I'm going to be much use to you.' And then: 'What's wrong with your eyes?'

A figure stepped through a gash in one wall. His night-vision goggles hung around his neck and the flashlight rigged to his gun played across us, coming to rest on my face. His chameleoflage stammered towards compatibility with the interior.

I blasted his guts open.

'There's nothing wrong with my eyes,' I said when the afterimage of my weapon discharge had dissolved to a thumb-shaped pink bruise in my visual field. I stepped over the corpse of the attacker, carefully refraining from placing my unshod foot in the spreading entrails. I walked over to the rifle rack, pulled down a huge but currently superfluous bosonic beam weapon – too heavy to be used against enemy this close – and tossed it onto Tanner's bunk. 'Nothing wrong with my eyes at all. Now use that as a crutch and start earning your pay. We'll get you a new foot if we get out of it, so just think of it as a temporary loss.'

Tanner looked from his wound to the gun and then back to the wound, as if weighing one against the other.

Then I moved.

I put my weight on the stock of the boser-rifle and tried to put the pain into some sealed compartment at the back of my head. My foot was ruined, but what Cahuella said was right. I *could* live without it – the blast had done a very professional job of cauterisation – and if I managed to survive the attack, obtaining a new foot would be a matter of a few weeks' discomfort. In terms of mortality, I had sustained worse injuries when I was regular soldier fighting against the NCs. But my mind didn't see it that way. What it saw was that part of me was simply not there any more, and it did not quite know how to process that absence.

Light – hard and blue and artificial – impaled the tent. Two of the enemy – I had counted three before the dead one shot me – were still out there. Our tent was big enough that it might look as if we were a larger force than we really were, so the other two might be laying down a suppressing fire before moving in to mop up anyone they had not already taken out.

I made my way over to the body, my vision darkening at the edges, as if seen through a tube of foreboding clouds. I knelt down until I could reach the dead man, unclipping his torch and taking his night-vision goggles. Cahuella had shot him blind, in near total darkness, and while the shot was a fraction low for my tastes, it had done the job. I remembered how, only a few hours earlier, I had watched him pump shots into the night, as if there was something there only he could see.

'They did something to you and Dieterling,' I said, clenching my teeth as I spoke and hoping that I was comprehensible. 'The Ultras . . .'

'It's nothing to them,' he said, his broad frame turning towards me like a wall. 'They all have it. They live in nearly total darkness on their ships, so that they can bathe in the glories in the universe more easily, when they've left sunlight behind. Are you going to live, Tanner?'

'If any of us do.' I snapped the night-vision goggles over my eyes and saw the room brighten in hues of choleric green. 'There wasn't much bloodloss, but I can't do anything about shock. That's bound to set in soon, and then I'm not going to be very much use to you.'

'Get yourself a gun, something useful at close range. We'll go and see what damage we can do.'

'Where's Dieterling?'

'I don't know. Maybe he's dead.'

Automatically, barely having to think about it, I tugged a compact pistol from the rack, flicking its ammo-cell to readiness and hearing the shrill whine as its condensers charged up.

Gitta screamed from the next partition.

Cahuella pushed through ahead of me and then stopped dead just beyond the drape. I nearly knocked him over, the stock of the boser-rifle scuffling against the floor as I tried to approximate walking. I had no need for the goggles now, since the room was already lit by the tent's glowlamp, which Gitta must have ignited. She was standing up in the middle of the space, clutching a dun-coloured blanket around her.

One of the attackers stood behind her, one hand drawing her head back by a clump of scalp-hair, the other holding a wickedly serrated knife to the convex whiteness of her throat.

She made no scream now. The only sounds she allowed herself were small and snatched, like someone choking.

The man holding her had removed his helmet. He was not Reivich, just some mildly competent thug who might have fought with or against me during the war, or against both sides. His face was lined and his black hair was tied back in a topknot, like a Samurai. He was not exactly grinning – the situation was too tense for that – but there was something in his expression which suggested he was enjoying it.

'You can stop or you can take a step closer,' he said, his rough voice accentless and surprisingly reasonable. 'Either way I'm going to kill her. It's just a matter of time.'

'Your friend's dead,' Cahuella said, needlessly. 'If you kill Gitta, I'll kill you as well. Except for every second she suffers, I'll make it an hour for you. How's that for generosity?'

'Fuck you,' the man said, and drew the blade across her throat. A caterpillar of blood formed beneath the track of the incision, but he had been careful not to draw too deeply. Good with his knife, I thought. How many ways had he practised to cut with such precision?

Gitta, to her credit, hardly flinched.

'I've got a message for you,' he said, lifting the blade slightly from her skin, so that the scarlet bloom on its edge was clearly visible. 'It's from Argent Reivich. Does that surprise you in any way? It shouldn't, because I understand you were expecting him. Only just not so soon.'

'The Ultras lied to us,' Cahuella said.

The man smiled now, but only briefly. The pleasure was all in his eyes, narrowed to ecstatic slits. I realised we were dealing with a psychopath and that his actions were essentially random.

There was not going to be a negotiated settlement.

'There are factions amongst them,' the man said. 'Especially between crews.

379

Orcagna lied to you. You needn't take it personally.' His fist tensed on the knife again. 'Now, would you be so good as to put down that gun, Cahuella?'

'Do it,' I whispered, still standing behind him. 'No matter how good your vision is, there's only a tiny area of him not covered by Gitta, and I doubt you're that confident of your aiming just yet.'

'Don't you know it's rude to whisper?' the man said.

'Do it,' I hissed. 'I can still save her.'

Cahuella dropped the gun.

'Good,' I said, still whispering. 'Now listen carefully. I can hit him from her, without harming Gitta. But you're in the way.'

'Talk to me, you fuck.' The man pushed the knife against her skin so that the blade depressed a valley of flesh without actually breaking it. It would only take a flick now and he would sever her carotid artery.

'I'm going to shoot through you,' I said to Cahuella. 'It's a beam weapon, so it's only the line of sight that matters. From the angle where I'm going to fire, I won't hit any vital organs. But be ready for it.'

The man's hand brought the knife deeper, so that the valley was suddenly rivened, and blood welled from its depths. Time slowed down, and I watched him begin to drag the knife across her throat.

Cahuella started to speak.

I fired.

The pencil-thin particle beam chewed through him, entering his back an inch or so to the left of his spine, in the upper lumbar region, around the twentieth or twenty-first vertebrae. I hoped I missed the subclavian vein, and that the beam angle would direct its energies between the left lung and the stomach. But it was not precision surgery, and I knew that Cahuella would have to count himself lucky if this did not actually kill him. I also knew that, if it were a question of dying to save Gitta, he would accept that wholeheartedly, and would even order me to make it so. I paid very little attention to Cahuella anyway, since Gitta's position effectively limited the rangle of angles I could select. It was simply a matter of saving her, no matter what it did to her husband.

The particle beam fired for less than a tenth of a second, although the ion trail lingered long after, in addition to the track it had seared on my vision. Cahuella fell to the ground in front of me, like a sack of corn dropped from the ceiling.

And so did Gitta, with a hole bored neatly in her forehead, her eyes still open and seemingly alert, and the blood still oozing from the partial throat-wound.

I had missed.

There was no avoiding that; no softening or sweetening of that one acidic message. I had meant to save her, but intention meant nothing. What mattered was the red weal above her eyes where I had hit her, meaning to hit the man holding a knife to her throat.

The beam had missed him completely.

I had failed. In the one moment where failure mattered most; in the one moment of my life where I actually thought I could win – I had failed. Failed myself, and Cahuella, by betraying the terrible burden of trust he had implicitly placed in me, without saying a word. His wound was serious, but with the proper attention, I had had little doubt that he would live.

But there was no saving Gitta. I wondered who was the luckier.

'What's wrong?' Zebra asked. 'Tanner, what's wrong? Don't look at me like that, please. I'm beginning to think you might actually do it.'

'Can you give me a good reason why I shouldn't?'

'Only the truth.'

I shook my head minutely. 'Sorry, but you've just given it to me, and it wasn't anywhere near enough.'

'It wasn't everything.' Her voice was quiet and somehow relieved. 'I'm not working for him any more, Tanner. He thinks I am, but I've betrayed him.'

'Reivich?'

She nodded, face down, so that I could barely see her eyes. 'Once you stole from me, I knew you were the man Reivich was running from. I knew *you* were the assassin.'

'It didn't take a great deal of deduction, did it?'

'No, but it was important to be sure. Reivich wanted the man isolated and removed from the picture. Killed, not to put too fine a point on it.'

I nodded. 'That would make sense.'

'I was meant to do it as soon as I had definite evidence you were the killer. That way Reivich would be able to put the matter out of his mind for good – he wouldn't have to worry that the wrong man had been killed and that the real assassin was still out there somewhere.'

'You had more than a few opportunities to kill me.' My hand softened on the gun now. 'So why didn't you?'

'I almost did.' Zebra was talking quicker now, voice hushed even though no one was remotely within earshot. 'I could have done it in the apartment, but I hesitated. You can't blame me. So then I let you take the gun and the car, knowing I could trace either.'

'I should have realised. It seemed easy at the time.'

'Credit me with more sense than to let that happen by accident. Of course, there was another way to trace you if that failed. You still had the Game implant.' She paused. 'But then you crashed the car, had the implant taken out. That only left the gun, and I wasn't getting a very clear trace from it. Maybe you damaged it in the car crash.'

'Than I called you from the station, after I'd visited Dominika.'

'And told me where you'd be later on. I hired Pransky to help me. He's good, don't you think? Admittedly his socials skills could use a little work, but you don't pay people like that for their charm and diplomacy.' Zebra took a breath and wiped a film of accumulated rain from her brows, exposing a strip of clean flesh beneath the caul of sooty water. 'Not as good as you, though. I saw you attack the Gamers – the way you injured three of them and then kidnapped the fourth, the woman. I had you targeted the whole time that was happening. I could have opened your cranium from a kilometre away, and you wouldn't have felt an itch before your brains hit the street. But I couldn't do it. I couldn't just kill you like that. And that's when I betrayed Reivich.'

'I felt someone watching me. I never guessed it was you.'

'And even if you had, would you have guessed I was a twitch of an eyelid away from killing you?'

'Eyelid-triggered sniper's rifle? Now what would a nice girl like you be doing with something like that?'

'What now, Tanner?'

I withdrew my empty hand from my pocket, like a conjuror whose trick had gone spectacularly wrong.

'I don't know,' I said. 'But it's wet out here and I need a drink.'

THIRTY-ONE

Methuselah looked very much the same as when I had last seen him, floating in his tank like a monstrous piscine iceberg. There was a small crowd around him, just as before – people who would linger for a few minutes at the marvel of the age before realising that, really, all it was was a large old fish, and that, size apart, there was really nothing about Methuselah which was intrinsically more interesting than the younger, leaner, nimbler koi which thrived in the ponds. Worse than that, in fact, since the one thing I noticed was that no one turned away from Methuselah looking quite as happy as when they had arrived. Not only was there something disappointing about the fish, there was something ineluctably sad as well. Maybe they were too scared that in Methuselah they glimpsed the inert grey hulk of their own futures.

Zebra and I drank tea, and no one paid us any attention.

'The woman you met – what was her name again?'

'Chanterelle Sammartini,' I said.

'Pransky never explained what happened to her. Were you together when he found you?'

'No,' I said. 'We'd argued.'

Zebra did a creditable double-take. 'Wasn't arguing part of the bargain? I mean, if you kidnap someone, don't you generally assume that there's going to be some arguing?'

'I didn't kidnap her, no matter what you think. I invited her to take me to the Canopy.'

'With a gun.'

'She wasn't going to accept the invitation otherwise.'

'Good point. And did you keep this gun on her the whole time you were up here?'

'No,' I said, not entirely comfortable with this line of debate. 'No, not at all. It turned out not be necessary. We found we could tolerate each other's company without it.'

Zebra arched an eyebrow. 'You and the Canopy rich kid actually hit it off?'

'After a fashion,' I said, feeling oddly defensive.

From across the atrium, Methuselah flicked a pelvic fin and the sudden-ness of the gesture – no matter how feeble or involuntary – generated a mild *frission* amongst the onlookers, as if a statue had just twitched. I won-dered what kind of synaptic process had triggered that gesture, whether there was any intention behind it, or whether – like the creaking of an old house – Methuselah occasionally just moved, no closer to thought than wood.

'Did you sleep with her?' Zebra asked.

'No,' I said. 'Sorry to disappoint you, but there just wasn't time.'

'You're not comfortable talking about this, are you?'

'Would you be?' I shook my head, as much to clear it of confusion as to deny anything deeper about my relationship with Chanterelle. 'I expected to hate her for what she did; the way she played the game. But as soon as I started talking to her I realised it wasn't that simple. From her point of view there was nothing barbaric about it at all.'

'Nice and convenient, that.'

'I mean she didn't realise – or believe – that the victims were not the kind of people she'd been told they were.'

'Until she met you.'

I nodded carefully. 'I think I gave her pause for thought.'

'You've given us all pause for thought, Tanner.' And then Zebra drank what remained of her tea in silence.

'You again,' the Mixmaster said, in a tone which conveyed neither pleasure nor disappointment, but a highly refined amalgam of the two. 'I had imagined that I had answered all your questions satisfactorily during your last visit. Evidently I was mistaken.' His heavy-lidded gaze alighted on Zebra, a twinge of non-recognition disturbing the genetically enhanced placidity of his expres-sion. 'Madame, I see, has had a considerable makeover since the last occasion.'

It had been Chanterelle, of course, but I decided to let the bastard have his amusement.

'She had the number of a good bloodcutter,' I said.

'And you emphatically didn't,' the Mixmaster said, sealing the outer door of his parlour against other visitors. 'I'm talking about the eyework, of course,' he said, ensconcing himself behind his floating console while the two of us stood. 'But why don't we dispense with the lie that this work had any connection with bloodcutters?'

'What's he talking about?' Zebra asked, entirely with justification.

'A small internal matter,' I said.

'This gentleman,' the Mixmaster said, with laboured emphasis on the last word, 'visited me a day ago, to discuss some genetic and structural anomalies in his eyes. At the time he claimed that the anomalies were the result of inferior intervention by bloodcutters. I was even prepared to believe him, though the edited sequences bore none of the usual signatures of bloodcutter work.'

'And now?'

'Now I believe that the changes were done by another faction entirely. Shall I spell it out?'

'Please do.'

'The work bears certain signatures which suggest that the sequences were inserted using the genetics techniques common to Ultras. Neither more nor less advanced than bloodcutter or Mixmaster work – just different, and highly individual. I should have realised much sooner.' He allowed himself a smile, obviously impressed by his own deductive skills. 'When Mixmasters perform a genetic service, it's essentially permanent, unless the client specifies otherwise. That doesn't mean that the work isn't reversible, in most cases – it just means that the genetic and physiological changes will be stable against reversion to the older form. Bloodcutter work is the same, for the simple reason that bloodcutter sequences are generally bootlegged from Mixmasters, and the 'cutters haven't the ingenuity to embed obsolescence into those same sequences. They steal code, but they don't hack it. But Ultranauts do things rather differently.' The Mixmaster cradled his long and elegant fingers before his chin. 'Ultras sell their services with an in-built obsolescence; a mutational clock if you will. I'll spare you the details; suffice to say that, within the viral and enzymic machinery which mediates the expression of the new genes inserted into your own DNA, there is a time-keeping mechanism, a clock which functions by counting the accumulation of randomness in a strand of foreign reference DNA. Needless to say, once these errors exceed a pre-defined limit, cellular machinery is unshackled which suppresses or corrects the altered genes.' Again the Mixmaster smiled. 'Of course, I'm simplifying tremendously. For a start, the clocks are set to trigger gradually, so that pro- duction of the new proteins and the division of cells into new types doesn't cease suddenly. Otherwise it could be fatal – especially if the changes allowed you to live in an otherwise hostile environment, like oxygenated water or an ammonia atmosphere.'

'You're saying Tanner's eyes were touched by Ultras?'

'You catch on extraordinarily swiftly. But there's rather more to it than that.'

'There generally is,' I said.

The Mixmaster danced his hands over the console, fingers plucking at invisible harp strings, causing reams of genetics data to spring into the air, particular sequences of Ts and As and Gs and Cs highlighted and cross-linked to a series of physiological and functional maps of the human eye and the associated brain regions of visual comprehension. He looked like a wizard suddenly accompanied by ghostly – and gory – familiars.

'Something very odd has happened here,' the man said, his fingers ceasing their too-dexterous dance. He sketched a particular block of base-pairs, the cross-linking rungs of DNA. 'These are the pairs which are allowed to grow progressively more random; the internal clock.' His finger moved to another highlighted block which looked superficially identical. 'And this is the reference map, the unmutated DNA. It's by comparing these – by noting the number of mutational changes – that the clock is driven.'

'There don't seem to be very many changes,' Zebra said.

'A few statistically minor point deletions or frame shifts,' the Mixmaster said. 'But nothing significant.'

'Meaning what?' I asked.

'Meaning that the clock has not had very long to run. The two sets of DNA have hardly begun to diverge.' His eyes narrowed. 'That means that the work was done very recently; definitely within the last year, and perhaps only a few months ago.'

'Why is that a problem?' Zebra asked.

'Because of this.' Now his finger moved across a densely tangled blob, rendered in lilac. 'This is a transcription factor; a protein that regulates the expression of a particular set of genes. It is not, however, a normally occurring human protein. Its only function – and it has been engineered for this purpose – is to suppress the newly inserted genes in your eye. It should not be present in large quantities until the mutational clock has been triggered. Yet I found it in abundance.'

'Could the Ultras have deceived Tanner?'

The Mixmaster shook his head. 'Not likely. There'd be no economic gain in doing so. The genetics changes would still have been made, so it's not as if it would be cheaper for them to reset the clock. In fact it would harm their longterm profits, because Tanner – if that's your name – would have sought the services of another crew.'

'I take it you have an alternative explanation?'

'I do, but you may not like it.' Once again he delivered a smile of utter salaciousness. 'It would be exceedingly difficult to reset the mutational clock to zero without triggering all sorts of secondary anti-tamper safeguards. Even for a Mixmaster. I could do it, but it would be far from trivial work. But the opposite procedure would be considerably simpler.'

'The opposite procedure?' I leaned forward, feeling that some kind of fundamental revelation was almost within my grasp. It wasn't a feeling I much enjoyed.

'Setting the clock forward, so that the new genes are switched off.' He said that, and then allowed himself a moment's contemplative silence, spinning the projected eyeball with the tip of one finger, a singularly macabre globe. 'It would be simpler because there would be no safeguards. It would never occur to the Ultras to protect against that kind of tampering, because it would only harm the client. Which is not to say it would be easy. It would, however, be an order of magnitude easier than setting the clock back. It could be attempted by any bloodcutter who understood the problem.'

'Go on.'

His voice took on a gravitas it had lacked a moment earlier, as if he had triggered his own mutational change to deepen the response of his larynx. 'For some reason, someone set your clock forward, Tanner.'

Zebra looked at me.

'You mean Tanner's changes are fading?' she asked. I realised that she still had no idea what form these changes took.

'That was probably the intention,' the Mixmaster said. 'Whoever did it was not entirely lacking in competence. Once the clock had been wound, the cells in your eye would have begun manufacturing normal human proteins, cell division following the normal blueprint.' He sighed. 'But whoever did it was either sloppy or hasty or both. They reset only a fraction of the clocks, and then imperfectly. There's a small war going on in your eye, between different components of the Ultra genetics machinery. Whoever tried to reset the clock thought they were turning the machine off, but all they really did was throw a spanner in its works.' A note of sorrow entered his voice. 'Such haste. Such dreadful haste. Of course, whoever it was more than deserved to fail. The question is why they thought it was worth doing in the first place.' His eyes opened in expectation, and I realised he thought I was going to give him an answer.

But I saw no sense in giving him that pleasure, much as I would have liked to. Instead I said, 'I want a scan. A full-body scan. You can do that, can't you?'

'It depends what you want it for; the kind of resolution you want me to achieve.'

'Nothing too fine. I just want you to look for something. Tissue damage. Internal. Wounds which may or may not have healed.'

'I can but try,' the man said, gesturing to the couch, a skatelike scanning device already gliding down from the ceiling.

It did not take very long. In all honestly, I would have been surprised if the Mixmaster scan had revealed anything other than what I was dreading and expecting. It was just a question of seeing it revealed in the cold indices of a readout; just a question of finally burying any residual traces of denial – and, for that matter, hope, which might have remained.

The skate imaged my body core, learning my inner secrets via a manifold of sensory techniques. The machine was really just a highly modified form of trawl, adjusted to cope with the cellular and genetic structure of the whole body, rather than the specialised flavours of neural tissue alone. Given time, it could resolve matter down to the atomic level; right to the border of quantum fuzziness, but there was no need for such precision now, and the scan was commensurately rapid.

And what it showed chilled me to the core. Something which should have been there was missing.

Something which should have been missing was there.

THIRTY-TWO

'You look like you've seen a ghost,' Zebra said.

She had forced me to sit down in the atrium and drink something hot and sweet and nondescript.

'You can't begin to imagine.'

'What was so bad, Tanner? It must have been something you were expecting, or you wouldn't have asked the Mixmaster to give you the scan.'

'Let's say fearing, rather than expecting, shall we?'

I didn't know where or when to begin, or even with whom. Ever since arriving around Yellowstone my memories had been damaged, and I'd had the added complication of the indoctrinal virus to deal with. The virus had given me unwelcome glimpses into the psyche of Sky Haussmann, and yet at the same time aspects of my own past had begun to come back into focus; who I was; what I was doing; why I wanted to kill Reivich. All of those things, disturbing as they'd been, I could have come to terms with. But it hadn't stopped there. It hadn't even stopped when I started thinking and feeling my way through Sky's past; vouchsafed secrets no one else knew about his crimes. Nor had it stopped when I started having confused thoughts about Gitta; remembering her from Cahuella's viewpoint rather than my own.

Even that I could have begun to rationalise, with some effort. Contamination of my own memories by Cahuella's? Well, it was possible. Memories could be recorded and transferred, after all. I couldn't begin to imagine why some of Cahuella's experiences should have become intermingled with my own, but it wasn't unthinkable that it had happened.

But the truth – the truth that I was beginning to glimpse – was more disturbing than that.

I wasn't even wearing the right body.

'It isn't easy to explain,' I said.

Zebra answered in a hiss, 'People don't just walk into Mixmaster parlours and ask to be scanned for internal tissue damage – not unless they half expect to find something.'

'No, I . . .' I stopped. Had I imagined it, or had I just seen that face again, near the mingling crowds around Methuselah? Perhaps now I was really hallucinating, pushed over the edge by what the Mixmaster had shown me. Perhaps it was my destiny to see Reivich everywhere I looked now, no matter what the circumstances.

'Tanner . . . ?'

I dared not look any deeper into the crowd. 'There should have been something there,' I said. 'A wound which should have been present, but wasn't. Something which happened to me once. It was healed . . . but nothing heals that perfectly.'

'What type of wound?'

'My memories tell me I lost a foot. I can tell you exactly how it happened; exactly how it felt. But there's no sign of the injury.'

'Well, the regrowth procedure must have been very sophisticated.'

'What about the other wound, then? A wound the man I was working for sustained at the same time? He took a beam-weapon discharge right through him, Zebra. *That* showed up.'

'You're losing me, Tanner.' She looked around, her gaze catching on something or someone for an instant before returning to me. 'Are you trying to tell me you're not who you think you are?'

'I'm giving it some serious consideration, let's say that much.' I waited a moment, then added, 'You've seen him too, haven't you?'

'What?'

'Reivich. I just saw him; for a moment I thought I might be imagining him. But I wasn't, was I?'

Zebra opened her mouth to say something – a denial, quick and fluid, but it just didn't come. Her veneer had cracked. 'Everything I told you is true,' she said quietly, when words returned. 'I'm not working for him any more. But you're right. You *did* just see him.' After a pause, she said, 'Except that isn't really Reivich.'

I nodded; I'd half guessed the truth already. 'A lure?'

'Something like that, yes.' She consulted her tea. 'You knew there'd be time for him to change his appearance as soon as he arrived in the city. In fact, it would be the only sensible thing for him to do. And that's exactly what he did. The real Reivich is out there now, somewhere in the city, but you'd need to take a tissue sample, or get him under a Mixmaster scanner before you'd know for sure. And even then you might not be certain. They can change everything, you know, given time. Even Reivich's DNA might not betray him, given enough money.' Zebra paused. Out of the corner of my eye I could see the man, still hovering at the fringe of the crowd gathered round the big fish. It was him, yes – or at least an extremely good facsimile. Zebra said, 'Reivich knew his cover was good, but he still wanted to flush you out. That way he could sleep at night and – if he wished – revert to his old appearance and identity.'

'So he persuaded someone to assume his shape.'

'There was no persuasion involved. The man was more than willing.'

'Someone with a death wish?'

She shook her head. 'No more than any other immortal in the Canopy. His name is Voronoff, I believe, although I don't know for sure, since I was never that close to Reivich. You won't have heard of Voronoff, but his name's fairly well-known in Canopy circles. He's one of the most extreme Gamers; someone for whom the hunt was always going to be too tame. He's good, too – or else he wouldn't still be alive.'

'You're wrong,' I said. 'I have heard of Voronoff.'

I told her about the man I had seen jumping into the mist in the Chasm, when Sybilline had taken me to the restaurant at the end of the stalk.

'That makes sense,' she said. 'Voronoff's into anything involving extreme personal risk, provided there's a large element of skill involved. Dangerous sports, anything which gives a genuine adrenalin kick, and which forces him to confront the thin border between mortality and his own longevity. He would never stoop to hunting now; he'd just regard it as an amusement, not a real game. Not because of its unfairness, but because there's no personal risk to the participants.'

'Except for one participant, of course.'

'You know what I mean.'

She was silent for a moment before continuing, 'People like Voronoff are extremists. For them the usual methods of controlling boredom just don't work any more. It's like they developed a tolerance for it. They need something stronger.'

'And putting himself in the firing line was just the ticket.'

'It was controlled. Voronoff had a network of spies and informers keeping track of you. When you first thought you'd seen him, he'd already seen you.' She swallowed. 'The first time, he kept Methuselah between you and himself. It wasn't any accident. He was more in control than you ever realised.'

'It was a mistake, though. He made it too easy. He made me wonder what was going on.'

'Yes,' Zebra said, knowingly. 'But by then it was far too late to stop him. Voronoff was out of our control.'

I looked into her faintly striped face, not needing to prompt her further. She said, 'Voronoff liked his role too much. It suited him too well. For a long time he acted the way he was meant to – keeping a discreet distance; never letting you see him. The idea was that he would plant a trail of clues which would lead you to him, but in such a way that you thought you'd done all the work yourself. But he wanted more than that.'

'More danger.'

'Yes.' She said it with deep finality. 'Laying down clues and waiting for you to follow them wasn't enough for Voronoff. He started to make himself more prominent – placing himself at ever-greater risk, but always maintaining an edge of control. That's why I said he's good. But Reivich didn't like it, for obvious reasons. Voronoff was no longer serving him. He was serving himself; finding a new way to stave off the boredom. And I think it worked, being in that role.'

'Not for me it didn't.'

I stood up, almost upsetting the table as I did so. And one hand was already beginning the journey to my pocket.

'Tanner,' Zebra said, quickly, reaching for the hem of my coat as I stepped away from her, 'killing him won't change a thing.'

'Voronoff,' I said, at the top of my voice – not actually shouting it, but projecting like a actor of great reknown. 'Voronoff – turn around and step away from the crowd.'

The gun gleamed in my hand, and now people began to notice it for the first time.

The man who looked like Reivich met my gaze and managed not to look too surprised. But he was not the only one who met my gaze. I had managed to get everyone's attention by now, and those who were not trying to read my expression were fixated by the gun. If the hunt was as endemic amongst Canopy dwellers as I had been led to believe, many of these people would have seen and handled weapons of far greater potency than the pistol I hefted now. But never in a place as public as this; never with such crass vulgarity. Judging by the looks of shock and bewilderment and revulsion I saw, I might as well have been pissing on the ornamental lawn which fringed the koi pond.

'Maybe you didn't hear me, Voronoff.' I sounded sweetly reasonable to my own ears. 'I know who you are and what this is all about. If you know anything about me you'll also know that I'm fully capable of using this.' I had the gun aimed in his direction now, double-handed stance with my feet slightly spread.

'Drop it, Mirabel.'

It was not a voice I had heard recently, nor had it come from the crowd. I felt a touch of soft metallic cold against the nape of my neck.

'Are you deaf? I said drop the piece. Do it fast or your head'll be following it down.'

I started lowering the piece, but that wasn't good enough for the speaker standing behind me. He increased the pressure against my neck in a manner which strongly suggested it would be in my best interest to let the gun drop.

I did.

'You,' the man said, evidently addressing Zebra. 'Kick the gun to me, and don't even think about trying anything creative.'

She did as she was told.

I saw a hand reach out in my peripheral vision and snatch the gun from the ground; the pressure of the weapon against my neck changed slightly as the man knelt. But he was good; I could tell that, so – like Zebra – I wasn't tempted to even think about trying anything creative. That was good, because I was all out of creativity.

'Voronoff, you fool,' said the voice. 'Look what you nearly got us into.' And then I heard clicking sounds as the gun was inspected, followed by a tut of amusement from the hidden speaker, whose voice I almost recognised. 'It's empty. The damn thing was empty all along.'

'News to me,' I said.

'I did it,' Zebra said, shrugging. 'You can't blame me, can you? I had a feeling you might end up pointing it at me, so I just took a precaution.'

'Next time, don't bother,' I said.

'Not that it exactly mattered,' Zebra said, doing a poor job of masking her annoyance. 'You never even tried to fire the fucking thing, Tanner.'

I angled my eyes upwards, as if I was trying to look behind my own head. 'Are you involved with this clown?'

That got me an acute stabbing pain between the ears. The man said, projecting his voice out to the people who were staring at us, 'All right; this is Canopy security; the situation is under control.' I saw a flash of identity in my peripheral vision; a leatherbound card embossed with scrolling data which he waved at the crowd.

It seemed to have the desired effect; about half the people drifted away and the others tried to pretend that they had never really been interested in what was going on. The pressure eased and the man sidled around to my front, pulling up a seat for himself. Voronoff had also joined us, the exact facsimile of Reivich disporting himself opposite me with a scowl of displeasure written across his face.

'Sorry for spoiling your little game,' I said.

The other man was Quirrenbach, although he had changed his appearance since our last encounter, looking meaner, leaner and a great deal less patient and bewildered. The gun in his hand was small and dainty enough to have been a gimmicky cigarette-lighter.

'How's the symphony coming on?'

'That was a very sneaky thing you did, Mirabel; leaving me like that. I suppose I should thank you for returning the money that you made on my experientials, but you'll excuse me if I don't overwhelm you with a flood of gratitude.'

I shrugged. 'I had a job to do. You didn't figure in it.'

'How's that job looking now?' Voronoff said, still sneering at me. 'Time for a rethink, Mirabel?'

'You tell me.'

Quirrenbach flashed a quick grin at me, like an aggressive ape. 'Tough talk from someone who didn't even know his gun wasn't loaded. Maybe you're not quite the professional hotshot we've been led to believe.' He reached over and helped himself to my tea, maintaining eye contact all the while. 'How did you know he wasn't Reivich, by the way?'

'Have a guess,' Zebra said.

'I could kill you for betraying us,' Quirrenbach said to her. 'But right now I'm not sure I can muster the enthusiasm.'

'Why don't you start with Voronoff, dickhead?'

He looked at Zebra, then at the man disguised at Reivich, as if weighing the idea seriously. 'That really wouldn't do, would it?' Then his attention returned to me. 'We caused quite a stir back there, Mirabel. It won't be long before what passes for authority here comes to take a look, and I really don't think any of us want to be around when that happens.'

'So you're really not Canopy security?'

'Sorry to shatter your illusions.'

'Oh, don't worry about that,' I said. 'They were shattered quite some time ago.'

Quirrenbach smiled and stood up, the tiny little gun still nestling in his fist, as if with one spasm of his fingers he might crush it to shreds. He danced the barrel between Zebra and myself, holding his fake ID in the other hand like a talisman. Voronoff, meanwhile, produced a weapon of his own; between them they had us comprehensively covered. We walked through the crowd, Quirrenbach daring anyone to pay us anything more than glancing interest. Neither Zebra or myself made any attempt to resist or escape; it would not have been worth it.

Only three vehicles were parked on the landing ledge, cowled dark shapes glossy with rainwater, roof-mounted arms partially extended in readiness for flight, like three upturned dead spiders. One was the car in which Zebra and I had arrived. I recognised one of the other cars as well, but not the one to which Quirrenbach was leading us.

'Are you going to kill me now?' I asked. 'Because if you are, you could save yourself a lot of trouble by throwing me over the edge here. There's no need to spice up my last moments with a ride through the Canopy.'

'I don't know how I've managed without your brilliant shards of wit, Mirabel,' Quirrenbach said, with a long-suffering sigh. 'And, incidentally – not that you care – the symphony happens to be coming along rather splendidly, thank you.'

'That wasn't a cover?'

'Ask me about it in a hundred years.'

'If we're going to talk about people who hesitate to kill others,' Voronoff said, 'you might crop up in the discussion, Mirabel. You could have dropped me when we first met around Methuselah. I'm rather puzzled that you didn't at least try. And don't say there was a fish in the way. You may be many things, Mirabel, but sentimental isn't one of them.'

He was right: I had hesitated, much as I preferred not to admit it to myself. In another life – at least on another world – I would have dropped Reivich (or Voronoff) almost before I had mentally acknowledged their presence. There would have been no ethical debates about the value of an immortal fish.

'Maybe I knew you weren't the right man,' I said.

'Then again, maybe you just didn't have the nerve.' It was dark, but I caught the quick flash of Quirrenbach's grin. 'I know your background, Mirabel. We all do. You were pretty good, once, back on Sky's Edge. Trouble was, you just didn't know when to pack it in.'

'If I'm so washed up, why the special attention?'

'Because you're a fly,' Voronoff said. 'Sometimes they need swatting.'

The vehicle readied itself as we approached, a door opening in one side like a drooling tongue, plush steps set into its inner surface. A pair of heavies shadowed the door, packing indecently large weapons. Any lingering thoughts I had entertained of resistance vanished at that point. They were professionals. I had a feeling they wouldn't even allow me the dignity of jumping over the side; that if I tried it they would put a pair of slugs in my spine on the way down.

'Where are we going?' I asked, not sure if I really wanted to know the answer, or if I could even expect an honest reply.

'Space,' Quirrenbach said. 'For a meeting with Mister Reivich.'

'Space?'

'Sorry to disappoint you, Mirabel. But Reivich isn't in Chasm City at all. You've been chasing shadows.'

THIRTY-THREE

I looked at Zebra. She looked at me. Neither of us said anything.

The vehicle into which the heavies escorted us had the reek of newness, leather trim sweating sumptuousness. There was an isolated rear compartment with six seats and a moundlike central table, with soft musak filling the air and elegant neon designs worked into the ceiling. Voronoff and one of the heavies sat opposite us, weapons still at readiness. Quirrenbach and the other man entered the front compartment, visible only as smoky shadows through the partition.

The car rose very smoothly, with a soft snicking from the roof arms, like someone crocheting at great speed.

'What did he mean, space?' I asked.

'A place called Refuge. One of the high orbital carousels,' Voronoff said. 'Not that it makes any real difference to you. I mean, it's not as if you're just tagging along for the ride, is it?'

Someone had mentioned Refuge since my arrival in the city, but I could not quite place the reference.

'What happens when we get there?'

'That's for Mister Reivich to know and you to find out. You might call it negotiation. But don't expect to take too many bargaining chips to the table, Mirabel. From what I hear, you're all cleaned out.'

'I've still got a few surprises up my sleeve.' But I sounded about as convincing as a drunk tramp boasting of his sexual prowess. Through the side windows I watched the hovering crystalline mass of Escher Heights recede, and – not inconsequentially – I saw the other car, the vehicle which did not belong to Zebra, unfurl its arms to maximum extension and commence following us at a polite distance.

'What now?' I asked, ignoring the heavy. 'Your game's up, Voronoff. You're going to have to find a new mode of pleasure.'

'It isn't about pleasure, you idiot. It's about pain.' He leaned forward, imposing his bulk across the table. He looked like Reivich, but his body language and manner of speaking was all wrong. There was no hint of a Sky's Edge accent and his physicality would have been alien to Reivich's aristocracy. 'It's about pain,' he repeated. 'Because pain is what it keeps away. Do you understand?'

'Not really, but go ahead.'

'You don't usually think of boredom as something similar to pain. That's because you've only been exposed to it in relatively small doses. You don't know its true colour. The difference between the boredom you know and the boredom I know is like the difference between touching snow and putting your hand in a vat of liquid nitrogen.'

'Boredom isn't a stimulus, Voronoff.'

'I'm less sure,' he said. 'There is, after all, a part of the human brain which is responsible for the sensation we call boredom. You can't argue with that. And it must logically be made active by some external stimulus, just like the brain centre for taste or sound.' He raised a hand. 'I anticipate your next point. That's one of my talents, you see – anticipation. You might say it's sympto-matic of my condition. I'm a neural net which is so well-adapted to its input that it hasn't evolved in years. But to return to the point in hand. You were doubtless going to say that boredom is an absence of stimulus, not the presence of a particular one. I say there is no difference; that the glass is both half empty and half full. You hear silence between notes; I hear music. You see a pattern of black on white; I see a pattern of white on black. More than that, in fact – I see both.' He grinned again, like a maniac who had been chained in a dungeon for years and was now having a meaningful conversation with his own shadow. 'I see everything. You can't help it when you reach my – what shall I call it? – depth of experience?'

'You're quite mad, aren't you?'

'I've *been* mad,' Voronoff said, apparently not taking it as an insult. 'I've been through madness and come out the other side. Now being mad would bore me as much as sanity.'

I knew he was not mad, of course – at least not screamingly insane. If he had been, he would have been no use to Reivich as a lure. Voronoff had to have some residual grasp on reality. His mental state was almost certainly unlike anything I had ever experienced – and I had certainly known boredom – but it would be lethal to assume he was in anything other than absolute control of his faculties.

'You could end it all,' I said, helpfully. 'Suicide can't be the hardest thing to arrange in a city like this.'

'People do,' Zebra said. 'People like Voronoff. They don't call it suicide, of course. But they suddenly take an unhealthy interest in activities with a very low survival-probability, like diving into the gas giant or saying hello to the Shrouders.'

'Why not, Voronoff?' And then it was my turn to smile. 'No, wait. You almost did it, didn't you? Posing as Reivich. You were hoping I'd kill you, weren't you? A way out of the pain with something approaching dignity. The wise old immortal gunned down by the out-of-town thug, just because he happened to take on the persona of a murderous fugitive?'

'With no bullets? That'd be a trick worth dying to see, Mirabel.'

'Good point.'

'Except,' Zebra said, 'you realised you liked it too much.'

Voronoff looked at her with ill-concealed venom. 'Liked what too much, Taryn?'

'Being hunted. It actually eased the pain, didn't it?'

'What would you know about the pain?'

'No,' I said. 'Be honest, Voronoff. She's right, isn't she? For the first time in years you actually remembered what it was like to live. That's why you started taking stupid risks – to keep that buzz alive. But nothing was good enough, was it? Even jumping into the chasm was just mildly amusing.'

He looked at us with new eagerness. 'Have you ever been hunted? Have you any idea what it's like?'

'I'm afraid I have had that pleasure,' I said. 'And fairly recently, too.'

'I'm not talking about your little hunting games,' Voronoff said, spitting the words with total contempt. 'Scum in pursuit of scum – present company excepted, of course. When they hunted you, Mirabel, they stacked the odds so heavily in their favour they might as well have blindfolded you and put a slug through your head before they even let you run.'

'Funnily enough, I would have almost agreed with you at the time.'

'But it could have been different. They could have made it fair. Let you get further away before they came after you, so that your death wasn't absolutely inevitable. Allowed you to find your hiding places and use them. That would have made a difference, wouldn't it?'

'Almost,' I said. 'Of course, there would have been the small matter that I never volunteered for it.'

'Maybe you would have, too. If it was worth it. If there was a prize. If you thought you could make it through the game.'

'What was your prize, Voronoff?'

'The pain,' he said. 'Its absolution. For a few days at least.'

I started to answer him, probably. I think I did, anyway. It might have been Zebra, or it might have been the taciturn heavy with the bludgeon-sized gun. All I remember with any clarity is what happened several seconds later, the intervening moments neatly edited from memory. There must have been a pulse of light and heat, at first, as the other car opened fire on us. Then there would have been a blast of eardrum-piercing sound as the shockwave of the beam weapon slammed through the flensed-open cabin, followed by an explosion of metal and plastic and composites as the car's innards eviscerated themselves in a hot cloud of fused machinery. Then we would have dropped, as the shattered roof-mounted arms, amputated and twisted by the attack, lost their grip on the cables.

A second or so later our descent was arrested, violently, and that was when, approximately, something like normal consciousness resumed. My first memory – before the pain hit – was that the car was upside down, with the moundlike table now dimpling down from the ceiling, and the neon-patterned floor evincing a gaping, jagged hole, through which the lower reaches of the city – the festering complexity of the Mulch – was far too clear, and far too far below.

The heavy was gone, except for his gun, which was rattling to and fro on the new floor as the car lurched and swayed, adjusting to its precarious new equilibrium. The heavy's hand was still present, clasped around the gun. It had been neatly severed by shrapnel. Seeing the bony details of the wrist reminded me of the absence of my foot in the tent, after we had been ambushed by Reivich's people; the way I had pawed at the stump and held my blood-drenched palm to my face, in abject denial that a part of me had been removed, like a strip of annexed territory.

Except – as I now knew – none of that had happened to me.

Zebra and I had tumbled into one corner of the cabin, thrown together in an untidy embrace. There was no sign of Voronoff – or any parts of Voronoff. I was being assailed by waves of pain, but as I began to pay particular attention to my discomfort, I decided there was nothing sharp enough to be actual broken bones.

The car swayed and creaked. It was remarkably quiet, apart from our breathing and the soft moaning which came from Zebra.

'Tanner?' she said, opening her eyes to pained slits. 'What just happened?'

'We were attacked,' I said, realising that she had had no knowledge of the other vehicle; that she had not been expecting anything at all, whereas I had been mentally tensed for some kind of intervention. 'A heavy beam weapon, probably. I think we're stuck in the Canopy.'

'Are we safe?' she asked, wincing as she untangled one limb. 'No; wait. Stupid question. *Incredibly* stupid question.'

'Are you hurt?'

'I umm . . . just a moment.' Her eyes, glazed as they were, conspired to glaze a degree more, for an instant. 'No; nothing that can't wait for a few hours.'

'What did you just do?'

'Checked my body-image for damage.' She said it dismissively. 'How about you, Tanner?'

'I'll make it. Assuming any of us makes it.'

The car lurched, slipping vertically downwards before something arrested its progress, shakily. I tried to keep my gaze away from the maw in the floor, but if anything, the Mulch looked further away than ever, like a street map held at arm's length. A few of the lowermost merged limbs of the Canopy intersected the view, but they were spindly and uninhabited, and served only to enhance the sense of tremendous height. Shadows moved beyond the smoky partition, and the vehicle budged again.

'Someone will rescue us,' Zebra said. 'Won't they?'

'Someone may not want to intervene in what is clearly a private matter.' Then I nodded at the partition. 'At least one of them is alive in there. I think we'd better move before they do anything we might regret, like shooting us.'

'Move where, Tanner?'

I looked down at the gap in the floor. 'We're not exactly spoilt for choice, are we?'

'You're mad.'

'Just possibly,' I said, kneeling at the edge of the hole, spreading my arms wide around the rim and preparing to lower my head through it. 'But I find it goes with the territory, Zebra.'

I lowered myself through the aperture until my feet found purchase against the gnarled top-surface of the Canopy branch against which we'd come to rest. It was a narrow branch; we were very close to its extremity, where it tapered to a fine, tendrilled point, like the nub of an onion. Once I had my balance, I reached up and helped Zebra through, though with the extreme elongation of her limbs, she hardly needed my assistance.

Zebra looked up, appraising the looming bulk of the ruined vehicle. What had been the roof was a mass of scorched and melted components, only one of the telescopic arms remaining, which was the arm which was holding the vehicle in place, clutching precariously and twistedly at a somewhat higher branch. It looked like it would take very little more than a breeze to send the whole mass careering down to the Mulch. Quirrenbach and the other heavy, who'd been in the forward compartment, were inside, but they were struggling with the door, which was wedged against a protrusion from the branch.

'Voronoff's still alive,' I said, gesturing a little distance up the branch, where it thickened. He was crawling along it, slowly but methodically, and I decided the branch must have broken an otherwise unintentional fall.

'What are you going to do?'

'Nothing,' I said. 'He won't get very far.'

The shot was precise and surgical; sufficient yield to make a point, yet not enough to risk cutting through the branch. It made Voronoff stop in his tracks, but for a moment he did not look back in our direction.

Zebra looked up, into the overlying mass of structural branches, where the figure who had fired the shot was standing. She stood with her hips slightly canted to one side, the stock of a heavy rifle resting against the convexity of one thigh.

Chanterelle shouldered the weapon, then commenced climbing down via an improvised staircase of linking branches. Above, her car was parked intact, and three other dark-clad figures had spilled out onto the branch. They were covering her as she worked her way down to our level with even larger and nastier weapons.

It was a small thing at first; just a smudge of phosphors on the deep radar screen. But it signified volumes. For the first time since leaving the Flotilla they had encountered something that lay behind them; something other than light years of empty space. Sky turned up the beam intensity and focused the phased-array on the specific region where the echo had come back from.

'It's got to be it,' Gomez said, leaning over his shoulder. 'Got to be the *Caleuche*. There can't be anything else out there.'

'Maybe we're just seeing another piece of discarded junk,' Norquinco said.

'No.' Sky watched as the phased-array teased out details, turning the smudge into something with density and shape. 'It's much too big for that. I think it is the ghost ship. Nothing else that big could be trailing us.'

'How big is it, exactly?'

'Wide enough,' Sky said. 'But I can't get an estimate of the length. She's keeping her long axis aligned with us, just as if she still has some navigational control.' He tapped keys, squinting as more numbers popped up next to the echo. 'Width is spot-on for a Flotilla ship. Same profile too – the radar's even picking out some asymmetries which line up with where we'd expect the antennae clusters to be on the forward sphere. She doesn't seem to be rotating – they must have sapped her spin for some reason.'

'Maybe they got bored with gravity. How far away is she?'

'Sixteen thousand klicks. Which, considering we've come half a light second, isn't bad. We can reach her in a few hours at minimal burn.'

They debated it for a few minutes, then agreed that a quiet approach made the best sense now. The fact that the ship had kept herself aligned with the Flotilla meant that it was no longer possible to think of her as a drifting, dead hulk. She still had some autonomy. Sky doubted that there could be living crew aboard her, but it must now be considered a real – if remote – possibility. At the very least, automated defence systems might be functioning. And they might or might not take kindly to the swift, unannounced approach of another ship.

'We could always announce ourselves,' Gomez said.

Sky shook his head. 'They've been following us quietly for the best part of a century without ever making any attempt to talk to us. Call me paranoid, but I think that just might suggest they're not particularly interested in visitors, whether they announce themselves or not. Anyway, I don't believe for one minute that there's anyone aboard. She has some systems still running, that's all – just enough to keep her antimatter safe and make sure she doesn't drift too far from the Flotilla.'

'We'll know soon enough,' Norquinco said. 'As soon as we get within visual range. Then we can take a look at the damage.'

The next two hours passed agonisingly slowly. Sky modified their approach trajectory to take them slightly to one side, so that the phased-array could begin to pick out some elongation in the radar echo. The results, when they came in, were no surprise: the *Caleuche* fitted the profile of a Flotilla ship almost exactly, except for some small but puzzling deviations.

'Probably damage marks,' Gomez said. He looked at the radar echo, bright now, and the absence of anything else on the screen only served to emphasise how isolated they were. There had not even been any response from the rest of the Flotilla; no sign that any of the other ships had noticed anything going on. 'You know,' he said, 'I'm almost disappointed.'

'You are?'

'At the back of my mind I kept wondering if it wouldn't turn out to be something stranger.'

'A ghost ship isn't strange enough for you?' Sky adjusted the course again, swinging them around to approach the ship from the other side.

'Yes, but now that we know what it is, so many possibilities are ruled out. You know what I used to think it might be? Another ship sent out from home, much later than the Flotilla – something a lot faster and more advanced. Sent here to follow us at a safe distance – maybe just to observe us, but perhaps to step in and help us if anything went seriously wrong.'

Sky did his best to look contemptuous, but secretly he shared some of Gomez's feelings. What if it got worse, he thought? What if the *Caleuche* turned out to have no useful supplies on her at all, and no safe way of exploiting her antimatter? Just because something had spawned a myth did not automatically mean it had to contain anything of substance. He thought of the original *Caleuche*: the ghost ship which was to supposed to haunt the waters of southern Chile, the dead aboard her trapped in an eternal and grisly celebration, sending mournful accordion music out across the waves. But whenever the real *Caleuche* was sighted, it always had the magical ability to turn into a seaweed-infested lump of rock or a piece of driftwood.

Maybe that was all they were going to find now.

The final hour passed as slowly as those that had preceded it, but at the end of that time they were rewarded with their first faint glimpse of the ghost ship. It was a Flotilla vessel all right – they might have been approaching the *Santiago*, except that the *Caleuche* had no lights on her at all. They could only see her by shining the shuttle's searchlights, and by the time they had come closer – to within a few hundred metres of the drifting ship's hull – they could pick out details just one tantalising spot at a time.

'Command looks intact,' Gomez said as the searchlight tracked across the huge sphere at the front of the ship. The sphere was dotted with dark windows and sensor apertures, with comms antennae protruding from circular pits, but there was no sign of any inhabitation or power. The front hemisphere of the globe was pored with countless tiny impact craters, too, but that was also the case for the *Santiago*, and at first glance this ship seemed not to have suffered any more damage than that.

'Take us further down the spine,' Gomez said. Norquinco, behind them, was busying himself with more schematics of the old ship.

Sky tapped the thrusters lightly, sending them cruising slowly past the command sphere and then the cylindrical module that followed it, the one that would have held the *Caleuche*'s own shuttles and freight stores. Everything looked exactly as it should have done. Even the entry ports were situated in the same places.

'I'm not seeing any major damage,' Gomez said. 'I thought the radar showed—'

'It did,' Sky said. 'But the damage was all on the other side. We'll loop around to the engine section and come back up.'

They tracked slowly down the spine, the searchlights revealing circles of bright detail amidst greater darkness. Sleeper module after sleeper module passed by. Sky had started counting them, half expecting that some might be missing, but after a while he knew there was no point. They were all still present and correct; the ship – apart from the minor abrasive weathering – was still exactly as she had been when launched.

'There's something about her, though,' Gomez said, squinting. 'Something that doesn't look quite right.'

'I don't see anything out of place,' Sky said.

'She looks normal enough to me, too,' Norquinco said, looking up momentarily from the far more interesting prospect of his data schematics.

'No, she doesn't. She looks like she's not quite in focus. Can't you see that as well?'

'It's a contrast effect,' Sky said. 'Your eyes can't deal with the difference in illumination between the lit and unlit parts.'

'If you say so.'

They continued in silence, not really wanting to acknowledge that what Gomez had said was true and that there *was* something not quite right about the *Caleuche*. Sky remembered what Norquinco had told him about the ghost ship story; how it was said that the old sailing ship had been able to surround itself with mist so that no one ever saw it clearly. Thankfully, Norquinco refrained from reminding him of that. It would have been about all he could take.

'There's no infra-red from the sleeper berths,' Gomez said eventually, when they were most of the way down the spine. 'I don't think that's a good sign, Sky. If the berths were still operational, we'd see the infra-red from the cooling systems. You can't keep something cold without making heat somewhere else. The *momios* can't still be alive.'

'Then cheer up,' Sky said. 'You wanted a ghost ship; now you've got one.'

'I don't think there are ghosts on it, Sky. Just a lot of dead people.'

They passed the end of the spine, where it coupled to the propulsion unit. They were closer now – only ten or fifteen metres from the hull – and the details should have been pin-sharp, but there was no denying what Gomez had pointed out. It was as if the ship was being seen behind a screen of slightly mottled glass, blurring every edge except the one between the ship and space. It was as if the ship had melted slightly and then resolidified.

It wasn't right.

'Well, there's no sign of major damage to the propulsion section,' Gomez said. 'The antimatter must still be inside, kept penned on residual power.'

'But there's no sign of any power at all. Not a single running light.'

'So she's turned off every non-essential system. But the antimatter *has* to be inside her, Sky. That means whatever happens here, our journey won't have been completely in vain.'

'Let's see what she looks like on the other side. We know there's something wrong with her there.'

They curved around, executing a hairpin turn beyond the gaping mouths of the exhaust vents. Gomez was right, of course – the antimatter had to be there, and that had never been in doubt. Had her engines exploded the way the *Islamabad*'s had done, there would have been nothing left at all except for a few unusual trace elements added to the interstellar medium. There must still be enough antimatter inside her to slow down the whole ship, and all the containment systems must still be operating normally. Sky's people could use that antimatter. They could either experiment with it in place, testing the *Caleuche*'s engines in ways they would never have risked with their own ship – thereby finding a way to squeeze more efficiency from them – or they could use the ghost ship as a single huge rocket stage, tethering it to the *Santiago* and enormously boosting their deceleration curve, before discarding the *Caleuche* at some still significant fraction of the speed of light. But there was a third way that appealed to Sky more than either of those two possibilities: gain experience with the handling of antimatter aboard the ghost ship, and then transfer only the reservoir back to the *Santiago*, where it could be connected up to their own fuel supply. That way, no fuel would be wasted decelerating dead mass – and the whole thing could be kept reasonably secret as well.

Now they turned around and began to track up the other side. The radar scans had forewarned them that there would be some kind of asymmetry; something different about this side of the ship, but when they saw what it was they had trouble believing their eyes. Gomez swore softly, Sky echoing the sentiment with a slow nod. All along her length, from the bulbous command sphere to the rear of the propulsion section, the ship's side had erupted outwards in a queasy leprous mass: a froth of globular blisters packed as dense as frogspawn. They studied it wordlessly for at least a minute, trying to rationalise what they saw with what they believed the sixth ship to be.

'Something strange happened here,' Gomez said, the first to speak. 'Something very, very strange. I'm not sure I like it, Sky.'

'You think I like it any more than you do?' Sky answered.

'Take us away from the hull,' Norquinco said, and for once Sky obeyed him without question. He tapped the thrusters, pushing the shuttle out to two hundred metres. They waited silently until they could get a better look at the ghost ship. The more he looked at it, the more it looked like blistered flesh, Sky thought, or possibly badly healed scar tissue. It certainly did not look like anything he would have expected.

'There's something up ahead,' Gomez said, pointing. 'Look. Tucked away near the command sphere. It doesn't seem to be part of her.'

'It's another ship,' Sky said.

They crept closer, nervously probing the dark mass with searchlights. Almost lost within the bubbled explosion of fleshlike hull was a much smaller, intact spacecraft. It was the same size as their shuttle – the same basic shape, in fact. Only its markings and details were different.

'Shit. Someone got here ahead of us,' Gomez said.

'Perhaps,' Sky said. 'But they could have been here for decades.'

'He's right,' Norquinco said. 'I don't think it's one of ours, though.'

They crept closer to the other shuttle, wary now of a trap, but the other ship looked equally as dead as the much larger craft alongside it. It was guyed to the *Caleuche* – moored to her hull by three lines which had been fired into the hull with penetrating grapples. That was standard emergency equipment on a shuttle, but Sky had never expected to see it used in this fashion. There were intact docking hatches on the *Caleuche*'s far side – why had the shuttle not used those?

'Bring us in nice and slowly,' Gomez said.

'I'm doing it, aren't I?' But docking with the derelict shuttle was much harder than it looked – their own thrusters kept blowing it away. When the two ships did finally come together, it was with a good deal more violence than Sky would have wished. But the hatch seals held, and he was able to divert some of their own power to the other craft, booting up its own systems which must only have been sleeping. It felt too easy, but the shuttles had always been designed for complete compatibility across the docking systems of all the ships.

Lights stammered on and the airlock began to establish equal pressure on either side of the lock.

The three of them suited up and strapped on the specialised sensors and comms equipment they had brought along for the expedition, and then each took one of the security-issue machine-guns with torches strapped to them which Sky had appropriated. With Sky leading they floated through the connecting tunnel until they were emerging in a well-lit shuttle cabin superficially similar to the one they had left. There were no cobwebs or floating veils of dust to suggest that any time at all had passed since the shuttle had been vacated. A few status displays had even come back online.

There was, however, a body.

It was spacesuited, and very obviously dead – although none of them wanted to look at the grinning skull behind the faceplate longer than necessary. But the figure seemed not to have died violently. It was seated calmly in the pilot's position, with the two arms of the spacesuit folded across its lap, gloved fingers touching as if in quiet prayer.

'Oliveira,' said Gomez, reading the nameplate on the helmet. 'That's a Portuguese name. He must have come from the *Brazilia*.'

'Why did he die here?' said Norquinco. 'He had power, didn't he? He could have made it back home.'

'Not necessarily.' Sky pointed to one of the status displays. 'He might have had power, but he certainly didn't have any fuel. He must have burned it all getting here in a hurry.'

'So what? There must still be dozens of shuttles inside the *Caleuche*. He could have ditched this one and taken another one back.'

Gradually they formed a working hypothesis to explain the dead man's presence. No one had heard of Oliveira, but then again he *was* from another ship and he would certainly have vanished many years ago.

Oliveira must have learned about the *Caleuche* as well, perhaps in the same way Sky had: a slow accretion of rumour which had eventually hardened into fact. Like Sky, he had decided to go back and see what the ghost ship had to offer, perhaps hoping to score some massive advantage for his own crew, or – just possibly – himself. So he had taken a shuttle, secretly, one presumed, but he had also decided to make the dash at a high fuel expenditure. Perhaps he was forced into this strategy by a narrow window in which his absence would not be noticed. It must have seemed a reasonable risk to take. After all, as Gomez had said, there would be fuel supplies aboard the *Caleuche* – other shuttles, for that matter. Getting back ought not to have proved problematic.

Yet evidently it had.

'There's a message here,' Norquinco said, peering over one of the read-outs.

'What?'

'Like I said. A message. From, um, him, I presume.' Before there was any time for Sky to ask him, Norquinco had called up the message, translated it through several software protocols and then piped it through to their suits, with the audio track playing over the normal comms channel and the visual component projected as a head-up display, making Oliveira's ghostly form seem to join them in the cabin. He was still wearing the same suit he had died in, but now he had the helmet visor raised over the helmet's crown so that they could see his face properly. He was a young-looking man with dark skin and a look in his eyes of both horror and profound resignation.

'I think I'm going to kill myself,' he said, speaking Portuguese. 'I think that's what I'm going to do. I think it's the only sensible course of action. I think, in my circumstances, that's what you would have done. It won't take any great courage on my behalf. There are a dozen painless ways to kill yourself in a spacesuit. Some of them are better than painless, I'm told. I'll know soon enough. Let me know if I died with a smile on my face, won't you? I hope I do. Anything else just wouldn't be fair, would it?'

Sky had to concentrate to follow the words, but it was not insurmountably difficult. As security officer it had been his duty to have a good grasp of the Flotilla's other languages – and Portuguese was a lot closer to Castellano than Arabic.

'I'm going to assume that you – whoever you are – have come here for much the same reason I did. Sheer, unadulterated greed. Well, I can't really blame you for that – and if you've come here for some infinitely more altruistic reason, you must accept my very humble apologies. But somehow I doubt it. Like me, you must have heard about the ghost ship and wondered what she had on board worth plundering. I just hope that you didn't make quite the same miscalculation I did, concerning her fuel supplies. Or maybe you did, and you already understand exactly what I'm talking about, because you've been inside her. And if you do need the fuel, and you haven't been inside her yet, well – I'm sorry – but you have something of a disappointment coming. If that's quite the word I'm looking for.' He paused, glancing down at the top of his suit's life-support tabard. 'Because she isn't quite what you thought she is. She's infinitely less. And infinitely more. I should know. I've been inside her. We both have.'

'Both?' Sky said, aloud.

It was as if the man had heard him. 'Or maybe you haven't found Lago yet. Did I mention Lago? I should have – my mistake. He used to be a good friend of mine, but now I think he's the reason I'm going to kill myself. Oh, I can't get home without fuel, I know that – and if I asked for help, I'd be executed for coming here in the first place. Even if the *Brazilia* didn't hang me, the other ships would. No – there's really no way out. But like I said, it's Lago that really has me convinced. Poor, poor Lago. I only sent him to look for fuel. I'm really so very sorry.' Suddenly, as if snapping out of a muse, he seemed to look all of them in the eye individually. 'Did I tell you the other thing? That if you can, you should leave immediately? I'm not sure I did.'

'Turn the fucking thing off,' Sky said.

Norquinco hesitated, then obeyed, leaving Oliveira's ghost hanging there with them, frozen in the middle of his soliloquy.

THIRTY-FOUR

'Get out,' Chanterelle said when the forward door had opened and Quirrenbach's bruised and bloodied face had looked out. 'You too,' she said, pointing the barrel of her gun at the other heavy, who – unlike his associate – was still conscious.

'I think I owe you thanks,' I said, doubtfully. 'You were hoping I'd survive that attack, weren't you?'

'It occurred to me you might. Are you all right, Tanner? You look a bit on the pale side.'

'It'll pass.'

Chanterelle's three friends, who had maintained a surly detachment, had Voronoff; he was already safely aboard Chanterelle's car, nursing a shattered wrist. They'd given me barely more than a sideways glance, but I couldn't blame them for that. The last time we had met had been when I put bullets through their legs.

'You're in grave trouble,' Quirrenbach said, once we were in the car and he had Chanterelle's undivided attention. 'Whoever you are.'

'I know who she is,' Voronoff said, gazing down at his wrist while the car deployed a little servitor to tend the wound. 'Chanterelle Sammartini. She's a hunt player. One of the better ones, whatever that means.'

'How the hell would you know?' Quirrenbach said.

'Because she was with Mirabel the night he tried to take me down. I had her checked out.'

'Not very thoroughly,' Quirrenbach said.

'Piss off. You were meant to be shadowing him, in case you forgot.'

'Now, now, boys,' Zebra said, the gun resting casually on her knee. 'Just because they've taken your big guns from you, no need to squabble.'

Quirrenbach stabbed a finger at Chanterelle. 'Why the hell is Taryn still holding a gun, Sammartini? She's one of us, in case you didn't realise.'

'According to Tanner she stopped working for you some time ago.' Chanterelle smiled. 'Frankly, I'm not surprised.'

'Thanks,' Zebra said, guardedly. 'I'm not sure why you trust me, though. I mean, I definitely wouldn't.'

'Tanner said I should. Tanner and I have had a few points of disagreement, but I'm prepared to take his word on this one. Can I trust you, Zebra?'

She smiled. 'You're not exactly spoilt for choice, are you?' Then added, 'Well, Tanner – what happens now?'

'Exactly what Quirrenbach had in mind all along,' I said. 'A trip to Refuge.'

'You're joking, aren't you? It has to be a trap.'

'It's also the only way I'll ever end this. Reivich knew that as well, didn't he?'

Quirrenbach said nothing for a few moments, as if uncertain of whether he had won, or had in fact lost beyond all hope of redemption. Then, weakly, he said, 'We'll need to go to the spaceport, then.'

'Eventually, yes.' Now it was my turn to play games. 'But there's somewhere I want to go first, Quirrenbach. Somewhere closer. And I think you know how to take me there.'

I pulled out the vial of Dream Fuel which Zebra had given me; spent now. 'Ring any bells?'

I hadn't known for certain that Quirrenbach would be any closer to the Dream Fuel production centre than Vadim, but it was a reasonable guess. Vadim had carried supplies of the drug, but his little empire of extortion was restricted to the Rust Belt and its orbital environs. Only Quirrenbach moved freely between Chasm City and space, and the chances were therefore good that Quirrenbach brought the vials up with him on a recent visit.

Which meant Quirrenbach might know where the source was.

'Well?' I said. 'Am I warm?'

'You don't know what you're getting into, Tanner. No idea at all.'

'You just let me worry about that. You worry about taking us there.'

'Taking us where?' Chanterelle asked.

I turned to her. 'I made a deal with Zebra that I'd continue the investigations her sister was making when she vanished.'

Chanterelle looked at Zebra. 'What happened?'

Zebra spoke quietly. 'My sister asked one too many awkward questions about Dream Fuel. Gideon's goons got to her, and I've wanted to know why ever since. She wasn't even trying to close them down, just to find out more about the source.'

'It most certainly won't be what you're expecting,' Quirrenbach said, looking at me beseechingly. We were brachiating away from Grand Central Station, where we'd dropped off Voronoff and the heavies. 'For pity's sake, Tanner. See sense. There's no need for you to embark on some personal crusade, especially given that you're an outsider. You have no need – or right, for that matter – to meddle in our affairs.'

'He doesn't need one,' Zebra said.

'Oh, spare me the righteous indignation. You use the substance yourself, Zebra.'

She nodded. 'And so do a few thousand other people, Quirrenbach. Largely because we haven't got much of a choice.'

'There's always a choice,' he said. 'So the world looks a little bleaker without implants? Fine; learn to live with it. And if you don't like that, there's always the hermetic approach.'

Zebra shook her head. 'Without implants we start dying of old age; most of us anyway. With them we've got to live half a life cowering inside machines. Sorry, but that's not what I call much of a choice. Not when there's a third way.'

'Then you have precisely no moral grounds for objecting to the existence of Dream Fuel.'

'I'm not objecting, you tedious little man. I just want to know why the stuff isn't easier to get hold of, when we need it so badly. Every month it gets harder to find; every month I end up paying Gideon – whoever he might be – a little more for his precious elixir.'

'Such is the nature of supply and demand.'

'Shall I hit him for you?' Chanterelle said brightly. 'It'd be no trouble at all.'

'That's very generous of you,' Zebra said, evidently pleased that she and Chanterelle had found some common ground. 'But I think we want him conscious for the time being.'

I nodded. 'At least until he gets us to the manufacturing centre. Chanterelle? Are you still sure you want to come with us?'

'I'd have stayed at the station if I wasn't, Tanner.'

'I know. But it'll be dangerous. We might not all walk out of this.'

'He's right,' Quirrenbach said, who must still have hoped that I could be talked out of this. 'I'd give the matter some serious thought if I were you. Wouldn't it make more sense to come back later, with a properly prepared squad; even something vaguely resembling a plan?'

'What, and miss having your undivided attention?' I said. 'It's a big city, Quirrenbach, and an even bigger Rust Belt. Who's to say I'd ever see you again if we agreed to postpone this little trip?'

He snuffled. 'Well, you still can't force me to take you there.'

I smiled. 'You'd be surprised. I could force you to do just about anything if I wanted to. It's really just a matter of nerves and pressure points.'

'You'd torture me, is that it?'

'Let's just say I'd apply some very convincing arguments.'

'You bastard, Mirabel.'

'Just drive, will you?'

'And watch *where* you're driving,' Zebra said. 'You're taking us way too low, Quirrenbach.'

She was right. We were skirting the Mulch now, skimming only a hundred or so metres above the tops of the highest slums – and the ride consisted of sickening undulations due to the lack of threads at this altitude.

'I know what I'm doing,' Quirrenbach said. 'So just shut up and enjoy the ride.'

Suddenly we were skimming down a slum canyon, descending a single long thread that vanished into murky, caramel-brown water at the canyon's end. Fires burned in the ramshackle structures either side of us and steam-powered boats huffed and puffed out of our way as the cable-car approached the waterline.

'I was right, wasn't I,' I said to Quirrenbach. 'You and Vadim were a team, weren't you?'

'I think the relationship might be better characterised as one of master and slave, Tanner.' He worked the controls with quite some skill, retarding our descent the instant before we hit the muddy water. 'That act of Vadim's – the big, stupid thug? It wasn't an act.'

'Did I kill him?'

He rubbed at one of his own bruises. 'Nothing Dream Fuel couldn't fix, in the end.'

I nodded. 'That's more or less what I thought. So what is it, Quirrenbach? You must know. Is it something they synthesise?'

'That depends what you mean by synthesise,' he said.

'So he went mad,' Sky said. 'He got stuck here and knew there was no way he could get back home safely. There isn't any mystery to that.'

'Do you think Lago was real?' asked Gomez.

'Maybe. It doesn't really matter. We still have to go in, don't we? If we find the man, we'll know that much is true. Look,' Sky did his best to sound reasonable, 'what if he killed Lago? They might have had some argument, after all. Maybe it was killing his friend that drove him insane.'

'Assuming, of course, that he was insane,' Gomez said. 'And not simply a perfectly rational man who'd had to confront something terrible.'

They decoupled from Oliveira's shuttle a few minutes later, leaving the dead man inside as they had found him. Cautiously, with gentle taps of thrusters, they flew around to the undamaged side of the Flotilla ship.

'The damage is confined totally to the other side,' Gomez said. 'It doesn't look like the kind of hull scorching the *Santiago* sustained when the *Islamabad* blew up, but the geometric extent is similar, wouldn't you say?'

Sky nodded, remembering his mother's shadow burned into the side of the hull. Whatever had happened to the *Caleuche* had been shockingly different, but it was clearly symptomatic of damage of some sort.

'I don't see how there can be a connection,' he said.

There was a chime from the console – one of the automated warning systems Norquinco had rigged up. Sky glanced towards the other man. 'What is it? Do we have a problem?'

'Not a technical one, but, um, still a problem. Someone's just scanned us with a phased-array.'

'Where did it originate from? The Flotilla?'

'That direction, but not precisely. I think it must be another shuttle, Sky – making a similar approach to the one we used.'

'Probably following our thrust trail,' Gomez said. 'Well – how long have we got?'

'I can't tell you, not without bouncing a radar beam off them as well. Could be a day; could be six hours.'

'Shit. Well, let's get in and see what we can find.'

They had moved around to the undamaged side of the command sphere now and were casting around for a suitable docking port. Sky did not want to try and land inside the *Caleuche*, but there were still plenty of surface points where the shuttle could have anchored itself for a quick crew transfer. Normally the larger ship would have responded to the shuttle's approach by activating one of the ports; guidance lights would have begun to shine and the port would have extended restraining clamps to guide the shuttle home the last few metres. If there had been any power left at all inside her, those docking mechanisms should still have woken up, even after decades of inactivity. But though the shuttle chirped its approach signal, nothing happened.

'All right,' Sky said. 'We'll do what Oliveira did: use the grapples.'

He positioned the shuttle over a docking port and let the grapples whip away and bury themselves silently in the *Caleuche*'s hull. Then the shuttle began to pull itself in, like a spider ascending a strand of cobweb. The grapples did not appear to have anchored themselves firmly – they began to give, like hooks in flesh – but they would hold for now. Even if the shuttle broke loose from its mooring while they were inside the larger ship, the shuttle's autopilot would prevent it from drifting away.

Still suited up, they moved to the airlock again and cycled through to vacuum. Sky's positioning had been excellent; their own docking seal was exactly aligned with the ship's, with the manual controls set to one side in a recessed panel. Sky knew from his experience on the *Santiago* that the airlocks were well-designed; even if no one had opened it in years, the manual opening controls should still function perfectly.

It was simple. There was a lever you turned by hand, and that would crank aside the outer door. Once inside the exchange chamber, there would be a more comprehensive panel with pressure gauges and controls to allow the space to be flooded with air from within the ship. If there was no pressure on the other side, the door would allow him to pass even more easily.

He reached out his gloved hand, ready to grasp the lever. But as soon as his fingers closed around the metal he knew something was wrong.

It didn't feel like metal at all.

It felt like meat.

412

Even as he was registering that, another part of his mind had sent the signal to his hand to apply the twisting motion that would begin to crank the door aside. But the lever was incapable of being rotated. Instead, it just deformed in his hand, stretching as if made out of jelly. He looked closer, nearly pressing his faceplate against the panel. Now that he could see it properly, it was obvious why the lever would never work: it blended in to the rest of the panel. In fact, all the controls were like that; merging seamlessly with the background. He looked at the door, carefully now. There was no seam between it and its frame – only a smooth continuation.

It was as if the *Caleuche* was made of grey dough.

The cable-car had become just another vessel on the brown ooze of the Mulch river. Quirrenbach was using the car's arms to propel it along against the sluggish flow, reaching out on either side to brush against the overhanging slums. He had obviously done it many times before.

'We're approaching the edge of the dome,' Zebra said, pointing ahead and up.

She was right. One of the merged domes of the Mosquito Net came down here, with the slums scraping against its filthy brown surface. It was hard to believe that overhanging, sloped ceiling had ever been transparent.

'The inner or outer edge?' I said.

'The inner,' Zebra said. 'Which means . . .'

'I know what it means,' I said, before she could answer. 'Quirrenbach's taking us towards the chasm.'

THIRTY-FIVE

The canyon grew darker as we approached the Net, the overhanging structures more precariously stacked above us until they arched over forming a rough-hewn tunnel dripping unspeakable fluids. Hardly anyone lived here, even given the squalid population pressure of the Mulch.

Quirrenbach took us underground; powerful lights glared from the front of the cable-car. Occasionally I saw rats moving in the gloom, but no sign of any people; human or pig. The rats had reached the city aboard Ultra ships – genetically engineered to serve aboard the ships as cleaning systems. But a few had escaped centuries ago, shrugging off their gloss of servitude, reverting to feral type. They scampered away from the bright ellipses cast by the cable-car's lights, or swam quickly through the brown water trailing vee-shaped wakes.

'What is it you want, Tanner?' Quirrenbach said.

'Answers.'

'Is that all? Or are you after your own private supply of Dream Fuel? Go on. You can tell me. We're old friends, after all.'

'Just drive,' I said.

Quirrenbach pushed us forward, the tunnel branching and bifurcating. We were in a very old part of the city now. Decrepit as this underground warren seemed, it might not have changed very much since the plague.

'Is this really necessary?' I said.

'There are other ways in,' he said. 'But only a few people know about this one. It's discreet, and it'll make you seem like someone with a right to get to the heart of the action.'

Presently he brought the car to a halt. I hadn't realised it, but Quirrenbach had steered it over a tongue of dry ground which rose out of the water near one stained and dilapidated wall, festered in grey mould.

'We have to get out here,' he said.

'Don't even think about trying anything,' I said. 'Or you'll become an interesting new addition to the décor down here.'

414

But I allowed him to lead us out anyway, leaving the cable-car parked on the mudspit. There were deep grooves in the ground where the skids of other cars had created impressions. Evidently we were not the first to use this landing place.

'Follow me,' Quirrenbach said. 'It isn't far.'

'Do you come here often?'

Now there was a note of honesty in his voice. 'Not if I can help it. I'm not a big player in the Dream Fuel operation, Tanner. Not a very large cog. I'd be a dead man if some people knew I was even bringing you this far. Can we make this a discreet visit?'

'That depends. I told you I wanted some answers.'

He had reached something in the wall. 'There's no way I can take you close to the centre of things, Tanner – start understanding that, will you? It just isn't possible. It's best if you go in alone. And don't even think about causing trouble. You'd need more than a few guns for that.'

'So what are you taking us to?'

But instead of answering, he yanked at something hidden in the slime-covered grime of the wall, hauling aside a sliding panel. It was almost above our heads; a rectangular hole two metres long.

Wary of tricks – like Quirrenbach using the hole as an escape route – I went first. Then I helped Quirrenbach up, and then Chanterelle. Zebra came last, casting a wary eye behind her. But no one had followed us, and the only eyes watching us depart belonged to the tunnel's rats.

Inside, we crawled, crouching, along a low, square steel-lined tunnel for what seemed like hundreds of metres, but which was probably only a few dozen. I had lost all sense of direction now, but part of my mind insisted that we had all along been approaching closer and closer to the edge of the chasm. It was possible that we were beyond the fringe of the Mosquito Net now. Above us, beyond only a few metres of bedrock, might have been poisonous atmosphere.

But eventually, just when my back was beginning to ache with something that went beyond discomfort into real, paralysing pain, we emerged into a much larger chamber. It was dark at first, but Quirrenbach turned on a matrix of ancient lights stapled to the ceiling.

Something ran from one end of the chamber to the other, emerging from one wall and vanishing into the other. It was a dull silver tube, three or four metres wide, like a pipeline. Jutting from it on one side, at an oblique angle, was what looked like a branch of the same tube: exactly the same diameter, but terminating in a smooth metal end-cap.

'You recognise this, of course,' Quirrenbach said, indicating the longer part of the pipe.

'Not exactly,' I said. I had expected one of the others to say something, but no one seemed any wiser than me.

'Well, you've seen it many times.' Then he walked up to the pipe. 'It's part of the city's atmospheric supply system. There are hundreds of pipes like this, reaching down into the chasm, down into the cracking station. Some carry air. Some carry water. Some carry superheated steam.' He knuckled the pipe, and now I noticed that there was an oval panel in the part which jutted out, more or less the same size as the panel which he had found in the wall. 'This one normally carries steam.'

'What is it carrying now?'

'A few thousand atmospheres. Nothing to worry about.'

Quirrenbach placed his hands on the panel and slid it aside. It moved smoothly, revealing a curve of dark green glass, framed by clean silver metal inset with controls. They were marked with a very old style of writing; words which were almost but not quite Norte.

Amerikano.

Quirrenbach tapped a few keys, and I heard a series of distant thumps. Moments later, the whole pipe thrummed as if sounding a monstrously low note. 'That's the steam flow being rerouted along another network, for inspection mode.'

He pressed a button and the thick green glass whisked aside, revealing a mass of bronze machinery, nearly filling the bore of the pipe. At either end it was all pistons and accordioned sections, festooned with pipes and metal whiskers, servo-motors and black suction pads. It was difficult to tell whether it was ancient – something from the Amerikano period – or much more recent, cobbled together since the plague. Either way, it didn't look very reliable. But in the middle of the machine was a skeletal space equipped with two large padded seats and some rudimentary controls. It made a wheeler look like an exercise in spaciousness.

'Start talking,' I said.

'It's an inspection robot,' Quirrenbach said. 'A machine for wriggling along the pipe, checking for leaks, weak spots, that kind of thing. Now it's . . . well, you figure it out.'

'A transportation system.' I studied it myself, wondering what were the chances of riding it and surviving. 'Clever, I'll give you that. Well – how long will it take to go where it goes?'

'I've ridden it once,' Quirrenbach said. 'It wasn't any picnic.'

'You didn't answer my question.'

'An hour or two to get down below the mist layer. Same time to come back. I don't advise that you spend too long when you get there.'

'Fine. I'm not planning to. Will I pass for someone in the know if I take this thing down?'

He eyed me over. '*Only* people in the know arrive via this route. With Vadim's coat you'll pass for a supplier, or at least someone in the loop – provided you don't open your mouth too much. Just tell whoever meets you that you've come to see Gideon.'

416

'Sounds like it couldn't be easier.'

'Oh, you'll manage. A monkey could run the machine. Sorry. No offence intended.' Quirrenbach smiled quickly and nervously. 'Look, it's easy. You won't have any trouble telling when you've arrived.'

'No,' I said. 'Especially as you're coming along for the ride.'

'Bad move, Tanner. Bad move.' Quirrenbach started looking around for moral support.

'Tanner's right,' Zebra said, shrugging. 'It would make a kind of sense.'

'But I've never been close to Gideon. They won't necessarily take me any more seriously than they take Tanner. What am I supposed to say when they ask why we're there?'

Zebra glared at him. 'Improvise, you spineless little shit. Say you heard some rumours about Gideon's health, and you wanted to check them out for yourself. Say there are stories about the quality of the final product reaching the streets. It'll work. It's the same kind of story that got my sister close to Gideon, after all.'

'You've no idea whether she got close at all.'

'Well, just do your best, Quirrenbach – I'm sure Tanner will be there to give you all the moral support you need.'

'I'm not doing it.'

Zebra waved her gun towards him. 'Want a rethink?'

He looked down the barrel of the gun, then at Zebra, his lips pursed. 'Damn you as well, Taryn. Consider your bridges well and truly burned, as far as our professional relationship is concerned.'

'Just get in the machine, will you?'

I turned to Zebra and Chanterelle. 'Take care. I don't think you'll be in any danger here, but keep an eye out in any case. I expect to be back within a few hours. Can you wait that long?'

Zebra nodded. 'I could, but I'm not planning to. There's enough room in that thing for three of us, if Chanterelle can hold the fort back here.'

Chanterelle shrugged. 'Can't say I'm exactly looking forward to spending a few hours up here on my own, but I think I'd rather be here than down there. I guess this is one you owe to your sister?'

Zebra nodded. 'She'd have done the same for me, I think.'

'Way to go. I just hope the trip's worth it.'

I spoke to Chanterelle now. 'Don't put yourself in any more danger than necessary. We can find our own way out of here if we have to, so if anything happens . . . you know where the car's parked.'

'Don't worry about me, Tanner. Just take care of yourself.'

'It's a habit of mine.' I slapped Quirrenbach on the shoulder, with all the hearty bonhomie I'd have liked to have felt. 'Well, are you ready? You never know. You might be inspired on the way down; something even more depressing than normal.'

He looked at me grimly. 'Let's get this over with, Tanner.'

Despite what Zebra had said, there was barely room for two people in the inspection robot, and it was a painful squeeze to accommodate a third. But Zebra's articulation was not fully human, and she had an uncanny ability to fold herself into what space remained, even if the process caused her some discomfort.

'I hope to God this isn't going to take too long,' she said.

'Start her up,' I told Quirrenbach.

'Tanner, there's still . . .'

'Just start the fucking thing up,' Zebra said. 'Or the only composing you'll be doing is decomposing.'

That did the trick; Quirrenbach pressed a button and the machine rumbled into life. It clunked its way along the pipe, moving like a slow mechanical centipede. The machine's front and back moved jerkily, the suction grips hammering the wall, but the part where we were seated travelled relatively smoothly. Though there was no steam in the tunnel now, the metal sides were hot to the touch and the air was like a steady belch from the depths of hell. It was cramped and dark except for the weak illumination from the basic controls placed in front of our seats. The pipeline walls were smooth as glacial ice, polished that way by the monstrous pressures of the steam. Though the pipe had started out horizontally, it soon began to curve, gently at first, and then to something that was not far off vertical. My seat was now a deeply uncomfortable harness from which I was hanging, constantly aware of the kilometres of pipe that fell away below me and the fact that all that was stopping me dropping into those depths was the suction pressure of the cups arrayed around the inspection robot.

'We're heading for the cracking station, aren't we?' Zebra said, raising her voice above the machine's hammering progress. 'That's where they make it, isn't it?'

'Makes a kind of sense,' I said, thinking about the station. That was where all the pipes came from: the city's great taproots. The station nestled deep in the chasm, lost under the perpetual mist layer. It was where titanic conversion machines sucked in the hot, raw gaseous poison rising from the chasm's depths. 'It's out of the way of any jurisdiction, and the people who crew it must have the kinds of advanced chemical tools they'd need to synthesise something like Dream Fuel.'

'You think everyone who works down there is in on the secret?'

'No; probably just a small clique of workers producing the drug, unknown to anyone else in the station. Isn't that the case, Quirrenbach?'

'I told you,' he said, adjusting a control so that our rate of progress increased, the hammering becoming a harsh tattoo. 'I was never allowed close to the source.'

'So how much do you know, exactly? You must know *something* about the synthesis process.'

418

'Why would it interest you if I did?'

'Because it doesn't make much sense to me,' I said. 'The plague made a lot of things stop working. Implants – complicated ones, anyway. Sub-cellular nano robots; medichines – whatever you want to call them. That was bad news for the postmortals, wasn't it? Their therapies usually needed some intervention by those little machines. Now they had to make do without.'

'And?'

'Suddenly something else shows up which almost does the job just as well. Better, in some ways. Dream Fuel's childishly easy to administer – it doesn't even need to be tailored to the person it's being used on. It heals injuries and it restores memories.' I thought back to the man I'd seen thrashing on the ground, desperate for a tiny drop of the scarlet stuff even though the plague had already subsumed half his body. 'It even confers protection from the plague for people who haven't discarded their machines. It's almost too good to be true, Quirrenbach.'

'Meaning what?'

'Meaning I'm wondering how something that *useful* ended up being invented by criminals. It would be hard enough to imagine it being created before the plague, even when the city still had the means to create wonderful new technologies. Now? There are parts of the Mulch where they haven't even got steam power. And while there might be a few high-tech enclaves in the Canopy, they're more interested in playing games than developing miracle cures. But that seems to be exactly what they've ended up with – even if the supply is currently a little tight.'

'It didn't exist before the plague,' Zebra said.

'Too much of a coincidence,' I said. 'Which makes me wonder if they might both have the same origin.'

'Don't flatter yourself that you're the first to have had that thought.'

'No, I wouldn't dream of it.' I scraped sweat from my brow, already feeling like I'd been in a sauna for an hour. 'But you have to admit the point is valid.'

'I wouldn't know. I don't profess any great interest in the matter.'

'Not even when the fate of the city might depend on it?'

'Except it wouldn't, would it? A few thousand postmortals, ten at the most. Dream Fuel may be a precious substance to those who've acquired a dependence on it, but for the majority it's of no consequence whatsoever. Let them die; see if I care. In a few centuries everything that's happened here will be little more than a historical footnote. I, meanwhile, have considerably larger and more ambitious fish to fry.' Quirrenbach adjusted some more controls, tapping a gauge here and there. 'But then I'm an artist. All this is mere diversion. You, on the other hand . . . I confess I really don't understand you, Tanner. Yes, you may now have some obligation to Taryn, but your interest in Dream Fuel was apparent from the moment we searched Vadim's cabin. By your own admission you came here to murder Argent Reivich, not to sort out a minor supply shortage in our sordid little drugs industry.'

'Things became a little more complicated, that's all.'

'And?'

'There's something about Dream Fuel, Quirrenbach. Something that makes me think I've seen it before.'

But there *was* a way in. Sky, Norquinco and Gomez located it by undocking and scouting around the ship for another thirty minutes, until they found the hole that Oliveira and Lago must have used to get inside. It was only a few tens of metres from where Oliveira's shuttle was parked; near the point where the spine connected to the rest of the ship. It was so small that Sky had missed it completely on the first pass, lost as it was amongst the blisterlike protuberances on the ship's ruined side.

'I think we should go back,' Gomez said.

'We're going in.'

'Didn't you listen to a word of what Oliveira said to us? And doesn't it worry you in the slightest that this ship appears to be made of something strange? That it looks like a crude attempt at copying one of *our* ships?'

'It worries me, yes. It also makes me even more determined to get inside.'

'Lago went inside as well.'

'Well, I guess we'll just have to keep a look-out for him, won't we?' Sky was ready now. He had not bothered removing his helmet since the last time he had gone through the airlock.

'I also want to see what's inside,' Norquinco said.

'One of us at least should stay aboard the shuttle,' Gomez said. 'If the ship that swept us with the radar gets here in the next few hours, it would be good to have someone ready to do something about it.'

'Fine,' said Sky. 'You just volunteered for the job.'

'I didn't mean . . .'

'I don't care what you meant. Just accept it. If Norquinco and I run into anything that needs your input, you'll be the first to know.'

They left the shuttle, using thruster harnesses to cross the short distance to the *Caleuche*'s hull. When they landed near the hole it was like touching down on a softly yielding mattress. They stood up, gripped to the ship by the adhesive soles of their shoes.

There was an obvious and vital question that Sky had almost managed not to ask himself, but now it must be dealt with. There was no way in his experience that the hull of a ship could be transmuted to this sponge-like state. Metal simply did not do that by itself – even if it had been exposed to the glare of an antimatter explosion. No; whatever had happened here was far beyond his experience. It was as if the ghost ship's hull had been replaced, atom by atom, by some new and disturbingly pliant substance which replicated the old details in only the broadest terms. There was shape and texture and colour, but no function, like a crude cast of the original ship. Was he even standing on the *Caleuche*, or was that just another flawed assumption?

Sky and Norquinco walked to the lip of the hole, poking the muzzles of their guns into the gloom. The lip was ragged and scorched with heat marks and had the puckered, wrinkled look of a half-closed mouth. A metre or two below the surface, however, the wall of the hole was lined with a thick, fibrous mass which glistened gently as their torchlight skittered across it. Sky thought he recognised that mass; it was a matrix of extruded diamond fibres embedded in epoxy, a quick-drying paste that could be used to repair hull punctures. Oliveira had probably located a weak spot on the *Caleuche* – he must have taken the time to make a density map before selecting this point – and had then used something to cut through, a laser torch or even the exhaust of his shuttle. Once he had bored the shaft, he had lined it with the spray-on sealant from his shuttle's emergency kit, presumably to prevent it collapsing shut.

'We'll go in this way,' Sky said. 'Oliveira must have found the most promising entry point; there's no sense in duplicating his effort when we've so little time to spare.'

They checked that the inertial compasses built into their suits were functioning accurately, defining their current position as a zero point. The *Caleuche* was neither spinning nor tumbling, so the compasses would prevent them getting lost once they were inside, but even if the compasses proved unreliable, they would be able to retrace their way to the wound in the hull, deploying a line as they went.

Sky halted in his thoughts, wondering why he had just thought of the hole in the hull as a wound?

They went in, Sky first. The hole led into a rough-walled tunnel which cut straight into the hull, threading down for ten or twelve metres. Normally by this point – had the ship been the *Santiago* – they would have passed right through the hull's outer integument and would be passing through a series of narrow service cavities, squeezing between the multitude of data-lines, power cables and refrigerant pipes; perhaps even one of the train tunnels. There were, Sky knew, points where the hull was more or less solid for several metres, but he was reasonably sure this was not one of them.

Now the sides of the shaft, or tunnel, or however he preferred to think of it, had become harder and more glossy – less like elephant hide and more like insect chitin. He shone his torch light ahead into the gloom, the beam sliding off the shining black surface. Then – just when it looked like it would end abruptly – the shaft jogged violently to the right. Fully suited, with the additional bulk of the thruster harness, it was an effort to squeeze round the bend – but at least the smooth-sided shaft would not snag his suit or rip away any vital component. He looked back and saw Norquinco following him, the other man's slightly larger bulk making the exercise even less easy.

But now the shaft widened out, and after it intersected with another the going became even easier. Periodically Sky stopped and asked Norquinco to ensure that the line was spooling out properly and that the line was still taut, but the inertial compasses were still functioning properly, recording their movements relative to the entry point.

He tried the radio. 'Gomez? Can you read me?'

'Loud and clear. What have you found?'

'Nothing. Yet. But I think we can say with some confidence that this isn't the *Caleuche*. Norquinco and I must be twenty metres into the hull, and we're still moving through what feels like solid material.'

Gomez waited for a few moments before answering. 'That doesn't make any sense.'

'No, not if we keep on assuming this is a ship like our own. I don't think it is. I think it's something else – something we definitely weren't expecting.'

'Do you think it came from home – that it's something they sent out after we left?'

'No. They've only had a century, Gomez. I don't think that's enough time to come up with something like this.' They slithered deeper. 'It doesn't feel like anything human. It doesn't even feel like we're inside a machine.'

'But whatever it is, it just happens to look exactly like one of our own ships from the outside.'

'Yes – until you get close. My guess is it altered its shape to mimic us; some kind of protective camouflage. Which worked, didn't it? Titus . . . my father . . . he always thought there was another Flotilla ship trailing us. That was disturbing, but it could be explained by some event which had happened in the past. If he'd known there was an alien ship following us, it would have changed everything.'

'What could he have done about it?'

'I don't know. Alert the other ships, perhaps. He would have assumed it meant us harm.'

'Maybe he was right.'

'I don't know. It's been out here an awfully long time. It hasn't done much in all those years.'

Something happened then – a noise that they felt, rather than heard, like the sonorous clang of a very large bell. They were floating through vacuum so the reverberation must have been transmitted through the hull.

'Gomez – what the hell was that?'

His voice came through weakly. 'I don't know – nothing happened here. But you're suddenly a lot fainter.'

After we had been descending for nearly two hours, I saw something below, far down the vertical pipeline.

It was a faint golden glow, but it was coming closer.

422

I thought about the episode I had just had. I could still taste Sky's fear as he entered the *Caleuche*; hard and metallic like the taste of a bullet. It seemed very much like the fear I was feeling myself. We were both descending into darkness; both of us seeking answers – or rewards – but also knowing that we were placing ourselves in great danger, with very little idea of what lay ahead. The way the episode resonated with my present experience was chilling. Sky had gone beyond simply infecting my mind with images. Now he seemed to be steering me, shaping my actions to commemorate his own ancient deeds; like a puppeteer whose strings stretched across three centuries of history. I clenched my fist, expecting that the episode would have caused blood to gush from my hand.

But my palm was perfectly dry.

The inspection robot continued its clunking descent. Nothing that Quirrenbach had done lately had made the machine move any faster. It was unbearably hot now and I reckoned none of us would have survived more than three or four hours before dying of heat exhaustion.

But it *was* getting lighter.

I soon saw why. Below us, but coming closer now, was a section of pipeline walled in filthy glass. Quirrenbach made the machine rotate so that none of us were easily visible by the time the robot began to descend through the transparent section. I still had a good view of the dark chamber we were moving through, a cavernous room infested with looming curved machinery: huge stovelike pressure vessels connected by networks of shiny intestinal tubing and festooned with slender catwalks. Rows of mighty turbines stretched away across the floor like sleeping dinosaurs.

We had reached the cracking station.

I looked around, wondering at the silent vastness.

'There doesn't seem to be anyone on duty,' Zebra said.

'Is this normal?' I asked.

'Yes,' Quirrenbach said. 'This part of the operation more or less runs itself. But I'd hated to have picked the one day when there was someone on duty who noticed the three of us coming down.'

Many dozens of pipes, much like the one I was descending, reached to the ceiling, a wide circular sheet of glass spoked by dark metal supports, and then rammed through it. Beyond it was only a stained soot-grey fog, for the cracking station lay deep in the chasm and was usually covered by the mist. Only when the fog parted momentarily, cleaved open by the chaotic thermals which spiralled up the chasm's side, could I see the immense sheer walls of planetary rock rising above. Far, far above was the antenna-like extension of the stalk, where Sybilline had taken me to watch the mist jumpers. That had been only a couple of days ago, but it felt like an eternity.

We were far beneath the city now.

The inspection robot continued its descent. I had expected that we would stop somewhere near the floor of the cracking chamber, but Quirrenbach carried us slowly below the turbine floor, into darkness again. Perhaps there was another chamber to the cracking station, below the one we had passed through. I managed to cling to this idea for a while . . . until I knew that we had descended much too far for that to be the case.

The pipe we were in reached completely through the cracking station.

We were going deeper still. The pipe made a few jogging changes of direction, almost threading sideways at one point, and then we were descending again. It was so hot now that it was an effort to stay awake. My mouth was so dry that just thinking of drinking a glass of cold water was too much like mental torture. Somehow I stayed conscious, however – knowing I would need clarity of mind when I arrived wherever the robot was taking me.

Another thirty or forty minutes, then I saw another light below me.

It looked like journey's end.

'You too. Norquinco – check the . . .' But even as he said it, Sky directed his torch back up the shaft they had come down, and he could see how the previously taut line was now beginning to drift, as if it had length to spare. It must have been severed somewhere further up the shaft.

'Let's get out now,' Norquinco said. 'We haven't come very far – we can still find our, um, way back.'

'Through solid hull? That line didn't cut itself.'

'Gomez has cutting equipment on the shuttle. He can get us out if he knows where we are.'

Sky thought about it. Everything that Norquinco said was correct, and any right-thinking person would now be doing their utmost to get back to the surface. Part of him wanted to do that as well. But another, stronger part was even more determined to understand what this ship – if it was a ship – actually meant. It was alien; he felt utterly sure of that now – and that meant it was the first evidence of alien intelligence any human being had ever witnessed. And – staggering though the odds were – it had latched itself onto his Flotilla, finding the slow, frail arks in the immensity of space. Yet it had chosen not to contact them, instead shadowing them for decades.

What would he find inside it? The supplies he had hoped to find aboard the *Caleuche* – even the unused antimatter – might be insignificant prizes compared to what really lay here, waiting to be exploited. Somehow or other this ship had matched velocities with the Flotilla, achieving eight per cent of lightspeed – and something made him certain that the alien ship had not found that in any way difficult; that achieving this speed had probably been trivially simple. Somewhere inside this worm-ridden solid black hull there had to be recognisable mechanisms which had pushed her up to her current speed, and which he might be able to exploit – not necessarily understand, he admitted that – but certainly exploit.

And perhaps, much more than that.

He had to go deeper. Anything less than that would be failure. 'We're carrying on,' he told Norquinco. 'For another hour. We'll see what we find in that time, and we'll be careful not to get lost. We still have the inertial compasses, don't we?'

'I don't like it, Sky.'

'Then think about what you might learn. Think of how this ship might work – its data networks; its protocols; the very paradigms underpinning her design. They might be exquisitely alien; as far beyond our modes of thinking as – I don't know – a strand of DNA is beyond a single-chain polymer. It would take a special kind of mind to even begin to grasp some of the principles which might be at play. A mind of unusual calibre. Don't tell me you aren't the slightest bit curious, Norquinco.'

'I hope you burn in hell, Sky Haussmann.'

'I'll take that as a yes.'

The inspection robot shunted itself into another branch of the pipe, just like the one where Quirrenbach had found it back on the surface. The hammering of the suction pads slowed, quietened and stopped, the maching ticking quietly to itself. We were in complete darkness and silence except for distant, thunder-like sounds of superheated steam roaring through remote parts of the pipe network. I touched the hot metal of the pipe with the tip of my finger and felt the faintest of tremors. I hoped that it didn't mean there was a wall of scalding, thousand-atmosphere steam slamming towards us.

'It's still not too late to turn back,' Quirrenbach said.

'Where's your sense of curiosity?' I said, feeling like Sky Haussmann goading Norquinco forwards.

'About eight kilometres above us, I think.'

That was when someone slid back a panel on the side of the pipe and looked at all three of us as if we were a consignment of excrement someone had sent down from Chasm City.

'I know you,' the man said, nodding at Quirrenbach. Then he nodded once at me and once at Zebra. 'I don't know you. And I certainly don't know you.'

'And I don't know you from shit,' I said, getting my own word in before the man who had opened the pipe could get the edge over me. I was already heaving myself out of the robot, relishing the chance to stretch my legs for the first time in hours. 'Now show me where I can get a drink.'

'Who are you?'

'The man asking you for a fucking drink. What's wrong? Did someone seal up your ears with pig shit?'

He seemed to get the message. I'd gambled that the man wouldn't be a major player in whatever operation was going on down here and that a large part of his job description would consist of taking abuse from visiting thugs a little higher up the food chain.

'Hey, no offence, man.'

'Ratko, this is Tanner Mirabel,' Quirrenbach said. 'And this is . . . Zebra. I phoned through to say we were on our way down to see Gideon.'

'Yeah,' I said. 'And if you didn't get the message, that's your fucking problem, not mine.'

Quirrenbach appeared impressed enough to want to join in. 'That's fucking right. And get the fucking man the . . . get the man the fucking drink he asked for.' He wiped a sleeve across his parched lips. 'And get me one too, Ratko, you, er, fucking little cocksucker.'

'Cocksucker? That's good, Quirrenbach. Really good.' The man patted him on the back. 'Keep on taking the assertiveness lessons – they're really paying off.' Then he looked at me with what was almost an expression of sympathy, a professional-to-professional thing. 'All right. Follow me.'

We followed Ratko out of the pipe room. His expression was difficult to read, since his eyes were hidden behind grey goggles sprouting various delicate sensory devices. He wore a coat patterned like Vadim's, but of shorter cut, its patches a little less rough and more lustrous.

'So, friends,' Ratko said. 'What brings you down here?'

'Call it a quality inspection,' I said.

'No one's complaining about quality, that I hear of.'

'Then maybe you haven't been listening too well,' Zebra said. 'The shit's getting harder and harder to track down.'

'Really?'

'Yeah, really,' I said. 'It's not just the Fuel shortage. There's a problem with purity. Zebra and I supply Fuel to a portfolio of clients all the way up to the Rust Belt. And we're getting complaints.' I tried to sound menacingly reasonable. 'Now – that *could* mean a problem somewhere in the chain of supply between here and the Belt – there are a lot of weak links in that chain, and believe me, I'm investigating them all. But it could also mean the basic product is getting degraded. Cut, watered, whatever you want to call it. That's why we're making this a personal visit, with Mister Quirrenbach's assistance. We need to see that there's still such a thing as high-quality Dream Fuel being manufactured in the first place. If there isn't, someone's been lying to someone else and there's going to be more shit hitting the fan than in a Force Ten shitstorm. Either way, it's bad news for someone.'

'Hey, listen,' Ratko said, holding up his hands. 'Everyone knows there are problems at source level. But only Gideon can help you with the why.'

I threw out a line. 'I hear he enjoys his privacy.'

'He doesn't have much choice, does he?'

I laughed, trying to make it sound as convincing as possible, without understanding what I was laughing at. But the way the man with the goggles had said it, he obviously thought he had made a joke of some kind.

'No, I guess not.' I changed the tone of my voice, now that he and I had established some shaky grounds for mutual respect. 'Well, let's put our relationship on a more friendly footing, shall we? You can put my doubts about the immediate quality of the product to rest by providing me with – how shall we say – a small commercial sample?'

'What's wrong?' Ratko said, reaching into his coat and handing me a small, dark-red vial. 'Got high on your own supply once too often?'

I took the vial, Zebra passing me her wedding-gun. I knew I had to do it; that only Fuel would enable me to unlock the final secrets of my past.

'You know how it is,' I said.

Sky and Norquinco pushed onwards, always keeping a wary eye on the inertial compasses. The shaft branched and twisted, but the head-up displays on their helmets always showed their positions relative to the shuttle, together with the route they had so far followed, so there was no real possibility of getting lost, even if they might encounter obstructions on the way out. The route they had taken led more or less to the middle of the ship, and now they were heading roughly forward, towards where the command sphere should be. They had been carrying on for perhaps five minutes when there was another bell-like reverberation, as if the entire hull had been struck like a gong. It seemed fractionally stronger this time.

'That's it,' Norquinco said. 'Now we're going back.'

'No, we're not. We lost the line already, and we already have to cut ourselves out. Now it just means we have some more to cut through.'

Reluctantly now, Norquinco followed him. But something was changing. Their suit sensors were beginning to pick up traces of nitrogen and oxygen instead of hard vacuum. It was as if air were slowly building up inside the shaft; as if the two clangs they had heard had been part of some immense alien airlock.

'There's light ahead,' Sky said when the air pressure had reached one atmosphere and begun climbing beyond it.

'Light?'

'Sickly yellow light. I'm not imagining it. It's like it's coming from the walls themselves.'

He turned off his torch light, ordering Norquinco to do likewise. For a moment they were in near darkness. Sky shivered, feeling again the old, never-entirely-vanquished terror of darkness which the nursery had instilled in him. But then his eyes began to adjust to the ambient illumination and it was almost as if they still had the torches on. Better, in fact, for the pale yellow light reached far ahead of them, revealing the tract of the tunnel for tens of metres.

'Sky? There's something else.'

'What?'

'I suddenly feel like I'm crawling downhill.'

He wanted to laugh; wanted to put Norquinco down, but he felt it too. Something was definitely pressing his body against one side of the shaft. It was soft now, but as he crawled further (and now it really was a kind of crawling), it increased in strength, until he felt almost as if he was back aboard the *Santiago*, with her spin-generated artificial gravity. But the alien ship had been neither spinning nor accelerating.

'Gomez?'

The answer, when it came, was incredibly faint. 'Yes. Where are you?'

'Deep. We're somewhere near the command sphere.'

'I don't think so, Sky.'

'That's what our inertial compasses say.'

'Then they must be wrong. Your radio emissions are coming from halfway down the spine.'

For the second time he felt terror, but now it had nothing to do with the absence of light. They had not been crawling for anywhere near the length of time needed to get that far down the ship. Had the hull somehow reshaped itself while they were inside, ferrying them helpfully along? The radio emissions must be correct, he thought – Gomez must have a reasonably accurate fix on their positions from signal triangulation, even though the mass of the intervening hull made his estimate imprecise. But that meant the inertial compasses had been lying almost as soon as they entered the ship. And now they were moving through some kind of static gravitational field; something intrinsic to the hull rather than an illusion created by acceleration or rotation. It appeared able to tug them in arbitrary ways depending on the geometry of the shaft. No wonder the inertial compasses had given false readings. Gravity and inertia were so subtly entwined that you could hardly bend one without bending the other.

'They must have complete control of the Higgs field,' Norquinco said, wonderingly. 'It's a pity Gomez isn't here. He'd have a theory by now.'

The Higgs field, Norquinco reminded Sky, was something that was believed to pervade all space; all matter. Mass and inertia were not actually intrinsic properties of the fundamental particles at all, but were simply effects of the drag imposed on them as they interacted with the Higgs field – like the drag imposed on a celebrity trying to cross a room full of admirers. Norquinco seemed to think that the builders of the ship had found a way to let the celebrity slip through unmolested – or to impede its progress even further. It was as if the builders could turn up or turn down the density of admirers, and restrict or enhance their ability to pester the celebrity. That was, he knew, a hopelessly crude way of imagining something that Gomez – and perhaps even Norquinco – might be able to begin to glimpse without layers of metaphor, seeing straight to the glistening mathematical heart of it, but for Sky it was sufficient. The builders could manipulate gravity and inertia as easily as they manipulated the sickly yellow light, and perhaps without giving it much more thought.

428

Which meant, of course, that his hunch had been right. If there was something aboard this ship which could teach him that technique, imagine what it could do for the Flotilla – or for the *Santiago*, anyway. They had been trying to shed mass for years, so that they could delay their deceleration to the last possible moment. What if they could just turn the *Santiago*'s mass off, like a light switch? They could enter Swan's system at eight per cent of the speed of light and come to a dead stand-still in orbit around Journey's End, cutting their speed in an instant. Even if nothing that dramatic was possible, any reduction in the ship's inertia – even if it were only a few per cent – would have been welcome.

The external air pressure was now well above one and a half atmospheres, although it was climbing less quickly now. It was warm, heavy with moisture and some other trace gases which, while harmless, would not have been present in the same ratios in the air Sky normally breathed. Gravity reached a plateau of half a gee; it occasionally ducked below that value, but it was never higher. And the sickly yellow light was now bright enough to read by. Now and then they had to crawl across an indentation in the floor of the shaft which was full of thick, dark liquid. There were traces of it everywhere: a bloodlike red smear sliming every surface.

'Sky? This is Gomez.'

'Speak up. I can hardly hear you.'

'Sky; listen to me. We'll have company within five hours. There are two shuttles approaching us. They know we're here. I risked a radar bounce off them to get a distance fix.'

Fine; by now he would probably have done the same thing himself. 'Leave it at that. Don't speak to them or do anything that would let them identify us as having come from the *Santiago*.'

'Just get out of there, will you? We can still make a run for it now.'

'Norquinco and I aren't done yet.'

'Sky, I don't think you realise—'

He broke off the link, more interested in what lay ahead. Something was coming towards them, moving down the same shaft. It transported itself with grublike oscillations of its fattened pink-white body, like a maggot.

'Norquinco?' he said, bringing his gun to the fore and pointing it down the shaft, 'I think someone's come to welcome us aboard.' He wondered how frightened he sounded.

'I can't see anything. No; wait – now I can. Oh.'

The creature was only the size of an arm; not really large enough to do either of them any physical harm. It lacked any obviously dangerous organs; no jaws that Sky could see. At the front was only a crownlike frill: translucent tendrils which waved ahead of the creature. Even if they had been venomous, he was still safe in his suit. The creature appeared to have neither eyes nor manipulative limbs. He repeated these reassuring observations to himself,

429

examined his state of mind and was slightly disappointed to find that he was still just as frightened as before.

But the maggot did not seem particularly frightened by the newcomers. It simply halted and waved its ghostly tendrils in their direction. The thing's pale pink segmented body blushed a deeper shade of red, and then an arterial red secretion oozed from between the segments, forming a fresh scarlet puddle beneath it. Then the puddle extended tendrils of its own, creeping forward as if running downhill. Sky felt his sense of what was vertical shift dizzyingly, as if there had been a local change in the direction of gravity. The red fluid trickled towards them like a scarlet tide, and then it was flowing up and around their suits. For a moment Sky felt that he had been turned upside down, and he was falling. The red veil passed over his faceplate, as if seeking a way into his suit. Then it passed.

Gravity returned to normal. Breathing hard, still terrified, he watched the puddle of red return to the maggot and then seep back into the creature. The maggot was red for a moment, then the blush slowly faded back to pink.

Then the maggot did something very odd, not turning itself in the shaft, but reversing itself; the tendrils retracting into the body at one end and popping out the other. The creature undulated back into the shaft's yellow depths. It was as if nothing at all had happened.

Then a voice spoke to them. It boomed through the walls at Godlike volume, and it sounded too deep to be human.

'It's good to have some company,' it said, in Portuguese.

'Who are you?' Sky said.

'Lago. Come and see me, please; it isn't very far now.'

'And what if we choose to leave you?'

'I'll be sad, but I won't stop you.'

The reverberations of the Godlike voice died down, all as it had been before the maggot had arrived. The two of them were breathing hard, as if they had just been sprinting. Long moments passed before Norquinco spoke. 'We're going back to the shuttle. Now.'

'No. We're going onwards, just as we told Lago we would.'

Norquinco gripped Sky's arm. 'No! This is insanity. Did you just erase what happened from your shortterm memory?'

'We were invited further into the ship by something which could already have killed us if it had that in mind.'

'Something which called itself Lago. Even though Oliveira . . .'

'Didn't actually say that Lago was dead.' Sky fought to hold the fear from his voice. 'Just that something had happened to him. Personally, I'm interested in finding out what that something was. And also anything else this ship, or whatever it is, might be able to tell us.'

'Fine. Then go ahead. I'm going back.'

'No. You're staying here, coming with me.'

Norquinco hesitated before answering. 'You can't force me.'

'No, but I can certainly make it worth your while.' Now it was Sky's turn to place his hand on the other man's arm. 'Use your imagination, Norquinco. There must be things here that could shatter every paradigm we've ever recognised. At the very least there must be things here that can get us to Journey's End ahead of the other ships, perhaps even give us a tactical advantage when they arrive behind us and start contesting territorial rights.'

'You're aboard an alien spacecraft and all you can think of is petty human issues like squabbles over land rights?'

'Believe me, those things won't seem so petty in a few years.' He grasped Norquinco's arm even tighter, feeling the layers of suit fabric compress beneath his grip. 'Think, man! Everything could stem from this one moment. Our whole history could be shaped by what happens here and now. We aren't small players, Norquinco; we're colossi. Grasp that, just for a instant. And start thinking of the kinds of rewards that come to men who make history happen. Men like us.' He thought back to the *Santiago*; of the hidden room where he kept the Chimeric infiltrator. 'I've already made longterm plans, Norquinco. My safety is guaranteed on Journey's End, even if events turn against us. If that should happen, I'd also arrange for your own safety, your own security. And if things didn't turn against us, I could make you a very powerful man indeed.'

'And if I should turn around now, and go back to the shuttle?'

'I wouldn't hold it against you,' Sky said softly. 'This is a terrifying place, after all. But I wouldn't guarantee you any sanctuary in the years that lie ahead.'

Norquinco dislodged Sky's grip from his arm, looking away until he had found his answer. 'All right. We go on. But we don't spend more than an hour in this place.'

Sky nodded, though the gesture was wasted. 'I'm pleased, Norquinco. I knew you were a man who'd see sense.'

They advanced. The going became easier now, as if the shaft was always sloping downwards – it hardly required any effort at all to slither down it. Sky thought of the way the red fluid had moved around him. The local control of gravity was so precise that the fluid had looked alive, flowing like a vastly accelerated slime mould. The creatures that had built the ship had learned to do far more than alter the Higgs field. They could play it like a piano.

Whatever they are, he thought – whether they were all like the maggot – they had to be millions of years in advance of humanity. The Flotilla must seem inexpressibly primitive to them. Perhaps they had not even been sure it was the product of intelligent thinking at all. And yet it had *interested* them.

The shaft opened out into a huge, smooth-walled cavern. They had emerged a little way up the side of one of its scalloped walls, but the place was so thick with cloying vapour that it was difficult to see the other side. The chamber was bathed in foetid yellow light and the floor was hidden beneath an enormous lake of red fluid which must have been many metres deep. There were dozens of maggots in the lake, some of them almost completely submerged. Many of them were of slightly different sizes and shapes to the one they had seen so far. Some were much larger than a man, and their end-tendrils included specialised appendages and, perhaps, sensory organs. One in particular was looking at Sky and Norquinco now, with a single human-looking eye on the end of a stalk. But by far the largest maggot sat in the middle of the lake, its pale pink body rising metres from the water; tens of metres long. It turned the end of its body towards them, a small crown of tendrils waving frondlike in the air.

There was a mouth beneath the frond; absurdly small against the size of the maggot. It was human in shape, fringed in red, and when it spoke – emitting an immense, booming voice – it formed human sound shapes.

'Hello,' it said. 'I'm Lago.'

I held the vial up to the light for a moment before slipping it into the breach. The way the red fluid twinkled, the way it flowed sluggishly one moment and then with blinding speed the next . . . it reminded me far too much of the red lake at the heart of the *Caleuche*. Except that there never was a *Caleuche*, was there? Just something much stranger, to which the ghost ship myth had attached itself like a parasite. And hadn't that memory of Sky's always been there, at the back of my mind? I had recognised Dream Fuel from almost the moment I saw it.

There was enough in that red lake to drown in, I thought.

I slammed the wedding gun against my neck and pushed the Fuel into my carotid artery. There was no rush; no hallucinogenic transition. Fuel was not a drug in that sense; it acted globally across the brain rather than hitting any single region. It wanted only to arrest cellular decay and to repair recent damage; bringing memories back into focus and re-establishing connective pathways that had recently been broken. It seemed to tap into a recent map of what *had* been, as if the body carried a lingering field which changed more slowly than the cellular patterns themselves. That was why Fuel was able to fix both injuries and memories just as easily, without the drug itself knowing anything about physiology or neuro-anatomy.

'Quality shit,' Ratko said. 'I only use the best myself, man.'

'Then you're saying that not everything that comes out of here is as good?' Zebra asked.

'Hey, like I said. One for Gideon.'

Ratko led the three of us along a series of twisting, makeshift tunnels. They had been equipped with lights and a rudimentary floor, but they were more or less bored through solid rock. It was as if the complex had been tunnelled back into the chasm wall.

'I keep hearing rumours,' I said. 'About Gideon's health. Some people think that's why he's letting the cheap stuff hit the streets. Because he's too ill to manage his own lines of supply.'

I hoped I had not said anything which would betray my ignorance of the true situation. But Ratko just said, 'Gideon's still producing. That's all that matters right now.'

'I won't know until I see him, will I?'

'He's not a pretty sight, I hope you realise.'

I smiled. 'Word gets around.'

THIRTY-SIX

While Ratko was leading us towards Gideon I allowed the next episode to happen. That was how it seemed, anyway: that now it was up to me when it happened, as if it were simply a case of digging through three-hundred-year-old memories, sorting them into something like chronological order and letting the next lot flood my mind. There was nothing jarringly unfamiliar about it any more. It was as if I half knew exactly what was going to happen, but just hadn't given the matter much recent thought, like a book I hadn't opened in a long time, but whose story could never completely surprise me.

Sky and Norquinco were climbing down from the shaft where they had emerged, negotiating the chamber's slippery, scalloped sides until they were standing near the shore of the red lake.

The maggot which rested in the lake, tens of metres away, had just introduced itself as Lago.

Sky steeled himself. He felt a tremendous sense of fear and strangeness, but he was convinced that it was his destiny to survive this place.

'Lago?' he said. 'I don't know. From what I gather, Lago was a man.'

'I'm also that which existed before Lago.' The voice, though loud, was calm and strangely lacking in menace. 'This is difficult to say through Lago's language. I am Lago, but I am also Travelling Fearlessly.'

'What happened to Lago?'

'That's also not easy. Excuse me.' There was a pause while gallons of red fluid gushed out of the maggot into the lake, and then gallons more flowed up into the maggot. 'That's better. Much better. Let me explain. Before Lago there was just Travelling Fearlessly, and Travelling Fearlessly's helper grubs, and the void warren.' The tendrils seemed to point out the cavern's sides and ceiling. 'But then the void warren was damaged, and many poor helper grubs had to be . . . there isn't any word in Lago's mind for this. Broken down? Dissolved? Degraded? But not lost fully.'

Sky looked at Norquinco, who had not said a word since entering the chamber. 'What happened before your ship was damaged?'

'Yes – ship. That's it. Not void warren. Ship. Much better.' The mouth smiled horribly and more red fluid rained out of the creature. 'It's a long time ago.'

'Start at the beginning. Why were you following us?'

'Us?'

'The Flotilla. The five other ships. Five other void warrens.' Despite his fear, he felt anger. 'Christ, it's not that difficult.' Sky held up his fist and opened his fingers one at a time. 'One. Two. Three. Four. Five. Understand? Five. There were five other void warrens, built by us – by people like Lago – and you chose to follow us. I'd like to know why.'

'That was before the damage. After the damage, there were only four other void warrens.'

Sky nodded. So it understood something of what had happened to the *Islamabad*, anyway. 'Meaning you don't remember it as well?'

'Not very well, no.'

'Well, do your best. Where did you come from? What made you latch onto our Flotilla?'

'There've been too many voids. Too many for Travelling Fearlessly to remember all the way back.'

'You don't have to remember all the way back. Just tell me how you got where you did.'

'There was a time when there were just grubs, even though there had been many voids. We looked for other types of grub but didn't find any.' Meaning, Sky assumed, that there had been a time when Travelling Fearlessly's people had crossed space, but not encountered any other form of intelligence.

'How long ago was this?'

'Ages ago. One and a half turns.'

Sky felt a chill of cosmic awe. Perhaps he was wrong, but he strongly suspected that the maggot was talking about rotations of the Milky Way; the time taken for a typical star at the current distance from the galactic centre to make one complete orbit. Each of those orbits would take more than two hundred million years . . . meaning that the grub's racial memory – if that was what it was – encompassed more than three hundred million years of space travel. The dinosaurs had not even been a sketch on the evolutionary drawing board three hundred million years ago. It was a span of time that made humans, and everything humans had done, seem like a layer of dust on the summit of a mountain.

'Tell me the rest.'

'Then we did find other grubs. But they weren't like us. Not like grubs at all, really. They didn't want to . . . tolerate us. They were like a void warren but . . . empty. Just the void warren.'

A ship with no living things aboard it.

'Machine intelligences?'

The mouth smiled again. It was quite obscene, really. 'Yes. Machine intelligences. Hungry machines. Machines that eat grubs. Machines that eat us.'

Machines that eat us.

I thought of the way the maggot had said that; as if all it amounted to was a mildly irritating aspect of reality; something that had to be endured but which could not really be blamed upon anyone. I remembered my revulsion at the thought of the maggot's defeatist mode of thinking.

No – not *my* revulsion, I told myself. Sky Haussmann's.

I was right – wasn't I?

Ratko led the three of us through the crudely excavated tunnels of the Dream Fuel factory. Now and then we passed through widened chambers, dimly lit, where workers in glossy grey coats leaned over benches so densely covered with chemical equipment that they resembled miniature glass cities. There were enormous retorts filled with litres of dark, twinkling blood-red Dream Fuel. At the very end of the production line, neat racks of filled vials waited ready for distribution. Many of the workers had goggles like those worn by Ratko, specialised lenses clicking and whirring into place for each task in the production process.

'Where are you taking us?' I said.

'You wanted a drink, didn't you?'

Quirrenbach whispered, 'He's taking us to see the man, I think. The man runs all this, so don't underestimate him – even if he does have quite an unusual belief system.'

'Gideon?' Zebra asked.

'Well, that's part of it,' Ratko said, obviously misunderstanding her.

We passed through another series of production labs, and then were led into a rough-walled office where an wizened old man lay – or sat, it wasn't immediately clear – before an enormous, battered metal desk. The man was in a kind of wheelchair: a brutish, black, armoured contraption which was simmering gently, steam whispering out of leaking valves. Feedlines reached from the chair back into the wall. Presumably it could be decoupled from them when he needed to move around, gliding on the skeletal, curved-spoke wheels from which his chair was suspended.

The man's body was hard to make out under its layers of aluminised blanketing. Two exquisitely bony arms emerged, the left placed across his thigh, the right toying with the army of black control levers and buttons set into one arm of the chair.

'Hello,' Zebra said. 'You must be the man.'

He looked at each of us in turn. The man's face was skin draped over bone, worn almost parchment-thin in places, so that he had a strangely translucent quality to him. But there was still an aura of handsomeness to him, and his eyes, when they finally looked in my direction, were like two piercing chips of interstellar ice. His jaw was strong, set almost contemptuously. His lips quivered as if he were on the verge of replying.

Instead, his right hand moved across the array of controls, depressing levers and pushing buttons with a dexterity that surprised me. His fingers, though they were thin, looked as strong and dangerous as the talons of a vulture.

He lifted his hand from the levers. Something started happening inside the chair, a rapid noisy clatter of mechanical switches. When the clatter stopped the chair began to speak, synthesising his words with a series of chime-like whistles which – if you concentrated – could be understood.

'Self-evidently. What can I do for you?'

I stared at him in wonder. I had been assuming that Gideon would be many things, but I had never imagined anything like this.

'You can fix us the drinks Ratko promised,' I said.

The man nodded – the movement was economical, to say the least – and Ratko went to a cupboard set into a rocky niche in one corner of the office. He came back with two glasses of water. I drank mine in one gulp. It didn't taste too bad, considering it had probably been steam only a little while earlier. Ratko offered something to Zebra and she accepted with clear misgivings, thirst obviously suppressing concerns that we might be poisoned. I put the empty glass down on his battered metal desk.

'You're not quite what I was expecting, Gideon.'

Quirrenbach nudged me. 'This isn't Gideon, Tanner. This is, well . . .' and then he trailed off before adding weakly, 'The man, like I said.'

The man punched a new set of orders into the chair. There was more clattering – it went on for about fifteen seconds – before the voice began to pipe out again, 'No, I'm not Gideon. But you've probably heard of me. I made this place.'

'What,' said Zebra. 'This maze of tunnels?'

'No,' he said, after another pause while the chair processed the words. 'No. Not this maze of tunnels. This whole city. This whole planet.' He had programmed a pause at that point. 'I am Marco Ferris.'

I remembered what Quirrenbach had just told me about the man having an unusual belief system. Well, this certainly fitted the bill. But I couldn't help but feel some sneaking empathy with the man in the steam-driven wheelchair.

After all, I wasn't exactly sure who I was any more.

'Well, Marco,' I said. 'Answer a question for me. Are you running this place, or is Gideon in charge? In fact, does Gideon even exist?'

The chair cluttered and clacked. 'Oh, I am definitely running this place, Mister . . .' He dismissed my name with a minute wave of his other hand; too much trouble to stop mid-sentence and query me. 'But Gideon is here. Gideon has always been here. Without Gideon, I would not be here.'

'Well, why don't you take us to see him?' Zebra said.

'Because there is no need. Because no one gets to see Gideon without excellent reason. You do all your business through me, so why involve Gideon? Gideon is just the supplier. He doesn't know anything.'

'We'd still like a word with him,' I said.

'I'm sorry. Not possible. Not possible at all.' He backed the chair away from the desk, the huge curved-spoke wheels rumbling on the floor.

'I still want to see Gideon.'

'Hey,' said Ratko, stepping forward to interpose between myself and the man who thought he was Marco Ferris. 'You heard the man, didn't you?'

Ratko moved, but he was an amateur. I dropped him, leaving him moaning on the floor with a fractured forearm. I motioned to Zebra to lean down and help herself to the gun Ratko had been about to pull. Now we were both armed. I pulled out my own weapon, while Zebra aimed the other gun at Ferris, or whoever the man really was.

'Here's the deal,' I said. 'Take me to Gideon. Or take me to Gideon weeping in agony. How does that sound?'

He pushed and tugged at another set of controls, causing the chair to unplug itself from its steam feed-lines. I suppose there could have been weapons set into the chair, but I didn't think they would be fast enough to do him much good.

'This way,' Ferris said, after another, briefer period of clattering.

He took us along more tunnels, spiralling downwards again. The chair propelled itself along with a series of rapid puffs, Ferris steering it expertly through narrow chicanes of rock. I wondered about him. Quirrenbach – and perhaps Zebra – appeared to accept that he was delusional. But then if he wasn't who he claimed, who was he?

'Tell me how you got here,' I said. 'And tell me what it has to do with Gideon.'

More clattering. 'That's a long story. Luckily it's one I've often been asked to recount. That's why I have this pre-programmed statement ready.'

The chair clattered some more and then the voice recommenced: 'I was born on Yellowstone, created in a steel womb and raised by robots. That was before we could transport living people from star to star. You had to be grown from a frozen egg cell; coaxed to life by robots that had already arrived.' Ferris had been one of the Amerikanos; that much I knew already. That period was such a long time ago – before even Sky Haussmann's time – that, in my mind at least, it had begun to blend into a general historical background of sailing ships, conquistadors, concentration camps and black plagues.

'We found the chasm,' Ferris told me. 'That was the odd thing. No one had seen it from Earth's system, even with the best instruments. It was too small a feature. But as soon as we started exploring our world, there it was. A deep hole in the planet's crust, belching heat and a mixture of gases we could begin to process for air.

438

'It made very little sense, geologically. Oh, I've seen the theories – how Yellowstone must have been tidally stressed by an encounter with the gas giant in the recent past, and how all that heat energy in her core has to percolate to the surface, escaping through vents like the chasm. And perhaps there's some truth in that, though it can't be the whole story. It doesn't explain the strangeness of the chasm; why the gases are so different to the rest of the atmosphere: warmer, wetter, several degrees less toxic. It was almost like a calling card. That, in fact, is exactly what it was. I should know. I went down into it to see what was at the bottom.'

He had gone in with one of the atmospheric explorers, spiralling deeper and deeper into the chasm until he was well below the mist layer. Radar kept him from smashing into the sides, but it was still hazardous, and at some point his single-seat craft had suffered a power lapse, causing it to sink even deeper. Eventually he had bottomed out, thirty kilometres beneath the surface. His ship had landed on a layer of lightly packed rubble which filled the entire floor of the chasm. Automated repair processes had kicked in, but it would take tens of hours before the ship could carry him back up to the surface.

With nothing better to do, Ferris had donned one of the atmosphere suits – designed to cope with extremes of pressure, temperature and chemistry – and had begun exploring the layer of rubble. He called it the scree. The warm, wet, oxygen-rich air was steaming up through the gaps in the rocks.

Ferris scrambled down, finding a route through the rubble. It was perilously hot, and he could have fallen to his death many times, but he managed to keep his footing and negotiate a route which took him down hundreds of metres. The rubble pressed down on the layers below, but there were always gaps he could squeeze through; places where he could anchor pitons and lines. The thought of dying was with him always, but it was only ever an abstract thing. None of the first-born Amerikanos had ever had to understand death; they'd never had to watch people grow older than themselves and die. It was something that they did not grasp on a visceral level.

Which was good. Because if Ferris had understood the risks a little better, and understood exactly what death entailed, he probably would not have gone as deeply into the scree as he had.

And he would never have found Gideon.

They must have expanded through space until they met another species, Sky thought – some kind of robot or cyborg intelligence.

Gradually, tediously, he got something resembling a coherent story out of Travelling Fearlessly. The grubs had been a peaceable, innocent starfaring culture for many millions of years until they had run into the machines. The grubs had expanded into space for arcane reasons of their own which Travelling Fearlessly was not able to explain, except to convey that they had little to do with curiosity or a need for resources. It seemed to be simply what

439

grubs *did*; an imperative which had been hardwired into them in evolutionary antiquity. They had no overwhelming interest in technology or science for their own sakes, seeming to get by on techniques they had acquired so long ago in racial memory terms that the underlying principles had been forgotten.

Predictably, they had not fared well when their outlying colonies had encountered the grub-eating machines. The grub-eaters began to make slow incursions into grub space, pressuring the aliens to modify behaviour patterns that had been locked rigid for tens of millions of years. To survive, the grubs first had to grasp that they were being persecuted.

Even that took a million years to sink in.

Then, with glacial slowness, they began, if not to fight back, then at the very least to develop survival strategies. They abandoned their surface colonies and evacuated themselves entirely into interstellar space, the better to hide from the grub-eaters. They constructed void warrens as large as small planets. By and by they encountered the harried remnants of other species who were also being persecuted by the eaters, though they had a different name for them. The grubs appropriated technologies as it suited their needs, usually without bothering to understand them. Control of gravity and inertia had come from a symbiotic race called the Nestbuilders. A form of instantaneous communication had been bequeathed by a culture who called themselves the Jumper Clowns. The grubs had been sternly admonished when they had asked if the same principles might be extended to instantaneous travel. To the Jumper Clowns there was a fine, blasphemous line between faster-than-light signalling and travel. The one was acceptable within tightly specified parameters of usage. The other was an unspeakable perversion; a concept so distasteful that it caused refined Jumper Clowns to shrivel up and die in revulsion.

Only the most uncouth of young species failed to grasp this.

But for all the technologies that the grubs and their loose allies held, it was never enough to beat the machines. They were always swifter; always stronger. Now and then there were organic victories, but the general drift of things was always such that the grub-eaters would win.

Sky was thinking about that when Gomez called him again. The urgency in his voice was obvious despite the weakness of the signal.

'Sky. Bad news. The two shuttles have launched a pair of drones. They might just be cameras, but my guess is they'll have anti-collision warheads on them. They're on high-gee trajectories and they'll reach us in about fifteen minutes.'

'They wouldn't do it,' Norquinco said. 'They wouldn't attack us without first finding out what's going on here. They'd run the risk of destroying a whole Flotilla ship which has, um, survivors and supplies on it, just like we thought it would have.'

'No,' Sky said. 'They'd do it – if only to stop us getting hold of whatever they think's on her.'

'I don't believe it.'

'Why not? It's exactly what I'd do.'

He told Gomez to sit tight and killed the link. The fraction of a day he had imagined they would have to themselves had now compressed down to less than a quarter of an hour. It was probably not enough time to make it back to the shuttle and get away, even if there had been no obstructions to cut through. But there was still time to do something. Time, in fact, to hear the rest of what Travelling Fearlessly had to say. It might make all the difference. Trying not to think of the minutes ticking away, and the missiles haring closer, he told the grub to continue his story.

The grub was happy to oblige.

'Gideon,' the man in the chair said, after he had curtailed the telling of his story with an abrupt sequence of commands.

We had arrived in a natural cavern, high up on one side of a concave rock face. There was a ledge here, large enough to accommodate the wheelchair. I thought of pushing Ferris over the edge, but there was a sturdy-looking safety rail, uninterrupted except for a point where it allowed entrance to a caged spiral staircase that led all the way down to the chamber's floor.

'Fuck,' Quirrenbach said, looking over the edge.

'You're getting the hang of it,' I said.

I would have been as shocked as Quirrenbach, I suppose – except that I'd been forewarned by what Sky had found inside the *Caleuche*. There was another maggot down there – bigger even than the one Sky had seen, I thought – but it was alone; there were no helper grubs with it.

'This wasn't quite what I was expecting,' Zebra said.

'It's not what anyone's ever expecting,' the man in the chair said.

'Someone please tell me what the fuck that thing is,' Quirrenbach said, like someone hanging very grimly onto the last tattered shred of sanity.

'Much what it looks like,' I said. 'A large alien creature. Intelligent, too, in its own special way. They call themselves the grubs.'

Quirrenbach spoke through clenched jaw, the words emerging one at a time. 'How. Do. You. Know.'

'Because I had the pleasure of meeting one before.'

'When?' Zebra asked.

'A long, long time ago.'

Quirrenbach sounded like a man on the edge of a nervous breakdown. 'You're losing me, Tanner.'

'Believe me, I'm not quite sure I believe it all myself.' I nodded at Ferris. 'You and him – the maggot – you have quite a relationship going, don't you?'

The chair clattered. 'It's really rather simple. Gideon gives us something we need. I keep Gideon alive. What could be fairer than that?'

'You torture it.'

'Sometimes he needs encouragement, that's all.'

441

I looked down at the maggot again. It rested in a metal enclosure, a steep-sided bath that was knee-deep in brackish dark fluid, like squid ink. He was chained in place, and all around him loomed scaffolding and catwalks. Obscure, industrial-looking machines waited on gantries to be moved over the maggot. Electrical cables and fluid lines plunged into him at various points along his length.

'Where did you find him?' Zebra said.

'Here, as it happens,' Ferris told her. 'He was inside the remains of a ship. It had crashed here, at the base of the chasm, maybe a million years ago. A million years. But that's nothing to him. Though damaged and incapable of flight, the ship had kept him alive, in semi-hibernation, for all that time.'

'It just crashed here?' I said.

'There was more to it than that. It was running away from something. What, I've never really found out.'

I interrupted the sequence of sounds emanating from the chair. 'Let me guess. A race of sentient, killer machines. They'd been attacking his race – and others – for millions of years themselves; harrying them from star to star. Eventually the grubs were pushed back into interstellar space, cowering away from starlight. But something must have driven this one here – a spying mission or something.'

He punched a new statement into the chair, which piped, 'How would you know all this?'

'Like I just told Quirrenbach: me and the maggots go back a long, long way.'

I retrieved Sky's memory of what his grub had told him. The fugitive species learned that to survive at all they had to hide, and hide expertly. There were pockets of space where intelligence had not arisen in recent times – sterilised by supernova explosions, or neutron star mergers – and these cleansed zones made the best hiding places. But there were dangers. Intelligence was always waiting to emerge; new cultures were always evolving and spilling into space. It was these outbreaks of life which drew the predatory machines. They placed automated watching devices and traps around promising solar systems, ready to be triggered as soon as new spacefaring cultures stumbled upon them. So the grubs and their allies – the few that remained – grew intensely paranoid and watchful for the signs of new life.

The grubs had never really paid much attention to Earth's system. Curiosity was still something that required an effort of will for them, and it was not until the signs of intelligence around Earth became blatant that the grubs forced themselves to become interested. They watched and waited to see if the humans would make any forays into interstellar space, and for centuries, and then thousands of years, nothing happened.

But then something *did* happen, and it was not auspicious.

What Ferris had learned from Gideon dovetailed exactly with what Sky had learned aboard the *Caleuche*. Ferris's grub had been chased for hundreds of light years – across centuries of time – by a single pursuing enemy. The enemy machine moved faster than the grub ship, able to make sharper turns and steeper decelerations. The enemy made the grubs' mastery of momentum and inertia look hamfisted in the extreme. Yet, fast and strong as the killing machines were, they had limitations – it might have been more accurate to call them blindspots – which the grubs had carefully documented over the millennia. Their techniques of gravitational sensing were surprisingly crude for such otherwise efficient killers. Grub vessels had sometimes survived attacks by hiding themselves near – or within – larger camouflaging masses.

Finding the yellow world, with the killing machine closing on him fast, Gideon had seen his chance. He had located the deep geologic feature with an emotion as close to blessed joy as his neurophysiology allowed.

On the approach, the enemy had engaged him with long-range weapons. But the grub had hidden his ship behind the planet's moon, the salvo of antimatter slugs gouging a chain of craters across the moon's surface. The grub had waited until the moon's position allowed him to make a rapid, unseen descent into the atmosphere and then into the chasm, the potential hideaway he had already scouted from space. He had enlarged and deepened it with his own weapons, burrowing further and further into the world's crust. Fortunately, the thick, poisonous atmosphere camouflaged most of his efforts. But on the way in he had made a terrible error, brushing the sheer walls with his projected skein of armouring force. A billion tonnes of rubble had come crashing down, entombing him when he had meant only to hide until the killing machine moved on to seek another target. He had expected to wait perhaps a thousand years, at the longest – an eyeblink in grub terms.

It had been considerably longer than that before anyone came.

'He must have wanted you to find him,' I said.

Ferris answered, 'Yes. By then he figured the enemy must have moved on. He was using the ship to signal his presence, altering the ratios of gases in the chasm. Warming them, too. He was sending out other signals too – exotic radiation. But we didn't even detect that.'

'I don't think the other grubs did either.'

'For a long time, I think they kept in touch. I found something in his ship – something that didn't seem to be part of it, intact where all else showed signs of great antiquity and loss of function. It was like a glittering dandelion ball about a metre wide, just floating in its own chamber, suspended in a cradle of force. Quite beautiful and mesmerising to look at.'

'What was it?' Zebra asked.

He had anticipated her question. 'I tried to find out for myself, but the results I got – based on the extremely crude and limited tests I was capable of running – were contradictory; paradoxical. The thing seemed to be astonishingly dense; capable of stopping solar neutrinos dead in their tracks. The way it distorted light-rays around itself suggested the presence of an immense gravitational field – yet there was nothing. It simply floated there. You could almost reach out and touch it, except that there was a barrier all around it that made your fingers tingle.' All the while that he had been speaking, Ferris had been entering another sequence of commands into his chair, his fingers moving with the effortless speed of an arpeggiating pianist. 'I did eventually learn what it was, of course, but only by persuading the grub to tell me.'

'Persuasion?' I said.

'He has what we may think of as pain receptors, and regions of his nervous system that produce emotional reactions analogous to fear and panic. It was only a matter of locating them.'

'So what was it?' Zebra asked.

'A communicational device, but a very singular one.'

'Faster than light?'

'Not quite,' he answered me, after the usual pause. 'Certainly not in the sense that you'd recognise it. It doesn't transmit or receive information at all. It – and its brethren aboard other grub vessels – don't need to. They already contain all the information which ever *would have been* received.'

'I'm not sure I understand,' I said.

'Then let me rephrase what I've just said,' Ferris said, who must have had a reply already queued up. 'Each and every one of their communicational devices already contains every message that would ever need to be communicated to the vessel in question. The messages are locked inside it, but are inaccessible until the scheduled moment of release. Somewhat in the manner of sealed orders on an old-time sailing ship.'

'I still don't follow,' I said.

Zebra nodded. 'Me neither.'

'Listen.' The man – with what must have been considerable expenditure of effort – leaned forward in his seat. 'It's really very simple. The grubs retain a record of every message they would have sent, across all their racial history. Then, deep in their future – deep in what is still *our* future – they merge the records into *something*. What, I've never really understood – just that it's some kind of hidden machinery distributed throughout the galaxy. I confess the details have always eluded me. Only the name is clear, and even then the translation is probably no more than approximate.' He paused, eyeing us all with his peculiarly cold eyes. 'Galactic Final Memory. It is – or will be – some kind of vast, living archive. It exists now, I think, only in partial form: a mere skeleton of what it will be, millions or billions of years from now. The point, nonetheless, is simple. The archive – whatever it is – transcends time. It keeps in touch with all the past and future versions of itself, down to the present epoch and deeper into our past. It's constantly shuffling data and up and down, running endless iterations. And the grubs' communicational device is, as near as I understand it, a chip off the old block. A tiny fragment of the archive, carrying only time-tagged messages between the grubs and a handful of allied species.'

'What's to stop the grubs reading messages earlier than they were sent, and figuring out how to avoid future events?'

Again, Ferris had seen that one coming. 'They can't. The device's messages are all encoded – without the key, you can't get at them. That's the clever part. The key itself, so far as the grub understood it, would appear to be the instantaneous gravitational background radiation of the universe. When the grubs put a message into the communicational device – this is how they store them, as well – the device senses the gravitational heartbeat of the universe – the ticks of pulsars spiralling towards each other; the low moans of distant black holes devouring stars at the hearts of galaxies. It hears them all, and creates a unique signature: a key with which it encrypts the incoming message. Every device carries those messages, but they can't be read out until the device satisfies itself that the gravitational background is the same. Or *nearly* the same – it has allow for the spatial position of the message recipient, of course. That gives the devices an effective range of a few thousand light-years, apparently – once they get separated beyond that distance, they just don't recognise the background signature as being correct any more. And any attempt to fake that background, to try and predict what the future gravitational signature of the universe will be like, based on the known contributions – well, it never seems to work. The devices just fold up and die, apparently.'

For centuries, then, the grub must have been able to keep in some kind of contact with its remote allies. Then it had begun to approach the message-store limit of its own communicational device and had begun to transmit only sparingly. The enemy, it was said, had access to those messages as well – their own copies of the devices – so there was always a danger in using them. The creature had imagined that it had been lonely before, when it was being chased, but now it began to understand that it had never really known solitude. Solitude was a hard crushing force, akin to the mountains of rock above it. Yet it had stayed sane, allowing itself to talk to its allies every few tens of years, maintaining a fragile sense of kinship, that it still played a small role in the greater arena of grub affairs.

But Ferris had removed the grub from its ship, severing it with the communicational device. That must have been the start of the creature's true descent into grub madness.

'You milk it, don't you?' I said. 'Milk it for Dream Fuel. And more than that. You use its terror and loneliness. You distil those impressions and sell them.'

Ferris piped, 'We've got probes sunk into his brain, reading his neural patterns. Run them through some software up in the Rust Belt, and we get to distil it into something a human can just about handle.'

'What's he talking about?' Zebra asked.

'Experientials,' I said. 'The black kind, with a small maggot motif near the top. I tried one, as a matter of fact. I didn't know quite what to expect.'

'I've heard of them,' Zebra said. 'But I've never tried one, and I wasn't even sure they weren't an urban myth.'

'No, they're for real.' I remembered the welter of emotions that the experiential had fed into my brain, when I'd tried it aboard the *Strelnikov*. The predominant feelings had been of awful, crushing claustrophobia and fear – yet underpinned with the gut-churning sense that no matter how oppressive the claustrophia was, it was preferable to the predator-haunted void beyond. I could still taste the terror that the experiential had instilled in me; subtly alien in flavour, yet recognisable for all that. At the time I'd had trouble under-standing why people would pay to experience something like that, but now it all made much more sense. It was all about extremes of experience; anything that would blunt boredom's edge.

'What does he get for doing it?' Zebra asked.

'Relief,' said Ferris.

I saw what he meant. Down in the black slime which filled the tank, grey-suited workers were sloshing around with what looked like huge cattle-prods. They were knee-deep in the black stuff. Now and then one of them would run the tip of his prod across the grey side of the maggot, causing a shiver of pain to run along its blimplike length. Pale red stuff squirted out of pores in his mottled silvery skin. One of the workers moved to catch it in a flask.

At the other end, a high, shrill squeal sounded from his mouth parts.

'I guess he isn't making Dream Fuel like he used to,' I said, feeling sickened. 'What is it? Some kind of organic machinery?'

'I suppose so,' Ferris answered, managing to convey the minimum of interest as he did so. 'He brought the Melding Plague here, after all.'

'Brought it?' Zebra said. 'But he's been here thousands of years.'

'Yes. And for all that time he was dormant, until we arrived, scurrying around on the surface with our pathetic little settlements and cities.'

'Did he know he had it?' I asked.

'I very much doubt it. The plague was probably something he carried without even knowing it; an old infection to which he had long since adapted. Dream Fuel might have been only slightly younger; a protection they evolved or engineered for themselves: a living stew of microscopic machines con-stantly secreted by their bodies. The machines were immune to the plague and held it in check, but they did much more than that. They healed and nourished their host, conveyed information to and from his secondary grubs . . . eventually, I think, it became so much a part of them that they could no longer have lived without it.'

'But somehow the plague reached the city,' I said. 'How long have you been down here, Ferris?'

'The better part of four interminable centuries, ever since I discovered him.

The plague meant nothing to me, of course – I had nothing in me that it could harm. Conversely, his Dream Fuel – his very blood – kept me alive, without access to any other life-extension procedures.' He fingered the silver blanket over his frame. 'Of course, the ageing process has not been totally arrested. Fuel is beneficial, but it is emphatically no miracle cure.'

I asked, 'Then you've never seen Chasm City?'

'No – but I know what happened.' He looked hard at me; I felt my body temperature drop under the scrutiny of his gaze. 'I prophesied it. I knew it would happen; that the city would turn monstrous and fill itself with demons and ghouls. I knew that our cleverest, swiftest and tiniest machines would turn against us; corrupting minds and flesh; bringing forth perversities and abominations. I knew there would come a time when we would have to turn to simpler machines; to older and cruder templates.' He raised a finger, accusingly. 'All this I foresaw. Do you imagine that I engineered this chair in a mere seven years?'

At the other end of the maggot I saw a worker leaning from a catwalk with something that looked like a chain-saw. He was carving off a huge iridescent scab from the back of Gideon.

I looked at the mottled patch on my coat.

'That's good, Ferris,' Zebra said. 'You mind if I ask you one final question, before we get on our way?'

He punched his answer into the chair. 'Yes?'

'Did you prophesy this?'

Then she took out her gun and shot him.

On the way back up I thought about what Ferris had shown me and what I had learned from Sky's memories.

The grubs had observed a massive release of energy in the vicinity of the Earth system: five sparks of fire which bore the signature of matter-antimatter annihilation. Five void warrens being pushed up to a speed which would cause no indignation to the Jumper Clowns: a mere eight per cent of light. It was, nonetheless, quite an achievement considering that the primates had still been bashing each other around with bones only a million years earlier.

By the time the five human ships were noticed, the grubs had suffered terrible losses themselves. Their once mighty void warrens had been smashed and shattered by skirmishes with the enemy. In a period which the long-lived grubs looked back upon with sorrow, the warrens had been sundered; split into tinier, nimbler sub-warrens. The large grubs were social creatures and the sundering caused them immense pain, even though they were able to stay in limited contact with their siblings using the Jumper Clown's superluminal signalling system.

Eventually, one of the sub-warrens latched onto the five human ships. The sub-warren reshaped itself to match one of the ships it was following.

447

Statistical analysis of ten million years of encounters had shown that the tactic benefited the grubs in the long run, even though it could be disastrous in any single meeting.

Travelling Fearlessly's plan was simple enough in grub terms. He would study the humans and decide what must be done about them. If they showed signs of expanding massively into this volume of space, creating the kind of disturbance which the eaters would find it hard to miss, then it might prove necessary to cull them. Amongst the surviving species, there were some which had taken it upon themselves to perform such painful-but-necessary cullings.

Travelling Fearlessly hoped that it would not come to that. He hoped that the humans would remain a low-level nuisance that did not require immediate culling. If all they planned to do was settle one or two immediate solar systems, they could probably be left alone for now. Culling was itself an act which ran the risk of attracting eaters, so it was never to be performed unless there was excellent reason. As decades passed and the humans made no move, hostile or otherwise, Travelling Fearlessly moved the void warren closer and closer to the cluster of human ships. Perhaps the thing to do was make his presence known; establish dialogue with the humans and explain the awkwardness of the situation. The grub had been working out how to make the first move when one of the ships had blown up.

The explosion was consistent with the complete detonation of several tonnes of antimatter. Travelling Fearlessly's void warren had caught much of the blast, damaging the ship's camouflage integument and killing many of the grubs who had been working near the skin. Their death agonies had reached Travelling Fearlessly through their secretions. He had absorbed what he could of their individual memories, even as the wounded helper grubs were dissolved back down into their organic constituents.

In pain, with half his memories lacerated, Travelling Fearlessly had moved the void warren away from the Flotilla.

But someone had noticed. Oliveira and Lago had arrived shortly afterwards, not really sure what to expect, half believing the old story of a ghost ship; a sixth original member of the Flotilla which had been expunged from history.

That, of course, was not what they had found.

Oliveira had sent Lago in first, to find the fuel they needed to get back, and Lago had quickly realised that he was not in any human ship. When the helper grubs had brought him to Travelling Fearlessly's chamber, things had gone poorly. Travelling Fearlessly had only been trying to help the creature by pointing out that he did not need to use his spacesuit; that they both breathed the same air. But perhaps the way he had done this – by having helper grubs eat the man's suit away – had, in hindsight, not been ideal. Lago had become upset and had begun to hurt the helper grubs with the cutting torch. As the fire burned the helpers, Travelling Fearlessly drank in their agonised secretions as if the pain was his own.

It was unpleasant, but he had no choice but to dismantle Lago. Lago, of course, hadn't taken to that very enthusiastically either, but by then it was too late. The helper grubs had detached most of his extremities and the more interesting components from inside Lago, learning how the various bits of him worked and fitted together, before dissolving his central nervous system into the secretion. Travelling Fearlessly had ingested as many of Lago's memories as he could make sense of. He had learned how to make the same kinds of sounds as Lago, and how to impart meaning to those sounds, and – copying Lago – he had made a mouth for himself. Other grubs had copied Lago's sensory organs, or even incorporated bits of him into themselves.

Now, having come to a greater understanding, Travelling Fearlessly understood why Lago had not taken well to his first view of the maggot-ridden chamber. He felt sorry for what he had been forced to do to Lago and tried to make amends by using as much of Lago's memory and component parts as he could.

He was sure the humans would appreciate this gesture.

'After Lago came, it was very lonely again,' the mouth said. 'Much lonelier than before.'

'You didn't grasp loneliness until you ate him, you fucking stupid maggot.'

'That is . . . possible.'

'All right – listen to me carefully. You've explained to me that you feel pain. Good. I needed to know that. You presumably have a well-developed instinct for self-preservation, too, or you wouldn't have survived until now. Well, I have a harbourmaker with me. If you don't understand the concept, look it up in Lago's memory. I'm sure he knew.'

There was a pause while the maggot shifted uncomfortably; red fluid sloshing around like seawater under a beached whale. Harbourmakers were nuclear warheads; equipment carried by the Flotilla to assist in the development of Journey's End.

'I understand.'

'Good. Perhaps you can use that gravity trick to stop it from working, but I'm willing to bet that you can't generate arbitrarily strong fields that easily, or you'd have used something similar to immobilise Lago when he started giving you difficulties.'

'I told you too much.'

'Yes, you probably did. But I still want to know more. About this ship, mainly. You were engaged in a war, weren't you? You may not have been winning it, but my guess is you wouldn't have survived until now without weapons of some description.'

'We don't have weapons.' The grub's mouth looked affronted. 'Only armouring skein.'

'Armouring skein?' Sky thought about it for a few moments, trying to get his head into the grub's mode of thinking. 'Some kind of projected force technology, is that it? You can put up some kind of field around this ship?'

449

'We could, once. But the necessary parts were damaged when the fifth void warren was destroyed. Now only a partial skein can be created. It's no use at all against an adept enemy like the grub eaters. They see the holes.'

'All right, listen to me. Do you sense the two small machines approaching us?'

'Yes. Are they also friends of Lago?'

'Not quite.' Well, the shuttle crews might be, he thought – but they were very unlikely to be friends of Sky Haussmann, and that was all that really mattered. 'I want you to use your skein against those machines – or I use the harbourmaker against *you*. Is that clear?'

The grub seemed to understand. 'You want me to destroy them?'

'Yes. Or I'll destroy you.'

'You wouldn't do that. It would kill you.'

'You don't understand,' Sky said amicably. 'I'm not Lago; I don't think like him, and I certainly don't act like him.'

He selected one of the nearer grubs and unloaded part of the machine-gun's clip into the creature. The slugs punched thumb-sized holes in the creature's pale-pink integument. He watched the red stuff drain out and then heard an awful shrill cry come from some part of the creature. Except he was wrong about that, now that he paid attention. The shrill cry was coming from the large grub; not the one that he had shot.

He watched the injured one collapse down into the sea of red, until only part of it was showing. Several other helper grubs undulated towards it and began to prod it with their feelers.

Gradually, the keening sound of anguish died down to a low moan.

'You hurt me.'

'I was just making a point,' Sky said. 'When Lago hurt you, he hurt you indiscriminately because he was scared. I'm not scared. I hurt you because I want you to know exactly what I'm capable of.'

A couple of helper grubs were thrashing their way ashore only metres from where Sky and Norquinco were standing.

'No,' Sky said. 'Don't come any closer or I'll shoot another one – and don't try any funny tricks with gravity, or I'll make the harbourmaker go off.'

The grubs halted, their fronds waving hysterically.

The yellow light – the light that bathed the whole chamber – died for a second. Sky was not expecting darkness. For an instant the terror of it was total. He had forgotten that the grubs controlled the light. In darkness, they could do almost anything. He imagined them emerging from the red lake, dragging him into it by his heels. He imagined being eaten by them, the way Lago had been. There might come a point where he could no longer tell the harbourmaker to go off; could no longer erase his own agony.

Perhaps he should do it now.

But the yellow light returned.

'I did as you asked,' Travelling Fearlessly said. 'It was hard. It took all our power to push the skein out to that distance.'

'Did it work?'

'There are two more out there – smaller void warrens.'

The shuttles. 'Yes. But they won't be here for a little while. Then you can do the same trick again.' He called Gomez. 'What happened?'

'The probes just blew up, Sky – like they'd hit something.'

'Nuclear?'

'No. They weren't carrying harbourmakers.'

'Good. Stay where you are.'

'Sky – what the hell is going on inside there?'

'You don't want to know, Gomez – you really don't want to know.'

He had to strain to pick out the next question. 'Did you find – what was his name? Lago?'

'Oh yes, we found Lago. Didn't we, Lago?'

Now Norquinco was speaking. 'Sky. Listen. We should go now. We don't have to kill the other people. We don't want to start a war between the ships.' He raised his voice, his helmet speaker booming out across the red lake. 'You can protect us in other ways, can't you? You could move us; move this whole ship – this whole void warren, to safety? Out of the range of the shuttles?'

'No,' Sky said. 'I want those shuttles destroyed. If they want a war between the ships, they'll get one. We'll see how long they last.'

'For God's sake, Sky.' Norquinco reached out to him, as if to grasp him. Sky stepped away and lost his footing on the chamber's hard and slick surface. Suddenly he was toppling over; falling backwards into the red brine. He landed on his backpack, half submerged in the shallows. The red liquid sloshed across his faceplate with strange eagerness, as if seeking a way into his suit. Out of the corner of his eye he saw two helper grubs undulating towards him. Sky thrashed, but he could not get a grip on any surface to lift himself out, let alone stand up.

'Norquinco. Get me out.'

Norquinco moved cautiously to the edge of the red lake. 'Maybe I should leave you there, Sky. Maybe that would be the best thing for all of us.'

'Get me out, you bastard.'

'I didn't come here to do any evil, Sky. I came here to help the *Santiago* – and maybe the rest of the Flotilla.'

'I have the harbourmaker.'

'But I don't think you have the courage to let it off.'

The grubs had reached him now – two and then a third he had not seen approaching. They were poking and prodding him with differently shaped clusters of appendages, exploring his suit. He thrashed, but the red fluid seemed to be thickening, conspiring to hold him prisoner.

'Get me out, Norquinco. That's your last warning . . .'

Norquinco still stood over him, but he had not come any closer to the edge. 'You're sick, Sky. I've always suspected it, but I never saw it until now. I really don't know what you're capable of.'

Then something he had not been expecting happened. He had stopped thrashing because it was almost too much effort, and now he was being lifted out of the red fluid, the fluid itself seeming to elevate him, while the grubs pushed him gently. Shivering with fear, he found himself on the shore. The last traces of the red fluid raced off him.

For a moment, wordlessly, he stared at Travelling Fearlessly, knowing that the grub sensed his attention.

'You believe me, don't you. You won't kill me. You know what it would mean.'

'I don't want to kill you,' Travelling Fearlessly said. 'Because then I'd be lonely again, like I was before you came.'

He understood, and the understanding itself was vile. It still cherished his company even after he had inflicted pain on it; even after he had murdered part of it. The thing was so desperately lonely that it even desired the presence of its torturer. He thought of a small child screaming in absolute darkness, betrayed by a friend that had never properly existed, and – while at the same time hating it absolutely for its weakness – did at least understand.

And that made his hatred all the more intense.

He had to kill another grub before he persuaded Travelling Fearlessly to destroy the two approaching shuttles, and this time it was not just the murder of the grub that agonised the creature. Generating the skein seemed to pain it as well, as if the grub could sense the ship's damage.

But by then it was over. He could have stayed; could have kept torturing the grub until it told him all it knew. He could have forced the grub to show him how the ship moved, and found out whether it was capable of taking them to Journey's End quicker than the *Santiago*. He could even have considered bringing some of the *Santiago*'s crew here, aboard the void warren – living in its endless tunnels, forcing the grubs to adjust the air mix and temperature until it suited human tastes. How many could the alien ship have supported – dozens, or hundreds? Perhaps even the *momios*, if they were woken? Maybe some of them would have had to be fed to the helper grubs to keep them happy, but he could have lived with that.

But he decided, instead, to destroy the ship.

It was simpler by far; it freed him from negotiating with the grub; freed him from the sense of revulsion he felt when he recognised its loneliness. It also freed him from running the risk of the void warren ever falling into the hands of the other Flotilla vessels.

'Let us leave,' he told Travelling Fearlessly. 'Clear a route right to the surface, near where we came in.'

He heard sonorous clangs as passageways were rerouted; airlocks opening and shutting. A breeze caressed the red water.

'You can leave now,' the grub told him. 'I'm sorry that we had a disagreement. Will you come back soon?'

'Count on it,' Sky said.

Later, they pulled away in the shuttle. Gomez still had no idea what had happened; no idea why the approaching forces had simply blown up.

'What did you find in there?' he asked. 'Did anything that Oliveira said make sense, or was he just insane?'

'I think he was insane,' Sky said. Norquinco made no comment; they had barely spoken at all since the incident by the lake. Perhaps Norquinco thought it would slip from his memory if it was not remarked upon – an understandable lapse of nerve in a tense situation. But Sky kept replaying the fall in his mind; remembering the red tide fingering his faceplate; wondering how many molecules of it had actually slipped through.

'What about the medical supplies – did you find anything? And did you get any idea what happened to her hull?'

'We found out a few things,' Sky said. 'Just get us away from here, will you? Max thrust.'

'But what about the propulsion section? I need to look at the containment; need to see if we can get that antimatter . . .'

'Just do it, Gomez.' He offered a comforting lie. 'We'll come back for the antimatter another time. She isn't going anywhere.'

The void warren pulled away from them. Gomez looped them around to her intact side, then kicked in the shuttle's thrusters. Once they had moved two or three hundred metres from her, it was impossible to tell that she was anything other than what she seemed to be. For a fleeting instant Sky thought of her again as the *Caleuche*: the ghost ship. They had been so wrong; so utterly wrong. But no one could blame them for that – the truth, after all, had been far stranger.

There would be trouble, of course, when they returned to the Flotilla. One of the other ships had sent their own shuttles here, which meant that Sky would probably face recrimination; perhaps even some kind of tribunal. But he had planned for that, knowing that, with shrewdness, he could use the moment to his advantage. The trail of evidence he had created with Norquinco's help would, when revealed, point to Ramirez as having orchestrated the expedition to the *Caleuche*, with Constanza part of the conspiracy. Sky would be revealed as none other than an unwitting stooge of his Captain's megalomaniac schemes. Ramirez would be removed from the Captaincy; perhaps even executed. Constanza would certainly be punished. There would, needless to say, be very little doubt in anyone's minds as to who should succeed Ramirez in the Captaincy.

Sky waited another minute or so, not daring to leave it longer than that in case Travelling Fearlessly suspected what was going to happen and tried to prevent it in some way. Then he made the harbourmaker go off. The nuclear flash was bright and clean and holy, and when the sphere of plasma had spread itself thin, like a flower whose bloom turned from blue-white to interstellar black, there was nothing left at all.

'What did you just do?' Gomez said.

Sky smiled. 'Put something out of its misery.'

'I should have killed him,' Zebra said, as the inspection robot neared the surface.

'I know how it feels,' I said. 'But we probably wouldn't have been able to walk out if you had.' She had aimed for his body, but it had never been very obvious where Ferris ended and his wheelchair began. Her shot had only damaged his support machinery. He had moaned, and when he'd tried to compose a sentence the inner workings of the chair had rattled and scraped before delivering a scrambled sequence of piped sounds. I suspected it would take a lot more than one ill-judged shot to kill a four-hundred-year-old man whose blood was almost certainly supersaturated with Dream Fuel.

'So what good did that little jaunt do?' she asked.

'I've been asking myself the same question,' Quirrenbach said. 'All we know now is a little more about the means of production. Gideon's still down there, and so's Ferris. Nothing's changed.'

'It will,' I said.

'Meaning what?'

'That was just a scouting expedition. When all this is over, I'm going back there.'

'He'll be expecting us next time,' Zebra said. 'We won't be able to breeze in so easily.'

'We?' Quirrenbach said. 'Then you're already committed to this return trip, Taryn?'

'Yes. And do me a favour. Call me Zebra from now on, will you?'

'I'd listen to her if I were you, Quirrenbach.' I felt the inspection robot begin to tilt over back to the horizontal as we approached the chamber where I hoped Chanterelle would still be waiting. 'And yes, we're going back, and no, it won't be so easy the second time.'

'What do you hope to achieve?'

'As someone close to me once said, there's something down there that needs to be put out of its misery.'

'You'd kill Gideon, is that it?'

'Rather than live with the idea of it suffering, yes.'

'But the Dream Fuel . . .'

'The city will just have to learn to live without it. And whatever other services it owes to Gideon. You heard what Ferris said. The remains of Gideon's ship are still down there, still altering the chemistry of the gases in the chasm.'

454

'But Gideon isn't in the ship now,' Zebra said. 'You don't think he's still influencing it, do you?'

'He'd better not be,' Quirrenbach said. 'If you killed him, and the chasm stopped supplying the city with the resources it needs . . . can you honestly imagine what would happen?'

'Yes,' I said. 'And it would probably make the plague look like a minor inconvenience. But I'd still do it.'

Chanterelle was waiting for us when we arrived. She opened the exit hatch nervously, studying us for a fraction of a second before deciding that we were the ones who had gone down. She put aside her weapon and helped us out, each groaning at the relief of no longer being inside the pipe. The air in the chamber was far from fresh, but I gulped in exultant lungfuls.

'Well?' Chanterelle said. 'Was it worth it? Did you get close to Gideon?'

'Close enough.' I said.

Just then something buried in Zebra's clothes began to chime, like a muffled bell. She handed me her gun and then fished out one of the clumsy, antique-looking phones which were the height of modernity in Chasm City.

'Must have been trying to reach me the whole time we were coming up the tube,' she said, flipping open the viewscreen.

'Who is it?' I asked.

'Pransky,' Zebra said, pushing the phone against her ear, while I told Chanterelle that the man was a private investigator who was peripherally involved in all that had happened since my arrival. Zebra spoke to him in a low voice, one hand cupped round her mouth to muffle the conversation. I couldn't hear anything that Pransky was saying, and only a half of what Zebra said – but it was more than enough to get the gist of the conversation.

Someone, presumably one of Pransky's contacts, had been murdered. Pransky was at the crime scene even as he spoke, and from the way Zebra was talking to him, he sounded agitated; like it was the last place in the world he wanted to be.

'Have you . . .' She was probably about to ask him if he'd alerted the authorities, before realising that where Pransky was, there was no such thing as law; even less than in the Canopy.

'No, wait. No one has to know about this until we get there. Stay tight.' And with that, Zebra cuffed the phone shut, returning it to her pocket.

'What's up?' I asked.

'Someone's killed her,' Zebra said.

Chanterelle looked at her. 'Killed who?'

'The fat woman. Dominika. She's history.'

THIRTY-SEVEN

'Could it have been Voronoff?' I asked as we approached Grand Central Station. We had left him at the station before going down to see Gideon, but killing Dominika didn't seem to fit in with what I knew about the man. Killing himself, perhaps, in an interesting and boredom-offsetting manner, but not a well-known figure like Dominika. 'It doesn't seem like his style to me.'

'Not him, and not Reivich either,' Quirrenbach said. 'Though only you can know that for sure.'

'Reivich's no indiscriminate killer,' I said.

'Don't forget Dominika made enemies easily,' Zebra said. 'She wasn't exactly the best person in the city at keeping her mouth shut. Reivich could have killed her for talking about him.'

'Except we already know he isn't in the city,' I said. 'Reivich is in an orbital habitat called Refuge. That was true, wasn't it?'

'To the best of my knowledge, Tanner, yes,' Quirrenbach said.

There was no sign of Voronoff, but that was hardly to be expected: when we'd let him go, I'd never seriously expected him to stay there. Nor had it mattered. Voronoff's role in the whole affair was incidental at best, and if I ever did need to speak to him again, his celebrity would make it easy enough to track him down.

Dominika's tent looked exactly as I remembered it, squatting in the middle of the bazaar. The flaps were drawn, and there were no customers in the vicinity, but there was nothing to suggest that a murder had taken place here. There was no sign of her helper trying to drag anyone into the tent, but even that absence was not especially noticeable, since the bazaar itself was remarkably subdued today. There must not have been any arriving flights; no influx of willing customers for her neural excisions.

Pransky was waiting just beyond the door, peering through a tiny gap in the material.

'You took your time getting here.' Then his funereal gaze assimilated

Chanterelle, myself and Quirrenbach, and his eyes widened momentarily. 'Well, well. A veritable hunting party.'

'Just let us in,' Zebra said.

Pransky held the door open and admitted us into the reception chamber where I had waited while Quirrenbach was on the slab.

'I must warn you,' he said softly. 'Everything is exactly as I found it. You won't like what you're about to see.'

'Where's her kid?' I asked.

'Her *kid*?' he said, as if I had used some piece of obscure street argot.

'Tom. Her helper. He can't be far away. He might have seen something. He might also be in danger.'

Pransky clicked his tongue. 'I didn't see any "kid". There was more than enough to occupy my mind. Whoever did this was . . .' He trailed off, but I could imagine what his mind was dealing with.

'It can't be local talent,' Zebra said, in the silence which followed. 'No one local would waste a resource like Dominika.'

'You said the people after me weren't local.'

'What people?' Chanterelle said.

'A man and a woman,' Zebra answered. 'They paid a visit to Dominika, trying to trace Tanner. They definitely weren't from the city. An odd couple, as far as I can tell.'

I said, 'You think they came back and killed Dominika?'

'I'd say they're fairly near the top of possible suspects, Tanner. And you still have no idea who they might be?'

I shrugged. 'I'm a popular man, evidently.'

Pransky coughed. 'Maybe we should, um . . .' He gestured with one grey hand towards the inner chamber of the tent.

We stepped through, into the part of the tent where Dominika performed her operations.

Dominika was floating on her back, half a metre above her surgical couch, suspended in that position by the steam-powered, articulated-boom suspended harness which encased her lower half. The harness's pneumatics were still hissing, gentle fingers of vapour rising towards the ceiling. Top-heavy, she had canted back to an angle where her hips floated higher than her shoulders. The head of someone thinner than Dominika would probably have lolled to one side, but the rolls of fat around her neck kept her face pointed at the ceiling, and her eyes were wide open, glazed white, her jaw hanging slackly open.

Snakes covered her body.

The largest of them were dead, draped across her girth like patterned scarves, their inanimate bodies reaching to the bed. There was no doubting that they were dead; they'd been slit along the belly with a knife, and their blood had painted ribbons on the couch. Smaller snakes were still alive, coiled across her

457

belly, or the couch, although they hardly moved even when I approached them, which I did with exquisite caution.

I thought of the snake sellers I had seen in the Mulch. That was where these animals had come from, purchased solely to provide detail to this tableau.

'I told you you wouldn't like it,' Pransky said, his voice cutting through the stunned silence of our party. 'I've seen some sick things in my time, believe me, but this must be . . .'

'There's a method to it,' I said, softly. 'It's not as sick as it seems.'

'You must be insane.' Pransky had said it, but I had no doubt that the sentiment was felt by the others present. It was hard to blame them for that, but I knew what I was saying was right.

'What do you mean?' Zebra asked. 'A method—'

'It's meant as a message,' I said, moving around the levitating corpse so that I could get a better look at her face. 'A kind of calling-card. A message to me, actually.'

I touched Dominika's face, the slight pressure of my hand making her head turn to one side, so that the others could see the neat wound bored into the middle of her forehead.

'Because,' I said, voicing what I knew to be the truth for the first time, 'Tanner Mirabel did it.'

Somewhere near my sixtieth birthday – though I had long since ceased to mark the passage of time (what was the point, when you were immortal?) and had doctored ship's records to obscure the details of my own past – I knew that the time had come to make my move. The choice of time was not really mine, forced upon me by the mechanics of our crossing, but I could still let the moment pass if I wished, forgetting about the plans which had occupied my mind so thoroughly for half my life. My preparations had been meticulous, and had I chosen to abandon them, my plans would never have come to light. For a moment I allowed myself the bittersweet pleasure of balancing vastly opposed futures: one in which I was triumphant; one in which I submitted meekly to the greater good of the Flotilla, even if that meant hardship for my own people. And for the tiniest of moments I hesitated.

'On my mark,' said Old Man Armesto of the *Brazilia*.

'Deceleration burn ignition in, twenty seconds.'

'Agreed,' I said, from the vantage point of my command seat, poised high in the bridge. Two other voices echoed me with tiny timelags; the Captains of the *Baghdad* and the *Palestine*.

Journey's End lay close ahead, its star the brighter of the 61 Cygni pair, a bloodshot lantern in the night. Against all the odds, against all the predictions, the Flotilla had crossed interstellar space successfully. The fact that one ship had been destroyed did not taint that victory in the slightest degree. The planners who had launched the fleet had always known that there would be losses. And those losses, of course, had not been confined solely to that ship. Many of the *momio* sleepers would never see their destination. But that, too, had not been unexpected.

It was, in short, a triumph, however one looked at it.

But the crossing was not yet finished; the Flotilla still at cruise velocity. Though only the tiniest of distances remained to be crossed, it was the most significant part of the journey. That, at least, was not something the planners had ever guessed. They had never predicted the depth of disharmony that would creep into the enterprise over time.

'Ten seconds,' said Armesto. 'Good luck to all of us. Good luck and Godspeed. It'll be a damned close race now.'

Not as close as you think, I thought.

The remaining seconds counted down, and then – not quite synchronously – three suns blazed in the night where an instant before there had been only stars. For the first time in a century and a half the engines of the Flotilla were burning again – wolfing down matter and antimatter and spewing out pure energy, beginning to whittle down the eight per cent of light velocity which the Flotilla still had.

Had I chosen otherwise, I would have heard the great structural skeleton of the *Santiago* creak as the ship adjusted itself to the stress of deceleration. The burn itself would have been a low, distant rumble, felt rather than heard, but no less exhilarating for that. But I had made my decision; nothing had changed.

'We have indications of clean burns across the board . . .' said the other Captain, before a note of hesitation entered his voice. '*Santiago*; we have no indication that you have initiated your burn . . . are you experiencing technical difficulties, Sky?'

'No,' I said, calmly and crisply. 'No difficulties at this moment.'

'Then why haven't you initiated your burn!' It was less a question than a scream of indignation.

'Because we're not going to.' I smiled to myself; the cat was well and truly out of the bag. The crux point had been passed; one possible future selected and another discarded. 'Sorry, Captain, but we've decided to stay in cruise mode a little longer.'

'That's madness!' I swore I could hear Armesto's spittle spraying against the microphone like surf. 'We have intelligence, Haussmann – good intelligence. We know damn well that you haven't made any engine modifications that we haven't made as well. You have no means of reaching Journey's End ahead of us! You have to initiate burn now and follow the rest of us . . .'

I toyed with the armrest of my seat. 'Or what, exactly?'

'Or we'll . . .'

'Do nothing. We all know it's fatal to turn off those engines once they're burning antimatter.' That was true. Any antimatter engine was ferociously unstable, designed to keep burning until it had exhausted all its reactant, supplied from the magnetic-confinement reservoir. The whispering engine techs had a technical name for the particular magnetohydrodynamic instability which prevented the flow from being curtailed without leakage, but all that mattered was the consequence: the fuel for the deceleration phase had to be stored in a completely separate reservoir from that which had boosted the ship up to cruise speed. And now that the other three ships had initiated burn, they were more or less committed to it.

By not following them, I had betrayed a terrible trust.

'This is Zamudio of the *Palestine*,' said another voice. 'We have stable flow here, green lights across the board . . . we're going to attempt a mid-burn shutdown before Haussmann falls too far ahead of us. We may never get as good a chance as this.'

'For God's sake, don't do it!' said Armesto. 'Our own simulations say a shutdown has only a thirty per cent chance of . . .'

'Our sims say it's better than that . . . marginally.'

'Hold on, please. We're sending you our technical data . . . don't make a move until you've seen it, Zamudio.'

They debated the matter for the next hour, tossing simulations back and forth, arguing about the interpretation. They thought that their conversations were private, of course, but my agents had long ago placed bugs on the other ships, just as I assumed they had bugged my own. I listened, quietly amused, as the arguments grew more frantic and rancorous. It was no small matter, to risk an antimatter detonation after a century and a half of travel. Under ordinary circumstances they would have extended their debate for months, perhaps even years, weighing the significance of every small gain against every possible death. But all the while they were slowing down, with the *Santiago* pulling triumphantly ahead of them, and every instant that they delayed made that distance worse.

'We've talked enough,' Zamudio said. 'We're initiating shutdown.'

'Please, no,' Armesto said. 'At least let us think about it for a day, will you?'

'And let that bastard creep ahead of us? Sorry, but we're already committed to a shutdown.' Zamudio's voice became businesslike as he read status variables aloud. 'Damping thrust in five seconds . . . bottle topology looks stable . . . constricting fuel flow . . . three . . . two . . . one . . .'

What followed was only a howl of static. One of the new suns had suddenly turned nova, outshining its brethren. It was a white rose, edged in purple which shaded to black. I stared at it wordlessly, marvelling at the hellfire. A whole ship gone in an eyeblink, just the way Titus had told me the *Islamabad* had died. There was something cleansing about that white light . . . something bordering on the pious. I watched as it faded. A breath of hot ions slammed into my own ship, a ghost of what had been the *Palestine*, and for a moment the status displays across the bridge quavered and ran with static, but the ships of the Flotilla were now so far apart that the demise of one could not harm the others.

When comms returned, I heard the voice of the other Captain speaking. 'You bastard, Haussmann,' Armesto said. 'You did that.'

'Because I was cleverer than any of you?'

'Because you lied to us, you piece of shit!' Now I recognised the voice of Omdurman. 'Titus was worth a million of you, Haussmann . . . I knew your father. Compared to him you're just . . . nothing. Dirt. And you know what the worst of it is? You've killed your own people as well.'

'I don't think I'd be quite that stupid,' I said.

'Oh, don't count on it,' Armesto said. 'I told you our intelligence was good, Haussmann. We know your ship like our own.'

'We have intelligence too,' Omdurman said. 'You haven't got any damned tricks up your sleeve. You'll have to start slowing down or you'll overshoot our destination; come to dead-stop in interstellar space.'

'It's not going to happen like that,' I said.

This was nothing like the way I had planned it, but sometimes you just had to abandon the precise letter of the plan, following instead the broad outline; hearing the grand shape of a symphony rather than the individual notes. With Norquinco's assistance I had made some modifications to my command seat. I flipped up a cover set into the black leather of the armest, unfolding a flat, button-studded console which I placed across my lap. My fingers skated across the matrix of buttons, bringing up a map. It was the cactus-like schematic of the ship's spine, showing the sleepers and their corporeal status.

Over the years, I had worked very diligently to separate the wheat from the chaff.

I had made sure that as many of the dead as possible were collected together in their own sleeper rings, studded along the spine. It had been laborious work at first, for the sleepers died not according to my neatly devised plans but in ways that were annoyingly random. At first, anyway. Then I had begun to get the magic touch. I needed only to wish that certain *momios* would die and it seemed to happen. Of course, there were rituals that needed to be performed for the magic to work properly. I had to visit them, touch their caskets. Sometimes (though it seemed to me that I worked unconsciously) I would make tiny adjustments to the settings of their support systems. It was not that I deliberately set out to harm them . . . but in some way that I could not quite fathom, my handiwork was always sufficient to bring about that end. In truth, it *was* magic.

And it had served me powerfully. The dead and the living were now quite separated. One whole row of sleeper rings – sixteen of them, holding one hundred and sixty caskets – was now occupied solely by the demised. Half of another row; another eight-six dead. A quarter of the sleepers were gone now.

I tapped the sequence of commands which I had long ago committed to memory. Norquinco had given me that sequence, after years of covert work. It had been a stroke of genius, recruiting him to the cause. According to all the technical manuals, and the best expert advice, what I was about to do should not have been possible, prevented by a slew of safety interlocks. Over the years, as he had slowly worked his way through the hierarchy of the audit team, Norquinco had found ways around every supposedly watertight failsafe, concealing his labours by stealth and cunning.

And with the work Norquinco had grown in confidence. At first, I had been surprised by this transformation, until I realised that it had always been inevitable, once the man had been ensconced into the audit team. Norquinco had been forced to go through the motions of functioning in a normal human environment, rather than his usual studied isolation. As he had risen to a position of seniority in the team, Norquinco had moulded himself to the role with worrying adaptability. There came a point when I no longer had to intervene in Norquinco's promotions.

But I'd never really forgiven him for his betrayal aboard the *Caleuche*.

We met only periodically; each time I noticed an incremental increase in Norquinco's cockiness. At first, it had been easy to dismiss. The work was proceeding apace, Norquinco's reports detailing each layer of safeguards which he had breached. I had demanded demonstrations to show that the work had really been done, and Norquinco had obliged. I had had no doubt that the task would be completed to my satisfaction by the time I needed it.

But there *had* been a glitch.

Four months earlier, after the last layer of safeguard machinery had been bypassed, the work, to all intents and purposes, was complete. And suddenly I understood why Norquinco had been so obliging.

'The technical term for the arrangement I am about to propose,' Norquinco said, 'is, I believe, blackmail.'

'You're not serious.'

We had met alone along the spine corridor, near node seven, during one of our inspection tours. 'Oh, I'm very serious, Sky. You realise that now, don't you?'

'I'm getting the picture.' I looked along the corridor. I thought I could see a pulsing orange glow somewhere down it. 'What exactly is it you want, Norquinco?'

'Influence, Sky. The audit squad isn't enough now. It's a dead-end job for computer geeks. Technical work just doesn't interest me any more. I've been aboard an alien spacecraft. That changes one's expectations. I want something more challenging. You promised me glories when we were aboard the *Caleuche*; I haven't forgotten. Now I want some of that power and responsibility.'

I chose my words carefully. 'There's a world of difference between hacking some software and running a ship, Norquinco.'

'Oh, don't patronise me. I do realise that, you arrogant bastard. That's what I said about wanting a challenge. And don't think I want your job either – not yet, anyway. I'll let the law of natural succession work for me there. No; I want a senior officer's position – one echelon below you will do nicely. A cushy position with excellent prospects for when we make landfall. I'll carve up a little fiefdom for myself on Journey's End, I think.'

'I think you're reaching, Norquinco.'

'Reaching? Yes, of course I'm reaching. Otherwise blackmail wouldn't have to come into it.'

The orange glow down the corridor had grown closer, accompanied by a faint rumbling. 'Getting you onto the audit team was one thing, Norquinco. You at least had the right background. But there's no way I can get you into any officer's position – no matter how many strings I pull.'

'That's not my problem. You're always telling me how clever you are, Sky. Now all you have to do is use some of that cleverness; use your skill and judgement to find a way to get me into an officer's uniform.'

'Some things just aren't possible.'

'Not for you, Sky. Not for you. Or are you going to disappoint me?'

'If I can't find a way . . .'

'Then everyone else will find out about your little plan for the sleepers. Not to mention what happened with Ramirez. Or Balcazar, for that matter. And I haven't even mentioned the grub.'

'You'll be implicated too.'

'I'll say I was only following orders. It was only recently that I realised what you had in mind.'

'You knew all along.'

'But no one will know that, will they?'

I was about to answer, but the noise of the approaching freight transport would have forced me to raise my voice. The string of pods was rumbling towards us along its rail, returning from the engine section. Wordlessly, the two of us walked backwards until we had reached one of the recesses which allowed us to stand aside as the train slid by. The trains, like much else on the *Santiago*, were old and not particularly well cared-for. They functioned, but much non-essential equipment had been removed from them for use elsewhere, or not fixed when it malfunctioned.

We stood silently shoulder to shoulder as the train neared us, filling the corridor completely except for a narrow gap either side of its blunt body. I wondered what was going through Norquinco's mind at that exact moment. Did he seriously imagine that I would take his blackmail proposal seriously?

When the rumbling string of pods was only three or four metres away, I pushed Norquinco forward, so that he went sprawling onto the rail.

I saw the man's body get pushed violently forward until I could no longer see it. The train continued for a few moments and then slowed down, but not with any great urgency. By rights the transport should have stopped the instant it detected an obstacle in its path, but that was undoubtedly one of the functions which had stopped working years ago.

There was a hum of labouring motors and the smell of ozone.

I squeezed out of the recess. It was difficult, and would have been impossible had the train been in motion, but there was just enough room for me to push past the string of pods until I reached the front. I hoped that my actions would not dislodge something and allow the train to continue, or I would certainly be crushed.

I reached the front, expecting to see Norquinco's mangled remains squashed between the train and its rail.

But Norquinco was lying beside the rail. His toolkit lay crumpled under the front of the train.

I knelt down to examine the man. He had received a glancing impact to the head which had broken the skin, blood pouring out copiously, but the skull did not seem to be fractured. He was still breathing, though unconscious.

I had an idea. Norquinco was now inconvenient to me, and would have to die at some point – probably sooner rather than later – but what I had just thought of was too tempting, too poetic, to ignore. It would be dangerous, however, and I would need not to be disturbed for some time – at least thirty minutes, I judged. By then the lateness of the shipment would be all too obvious. But would anyone do anything about it immediately? I doubted it; from what I had gathered, the trains were no longer very reliable at the best of times. It made me smile. I had become emperor of this miniature state, but the one thing I had not done was make the trains run on time.

Ensuring that the toolkit was still blocking the train, I picked up Norquinco and carried him upship towards node six. It was hard work, but at sixty I had the physique of a thirty-year-old man and Norquinco had lost much of his youthful weight.

Six sleeper rings were connected to this node: sixty sleepers, some of them dead. I racked my memory, recalling as best as I could the ages and sexes of the passengers. There were, I felt sure, at least three amongst those sixty who could pass as Norquinco – especially if the accident was restaged in such a way that the man's facial features were crushed beyond recognition by the train.

I worked my way towards the skin of the ship. I was sweating and short of breath by the time I reached the berth where I judged the best candidate to lie. This was one of the frozen living, I saw, and that suited my plans excellently. With Norquinco still unconscious, I accessed the casket controls and set about warming the passenger. Normally the process would have taken several hours, but I had no interest in limiting cellular damage. No one would autopsy the corpse when it was found under the train, and there would be no reason to think that I had swapped the body.

My personal comm bracelet chimed. 'Yes?'

464

'Captain Haussmann? Sir, we have a report of a possible technical malfunction with a train in spine corridor three, near node six. Should we send a breakdown team along to check it out?'

'No, no need for that,' I said, with what I hoped was not undue haste. 'I'll check it out myself. I'm near enough.'

'You sure about that, sir?'

'Yes, yes . . . no sense in wasting effort is there?'

When the passenger was warm – but now brain dead – I lifted him from the casket. Yes; he was passably close in build to Norquinco, with the same hair colour and skin tone. To the best of my knowledge, Norquinco had no romantic connections with anyone else on the *Santiago* – but even if he had, his lover was not going to be able to tell them apart once I was done.

I lifted Norquinco and placed him in the casket. The man was still breathing – once or twice he had even moaned before slipping back into unconsciousness. I stripped him naked and then arranged the web of biomonitors across his body. The inputs adhered automatically to his skin, adjusting themselves minutely. Some would burrow neatly beneath his skin, worming towards internal organs.

A series of lights flicked to green across the fascia of the casket, signifying that the unit had accepted Norquinco. The lid closed.

I studied the main status panel.

Programmed sleep time was another four years. By then the *Santiago* would have already made orbit around Journey's End and it would be time for the sleepers to warm and step onto their new Eden.

Four years suited my plans, too.

Satisfied, I readied myself for the difficult task of lugging the other passenger back to the spine corridor. First, however, I had to dress the barely warm corpse in the clothes I had just taken from Norquinco.

When I reached the spine I positioned the man ten metres ahead of the train, which was still straining against its obstruction, filling the air with the smell of burning armatures. Then I found a heavy, long-handled wrench from a recessed stores locker. I used the wrench to pulp the man's face into unrecognisability, feeling the bones crack like lacquer beneath each blow. Then I went back to the train and delivered a series of swiping strikes to the jammed toolkit, until it sprang free.

The train, no longer obstructed, began to pick up speed immediately. I had to run ahead of it to avoid being pulped against the wall. I stepped gingerly over the dead man and then retired to a safety alcove, watching with detached fascination as the string of freight pods gathered speed. It hit the man and snowploughed him along, mangling him in the process.

Finally, some distance down the corridor, the train came to a standstill.

I crept behind it. I had been through this before, half an hour earlier, and had been mildly surprised when I had found that Norquinco was only knocked out. That had, of course, been a blessing in disguise . . . but now there was to be no disappointment. The train had done its work creditably. Now, rather than the crushed toolkit, what made it stop was some sluggishly responding safety-mode . . . but it had been much too late to save the passenger.

I lifted my sleeve and spoke into my comms bracelet. 'Sky Haussmann here. I'm afraid there's been a terrible, terrible accident.'

That had all been four months ago; a regrettable coda to our relationship, but Norquinco had, ultimately, not let me down. I assumed so, at least – and would know for sure in a few moments.

On the main viewscreen was a view looking down the spine of the *Santiago* from a vantage point a few metres above the hull. It was an exercise in vanishing points, crisp perspectives that would have thrilled a Renaissance artist. The sixteen sleeper rings containing the dead marched away, diminishing in size, foreshortened towards ellipses.

And now the first and closest of them began to move, kicked loose by a series of pyrotechnic charges studded around the ring. The ring uncoupled from the hull and drifted lazily away from it, tipping slowly to one side as it moved. Umbilicals stretched between ship and ring to breaking point and then snapped cleanly, whiplashing back. Frozen gases trapped in severed pipes erupted in crystal clouds. Somewhere, alarms began to sound. I heard them only dimly, though they seemed to be causing considerable consternation amongst my crew.

Behind the first ring, the second was breaking loose as well. The third trembled and shucked itself loose from its moorings. All along the spine the pattern was repeated. I had arranged it well. I had thought to have all the rings blow their separation charges at once, so that they would drift away in clean, parallel lines, but there was no poetry in that. It pleased me instead to stagger the releases, so that the rings seemed to follow each other, as if obeying some buried migratory instinct.

'Do you see what I'm doing?' I asked.

'I see it well enough,' the other Captain said. 'And it sickens me.'

'They're dead, you fool! What do they care now, if they're buried in space or carried with us to Journey's End?'

'They're human beings. They deserve to be treated with dignity, even if they're dead. You can't just throw them overboard.'

'Ah, but I can, and I have. Besides – the sleepers hardly matter. What they mass is inconsequential compared to the mass of the machines that accompany them. We have a real advantage now. That's why we'll stay in cruise mode longer than you.'

'One quarter of your sleepers isn't much of an edge, Haussmann.' The other Captain had obviously been doing his homework. The kind of calculations I had run could not have been far from his own thoughts. 'What kind of lead does that give you over us when you make orbit around Journey's End? A few weeks at best?'

'It'll be enough,' I said. 'Enough to select the plum landing sites and get our people down there and dug in.'

'If you have anyone left. You killed a lot of those dead, didn't you? Oh, we know what kind of losses you should have run, Haussmann. Your death-rate should not have been much higher than our own. We had intelligence, remember? But we've only lost one hundred and twenty sleepers ourselves. The same goes for the other ships. How did you become so careless, Haussmann? Was it that you wanted them to die?'

'Don't be silly. If it suited my purposes to have them die, why wouldn't I have killed more of them?'

'And try and settle a planet with a handful of survivors? Don't you know anything about genetics, Haussmann? Or incest?'

I started to say that I had thought of that as well, but what was the point of letting the bastard know all my plans? If his intelligence was as good as he claimed, let him find these things out for himself.

'I'll cross that bridge when I reach it,' I said.

Zamudio was the one who finally gave the others a temporary edge – even if it probably wasn't in quite the way he would have planned. But the *Palestine*'s Captain must have thought he stood a very good chance of damping his antimatter flow, or else he would not have tried stopping his engine.

The explosion had been as hard and radiantly white as I remembered from the day in the nursery when the *Islamabad* had gone up.

But the next day, something unexpected happened.

In the instants before Zamudio's ship had blown up, it had still been transmitting technical data to its two allies, both locked in the same deceleration burn that Zamudio had tried unsuccessfully to abort. I could guess that much myself, even though I was not directly privy to that flow of information. That was the other odd thing. The rest of the Flotilla had become grudgingly united against me. I hadn't really expected that, but in hindsight I should have realised that it would happen. I had given the bastards a common enemy. In a way, it was to my credit. There was only one of me, yet I had raised such fear in the other Captains that they had thought it best to amalgamate against me, despite all that had happened between them.

And now this – Zamudio clawing back from the grave.

'That technical data was more useful than he realised,' Armesto said.

'It didn't do Zamudio much good,' I said.

By now there was an appreciable redshift between my ship and the other two Flotilla craft, beginning to fall behind me as they decelerated. But the communications software effortlessly removed all distortion, save for the increasing timelag which accompanied the break-up of the Flotilla.

'No,' Armesto said. 'But in their sacrifice they gave us something tremendously valuable. Shall I explain?'

'If it pleases you,' I said, with what I hoped was a convincing show of boredom.

But rather than being bored, I was actually a little scared.

Armesto told me about the technical data, squirted across from the *Palestine* until the last nanosecond before it detonated. It concerned the attempts that had been made to shut down the flow of antimatter. It had always been known that the procedure was almost bound to be fatal, but until then the precise failure mode had been unclear, glimpsed only fleetingly in computer simulations. There had been speculation that if the failure mode could be understood sufficiently well, it might even be possible to counteract it by subtle manipulation of the fuel-flow. It was nothing that could be tested in advance. Now, however, a kind of test had been made for them. The telemetry from the ship had ended just after the failure mode had begun to arise, but it still probed closer into that instability régime than any carefully harnessed laboratory test or computer simulation.

And it had taught them well.

Enough information could be extracted from those numbers to guess how the failure mode must have evolved. The numbers, fed into the on-board simulations devised by the propulsion teams, hinted at a strategy for containing the imbalance. Tweak the magnetic bottle topology slightly and the injection stream could be neatly curtailed with no risk of normal-matter blowback or antimatter leakage. It was still, of course, hellishly risky.

Which did not stop them trying it.

My ship was falling ahead of the *Brazilia* and the *Baghdad*, and those latter two ships had flipped over to bring their engines forward for the deceleration phase. The bright spikes of those antimatter torches pin-pricked the minutely redshifted hemisphere of sky to the rear of the *Santiago*, like a pair of hot blue sibling suns. The thrust beams of the two deceleration ships were not to be underestimated as potential weapons, but neither Armesto or Omdurman would have the nerve to sweep their torches over my ship. Their argument was with me, not with the many viable colonists I still carried. Equally, I could consider igniting my own engine and dousing one of the two laggard ships with the *Santiago*'s exhaust – but the other vessel would almost certainly take that as a incitement to kill me, whether or not I still carried passengers. My simulations showed that I would not be able to realign my own flame before the other ship took me out in a single baptism of hellfire.

Not an option, I thought . . . and that meant I would have to live with those two enemies unless I found another way of destroying them. I was still considering the possibilities when, in perfect synchrony, the two drives flames to the rear winked out.

I waited, breath held, for the twin blossoms of nuclear light which would signify that the antimatter drives had malfunctioned during shutdown.

But they never came.

Armesto and Omdurman had succeeded in quenching their flames, and now they were coasting with me, albeit with the lower velocities they had gained during the time they were decelerating.

Armesto contacted me. 'I hope you saw what we just did, Sky. That changes everything, doesn't it?'

'Nowhere near as much as you'd like to think.'

'Oh, don't play games. You know what it means. Omdurman and I now have the ability to turn on our engines for however short a time we want. You don't. That makes all the difference.'

I mulled this over. 'It changes nothing. Our ships still have almost the same relative rest-mass as they did a day ago. You are still obliged to continue decelerating now if you want to make orbit around 61 Cygni-A. My ship's lighter by the mass of the sleeper rings I ejected. That still gives me the edge over you. I'm staying in cruise mode until the last minute.'

'You're forgetting something,' Armesto said. 'We have our dead as well.'

'It's too late to make a difference. You're cruising slower than me. And you said it yourself – you never sustained as many casualties as we did.'

'We'll find a way to make the difference, Haussmann. You're not getting ahead of us.'

I looked at the long-range displays, which showed the vastly magnified dots of the other two ships. They were flipping over again, slowly but surely. I watched the dots elongate into thin lines, then contract again.

And then the dots were haloed by twin auras of exhaust radiation.

The two other ships were rejoining the chase.

'It's not over,' Armesto said.

A day later, I watched the dead drift away from the other two ships.

It was twenty-four hours since Armesto and Omdurman had resumed the chase, demonstrating their ability to control their drive flames in a manner that was not yet within my grasp. The death of the *Palestine* had been a blessing in disguise for them . . . even if the better part of a thousand colonists had been killed in the process.

Now the other two ships were moving at the same relative speed as the *Santiago*, once again cruising towards Journey's End. And they were trying very hard to beat me at my own game. There was a kind of inevitability to this, of course. My ship was still less massive than theirs . . . which meant they would have to shed mass if they wanted to follow the same cruise/deceleration curve as I did.

Which meant throwing their own dead into space.

There was nothing elegant about the way they did it. They must have worked overnight to smash through the same countermeasures which it had taken Norquinco nearly his entire life to circumvent . . . but they had the advantage over Norquinco in that they were not trying to complete this work in secret. Aboard the *Brazilia* and the *Baghdad*, every hand must have been turned towards that goal, working furiously. I almost envied them. So much easier when there was no need to work covertly . . . but so infinitely less elegant, too.

On the high-magnification image I watched sleeper rings peel off randomly from the two other ships, more like autumn leaves falling from a tree than anything orchestrated. The image resolution was too poor to be sure, but I suspected there were actually space-suited teams crawling around outside those ships with cutting tools and explosives. They were dislodging the sleeper rings by brute force.

'You still can't win,' I told Armesto.

Armesto deigned to reply, though I'd half expected the other ships to maintain radio silence from here on in. 'We can and we will.'

'You said it yourself. You don't have as many dead as us. No matter how many you throw away, it'll never be sufficient.'

'We'll find a way to make it sufficient.'

Later, I guessed at what kind of strategy that might be. No matter what happened next, the ships were no more than two or three months from Journey's End. With carefully rationed supplies, some colonists could be woken ahead of schedule. The revived *momios* could be kept alive on board the ship with the crew, albeit in conditions which would border on the dehumanising, but it might be sufficient. Every ten colonists that were woken meant a sleeper ring which could be ejected, and a concomitant reduction in ship's mass, allowing a sharper deceleration profile.

It would be slow and dangerous – and I expected that they would lose perhaps one in ten that they tried to revive under such sub-optimal conditions – but it might be just enough to offset the mass difference.

Enough to give them, if not an edge over me, than at least parity.

'I know what you intend,' I told Armesto.

'I doubt it very much,' the old man answered.

But I soon saw that he was right. After the initial flurry of sleeper ring ejections, there followed a pattern: one ejection every ten hours or so. That was exactly what I would have expected, ten hours to thaw every colonist in a ring. There would only be a handful of people on each ship with the expertise to do that, so they would have to work sequentially.

'It won't save you,' I said.

'I think it will, Sky . . . I think it will.'

Which was when I knew what had to be done.

THIRTY-EIGHT

'What do you mean, you killed her?' Zebra asked, the five of us still studying the grotesque tableau of Dominika's death.

'That's not what I said,' I answered. 'I said Tanner Mirabel killed her.'

'And you are?' Chanterelle said.

'If I told you, I'm not completely sure you'd believe me. As a matter of fact I'm having a little trouble dealing with it myself.'

Pransky, who had been listening to our exchange, raised his voice and spoke with solemn surety. 'Dominika's still warm. And rigor mortis hasn't set in yet. If your whereabouts can be accounted for over the last few hours – which I suspect is strongly the case – you're hardly a prime suspect.'

Zebra tugged at my sleeve. 'What about the two people I said were after you, Tanner? They acted like outsiders, according to Dominika. They might have killed her for snitching about them.'

'I don't even know who they are,' I said. 'At least, I can't be sure. Not about the woman, anyway, but I'm willing to hazard a guess about the man.'

'Who do you think it is?' Zebra said.

Quirrenbach cut in, 'I really don't think we should spend too long here; not unless you want to tangle with what passes for authority here. And believe me, that's not especially high on my agenda.'

'Much as it grieves me to agree with him,' Chanterelle said, 'he has a fairly good point, Tanner.'

'I don't think you should call me that any more,' I said.

Zebra shook her head slowly. 'Who do we call you, then?'

'Not Tanner Mirabel, anyway.' I nodded at Dominika's body. 'It must have been Mirabel who killed her. The man who's following me is Mirabel. He did this; not me.'

'This is insane,' Chanterelle said, to general nods of agreement, although no one much looked like they were enjoying proceedings. 'If you're not Tanner Mirabel, then who are you?'

'A man called Cahuella,' I said, knowing that this was only half of the truth.

Zebra placed her hands against her hips. 'And you didn't feel like telling any of us this until now?'

'Until recently I didn't realise it.'

'No? Just slipped your mind, did it?'

I shook my head. 'I think Cahuella altered my memories – his memories – to suppress his own identity. He needed to do it temporarily, to escape from Sky's Edge. His own memories and face would have incriminated him. Except when I say "he", I mean "me", really.'

Zebra squinted at me, as if trying to tell if her earlier judgements had been fatally incorrect. 'You actually believe this, don't you?'

'It's taken me a little while to come to terms with it, believe me.'

'He's clearly snapped,' Quirrenbach said. 'The odd thing is, I assumed it would take rather more than the sight of one dead fat woman to push him over the edge.'

I punched him. It was quick; I allowed him no warning at all, and in any case, under the permanent threat of Chanterelle's gun, he was in no position to fight back. I watched him fall, slipping on the floor which was slick with some spilled medical fluid, one hand rising to nurse his jaw before he even hit the ground.

Quirrenbach slipped into the shadow beneath the couch, yelping as he made contact with something.

For a moment I wondered if he had touched a snake which had found its way to the floor. But instead, something much larger emerged from the shadow. It was Dominika's kid, Tom.

I reached a hand out towards him. 'Come here. You're safe with us.'

She had been killed by the same man who had visited her before, asking questions about me. An offworlder, yes – much like you, Tom said, casually at first, and then repeating himself in a tone that was altogether more suspicious. Not just much like Tanner – but very like him indeed.

'It's all right,' I said, putting a hand on his shoulder. 'The man who killed Dominika only looked like me. It doesn't mean I'm him.'

Tom nodded his head slowly. 'You no sound like him.'

'He talked differently?'

'You talk fancy, mister. The other man – the man who look like you – he don't use so many words.'

'The strong silent type,' Zebra said. Then she drew the kid away from me, wrapping her long lean limbs around him protectively. I was touched, for a moment. It was the first time I had seen any hint of compassion shown by someone from the Canopy for a Mulch-born; the first time I had seen any hint that either party regarded the other as human. Of course I knew what Zebra believed – that the game was evil – but it was another matter to see that belief

472

acted out in a simple gesture of giving comfort. 'We're sorry about Dominika,' she said. 'You have to believe it wasn't us.'

Tom sniffed. He was upset, but the shock of her death had yet to set in, and he was still reasonably coherent and eager to help us. At least I hoped it was because the shock had not set in; the other possibility – that he was just immunised against that kind of pain – was too unpleasant to contemplate. I could handle it in a soldier, but not in a kid.

'Was he alone?' I asked. 'I was told that two people were looking for me; a man and a woman. Do you know if this was the same man?'

'Same guy,' the kid said, turning his face away from the suspended corpse of Dominika. 'And he not alone this time either. Woman with him, but she no look happy this time.'

'She looked happy the first time?' I said.

'Not happy, but . . .' The kid faltered, and I could see that we were making unreasonable demands on his vocabulary. 'She look like she comfortable with guy; like friends. He nicer then – more like you.'

It made sense. The first time he'd paid a trip to Dominika's would have been a fishing trip; gathering what information he could about the city and – hopefully – where he could find the man he wanted to kill, whether that man was me or Reivich or both of us. It might have made sense to kill Dominika there and then, but he must have suspected she could be of use to him in the future. So he had let her live, until he returned, with the snakes he must have bought in the bazaar.

And then he had killed her in a manner which he knew would speak to me; a private code of ritual murder which opened seams into the heart of my being.

'The woman,' I said. 'She was offworld too?'

But Tom seemed no wiser than I about that.

Using Zebra's phone, I called Lorant, the pig whose kitchen I had half-destroyed during my descent from the Canopy, an eternity ago. I told him I had a final huge favour to ask of him and his wife, which was only that they look after Tom until things quietened down. A day, I said, although in truth I plucked the figure from my head at random.

'I look after myself,' Tom said. 'No want stay with pig.'

'They're good people, trust me. You'll be much safer there. If word gets out that someone witnessed Dominika being killed, the same man will come back. If he finds you, he'll kill you,' I said.

'I always got to hide?'

'No,' I said. 'Only for as long as it takes for me to kill the man who did this. And believe me, I'm not planning on spending the rest of my life doing it.'

The concourse was still quiet when we left the tent, meeting the pig and his wife just beyond the cataract of greasy rain which fell endlessly down the building's overhung side, like a curtain of yellowing calico. The kid went with them, nervously at first, but then Lorant scooped him aboard and their balloon-wheeled vehicle vanished into the murk like an apparition.

'He'll be safe, I think,' I said.

'You think he's in that much danger?' Quirrenbach said.

'More than you can imagine. The man who killed Dominika isn't exactly overburdened with a conscience.'

'You sound like you know him.'

'I do,' I said.

Then we returned to Chanterelle's car.

'I'm confused,' Quirrenbach said, as he climbed into the vehicle's bubble of dryness and light. 'I don't know who I'm dealing with any more. I feel like you've just pulled the carpet from under me.'

He was looking at me.

'All because I found the dead woman?' Pransky said. 'Or because Mirabel has started going mad?'

'Quirrenbach,' I said, 'I need to know of places where someone might buy snakes; probably not far from here.'

'Did you hear anything of what we just said?'

'I heard,' I said. 'I just don't want to talk about it right now.'

'Tanner,' Zebra said, then stopped herself. 'Or whoever you say you are. Does this business about your name have anything to do with what the Mixmaster told you?'

'That wouldn't by any chance be the same one you visited with me, would it?' It was Chanterelle speaking now, and it was all I could do to nod, as if in that gesture I made my final acceptance of the truth.

'I know some local snake sellers,' Quirrenbach said, almost to ease the tension. He leant forward, over Zebra's shoulder, and fed orders into the car. It lifted smoothly, quickly spiriting us above the stench and chaos of the rain-sodden Mulch.

'I had to know what was wrong with my eyes,' I told Chanterelle. 'Why they seemed to have been tampered with genetically. What the Mixmaster told me when I returned with Zebra was that the work had probably been done by Ultras, and then undone – crudely, as it happened – by someone else; someone like the Black Geneticists.'

'Go on.'

'That wasn't quite what I wanted to hear. I'm not sure what I was expecting, but it wasn't to find out that I must have been in some way complicit in the act.'

'You think you willingly did this to your eyes?'

I nodded. 'It wouldn't be without its uses. Someone with an interest in hunting, perhaps, might consider it. I can see very well in the dark now.'

'Who?' Chanterelle said.

'Good question,' Zebra echoed. 'But before you answer it, what about the full-body scan you had when we visited the Mixmaster? What was the significance of that?'

'I was looking for evidence of old injuries,' I said. 'Both wounds were inflicted at about the same time. I was rather hoping to find one and rather hoping not to find the other.'

'Any particular reason why?'

'Tanner Mirabel had a foot shot off by Reivich's gunmen. The foot could have been replaced by an organic prosthesis, or a cultured copy cloned from his own cells. But either way it would need to be surgically attached to the stump. Now, maybe with the best medical skills available on Yellowstone, that kind of work could be done invisibly. But not on Sky's Edge. There'd be plenty of microscopic evidence – signs which should have easily shown up in a Mixmaster scan.'

Zebra nodded, accepting that much. 'Maybe that's true. But if you're not Tanner – as you claim – how do you know it ever happened to him?'

'Because I seem to have stolen his memories.'

Gitta dropped to the floor of the tent at almost the same moment as Cahuella.

Neither of them made much of a sound. Gitta had died – in as far as it mattered – the instant the beam from my weapon reached into her skull and turned her brain tissue into something resembling funereal ash; barely enough of it to cup in your hands and watch slipping in grey streams between your fingers. Her mouth opened slightly wider, but I doubted that she'd had any time to register my actions before thought itself failed. I hoped – devoutly – that the last thing Gitta thought, literally, was that I was about to do something which would save her. As she fell, the gunman's knife etched deeper into her throat, but by then there was nothing left of her capable of feeling pain.

Cahuella – impaled by the beam which should have spared Gitta and killed the guard – exhaled softly, like the last sigh of someone falling gratefully into sleep. He had lost consciousness with the shock of the beam's passage; a small mercy for him.

The gunman lifted his face to me. He did not understand, of course. What I had done had made no conceivable sense. I wondered how long it would take before he realised that the shot which had killed Gitta – with such geometric precision, bored straight through the forehead – had in fact been intended for him. How long would it take him before he realised the simple truth, which was that I was not quite the crack shot I had dared to imagine, and that I had killed the one person I was striving to save.

There was a moment of strained silence, during which time he might have come halfway to that realisation.

I did not give him time to finish the journey.

And this time, I neither missed nor stopped shooting when the task was obviously done. I emptied an ammo-cell into the man, and kept firing until the barrel was a cherry-red glow in the tent's dim light.

For a moment I stood with three ostensibly dead bodies at my feet. Then some soldiering instinct snapped into play and I moved again, assimilating what I could.

Cahuella was breathing, though profoundly unconscious. I had reduced the Reivich gunman into an object lesson in cranial anatomy. I felt a spasm of remorse, guilt at having taken his execution well beyond any sensible limit. It was, I suppose, the last twitch of a dying professional soldier. In the exhaustion of that ammo-cell I had crossed some threshold into some less clinical realm where there were even fewer rules, and where the efficiency of a kill counted for infinitely less than the measure of hatred expended.

I put down the gun and knelt closer to Gitta.

I had no need of the medical kit to tell she was dead and irretrievably so, but I did it anyway: running the pocket neural imager across her head, watching as the little embedded screen turned red with messages of fatal tissue damage; deep cerebral injury; extensive cortical trauma. Even if we had a trawl in the tent, it would not have been able to skim her memories and thereby capture a ghost of her personality. I had ensured that she was too severely harmed for that; that the very biochemical patterns themselves were lost. I kept her alive, anyway: strapped a life-support cuirass across her chest and watched as it gave lie to the notion she was dead, colour flowing back into her cheeks as blood circulation resumed. It would keep her body intact until we got back to the Reptile House. Cahuella would kill me if I did anything less than that.

I turned to him, finally. His injuries were almost trivial; the beam had cut through him, but the pulse had been extremely brief and the beam width at its narrowest focus. Most of the internal damage would have been caused not by the beam itself but by the explosive vaporisation of water trapped in his cells, a series of tiny scalding concussions tracing the beam path. Cahuella's entrance and exit wounds were so small they were hard to find. There should not be any internal bleeding; not if the beam had cauterised as it gnawed through him, as I intended. There would be harm yes . . . but I had no reason to suppose he would not survive, even if the best I could do for him here was maintain his current coma with another cuirass.

I strapped the device on, left him resting peacefully next to his wife, then grabbed the gun, palmed in a fresh ammo-cell and secured the perimeter again, supporting myself with the improvised crutch of another rifle, trying not to think about what had been done to my foot, while knowing – on a level of abstract detachment which was anything but reassuring – that it was nothing that could not be fixed, given time.

It took me five minutes to satisfy myself that the rest of Reivich's men were dead; as were almost all of our own except for Cahuella and myself. Dieterling was the only lucky one of us; the only one who had taken a minor wound. It looked worse than it was, and because the head-grazing shot had put him into unconsciousness, the enemy had assumed he was dead.

An hour later, close to collapse myself, blackouts fogging my vision like the awesome thunderhead which had preluded the night's storm, I managed to get Cahuella and his wife into the vehicle. Then I managed to get Dieterling awake, though he was weak and confused by blood-loss. At times, I remember, I screamed aloud because of the pain.

I slumped into the control seat of the vehicle and started it moving. Every part of me was fighting an agonised war to drag me into sleep, but I knew I had to move now – and start moving south – before Reivich sent another attack squad; something he would surely consider if the last squad failed to return on time.

Dawn seemed an eternity away, and when finally pinkish daylight oozed over the now cloudless seaward horizon, I had already hallucinated its coming a dozen times. Somehow I got us back to the Reptile House.

But it would have been better for everyone if I had never made it.

THIRTY-NINE

We stopped at three snake sellers before we found one who knew who we were talking about: a stranger – evidently offworld – who had bought enough snakes for the keeper to be able to shut up shop for the rest of the day. That had been yesterday: the man had obviously planned Dominika's murder long before her actual execution.

The man, the snake seller said, looked a lot like me. Not precisely, but the resemblance was strong if you squinted, and we both spoke with a similar accent, even though the man was far less loquacious.

Of course we spoke similarly. We were not just from the same planet. We were from the same Peninsula.

'What about the woman who was with him?' I asked.

He had not mentioned a woman, but there was something in the way he fingered the extremities of his waxed moustache which told me I was right to ask.

'Now you're beginning to take up my time,' he said.

'Is there anyone or anything in this city which can't be bought?' I said, slipping him a note.

'Yeah,' the man said, laughing quietly. 'But I'm not it.'

'What about the woman?' I asked, eyeing a caged snake the colour of spearmint. 'Describe her.'

'Don't have to, do I? Don't they all look the same?'

'Don't who all look the same?'

He laughed, louder this time, as if he found my ignorance hysterical. 'The Mendicants, of course. Seen one, seem 'em all.'

I looked at him in horror.

I had made a call to the Mendicants the day after I arrived in Chasm City. I was trying to reach Sister Amelia; to ask her what – if anything – she knew about Quirrenbach. I had not been able to get through to her; had instead spoken to

Brother Alexei and his black eye. But I had been told that she was as interested in seeking me as I was her. The remark had not meant much at the time. But now it detonated in my skull like a starshell.

Sister Amelia was the woman with Tanner.

Zebra's contacts had not even hinted that the woman was from the Mendicant order. The snake seller, on the other hand, was sure. Maybe I was wrong in assuming that the other woman was always Amelia. But I thought otherwise. I figured she had to be slipping in and out of disguise; either deliberately, or because she just wasn't thorough enough in maintaining whatever new identity she had concocted.

What was her part in this?

I had trusted her implicitly after my revival. I had allowed her to help my mind heal after the identity-shattering processes of reefersleep. And in the whole time I had spent in the Mendicant habitat, nothing she had done had given any hint that my trust was anything other than well-placed.

But how much did she trust me?

Tanner – the *real* Tanner – might have come through Hospice Idlewild after me. He must have come through on the same ship from Sky's Edge, his revival delayed a little after my own, just as my own had been delayed a little after that of Reivich. But I had already used the name Tanner Mirabel, which meant that Tanner had to be travelling under an identity other than his own. Unless he wanted to sound screamingly insane, his mind pulverised by adverse reefersleep trauma, he would not have advertised his real name too quickly. Better to keep up the lie and let the Mendicants think he was someone else.

It was getting confusing. Even I was getting confused. I tried not to think how this must look to Zebra, Chanterelle and the others.

I was *not* Tanner Mirabel.

I was . . . something else. Something hideous and reptilian and ancient which my mind recoiled from, but which I could not really continue to ignore. When Amelia and the other Mendicants had revived me, I had been travelling under Tanner's name and I also carried what appeared to be his memories, skills and – more importantly – the knowledge of his immediate mission. I had never thought to question any of it; everything had seemed correct. Everything had seemed to fit in place.

But all of it had been false.

We were still talking to the snake seller when Zebra's phone chimed again, a noise almost lost in the ceaseless susurration of rain and the hissing of caged reptiles. She took the phone from her jacket, staring at it suspiciously without actually answering it.

'It's coming in on your name, Pransky,' Zebra said. 'But you're the only person who knows that number, and you're standing right next to me.'

'I think you should be very careful before answering that call,' I said. 'If it's from who I think it is.'

Zebra cuffed the phone open; Pandora opening the lid of her box, fearful of what might lie within. Speckles of rain dimpled the screen, like a parade of tiny glass beetles. Zebra lifted the phone to her face and said something quietly.

Someone answered her. She said something back – her tone uncertain – and then turned her face to mine.

'You were right, Tanner. It's for you.'

I took the phone from her, wondering how something so innocent could contain so much evil. Then I looked into a face which was very much like my own.

'Tanner,' I said quietly.

There was an appreciable delay before the man answered, amusement in his voice. 'Are you asking or telling?'

'Very funny.'

'I've got something to tell you, you know.' The voice was faint, backdropped by sounds of machinery. 'I don't know if you've quite put the pieces together yet.'

'I'm beginning to.'

Another delay. Tanner was in space, I realised – somewhere near Yellowstone, but appreciable fractions of a light-second away from low-orbit; probably out near the belt of habitats where the Mendicants held tenancy. 'Good. I won't insult you by using your real name; not just yet. But this much I will tell you.'

I felt myself stiffen.

'I've come to do what Tanner Mirabel does, which is to complete something he started. I've come to kill you – just as you came to kill Reivich. Symmetric, don't you think?'

'If you're in space then you're already going in the wrong direction. I know you were here before. I found your calling card with Dominika.'

'Nice touch with the snakes, wasn't it? Or haven't you quite figured that part out yet?'

'I'm doing my best.'

'I'd love to chat, I really would.' The face smiled. 'And maybe we'll still get the chance.'

I knew it was bait, but I fell for it anyway. 'Where are you?'

'On my way to an engagement with someone dear to your heart.'

'Reivich,' Quirrenbach said quietly, and I nodded, remembering how Quirrenbach had claimed to be taking us into space – for a meeting with Reivich – before Chanterelle rescued us.

One of the high carousels, he had said. A place called Refuge.

'Reivich doesn't figure in this,' I said. 'He's an accessory; nothing more. This

480

is only about you and me. We don't have to make it any more than it already is.'

'Quite a change of tune from a man who was intent on killing Reivich up to only a few hours ago,' Tanner said.

'Maybe I'm not the man I thought I was. But why do you have to go after Reivich?'

'Because he's an innocent.'

'What does that mean?'

'It means he'll bring you to me.' Tanner's smile flashed on the screen, daring me to find fault with his logic. 'I'm right, aren't I? You came here to kill him, but you'd rather *save* him than have me do the job for you.'

I had no idea how I felt, in all truth. Tanner was forcing me to confront questions I had skirted around until now while I dealt with the schism in my memories. But that schism had opened into a cleft which had ripped my past from me and left something poisonous in its place. If I was Cahuella – and everything now pointed to that – then I hated myself to the core.

But I could not hate Tanner any less. He had killed Gitta.

No: *we killed her.*

The thought – the crushing logic of it – hit home. We shared memories now, whole intermingled strands of past. Tanner's memories were not truly mine, but now that I'd carried them in my head, I could never be entirely free of their influence. He had killed Gitta; now I carried the memory of having done it myself; the memory of having killed the most precious entity in my universe. But it was worse; far worse than that. Tanner's crimes were nothing compared to those that I'd suppressed; buried in the memories I had hidden beneath Tanner's, but which were now upwelling into my consciousness. I still felt like Tanner; still felt that his past was the right one, but I'd glimpsed enough of the truth to know that this was only an illusion which would grow less and less convincing with time; that it was Cahuella's past and memories which really belonged in this body. And even that was not the end of it, for Cahuella himself was only a kind of shell, overlaying an even deeper set of memories.

I didn't want to think about that, but I could see the way things were headed.

I had stolen Tanner's memories; made myself think – temporarily – that I was really him. Then – as I began to shrug aside this disguise – began to suffer the effects of the indoctrinal virus, catalysing the release of even deeper layers of memory; glimpses into my hidden history; one that went back centuries.

Back to Sky Haussmann.

Something gave in me as the full realisation of what I was sunk in. My knees buckled; I dropped to the rain-slicked ground and felt the urge to vomit. I had dropped the phone; now it lay beside me, up-ended so that I could still see Tanner's face, his expression quizzical.

'Something the matter?' he asked.

I spoke into the phone.

'Amelia,' I said, at first barely a whisper, then repeating her name more audibly. 'She's with you, isn't she? You tricked her.'

'Let's just say she's been very useful to me.'

'She doesn't know what you mean to do, does she?'

Tanner seemed to find this amusing. 'She's a very trusting soul. She had her doubts about you, you know. Apparently, after you'd discharged yourself from the Mendicants, she became aware of certain irregularities in your genetic code – evidence of what she naturally thought was congenital illnesses. She tried to contact you, but you were already becoming a very slippery customer.' Tanner smiled again. 'By then I'd revived and recovered my faculties. I remembered who I was and why I was on that flight from Sky's Edge. That I was after you, because you'd stolen my identity and memories. Of course, I didn't let Amelia know any of that. I just told her that you and I were brothers and that you were just a little confused. A little harmless deception. You can't blame me for it.'

No; that was true enough. I had also lied to Amelia; hoping that she'd give me a lead on Reivich.

'Let her go,' I said. 'She's nothing to you.'

'Oh, but she's much more than that. She's another reason to bring you here. Another reason why we should meet, Cahuella.'

His face was frozen for a moment, then the link terminated, leaving us standing in the rain. I passed the phone back to Zebra.

'What about the other injury?' she asked, as we scudded back across the city in her car. 'You said Tanner had lost a foot, and now there was no evidence of that ever happening. But that wasn't the only thing you had the Mixmaster look for.' She shook her head. 'You know, I want to keep calling you Tanner. It isn't easy, you know – talking to someone who denies their own name.'

'Believe me, it isn't easy from my side of the conversation, either.'

'Tell us about the other injury, then.'

I drew in breath. This was the hardest part of all. 'Tanner shot someone once. A man who he was working for. A man called Cahuella.'

'Nice of him,' Chanterelle said.

'No; it wasn't like that. Tanner was actually doing this man a favour when he shot him. It was a hostage situation. Tanner had to fire a weapon through the man to . . .' My voice gained a crack, 'to kill one of the gunmen, who had Cahuella's wife at knifepoint. It wasn't going to kill Cahuella. Tanner knew that with the angle of the beam, it wouldn't seriously injure the man.'

'And?'

'Tanner made the shot.'

Zebra said, 'And it worked?'

In my mind's eye I watched Gitta fall to the floor, not via the knifeblade, but through Tanner's errant shot. 'The man lived,' I said, after a few moments.

482

'Tanner's knowledge of anatomy was faultless. It came from being a professional killer, you see. They teach assassins which organs they need to hit to ensure a kill. But the knowledge can just as easily be inverted; to find the safest route for a beam to take through a body.'

'You make it all sound so surgical,' Chanterelle said.

'That's just what it was.'

I told them the Mixmaster's scan had found a healed, elongated wound running through my body, consistent with a beam weapon entering my back and exiting my abdomen, at a positive angle. The wound had shown up on his scan like the dissipating vapour trail of an aircraft.

'But that means . . .' Zebra started to say.

'Shall I spell it out for you? It means I'm the man Tanner Mirabel was working for. Cahuella.'

'This gets worse,' Quirrenbach said.

'Hear him out,' Zebra said. 'I was there when we visited the Mixmaster, remember. He isn't making all of this up.'

I turned to Chanterelle. 'You saw the genetic changes which had been worked on my eyes. Cahuella had that done to himself; it was work he paid the Ultras to perform on him. Hunting was a hobby of his.'

But there was more to it than that, wasn't there? Cahuella wanted to be able to see at night because he hated darkness, hated the memory of being small and alone and forgotten, waiting in the nursery.

'You're still talking of Cahuella like he's some third person,' Zebra said. 'Why. Aren't you sure that you're him?'

I shook my head, remembering kneeling in the rain; every absolute blasted away. That sense of total dislocation was still there, but in the intervening time I'd contained it; built a scaffold around it, a structure – however rickety – which would at least allow me to function in the present.

'Circumstantially, yes. But if I have his memories, they're fragmented – no more clear than Tanner's.'

'Let's get this straight,' said Quirrenbach. 'You haven't got a fucking clue who you are, is that it?'

'No,' I said, admiring my own calm. 'I'm Cahuella. I'm completely sure of it now.'

'Tanner wants you dead?' Zebra said, as we left Chanterelle's car at the perimeter of the station concourse. 'Even though you and he used to be close?'

Images of a white room – of a man crouched naked on its floor – flashed across my mind's eye like glimpses in a strobe light, gaining tiny increments of clarity with each repetition.

'Something very bad happened,' I said. 'The man I am – Cahuella – did something very bad to Tanner. I'm not sure I blame Tanner for wanting revenge.'

'I don't blame him, or you, or whoever it was,' Chanterelle said. 'Not if you – Tanner – shot him.'

She frowned, but I couldn't blame her for that. Keeping track of these shifting layers of identity and memory was like holding the weave of a complex tapestry in mind.

'Tanner missed,' I said. 'His shot was meant to save Cahuella's wife, but he ended up killing her instead. I think it may have been the first and last mistake of his career. Not bad, when you think about it. And everything he did was in the heat of the moment.'

'You sound like you don't really blame him for coming after you,' Zebra said.

Our group trooped into the concourse, which was noticeably busier than when we had last been here, only a few hours before. Nothing resembling officialdom had yet claimed Dominika's tent, although there were also no customers anywhere near it. I presumed her body was still alive, still suspended above the couch where she worked her acts of neural exorcism; still gilded by snakes. Word of her death must surely have spread far into the Mulch by now, but the sheer illegality of it – cutting against all the unspoken laws of who could and could not be touched – still served to enforce a zone of exclusion around the tent.

'I don't think anyone would blame him,' I said. 'Because what I did to him . . .'

The white room returned – except this time I shared the perspective of the crouched man; felt his nakedness and his excruciating fear; a fear that opened up rifts of emotion he'd never imagined before, like a man glimpsing hallucinogenic new colours.

Tanner's perspective.

The creature stirred in the alcove, uncoiling itself with languid patience, as if – in some simple loop of its tiny brain – it *understood* that its prey was not going anywhere in a hurry.

The juvenile was not a large hamadryad; it must have been birthed from its tree-mother in the last five years, judging by the roseate hue of its photovoltaic hood, furled around its head like the wings of a resting bat. They lost that colour as they neared maturity, since it was only fully grown hamadryads which were long enough to reach the tree tops and unfurl their hoods. If the creature was allowed to grow, in a year or two the roseate shade would darken to a spangled black: a dark quilt studded with the iridophore-like photovoltaic cells.

The coiled thing lowered itself to the floor, like a bundle of stiff rope tossed from a ship to the quayside. For a moment it rested, its photovoltaic hood opening and closing softly and slowly, like the gills of a fish. It was very large indeed, now that he could see it more closely.

He had seen hamadryads dozens of times in the wild, but never closely, and never in their entirety; only a glimpse between trees from a safe distance. Even though he had never been near one without possessing a weapon which could easily kill it, there had never been an encounter which was not without a little fear. He understood. It was natural, really: the human fear of snakes, a phobia written into the genes by millions of years of prudent evolution. The hamadryad was not a snake, and its ancestors did not remotely resemble anything which had ever lived on Earth. But it looked like a snake; it moved like a snake. That was all that mattered.

He screamed.

FORTY

'You may have let me down in the end,' I said, mouthing a silent message to Norquinco, who was far beyond any means of hearing me, 'but I can't deny that you did an exemplary job.'

Clown smiled at that.

'Armesto, Omdurman? I hope you're watching this. I hope you can see what I am about to do. I want it to be clear. Crystal clear. Do you understand?'

Armesto's voice came though after the timelag, as if halfway to the nearest quasar. It was faint because the other ships had sloughed all non-essential communications arrays: hundreds of tonnes of redundant hardware.

'You've burned all your bridges, son. There's nothing left for you to do now, Sky. Not unless you manage to persuade any more of your viables to cross the River Styx.'

I smiled at the classical reference. 'You still don't seriously think I murdered some of those dead, do you?'

'No more than I think you murdered Balcazar.' Armesto was silent for a few moments; silence broken only by static; cracks and pops of interstellar noise. 'Make of it what you want, Haussmann . . .'

My bridge officers looked awkwardly at him when Armesto mentioned the old man, but none of them were going to do more than that. Most of them must have already had their suspicions. They were all loyal to me now; I had bought their loyalty, promoting non-achievers to positions of prominence in the crew hierarchy, just as dear Norquinco had tried to blackmail me into doing. They were weak, for the most part, but that did not concern me. With the layers of automation Norquinco had bypassed, I could practically run the *Santiago* myself.

Perhaps it would come to that soon.

'You've forgotten something,' I said, enjoying the moment.

Armesto must have been confident that nothing had been forgotten, beginning to think that the chase was winnable.

486

How wrong he was.

'I don't think I have.'

'He's right,' came the voice of Omdurman on the *Baghdad*, similarly faint. 'You've used up all your options, Haussmann. You don't have another edge.'

'Except this one,' I said.

I tapped commands into my seat command console. Felt, subliminally, the hidden layers of ship subsystems bend to my will. On the main screen, looking along the spine, was a view very similar to the one I had seen when I had detached the sixteen rings of the dead.

But it was different now.

Rings were leaving all along the spine, around all six faces. There was still a harmony to it – I was too much of a perfectionist for anything else – but it was no longer an ordered line of rings. Now, every other ring amongst the eighty remaining was detaching. Forty rings broke away from the spine of the *Santiago* . . .

'Dear God,' said Armesto, when he must have seen what was happening. 'Dear God, Haussmann . . . No! You can't do that!'

'Too late,' I said. 'I'm already doing it.'

'Those are living people!'

I smiled. 'Not any more.'

And then I turned my attention back to the view, before the glory of what I had done had passed. Truly, it was beautiful to watch. Cruel, too – I admitted that. But what was beauty without a little cruelty at its heart?

Now I knew I'd win.

We took the Zephyr to the behemoth terminal, the train hauled by the same huge, dragonlike locomotive that had brought Quirrenbach and me into the city only a few days earlier.

Using what little reserves of currency I had left, I bought a fake identity from one of the marketeers, a name and a cursory credit-history just about robust enough to get me off the planet and – if I was lucky – into Refuge. I had come in as Tanner Mirabel, but I did not dare try and use that name again. Normally it would have been a matter of reflex for me to pull a false name out of the air and slip into that disguise, but now something made me hesitate when selecting my new identity.

In the end, when the marketeer was about to lose his patience, I said, 'Make me Schuyler Haussmann.'

The name meant almost nothing to him, not even the surname worthy of comment. I said the name to myself a few times, becoming sufficiently familiar with it that I would act with the right start of recognition if my name came over a public address system, or if someone whispered it across a crowded room. Afterwards, we booked ourselves onto the next available behemoth making the haul up from Yellowstone.

'I'm coming, of course,' Quirrenbach said. 'If you're serious about protecting Reivich, I'm the only way you're going to get anywhere near him.'

'What if I'm not serious?'

'You mean what if you might still be planning to kill him?'

I nodded. 'You've got to admit, it's still a possibility.'

Quirrenbach shrugged. 'Then I'll simply do what I was always meant to do. Take you out at the earliest opportunity. Of course, my reading of the situation is that it won't come to that – but don't imagine for a moment that I wouldn't do it.'

'I wouldn't dream of it.'

Zebra said, 'You need me, of course. I'm also a line to Reivich, even if I was never as close to him as Quirrenbach.'

'It might be dangerous, Zebra.'

'What, and visiting Gideon wasn't?'

'Fair point. And I'll admit I'm grateful for any help I can get.'

'Then you'll want me as well,' Chanterelle said. 'After all, I'm the only one of us here who really knows how to hunt someone down.'

'Your gaming skills aren't in question,' I said. 'But it won't be like a hunt. If I know Tanner – and I'm afraid I may know him as well as he knows himself – he won't be following any rulebook.'

'Then we'll just have to play dirty before he does, won't we.'

For the first time in ages I laughed a laugh that wasn't totally insincere.

'I'm sure we can rise to the occasion.'

Quirrenbach, Zebra, Chanterelle and I lifted an hour later; the behemoth making one arcing swoop over Chasm City before lofting itself into the lowering clouds, twisted like phantasms by the collision between Yellowstone's relentless winds and the belching updraft of the chasm itself. I looked down and the city looked tiny and toylike, the Mulch and the Canopy hardly separated at all, compressed into one tangled and intricate urban layer.

'Are you all right?' Zebra said to me, returning to our table with drinks.

I turned away from the window. 'Why?'

'Because you almost look like you miss the place.'

When the journey was almost over; when the success of what I had planned was becoming apparent – when, openly, they were beginning to talk of me as a hero – I visited my two prisoners.

In all the years, no one had ever located the chamber deep inside *Santiago*, though some – Constanza in particular – had come close to guessing that it must exist. But the chamber drew only parsimoniously from the ship's power and life-support systems grid, and even Constanza's undoubted skill and persistence had not been sufficient to bring its location to light. Which was good, for although the situation was less critical now, there had been long years in which the chamber's discovery would have ruined me. Now, however, my situation was secure; I had enough allies to weather minor scandals, and I had dealt effectively with most of those who stood against me.

Technically, of course, there were three prisoners, although Sleek did not really fit into the latter category. His presence had merely been useful to me, and – irrespective of how *he* viewed it – I did not view his incarceration as a genuine punishment. As ever upon my arrival he flexed within his tank, but lately he only moved sluggishly, his small dark eye only dimly registering my presence. I wondered how much of his earlier life he remembered, confined in a tank that was oceanically vast compared to the one where he had been for the last fifty years.

'We're nearly there, aren't we?'

I turned around, surprised after all this time to hear the croak of Constanza's voice.

'Very nearly,' I answered. 'I've just seen Journey's End with my own eyes, you know – as a fully formed world, not just a bright star. It's really quite wonderful to see it, Constanza.'

'How long has it been?' She tried to look at me, straining against her constraints. She was tied to a stretcher which had been cranked to an angle of forty-five degrees.

'Since I brought you here? I don't know – four, five months?' I shrugged, as if the matter had barely occupied my thoughts. 'It doesn't really matter, does it?'

'What did you tell the rest of the crew, Sky?'

I smiled. 'I didn't need to tell them anything. I made it look as if you'd committed suicide by jumping out of one of the airlocks. No need to provide a body that way. I just let the others draw their own conclusions.'

'They'll figure out what happened one day.'

'Oh, I doubt it. I've given them a world, Constanza. They want to canonise me, not crucify me. I don't see that changing for a very long time.'

She had always been problematic, of course. I had discredited her after the *Caleuche* incident, bringing to light a trail of faked evidence which placed her in the same conspiratorial frame as Captain Ramirez. That was the end of her career in security. She had been lucky to avoid execution or imprisonment, especially in the desperate days that had followed the detachment of the sleeper modules. But Constanza had never ceased to give me cause for concern, even when she had been demoted to menial work. The crew as a whole were willing to accept that the detachment had been a desperate but necessary act; a conclusion I pushed them towards, via propaganda and lies concerning the other ships' intentions. I did not even think of it as a crime myself. Constanza thought otherwise, and spent her last years of liberty trying to unravel the labyrinth of misinformation I had recently woven around myself. She was always probing into the *Caleuche* incident; protesting that Ramirez had been innocent, and she insisted on wild speculation about the manner in which Old Man Balcazar had really died; that his two medics had been wrongfully executed. At times, she even raised doubts about the way Titus Haussmann had died.

Finally, I decided I had to silence her. Faking her suicide required only a little preparation, as did bringing her to the torture chamber unseen by anyone else. She had spent most of that time drugged and restrained, of course, but I had allowed her little windows of lucidity now and again.

It was good to have someone to talk to.

'Why did you keep him alive for so long?' Constanza said.

I looked at her, marvelling at how aged she had become. I remembered when we had both stood against the glass of the large dolphin tank; near-equals.

'The Chimeric? I knew he'd come in useful, that's all.'

'To torture?'

'No. Oh, I saw that he was punished for what he'd done, but that was only the start of it. Here. Why don't you take a better look at him, Constanza?' I adjusted the angle of her stretcher, until she faced the infiltrator. He was completely mine now, and did not require restraining at all. Nonetheless – for my peace of mind – I kept him chained to the wall.

'He looks like you,' Constanza said wonderingly.

'He has twenty additional facial muscles,' I said, with paternal pride. 'They can pull the flesh of his skin into any configuration he wants, and hold it there. And he hasn't aged much since I brought him here. I think he can still pass for me.' I rubbed my face, feeling the rough texture of the cosmetics I wore to offset my unnatural youthfulness. 'And he'll do anything – anything – that I ask of him. Won't you, Sky?'

'Yes,' the Chimeric answered.

'What are you planning? To use him as a decoy?'

'If it comes to that,' I said. 'Which, frankly, I doubt.'

'But he only has one arm. They'll never mistake him for you.'

I wheeled Constanza back into the position she had been in upon my arrival. 'That's not an insurmountable problem, believe me.' I paused and produced a huge, long-needled syringe from the kit of medical instruments I kept next to the God-Box, the device I had used to smash and remake the infiltrator's mind.

Constanza saw the syringe. 'That's for me, isn't it?'

'No,' I said, moving over to the dolphin tank. 'It's for Sleek. Dear old Sleek, who has served me so loyally over the years.'

'You're going to kill him?'

'Oh, I'm sure he'd regard it as a mercy by now.' I unlatched the top of his tank, wrinkling my nose at the appalling smell of the brackish water in which he lay. Sleek flexed again, and I put a calming hand across his dorsal region. His skin, once as smooth and glossy as polished stone, was now like concrete.

I injected him, pushing the needle through an inch of fat. He moved again, almost thrashing, and then became stiller. I looked at his eye, but it looked as expressionless as ever.

'He's dead, I think.'

'I thought you'd come to kill me,' Constanza said, unable to keep the nervous relief from her voice.

I smiled. 'With a syringe like that? You must be joking. No; this one's for you.'

I picked up another one; smaller this time.

Journey's End, I thought, gripping the support strut in the *Santiago*'s free-fall observation blister. It was an apt name. The world hung below me now, like a green paper lantern lit by a dimming candle. Swan, 61 Cygni-A, was not a bright sun, and even though the world was in a tight orbit around the dwarf, daylight here was not the same thing that Clown had shown me in pictures of Earth. It was a sullen, paltry kind of illumination. The star's spectrum was acutely red, even though it still looked white to the naked eye. But none of this was surprising. Even before the Flotilla had left home, a century and a half earlier, they had known how much energy the world would receive in its orbit.

Deep in *Santiago*'s cargo hold, too light to have ever been worth sacrificing, was a thing of diaphanous beauty. Teams were preparing it even now. They had extracted it from the starship, anchored it to an orbital transfer tug and towed it beyond the planet's gravitational field, out to the Lagrange point between Journey's End and Swan. There, stationed by minute adjustments of ion-thust, the thing would float for centuries. That at least was the plan.

I looked away from the limb of the planet, towards interstellar space. The other two ships, the *Brazilia* and the *Baghdad*, were still out there. Current estimates placed their arrival three months in the future, but there was an inevitable margin of error.

No matter.

The first wave of shuttle flights had already made several return trips to and from the surface, and many transponder-equipped cargo packages had already been dropped, ready to be found in a few months' time. A shuttle was descending now, its deltoid shape dark against a tongue of equatorial land-mass which the geography section was calling the Peninsula. Doubtless, I thought, they would come up with something less literal given a few more weeks. Five more flights would be all it took to get all the remaining colonists down to the surface. Another five would suffice to transport all the crew and the heavy equipment which could not be dropped via cargo packages. The *Santiago* would remain in orbit, a skeletal hulk denuded of anything remotely useful.

The shuttle's thrusters fired briefly, kicking it onto an atmospheric insertion course. I watched it dwindle until it was out of sight. A few minutes later, near the horizon, I thought I saw the glint of re-entry fire as it touched air. It would not be long before it was on the ground. A preliminary landing camp had already been established, near the southern tip of the Peninsula. Nueva Santiago, we were thinking of calling it – but again, it was early days.

And now Swan's Pupil was opening.

It was too far away to see, of course, but the angstrom-thin plastic structure was being unfurled at the Lagrange point.

The placement was almost perfect.

A torch beam seemed to fall on the sombre world below, casting an ellipsoidal region of brightness. The beam moved, hunting – reshaping. When they had adjusted it properly, it would double the solar illumination falling on the Peninsula region.

There was life down there, I knew. I wondered how it would adjust to the change in ambient light, and found it hard to stir up much enthusiasm.

My communications bracelet chimed. I glanced down, wondering who amongst my crew would have the nerve to interrupt this moment of triumph. But the bracelet merely informed me that there was a recorded message waiting for me in my quarters. Annoyed – but nonetheless curious – I pushed myself out of the observation blister, through a gasket of locks and transfer wheels, until I reached the main, spinning part of our great ship. Now that I was in a gravitational zone, I walked freely, calmly, not allowing the faintest hint of doubt to show on my face. Now and then crew and senior officers passed me, saluting; sometimes even offering to shake my hand. The general mood was one of utter jubilation. We had crossed interstellar space and arrived safely at a new world, and I had brought us here before our rivals.

I stopped and talked with some of them – it was vital to cement alliances, for troubled times lay ahead – but all the while my mind was on the recorded message, wondering what it could mean.

I soon found out.

'I assume by now you've killed me,' Constanza said. 'Or at the very least made me disappear for good. No; don't say a word – this isn't an interactive recording, and I won't take very much of your precious time.' I was looking at her face on the screen in my quarters: a face that looked fractionally younger than the last time I had seen her. She continued, 'I recorded this some time ago, as you've probably gathered. I downloaded it into the *Santiago*'s data network and had to intervene once every six months to prevent it being delivered to you. I knew that I was an increasingly sharp thorn in your side, and thought the chances were good that you would find a way of getting rid of me before too long.'

I smiled despite myself, remembering how she had demanded to know how long I had held her prisoner.

'Well done, Constanza.'

'I've ensured that a copy will reach a number of senior officers and crew, Sky. Of course, I don't really expect that I will taken seriously. You'll have certainly doctored the facts surrounding my disappearance. That doesn't matter; it's enough that I've sown a seed of doubt. You'll still have your allies and admirers, Sky, but don't be surprised if not everyone is prepared to follow your leadership with blind obedience.'

'Is that all?' I said.

'There's one final thing,' she said, almost as if she had expected me to speak at that point. 'Over the years, I've amassed a great deal of evidence against you, Sky. Much of it is circumstantial; much of it open to different shades of interpretation, but it's a life's work and I'd hate to see it go to waste. So – before I recorded this message – I took what I had and concealed it in a small, hard-to-find place.' She paused.

'Have we reached orbit around Journey's End yet, Sky? If so, there's little point trying to find the materials. By now they're almost certainly on the surface.'

'No.'

Constanza smiled. 'You can hide, Sky, but I'll always be there, haunting you. No matter how much you try and bury the past; no matter how effectively you remake yourself as a hero . . . that package will always be there, waiting to be found.'

Later, much later, I stumbled through the jungle. Running was difficult for me, but that had very little do with my age. The hard part was keeping my balance with only one arm, my body always forgetting that necessary asymmetry. I had lost the arm in the very earliest days of the settlement. It had been a dreadful accident, even though the pain of it was only an abstract memory now. My arm had been incinerated; burned to a crisp black stump when I held it in front of the wide muzzle of a fusion torch.

Of course, it hadn't been an accident at all.

I had known for years that I might have to do it, but had kept delaying it until we were down on the planet. I had to lose the arm in such a way that no medical intervention could save it, which ruled out a neat, painless severing operation. Equally, I had to be able to survive the loss of it.

I had been hospitalised for three months after the accident, but I had pulled through. And then I had began to resume my duties, word escaping around the planet – and out to my enemies – of what had happened. Gradually it had settled into the mass consciousness that I only had one arm. Years had passed and the fact had become so obvious that it was barely mentioned any more. And no one had ever suspected that losing the arm was just a tiny detail in a greater plan; a precaution set in place years or decades before it might become useful. Well, now the time had come when I could be thankful for that forethought. I was a fugitive now, even as I approached my eightieth birthday.

Things had gone well enough in the early years of the colony. Constanza's message from the grave had taken the shine off for a while, but before very long the people's need for a hero had overridden any nagging doubts they might have had about my suitability for the role. I had lost some sympathisers, but gained the general goodwill of the mob, a trade-off I considered acceptable. Constanza's hidden package had never come to light, and as time passed I began to suspect that it had never existed; that the whole thing had been a psychological weapon designed to unnerve me.

Those early days were heady times. The three months' good grace which I had given the *Santiago* had been enough time for us to establish a network of small surface camps. We had three well-fortified main settlements by the time the other starships braked into orbit above them. Nueva Valparaiso, near the equator (it would make a fine site for a space elevator one day, I thought) was the latest. Others would follow. It had been a good start, and it had seemed unthinkable then that the people – with a few loyal exceptions – would turn so viciously against me.

Yet they had.

I could see something ahead, through the dense-packed rainforest foliage. A light. Definitely artificial, I thought – perhaps the allies I was supposed to be meeting. I hoped that was the case anyway. I did not have many allies now. The few left in the orthodox power structure had managed to break me out of custody before the trial, but they had not been able to assist me in reaching sanctuary. Very probably those friends would be shot for their treason. So be it. They had made the necessary sacrifice. I had expected nothing less.

At first it had not even been a war.

The *Brazilia* and the *Baghdad* had arrived in orbit, confronted by the skeletal hulk of the old *Santiago*. For long months nothing had happened, the two allied ships maintaining a chill observational silence. Then they had launched a pair of shuttles on trajectories which would bring them down in the Peninsula's northern latitudes. I had wished I could have saved a speck of antimatter in the old ship, just to fire up its engine for a moment, and to douse the shuttles with that killing lance. But I had never learned the trick of shutting down an antimatter reservoir.

The shuttles had come down, then made further flights back up to orbit, ferrying down sleepers.

More long months of waiting.

And then the attacks had begun: skirmish squads moving down from the north, striking against the *Santiago*'s nascent settlements. So what that there were barely three thousand people on the whole planet. It was enough for a small war . . . and it had been quiet at first, giving both sides time to dig in, consolidate . . . breed.

Not really a war at all.

But my own side were still trying to have me executed for war crimes. It was not that they were interested in peace with the enemy – too much had happened for that – but they certainly blamed me for bringing about the whole situation. They would kill me and then return to the fray.

Ungrateful sons of bitches. They had twisted everything now. They had even changed the name of the planet, as a kind of joke. Not Journey's End any more.

Sky's Edge.

Because of the edge I had given them to be the first to arrive.

I hated it. I knew what they meant by it: a sick acknowledgement of the necessary crime; a reminder of what had brought them here.

But the name was sticking.

Now I paused; not merely to catch my breath. I had never really liked the jungle. There were rumours of things in it – large things which slithered. But no one I trusted had ever seen one. Just stories then – that was all.

Just stories.

But I was still lost. The light I had seen earlier was gone now. It might have been obstructed by a thick patch of trees . . . or perhaps I'd imagined it all along. I looked around me. It was very dark, and everything looked the same. The sky was blackening overhead – 61 Cygni B, normally the brightest star in the sky apart from Swan, was below the horizon – and the jungle would soon just be a darkening extension of that blackness.

Perhaps I was going to die here.

But then I thought I saw movement far ahead, a milky shape which I at first assumed was the same patch of light I'd seen earlier. But this milky shape was much closer – approaching me, in fact. It was man-shaped and it was stepping towards me through the overgrowth. It shone, as if imbued with its own inner luminosity.

I smiled. I recognised the shape now. I shouldn't have been afraid. I should have remembered that I was never truly alone; that my guide would always appear to show me the way forward.

'You didn't think I'd forget you, did you?' Clown said. 'Come on. It's not far now.'

Clown led me on.

It had not been my imagination; not completely. There was a light ahead, gleaming through the trees like spectral fog. My allies . . .

By the time I reached them Clown was no longer with me. He had faded away like a retinal burn. That was the last time I ever saw him – but he had done well to bring me this far. He had been the only trusted friend of my life, even though I knew that he was just a psychological figment, a subconscious entity projected into daylight, born from memories of the tutelary persona I had known in the nursery aboard the *Santiago*.

What did that matter?

'Captain Haussmann!' called my friends through the trees. 'You made it! We were beginning to think the others hadn't managed . . .'

'Oh, they played their parts well,' I said. 'I imagine they've been arrested by now – if they haven't already been shot.'

'That's the odd thing, sir. We are hearing reports of arrests – and they're saying they've recaptured you.'

'That wouldn't make any sense, would it?'

But it *would*, I thought – if the man they thought they had recaptured only looked like me; if the man only looked like me because buried beneath the supple skin of his face was an armature of twenty additional muscles which allowed him to mimic almost anyone. He would talk and act like me too, as he had been conditioned over years to do so; trained to think of me as his God; his only desire to obey me selflessly. And the missing arm? Well, that was a dead giveaway, wasn't it? The man they had arrested looked like Sky Haussmann and was missing an arm as well.

There couldn't be any doubt that they had recaptured me. There'd be a trial, of sorts, during which the prisoner might appear incoherent – but what more would they expect from an eighty-year-old man? He was probably going senile. The best thing would be to make some kind of example of him; something as public as possible. Something no one was going to forget in a hurry, even if it bordered on the inhumane. A crucifixion might fit the bill.

'This way, sir.'

There was a vehicle waiting in the pool of light, a tracked surface rover. They bundled me aboard it and then we sped through the forest trail. We drove through night for what felt like hours, always further and further away from anything resembling civilisation.

Eventually they brought me to a large clearing.

'Is this it?' I said.

They nodded in unison. I knew the plan by then, of course. The climate was against me now. It was not a time for heroes – they preferred to redefine them as war criminals. My allies had sheltered me until now, but they had not been able to stop my arrest. It had been all they could do to spring me from the makeshift detention centre in Nueva Iquique. Now that my double had been recaptured, I would have to disappear for a little while.

Here in the jungle they had devised a means to protect me for good; no matter how the fortunes of my allies in the main settlements waxed and waned. They had buried a fully-functioning sleeper berth here, with the power supply to keep it working for many decades. They thought there was a risk involved in using it, but they also thought I was really eighty years old. I figured the risk was a lot less than they imagined. By the time I was ready to wake up – I'd give it a century at the very least – my helpers would have access to much better technology. It wouldn't be a problem to revive me. It probably wouldn't even be a problem to repair my arm.

All I had to do was sleep until the right time. I would be tended across the decades by my allies – just as I had tended the sleepers who rode the *Santiago*.

But with infinitely more devotion.

They hitched the surface rover to something buried beneath overgrowth – a metal hook – and then pulled the vehicle forward, dragging aside a camouflaged door set into the clearing's floor, revealing steps sinking down into a well-lit, clinically clean chamber.

Helped by two of my people, I was escorted down the stairs, until I reached the waiting sleeper-casket. It had been refurbished since it had carried someone from Sol system, and it would suit my needs excellently.

'We'd best get you under as soon as possible,' said my aide.

I smiled and nodded at the man, and then allowed him to slip a hypodermic into my arm.

Sleep came quickly. The last thing I remembered, just before it closed over me, was that when I woke up I would need a new name. Something that no one would ever connect to Sky Haussmann – but which, nonetheless, would provide me with some tangible link to the past. Something that only I knew the meaning of.

I thought back to the *Caleuche*, remembering what Norquinco had told me about the ghost ship. And I thought about the poor, psychotic dolphins aboard the *Santiago*; of Sleek in particular; of the way his hard, leathery body had thrashed as I pushed poison into him. There had been a dolphin with the ghost ship, too, but for a moment I couldn't remember its name, or even be certain that Norquinco had told me. I would find out when I woke, I thought.

Find out and use that name.

FORTY-ONE

Refuge was a kilometre-long blackened spindle, unrelieved by exterior lights; visible only by the way it occluded background stars and the silvery spine of the Milky Way. Very few other ships were seen coming or going, and those that we saw were just as dark and anonymous as the habitat. As we vectored in, one end of the spindle opened out in four triangular segments, like the highly adapted jaw of an eyeless marine predator. Insignificant as plankton, we drifted in.

The berthing chamber was just large enough to take a ship like ours. Docking clamps folded out, followed by concertina-like transfer tunnels, mating with the airlocks spaced around the equatorial belt of the ship's main sphere.

Tanner's here, I thought. From the moment we stepped into Refuge, he might be on the point of killing me and anyone who got too close to our little vendetta.

It wasn't something I was going to forget easily.

Refuge sent armed drones into the ship, gloss-black spheroids bristling with guns and sensors which swept us for concealed arms. Of course we'd brought none with us; not even Yellowstone's security was sloppy enough for that. By the same token, I hoped that Tanner had also come in unarmed – but I wasn't counting on it.

With Tanner, you didn't count on anything.

The robots betrayed a level of technology appreciably more advanced than anything I'd encountered since my revival, with the possible exception of Zebra's furniture. Presumably unaugmented humans were not considered a serious transmission risk, but it might have been the case that we would have been denied entry if one of us had been carrying a Plague-susceptible implant. Human officials moved in once the robots had completed the preliminary work, carrying significantly less brutal-looking guns, weapons which they toted with an air of embarrassed apology. They were excessively polite and I began to understand why.

No one gets here without an invitation.

We had to be treated like the honoured guests that we were.

'I called ahead, of course,' Quirrenbach said, while we waited in the airlock for our documents to be processed. 'Reivich knows we're here.'

'I hope you warned him about Tanner.'

'I did what I could,' he said.

'What does that mean?'

'It means Tanner's definitely here. Reivich won't have turned him away.'

I was sweating as it was; worried that my fake identity would not be enough to get me into Refuge. But now the sweat on my brow turned into droplets of ice. 'What in hell's name is he playing at?'

'Reivich must feel that he and Tanner still have some business to attend to. He'll have invited him.'

'He's insane. Tanner might kill him just for kicks, even if his real argument's with me. Don't forget my own imperative was to complete a mission; to keep my word that I'd track down Reivich. I don't know whether that impulse came from Tanner or Cahuella. But I wouldn't like to stake my life on it.'

'Keep your voice down,' Quirrenbach said. 'Those robots will have sprayed listening devices over every square angstrom of this room. You're not here for a spot of quiet bloodshed, remember.'

'Strictly tourism,' I said, grimacing.

The armoured outer door reopened, rust flakes chipping in free-fall from its hinges.

A third-tier official came in, not even armed this time, nor clad in muscular armour. He wore a look of pained evasiveness, homing in on me like a heat-seeking slug. 'Mister Haussmann? I'm sorry to inconvenience you, but we're experiencing an administrative problem in processing your application for entry into Refuge.'

'Really?' I said, trying to sound remotely surprised. I could hardly complain: Sky Haussmann had got me out of Yellowstone's atmosphere, which was all that could be reasonably expected of him.

'I'm sure it's nothing serious,' the official said, sincerity chiselled into his face. 'We frequently experience conflict between our records and those of the rest of the system; it's to be expected after the recent unpleasantness.'

Recent unpleasantness. He was talking about the Plague.

'I'm sure the matter can be resolved with a slightly more thorough examination, a few physiological cross-checks; nothing too complicated.'

I bridled. 'What kind of physiological cross-check, exactly?'

'A retinal scan, that kind of thing.' The official was snapping his fingers at something or someone beyond our view. Almost immediately another robot entered the airlock, a dove-grey sphere politely devoid of any nasty weapons, bearing the Mixmaster sigil.

'I'm not submitting to a retinal scan,' I said, as reasonably as I could. I knew it wouldn't take a machine to spot the oddity of my eyes. A human barely had to glance at me in the right light to see there was something strange about the way I looked back at them.

My remark had the same effect on the official as a slap across the cheek, causing an almost tangible blanching. 'I'm sure we can come to some kind of arrangement . . .'

'No,' I said. 'I very much doubt that, I'm afraid.'

'Then I'm afraid—'

Quirrenbach stepped between us. 'Let me handle this,' he mouthed, before speaking aloud to the man. 'Excuse my colleague; he's a little nervous around officialdom. There's been an honest mistake, as I'm sure you appreciate. Will you accept the word of Argent Reivich?'

The man looked flustered. 'Of course . . . provided I have his guarantees . . . and that it's in person . . .'

He hadn't needed to ask who Argent Reivich was, I noticed.

Quirrenbach snapped his fingers at me. 'Stay here; I'll square things with him. It shouldn't take more than half an hour.'

'You're going to ask Reivich to sign me in?'

'Yeah,' Quirrenbach said, without a hint of humour. 'Ironic, isn't it.'

I didn't have to wait long.

Reivich appeared on a screen in the holding pen where the Refuge officials held those pending a decision on entry. It was not too much of a shock to see his face, since I had already met Voronoff, who looked exactly the same. But there was something unique about the real Reivich; some essence Voronoff had not succeeded in capturing. It was nothing I could quite place. I suppose it was just the difference between someone playing a game – however earnestly – and someone whose intentions are deadly serious.

'This is quite a turn-up,' Reivich said. He looked pale but healthy, a white tunic with a high collarless neck his only visible item of clothing. He was backdropped by a mural of interlocking algebraic symbols, denoting part of the mathematic theory of Transmigration. 'You asking me for entry, and me agreeing to it.'

'You let Tanner in,' I said. 'Are you sure that was wise?'

'No, but I'm sure it'll prove interesting. Assuming he's who you say he is, and you're who you say *you* are.'

'One or both of us might want to kill you.'

'Do you?'

It was an admirable question; straight to the point. I gave him the dignity of appearing to think it over before answering. 'No, Argent. I did once, but that was before I knew who I was. Finding out you're not who you think you are does rather change one's priorities.'

'If you're Cahuella, then my men killed your wife.' His voice was thin and reedy, like a child's. 'I'd have thought you were even more keen to have me killed.'

'Tanner killed Cahuella's wife,' I said. 'The fact that he thought he was going to save her doesn't really alter things.'

'Are you Cahuella or not, in that case?'

'I might have been, once. Now Cahuella doesn't exist.' I looked hard into the screen. 'And frankly, I don't think anyone's going to mourn him, are they?'

Reivich pursed his lips distastefully. 'Cahuella's weapons butchered my family,' he said. 'He sold arms which murdered my loved ones. For that I could gladly have tortured him.'

'If you'd killed Gitta, that would have been more torture than you could ever have inflicted on him with knives and electrodes.'

'Would it? Did he really love her that much?'

I examined my memories, in the hope of answering him. In the end all I could offer was, 'I don't know. He was a man capable of a lot of things. All I do know is that Tanner loved her at least as much as Cahuella.'

'But Gitta did die. What did that do to Cahuella?'

'It made him very hateful,' I said, thinking back to the white room, which still lingered slightly beyond recall, like a nightmare not quite brought to mind after waking. 'But he took that hatred out on Tanner.'

'Tanner lived though, didn't he?'

'Some part of him,' I said. 'Not necessarily any part we'd call human.'

Reivich was silent for a minute, the difficulty of our meeting obviously weighing hard on him. Finally he said, 'Gitta. She was the only innocent in any of this, wasn't she? The only one who didn't deserve any of it.'

There was no arguing with that.

The hollow interior of Refuge was locked in perpetual gloom, like a city in blackout. Unlike the gloom of Chasm City, this was deliberate; a state of affairs willed into being by the groups which claimed tenancy here. There was nothing resembling a native ecology. The interior was unpressurised apart from trace gases, and every square inch of the walls was occupied by sealed, windowless structures, linked by an intestinal tangle of transit tubes. The dimly glowing tubes were the only source of illumination, which wasn't saying much – and if it had not been for the enhanced biology of my eyes, I doubted that I'd have been able to see anything at all.

Yet the place hummed with a sense of barely managed power; a constant subliminal rumble which transmitted itself into the bones. The balcony we stood on was sheeted over with airtight glass, but even so I had the feeling that I was standing in the corner of a vast, shadowy turbine room in which every generator was spinning at full tilt.

Reivich had given the authorisation for Refuge security to let me in, provided my party were escorted to him. I had misgivings about this – it was too much out of my control – but we had absolutely no choice but to comply with Reivich's wishes. This was where the chase ended – on his territory. And by sleight of hand, it was no longer Reivich who was being chased.

It might have been Tanner.

Maybe it was me.

Refuge was sufficiently small that there was no real drawback in walking from point to point within its interior; a fact aided by the relatively weak artificial gravity which the habitat's lazy spin imparted. We were led into one of the connecting tunnels: a three-metre-wide tube fashioned from thick smoky glass, with intermittent glass irises spaced along its length, dilating open and shut to allow us passage and to make abundantly clear the fact that we were being shepherded, like food passing along the gullet. The walk took us further along the main axis of the spindle, gravity rising as we descended from the endcap, but never reaching anything like one gee. The unlit structures of Refuge towered over us like canyon walls at night, and there was no sense whatsoever that anyone else inhabited the place. The truth was that the kind of clientèle which Refuge serviced were the kind of people who demanded absolute discretion, even from others like themselves.

'Has Reivich been mapped yet?' I asked, realising that it was an obvious question which so far hasn't occurred to me. 'After all, that's why he's here.'

'Not yet,' Quirrenbach said. 'There are all sorts of physiological tests which need to be made first, to ensure that the mapping is optimised – cell membrane chemistry, neurotransmitter properties, glial cell structure, blood-brain volume, that kind of thing. You only get one shot at it, you see.'

'Reivich's going for the full destructive scan?'

'Something very close to it. It's still the way to get the best resolution, they say.'

'Once he's scanned, he won't have to worry about an irritation like Tanner.'

'Not unless Tanner follows him.'

I laughed – before I realised that Quirrenbach wasn't making a joke.

'Where do you think Tanner's now?' Zebra said, walking to my left, her heels clicking on the floor, her elongated reflection like dancing scissors in the wall's reflection.

'Somwhere Reivich has his eye on him,' I said. 'Along with Amelia, I hope.'

'Is she really to be trusted?'

'She might be the only person who hasn't betrayed one of us,' I said. 'At least not intentionally. But I'm sure of one thing. Tanner's stringing her along only until she ceases to be of use to him. Once that moment comes – and it might be soon – she'll be in very great danger.'

Chanterelle said, 'You came here to save her?'

For a moment I wanted to answer in the affirmative; to dredge up some tiny crumb of self-respect and pretend that I was a human being capable of something other than wickedness. And maybe it wouldn't have been entirely untrue – maybe Amelia was a large part of the reason I'd come here, knowing it was everything that Tanner wanted. But she wasn't the largest part, and the last thing I felt like doing was lying any more, least of all to myself.

'I came here to end what Cahuella started,' I said. 'It's as simple as that.'

The smoked-glass tunnel wound its way up again, towards the far endcap of Refuge, and then punched its way into the lightless side of one of the looming airtight structures. At the end of this particular stretch of tunnel was another iris, currently sealed. But this one was gloss-black, and it was impossible to see what lay beyond it.

I walked up to it and pressed my cheek against the unyielding metal, straining to hear something.

'Reivich?' I called. 'We're here! Open up!'

The door irised open, more ponderously than those we'd passed through earlier on.

Cool green light streamed through the opening arcs, bathing us in its insipidity. Suddenly the fact that I didn't have a weapon – that none of us were armed – hit home. I might die in a second, I thought – and probably not even know it when it happened. I had allowed myself to be admitted into the lair of a man who had everything to fear from me, and no reason in the universe to trust me. Did that make Reivich or myself the bigger fool? I couldn't begin to guess. All I knew was that I wanted to get out of Refuge as quickly as possible.

The door opened fully, revealing a bronze-walled antechamber, with vivid green lamps hanging from the ceiling. Bas-relief gold symbols scurried around the walls, iterating similar mathematical statements to those I had seen when I'd spoken to Reivich; the incantations which could shatter a mind into ones and zeros; pure number.

There was no doubt that he was here.

The door closed behind us and another irised ahead, revealing a much larger space, like the inside of a cathedral. The room was bathed in golden light, yet its extremities were so far away that they were lost in shadow. I could see the slight curvature of Refuge's floor, an effect accentuated by the interlocking bronze and silver chevrons which patterned the floor.

The air smelled of incense.

A man sat in the distance, in the middle of a pool of brighter light shafting from a stained-glass window far above. He sat facing away from us, in a high-backed chair of ornate construction, wreathed in gold. A trio of slender bipedal servitors stood a few metres from the chair, presumably awaiting instructions. I studied the shape of his head, almost lost in shadow itself, and knew that I was standing behind Reivich.

I remembered when I thought I had seen him, near the immortal fish in Chasm City. How quickly I had reacted, slipping out my gun and chasing around the fish tank to confront and kill him. I was sure that I would have done so if Voronoff had not been a second faster than I.

Now I didn't feel any pressing need to kill him.

A voice, like sandpaper rasping against sandpaper, said, 'Turn me around so that I may face my guests, please.' The statement itself was a laboured thing, punctuated by wheezes and words less spoken than whispered.

One of the servitors stepped forward, treading with the inhuman silence of their kind, and swivelled Reivich around.

What faced us was not what I was expecting.

It was not possible . . .

Reivich looked like a corpse: a cadaver briefly animated by the application of electrical puppetry. He did not look like anything living. He did not look like anything which had a right to speak, or to be able to curve his mouth in the semblance of a smile.

He reminded me of a less healthy version of Marco Ferris. We could see only his head and the tips of his fingers. The rest of him was lost beneath a thick quilted blanket, from which trailed medical feedlines, curving around into a compact life-support module clamped to one arm of the chair, a smaller version of the cuirass which I had used to keep Gitta 'alive' while I returned her body to the Reptile House. His head was little more than a skull around which skin had been draped; skin which was mottled black where it wasn't already a shade of bruised purple. His eyesockets had been enucleated; fine cables trailed from the darkness between his lids, running into the same life-support module. There were only a few wisps of hair left on his crown, like the few trees which will always remain standing directly under an airblast. His jaw hung slackly open, his tongue a black slug filling his mouth.

He raised a hand. Apart from a few liver spots, it was that of a much younger man.

'I see you're disturbed,' Reivich said.

I realised now that the voice didn't come from him at all, but from the life-support module. It still sounded feeble. Presumably even the act of subvocalising was an effort to him.

'You did it,' Quirrenbach said, stepping closer to the man he still worked for. 'You took the scan.'

'Either that or I didn't get enough sleep last night,' Reivich said, his voice like wind. 'On balance I'm inclined to think the former.'

'What happened?' I asked. 'What went wrong?'

'Nothing went wrong.'

'You shouldn't look like this,' Quirrenbach said. 'You look like a man on the edge of death.'

'Perhaps because I am.'

'The scan failed?' Zebra said.

'No, Taryn, it didn't. The scan was a complete success, I'm told. My neural structure was acquired flawlessly.'

'You did it too soon,' Quirrenbach said. 'That's right, isn't it? You couldn't wait for the all the medical checks. And this is what it did to you.'

Reivich's head approximated a nod. 'People like myself, and Tanner – and yourself,' he said, directing his gaze at me, 'lack medichines. Almost no one on Sky's Edge has it in their cells, except for the very few who were able to afford the services of the Ultras. And even those that could often chose some other kind of longevity procedure.'

'We had other things to concern us,' I said.

'Of course we did. Which is why we dispensed with such luxuries. The trouble was, I'd need medichines to protect my cells against the effect of the scan.'

'The old style? Hard and fast?' I said.

'The best, if you listen to the theorists. Everything else is a compromise. The simple fact is that if you want to get your soul into the machine – and not just some blurred impression – you have to die in the process. Or at least suffer what would ordinarily be lethal injury.'

'So why didn't you protect yourself with medichines?' Quirrenbach said.

'There wasn't time to do it properly. Medichines have to be carefully matched to the user, and introduced into the body slowly. Otherwise the effect is massive toxic shock. You die before the medichines can aid you.'

'If you used Sylveste's equipment,' I said carefully, remembering what I'd been told of those experiments, 'you shouldn't even be breathing.'

'It was an updated process, based on Sylveste's original work. But you're right – even allowing for technical refinements, I should be quite dead. As it happens, I was administered with enough broad-spectrum medichinery to survive the scan – at least temporarily.' He waved his hand at the life-support module and the three attendant servitors. 'Refuge supplies these machines. They're trying to stabilise the cellular damage and introduce more refined variants of medichines, but I suspect they're only doing it out of obligation.'

'You think you're going to die?' I said.

'I feel it in my bones.'

I tried to imagine what it would have been like for him; that agonising instant of neural capture, like being caught in the glare of the brightest flare imaginable; a radiance which shone beneath the skin, into the marrow itself, turning him into a smoky glass sculpture of himself, for that piercing instant.

The rapid analytic beams of the scan, focused down to cellular-resolution, would have swept through his brain at a speed only fractionally faster than the speed of synaptic impulses, keeping slightly ahead of the cortical messages proclaiming the havoc spreading through his mind. By the time the scan reached his brain-stem, no information would have yet reached that part

505

regarding the disruption being suffered by the layers of his mind situated above. Because of that slight edge, the overall snapshot of his brain would have been completely normal, apart from the slight blurring caused by the finite spatio-temporal resolution of the process. The scan would have been finished before Reivich had recognised that it had begun – and by the time his mind began to keel over under the shock of the procedure, whole neural routines crashing into coma, it would not matter at all.

He would have been captured.

And even the damage *should not have mattered*; should not have been anything which the medichines could not have repaired, almost as swiftly as the injuries took place. Like shelling a building, dislodging bricks, but with a team of fanatical builders inside, putting right the harm before the next shell arrived . . .

But Reivich had never taken that path.

Reivich had opted to die; had opted to suffer assault on every cell in his brain and surrounding tissue, but knowing that, no matter what the consequences for his physical body, his essence would remain, captured for eternity and – at last – recorded in a form which could not be erased by anything as trivial as assassination or war.

Part of him had made it.

But not the part we were looking it.

'If you're going to die,' I said, 'if you accept that it's inevitable – and that you must have known this would happen before the scan – why didn't you just die in the scan?'

'I did,' Reivich said. 'By at least a dozen medical criteria which would satisfy courts of law in other systems. But I also knew that Refuge's machines could bring me back to life, albeit transiently.'

'You could have waited,' Quirrenbach said. 'Another few days, and they could have matched your medichine requirements perfectly.'

Reivich's bony shoulders moved beneath the quilt; a shrug. 'But then I would have been forced to accept a less accurate scan, in order to give the medichines a chance to function. *It wouldn't have been me.*'

'I don't suppose Tanner's arrival had anything to do with it?' I asked.

Reivich seemed to find that amusing; the curve of his smile increasing minutely. Soon, I thought, we would all see the real smile beneath his face; the one written in bone. He could not have very long left now.

'Tanner made my choice rather easier,' Reivich said. 'I won't dignify him with any influence on my circumstances beyond that.'

'Where is he?' Chanterelle asked.

'He's here,' the withered creature in the chair said. 'He's been here – in Refuge – for more than a day. We haven't met yet, though.'

'You haven't *met*?' I shook my head. 'What the hell's he been up to since he arrived, in that case? And what about the woman with him?'

506

'Tanner underestimated my influence here,' Reivich said. 'Not just here in Refuge, but in the vicinity of Yellowstone as a whole. You did too, didn't you?'

'Forget me. Let's talk about Tanner. He's a much more interesting subject.'

Reivich's fingers caressed the edge of the quilt. One hand remained entirely concealed beneath it – assuming there *was* another hand. I tried to reconcile this apparition with the young aristocrat I had been following, but there was nothing they seemed to have in common. The machine even stripped Reivich of his Sky's Edge accent.

'Tanner came to Refuge intending to kill me,' he said. 'But his main reason for coming here was to draw you from the shadows.'

'You think I don't know that?'

'I'm rather surprised you came, put it like that.'

'Tanner and I have unfinished business.'

'Such as?'

'I can't let him kill you, even as an incidental detail. You don't deserve it. You acted in revenge – stupidly, even – but not dishonourably.'

The head canted forward again, this time in mute acknowledgement of what I had just said. 'If Cahuella hadn't tried to ambush my squad, Gitta would never have died. And he deserved worse than he got.' The eyeless sockets lifted to me, as if some reflex demanded that he 'look' in the direction of whoever he was addressing, even though his vision was undoubtedly being relayed from some hidden camera situated in the chair. Reivich said, 'But of course, it's you I'm talking to, isn't it. Or do you still pretend otherwise?'

'I don't pretend anything. I'm just not Cahuella. Not any more. Cahuella died the day he stole Tanner's memories. What's left is . . . someone else. Someone who didn't exist before.'

An eyebrow raised above one of the enucleated sockets. 'A better man?'

'Gitta asked me a question once. How long would you have to live; how much good would you need to do, to compensate for one act of pure evil you'd committed as a younger man? It struck me as an odd question at the time, but I understand now. She knew, I think. She knew exactly who Cahuella was; exactly what he'd done. Well, I don't know the answer to that question, even now. But I think I'm going to find out.'

Reivich seemed unimpressed. 'Is that the entirety of your unfinished business with Tanner?'

'No,' I said. 'The woman with him. Amelia. She's a Mendicant, no matter what disguise she's travelling under. I believe Tanner will kill her the instant she ceases to be of use to him.'

'You came to save her, putting yourself in danger? How gallant.'

'Gallantry doesn't come into it. It's . . . human goodness.' The words sounded completely alien to me, but I wasn't ashamed of speaking them. 'Maybe this place could use a little more of it, don't you think?'

'You'd kill him – the man whose memories you carry? Isn't that a little close to suicide?'

'I'll worry about the ethical problems when I've cleaned the blood up.'

'I admire your clarity of mind,' Reivich said. 'It makes what's about to happen all the more interesting.'

I tensed. 'What are you talking about?'

'I told you Tanner was here, didn't I? I meant here; literally *here*. I've had him entertained at my pleasure until you arrived.'

A rectangle of deeper shadow interrupted the gloom behind Reivich. From out of it stepped a man who looked very much like myself.

FORTY-TWO

Once again I felt the spasm of need; the soldier's instinct to reach for an instrument of death. But there was nothing to hand, and in any case, for all my bravado, I knew that the one thing that I would not be able to do would be to kill Tanner Mirabel in cold blood. It would be too much like shooting myself.

Sister Amelia of the Ice Mendicants came behind him, emerging from the darkness into the chamber's glade of golden light. She was no longer dressed as a Mendicant – her clothes were functionally dowdy – but she was unmistakable. She wore a symbolic snowflake pendant around her neck.

Tanner stepped forward until he towered over Reivich's seat. Dressed in a dark greatcoat which almost reached the floor, he was taller than I had been expecting – an inch or so above me – and deported himself differently: a swagger which was just one element of a bodily choreography we barely shared, for all our physical similarity. We did not exactly look like twins, but we could have been brothers, or the same man seen in different illumination, where the changed aspects of shadows subtly differentiated our characters. There was a cruel set to Tanner's face which I thought I had never seen in my own, but maybe I had just not looked in the mirror at the right times.

Amelia was the first to speak. 'What's going on? I don't understand.'

'Good question,' Tanner said, placing a gloved hand on the high, scrolled back of Reivich's chair. 'Very good question indeed.' Then he peered over the back of the chair until he was looking down into the sightless face of the man he had come to kill. 'Any time you feel like answering that, you go ahead and do it, handsome.'

'You realise who I am, then?' Reivich said.

'Yeah. You went for the quick and dirty, obviously. Let me guess. Extensive neural, cellular and genetic trauma. The goons here probably buffered you with medichines, but that would have been like trying to shore up a collapsing building with drinking straws. I'd say – judging by the look of things – you've probably only got a few hours left, maybe not even that. Am I right?'

'Unerringly so,' Reivich said. 'I hope that gives you some consolation.'

'Consolation for what?' Tanner was fingering Reivich's head now, tracing it as one might trace the texture of an antique globe.

'You arrived too late to kill me.'

'I could make amends.'

'Very good. But what use would it be? You could crush this body of mine and I'd thank you for it with my dying breath. Everything that I am – everything I ever knew or felt – is preserved for eternity.'

Tanner stepped back. His tone was businesslike now. 'The scan was successful?'

'Entirely. I'm running even as we speak, somewhere in Refuge's vast distributed architecture of processors. Backup copies of me have already been transmitted to five other habitats even I can't name. You could detonate a nuclear weapon in Refuge and it wouldn't make a blind bit of difference.'

It was obvious now that the version of Reivich I had spoken to only an hour earlier had been the scanned copy. The two were playing a game together; co-conspirators. Reivich was right. Nothing that Tanner could do now would have any meaning. And maybe that did not matter to Tanner, since in drawing me here, he'd already achieved his primary aim.

'You'd die,' Tanner said. 'You expect me to believe that doesn't matter to you?'

'I don't know what you believe. Frankly, Tanner, it's of no real interest to me either way.'

'Who are you?' Amelia said, incomprehension flooding her face. I realised that even until now, he'd maintained her trust, concealing the true nature of his mission. 'Why are you talking about killing?'

'Because it's what we do,' I said. 'We've both lied to you. The difference is I never had any plans to kill you.'

Tanner reached for her. But he was not quite fast enough; too keen to linger around Reivich. Amelia padded across the floor's chevrons, bewilderment on her face. 'Please tell me what's going on!'

'No time,' I said. 'You just have to trust us. I lied to you and I'm sorry – but I wasn't myself when I did it.'

Chanterelle said, 'You'd better believe him. He risked his life to come here, and it was mainly to save you.'

'She's telling the truth,' Zebra said.

I looked into Tanner's eyes. He was still stationed behind Reivich's chair. The three servitors stood inert, as if oblivious to all that was happening around them.

'There's just one of you, Tanner,' I said. 'I think your number's finally up.' I turned to the others. 'We can take him, if you let me lead. I've got his memories. I'll anticipate every move he makes.'

Quirrenbach and Zebra flanked me, Chanterelle slightly to my rear, while Amelia retreated further behind us.

'Be careful,' I whispered. 'He might have smuggled a weapon into Refuge, even if we didn't.'

I took two steps closer to Reivich's throne.

Something moved under the quilt. His other hand, unseen until now, emerged from darkness, clutching a tiny jewelled gun. He levelled it with impressive speed, all frailty gone in the instant of aiming, and squeezed off three shots. The projectiles slammed past me, leaving silver smears on my retina.

Quirrenbach, Zebra and Chanterelle dropped to the floor.

'Remove them,' Reivich croaked.

The servitors came to life, all three of them gliding silently past me like ghosts, before kneeling down to pick up the bodies. They carried them away from the light, like spirits returning to the dark of a forest, laden with trophies.

'You piece of shit,' I said.

'They'll live,' Reivich said, returning his hand beneath the quilt. 'They're just tranquillised.'

'Why?'

'I was wondering the same thing myself,' Tanner said.

'They spoilt the symmetry. Now it's just the two of you, don't you see? The perfect conclusion to your hunt.' He tilted his skull towards me. 'You must admit, the simplicity is appealing.'

'What is it you want?' Tanner said.

'What I want is what I already have. The two of you in the same room. It's been a while, hasn't it?'

'Not long enough,' I said. 'You know more than you admitted, don't you?'

'Let's just say that the intelligence I gained before leaving Sky's Edge was intriguing, to say the least.'

'Maybe you know more than me,' I said.

Reivich poked the nozzle of the gun from under the quilt again, this time directing it back towards Tanner. His aim was no more than approximate, but it seemed to have the desired effect, causing Tanner to step away from the chair until we were equidistant from it. Then he said, 'Why don't the two of you tell me what you remember? Then I'll fill in the gaps.' He nodded at Tanner. 'You can start, I think.'

'Where would you like me to begin?'

'You can start with the death of Cahuella's wife, since you brought it about.'

I felt a weird instinct to defend him. 'He didn't kill her deliberately, you shit. He was trying to save her life.'

'Does it matter?' Tanner said, contemptuously. 'I just did what I had to do.'

'Unfortunately you missed,' Reivich said.

Tanner seemed not to hear. He was speaking now, recounting what he remembered. 'Maybe I missed; maybe I didn't. Maybe I knew I'd rather kill her than have her live without her being mine.'

'No,' I said. 'That isn't how it happened. You tried to save her . . .'

But I wondered if I really knew.

Tanner continued, 'Aftewards, I knew Gitta was finished. I could save Cahuella, though. His injuries weren't that bad. So I kept them both on life-support until I got back to the Reptile House.'

I nodded involuntarily, remembering the hellish length of the journey back through the jungle, suppressing the pain of my own severed foot. *Except it never happened to me . . . it happened to Tanner, and I only knew about it from his memories . . .*

'When I got back I was met by some of Cahuella's other staff. They took the bodies from me and did what they could for Gitta, even though they knew it was pointless. Cahuella was in a coma for a few days, but he came round eventually. He didn't remember too much of what had happened, though.'

I remembered waking after a long and dreamless sleep, choked by fever, consumed with the knowledge that I'd been *impaled*. And remembered not remembering what had happened. I called for Tanner, and was told that he was injured but alive. No one mentioned Gitta.

'Tanner came to see me,' I said, taking over the narrative. 'I saw that he had lost a foot, and knew that something very bad had happened to us. But I hardly remembered anything, except that we had gone north to set up an ambush for Reivich's party.'

'You asked for Gitta. You remembered she'd been with us.'

Fragments of that long-forgotten conversation were coming back to me now, as if recalled through layers of gauze.

'And you told me. Everything. You could have lied – made up some story which protected you; said that Reivich's man had killed her – but you didn't. You told it exactly as it happened.'

'What would have been the point?' Tanner said. 'You'd have remembered it all eventually.'

'But you must have known.'

'Must have known what?' Reivich said.

'That I'd kill you for it.'

'Ah,' Reivich said, a soft phlegmatic chuckle emerging from his life-support module. 'Now we're almost there. The crux of it all.'

'I didn't think you'd kill me,' Tanner said. 'I thought you'd forgive me. I didn't even think I'd *need* forgiveness.'

'Maybe you didn't know me quite as well as you thought.'

'Maybe I didn't.'

Reivich tapped his empty hand against the ornate armrest of his chair, his blackened nails clicking against the metalwork. 'So you had him murdered,' he said, addressing me. 'But in a manner tailored to your own obsessions.'

'I don't really remember,' I said.

And it was almost the truth.

I recalled looking down on Tanner, imprisoned within that ceilingless white enclosure. I remembered the way he slowly became aware of his predicament; aware that he was not alone. That something else shared the space with him.

'Tell me what you remember,' Reivich said, turning to Tanner.

His voice was as flat and devoid of emotion as Reivich's synthetic tones. 'I remember being eaten alive. It's not something you forget in a hurry, believe me.'

And I remembered how the hamadryad had died almost instantly, killed by the alien poisons which every human carried; a fatal clash of metabolisms. The creature had spasmed and curled like a loose firehose.

'We slit it open,' I said. 'Removed Tanner from its throat. He wasn't breathing. But his heart was still beating.'

'You could have ended it there and then,' Reivich said. 'A knife to the heart, and it would have been over. But you had to take one more thing from him, didn't you?'

'I needed his identity. His memories, particularly. So I had him kept alive on a cuirass while a trawl was prepared.'

'Why?' Reivich said.

'To chase you. I knew by then that you'd left the planet; that you'd soon be aboard a lighthugger making the run to Yellowstone. I'd punished Tanner. Now I had to do the same to you, for Gitta's sake. But I needed to become Tanner to do it.'

'You could have become anyone on the planet.'

'His skills suited me. And I had him to hand.' I paused. 'It was never meant to be permanent. I suppressed my own identity just long enough to get aboard the ship. Tanner's memories were meant to fade gradually. They'd remain as a residue – as they do now – but distinct from my own.'

'And your other secrets?'

'My eyes? That was something I had to hide. It worked, too. But now they've returned to their altered state. Maybe that was how I meant it to happen.'

'You still don't remember all of it,' Reivich said, smiling horribly. 'There was more to it, you know. More than just the eyes.'

'How would you know?'

He raised a hand, tapping what remained of his teeth in an odd gesture of knowing. 'You forget. I'd already persuaded the Ultras to betray you to me. Finding out the rest of what they did to you was simple enough.' He smiled again. 'I had to know who I was dealing with, you see. What you were capable of.'

'And now you know?'

'I think you're a man who might surprise even himself, Cahuella. Except you claim you're not him, of course.'

'I hate him as much as you do,' I said. 'I've seen things from Tanner's perspective. I know what he did to him. He isn't me.'

'So you share sympathies with Tanner?'

I shook my head. 'The Tanner I know died in a pit. It doesn't matter that something survived. It isn't him. It's just a monster Cahuella made.'

Tanner sneered. 'You think you can kill me?'

'I wouldn't have come here if I didn't.'

Tanner moved forward quickly, approaching the chair. He was going to kill Reivich; I knew it. But Reivich was ahead of him; he had the gun out and drawn before Tanner had taken more than two paces. 'Now, now,' he said. 'What's the point of you two settling your differences if you do it without an audience?'

I remembered Amelia, somewhere in the shadows. I wondered what she made of all this.

Tanner took a step back, raising his empty gloved palms. 'I suppose you're wondering how I survived,' he said, to me.

'It had crossed my mind.'

'You should never have left me alive, even if I was only kept that way by the cuirass.' He shook his head pitifully. 'You couldn't do it; not after the snake failed you. So you told one of your men to do it for you, while you got the hell away from the Reptile House.'

What he said was true, although it was only in his telling that my memories crystallised into surety. 'I headed south,' I said. 'Towards a camp occupied by NC defectors. They had surgeons with them. I knew they'd be able to suppress the work the Ultras had done on me, camouflage my genes and make me look like Tanner. I always intended to return to the Reptile House before leaving the planet.'

'But you never got the chance,' Reivich said. 'The NCs reached the Reptile House while you were away with Dieterling. They killed most of your people, except for Tanner, for whom they had a grudging respect. They brought him back to consciousness.'

'Bad mistake,' Tanner said. 'Even without a foot, I took their weapons and killed them all.'

I remembered none of that, not even faintly. *Of course not* – those events had happened after Tanner had been trawled; after I had stolen his memories.

'What happened next?' I asked.

'I had a month to get aboard the lighthugger, before it left orbit.' Tanner angled himself down and scratched his ankle under his greatcoat. 'I wasn't far behind. I got my foot fixed and came after you. I killed Dieterling, you know – how else do you think I got so close to him? Walked up to him in the wheeler and popped him.' He made the gesture, as if he was re-enacting the murder.

514

It was a classic piece of misdirection.

When Tanner rose to his full height, he did so in a movement swift and fluid. A knife arced from his hand, executing a faultlessly computed trajectory across the room. His aim was perfect – he'd even allowed for the coriolis drift caused by Refuge's lazy rotation.

The knife buried itself in the back of Reivich's head.

A digital moan came from the life-support module; an artificially stable note which kept up even when Reivich's head tilted lifelessly forward on his chest. The gun slipped from his hand and clattered on the floor. I made a move for it, knowing this was probably my only chance to achieve at least parity with Tanner.

But he was faster. He sent me flying, my spine cracking against the floor in a fall which blasted the air out of my lungs. Tanner's foot kicked the gun by accident, sending it skittering into the twilight between the pool of golden light and the shadows encompassing it.

Tanner reached for the knife and retrieved it from Reivich's skull, mono-molecular blade shimmering with prismatic patterns, like a skein of oil on water.

He won't risk throwing the knife, I thought. *If he missed, he'd lose his only weapon* . . .

'You're finished, Cahuella. This is where it ends.'

He had the knife in one hand, balanced gingerly in his gloved palm. With the other hand he reached around the front of Reivich's face and snapped the optical feeds from his eye-sockets, each line trailing ropy filaments of congealing blood.

'It ended for you a long time ago,' I said, stepping forward into his radius of attack. He swept the knife through the air, the blade scything silver arcs, parting the air so surgically that its passage was totally silent.

'Then what does that make you?' Tanner pushed Reivich's body out of the chair, the thin, quilt-shrouded figure falling to the floor like a bag of dried wood.

'I don't know,' I said. 'But I'm nothing like you.'

I tried to time the angle of his swipes with the knife, trying to focus on those specific Tanner memories which would serve me now; what he knew about combat in close quarters.

It was impossible. There was no way I could get an edge on him – and he had the advantage that he didn't have to fight to retrieve those memories. They came unbidden, deep as reflex.

I lunged, hoping to twist his free arm, to unbalance him before he could bring the blade to bear.

My timing was off.

I didn't feel the cut itself; only the cold which seeped in after it. I dared not look down, but in my peripheral vision I could see the gash in my chest, right through my clothing. It was not nearly deep enough to kill me – not even down to the ribs – but that was only luck on my part. Next time, he would have me. I was sure of it.

'Tanner!'

It was not my voice. It was Amelia, calling from the shade. I saw her, half lost in darkness, reaching out to me.

Of course. To her I was still Tanner. She had no other name for me.

She had Reivich's gun.

'Throw it to me!' I shouted.

She threw it. The gun slammed into the floor, then skidded for metres, chips of its jewelled husk flaking off.

I spun from Tanner and ran for the gun.

I fell to my knees, sliding until I was within reach of the gun. My hand closed on the grip.

Tanner's knife flew through the air and slammed into my hand. I dropped the gun, yelling in pain, seeing the point of the knife jutting from my palm like the sail of a yacht.

Tanner ran towards me, his footfalls racing into the echoless gloom. Tears clouding my eyesight, I picked up the gun with my other hand and tried to aim it at him.

I squeezed off a shot, feeling the delicate recoil of the gun. The blur of the projectile glistened past Tanner, missing him by inches. I re-aimed and squeezed the trigger again.

The gun did nothing.

Tanner crashed into me, kicking the useless weapon away for good measure. Forcing me to the ground, kneeling over me like a victor, he wrestled with me while I tried to stab him with the edge of the knife projecting from my palm.

Tanner caught my wrist above my impaled hand and smiled for a second. He'd won now. He knew it. It was just a question of removing the blade from my palm and turning it against myself.

Out of the corner of my vision I saw Reivich's slumped corpse, his mouth agape, his few teeth catching the golden glow of the chamber.

I remembered him tapping his teeth.

And finally remembered the other thing Cahuella had bought from the Ultras; the transformation that went deeper than vision; the hunter's aid he had never mentioned to Tanner Mirabel.

What use is it to hunt in the night, if you can't kill what you catch?

I opened my jaw wide; wider than strict human anatomy allowed. I seemed to find a muscle inside myself that I had not known was there before; a muscle anchored high in the roof of my mouth. Something cracked in my jaw, painlessly.

With my good arm I cradled Tanner's head, turning his face to mine while he struggled with the knife, thinking it would do him some good.

He looked into my mouth, and must have seen it then.

'You're dead,' I said. 'It wasn't just snake-vision I bought from them, you see.'

I felt my venom glands activate, pumping poison along the microfine channels bored through my articulated fangs.

And drew Tanner to me, like the final embrace of a long-lost brother.

And bit deep into his neck.

EPILOGUE

For a long time I just stood looking out the window.

The woman who was sitting in my office must have thought I'd forgotten she was there. I could see her face reflected in the floor-to-ceiling glass, still waiting for an answer to the question she had just asked. I hadn't forgotten her or her question. I was just wondering how something that had once seemed so strange could now seem so familiar.

The city hadn't changed much since my arrival.

It had to be me, then.

The window was spattered by rain falling from the Mosquito Net, hard diagonal slashes of it. They said it never really stopped raining in Chasm City, and maybe that was true, but it missed the nuances that rain was capable of. Sometimes it came down straight and soft like a cool mist, alpine clean. Sometimes, when the steam dams around the chasm opened and sent pressure changes squalling across the city, it came at you sideways, lashing and acid-tongued, like defoliant.

'Mister Mirabel . . .' she said.

I turned back from the window. 'I'm sorry. I got caught up in the view. Where were we?'

'You were telling me about Sky Haussmann, how you think he . . .'

She had heard most of what I was willing to tell anyone by then; how I believed Sky had emerged from hiding and remade a new life for himself as Cahuella. I suppose it was odd that I was speaking of these things at all – much less to a prospective recruit – but I'd liked her and she'd been more than usually willing to listen to me. We had finished a few pisco sours – she was from Sky's Edge as well – and the time had slipped by.

'Well?' I asked, interrupting her. 'How much of it are you prepared to believe?'

'I'm not sure, Mister Mirabel. How would you have found all this out, if you don't mind my asking?'

'I met Gitta,' I said. 'And she told me something which makes me think Constanza was telling the truth.'

'You think Gitta found out who Cahuella was, before anyone else?'

'Yes. There's a good chance she stumbled on Constanza's evidence, and that led her to Cahuella, even though it was at least two centuries since Sky had supposedly been executed.'

'And when she found him?'

'She was expecting a monster, but that wasn't quite what she got. He wasn't the same man Constanza had known. Gitta tried to hate him, I think, but couldn't.'

'What do you think made her certain she'd found him?'

'His name, I think. He took it from the legend of the *Caleuche*, the ghost ship. Cahuella was its dolphin; a link to his past he couldn't quite sever.'

'Well, it's certainly an interesting theory.'

I shrugged. 'Probably no more than that. You'll hear stranger stories if you spend any time here, believe me.'

She was a recent arrival to Yellowstone; like me a soldier, but one who had been sent here not on some errand but because of a clerical error.

'How long have you been here, Mister Mirabel?'

'Six years,' I said.

I looked to the picture window. The view across the city had not changed greatly since I had returned from Refuge. The thicket of the Canopy stretched away like a section through someone's lung: a convoluted black tangle against the brown backdrop of the Mosquito Net. They were talking about cleaning it next year.

'That's a long time, six years.'

'Not for me.'

Saying that, I thought about the time when I had come round in Refuge. I must have slipped beneath consciousness through the blood I had lost from the wound Tanner had inflicted on me, even though I had barely felt it at the time. My clothes had been slit open, a turquoise medicinal salve applied to the suture-like gash where his knife had passed through. I was lying on a couch, with one of the slender servitors eyeing me.

I was a mass of bruises, and each breath hurt. My mouth felt strange, as if it no longer belonged to me.

'Tanner?'

It was Amelia's voice. She moved into focus next to me, her face angelic, just as she had looked on the day of my revival in the Mendicant habitat.

'That isn't my name,' I said, startled when my voice came out perfectly normally, apart from a slight rasp of fatigue. My mouth did not feel like it should be capable of anything as subtle as language.

'So I gather,' Amelia said. 'But it's the only one I know you by, so it will have to suffice for now.'

I was too weak to argue, and not even sure I wanted to.

'You saved me,' I said. 'I owe you a debt of thanks.'

'You seemed to save yourself,' she said. The room was much smaller than the one where Reivich had died, but it was illuminated in the same shade of autumnal gold and the walls were chiselled with the same intricate mathematics that I had seen elsewhere in Refuge. The light played on the snowflake she wore around her neck. 'What happened to you, Tanner? What happened to make you capable of killing a man in that way?'

Her question sounded accusatory, except for the tone in which it was delivered. She was not blaming me, I realised. Amelia appeared to recognise that I was not necessarily responsible for the horrors of my own past, any more than a waking man is responsible for the atrocities he commits in his sleep.

'The man I was,' I said, 'was a hunter.'

'The man you were talking about? The man called Cahuella?'

I nodded. 'He had snake genes inserted into his eyes, amongst other tricks. He wanted to be able to hunt any creature in the dark on equal terms. I thought that was as far as it went. I was wrong about that.'

'But you didn't know?'

'Not until it was time. Reivich knew, though. He knew Cahuella had venom glands, and the means to deliver the venom into a host. The Ultras must have told him.'

'And he tried to tell you?'

I moved my head up and down on the pillow. 'Maybe he wanted one of us to live more than the other. I just hope he made the right choice.'

'Of course he did,' Zebra said.

I turned around – painfully – to see her standing on the other side of the bed. 'Reivich told the truth, then,' I said. 'About the gun. You were only put to sleep.'

'He wasn't a bad person,' Zebra said. 'He wouldn't have wanted anyone harmed except the man who killed his family.'

'But I'm still alive. Does that mean he failed?'

She shook her head slowly. She looked radiant in the golden light, and I realised that I wanted her intensely, no matter how we had betrayed each other or what lay in the future; no matter that I did not even have a name by which she could call me. 'I think he got what he wanted, in the end. Most of it, anyway.'

There was something in her voice which told me she was not telling me everything she knew. 'What do you mean by that?'

'I don't suppose anyone's told you,' Zebra said. 'But Reivich lied to all of us.'

'About what?'

'His scan.' She looked towards the ceiling, the lines of her face defined in golden highlights. Her skin stripes were still faintly visible. 'It was a failure. It was done too hastily. He wasn't captured.'

I went through the motions of registering disbelief, even though I could tell Zebra was telling the truth.

'But it can't have failed. I spoke to the copy after he'd been scanned.'

'You *thought* you did. Apparently it was just a beta-level simulation, a mockup of Reivich programmed to mimic his responses and make you think the scan had been successful.'

'Why, though? Why did he feel the need to pretend it had worked?'

'I think it was for Tanner's benefit,' she said. 'Reivich wanted Tanner to think everything had been in vain; that even killing Reivich's physical body was a meaningless gesture.'

'Except it wasn't,' I said.

'No. Reivich would have died anyway, sooner or later – but it was really Tanner that did it.'

'And he knew, didn't he? The whole time we were with Reivich, he knew he was going to die, and the scan had failed.'

'Does that mean he won?' Zebra said. 'Or did he lose everything?'

I reached out and took her hand and squeezed it. 'It doesn't matter now. None of it matters now. Tanner, Cahuella, Reivich – they're all dead.'

'All of them?'

'All of them that really matters.'

And then I looked up into the sourceless gold light, for what seemed like an eternity, until Zebra and Amelia left me alone. I was tired; the kind of absolute weariness that feels too much a burden to escape through sleep. Sleep did come, though, eventually. And with it dreams. I had hoped it would be otherwise, but with dreaming came the white room, and the pristine horror of what had happened there; what had happened to me; what I had inflicted on myself.

Later – much later – I returned to Chasm City. It was a long journey back, and it was interrupted by a stopover at the Mendicant habitat, where I returned Amelia to her duties. She had taken it all remarkably well, and when I offered to help her in some way – not really knowing how I could – she deflected all such intentions and asked only that I make a donation to the Ice Mendicants when I was able to.

I promised her I would. It was a promise I held to.

Quirrenbach, Zebra and I arranged a meeting with Voronoff upon our return to the Canopy.

'It's about the Game,' I said. 'We're proposing a major restructure of the whole operation.'

'Why do you imagine it could interest me?' Voronoff yawned.

'Hear us out,' Quirrenbach said, and started to explain the framework the three of us had worked out since our time in Refuge. It was complex, and for a while we did not seem to be getting through to to Voronoff. But gradually comprehension dawned.

He listened to what we had to say.

And finally he said that he liked our ideas. That maybe it could be made to work.

We proposed a new form of the hunt; something we would call Shadowplay. In essence it would be similar to the old, underground Game which the city had spawned since the Plague. But in every detail it would be radically different, not the least of which would be legality. We would take the Game into the limelight, establish sponsorship rules and a framework which guaranteed coverage and commentary to whoever wanted the vicarious thrill of a manhunt. Our chasers would be more than just rich kids looking for a night's quick thrill. They'd be hand-trained experts; hunter-assassins. We'd school them in professionalism and construct elaborate personae around them, cults of personality which would elevate the Game to the status of art. We would recruit from the best existing players, of course. Chanterelle Sammartini had already agreed to be our first employee. I had no doubts that she would fit the role perfectly.

But we would change more than just the hunters.

No victims this time. The hunted would be *volunteers*. It sounded insane, but this was the part Voronoff quickly warmed to.

There would be no prize for the survivors other than survival itself. But with it would come immense prestige. We would have all the volunteers we needed: drawn from the vast pool of bored, affluent near-immortals who filled the Canopy. In the revised form of the Game, they would have finally found a way to inject a controlled edge into their lives. They'd sign contracts with us, detailing the terms of a particular contest: the duration, the permitted range of play and the types of weapon allowed by the assassin. All they would need to do was stay alive until the contract expired. They would be famous and envied. Others would follow, anxious to do a little better: a longer contract; more challenging terms of play.

We would use tracking implants, of course – but they would not function in the same way as the device Waverly had installed in my skull, and which Dominika had so kindly removed at short notice. Assassin and hunted would carry matched pairs, and they would be primed to activate and transmit only when within a certain range of each other – again, covered by the terms of the contract. Both parties would know when that happened – a ringing tone in the skull, or something similar. And in that final hour of the chase, media would be allowed to descend for the first time, witnessing the end – however it played out.

Voronoff joined us, eventually. He was our first customer.

We called our company Omega Point; soon there were others, and we welcomed the competition. Within a year of operation, we had pushed the memory of the old hunt into oblivion. It was not a part of the city's history that anyone wanted enshrined. And that was the way it happened.

At first, we were careful to allow our clients to survive the terms of their contracts, for the most part. Our assassins would lose their trail at the critical moment or misfire whatever single-shot weapon had been specified in the contract. It was a way of building up an initial client list, so that our name would spread more rapidly.

Once that began to happen, we got serious. Now it was for real; now they really did have to fight to stay alive for the duration.

And the majority managed it. The odds on being killed during a game of Shadowplay fluctuated somewhere around thirty per cent – safe enough so that players were not actively discouraged from participation, no matter how bored – but with enough of an edge to make survival, winning, something to be prized.

Omega Point became very rich indeed. Within two years of my arrival in Chasm City I counted myself amongst the hundred wealthiest individuals – corporeal or otherwise – in the whole Yellowstone system.

But I never forgot the pledge I had made to myself, during the long journey up to Refuge.

That if I survived, I would change everything.

With Shadowplay, I had started. But it was not enough. I had to alter the city totally. I had to destroy the system that had allowed me to flourish; to unbalance the unspoken equilibrium between Mulch and Canopy. I began by recruiting my newest hunters from the Mulch itself. There was no real risk to myself in doing this, for the Mulchers were as adept at the art as anyone I'd find in Canopy – and just as receptive to the training methods I advocated.

Just as the game had made me rich, I made my best players wealthy beyond their dreams. And watched as some of that wealth seeped back into the Mulch.

It was a small start. It might take years – decades, even – before there was a noticeable change to the hierarchy in Chasm City. But I knew it would happen. I had promised myself that it would. And though I had broken promises in the past, I was never going to do it again.

After a while, I began to call myself Tanner again. I knew it was a lie; that I had no right to that name; that I had stolen memories and then life itself from the man who really was Tanner Mirabel.

But what did any of that matter?

I thought of myself as the custodian of his memories; all that he had been. He had not exactly been a good man, not by any reasonable definition of the word. He had been callous and violent, and he had approached the arts of science and murder with the studied distance of a geometer. Yet he had never been truly evil, and in the moment which effectively sealed his life – when he shot Gitta – he had been trying to do something good.

What had happened to him afterwards; what had happened to turn him into a monster – none of that mattered. It did not tarnish what Tanner had been before.

It was, I thought, as good a name as any. And there would never be a day when it felt like any name but my own.

I decided not to fight it.

I realised that I had slipped into another reverie. The woman in my office was waiting for me to say something.

'Well, do I get the job or not?'

Yes, she probably did, but there would be other candidates to see before I made my final decision. I stood up and shook her small, lethal hand. 'You're certainly near the top of the list. And even if you don't get the position we've discussed, there's another reason I might want to keep your name on file.'

'Yes?'

I thought about Gideon; still imprisoned down there after all these years. I had vowed that I would go down into the chasm again – if only to kill him – but the time had never been right. I knew he was still alive, since Dream Fuel was still reaching the city, albeit in tiny, sought-after quantities. There was still a perverse trade to be had in selling his terrors, distilled into a format humans could just assimilate. But he must surely be close to death now, and there could not be very much time left before my vow would become meaningless.

'Just an operation I might have in mind; that's all.'

'And when would that be?'

'A month or so from now; maybe three or four.'

She smiled again. 'I'm good, Mister Mirabel. You'd better hope I don't get poached by someone else in the meantime.'

I shrugged. 'If it happens, it happens.'

'Well, who knows.'

We shook hands again, and she began walking towards the door. I looked out the window; dusk was settling in now, lights burning in the Canopy; cable-cars tiny motes of light swinging through the eternal brown twilight. Down below, like a plain strewn with campfires, the lamps and night markets of the Mulch reflected a sullen red glow towards the Net. I thought of the millions of people who had found a way to think of this city as home, even after the transformations it had been through since the Plague. It was thirteen years ago, after all. There were adults down there who had no real memories of what the place had been like before.

'Mister Mirabel?' she said, hesitating at the door. 'One other thing?'

I turned around and offered a polite smile. 'Yes?'

'You've been here longer than I have. Did there ever come a point when you actually liked this place?'

'I don't know,' I said, shrugging. 'I just know one thing.'

'Which is?'

'Life's what you make it.'